SPECIAL OPS SHIFTERS: L.A. FORCE

THE COMPLETE SERIES COLLECTION

MEG RIPLEY

SHIFTER NATION

Disclaimer

This book is intended for readers age 18 and over. It contains mature situations and language that may be objectionable to some readers.

CONTENTS

SECRET BABY FOR THE SOLDIER BEAR

SPECIAL OPS SHIFTERS: L.A. FORCE

1

GABE VINSON SCANNED THE DUSTY PARKING LOT JUST BEFORE HE STEPPED into the bar. It was a force of habit that he doubted he'd ever be able to drop. His time with the Delta Force had kept him constantly vigilant. Sure, there didn't seem to be any threat from this place. Vance wouldn't have invited him there if that were the case. Gabe smiled, thinking of some of the times they'd shared before Gabe had moved on to Delta and reconsidered. *Or maybe he would have...*

He found his old friend at the bar and slid onto the stool next to him. He glanced at the chalkboard menu on the wall and the clean tables scattered around the place. "This isn't quite like the shit holes we used to frequent."

Vance laughed and took a sip of his beer. "Yeah, it's a little cleaner than those. And hey, you won't get any sand in your whiskey here." He gestured at the barkeeper to pour Gabe a drink. "How are you holding up?"

"Well enough," Gabe said with a sigh, scratching his fingers through the short beard he'd grown out ever since his medical discharge. "You know how it is. You think when you get out that everything will have stayed the same, but it's all different. All the girls you used to date have gotten married and had kids. Some of them even married your buddies, so they're not interested in going out, either. Your family wants you to come visit, but they don't know how to talk to you anymore. And even though they say they want to hear what you've been up to, you can only tell them so much." He nodded at the bartender for the shot of whiskey and took a sip, enjoying the burn.

"I'm sure it's even worse for you. The Delta Force doesn't fuck around with that sort of stuff," Vance agreed. "I'm mighty glad you made your way back around through Dallas, though. There's something I wanted to talk to you about. You said you were trying to figure out what to do with yourself now that you're out."

"Right." Gabe knew that Vance was a member of the Special Ops Shifter Force, a group of veteran soldiers with special skills on top of their ability to shift. It was supposed to be a secret, and it still was when it came to the human population, but the more work the Force did, the more word spread about them throughout the shifter community. Right now, they'd essentially achieved rumor status. It sounded like just the kind of work Gabe would enjoy, but it wasn't as though the Force just stuck a 'Now Hiring' sign in the window when they had a vacant spot.

Vance looked casually over his shoulder. The bar was loud, and no one had been rude enough to sit down right next to them. "Well, have you decided where you want to live?"

Gabe let out a snort of laughter. "One place is about as good as another to me as long as it's stateside. I came from a military family, so I've never been in one spot for very long."

"How do you feel about Los Angeles?"

"L.A.?" The grizzly tossed back the rest of his drink and let is swirl on his tongue as he thought about it. "I guess that would be all right. Just like any other city, right?"

The cowboy tipped his head from one side to the other. "Sort of. It's got a hell of a lot of people in it, and a decent percentage of them just happen to be shifters. There are more of them than the local conclave has been able to keep track of, actually, and it's recently come to light that some of them are forming gangs. It could be incredibly dangerous for shifters as a whole if this is allowed to get out of hand."

"What exactly do you want me to do about it?" Gabe had spent his entire military career trying to hide his true identity from anyone who was pure human, and the other soldier shifters he managed to find were few and far between. The idea of connecting with so many more people like himself was an intriguing one.

"Not just you, but a group. See, the SOS Force was started in Washington, D.C. by Dr. Drake Sheridan, a Special Forces Medical Sergeant. As the need for the Force expanded across the country, the Dallas unit was formed. After you came to see me on the ranch, I talked a bit with the guys in Dallas and with Drake himself. It seems that we may need to start up yet another unit, this time in L.A. We'll have to find all the right people to staff it, all shifters, all former Special Ops." Vance pointed at him with the mouth of his beer bottle, his eyes steady. "I've recommended you."

Gabe lifted his empty glass to get the bartender's attention. He watched the liquid swirl in the glass for a long minute as he thought. Gabe was the type of man who liked to take action. Not only did he not mind being busy, he lived for it. There was nothing worse than sitting around idly, and even in the Delta Force, he'd had his share of that. This could be one hell of an opportunity, and he didn't think he could dare pass it up. "You've got yourself a recruit, Vance."

"Hell, yeah!" Vance rang his beer against Gabe's glass. "We'll be working on a list of other potential members, and we'll get you set up with a headquarters building out there in L.A. Garrison, who's part of the D.C. unit, is great with construction, so you'll have everything you need."

Gabe smiled. When that mortar had blown him up and left his ribs peppered with shrapnel, he thought he'd lost everything. His job and the missions he'd worked so hard on for the U.S. Army had all gone down the drain and left him with no direction and no future.

But he was about to have it all back and more.

———

IN THEORY, commercial flights should be downright luxurious compared to the planes he'd been on with the Army. The seats were more comfortable, someone brought a snack and a drink, and the chances of having to jump out the side door were pretty minimal. Even with a normal landing, there was no concern about having to head straight off to war.

But being seated in front of a small child who couldn't sit still and continuously kept kicking his seat made Gabe wish he was flying with good old Uncle Sam again. The talkative man to his right wasn't making things any better.

"Ah, the good old city of Los Angeles," he announced in a voice worthy of a cheesy game show. He ran a hand through his bleached hair and flashed a blinding white grin. "Is this your first time?"

Gabe nodded. He'd gotten used to talking to all sorts of people in his work with the Delta Force, learning to connect, despite cultural and lingual differences. So many locals from the various countries he'd worked in had been kind and welcoming, but this character was something else. "Yes, it is."

"Whoa, baby! You're in for a real treat. You haven't traveled *at all* if you haven't been to the City of Angels."

Gabe stifled a laugh. This sleaze with a fake spray tan would've shit his pants if he'd hopped a plane to some of the places he'd seen. "You don't say."

"I have to ask: are you here for business or pleasure?" He nudged Gabe's elbow on the narrow armrest suggestively.

"Business," Gabe quickly affirmed. "I'm here for a new job."

"Oh, you're moving here? Even better. Tell me, where are you from?" The man was leaning forward, grinning enthusiastically as he waited for Gabe's answer.

There was no point in trying to ignore him now. Gabe had baited the bear, and now he had to stay for the rest of the circus. "A little bit of everywhere, actually." He'd moved around enough in his life, both as a child and an adult, that he didn't have a place he could call his hometown.

"Well, let me tell you, the nightlife here is crazier than you could ever imagine. Hell, there's plenty to do during the day, too. I'm sure you'll start with all the touristy stuff. Everyone does. You check out the beach and the museums and the shopping, but the more you look, the more you find. I swear, you could do something different every day and never run out of new things to do. The clubs are absolutely wild, and there are gorgeous babes around every corner."

"Great." Gabe didn't really care. He had work to do, and that was far more important than drinking too much or getting himself in trouble with a woman.

The man nudged him once again. "Come on, man. A young guy like you? You've got to be excited about being surrounded by chicks with the best tit jobs in the entire world. Seriously, the honeys are absolutely dynamite!"

What year was this guy from anyway? "I'm good, man."

"You married or something? I mean, not like that should matter." He chuckled as though they shared some stupid inside joke.

He could make conversation all he needed, but Gabe wasn't interested in sharing details about his personal life with a stranger. The guy had no idea how these sorts of things worked for men like Gabe. Shifters were attracted to plenty of people, sure. They had relationships that came and went like anyone else. But that was nothing compared to the feeling of finding one's true mate, that deep and spiritual moment when two souls that had been created for each other were finally in the same space and could feel each other in their blood. He'd felt that once, but he'd had other obligations that had pulled at him harder.

Fortunately, the crackling sound from the overhead speaker kept him from having to respond. "Ladies and gentlemen, if you look out the left side of the aircraft, you can see we're approaching the city of Los Angeles. Please take your seats and fasten your seatbelts. We'll be landing as soon as possible. Thank you."

Gabe turned to the window. Sure enough, the baked wilderness of the Mojave had changed into verdant mountains embracing a sprawling city. The plane bobbed and dipped in the air as the pilot changed direction, bringing more and more of the city into focus. The massive skyscrapers were the easiest to spot, and the gridded blocks that surrounded them slowly coalesced into numerous homes with turquoise swimming pools and businesses. Another turn of the plane brought the ocean into view, with miles and miles of beach showing as a crisp white line.

Los Angeles, even from the air, was clearly bustling with life. Gabe peered down at it, wondering just how many shifters made up its population. If Vance had been right when he'd mentioned there were more shifters in L.A. than anywhere else in the country, Gabe would have more than enough to do.

An hour later, when he'd made it through baggage claim and had taken an Uber to his hotel, Gabe spotted two men seated in the lobby. They watched him as he checked in, one of them leaning over to whisper to the other. They were shifters, he could tell. In the short time that he'd been in the city, he'd already encountered quite a few of them.

A knock came on his hotel room door as he was getting settled in. Gabe turned away from his suitcase and looked through the peephole to find the same two men he'd noticed in the lobby. One of them was tall and dark with green eyes and a broad physique. The other was only slightly slimmer, his dirty blonde hair combed back and his clothes neatly pressed. He looked familiar, but Gabe couldn't quite place him.

Gabe wasn't one to hide, though he knew there was a chance the two strangers were after him. He'd made plenty of enemies by the time he'd left the Delta Force. You couldn't fight terrorism or carry out the most dangerous missions on the planet without pissing a few people off here and there. For all he knew, these two men were either seeking revenge for his former work or trying to prevent him from ever getting to his first day on the new job. He checked the pistol tucked into the back of his waistband and opened the door.

The first man grinned as he stuck out his hand. "Gabe Vinson, I'm Garrison Stokes from the D.C. unit. This is Hudson Taylor. May we come in?"

Gabe shook their hands and opened the door wider, laughing a little at himself for thinking they could be anything other than the Special Ops Shifter Force members sent to meet him. He was just too eager for action, and the idea of languishing in a hotel room hadn't appealed to him the way it did to most people. "Of course. It's nice to meet you. Vance told me a lot about you."

"All shitty things, I'm sure," Garrison joked. He took a seat in one of the chairs near the window, his large body folding into it. "You're the first one to get here. We're still working on the rest of the recruits, but we didn't want to wait to get started. I take it you know what you're in for?"

"The general idea, at least. Shifters have problems that can't always be solved by the human authorities or even our own conclaves, and that's when we step in." Gabe remained standing, eager to move, but glad that things were getting started.

"Pretty much," Hudson agreed. "There's no real limit to the types of missions we run, either. We've protected important people, settled arguments within clans or among them, and even hashed some things out between conclaves themselves. I have to say that when we started the D.C. unit with Drake, I didn't think we'd be that busy. The next thing I knew, we were flying all over the country."

"And now there will be one more part of the country that's taken care of," Gabe added. He didn't know this city or its people, but he liked the idea of protecting them. "That all sounds good to me. What do we do first?"

"First, we find a place to use for headquarters. We can't do much of anything unless there's a building to work out of. Hudson here is in charge of all our communications equipment, and we'll need a place to put it."

Now Gabe knew why the blonde man looked familiar. "You're not Hudson Taylor of Taylor Communications, are you?" He'd heard a lot about the telecom corporation in the news and all the massive efforts its wealthy owner was making to ensure connectivity throughout the entire world. He was rumored to be an absolute genius when it came to the latest innovations in the tech industry.

"For better or worse," Hudson said with a smile. "I'm excited to show you everything we've already established with the other units. I'll be sure to have everything set up so we can have remote meetings among all the units if necessary."

"Great. So we'll need space for meetings. What else are we looking for in a headquarters building?"

"It's always tricky finding just the right place. We want something big enough to house not only a meeting space, but enough living quarters for everyone involved. Some of the team members might choose to stay in their own housing, but I think it's important that we have enough space in case anything disastrous should happen. In Dallas, we managed to find a place that had been some sort of showroom. There was a lot of empty space that I could convert and use the way we needed to. Something like that would be ideal."

"And I imagine it needs to blend in with the surroundings," Gabe added.

Hudson nodded. "Absolutely. There will be four of you, so we know we need at least that many apartments within the HQ building. The new comm officer will need to work closely with Hudson, and our med sergeant can do all the exams since Drake can't be here. That just leaves Amar and Jude. We don't have any information about your immediate families yet, though."

Gabe understood what they were asking, and he shook his head. "It's just me."

"I've got a few places lined up to evaluate this afternoon if you'd like to come along," Garrison offered. "There's nothing for us to do until everyone else gets here, anyway."

"Sure. Let's go." Now more than ever, Gabe was desperate for something to do. Checking out buildings for sale would give him the chance to see more of the city while also getting to know some of the men he'd be working with for the foreseeable future, even if it was only by long distance.

Garrison drove as they checked out the first place, an ample office space that took up one level of a massive glass building, but Gabe's mind was on anything but real estate. Somehow, the question of whether or not he lived alone had struck a chord with him. Growing up, Gabe had been incredibly close to his mother. His father had left when Gabe was just a kid, leaving her to raise her three cubs on her own. Gabe had immediately taken up the position of man of the house, but at first, he had no idea how to do it. He didn't know how to provide for them, and he wasn't even old enough to learn that lesson.

It hadn't really hit home for him until he'd gotten out of bed one night when he couldn't sleep. Gabe could still see the memory clearly instead of all the palm trees and glittering glass around him. His mother sat at the kitchen table with papers spread all around her. Her back was hunched over, and at first, Gabe thought she'd fallen asleep. But then he'd noticed her shoulders shaking and heard the sound of her weeping.

"Oh, Gabe," she'd said when he came forward and put his arm around her shoulders. "There are many things I hope for you and your sisters, but the one thing I want for you most of all is not to have to choose between feeding your family and paying your bills."

Gabe's mind had drifted to the pantry, which he knew was nearly empty. His sisters had been complaining about it earlier in the day, and so had he. Guilt washed over him.

"Life isn't easy, Gabe," his mother had continued. "And kids are wonderful, but they're also very expensive. I want you to make me a promise."

He was only ten; he didn't know what to make of any of this. Gabe had never seen his mother cry unless they were watching a sad movie. She hadn't told him she couldn't pay the bills, and in that moment, he wished she hadn't. He didn't know what it meant or what he should be doing about it, but he didn't feel he could ask, either. "All right."

"Promise me you will never start a family and then leave them behind. Family always takes care of family. It might not be easy. We won't always get along and agree on everything. But you must always take care of your family." Her dark eyes, eyes he hadn't inherited from her, implored him to do as she asked.

"Okay." He hadn't known what he was agreeing to at the time; Gabe only wanted to make his mother feel better. In time, he'd come to understand that she meant she didn't want him to make the same mistakes his father had. At the moment, though, he'd understood it in a completely different way.

Within a week, Gabe had a job delivering papers. It meant getting out of bed before the sun came up, taking his bike across town to fold and stack his newspapers for the day, and feeling like he'd had a complete workout before he'd even started school. He got home just in time to help his sisters get ready, something that always seemed to take a few of the worry lines out of his mother's face.

At the end of his first week, he once again found her at the kitchen table with her bills spread out on the battered surface. He set his pay down in the middle of all of it, a smile on his face.

"What's this?"

"It's what I earned this week, and I'll do the same again next week. Mr. Robinson even gave me a tip." He'd felt so proud of himself, knowing he was keeping his promise to his mother.

"No, sweetheart." She gently pushed the cash back toward him. "That's not right. You keep your money."

He'd stared at those crumpled bills, bewildered and confused. "But there are bills to pay. I want to help, Mom. I can do this."

She pressed her lips together, still uncertain, but finally, she nodded. "All right. You have enough here to take care of this one."

He watched as she filled out the payment slip and put it along with the money in an envelope. Gabe went to bed that night knowing he was a real man, one who took care of his family the way he should. And from that point on, he'd never looked back.

"What do you think?"

"Hmm?" Gabe had let himself get so lost in his thoughts that he'd hardly paid attention as they toured the building.

Garrison gave him a look. "I was asking what you think of the place. We can do whatever we want with this floor when it comes to remodeling and such, but being in a district full of office spaces might pose a problem."

He looked around, suddenly realizing he'd come a long way without paying a lick of attention. He hadn't officially started his new job with the SOS Force, and already he was failing. "I agree. Something a little more out of the way might be better."

They followed the realtor to another building that they wouldn't have to share with anyone, but it was still located at a major intersection. Another warehouse had ample space and wasn't too close to traffic, but it didn't meet Garrison's expectations on something he could make habitable.

The realtor, Mrs. McKeal, stood on the sidewalk flicking through listings on her tablet, her long fake nail tapping faintly against the screen each time. "I think I have one more place. It might not be quite what you're looking for, as it's currently a residential building, but if you're running a private business that doesn't require a lot of foot traffic, I think you'll be okay." She'd seemed a bit sour over the fact that they didn't like anything yet.

Garrison nodded. "We're open to anything."

"Okay, but it's a little expensive."

Her sedan slid through a gate and into the driveway of a sleek and modern house. It didn't look like much from the road, but the fact that it butted up against state park land was certainly a bonus. He got out of the rental car and smiled, finally starting to feel good about moving there.

"We're looking at six bedrooms and seven baths," Mrs. McKeal announced as she let them in through the front door. "It's just over four thousand square feet. This is the perfect place if you like to be outdoors with the number of patios and outdoor living places it features. Here." She strode through the main room, sailing past the fireplace and the twelve-foot ceilings toward the back of the house.

At the push of a button, large sections of the back wall began to move. They receded into themselves like pocket doors, making the living room more of an outdoor space with not so much as a door separating them from the private pool out back.

It was impressive, and it was certainly a nicer place than Gabe had ever lived before, but what intrigued him most was when they made their way up to the second floor.

"Like I mentioned, there are a lot of outdoor spaces," Mrs. McKeal reminded them before opening a patio door with a flourish.

Gabe stepped out, warm fingers of sunshine brushing against his skin as he took in the scenery. The wild hills, with their scrubby brush and soaring trees, were calling to him already. The grizzly bear that lived inside him lashed and growled, demanding that he shift immediately and jump over the rail. He'd make it safely to the ground, and then it would only be a short run before he was in those hills that called to him.

When he turned back to the senior SOS Force members, Hudson and Garrison were discussing details while Mrs. McKeal stepped into the other room to answer a phone call. "It's not the norm," Hudson admitted, "and I'm certainly jealous compared to the space we get to call HQ. But there's no doubt you can fit plenty of people in here. Even if one of the recruits has a mate or a family, I think we can make it work."

Garrison nodded. "The layout of the house certainly lends itself to be used the same way as our other buildings. All the common areas like the kitchen and the living room are centralized and the bedrooms are already made like suites with their own bathrooms. I don't think we can go wrong. Gabe? You're the one who's going to be living here."

He grinned as he gestured over his shoulder to the gorgeous scenery. "You're damn right I am."

2
———————

"DR. CRUZ, WE'VE STILL GOT A LINE ALL THE WAY OUT THE FRONT DOOR. What do you want me to do?"

Emersyn finished washing her hands and looked up at the clock. It was nearly closing time, and she had to get home to Lucas. Melody was with him, and she never complained when Emersyn showed up late, but that didn't mean she wanted to take advantage of her best friend if she could avoid it. She sighed. It was so hard to make the right decisions. "Cold and flu season is hitting so hard already this year. I'm willing to see them if you're willing to keep helping me corral them, but we'll have to cut the line off where it's at or we'll never get out of here."

Louise nodded soberly. "You know I can handle it. This is a vacation compared to all those nights I worked in the ER. I'll check in with Wendy, but I don't think she'll mind." She headed back to the exam rooms to continue setting up patients.

Knowing she had her staff working with her always made things better, but Emersyn still felt her forehead wrinkle with concern as she sent a text to Melody to let her know she'd be late once again. Then she headed down the hall toward the next exam room. "Good afternoon, Mr. Bridges. I understand you're feeling pretty rough."

The old man sat on the end of the exam table, his feet dangling like a small child's, even though he was taller than she was. His gray hair stuck out in all directions, but his beard had been smoothed down by his nervous habit of running his hand down his face. He nodded.

"Tell me about some of your symptoms." Emersyn washed her hands once again and then donned a pair of nitrile gloves before taking his temperature and checking out his eyes, nose, and ears.

"I think I have a fever," he replied. His voice was hoarse, but it had been like that for as long as Emersyn had known him. "I'm really cold, and then I'm really hot. And my body hurts. And my throat."

"Sounds like you're a bit congested, too." She made a few notes about his exam as she ignored the powerful odor that emanated from Mr. Bridges. At a free clinic in the heart of the city, not all of her patients had the opportunity to get cleaned up before a doctor's appointment.

"Yeah." His hand moved of its own volition through his beard.

Emersyn knew that touching his face all the time was probably not going to do him any favors when it came to getting sick, but it was a nervous habit he wasn't likely to get rid of anytime soon. "We'll need to do a quick swab to verify it, but I'm pretty sure you've got the flu. Once we have that result, I can get you a prescription."

Mr. Bridges shook his head quickly, alarm brightening his eyes. "I don't have any money."

She smiled and laid a hand on his arm. "That's okay. You're on Medi-Cal, remember? The state covers everything you need."

"Oh. Right." He nodded, but he didn't seem to quite understand. Emersyn suspected he'd had a stroke at some point, a small one that hadn't affected him too much physically. She'd attempted to get him to a hospital that could check it out for him, but he refused to see anyone but her.

"That means everything will be taken care of. You don't have to pay for your exam here with me this evening, and you don't have to pay for any medicine. Okay?"

She found the relief she was looking for as she searched his face. His shoulders relaxed, and he no longer looked like a hunted animal. "That's wonderful. Thank you, Dr. Cruz."

"You're very welcome. I'll just go get the test kit and I'll be right back." Emersyn stripped off her gloves, but she turned back to her patient as she reached for the doorknob. "Mr. Bridges, do you have a place to sleep tonight?"

His hand dropped to his lap, and his lower lip turned up. Emersyn always had a soft spot for sweet old men, and she blinked to keep herself from tearing up at the sight of him. "No. The shelter's full."

"I thought you had a place with them in their transitional program?" There were only so many spots available in that particular program, which helped homeless people like Mr. Bridges get back on their feet, get jobs, and be able to care for themselves. Getting a spot with them was a big deal.

"I was," the old man admitted. "But I saw a young woman and her two kids come into the soup kitchen, and I overheard her telling one of the workers she had no place to go. I told Ms. Joann that she could have my spot."

Emersyn pressed her hand against her chest, feeling her heart break. Here was this man, out on the streets in a cruel world, elderly and ill, yet he gave up the one good thing he had going to care for someone else. It was people like him who kept her working there day after day when she could've earned so much more if she went to one of the hospitals. "Mr. Bridges, that's so sweet of you. I'm going to place a few calls and see if I can get you in somewhere else."

She left the exam room and closed the door behind her. Now it would be that much longer before she got home. It was so difficult making these decisions, knowing that many times she was choosing between her son and the people in the community she cared for so much. But there was no question on this one. Mr. Bridges needed and deserved her help, and she'd do everything she could to make sure he got it.

———

"I'M SO SORRY," Emersyn said as she walked through the doorway of Melody's apartment. "Things have just been so crazy at the clinic, and I can't bear to send anyone away and tell them to come back tomorrow. Not when they already have so little." She scooped her son out of her friend's arms, happy to feel the comforting weight of his little body.

At almost a year old, Lucas was beginning to show so much personality. He could speak a few words, but he mostly preferred a long string of chatter that sounded like absolute music to Emersyn's ears. He let out a long string of it now as he gestured wildly with his arms.

"Are you telling me all about your day?" Emersyn asked with a smile, "or are you tattling on Aunt Melody?"

Melody tickled Lucas's back. "I'm pretty sure he teaches me more than I teach him. I keep trying to show him how to add and subtract, but he refuses to lift a finger and help me with my work." A book-keeper who worked from home, Melody was the perfect person to watch Lucas all day—especially because she was a shifter, too.

Lucas turned in Emersyn's arms and reached for Melody's glasses, causing his babysitter to quickly yank her head back. He'd already broken one pair out of sheer curiosity.

"I really am sorry," Emersyn repeated. "I hope he hasn't been keeping you from your work too much lately."

Melody shook her head, her curly auburn ponytail swaying along with it. "No, he's fine. It's nice to have some company while I'm stuck here by myself all day. He keeps me entertained." She held Lucas's hand to keep him from grabbing her glasses again and gave him a loud kiss on the cheek, eliciting a giggle from the little boy.

"So, has he...?" Emersyn trailed off, knowing Melody already understood what the question was.

Her friend shook her head. "Nothing yet. It'll come."

"I know." Emersyn felt a distinct mixture of relief and worry at the answer. Emersyn looked like a typical human, and most of the time, she felt like it. But the panther that lived inside her made her completely different. It usually only showed itself when her emotions got out of control, and with years of practice, she didn't need to bring it out very often at all. Lucas's father was a shifter, too, but not a panther. She anxiously awaited the day he'd first show signs of what animal hid inside him, but it had yet to come. She worried that perhaps some-thing had been incompatible between her and his father and that Lucas would never actually come to know his inner beast, but she worried even more that she'd miss the moment while she was at work.

"Here's his bag. He's running a bit low on diapers, but don't worry about restocking. I need to get out and go to the store tomorrow anyway, and I'll just pick some up."

Emersyn took the diaper back and shook her head. "No way. You already do so much for us."

Melody raised one dark eyebrow above the frame of her glasses. "It's fine, really. You're not going to have the chance to go. I've got to get some groceries, and Lucas always attracts lots of attention in the store. It'll be good for the little guy and me to get out together."

"Okay, but at least let me know how much you spend so I can reimburse you," Emersyn insisted.

She looked like she wanted to argue, but she knew better. "Fair enough. Oh, and Lucas already had his dinner. I've got some leftovers if you want to take some home."

"No, that's okay. I've got some things at my place. Thanks again, Mel. I'll see you in the morning." Emersyn, with her sweet baby boy in her arms, made the short walk back to her apartment. She'd been very fortunate in getting a place that had been recently remodeled in an older building. That meant the rent was relatively inexpensive, but the walls were freshly painted and the old wooden floors were sanded smooth. There was a certain comfort that came along with it, even though deep down, she knew it wasn't permanent. Nothing had been permanent in her life ever since she'd enlisted at eighteen, and her post-military life hadn't been much different.

She took the stairs, wanting the exercise even after a long day at work, but she was startled to find a figure leaning casually in the corner near her apartment door. Emersyn immediately took a step back, securing Lucas to her hip with one hand while she readied her claws with the other.

"Take it easy," the figure said as it stepped out of the shadows. "I mean, I know it's been a long time since we've seen each other, but it's just me."

"Leona?" Emersyn's jaw dropped as she took in the blonde hair and intelligent brown eyes that had once been more familiar than her own face. She grinned, running forward to hug her old friend. "Oh my god, I can't believe it's you!"

Leona hugged her back. "In the flesh! I was starting to think I'd shown up at the wrong place. I was going to send a search party after you."

"The clinic is pretty overwhelmed right now, and I couldn't just leave. If I had any idea you were coming, I'd have called and told you. Why are you here, anyway? And how's the leg?" She dug around in her pocket for her key.

"Oh, it's fine. I knew it would be." They stepped into the apartment and Leona did a little jig to prove her point. The two of them had served in the same unit as Green Berets, and Emersyn was the one who tended to Leona's leg when she'd accidentally stepped on an IED. The fact that she was a shifter meant she would heal far more quickly and efficiently than any typical human, but since none of the others could know her true identity, the injury had left her with a medical discharge. "I see you've been keeping yourself occupied since we last parted ways." Leona gestured at the bundle in Emersyn's arms.

Lucas had fallen asleep on the walk home, his eyelashes resting angelically on his chubby little cheeks. Emersyn's heart burst with love for him, as it did so many times each day. It was impossible not to be absolutely crazy about him. She laid him down gently in the playpen in the living room. "Yeah, you could say that. This is Lucas."

"So tell me everything. It's been so long since I've seen you, and we have a lot to catch up on." Leona parked herself on the couch, as comfortable as if she'd been coming over every Tuesday night for the last six months.

Emersyn caressed Lucas's forehead with her fingertips, watching him sleep. She had a feeling there was something more to this visit than a mere social call, but she knew Leona well. She was a forthright woman, one who didn't take shit from anybody. She also didn't beat around the bush unless she thought it was really necessary. The best bet was to be patient for the moment. "I thought I was in love," she finally said, straightening. "We got a new guy in our unit. He was hot, of course, and always ready to step into whatever action was going on. I thought I knew everything, and when I felt the click between us, I just knew it was meant to be. That pull was so strong, and I thought for sure we were mates." She crinkled her brows as the memory came up before her, still so clear. He'd been like a dream, a real-life action hero who'd swooped in. He was brave and incredibly capable, and yet he had just enough humility to keep him from being cocky. He'd been so perfect.

"I see," Leona replied, smiling. "And so now it's happily ever after?" She looked around as though she expected him to pop out from one of the other rooms.

"Not exactly. He had bigger plans and transferred to another unit. I haven't seen him since then." She crossed the room and sat next to her old comrade.

Leona was staring at her, openly shocked. "You mean he doesn't come around to see Lucas? Tell me he at least sends child support."

"No. He doesn't even know Lucas exists." Emersyn sighed. "Don't look at me like that. I know how you are. If you were in the situation, you'd march right up to whomever you'd been involved with and lay it right out for them. But I don't think that would work well for us. He had ambitions for his career. I knew that, and I'm not going to kid myself into thinking he would just automatically step up to be a good father. I didn't even know I was pregnant when he left, and I was stuck making plenty of decisions on my own from the very beginning."

It hadn't been easy. From the moment she suspected her pregnancy, Emersyn had been forced to figure out what she was going to do with the rest of her life. She'd wanted nothing more than to stay in the service. That had always been her life's dream. But an infant shifter was a mighty dangerous thing among humans. The government would separate her unless she could prove that she could take care of the child even when she was on duty. That only made sense, of course, but it wasn't as though Emersyn could leave her child with any typical daycare. What would happen when he shifted and a human saw? She'd been lucky enough to have a commanding officer who was a shifter, one who was able to push the right paperwork through and get her discharged without too much hassle.

Emersyn shook her head. "Trust me, it's easier to just do this on my own." That was what she'd told herself a hundred times, anyway. All those late nights and early mornings, all the laundry, the teething. It was so tough, and she often envied other mothers who had someone at their side. On the other side of that token, she knew that simply having a mate didn't mean he'd be willing to help.

"Wow." Leona let out a low whistle. "That's got to be really hard on you. I had no idea. And you're working full-time, too?"

"Of course." Emersyn smiled, thinking about Mr. Bridges and how grateful he'd been when she told him she'd gotten him into a shelter for the night. "It's tough, but it's not like I can just quit and stay home all day."

Leona swiped a hand across her forehead. "And I assume between Lucas and your job you're not dating anyone?" she asked with a smile.

Emersyn laughed. "Not by a long shot. I think I'm still messed up over thinking I'd found *the one,* then having the rug pulled out from under me. I just can't imagine what it'd be like to get involved with someone, and have Lucas get attached to him, only to have him up and leave again."

"You don't know that it would work like that," Leona countered gently. "Wow. There's so much that has happened. I'm not even sure what to say."

"How about telling me why you're actually here?" Emersyn challenged. She rose and went to the fridge, pulled out a bottle of pinot grigio and poured a glass for each of them. She certainly needed it after that long day at work, and she rarely got a chance to just sit and relax with an old friend. "Don't get me wrong. I love seeing you, and I'm so glad you're here, but I don't think you'd come all this way just to say hello. Where are you living these days, anyway?" It seemed that anyone who was used to the military life of moving from one place to another often ended up doing the same thing once they left the service.

"I'm in the D.C. area. My family is near there, and now my job is, too." Leona accepted the glass of wine, a slight smile curving her lips.

"What?" The smile was contagious, and even though Emersyn only had one sip of wine, she was already feeling a slight buzz. "If you've got something to tell me, then just do it."

"Okay. Have you heard of the SOS Force?"

Emersyn shook her head. "I don't think so. Is that a new show on Netflix or something?"

Leona laughed. "No, but sometimes it feels like one. It's a group of former special forces shifters who work to help settle issues for conclaves and clans. Obviously, people like us have problems that the human organizations can't help us with. That's when the Force steps in."

"And that's what you do?" Emersyn rested her glass on her knee.

"Yeah. The Force is supposed to be kept confidential to protect both us and other shifters, but of course, word starts to spread after a while. We started getting enough calls that we even had to start up a second unit in Dallas just because we weren't able to get out to everyone who needed us. It cut down on some of our travel expenses, too." She spoke casually, as though she was working with a small retailer that had managed to open a second shop on the other side of town.

"Leona, that's so impressive! I mean, I'm not surprised. You were always one of the best soldiers I ever worked with. But it's certainly exciting. You must love it!" Emersyn could easily see her old friend fitting into that role. Leona was fierce and fearless.

"And you really haven't heard of us?" the lioness questioned.

Emersyn shook her head. "I've been pretty involved between Lucas and work. If it weren't for the fact that I'm constantly waiting to see what animal he might shift into, I don't even know that I'd remember I'm a shifter." As she thought about it, she reached inside for her panther. It was quiet and restful, certainly there, but not so prevalent as to be a force she had to battle with.

Savoring her wine, Leona gave her friend a meaningful glance. "How would you like to get back in touch with that side of yourself?"

"What exactly are you suggesting?"

Leona set her glass on the coffee table and turned fully toward Emersyn. "The Force is starting up a third unit right here in Los Angeles. We've taken note of a lot of issues going on around here. Some of them are between different clans and conclaves, which is pretty normal, but now we've gotten word about some biker gangs of shifters, too. It could be a really big deal. Sure, we could just swoop in and try to fix it quickly, but we have our doubts as to how well that would actually keep the situation quelled. The best decision is to have a permanent group in this area to serve the massive shifter population here."

Now Emersyn was starting to understand. "I see. So you've been chosen to come out here and get it all set up. I want you to know you're more than welcome to stay here. I know something like the Force probably has enough money to put you up in some nice hotel, and the only thing I've really got is a couch, but it's all yours if you want it."

Leona shook her head. "I'm not about to put you out. And you're not wrong. I'm here to help get the L.A. unit going, but I'm also here to recruit you."

"What?" The smile faded from Emersyn's face, replaced by shock. "Me? Why the hell would you want me?"

"Why *wouldn't* we?" Leona countered with a laugh. "You're one of the best doctors I know, and we definitely need a med sergeant on this team. You know as well as I do that shifters just aren't the same inside as humans. If something happens to one of the team members, we need a trained medic to get them taken care of. The Dallas unit is lucky enough to have an entire shifter hospital at their disposal, but we need to make sure our team members are taken care of, no matter what happens."

"A shifter hospital?" This was all so overwhelming. "I really must be out of touch. I had no idea."

"So, what do you say?" Leona pressed.

Emersyn let out a breath through pursed lips and stood up. She paced across the room to the sliding glass doors that led onto a small patio, the tiny bit of outdoor space they were afforded at this apartment. She stared through the glass over the city. "This is big, Leona. I don't even know what to say."

"Just say yes," Leona urged. "You'd be great, which is exactly why I'm recruiting you for it. I was asked if I had any personal recommendations for the L.A. unit, and you were the first person who came to mind. You'd have all the adventure you could possibly want, and you'd get plenty of opportunities to remember who you really are."

Who I really am. The phrase rattled around in Emersyn's head. She wasn't even sure what that meant anymore. "I'm flattered, and it's certainly tempting. But I don't know if I can just up and leave my job. There are so many people who need me at the clinic. I'm not some rich doctor who sits back and collects insurance payments. I'm serving people who really need me, who have little or no coverage, who are afraid to go to the big hospitals because they don't want to be turned down or treated differently. It's not glamorous, but I don't think I can bear to just turn away from it."

"You don't have to." Leona joined her at the glass door, putting a gentle hand on her shoulder. "The Force can take up a lot of time. You might get sent out on a mission that takes a week or so, and in that case, you'd certainly need someone else who can work at the clinic in your place. But there are several of us who've kept our day jobs. We've got a rancher, a construction company owner, a VA doctor, you name it."

"Sounds like the shifter version of The Village People," Emersyn joked. Her eyes burned, tears threatening, and she blinked quickly. There was no need to get so emotional over this, but she felt her panther perking up and taking note. She was stirring inside, and she didn't know how to stop it.

"Yes," Leona laughed. "We've even got the head of a major tech corporation."

"Yeah? Who's that?"

"Hudson Taylor. My mate."

"What?" Emersyn turned to her friend, gripping her shoulders as her grin expanded. "Are you shitting me? Your mate is Hudson Taylor? *The* Hudson Taylor?"

"Yes, and he still spends just as much time tinkering around with all his geeky devices as he did before he joined the Force. He's in town right now, actually, because he's helping to set up the new headquarters building. You'll get to meet him, whether you decide to join or not."

Emersyn sighed. She looked over her shoulder at Lucas, still sleeping peacefully in his playpen. "I'd love the chance, Leona. I can't tell you how much I appreciate you thinking of me. You're right; I could make the clinic still work out. But the one thing I don't think I can manage is Lucas. I couldn't stay in the Army because of my pregnancy. I'm only able to work at the clinic because I have a good friend who works from home who watches him for me. I couldn't possibly ask her to watch him while I go frolicking off on missions, too. It wouldn't be fair."

Leona tapped her chin, the gleam in her eyes showing she was thinking. "Where does this friend of yours live?"

"In an apartment building just down the street. Why?"

"And you say she works from home? What does she do?"

"Melody's a bookkeeper. She's contracted with several companies."

"Uh huh. I see. So she's paying rent, and then you have to go back and forth to drop Lucas off and pick him up at the end of the day."

"Of course." Emersyn put a hand on her hip, finally getting impatient. "Let me in on what you're thinking. You're driving me nuts."

Leona turned, resting her back against the wall next to the door and tipping her head back. "Garrison—you'll meet him soon enough —set up the Dallas headquarters to include enough apartments for all the members. Some still choose to live in their current homes, but it's certainly convenient to have your work right down the hall. I'll have to check with him to see how big of a space he's found, but it seems to me like a built-in daycare service could be a really good thing for the Force."

Emersyn was already reeling from finding out about the Force and the fact that Leona wanted her for it, but now her head felt like it was going to explode. "You want to move Melody into the headquarters building? I don't know that she'd want to. I mean, she loves Lucas, but she still loves her bookkeeping, too. That's a big ask."

Leona shook her hand in the air. "That's just it. I'm not saying she'd have to quit what she's doing right now. I'm just saying she could do it in a different place. She can watch Lucas and do her work, but everything would be centralized. Melody would certainly have some incentive in that she wouldn't have to pay rent, and I know that's not cheap around here."

Leona let out a deep breath. This was all too good to be true. "All right, I'll talk to her. And I'll think about it myself."

The two women talked for a while longer, turning the conversation to catching up on old times. When Leona finally left, the apartment felt incredibly quiet and empty. Emersyn scooped a sleeping Lucas out of his playpen, smoothing down his hair and taking him into his room to change him into his pajamas. She was lucky that he'd always been such a good sleeper, and he only stirred mildly as she got him ready for bed.

Instead of laying him down in his crib, Emersyn stood in the middle of the room and just held him. There was something so comforting and sweet about his warmth and his weight. Moonlight invaded the room, casting a blue light over the nursery that she'd built so carefully for him there. "It's not easy being a mommy," she murmured. "Did you know that? I've always had to worry about whether or not I'm making the right decisions for you. From not saying anything to your father, to leaving the service, to taking the job at the clinic. It's already not fair to constantly have to make the choice between being here with you and the wellbeing of others. Now I have to choose again. Do I take up this opportunity of a lifetime, knowing you'll have a chance to grow up among other shifters and see just what your mother is capable of? Or do I stay here and try to raise you with the most normal life possible so that you can blend in with the humans more easily? I really don't know."

Regretfully, she laid him down in his crib, smoothing the sheets around him and planting a gentle kiss on his forehead. "I'll talk to Aunt Melody tomorrow," she whispered. "That'll help me figure all this out. I hope." She left the room, softly closing the door.

After a quick shower, she lay awake in bed. Emersyn felt as though she'd lived through several different lifetimes. Each stage of her life had been so different and separate from the last that sometimes it was hard to tie them all together and claim them as her own. Now, she was considering stepping into a whole new life, one she didn't know if she could handle.

3

Gabe sighed as he stepped out of the hotel shower, making a mental note to ask Garrison about the shower heads at the new headquarters. This was a very nice hotel, but someone had still gone cheap on the plumbing. He wanted to feel like he was washing up in a wild stream under a waterfall in the middle of nowhere, not standing under a leaky roof. Drying off and wrapping the towel around his hips, he stepped out of the bathroom to get dressed.

His phone rang irritably from the bedside, and Gabe glanced at the caller ID and answered. "Hey, Mom."

"Well, hey to you, too! I haven't heard anything from you in days. Are you all right?"

Gabe pulled a face. He'd seen the missed calls, and he'd genuinely meant to return them. "I'm sorry, Mom. I've just been really busy."

"Busy or not, the least you could do is send me a text to let me know you're alive. I thought now that you were out of the service I wouldn't have to worry about that, but I think you're worse than ever."

He sat down on the side of the bed and ran a hand through his damp hair. "I'm still getting used to the routine of civilian life. Is everything okay, though?" As busy as Gabe was, he always worried about his family. His mom and sisters were everything to him. They were the reasons for almost all of his decisions in life, and his mother's urgency at not being able to get a hold of him made him worry a little more.

"Oh, yes. We're fine. Nothing's really changed since you saw us last month. The only real difference is that Hope says she might let her rental agreement run out and move in with Rob. You know I'd much prefer they just get married, but she insists that's how people do things these days."

Gabe had to smile. Hope was his youngest sister, but she was the fiercest of the family. She was strong and independent, and there was no 'might' about her moving in with Rob. Their mother just didn't want to admit it. "I'm sure she'll be fine, Mom."

"Yes, that's what Hannah keeps telling me, too. Of course, she hasn't found anyone yet. She's too focused on her career. I admire that for what it is, but I'd like to think she'll be taken care of, no matter what happens."

Glancing at the clock, Gabe put the phone on speaker and started getting dressed. He didn't want to be late getting over to the new building to meet up with Hudson and Garrison. That wasn't the impression he wanted to make this early on in his new career. "She'll be fine. We'll all be fine. We've got each other, and that's never going to change, no matter who gets married or where we live." It was ironic that a woman whose husband had left her and never returned was so bent on her children finding love, but Gabe understood. She didn't want them to suffer through what she was most afraid of herself: being alone.

"I know. I'd like to take the credit and say I raised you all right, but I think you're just good-natured kids to start with. Anyway, the reason I was trying to get a hold of you is that I think I've found a job for you."

Gabe pulled his shirt down over his head and stared at his phone on the nightstand, sure he hadn't heard her right. "What?"

"I've found the perfect job for you. I know you were feeling a bit restless after you were discharged, and I know how much your career meant to you. I was talking to Glenda over at the bank the other day. Her husband works at that factory that makes electronics, and she told me they were hiring. People usually start out in general labor, but she thought with your experience in the Army, you might be able to get a higher position. It would at least be something you could work up to. The hours are good, they offer benefits, and it's right here in town."

He shook his head as he bent to put on his shoes. "Mom, that's really nice of you, but I don't need you to find me a job."

"You need to do something. I've seen those documentaries about veterans who end up just wandering around the country, and you deserve better than that. Besides, if you take this job, it means you can live right here with me. There's more than enough room now that your sisters have moved out." Mrs. Vinson's bird chirped happily in the background.

Gabe knew she meant well, and she was genuinely excited about the idea of one of her children coming back home to live with her. Most parents wouldn't like that idea, but his mother had never been like most parents. Gabe had no doubt she'd let him stay there, rent-free, indefinitely. Fortunately, he had another offer that was also rent-free. "Look, that sounds like it could be a nice job, but I've got a lead on something out here in Los Angeles that could be perfect for me."

There was a long pause on the other end of the phone. "Los Angeles?"

Oh, boy. This was going to be fun. "Mom, don't start."

"I'm just worried, Gabriel. I've heard about some of the trouble they've been having out there. I've tried to tell myself it's just a rumor, but that's hard to do when I know you're out there. Are you at least in a safe place? Tell me you aren't trying to get in with the police or something?"

"I'm safe, and I'm not joining the police force. It's something I'm excited about, but I can't tell you about it yet. Not until it's all official." Actually, Gabe knew he might never be able to tell his mother the complete truth about his new job. Vance had been very specific when he said they weren't supposed to talk about it. The rumors could and would spread, but as long as the information wasn't coming from their lips, it should stay well enough contained.

"Something else with the military, then?"

He flung his hand in the air. There wasn't a better answer. He didn't want to lie to his mother, but sometimes these things just happened. "Yeah."

"Hmm. Well, that doesn't make me feel much better. You know I just about had a heart attack when you had your incident."

"I know, Mom." It'd come as quite the surprise to Gabe, too. He and another comrade had been driving back onto the base, and they were supposed to be in safe territory. The two of them were talking and laughing, making plans for an upcoming leave of absence. But the Humvee lifted off the ground, metal and fire exploding all around them. Gabe had been driving at the time, as usual. His hands had gripped the wheel, an effort to hold onto something, and when the vehicle slammed back down onto the dusty earth, he still had his foot on the gas pedal. They'd shot off, heading into the gates on all four flats while pieces of the truck disintegrated around them. It wasn't until he'd gotten safely back onto the base that he'd even realized he was injured.

The docs out there hadn't exactly been kind or thorough. Gabe had heard rumors they'd been sent to that particular part of Iraq as a punishment more than anything, and after the treatment he'd gotten from them, he could see why. They'd done a quick x-ray before poking at the holes in his flesh, and then they'd pronounced with no compassion that the twisted bits of metal would be stuck inside his body forever. They were human doctors with no awareness of shifters and how they healed, and so he'd been left with medical discharge papers instead of a career.

"You sure about this job?" she pressed.

He checked the clock again. It was time to go. He had a full day of work ahead of him, and his mother's worries couldn't hold him up forever. Besides, he knew she wouldn't stop worrying, even if he moved back in with her. "Yeah. I'm sure. I've got to go, but I promise I'll give you a call again soon."

"Okay. I love you, Gabe."

"Love you, too, Mom." He hung up and headed downstairs, feeling like an asshole for making her worry. Maybe he could explain it all at some point; she would know that he not only had a chance at a great job, but one that was exactly what he wanted to do. The Delta Force had trained him for this, and all those years with the Army would've been a waste if he'd just signed up for some dull factory job. He'd never be happy with a gig like that.

He managed to pull up to the house right behind Hudson and Garrison, once again excited about this huge house that would become his new office. "Looks like the realtors move quickly around here," he remarked as he got out.

Garrison was swinging the keys in his fingers, grinning. "They do when they know there's a hefty commission on the line, and the housing out here sure isn't cheap. I don't think it hurt that the owners had already moved off to some island and were ready to unload this place. They even left most of the furniture."

As they stepped inside, Gabe couldn't help but think about how lucky he was. He'd been in the Army his entire adult life, and even the nicest housing didn't compare to this. There would be some dangerous missions ahead, from what everyone had told him, but in between it was going to be like a vacation. "Are the others coming soon?"

"Any minute," Hudson confirmed. "I should also be getting a good-sized shipment of new equipment to be installed from my corporate office. We've got a lot of work ahead of us, but I'd like to have our first official briefing by tomorrow."

"We could turn this dining room into a conference area," Gabe suggested. The enormous table that the previous owners had left behind would more than accommodate them.

Garrison nodded approvingly. "That works for me. There are plenty of outlets for all of Hudson's gadgets. Lots of room on the walls, too. He likes his big screens."

Hudson punched him on the arm. "So does everyone else, thank you very much. I'm just doing my best to make sure all three units can teleconference easily."

The three men began moving furniture around and making decisions about what to do with each room, and Gabe was busy holding a large screen up against the wall while Hudson fixed it in place when the rest of the recruits arrived an hour later.

"Come on into the living room and we'll all get to know each other a bit," Garrison offered.

Gabe followed him. It was a beautiful day, and the walls on the back of the house had been retracted to show off the pool and let in the sunshine. Four recruits filed into the room, but his eyes landed only on one of them. She was tall and beautiful, her dark hair cascading in a straight line down her back that was only broken by the curve of her shoulder. Her wide eyes scanned the room before landing on him, and he felt his entire body shudder in delight.

Emersyn. He blinked, sure that this was just a vision from another lifetime that had come back to haunt him. She couldn't possibly be there, yet she stood before him in the flesh. His bear was going wild, thrashing and clawing, urging him to stop fighting against the pull he felt even from across the other side of the room. It was *her,* damn it, and there was no reason not to leap right over the coffee table and wrap his arms around her.

But if she felt it, she gave no indication. She set down her medical bag and took the seat on the sofa that Garrison offered to her, calm, cool, and collected.

Gabe swallowed. Did she remember? Was it even possible to forget such a thing? Lovers came and went for young soldiers, full of life and the desire to live it despite not knowing what might happen the next day or even the next hour. Emersyn, though, was completely different. His body intrinsically remembered the way they'd felt together, the warmth of her skin against his, the curve of her hip in his hand, the way her back arched just like the cat she held inside her when he rubbed her the right way.

"For those of you who haven't met me yet, I'm Garrison. This is Hudson. Both of us are with the D.C. unit. I'll let you introduce yourselves."

Garrison's voice jarred Gabe back into the present instead of a sandy tent somewhere in the desert with Emersyn. With few other options, he sat down. He'd have to wait to catch up with Emersyn later. He barely listened as the others introduced themselves.

The first one to stand was a man with mahogany skin and jet-black hair. "My name is Amar. Garrison and his mate found me in their search for other dragon shifters in the world. Like the rest of you, I served in the Special Forces." He gave a brotherly smile to Garrison.

This part did catch Gabe's attention somewhat. He hadn't realized there were still dragons in the world, and he'd even wondered at times if their existence was purely a myth. That explained what was a little different about Garrison, though, and it couldn't hurt to have Amar as part of their unit. Dragons had to be incredibly powerful.

The next was Raul, a veteran Green Beret and communications sergeant, who had already started forming a bond with Hudson over all the gadgetry being brought into the house. Jude was next, and though Gabe recognized the bear inside him, his focus was still entirely on Emersyn.

She rose, just as graceful and wary as the panther inside her. Gabe knew he was staring, his eyes raking over her body, but he couldn't help himself. How long had it been since he'd seen her? It felt like forever, but she was no worse for the wear. His heart thundered as he realized the two of them might be living under the same roof from now on.

"I'm Emersyn Cruz. I was a medical sergeant with the Green Berets, and I currently work at a low-income clinic in the heart of the city. Garrison has informed me that I'll be handling most of the medical issues that arise here, including medical exams for baseline data. I'd like to make sure we get those taken care of as quickly as possible."

"Yes. I've got a room all set up for you whenever you're ready," Garrison replied. The smile he gave her was simply a courteous one, but Gabe felt a flash of jealousy ripple through his body.

He had only a moment to suppress it before he realized it was his turn. His tongue was thick in his mouth, his throat dry from finally seeing Emersyn again. "My name's Gabe. Delta Force. Medically discharged." He didn't even bother standing. It was funny how something as seemingly simple as introducing himself to a small crowd was more difficult than infiltrating enemy territory and kicking down doors that could lead to unknown danger.

The two senior Force members either didn't notice the tension in the room or they chose to ignore it for the moment. After all, this was the first time the five of them were meeting each other, and they couldn't be expected to get along like old comrades right away.

"As some of you may already know," Hudson said, "each Force unit acts like its own clan. For the most part, you'll live together, work together, and eat together. You'll have your own lives of course, and some of you may keep the jobs you currently have, but being in the Force is much more of a commitment than simply being roommates. In this clan-like model, you must have an Alpha. Since this isn't like a clan in the sense that there is no innate leader who was born into the position, we've decided that because he held the highest rank in the service, it should be Amar."

The man bowed his head. "Thank you. I'm honored."

Garrison continued the orientation. "Another element that echoes clan life is the bond that links you telepathically. Most of you come from different species, but there's an ancient form of dragon magic that can connect you despite this. We have to wait for the correct moon phase, but we'll perform this rite as soon as possible."

Gabe's throat tightened a little further. At one point, he'd felt Emersyn in his mind. This unique shifter ability could only happen amongst those who were related or who were bonded mates, and even then, it didn't work unless they were in their animal forms. There'd been few times when he and Emersyn had the chance to shift, but he still knew what it felt like to have her inside him in that most intimate of ways.

"There's a lot of work that still needs to be done on this building, but we'll have the first official briefing tomorrow morning at eight o'clock. For the moment, feel free to explore the house and decide which set of rooms you'd like for yourselves. I think you're all mature enough to handle that without having to draw straws," Hudson joked. "Afterwards, you can meet with Dr. Cruz for your exam."

Emersyn rose and followed Garrison to the east wing of the house, presumably toward the place he'd set up for her as a makeshift medical office. Again, Gabe felt that pang of jealousy. Garrison was a good-looking guy, and even though there had been some mention that the man had a mate, Gabe couldn't help but wonder just what the two of them might be talking about behind closed doors.

He shook his head at how ridiculous he was being and made his way through the house to claim a room. It didn't matter too much to him, though. He'd already seen the whole place when they'd come to check it out with the realtor, and all the rooms were equally nice. The only difference was the master bedroom, which of course he left for Amar. The man might have only been his Alpha for a few minutes, but Gabe understood the hierarchy of shifters just as anyone else did. He retrieved his bag from the car and dropped it in a random room, knowing that whichever one he picked would be fine.

Back downstairs, Emersyn and Garrison emerged from the medical exam room. No one else was there waiting, and so she waved him inside. "Might as well get started."

His bear hadn't calmed down from the moment he'd seen her walk in, and it was going absolutely crazy now. He barely registered the exam table Garrison had brought in or the stainless-steel cabinet where she kept her supplies. Gabe focused only on her back, watching the way she moved as she readied herself for the exam. "It's been a long time," he began.

She nodded. "It has."

"Of all the places we could've met up again, I didn't think it would be here. How did you end up on the Force, anyway?" There was so much more he wanted to say, and yet his brain was limiting him to the simplest of small talk.

Emersyn turned to him, her eyes cool as she swiped a thermometer gently across his forehead and checked the readout. "I served with one of the D.C. members, Hudson's mate. She recommended me."

"Why isn't she here today?"

"She had some other errands to run. Could you sit down?" Emersyn gestured toward the exam table.

He did as he was told. "I'm not surprised to hear you're running a clinic. You always had a soft touch." Gabe smiled at her as she pressed a stethoscope to his chest. He had no doubt she could feel the manic vibrations happening inside his ribcage at that moment, but he knew she wouldn't have forgotten what the two of them had shared together.

Emersyn didn't respond at first, and so he focused on her dark, glistening hair and the wide almond shape of her eyes as she listened to his heartbeat. After a minute, she flicked the earpieces down around her neck and turned around to make a note on her computer. "It's not a glorious job, but it's satisfying. I'm helping people, which is what I've always wanted to do."

"Emersyn." Her name tingled on his tongue. It had been so long since he'd said it. When she turned to him, he dared to reach out and take her hand, his bear demanding to make contact with his mate. "How crazy is this that we should end up here together, living in the same house, doing the same job? It's like fate was doing everything possible to bring us back together. I mean, it was worth getting blown up for."

"What?" Her eyes widened in alarm.

He lifted the hem of his shirt to show her the angry lines that were all that was left of his injury. After all, it wasn't as though she hadn't seen his chest before. Gabe scraped his teeth against his lower lip as Emersyn delicately traced her fingers over the scars. "Shrapnel? Did they at least get it out?"

"No, it's all still there. I'll never get through the airport without a hassle again. But let's not worry about that right now." He put his shirt down, his ursine half wanting to focus more on what was happening now—or could happen in the near future—than what had happened in the past.

Her face was touched with sadness. "Is that why you were discharged?"

"Yeah. Just recently, actually." She was beautiful as ever, and it was hard to keep his mind on any one thing for long. His bear was getting crazy enough now that it was no longer satisfied with being kept inside. He could feel the bristly brown hairs threatening to burst through his skin. To stave the beast off, he reached out and put his arms around Emersyn's waist. "Come on, Em. You can't ignore this forever. We were good together, weren't we?"

Her face was serious as she looked down at him, her back stiff, but then she smiled. "Yeah, we were." Emersyn's cheeks reddened, indicating she remembered some of those good times.

"And now here we are. No point in making ourselves suffer, right?" He tightened his grip on her waist, drawing her closer. Even with all their clothes on and a house full of people, Gabe could feel that pull. She was intoxicating; he couldn't resist her if he tried. "We couldn't expect things to work out while we were both still enlisted. Things were messy, and there was too much to deal with. But now..." Their lips were so close, he could feel the heat radiating from her body.

"Things *were* messy," she agreed as she pulled back, breaking his embrace. "You fucking *left*, Gabe."

Heat washed over his temples, but it was no longer the heat of desire. It was the hot panic of anxiety as she pulled away from him, an unexpected side effect that he didn't enjoy. Gabe remembered having a very familiar feeling when he'd made the decision to leave Emersyn behind and move on to the Delta Force. Something about it had felt incredibly wrong, but the paycheck that dangled within his grasp would go a long way toward making sure his sisters had college tuition without joining the service and his mother wouldn't have to get a second or third job to put food on the table. He pressed his lips together as he recalled the cavalier way he'd announced his departure. "A lot's changed since then."

"Yes, you're right." She turned slightly away from him, her eyes narrowing as she looked out the window. Emersyn pulled in a slow, deep breath. "More than you know, actually. Gabe, you and I have a son."

4

___

"WHAT DID YOU SAY?"

Emersyn's panther growled, swirling inside her. She hadn't meant to tell him, or at least not like that. She was no longer in control of her body or anything else, and she hadn't been from the moment she'd walked into that damn house. At first, she hadn't even known what was causing it and had written it off as nerves. After all, it'd been a long time since she'd started a new job, and the elite status of everyone else on the Force was certainly something to make her feel self-conscious.

But no. As soon as Gabe walked into the living room, she'd known it was him.

She'd spent the last year focusing on Lucas and her career so intently, her panther practically never made its presence known. But it was wild now, demanding answers.

Demanding *Gabe*.

She angrily tamped it back down again. It was unfair enough to feel the fated pull toward someone who'd already shown her he wouldn't be a reliable mate, but it was even worse to know that despite everything, she still responded to his presence in the same way.

"We have a son together." She folded her arms across her chest and refused to look at him. She didn't want to see the fear and anger that she knew she'd find in his eyes. "I found out I was pregnant after you left, and I was fortunate enough to arrange a discharge for myself.

I couldn't exactly stay in with a child on the way who could turn out to be either a panther or a bear. We all know how that would turn out."

"And you didn't even tell me?" His voice was a harsh whisper.

Emersyn flicked a hand in the air. "How could I? You'd already made it quite clear that you had bigger plans than sticking around with me, no matter what we felt for each other. The last thing I was going to do was track your sorry ass down just to beg you for child support."

"You wouldn't have... You could've... I'd have... Ugh!" His splutterings ended in a cry of frustration. "Emersyn, how could you seriously think that? I would've done so many things differently if I knew! And of course I would've helped with finances. I'm not a fucking deadbeat. You really think I'd be cool with just leaving you to raise our kid on your own?" He choked out the last words as he launched himself off the exam table and paced the room.

"It's easy to say that now. You had big ambitions, Gabe. We both knew that. It's not as though this really changes anything."

"Of course it does!" He stormed to her side of the room and spun her around to face him, his hands gripping her arms. "I can't believe you would think otherwise. This changes absolutely *everything*."

She shook her head, furious with herself for even saying anything. Emersyn had left Lucas with Melody for the day while she arranged her living situation, but he would be coming to headquarters soon enough. She'd been sure for just a moment that Gabe would know as soon as he saw those sweet little cheeks, but now that she'd opened her big mouth, she wished she'd just kept it shut and taken her chances. "No. Nothing has to change. You can keep living your life the way you want to."

"That's not right," Gabe growled. His grizzly was enraged, yet he was careful not to grip her too tightly.

"I don't need you," she asserted, pushing her chin into the air. "I've been doing just fine on my own, and the last thing I want is for you to come swooping in like you're some fucking hero, determined to save a day that doesn't need saving!" Emersyn twisted away from him. Only a few minutes earlier, she'd been tempted to fall right into his arms and relive those old trysts he'd alluded to. Now, she wished she could walk away and never see him again.

His jaw was tight, his blue eyes glittering. "Whatever you might think, Emersyn, I *will* be a part of my son's life. What's his name? Where is he? I want to meet him."

Emersyn sagged against the counter, feeling defeated. She'd messed everything up. She didn't want to be one of those women that parades men in and out of their children's lives. There was no doubt in her mind that Gabe would leave again, and that meant she'd put her son in the same position of heartache she'd been living in. She covered her face with her hands and closed her eyes, envisioning her sweet little boy. "His name is Lucas. He's at my friend's house for the day, but I'll be picking him up soon and he'll be staying here with me."

"Good. Let me know as soon as he arrives." The door whisked open and slammed shut as Gabe left.

Emersyn clenched her teeth and lifted her head, determined not to cry or show any other sign that he'd gotten to her. After all, she had other patients to see.

———

THE NEXT MORNING was even more tense than the initial meeting in the living room. Emersyn had discovered when she'd gone to bed that night that Gabe had chosen the bedroom suite right next to hers. Whether it was on purpose or not, she had no idea, but she hated it all the same. It was bad enough to be under the same roof, but sharing a wall was that much worse. Fortunately, Melody and Lucas had arrived late enough that the baby was already asleep, and that had put off the meeting she was dreading for just a little bit longer.

She'd hardly slept at all, which made it easy to roll out of bed at six. It was far earlier than it needed to be, considering she'd taken a few days off at the clinic and didn't have to commute to make the SOS Force meeting, but she figured it decreased her chances of running into Gabe in the kitchen.

"Holy cow," she whispered to Lucas, who rubbed his eyes sleepily. "This place is incredible. The Force must have a lot of money backing them." She took in all the sleek lines of the modern cabinets, the high-end appliances, and the retractable walls that could make this room an outdoor space as well. It was like nothing she'd ever seen before.

"They certainly do."

The voice behind her made her jump. Emersyn pressed her free hand to her chest as she turned to find Melody standing in the doorway, still in her pajamas. "I don't need any coffee now. I'm awake," she joked.

"Sorry about that." Melody ruffled Lucas's tuft of dark hair on her way to the coffee pot. "You don't look like you slept any better than I did. I take it things are still a little strained between you and Gabe?"

Emersyn had told her friend all the gory details when she'd arrived, and it'd felt so good to have someone she knew and trusted at her side. She made a mental note to thank Leona profusely for setting this up. "I don't really know, since I'm doing my best not to talk to him right now. Why didn't you sleep?"

"It's just a new place. I've been sleeping on that ratty old mattress and flat pillow for years, simply because I didn't want to spend the money on something new. I was so comfortable last night that I didn't know how to handle it." She reached for another mug. "Want some?"

"Yes, thank you." Emersyn settled Lucas into the highchair she'd brought along, which contrasted distinctly with the rest of the kitchen. "What did you mean a minute ago? I said the Force must have a lot of money, and you said they do."

"It can't come as any surprise, really. There are some very prominent people backing this organization. Hudson, for one. A quick search online shows that he's worth millions, and we know he pumps a lot into the Force." Melody opened several cabinets. "I might have to start doing some of the grocery shopping myself. I could really use some Pop-Tarts."

"And?" Emersyn had known Melody long enough to know there was more to the story than she'd already told.

"And," Melody said with a sly smile as she opened a box of doughnuts, "I spent some time talking with Hudson and Garrison. Initially, we were just talking about what my role would be here when it came to taking care of Lucas or any other children who might happen to be here. The conversation turned to what I actually do for a living, and they were much more interested in that. The Force members are a bit busy with their jobs and their missions, and they didn't have anyone to take care of the books."

Emersyn smiled despite her rough night. "Are you telling me you're part of the Force now, too?"

Mel lifted a shoulder. "I'd say I'm more like Force-adjacent. I'm certainly not on the same level as the rest of you. I just crunch the numbers in my spare time."

"That's so exciting!" Emersyn wrapped her arms around her friend. "I can't tell you how happy I am about all this. I've been questioning a lot of my decisions lately—both current and past—but having you here is going to be great. I love that I won't have to worry about Lucas no matter which job I'm working, and he adores you." Finding some cottage cheese and fruit, she began making breakfast for herself and her son.

"I adore him, too," she said in a singsong voice as she tickled his cheek. "And seriously, this house is amazing. There are six adults living here, plus three more staying temporarily, and yet it feels like we're the only ones. I don't think I've ever been in a place this big." She pointed a finger at Emersyn. "You better not quit now, because I can't possibly go back to that dinky apartment."

Emersyn laughed, but her joy faded as she thought of the possible reasons she just might leave. "That all depends on how things go with Gabe."

"I know. Well, I'm going to grab a shower while I can. Just bring Lucas by when you're ready." She polished off her doughnut and carried her coffee mug out of the kitchen.

A little while later, Emersyn held her shoulders stiff and straight as she walked into the dining room that was now a conference room. The others were filtering in as well, and she made sure she took a seat in between Raul and Jude so that Gabe couldn't possibly sit next to her. She imagined he wouldn't want to, considering how angry he'd been the night before, but he did manage to take up the spot directly across from her.

"Good morning, everyone. For those of you who didn't get a chance to meet her before, this is Leona." Hudson gestured to his side. "She's my mate and a vital part of the D.C. unit."

Leona gave a little wave to everyone and a wink to Emersyn.

"I appreciate how quickly this has all come together," he contin-ued, "and it's particularly important since we already have business to take care of here in Los Angeles. As you all know by now, there are great numbers of shifters living in the area. It makes sense, considering how dense the general population is here, anyway. We've started a registry system in Dallas to help us keep track of the actual shifter numbers. I suggest we get one up and running for this area as soon as possible, too. It helps not only determine what shifters are where, but who belongs to what clan and which conclave's jurisdiction. We're dealing with massive numbers compared to what we've had in the past."

Jude raised a finger in the air. "I'd be glad to head that up. I've done some similar things in the past."

"Great," Hudson said with an appreciative nod. "It could come in handy with the first mission."

"We're looking at an interesting development when it comes to clan activity," Garrison offered. "Many clans—or prides, or packs, as the case may be—operate pretty independently, as you know. It appears that some of them in this area aren't just extended family units that live and work together, but actual biker gangs. I don't want to sound biased against those types of organizations. I know some of them do some very charitable work in the world. But the ones we're seeing around here are getting violent. They're fighting with each other over turf, killing each other for status, and then exacting revenge on those who they feel wronged them. This is a problem for human gangs, but I'm sure you can imagine how much more complicated it gets when we start talking about shifters. They're bigger, stronger, and they have closer family ties and loyalties."

Emersyn listened, focusing the entirety of her attention on Garrison and Hudson. This was something completely unlike anything she'd ever done before, and she wasn't sure that she really qualified for these types of missions unless someone got hurt and needed medical attention. The major upside of it, though, was that it gave her something to think about besides Gabe.

Hudson once again took over the briefing, pulling up a map on one of the large screens. "These gangs are loosely associated with either the San Bernardino or the San Fernando Valley conclaves, or at least they should be according to where their clubhouses are located. From what we can tell, neither conclave really claims them under their jurisdiction. My guess is that's because they're causing so much trouble. What we need to do is get in there and see what's actually going on."

Garrison nodded. "Ideally, we'd wait until we have a chance to make sure you all have the telepathic link that lets you communicate with each other in shifter form. Hudson has some excellent comm devices, and he can go over those in detail with you later, but as I mentioned earlier, the moon isn't in the right phase. That means the initial part of the mission may be a little more dangerous than it would be otherwise."

Emersyn let out a long breath at the mention of that telepathic link again. It was something she hadn't anticipated. Even if she had known, she wouldn't have thought it was an issue because she never imagined that Gabe would've been part of the Force. But they were both there, and the rest of the members would soon enough be inside their heads. She cleared her throat.

The dragon raised an eyebrow. "Are you concerned about the safety of this procedure, Doctor?"

"No." She hadn't known Garrison for very long, but he was an easy man to trust. "I just thought I should mention that Gabe and I have already experienced that link."

The conference room fell silent. Even Leona stared at her, stunned by the revelation.

Hudson cleared his throat. "Well, the two of you certainly aren't from the same clan..."

Emersyn made a point not to look at Gabe. "No. We met before, in the service." There was so much more to that story. They weren't just good friends, and they weren't even two soldiers who happened to have a fling. It was so much more than that, but this wasn't the time or the place to go into it.

The D.C. members glanced at each other, and Garrison tapped his finger on the table. "I didn't realize that the two of you were... ahem. Anyway, we started out having a strict rule that Force members couldn't be involved with each other that way. That went out the window with Hudson and Leona, of course, so our concern right now would be that it doesn't become a problem."

She could feel Gabe's glare on her skin, but she kept her focus at the head of the table. "It won't be," she assured them. "It's been a long time, and I don't even know for sure that it's still there."

"I see."

Leona leaned forward, resting her elbows on the table. "I don't know how the two of you feel about this, but perhaps this would be a good time to test it. The first part of the plan is to send someone out to speak to each conclave. We don't need everyone to go, but if there's a chance the two of you still have the link, then it's a bit of a backup in case things go sideways."

There was no avoiding it now. Emersyn turned her head and met Gabe's stare head-on. He was hard as stone. Even in their human forms, when they shouldn't have been able to communicate with each other any more than anyone else, she could read his feelings. He was furious. Embarrassed, maybe. But he was still the same soldier she'd always known, and he was willing to do this. It was for the good of the shifter community, and no squabble between them was going to stop him from doing his duty. "That would be fine," she said.

"Good. That's settled. We'll get you all the information. Now let's go over a few other things, just basic protocol for the way we do things in the Force," Hudson continued.

Emersyn sat quietly through the rest of the meeting. She wanted the distraction of work, but it was impossible with Gabe in the same room. Already she was regretting agreeing to be his partner on this mission.

When the D.C. member dismissed them, Gabe caught her in the hallway. "How could you do that?" he growled.

She flicked her silky hair over her shoulder, keeping her eyes straight ahead. She wouldn't give him the satisfaction of showing him that he'd gotten to her. "Do what?"

"Tell them all about... *us*. That's personal."

Now she risked a glance at him, but she swiftly looked away again. He was going to make her lose her cool, and she needed to maintain as much of an advantage as possible. "It's my story to tell just as much as it is yours. I don't think you can claim it solely as your own."

"Okay, you've got me there. But I don't think they needed to know. You obviously don't want to have anything to do with me, so it's not like we have to worry about nepotism."

There was something hidden in those words, the implication that he did still want to have something to do with her. Gabe had certainly shown it the previous day when he'd come onto her. Emersyn had been tempted to give in. He was a gorgeous man, with that dark hair and those brilliant eyes, not to mention the strong jaw and wide shoulders. She'd made the equation to him and an action hero before, and it wasn't strictly based on the way he acted. But no. Handsome or not, that didn't make any difference when it came to him abandoning her.

"You heard Garrison. All five of us will be bonded like clan members soon enough. Don't you think they'll figure it out once we're in each other's heads? Personally, I don't know how much control I'm going to have when it comes to what information gets pushed through to them and what I keep to myself." Theoretically, shifters who had that link didn't automatically know every single thing about the others in their group. It was only the specific messages they pushed out to their brethren. But Emersyn hadn't had that type of experience in a long time, and she didn't think it was right to keep such a big secret from the men they were supposed to be working with for the foreseeable future.

"Fine. Okay. But I think we could've found a better way to tell them than just spring it on them. Now, what about Lucas?"

She pursed her lips. Just as it would be useless to hide their former relationship, it was also useless to keep Lucas from his biological father any longer. Emersyn had already opened her mouth, and there was no going back or denying it. If Gabe decided to break his son's heart, then she couldn't stop him. Her panther could kill him later, though. "All right. I'll get him from Melody. Wait here."

Leaving Gabe in the living room, she headed to Melody's room. "Hey. I need to borrow Lucas for a minute."

Her friend peered into her face. "Is it Gabe?"

"Yeah. It's always Gabe," she sighed as she hoisted the sweet little bundle on her hip. "We'll be back in a bit."

During the meeting, she'd managed to keep her panther fairly well in check. Maybe it was something about the work-like setting that had helped, because now that she was faced with not only dealing with Gabe alone but introducing him to his son, she wasn't sure she could keep her whiskers from piercing the skin of her cheeks. Sometime soon, she'd have to find a way to get outside and go for a good long run.

When she returned to the living room, Gabe was on the couch. He still had that angry look on his face, but his head snapped up when he heard her footsteps. His jaw slacked, and his eyes widened. He stood as though pushed from the couch cushions, and his feet quickly crossed the room as he reached out for the child.

"He doesn't really like strangers," she began, but she stopped when she saw there was no need. Lucas had been a good baby, but a rather clingy one. The few times she'd attempted to leave him with anyone other than Melody, he'd fussed inconsolably.

Somehow, Lucas must've known who was holding him. He easily went into Gabe's arms, suddenly that much smaller compared to the well-muscled man. His plump little hands reached out to explore the stubble on Gabe's chin, his mouth slackening as his interest grew.

"Hi, there," Gabe whispered, his voice cracking ever so slightly.

"You don't know it, but I'm your daddy. I'm sorry I hadn't met you before now." A tear rolled down his cheek as he pressed his lips to the back of Lucas's hand.

The baby giggled in delight, and then his investigation moved on to Gabe's nose and eyebrows. He smiled and wiggled happily.

"Yeah?" Gabe asked, falling easily into this primal conversation. "I like you, too. You're a handsome little thing, aren't you? Black hair like your mommy. And blue eyes like mine." He carried the boy off to the sofa, where he straddled him on his knee. "I can't stop looking at you, buddy. You're amazing."

Emersyn wasn't quite sure what to do with herself. She was used to being the one directly taking care of her son if she was in the room. She'd been doing it alone for so long, and she rubbed her hands nervously on her hips. Finally, she sat down across from them, not quite willing to leave them alone just yet. Gabe had left her, and he'd made decisions only for himself, but Emersyn had no doubt in her mind that he would treat their son with the care and love he deserved.

"Has he shown any signs of shifting yet? Do we know what he is?" Gabe spoke to her without breaking his gaze from Lucas, bounding his knee and smiling at the baby's happy reaction.

She didn't like that he was already referring to the two of them as 'we.' They might both be Lucas's parents, but that didn't mean they had any further unity than that. Still, it wasn't worth arguing about right now. "No, not yet. He'll be a year old in a couple of months. I'm hoping he'll start showing something soon."

"You've got some little teeth in there, don't you? Let me see those little teeth! Oh, they're so big! You're such a big boy!" Gabe put his big hands on Lucas's sides and lifted him into the air, his proud grin just as wide as the child's.

Emersyn knew she should be thrilled to see this. So many men refused to be active in their responsibility as fathers. She'd seen it countless times when single mothers came into her clinic, struggling to fulfill every role on their own. It was so hard to be the caregiver and breadwinner at the same time. *There's no telling just how far this will go,* she reminded herself. Just because Gabe was interested at the moment didn't mean he would stick around in the long term. He'd already proven that once.

5

"So tell me more about Melody." Gabe guided the car along the busy highway, keeping only some of his attention focused on the traffic. It was thick there, potentially worse than some of the driving he'd done overseas, yet he couldn't get his mind off his son.

Holding him for the first time had been magical. Gabe hadn't known exactly what to expect, but as soon as he'd seen Emersyn walk into the room with Lucas in her arms, he knew he wanted to do more than just see him. They'd spent over an hour together on the couch, just playing and being silly with each other, and Gabe couldn't take his eyes off him.

Emersyn folded her arms across her chest, her irritation rolling off in waves that reached him easily from the passenger seat. "I already told you, she's a good friend of mine. She's been watching Lucas since I could first get back to work after having him."

"Yes, you did say that. But I want to know more. I mean, this woman is spending a lot of time with my son. I think I deserve more than that."

Her dark eyes flashed as she turned to him. "Oh, I see. So you've known for a couple of days that you accidentally made a baby, and now you think you're some expert on parenthood? You think you know what's best for him? You might want Melody's mental health history and blood type, but I think I deserve a little more credit."

He gripped the wheel and tried to get a grip on his own emotions at the same time. She was right, in a way. Emersyn had been doing this alone, and clearly, Lucas hadn't suffered. Yes, he should've been able to have his father around, but he was obviously healthy and happy. "I'm not saying you aren't competent. I just want to know all the details. She's living under the same roof as I am and she's caring for my son."

"Then I suggest you take some time and get to know her. She's a great friend I met back in college, and now she's the bookkeeper for the Force. As you said, she's living with us now, so you should have plenty of time to chitchat. Yep, we're all just one big happy family." Emersyn had been nothing but irritable, and it was clear this was a trend that would continue.

"Look, you and I have to find some way to get along. You might not want me to be part of Lucas's life, but it's happening. I don't see any reason for us to fight, especially because that's only going to affect him. Then, of course, there's the Force. I admit it's strange that we've been put in this situation, but I'd like to think we're mature enough to handle it. Hell, the U.S. Army thought we were pretty damn mature, considering what they asked us to do." He'd been so excited to see Emersyn on that first day, imagining the simple pleasures of tumbling between the sheets together when they were so inclined. Things had gotten much more complicated than that, and fast.

"You're right," she relented, although he could still hear the reluctance in her voice. "It's just not easy."

"What can I do to make it better?"

When she looked at him this time, the sheer anger in her eyes had been replaced by surprise. "Well, I'm not sure. Maybe start by not treating me as though I suddenly don't know how to raise my own son."

He bit back the argument that he was just trying to help and that he had a lot of making up to do. "All right, I'm sorry. I'll try to be more aware of that."

They swung off the highway and into a suburban neighborhood full of small homes, white fences, and planted flowerbeds. Children played on the streets, scattering out of the way to accommodate traffic and then running right back onto the pavement. Gabe had never visited a conclave meetinghouse before, and he hadn't known exactly what to expect, but this wasn't it.

Finally, they pulled into the driveway of a sprawling ranch house at the end of a cul-de-sac. The brick siding and impeccable yard were a level above most of the surrounding homes, but not so much that it completely stood out. "Is this the right address?"

She shrugged. "It seems to be. Let's see what they have to say." Emersyn hopped out of the car before he could get his seatbelt off.

Gabe caught up to her just before they reached the front door. "Let's make sure we keep Hudson's instructions in mind. We just talk about the situation with the gangs and see what they have to say. We don't make any suggestions or try to tell them what to do. This is strictly an information-gathering mission."

Her lips tightened. "I know, Gabe. I can handle it. As far as I'm concerned, this is just like a difficult medical patient. You check the symptoms and go back to discuss treatment options with your team. If you whip out the big syringe, someone's gonna get scared." She lifted her fist and knocked boldly on the door.

Gabe felt an odd feeling wash over him as they waited on the front porch. He was suddenly incredibly aware of everything around them, from the copper-shrouded porch light overhead to the sound of a distant siren. It wasn't just awareness, though. It was a desire to grow bigger, to pull Emersyn under his arm and hustle her out of there before anything could happen. His bear let out a low growl, warning anyone who might try to harm her. He shuddered with the power of it all. Gabe hadn't felt that protective urge in a long time, and it didn't sit well with him that he should be feeling it for Emersyn right now.

The door swung open to reveal a short, burly man with tattoos. "Can I help you?"

"We'd like to speak with the conclave, please," Emersyn said politely.

The man's eyes narrowed. "I don't remember seeing you before. Are you in our jurisdiction?"

She smiled sweetly, even tipping her head slightly to the side. "Sort of. We're actually from the SOS Force."

"Huh." He looked each of them over for a moment before stepping back and opening the door wider. "Come on in. I'll see if they're available." He left them in the foyer while he stomped off through the house.

"I guess he must be one of the guards," Emersyn muttered. "It's funny. Garrison said he'd get in touch with each of the conclaves before we visited, but this man is acting like he's never heard of us before."

"So that gives you a good reason to flirt with him?"

"Excuse me?" Her eyes cut through him as her head snapped up.

Shit. He was treading on dangerous ground again. It was just so hard to control himself around her. It was his bear, and that couldn't really be helped. "I just think you shouldn't be overly nice, or they might think we're pushovers."

Her sideways glance was one of disbelief. "I don't think we need to worry about that. We've got plenty of fighting power if we need it, but for right now, there's nothing wrong with being diplomatic."

"We'll see." Gabe had his doubts about all of this.

The tattooed man reappeared, this time with another man the size of a mountain next to him. The newcomer had to duck to get through the doorway. His wide shoulders, dark hair, and thick beard only accentuated the look. "You must be Gabe and Emily," he said, extending his hand. "I'm Hunter, and I'm sorry. I almost completely forgot you were coming."

"That's all right, and it's Emersyn," she corrected, reaching out to take his hand and smiling up warmly at him.

"Emersyn, what an unusual and lovely name. Please, come on in." He gestured for them to follow him through the house. The side doorway that led to the living room held a plaque above it with an eagle carrying a flaming skull. Apart from that odd piece of décor, the rest of the open floor plan was fairly normal, plain even. The rest of the San Bernardino County conclave members were there waiting for them. It was a less formal arrangement than the Force had at their new headquarters, with the members lounging on sofas. The television was on, and Gabe noticed several of them were sipping whiskey and other liquors despite the early hour. He hadn't known exactly what to expect, but he wasn't sure this was it.

"Can I get you anything to drink?" Hunter's dark eyes glittered, focused entirely on Emersyn as he stepped over to the bar. "We've got just about anything you could want."

Gabe almost choked on the beast trying to come out of him. "We're fine for now, thanks," he answered before she could say anything different. He had a memory of her becoming particularly flirtatious after a few rounds, and it was already hard enough to deal with this. "We just want a chance to sit down and talk."

"By all means." Hunter gestured grandly to an unoccupied loveseat. "I understand you want to discuss the biker gang activity in the area."

"Exactly, yes," Gabe affirmed, glad that Emersyn had essentially been forced to sit right next to him. He took a certain amount of comfort in knowing she was within arm's reach, especially since he didn't know if he could trust these people yet. "We understand there have been quite a few casualties from gang activity, and we'd like to see what we can do to help."

The big man poured himself a rather large glass of whiskey before leaning casually against the bar. His obsidian beard split in a sardonic smile. "That's a nice idea, but I'm not sure what a small group of people could actually do to help."

Gabe could detect the challenge in that statement. "You might be surprised."

"Right. Sure." He took a sip of his whiskey but didn't seem bothered by the burn. "I've heard rumors about what the SOS Force is capable of. That's great, but you're still only a handful of people compared to these gangs. Some of them run deep, and their loyalty knows no bounds. They would gladly die for their Alpha, no reservations, no questions. They're incredibly violent."

"Do any of them consider themselves to be part of your constituency?" Emersyn asked.

"There's no clear answer on that. They're a little more wild than your average citizen. They do cause a lot of trouble, but the good thing is that it's mostly among themselves. Sure, every now and then someone happens to be in the wrong place at the wrong time, but their only true targets are each other. I'd say the biggest threat they pose to shifters around here is simply the fact that they create a terrible reputation for the area. People—humans and shifters alike, actually—don't feel safe going out."

"What do you think the right solution is?" Emersyn was sitting forward, ankles crossed, the poise of the perfect lady. It made Gabe nervous. She was too vulnerable, too tempting. Any one of these monsters might try something.

Hunter glanced at the rest of the conclave members, who seemed content with letting him run the show. "That's something we've discussed quite a bit, and no solution seems like the perfect one, but the general consensus is that we wipe them out."

Emersyn stiffened visibly. "You want to kill them?"

He flipped a large hand through the air as though waving away these lives that were such a problem. "They're a problem, a pest that needs to be extinguished. They're only important to each other. They don't vote, so it isn't as though the conclave members have any real reason to protect them. The fastest and easiest thing to do is eliminate them. We just haven't worked out the details yet."

The surging emotions in Gabe latched onto this idea. He was growing more feral by the minute and the idea of sinking his claws and teeth into someone was incredibly appealing. It was too easy to imagine himself diving in to just that sort of action. Feeling a shudder across his shoulders that indicated his bear was coming on, he suppressed it quickly. "And what about the San Fernando Valley conclave? Have you talked with them about any of this?"

The room erupted in laughter. "That wouldn't get us very far. They're not interested in anything we have to say, and even if they listened, they wouldn't like it. You could say they're a little more diplomatic about these things."

"Do you know what their solution to this situation is?" Emersyn asked.

"You strike me as the kind of woman who likes everyone to get along. It's a lovely idea, as lovely as you are, but it isn't going to happen. We like to take action, to cut down problems before they become a bigger ordeal. I haven't talked to them, but I have no doubt they want to take a more sensitive approach."

Gabe once again felt a wave of jealousy wash over him as Hunter focused on Emersyn. He wished she'd stop talking. Her good looks were already drawing too much attention, and that only increased when she opened her mouth. He stood up. "I appreciate you taking the time to discuss this with us. We'd like to spend some time talking with the San Fernando Valley conclave, and perhaps with some of the biker gangs themselves to see about getting this resolved."

Hunter lifted one thick eyebrow. "That's bold of you, but it's likely to get you killed."

"I think I can handle myself." This asshole had no idea who Gabe was. Many people had tried to kill him before, and none of them had succeeded yet. "We'll be in touch."

Emersyn gave him a look, but she also stood.

Hunter escorted them up the stairs. "I suggest you be careful," he warned. "There are plenty of people who would want to take out a group like the SOS Force, feeing they're just as violent and high-handed as the biker gangs are."

Gabe, at the front of the trio heading for the door, steeled his jaw. "I appreciate that, but we'll be fine."

"If you should need protection, I'm more than happy to offer my services."

Something in the man's voice had changed, and Gabe whirled around to find Hunter addressing Emersyn directly. He loomed over her, his eyes liquid and hungry, and there was no question as to his intentions.

Possession, jealousy, and that same urge to protect took over his body. Gabe had been holding it inside the best he could, but there was no patience left in his cells. He lurched toward them as his spine twisted and his jaws stretched, the jagged pain of his pointed teeth ripping through his gums. His skin shrank back as fur bristled forth. He reached the pair mid-shift, knocking each of them aside as he roared his anger. In full bear form, he filled the small room and stood taller than Hunter. He knocked the big man backwards, sending him crashing into the wall.

The other conclave members flooded up the stairs, headed by the tattooed man. "What the fuck?" He didn't wait for an answer before he shifted, his small form rapidly switching to that of a tiger in midair as he leaped at the offending intruder.

Gabe had the advantage on Hunter. His big paws held the man down by the shoulders, and he roared all of his anger and jealousy into the man's face. It didn't last long. The conclave president that they'd met with twisted and writhed to reveal his own inner bear. He flung Gabe aside and bellowed his fury as he attacked. They were a tumble of dark fur as they crashed through the living room, forcing the tiger to dodge out of the way.

Hardly able to see for all his frustration, Gabe operated on instinct alone. He swiped and bit, searching for the most vulnerable part of his opponent, ready for the kill. Everything he'd ever felt for Emersyn was on the surface now, bubbling and boiling. She was his, and if this asshole thought he could do anything to change it, then he would show him otherwise. The brilliant red of blood showing from among the dark forest of his hair satisfied him and drove him further on, making him all the more determined to inflict as much damage as possible. The bastard deserved it, and he was going to make it happen.

But Hunter was a strong man, and an even stronger bear. He lurched upward, smacking Gabe hard in the mouth with his shoulder. Sparks filled Gabe's vision, stunned momentarily as he reeled back. The other bear took advantage of the moment and threw himself down on top of Gabe, pressing a thick paw to his throat. The world collapsed inward as Gabe's vision tunneled, going black on the edges and bringing only what was directly in front of him to a sharp definition. His lungs fought for air, and his exerted muscles quickly weakened from the lack of oxygen. Though his brain demanded that he fight back and fight harder than ever before, the message wasn't getting to the rest of his body.

The brilliant red of Hunter's blood caught his attention, and Gabe watched as it trickled through his thick fur like water finding a path through the desert. The scent of it slipped just inside his lungs, and the instinct to survive revived his system. He planned his next move, knowing how difficult it would be to move at all and that he only had one chance. If he miscalculated or his muscles refused to cooperate, that could be the end of him.

With one hurtling move, Gabe reached across with his right paw and struck the arm that held him down. As he'd hoped, his claws raked through the opening wound, sending a crimson splatter through the air as Hunter bawled out his pain. He let go, and cold air came rushing back into Gabe's lungs. He followed the bigger bear across the room, pinning him down.

He was on top again and ready to let loose with a final blow when something sharp sank into his shoulder. It clamped down hard, piercing his thick skin, digging deep toward his shoulder blade. Gabe let out a furious roar, but it died on his lips as he turned to see the massive black cat who had a hold of him.

It was Emersyn. It'd been so long since he'd seen her in this form, but there was no denying it. Though she'd taken on the form of a panther, her deep brown eyes now a brilliant gold, he knew it was her. Her lips and teeth scraped against his skin in an erotic threat.

Let him go, or I'll leave you here, she told him through their telepathic link.

Gabe backed off, letting the other bear get up. He felt a deep sense of regret at such an action. The man had gone after his mate, a crime that was unforgivable as far as he was concerned. Hunter deserved severe injury if not death, but Emersyn herself had put a stop to it.

They returned to their human forms, and the room was full of nothing but heavy breathing for a moment. The tattooed man helped Hunter to his feet, and Gabe understood what he'd just done. "I'm sorry," he panted, adrenaline still flooding through his system. "I lost control."

The look on Hunter's face was ominous as he glanced back and forth between the two of them. "I didn't realize she was yours."

Emersyn let out an angry huff of breath, but she didn't argue the point. "We'll see ourselves out. I'm sorry for any trouble we caused you, and please know that we'd still like to work with you to resolve the gang issue." She moved pointedly toward the front door.

Gabe marched after her, not liking the idea of turning his back on the conclave members. As far as he was concerned, they were still a threat. He got behind the wheel of the car and headed out of the neighborhood. "I had a bad feeling about that conclave from the moment we walked in there. I didn't see or hear anything specific, other than the fact that they want to kill the gangs without remorse, but it was just one of those gut feelings. And can you believe that dickhead, hitting on you like that?" He could still see the scene clearly in his mind's eye, and he wouldn't forget it anytime soon.

"The only dickhead I can't believe is *you*," Emersyn retorted from the passenger seat. She ran her hands angrily through her hair, combing it with her fingers. "Hunter was a bit on the aggressive side, yes, but he wasn't hurting me. And it's not as though I can't take care of myself."

His fingers tightened on the wheel. How the hell had they gotten along so well before, when now they could hardly stand to be in the same room without arguing? "No offense, Em, but did you see the size of him? Even shifted, I'm not sure you could've held him off alone if he'd decided to attack you."

"Attacking is definitely not what was on his mind."

"Damn it!" He slammed his hand against the dashboard. "You're going to make me shift in the middle of the highway if you keep going on like that! Whether you like it or not, whether you think of us as mates or not, protecting you is part of my job as your comrade in the Force. Besides, I didn't hear you correct him when he said you were mine." There was something so wild in that phrase, in that notion that she belonged to him. He liked it in a primal way that he couldn't explain. Gabe was perfectly aware that modern society didn't see women that way, but it didn't matter when there was a massive beast inside him fighting so hard for it.

"I figured we'd have plenty of time to argue about it later, instead of continuing to botch our very first mission." Emersyn slammed her back against the seat, angry and stuck in the car. "Garrison and the others are relying on us to be mature about this...whatever this is between us...and I can't believe you're already trying to ruin it."

"Me?" Holy shit. How had this all turned around on him? "I saw the way you were looking at him, and I heard the way you talked to him. It's no wonder he was going after you."

"Excuse me?" Her dark eyes blazed with golden light, and he knew that her panther was just as restless as his bear. "Are you even hearing yourself? I was polite, and I didn't speak to him any differently than I would've talked to anyone else. That's so sexist of you to mistake kindness for flirtation."

"Even humans are animals to a degree," he reminded her. "There's biology at work here."

"That's a weak argument, even for a shifter. And instead of chastising and blaming me, you ought to be thanking me for saving your ass. I kept the rest of the conclave and the guard from joining in the fray. I can't even imagine what would've happened if this had gone any further than it did."

His lips tightened over his next argument. Gabe could come up with plenty of them, but he wasn't making any headway. Emersyn had a comeback for everything. He let go of his anger a little, remembering that was something he'd liked about her. As a woman in the military, she'd caught plenty of shit despite her training and the work she'd done. She'd been willing and able to dish it right back, and that ferocity had caught his attention just as much as those smoldering eyes of hers. He continued the rest of the drive in silence.

When they pulled back into the driveway, she finally spoke again. "Gabe, I can appreciate that you thought I might've been threatened in some way. I just think it should've been handled differently. It would make me feel a lot better if you gave me a chance to take care of myself —no matter if you're seeing me as a mate or a coworker—before you jump in to save me. I'm not a delicate little flower, but I do know how to make myself sound like one if it might benefit the mission."

He shut off the engine, keeping his thumb and finger on the key. If only he could make her understand that it wasn't that simple. They could assure the D.C. members that their past wouldn't interfere with the present, but there was a huge difference between saying those words and actually following through with the promise. Emersyn did things to him. Her soul reached out and touched his in a way that no one else's ever had. He couldn't just let her go, but it was clear that forcing the situation wasn't going to work, either. "Okay. I'll try."

"Thank you." She stepped out of the car and into the house.

He watched her go, his eyes gliding over the gentle sway of her hips that she'd always had, even when she was operating in the middle of the desert on a dangerous mission. Did the woman truly understand just how much she affected him?

6

THE MORNING DAWNED BRIGHT AND BEAUTIFUL OVER THE HILLS, BUT Emersyn couldn't appreciate it. She'd been up all night, and the day didn't promise to be any better. Lucas whined and fussed in her arms, unable to cope with the fever that developed just before midnight and kept both of them awake. He clung to his mother, his little fingers digging into her flesh with a deep need that he didn't quite understand and that even Emersyn couldn't quite satiate. He pinched her skin as he pressed himself as hard against her as he could, still not happy.

A gentle knock sounded on her door before Melody appeared. "Hey, I didn't see you in the kitchen, so I thought I'd check on you. Is everything okay?" She shut the door behind her, frowning at the baby in concern. "He looks miserable!"

"He is," Emersyn sighed. "I've checked him over, and I think it's just a virus. I've given him everything I can, but of course his symptoms only abate for a short time before they're back again. I haven't even been able to set him down to go to the bathroom." When she'd tried, his screams had been so loud, she was afraid he'd wake the entire place.

"Poor guy. You want to come see Aunt Melody?" She held out her hands, which Lucas normally went into so eagerly, but he only pressed his hot cheek against Emersyn's chest. "Wow, he really doesn't feel good."

"I hate to do it, but I think I'll have to call in sick. He obviously wants to be with me, and I can't head out on a mission if I know he's feeling this way. God, this has just been such a terrible start to this job." She wrapped her arms around her son and closed her eyes, wishing she could somehow make it all better.

"I never did get a chance to hear how things went with you and Gabe yesterday. It's funny. You'd think with us living in the same building we'd get to see each other more often, but the Force is keeping both of us pretty busy."

Emersyn made a disgusted sound. "Awful, actually. I wish we could just say we're both mature adults who can put the past behind us, but he made a complete ass of himself and a mess of the mission."

Melody sat down on a chair, ready for the gossip with bright eyes. "What happened?"

"He decided that the president was a little too interested in me. The jerk actually shifted and started a fight!" She sat down, once again recalling the horror that had flooded her system when she saw his half-bear, half-man form hurtling toward the two of them, his face twisted in anger. "I couldn't believe it. The two of them were fighting in the middle of their living room like beasts out in the wild. I could tell the rest of his conclave was about to jump in and help, and there's no telling what would've happened then. But I shifted myself, staved them off, and bit Gabe on the shoulder."

"Are you serious?" Melody clamped her hands over her mouth, but she couldn't stop her laugh.

"Unfortunately." She'd been so angry with him, and it'd seemed like the fastest way to stop him at the time. It had worked, and of course he'd recovered quickly, but that didn't make her any happier about it. "Then he had the nerve to argue with me in the car, still trying to say he was right."

Melody rolled her eyes and head to one side. "Well, the two of you had been mates. You told me what a pull he had on you, and we know how serious that is for people like us. We're lucky to experience it once in a lifetime. You can't completely blame him if he still feels something for you."

"Can't I?" Emersyn was still pissed off enough that she didn't want to give Gabe any allowances.

"Yes. It's not really a conscious decision, Em. Your body just tells you who the right person is, and it doesn't matter if you agree. At least, that's how I understand it. I've never been lucky enough to go through it myself."

"Or unlucky, as the case may be." She sighed. "You might be right. I don't know. I hope we find a way to get through it, that's all. For the time being, I just need to get through the day. Do you think you could hold onto Lucas long enough for me to go talk to Garrison? I feel like I should have this conversation in person." She'd already had to tell him all the details about their mission, and she hadn't missed the look of disappointment on his face. Surely, this news was going to give him even more doubts about how suitable she was for the Force.

"Of course."

Lucas fussed and cried as Emersyn put him in Melody's arms, and when he didn't settle down after being in the company of his caregiver, Emersyn knew she was making the right decision. She couldn't possibly leave him like this. She slipped out the door as quickly as possible and found Garrison in the kitchen. Fortunately, he was alone.

"Are you all right?" he asked, his brows drawing together in alarm as soon as he saw her.

"Yes, or at least mostly. Lucas is really sick, and I need to stay here with him today. I'm so sorry. I know this is bad timing, but I can't leave him." She felt a familiar pang of guilt in her stomach as she had to once again deal with choosing between work and her child.

"That's all right. I like to think the Force is pretty understanding about family life."

"Right." That was exactly why they'd allowed Melody to stay at the house, but she was glad he wasn't trying to make her leave Lucas even though a sitter was technically available. "Thank you again."

"Um, if you have a minute, I'd like to talk to you about yesterday." He held out a finger to stop her from running right back up the stairs.

"Sure." It was the absolute last thing she wanted to do, but she couldn't exactly say no.

Garrison rapped his knuckles on the kitchen counter. "Is there going to be a problem with you and Gabe? And before you answer that, know that this conversation won't go outside the two of us. I know you both said it would be fine when we were in the meeting, but it's different when you have an audience."

Emersyn picked up an orange from the bowl on the table and rolled it around in her hands. "I wish I knew how to answer that honestly. I think the two of us still need a little time to adjust to each other. Things didn't go well at all yesterday, and we argued quite a bit when we first got back in the car. But I think we were on a more amicable footing by the time we got home, and that makes me hopeful that we can get it worked out." There was certainly something to be said for the idea of both of them staying there, since it would make visitation a lot easier than traipsing back and forth across town.

"Okay. If you're sure. I don't want to put more pressure on you than you can handle." One corner of his mouth lifted in half a smile. "We're all former soldiers, and we've seen some serious shit, but I don't think it's anything compared to navigating relationships. If you need anything, just let me know."

"I will. Thank you." She snagged a cup of coffee before heading back upstairs.

"Is there anything you need?" Melody asked when she returned. Lucas had been fussing the entire time, and Emersyn had heard him all the way down the hall. "Breakfast?"

"That would be great." She should've grabbed something while she was downstairs, but she'd been in a rush to get back to Lucas. "And, if it's not too much hassle, could you go by the clinic and pick up some medication for me? I only had so much in my bag. I can send Louise a text and she can have it ready for you."

"Not a problem at all, and you know it," Melody replied. She frowned, studying Emersyn's face. "Is there something wrong? I mean besides Lucas, of course. That much is obvious."

With reassurances from Garrison, her baby boy back in her arms, and help from Melody, Emersyn knew she should be feeling much better about her life. But her old friend knew her better than anyone else, and she wasn't wrong. "Yeah. I just feel so conflicted. It's even worse than it was before. I already had a hard time working so much and feeling like I wasn't taking good enough care of Lucas. It's only gotten worse since I got here."

"That makes sense," Melody sympathized. "You've essentially taken on a second job, and it's going to take some time to adjust to it all. There's not much about your life that hasn't changed in the past week or so."

There was the new house and the new job, but there was so much more. "I think most of it is Gabe. I could deal with the rest if it weren't for him. I just don't know how to act around him. He's awoken my panther again. It'd practically been asleep for the longest time, yet I was able to shift just like that yesterday." She snapped her fingers in the air.

"Does that mean you feel more for him than you want to admit?" Melody challenged. "I mean, I know you're angry with him for leaving you like he did. But like I said, we can't always help the way we feel."

"I'm angry. I'm confused. I'm intrigued." Her body rippled with excitement from merely thinking about him, even though he was so good at ticking her off lately. The attraction between them was undeniable, and she was fighting so hard against it. The strangest part about it was that the harder she fought, the harder the universe was tugging them back together. Even now, her panther swirled anxiously inside her just knowing he was in the house. "It was so sweet seeing how he and Lucas interacted the other day, like they had an intrinsic bond just like Gabe and I do—or did. But then he turned around and did something absolutely infuriating."

Melody scratched her neck thoughtfully. "Most men are like that, Em. No one's perfect. Hell, he might be having just as much of a hard time dealing with your presence as you are with his, not to mention the news that he has a son."

"Whose side are you on, anyway?" Emersyn retorted.

"I'm just saying."

"I know." Melody liked to look at things from all sides, no matter what her actual opinion was. "And you're probably right. It's just a lot to deal with."

"Well, I'll get you some breakfast and head to the clinic. Just holler if there's anything else you need, since I'll be right next door after that. And take care of that sweet baby." Melody planted a kiss on Lucas's forehead before heading out the door.

The day dragged on as Emersyn worried both over Lucas and her new job. At one point in the afternoon, the boy finally settled down enough that she could sit on the couch with him, and she flicked on the TV to distract herself. The next thing she knew, she was waking up to a knock on the door. She yanked her head up. "Come in."

She'd assumed it was Melody, but Gabe was the one who came through the door. He walked right in, shutting the door behind him, and sat next to her on the couch. "How is he? Garrison said you stayed home with him. I talked to Melody for a few minutes in the kitchen before I left for the day, and she said you had things under control, but

I've been worried sick." He stroked a gentle finger down the sleeping baby's back.

"He's fine," she snapped, growing angry at his forwardness. She'd asked him twice to keep his distance and let her handle things, yet there he was again.

"What about you?" His blue eyes pierced hers as he turned his attention to her instead of Lucas. "You've got to be exhausted. Let me take him for a bit so you can rest." Without giving her a chance to argue, he put his arms around Lucas and lifted him from her lap.

The boy fussed at being disturbed, but he settled easily into his father's arms and nuzzled against his chest. His body relaxed visibly, and a hint of a smile pushed up his chubby cheeks.

As badly as she wanted to snatch him back, Emersyn wasn't going to do anything to disturb Lucas if he was happy. She realized just how tired her arms were from holding her son all day. "I'm okay," she replied quietly.

"I can stay with him if you need to take a shower or get some food or anything." He focused on the boy in his arms, rocking him gently and smiling at him.

"I don't think I even want to move," she replied honestly. The previous day had been tiring on an emotional level, the night hadn't been any better as she tried to soothe Lucas, and the day had tipped her over the edge of exhaustion. She was so tired, she was starting to feel sick herself, though she knew it wasn't the same fever that Lucas had. "I'm pretty sure I could just sit here for the rest of the day and stare off into space."

He gestured with his head toward the bed. "Go lay down for a bit and I'll take Lucas back to my place."

She frowned, not because she didn't trust Gabe with the baby, but because she didn't really want him to leave. By all logic, she should be taking full advantage of having someone there to help her, especially if it was someone Lucas was willing to be calm for. Was this what it was like for people who had mates by their sides all the time? Did they get a chance to rest, to eat, to just take a ten-minute shower in peace? Did they have someone to share all their decisions and worries with? Of course they did, and the idea was one she wanted more than she ever would've admitted out loud. "Why don't you tell me how things went today? I feel bad about missing out."

"Don't. You didn't have a choice, and everyone understands that.

Amar and I went to speak with the San Fernando conclave. As we were told, they were very different from the San Bernardino guys."

She turned away from him, wishing she could completely forget how things had gone with Hunter. "Were they willing to talk? Did they have a better solution?"

"Yes, and yes. They seemed a little hoity-toity at first, the polar opposite of Hunter and his crew, and their ideas were the complete opposite, too. They definitely want to address the issues with the biker gangs, but they do have some value for their lives. Their idea is simply to talk to the Alphas of the gangs and maybe even get them all together in the same room to work it out. Their approach is a stepped one that starts with talking and negotiating and escalates up to getting the police involved. Even at the worst, they don't agree with a blanket elimination like Hunter wants, but I'm not sure about asking law enforcement for help, either."

"No," Emersyn agreed, glad to have something to think about besides her sick child, who was still quite content in Gabe's arms. "That puts all shifters at risk. We don't know enough about these gangs yet, but if what Hunter said is true, then they're incredibly violent and they don't care who gets in the way. To me, that translates to them being a risk when it comes to protecting our secret."

"Right. If they feel threatened by the police, they might very well shift. That happens sometimes when our emotions get the better of us."

She looked up, seeing that those ultramarine eyes were focused on her once again. She rolled her shoulders, not entirely certain how to respond to him. Now that they were in the same room together, she could feel the bond between them like a silvery thread that extended through the air and touched each of their hearts. It incited their inner beasts, and she knew that despite how tired her human body was, her panther self was excited at having him there on her territory.

It was clear he was speaking about yesterday's incident. She'd been so reluctant to forgive him for what he'd done, but her conversation with Melody had made her start thinking about it in a different way. Maybe she could have a little more sympathy and compassion instead of just assuming none of this bothered him. After all, she was a doctor. "It happens. It's okay."

His grin transformed his face, and she looked away to keep it from showing up on her face as well. "I guess we're both still figuring out how we're going to do this. We've got a lot of catching up to do, and now we have the weight of the Force on our shoulders, too. It's going to take us some time, and I think we've both been too hard on each other."

Emersyn rubbed her lips together, pleasantly surprised at the sense of comfort that came with having him there. "I swear Lucas knows you're his father. He doesn't let just anyone hold him, especially when he's sick. He usually clings to me like a little leech." She reached over and gently cupped her hand over the baby's cheek, glad there was someone else in the world who made him feel good. Every child deserved as many people who loved them as possible.

"He just knows what a good mother you are." Gabe's eyes were velvety soft when he looked up at her. "Emersyn, I'm sorry for the things I've said; when I've made you feel like I'm judging you for your parenting skills. I'm not." He pulled in a deep breath. "I'm just trying to make up for lost time, I guess, and doing it in the wrong way. I feel so bad for you having to do this all on your own. I know it isn't easy, and I never would've left if I'd known."

His words meant so much to her. It was nothing more than a little cloud of sentences in the air, something fleeting that he could deny tomorrow, yet the power of it burrowed right down to her heart. All those sleepless nights, all that worrying, and in one moment, it could all be better. "It's okay."

"No, it's not. There's been a lot that's been put in perspective for me over the last few months. I thought a top-notch career was the be-all, end-all goal. I thought I was doing the right thing by climbing the ladder as high as I could, but it put me out of sight of what really mattered. I didn't know about Lucas, but I did know how important you were to me. I ignored that for all the wrong reasons, and I'm really sorry."

Tears burned the backs of her eyes. She blinked them away and let her gaze fall down into his arms. "He's asleep," she whispered.

"I'll put him to bed." With expert skill, Gabe rose from the couch without disturbing the baby and took him to the adjoining nursery. Emersyn leaned against the doorway, watching the care Gabe took with his son, and realized how heavy her heart had been.

When he rejoined her in the main room of her suite, Emersyn could no longer hold back her tears. They left hot rivers down her cheeks as she looked at him. "I'm sorry, too."

Seeing her crying, Gabe rushed to hold her in his arms. "For what?"

"For thinking the worst about you instead of just talking to you. For refusing to track you down and tell you about Lucas. You deserved better than that, and so did he. I denied you both because I was just so angry and scared, and it seemed easier to do it on my own than hope for help from someone else." She sobbed against his shoulder, clinging to him as the pain racked her chest.

His hand smoothed over her back. "I understand. We both made some mistakes, but it's not too late. We can still make up for them. We're here together now. Lucas has both of us. It's going to be all right."

"Is it? Every time I convince myself of that, everything changes." His body was so warm and strong, and his skin smelled of soap and sunshine. Emersyn wanted to bury herself into his chest and forget the rest of the world existed. Her panther purred its assent, pleased with the luxury of having someone else to lean on.

"You can't know how sorry I am that you've been doing this on your own. I know I already said it, but really." He lifted her chin from his shoulder to look her in the eyes and wiped the tears from her cheek with his thumb. "Emersyn, I don't want you to ever feel alone again."

Her heart lurched in her chest, and it headed directly for him. She couldn't say if she started it or if he did, but suddenly they were kissing. His lips were warm, soft, both consoling and enticing. A thrill of energy shot across her tongue and down her throat, racing through her body to reach her core. Her panther swirled and rippled inside, once again brought to life in a way she'd no longer thought possible. Where her hands had clutched at him for relief and reassurance, they now skimmed over his hard muscles in exploration.

Gabe tightened his grip on her waist, pressing her close against his body. He moved his lips from hers and skimmed her jawline back to her earlobe, giving it a nip before roving down her neck in an exotic line that ignited her very blood. "I've missed you so much," he whispered as he pulled the top of her blouse aside to kiss her collar bone. "I know what we had together, and what we can have if we only allow ourselves."

She hadn't permitted herself to fall into anything with abandon since she'd found out she was pregnant with Lucas. Every little thing, every moment, was a decision that had to be scrutinized and thought out before she took any action. Now, it was as though the weight of the world had been lifted off her shoulders. Emersyn didn't need to think about it. Her body refused to allow in any sort of logic and reasoning as she tipped her head back in sheer delight.

Gabe's hands slipped up her spine and he buried his fingers in her hair. His lips pressed to the very center of her collar bone before dipping downward. She leaned back, succumbing to him as he unbuttoned her shirt and explored the curves of her breasts that showed above her bra. His tongue dipped below the fabric and across her nipple. Emersyn shivered, wondering how she'd let herself go so long without this. It was as though she'd been in the desert, skirting widely around the oasis because she was too afraid of drinking the water and enjoying it too much. Now she dove in, lifting her leg to wrap around his thigh and keep him pressed against her. She could feel the hardness of his arousal, and she let out a gasp of desperation.

"Emersyn." Gabe straightened, heat filling his eyes. "If we keep going like this, I might not be able to control myself. I want to know that this is what you want, too."

Simply standing there and holding each other, Emersyn could feel him in the very marrow of her bones. She could sense not only his human side but his animal as well, fully aware of the way it moved inside him and controlled him. There was no one else like him. She needed him in the same way her body needed air, even though he was already making her forget how to breathe. "Yes," she replied, feeling the electricity in her lips as they drew close to his once again. "Please, yes."

They came together in a frantic clash of desperation. Gabe peeled back the thin film of her shirt and kissed a line down her ribs and hips as he freed her from the confines of her jeans. Emersyn skimmed her palms over each new chiseled muscle as she uncovered it, her body buzzing as she realized how close she was to finally fulfilling this craving that lived deep inside her.

She squealed in surprise as he spun her around and yanked her close to him. Gabe kissed and bit at her shoulder, his lips soft but his teeth pleasantly sharp. His hands glided around her waist and up to embrace the globes of her breasts.

Emersyn leaned against him as she tipped her head to the side to give him easier access. That stirring inside her that she'd been able to define so easily a moment ago as her panther was no longer separated from her human body. They were now one and the same as she reached behind her to wrap her fingers around his hardness, both of them hungry for the one thing that would bring them the ultimate satisfaction. His skin was velvety smooth, a contrast to the solidity underneath, and she stroked it for her own indulgence as much as his. Gabe returned the favor, one hand sliding down her stomach and down between her legs, his fingers moving expertly, confidently.

Any last bit of doubt dissolved as concentric circles of heat radiated from her core, enveloping her body in pure rapture. Emersyn leaned heavily on him as her knees lost their strength, sucking air in through her teeth as she reveled in this heady heaven. Her muscles twitched as he brought her to a crest of desire that climbed up and up and up until it seemed impossible to go any further into the sky before crashing back down and drenching her body in fire.

The bed was only a few feet away, but they tumbled to the floor together. Emersyn wrapped her legs around his waist, welcoming him as he filled her. She'd had her gratification, but Gabe's careful attention had left her primed and ready. The sensation of him inside her extended to her very soul. His cells lived between hers, and the two of them moved together in synchronized rhythm. Emersyn clutched at him, her breath ragged as her muscles clamped around him and drew him further in, demanding all he had to give and more.

Gabe was more than willing to give it, gripping her hips as he scraped his teeth along her neck. Then he was kissing her again, his tongue roving inside her mouth and gliding against her own, the texture of it at once foreign and familiar. His rhythm quickened as he expanded inside her, and she shivered around him as their bodies surrendered to each other.

7
_____

GABE STOOD ON THE BACK DECK, STARING OUT AT THE GORGEOUS mountain view. He'd been so interested in this house mostly because of this closeness to the wild lands, but now his interests had changed. Eventually, he would need to get out and go for a run in his true form, but his tryst with Emersyn had given him a sort of satisfaction he would never find even from filling his lungs with fresh air and expending his muscles until they burned.

A permanent grin had occupied his face the entire morning, and he didn't think it would go away any time soon. He didn't want it to. Emersyn was just...everything. She made the world stand out in sharp relief, a high definition view that he couldn't see when he was on his own. Being with her hadn't simply been a physical need that he wanted to satisfy. It had been a more deeply rooted desire than that. The physicality of it was incredibly nice, but it was merely symbolic of what he felt for her on a spiritual level. Emersyn was like coming home again.

The only problem was that he knew there were still so many things to explain to her. She deserved it, but he hadn't wanted to taint the purity of what they'd just experienced with dragging them back to the past once again. The right time would come, and he was more certain of that now than ever.

"I understand your son is feeling better today?" Amar stepped out onto the deck and leaned against the rail, his dark skin shining in the sun.

"Word travels quickly around here, doesn't it?" Gabe replied with a smile. "Yes. It's not a surprise, though. Emersyn is an excellent doctor."

"Good. We'll need one. Our missions could be incredibly danger-ous." He adjusted his elbows on the deck railing, admiring the beauty that surrounded them. "Speaking of missions, there's something I'd like to talk to you about."

"Sure." They could talk about anything he wanted. Gabe couldn't remember the last time he'd felt so good. He could take on the world.

"I just want to make sure all is well between you and Emersyn. I think you'll both be incredibly valuable assets to this team, and we need every bit of skill and experience we can get if we're going to actu-ally settle this issue with the biker gangs. I wouldn't want some old romance to get in the way."

Gabe's smile widened. It wasn't an old romance as far as he was concerned. As soon as he got the chance, he was going to let Emersyn know not only his past and the reason he'd left her, but how he felt about her now. They were meant to be together, and they'd both tried to deny it for too long. The fact that he'd heard her in his mind when he was fighting Hunter should've been evidence enough, but the time they'd spent together the previous day had proven it. "I know things got off to a bit of a rocky start, but I think we've worked it all out."

"You're certain? Because things would be very complicated for us if I had to constantly keep the two of you apart. Also, I read the report from your encounter with Hunter and the San Bernardino conclave." The disappointment was evident in his eyes.

"Yeah." Gabe ran a hand over the back of his neck. "I wish that hadn't happened. It wasn't professional, and it certainly didn't help our case. I lost control. Emersyn and I still had a lot of things to work out, and even though my fight with Hunter was uncalled for, I think it helped us bring things out in the open. We've talked a lot, and I think we're headed toward the right place."

"Good." Amar clapped him on the shoulder. "That's good to know. Especially since it's time for the third leg of our mission. We'll be split-ting into teams to go talk to the gangs themselves. Can I count on the two of you to work as a pair again?"

His cheeks were starting to hurt from smiling so much. "Absolutely. Not a problem at all."

"Great. I know we have Hudson's cell phones we can rely on for now, but I can't wait until we get the chance to be linked. I think we'll all be a lot safer when we're out in the field. Anyway, we'll go over all the details at the meeting. See you then." Amar headed back in the house.

Gabe remained on the deck for a moment, allowing himself a thrill of excitement in knowing that he and Emersyn would be heading out together once again. He had no doubt it would go better than it had the first time. It would also give him an opportunity to tell her how he really felt. He stepped back inside, rehearsing the right words in his head.

A couple of hours later in the car, Gabe moved his hand from where it rested on the gear shifter and rested it on Emersyn's knee. He felt her muscles contract and stiffen. "What's the matter?"

"Nothing," she said quietly.

"If you're worried about Lucas, he's fine. He was feeling much better this morning, and he seemed perfectly content to stay with Melody." Gabe hadn't been completely sure about Melody at first, simply because he didn't know her. But now he'd had the chance to see just how much she cared for the little boy and that the feeling was mutual. They were incredibly fortunate to have someone they trusted just down the hall.

"I know." She turned to look out the window, but her eyes were more distant than the scenery.

He moved his hands back to the steering wheel. There was clearly some sort of tension in the air, but he didn't know what had caused it. Only earlier that morning, Gabe had been completely sure of where their relationship was heading. Now he felt like he was driving in circles. "What is it, Emersyn? Is there something we need to talk about?"

She blew out a breath of air between pursed lips and looked down at her lap. "I guess so. I was going to wait until after we got back to headquarters. Right before a mission didn't seem like a good time, but I suppose it's got to happen sooner or later."

"What?" He was growing impatient with worry.

Emersyn glanced at him and then away. "This is going to be my last errand with the Force."

His heart came to a screeching halt in his chest. All the joy and hope he'd been feeling about the future dissipated. "What are you talking about?"

"I had my reservations from the start. I was worried about what to do with Lucas. I was worried about how I would balance the Force with the clinic. Those were enough to deal with, but now it's like everything's gotten more complicated. I don't know that I can handle it." She pressed the back of her hand to her lips.

"Do you mean...us?" He didn't really want to know the answer to that. Rather, he was terrified of what the answer would be.

She nodded.

Gabe felt like the wind had been knocked out of him. He'd been stupid enough to think that a fun little tumble meant something more. That sweet satisfaction of being with his soulmate had been intoxicating, but this sudden news made him feel like it was nothing more than a drinking binge followed by the worst hangover in the world. "Emersyn, I don't understand what's happening here. I thought everything had gone well. I thought..." He didn't want to say out loud what he'd thought. It would make him sound vulnerable and foolish in light of what she was saying.

"I thought so, too, okay? I saw that temptation to fall back into what we used to be, and I just jumped right in. I was jealous of the mothers who don't have to do it alone. I was worried that I might have made the wrong decisions for Lucas and that I needed someone to help me. I was tired and worried and I took the easy route. That doesn't mean it was the right one."

"Wow. That's pretty damn insulting."

"No." She flapped her hand impatiently in the air. "I don't mean for it to be. It's just that it was too easy to fall into your arms, whether it was the right thing to do or not."

"And why wouldn't it be the right thing?" It had certainly felt right to him.

"I don't know. It's hard to explain, okay?" She flipped her hands impatiently in the air once again, effectively brushing him off.

Gabe was boiling inside. He'd been about to tell her what a colossal mistake he'd made when he'd left her, and even why he'd made it. That was something he'd never opened up about, and seeing her raising Lucas by herself had made him realize that. Now, the only thing he actually realized was what a fool he'd been. "Damn it! I missed my turn."

"I'm sorry." Her words were choppy and choked. "I know this was a bad time. Like I said, I was going to wait until later."

"It's not like waiting would've made it any better." Gabe didn't know if he would've wanted to wait or not. It would've been nice to bask in the glow of what he thought was happening between them a little longer, but maybe not if it was only giving him false hope. "I'll just turn around."

"We have to make sure this doesn't impact the mission. It doesn't matter for me so much, since I'll be leaving, but I don't want our problems to mess up your career with the Force."

He realized this meant she would also be moving out of the shared house. "So that's it. I get, what, three days of having my son under the same roof, and then you're just going to take him away again?"

"I still have a lease on my apartment," Emersyn snapped. "We can arrange for visitation. It'll be fine."

The only thing that kept him from arguing further on that point was the fact that they'd arrived at the Flaming Skulls' clubhouse. The big brick building looked like it'd been a factory of some sort at one point, and it was certainly in the right part of town for it. "Let's just get this over with."

"Fine."

They stepped out of the car and up to the door. At one point, he'd been eager to go on this mission because he wanted to see how this particular gang lived. Now, he could care less. He just wanted to talk with them and head back home.

The door opened before they could knock, revealing a large man in a vest and a sleeveless t-shirt. He crossed his tattooed arms across his wide chest, accentuating his beer belly. His handlebar mustache frowned at them. "Can I help you?"

In this sense, the clans, the conclaves, and the gangs were all the same. They always had some hardhead at the front door to keep out the rabble. "We're here to speak to Grizz."

"Hmph. Wait here." He slammed the door in their faces, but he returned a minute later to guide them inside. Gabe didn't like how similar this was to their experience in San Bernardino.

Moving through an old garage area that was still used for the same purpose, Gabe took note of the motorcycles lined up along the walls. The gang also had top-of-the-line tools with which to work on them. It made Gabe wonder what kind of financial structure these guys had.

Were they selling drugs? Eliciting payments from local businesses in exchange for 'protection' the way the mob did? Money laundering? All were possible, but he knew he might never find out. They were simply there to talk about the gang's rivalry with other clans, and they weren't going to let him see the books.

From the garage, they entered a part of the factory that had been refinished into a bar. Neon signs hung between large posters of half-nude women and antique motorcycle parts. Both the ceiling and the floor were made of solid hardwood, stained a dark color that gleamed in the colored lights. A jukebox pounded out an old tune for the bikers that sat at tables or at the bar, some of them with their arms around scantily clad women who eyed him uncertainly. Gabe was surprised at how clean the place looked.

"Here you go, Grizz." The bouncer left them at the bar, where a large man worked away behind the counter. He eyed them carefully as he dispensed a beer and slid it down the slick wooden surface, but then he smiled. "So you're from the Force. It's funny. I heard such a thing existed, but I wasn't really sure. I suppose I should thank you for your service to the country."

Gabe noted the prominent American flag on the man's vest. "Thank you. And I appreciate you taking the time to speak with us. We're basically just trying to figure out how we can help settle some of the violence that's been happening in this area without inciting even more."

Grizz let out a roaring laugh that rolled like thunder through the bar. "Your diplomacy is duly noted, but I don't know how far it's going to get you. We've been living with the threat of violence at our backs all our lives. That goes way back, even before we had any formal conclaves in the area."

"Surely you agree this is a problem that needs to be addressed," Emersyn said. "I don't have all the statistics in front of me right now, but I've been working at a clinic downtown. I've seen the results. There shouldn't be any reason for so much brutality. We'd like to know what we can do to help."

Grizz smiled at her, but it was a different look than she'd received from Hunter. This man looked at her more like a daughter than anything else, as though he admired her eagerness but also knew it wouldn't really get her anywhere. "Sweetheart, that's a lovely idea. If there's anything I can do to help, then I will. But I can't say I have much hope for it. Your best bet is to let our gangs work it out on our own."

"Maybe if you just tell us a little about how you operate and what sorts of things you and the other gangs go to war over, perhaps we could map out actual boundaries, just like countries do when they're fighting over territory. Negotiations, contracts, that sort of thing." Gabe had been more involved in that sort of work when he was with the military than he'd ever anticipated and knew he had skills that could help.

The big man shook his head and laughed a little. "You have good intentions, I'll give you that. Excuse me for just a second." He moved down the bar to speak with one of his associates.

Emersyn's elbow nudged sharply into his arm. "Hey, do you see what I see?"

"What?"

"Check out the back of the Alpha's vest, and that plaque up on the wall. They've got the same symbol that was in the San Bernardino conclave's meeting house. An eagle holding a flaming skull."

He looked up where her eyes led him, and Gabe felt the blood drain from his body. He was sure that things like eagles and skulls were a pretty popular motif among bikers, and the name of this gang was the Flaming Skulls, but this was indeed the exact same symbol. It couldn't be a coincidence. "Looks like Hunter was lying to us. That's the only explanation I can come up with." The man had assured them he had no interest in the biker gangs and would rather systematically annihilate them than deal with them. Was that simply a red herring to lead them in the wrong direction?

"I'm just going to step outside and call Garrison." Emersyn pushed off the bar and turned back the way they'd come.

Gabe seized her elbow. He'd gotten caught up in their argument, and he'd ignored the fact that they might be heading into dangerous territory. Grizz and his members had made no move to harm them yet, but he didn't like the chances. "Just... be careful, okay?"

"Always." Several men turned to watch her walk out of the room toward the garage. One of them even dared to let out a low, apprecia-tive whistle.

Gabe heard it and felt his bear growing restless inside him again, but he couldn't make the same mistake as last time. He turned back to the bar just as Grizz was returning.

"Where'd your pretty little friend go?" the Alpha asked.

"She had an emergency phone call," he quickly explained. "Her son is sick." It killed him to say it that way, as though he didn't have anything to do with Emersyn or Lucas other than being her coworker. But there had been enough problems the last time they were out together and he'd tried to get possessive, so this was the better option.

"I'm sorry to hear that, but it's just as well she's gone. I hoped I'd get to talk to you alone, man-to-man. Women don't always understand how things are for us, am I right?" He leaned heavily on the bar.

Gabe smiled at that one. There was probably a lot he and Grizz wouldn't agree on, but given how much Emersyn had confused him lately, this was definitely one of them. "That's true enough."

"You see, our little gang here might look to the outside world like some troublemaking force, little more than a problem to be dealt with. I can appreciate that you want the area to be nice and peaceful, but I want you to understand right here and now that it's not going to happen. We have our reasons for not getting along with the other clans, and we're not going to change it just because you tell us to. I don't care that you were in the military or that you consider yourselves part of some elite group. You can't just give yourselves authority over us because you want to. My suggestion for you is to butt out while you still can."

His words only stirred Gabe's bear up all the more, but he could sense all the sets of eyes that were now focused on him. This entire room was filled with potential enemies if their Alpha simply gave the word. He wouldn't get out of it as easily as he had back in San Bernardino. Gabe held up his hands. "We're not here to cause trouble."

"Good, 'cause—" His next statement was interrupted by the door from the garage slamming open. The man with the handlebar mustache held Emersyn roughly by the hair as he dragged her toward the bar. "I caught this little bitch calling for backup. What do you want me to do with her, Grizz?"

The Alpha narrowed his eyes. "What the hell did you do that for?"

"Let her go," Gabe growled. It was coming. The shift was heading down the pipeline, and there was almost nothing he could do to stop it. He could feel the bear in his blood and bones, bracing itself to shove his human form out of the way and let it take care of business. "Let her go right this second, or I'm going to rip that dirty mustache right off your face and shove it down your throat."

The guard laughed. "You're pretty damn brave for someone who wandered in here alone. I'd like to see you try."

Emersyn's dark eyes were afire with rage as she struggled against the big man, her hands holding her hair to keep his grip from pulling too hard on her scalp. "What's the matter? Are you so threatened by a woman that you won't let me go?"

"Shut up, bitch." In one quick movement of his thick arm, he flung Emersyn aside. She toppled into an unoccupied table, taking it and the accompanying chairs to the floor with her.

Gabe let go. His human form melted away as his bear shot forward, expanding and mutating with such rapid force that it made him nauseous. He felt the thick strength of his paws as he dove forward from his position by the bar, the back half of his body catching up quickly as he finished the transition. His roar filled the room as he leaped for the guard, who was too startled to shift. Gabe's teeth sank into the beefy flesh of his neck. The salty taste of sweat reached his tongue as he clamped down, sending the man down to the floor.

Commotion rang out all around him as the rest of the gang followed suit. As soon as Gabe turned from the man he'd attacked, he found himself completely surrounded by other bears. They filled the room, their dark, greasy fur smelling strong in a space that was plenty large for humans but not so much for beasts. A few of them lumbered forward, ready for a challenge, but it was Grizz that Gabe kept his eyes on. The man was huge as a bear, as big as Hunter had been, and the scars that slashed through his fur showed just how many battles he'd taken on.

If he jumps, just make sure you protect your throat, said a voice inside his head. It was beautiful and silky despite the anger and fear in it. *I'll get him.*

Gabe could feel the mental link to Emersyn almost as well as he could hear it. He didn't need to turn around to know that she'd shifted but was staying under the wreckage of the table for the moment. She was planning a nice little surprise for any bears who hadn't been paying attention. *No. You just let me keep them occupied while you get out of here.*

You're crazy.

Yes. Crazy for her. Crazy for ever thinking that their experience together the night before could change anything about who they were now and what they wanted out of life. Crazy for taking this job instead of going home and working that factory position his mother had heard about. *Maybe. But there's no way we're going to get out of this alive. We're outnumbered by a long shot.*

I got through to Garrison.

This last message came through just as one of the lower members of the gang sprang for him. He missed Gabe's throat with his teeth, but the bulk of him hit Gabe's shoulder and sent the two of them skidding across the floor. Gabe felt the impact to his spine as they hit the door. He was on his side, and the other bear's weight was keeping his legs in place. Unable to use his claws, he reached up and gnashed his teeth toward the sensitive flesh of his throat. The bear yanked his head back to get out of the way, slamming his own nose against the exposed brick wall behind him. Gabe took advantage of the temporary stunning effect and thrust all his body weight upward, sending his foe tumbling to the floor as he rose on his four paws once again.

Are they coming? Were you able to tell them about the symbol? He could wait for another enemy to attack, but the adrenaline pumping through his system told him otherwise. Gabe barreled forward to take on the next one.

I didn't have a chance, but I think they'll come. They must've heard the scuffle when that asshole found me.

Gabe hoped she was right as he twisted and turned, locked in an embrace of death with his opponent. Big claws pressed against his flesh and teeth snapped in his ear as he sought purchase that would rip through the tough ursine skin and take the other bear down.

A high-pitched scream ripped through the air, sending a shiver down's Gabe's spine even though he knew exactly where it came from. He could feel the sound in his bones, telling him not only who had made it, but exactly where she was in proximity to him.

Emersyn had leaped onto one of the other tables, calling out a challenge. She hissed as one of the bears took her up on it, crouching her body as she prepared to jump. Gabe shoved his rival back and turned just in time to see the big black cat pounce. Her sharp claws easily drew blood, making inky runnels in the dark fur.

There was no more time to watch her in action as two more bears came at him. He struggled against their weight and strength as he mentally calculated just how many enemies they had in there and how many they could take out before they completely exhausted themselves. *Emersyn, I need you to know I'm sorry.*

Don't talk like you're going to die, she snapped. *The others are on their way. I know they are.*

It was certainly something to hope for, but Gabe wasn't counting on anything until he saw it. *You need to know I'm sorry whether we make it out of this or not. I never meant to hurt you by going away. And whatever I did to make you upset last night or this morning, then I'm sorry for that, too.* He crunched his teeth down on a furry brown ear, clamping them hard against the delicate skin until the combatant bellowed in pain. The second bear was trying to do the same to Gabe, though, and he let go in order to swat him back.

Emersyn was silent for a long time. It was only the fact that he could feel her presence—no words, but simply her—in his mind that kept Gabe from panicking and swirling around to find her. *It's fine.*

That wasn't much, but it would do for the moment. A swift smack of his paw landed just right, his claw scraping against the other bear's eye as the strength behind the blow turned his head. His foe staggered off, but there was another one in his place. Gabe was drowning in enemies. He backed up, and he could sense the excitement in the other bears as they thought he was retreating. But he was merely getting closer to Emersyn.

She was at his back sooner rather than later, the two of them fighting as the center of a spiral that simply couldn't last forever. They were outnumbered, and even the time it would take for someone to get there was too long.

There's one thing we have to agree on, no matter what else we have between us. Emersyn screamed again as she swiped and bit at the bear that had come after her.

Gabe could feel her muscles working, the force of her against his back. They were fighting together, defending themselves from the enemy. It was the stuff of dreams for a man like him, yet he couldn't help but feel this could also be the end. *What's that?*

Lucas. Emersyn shoved off the floor, jumping almost straight up into the air so that she came down on top of her enemy's head, her claws shredding his face. *One of us has to get out of here. For him. He's already gone through almost the first year of his life without both of his parents. He can't lose us. Not now.*

Thoughts of his son drove Gabe onward, renewing his strength and energy as he put down his head and barreled into the next man who dared to come forward. Grizz still wasn't one of them yet, standing back and watching his men do the work.

Before Gabe could answer, a door on the opposite end of the bar slammed open. Even in bear form, Gabe recognized Hunter. He charged into the room, his conclave behind him. A path cleared before Hunter as he headed straight for Gabe, revenge clear in his eyes.

He reeled back as the big bear hit him. Gabe's muscles were already tired, and this fight wasn't going to be the same as the one back at the San Bernardino conclave. Then, he'd been fresh and readily fueled by his urge to protect Emersyn. He still wanted to do that, but he knew it wouldn't be possible. He was losing already, and the fight had barely begun. The bear on top of him was gigantic, and he seemed to recover instantly from every blow and bite. *Yes,* he panted out in his mind, determined to let Emersyn know before the end that there was at least one thing they could agree on. *One of us has to survive for Lucas. And it should be you. Go! Please!*

I'm not leaving you!

A blur of black flickered across Gabe's vision. Hunter's head snapped back to combat the new challenger on his back, and he grunted in pain as she slashed her claws across his cheek. Gabe knew she was helping, but he also knew it was futile. They would never make it. Even if she ran for the door right now, some of the bears would follow. She would be faster, but they knew the place better and there were more of them.

An odd noise reached his ears as he was still pinned underneath Hunter. Gabe didn't know what it was at first. He ignored it as he snapped his teeth around Hunter's paws and ground them together, exuding just enough force to make the other bear yank his leg back. It gave him just enough of a chance to force him further back with his bodyweight and pull himself upright again. It wasn't a win, but it was victory enough to give him a little bit of hope back.

The noise sounded again. It stirred up the members of the gang, making them even snap at each other as they tried to figure out what was happening. It wasn't the scream of Emersyn's panther, nor was it the deep roar of a bear. The tinted windows behind the bar shattered as two massive beasts shot through them, their wings filling the air. Everyone in the room froze as two dragons, one onyx and one emerald, entered the room.

Gabe's heart lifted, knowing Emersyn was right. Garrison had understood what was happening, and the Force had their backs. The gap in the window admitted the brilliant light of the sun, and with it, Raul's wolf, Hudson and Leona's lions, and Jude's bear. They were still outnumbered, considering they were fighting both the biker gang and the conclave, but the odds of getting out alive were definitely ticking upward.

Amar and Garrison cleared the room of most of the gang with blasts of fire that sent bears running and sizzled the worn oak bar. Hunter and Grizz remained. Grizz attacked the newcomers, finally entering the fray, but he was taken down as swiftly as he came in when the rest of the Force easily overpowered him.

Hunter was younger and more determined. His fighting became more ferocious as he became desperate, and he used his weight more than his skill in one last effort at taking Gabe down. But Emersyn was at Gabe's side. They attacked as one, their muscles and their souls moving in sync as they fought for the Force, for Lucas, and for each other. Gabe's mouth filled with blood as they each landed a fatal bite to the big bear's throat and watched him fall to the floor in defeat.

8

Emersyn sat down hard on her chair in the conference room. They'd reassembled at headquarters, and though they'd had time to wash, tend any wounds that had made it through the shift back to their human forms, and eat to replenish their energy, there was still work to do.

She'd managed a few minutes to hold Lucas, moments that were infinitely more precious than they'd been before. The fight at the club- house had seemed to take forever, the threat of her death hanging over her head like a dark cloud. What would happen to Lucas if she died? Worse, what would happen if they both died? The logical part of her brain told her that Melody would take care of the boy, and that even the rest of the Force would help ensure that he was taken care of. But logic didn't have room to enter her brain when she was fighting so hard for her life.

"I know you're all exhausted from your efforts today." Garrison stood at the head of the table, his hair still damp from showering. Amar, Raul, and Jude had already been out on their individual missions when they'd gotten the call from Garrison to head to the clubhouse. Shifting and the fight had worn them all out completely. "I'd be more than happy to say we should all rest and gather ourselves before we continue, but it's apparent there's a lot more going on here than we originally thought."

Hudson nodded. "I managed to get some information out of a few of the lower members of the gang. Apparently, the San Bernardino conclave and the Flaming Skulls were working together. The conclave used the biker gang almost like their own personal army, deploying them anywhere they thought someone was fighting against their cause. Hunter and his group were no better than any other clan or gang who wants to take everything for themselves."

"Interesting that he proposed wiping the gangs out altogether," Gabe mused. "He must've done that to keep us off the trail of their connection."

"That's our best guess, too," Leona agreed. "The conclave and the Flaming Skulls are fairly well stamped out for now, but of course this puts us in the position of helping to create a new conclave and make sure any other gang activity is settled. I don't think we'll have any problem with that. The other gangs that you all met with today seemed on board to find a way to work together, and we'll no longer have Hunter's influence over them."

Garrison smiled as he looked around the table at each of them. "That also means we'll need to ensure our safety on any future missions by creating that telepathic link. The moon is just right tonight. Since we're lucky enough to be right up against the woods, I figured we'd just walk."

Amar was the most excited about this. "I'm eager to see this. I've heard tales of this ritual, but I've never seen it in person."

A thrill of intrigue shot through Emersyn's system, despite her sore muscles and tired joints. She hadn't seen anything like it, either. In fact, there was very little she knew about dragons at all.

"I'm happy to share it with you," Garrison replied genuinely. "It's not very often that I get to perform the ceremony, and it's even more rare to share it with one of my own brethren."

Emersyn had heard a few bits of conversation here and there about Garrison's search for any of the remaining dragon shifters on the planet. They were a very unusual breed, and she was eager to learn more about them as the time passed with the Force.

Garrison went over the basic procedure for the ceremony so they would all know what to expect when they reached the place he'd set up in the hilly lands behind the house, and then they all filed out the back door.

"So," Gabe said quietly at her shoulder as they walked out of the house and began leaving suburbia behind, "I take it you've changed your mind."

It was the kind of thing that should've been an incredibly hard decision. Staying with the Force or not was a life-changing choice. She'd wavered on it numerous times over the last week, weighing the benefits for Lucas against the greater good. "I was dead-set against it less than twenty-four hours ago," she admitted. "I felt that I was letting myself go down the wrong path because it was the easier one."

He lifted an eyebrow. "I'm not sure being on the Force could really be categorized as easy."

She laughed, thinking about just how challenging the missions were already proving to be, and that was with D.C. members there to help them get started. "True enough. But the other things that come along with it are easier. Having a place to live without worrying about rent and utilities. Having Melody right next door, and even you right across the hall." Her face heated. She hadn't wanted to tell him just how much he meant to her, but everything had changed that morning as they were fighting. "I've often thought about women who have men at their sides as they're raising children and that it must be better than doing it alone. I didn't want to stay with the Force just because I was tired of doing all the work by myself."

"I see." He was quiet again for some time as they trudged up the pathway that led into the hills. The stars stood out in the deepest parts of the sky where the light pollution didn't reach, illuminating their path.

Emersyn bit her lower lip, knowing they would need to talk about this more. There had most certainly been something between them, and they couldn't deny it considering the mental link they already had and that they would soon have with the others. Staying on the Force meant they would still have to deal with each other on a daily basis, but she didn't yet know what that would entail. Maybe they would be friends, or maybe they would just do their best to raise their son until he was of age, and then each move on with their lives. She didn't know, and she didn't even like to think about it. There was unknown territory ahead.

The woods parted to reveal a small clearing. Garrison had placed a pile of wood at the center of it, and he stood near it now. The new Force members did as they'd been told back in the conference room and filed around the edge of the clearing until they stood in a tight circle. Producing a knife from a sheath at his waist, Garrison handed it to Amar.

He turned the curved blade in his hands, running his finger over the handle that bent in the opposite direction, and let out a low whistle. "I've heard of these, in old stories my grandmother used to tell me. I didn't think it could be true, because I never thought a dragon would actually give up his claw for the sake of a knife."

"Are we ready?" Garrison asked.

The assembly nodded.

Amar began, using the knife to make a slash on each of his arms just above the wrists, just big enough to flow, but not so large as to create any permanent damage. Garrison had explained back at headquarters that although most wounds inflicted on shifters healed when they transformed, the magic in the knife kept the cut open until the ceremony was complete.

They passed the knife around. Emersyn tried to leave her medical training behind as she touched the blade, already dark with blood, against her skin. It was so sharp that she hardly felt a thing and was unsure that she'd even been successful until blood welled from the wound. Finished, she handed it to Gabe.

When they'd all done the first task, the knife was handed back to Garrison. "And now shift," he reminded them gently, doing so himself.

Emersyn pulled in a deep breath of clean air, and as she let it out, she also let her human body go. It was strange to still feel the cuts as her spine lengthened and her tail flicked through the night air. She twisted her head to one side as the bones of her skull cracked and bulged to accommodate the face of a panther. An electric thrill shivered over her body as short black fur bristled from her skin.

When she had fully transformed, Emersyn looked around. An emerald green dragon stood at the center of the circle, puffing out his chest to ignite the wood he'd put there. To her right stood Raul, now a glorious wolf. Amar was on the other side of him, his magnificent obsidian scales reflecting the glow of the firelight. Jude was next, his hulking bear form similar to that of Gabe next to her.

Emersyn focused on Gabe as they each spread their forelegs so that their wounds touched those on either side of them. She didn't know if she should feel comforted or more nervous in having him at her side for this ceremony. He incited both feelings in her on tremendous levels. But as she pressed her cut against his, Emersyn felt a spark of something enter her bloodstream.

Dragons were the only shifting species who could speak audibly when in their animal form, and Garrison did so now. But the words that came forth from his long tongue and sharp teeth weren't English. They rasped and scraped in the air as he chanted in the ancient language of his people, translating it for the rest of them when he was finished. "Our blood becomes one, flowing within each other. Bonded as brothers, our nexus strong."

For a second, Emersyn didn't feel anything more than the pulsating blood of the rest of the Force in her veins. Then a jolt shot through from Gabe, sizzling up her left arm and across her chest before discharging into Raul. She gasped, recovering just in time for it to come bursting through her system a second time. The waves surged through her body repeatedly, leaving her numb and limp in between, wondering if she was going to die.

Finally, the bursts of magic subsided, leaving everything eerily quiet in the clearing. *It is done,* intoned a deep voice in her head that could only be Amar.

Emersyn sat down heavily as she disengaged her forelegs from Gabe and Raul. She was all right. She'd lived, but this was so much more than she'd expected. Her link with Gabe had been more automatic, no more taxing than the typical rush of hormones that came from their physical bond.

Testing, testing. 1, 2, 3! Raul joked.

Is this thing on? Jude added.

You guys are going to be fun. Amar's voice was serious, but there was a hint of amusement in his brilliant gold eyes. *Let's try some one-on-one while we're at it.*

Emersyn wasn't surprised to find that the next one inside her head was Gabe. *Well, I guess not much has changed for us, right?*

But he was completely wrong. As soon as she heard him use their link, the last bit of energy left her body. Emersyn's vision tunneled away until she was seeing moving images of a past that wasn't hers. She didn't recognize the woman at a kitchen table, crying as she wrote out checks to pay the bills. Neither did she know the two young girls who grew up right before her eyes into beautiful young women. It didn't make sense, even though she could see it so clearly.

But then, the dreamlike images changed. They were flashes of military life, filled with heartache and worry. Emersyn began to understand, and as she did the pictures and the feelings that went with them became more clear. She was seeing it all from Gabe's perspective. Before, she'd known only what he wanted to put in her head, bits of conversation that were no different than conversing aloud. Emersyn sobbed as she felt the constant worry of Gabe wondering if his mother and sisters were going to be all right, if they would have enough to eat, if the girls would have clothes for the new school year or textbooks for college. She felt the stabbing pain of resentment as Gabe left to join the Delta Force, knowing the extra money would mean that much more he could send home to his family.

And then there was Lucas. Dear, sweet Lucas, looking up at his daddy with wonder and love. The pain in her chest was almost unbearable. She sobbed as she experienced his heartache not only at not being there for the baby, but not being there for her. He loved her. Gabe loved her so much that it shattered him inside every time he looked at her, and she'd completely destroyed him when she'd told him she wasn't going to stay with the Force. Hot tears ran down her cheeks and into the earth, but she didn't notice. She wasn't there in the clearing; she was in Gabe's past.

A hand on her shoulder brought her back. Emersyn looked up at Gabe, his own eyes shimmering with moisture. She'd been curled up on the ground, her face down and her paws around her head, but they were now hands. Emersyn hadn't even realized she'd shifted back. They all had, and they were looking at her with concern.

Garrison, also human again, knelt in front of her. "Emersyn, what happened? I've never seen anyone have a reaction like that. I'm sorry."

"I don't think it was you." She sniffed as she looked once more at Gabe. "I think it was us."

The dragon looked back and forth between them. "We'll give the two of you some time." He left the clearing, the others following him.

Emersyn scooted closer to the still-burning fire and wiped her cheeks with her hands. "I've never experienced anything like that. I could see everything. I had no idea that you'd sacrificed so much for your family and how much you worried about them. You never told me."

He sat down next to her, the flames casting an orange glow on his hair. "I don't really like to talk about it. It hurts, knowing that I can never do enough to make up for my father walking out."

Pain still radiated in her chest, and a new wave of tears spilled over her lashes. "Oh, Gabe. You don't have to make up for that. It wasn't your fault. And I so wish I'd known. All this time, I thought you'd chosen the Delta Force because you were more interested in your career than in me, and certainly more than a family. I was so convinced you'd abandon us, and now I understand that it was the complete opposite. I'm so sorry I hurt you."

His arm slipped around her as she cried into his shoulder. "It seems we've both made some mistakes, but we did them for all the right reasons. I know you mean it, Em, because the same thing just happened to me. Whatever bond we had was increased exponentially by that ceremony. I felt the rejection you felt when I left, your exhaustion on those sleepless nights with Lucas, your hopelessness at wondering if it would ever get easier, your despair at knowing if you were making the right choices for both him and you. I can't tell you how sorry I am for leaving you with that. I should've been honest. I should've told you what was really going on in my life."

It felt strange to smile at a time like this. She'd been crying so hard that the light from the fire was too much for her eyes, and her body was completely drained from both the outward battle earlier in the day and the inward one just now. But seeing inside each other's minds that way gave her so much perspective. "If we'd just been upfront with each other, none of this would've happened."

"True." He rested his chin on her head, his stubble scratching against her scalp pleasantly. "But maybe then we wouldn't be who we are. I like to think there's a reason for everything that happens in our lives, whether we understand it at the time or not. At least, that's what I always told myself when it came to my family. I liked to think that even though it hurt like hell when my father left, and it was even worse when I saw how it affected my mother, that there could be some sort of positive outcome."

Emersyn wiped her face again and sat up. "What kind of positive outcome do you think there is for us?" The question would've made her nervous at any other time, as she tested the waters to see what Gabe wanted for their future. She was only just starting to understand what she wanted.

He was silent for a time as he stared into the flames. "I thought it had to be all or nothing. We were either absolutely together, or we weren't anything more than two people who happened to have a child together. I'm starting to think it's not as black-and-white as that. Not for us, and maybe not for anyone."

The wisdom that had come from Garrison's ancient ceremony was remarkable, and Emersyn made a mental note to tell him so later. "We could take it slow," she suggested. "We know we're meant to be together in some way. The universe has already told us that. But we could take some of the pressure off ourselves, even though we've had a past."

His arm wrapped around her and pulled her close. "We could. I have to be honest, though, I'm not sure I'll know how to take it slow around you. You've got quite a power over me, Emersyn. I want to be with you all the time, when things are good or bad. I want to know you're safe, and that our son is safe. I want to wake up next to you and feel your warmth against my side."

A chill had settled into her body after the ceremony, but now it was being driven away by the heat of her desire. Gabe was right. They completed each other in a way that couldn't be described. They might not always agree, but there was no doubt in her mind that they belonged to each other in a primitive way that they couldn't deny.

His lips were as soft as the firelight when he bent forward, brushing them against her mouth experimentally once and then twice when she didn't protest. His hand cupped her jaw as he kissed her again, moving around to the nape of her neck as he deepened the kiss.

Emersyn's body and soul came alive like a flame, igniting at the fuel he provided. The sensation of their lips and tongues moving together was like an erotic dance, one that sent tingles of energy throughout her body to spark at her fingertips and nipples. She allowed him to pull her closer, knowing that he was right. It would be very hard to take it slow, and it would come in ways other than their physical need for each other. He grounded her and strengthened her, evidenced by the way her fatigue dissipated while she was in his arms.

"I want to see you." Slowly, so slowly it was almost painful, Gabe pulled off her clothes. He kissed each new facet of her body that he revealed, his lips tender and worshipful against her skin. His hands and lips traced her every curve. The warmth of the fire on one side and the cool of the night on the other sent an extra shiver down her spine, and Gabe's eyes sparked with amusement. "You keep doing that, and I won't be able to help myself. It's impossible to control myself around you, Emersyn."

She slowly closed her eyes and reached out to her panther. It was well aware of the current situation, panting and pacing, eager for what would come, but it was manageable. It'd nearly been wild when Gabe had started coming back around. It would never be completely domesticated, nor did she want it to be. That feral mix was the perfect solution for both of them.

"I think I understand," she said with a smile, leaning forward to return the favor. She stripped him of his clothing until they were both naked, exposed to the fire and the stars and each other. Emersyn pushed him back, crawling forward until she straddled him on her hands and knees.

Gabe gave her an inquisitive look. "I take it you want to make this quick?"

"Not by any stretch of the imagination." Emersyn ran her hands across his wide shoulders and down his chest, languishing in the strength which lay inert there for the moment but that she knew would come bursting forth whenever it was needed. Her fingers rippled down his abs and lower, and she moved down to take him in her mouth.

He gasped and tensed, but then relaxed with a moan as she slid her lips up and down his shaft. There was nothing more important to her right then than bringing him pleasure. She worked her tongue against his velvety soft skin, her body buzzing with delight every time he groaned or his hips bucked softly against her in encouragement. Every indicator of his satisfaction turned her on all the more, until Emersyn was burning so intensely with her need for him, she could hardly stand it.

Gabe seemed to understand, too, because when she raised her head, he took her by the waist and lifted her. They came together, the two of them truly one in so many ways. They had separate bodies, but those bodies were simply two parts of the same whole. Emersyn threw her head back, feeling her hair slide across her bare skin. Her entire body tingled with energy and love, forcing her toes to curl against his strong thighs. She pulsed against him, feeling him inside her and never wanting this moment to end.

His fingers stroked down her back, catching her hair and pulling it gently, sending vibrations through her scalp and down her spine. Her panther purred intensely, taking such great joy in this moment that it was as though the rest of the world didn't exist. She barely even gave thought to the threat of being caught out there by some late evening hiker. Let the whole world see, because this moment was too beautiful to hide.

Gabe ran his fingertips up her back, across her shoulders, and down her arms until he took her hands in his, entwining their fingers. He held her, and she felt as though she were floating. The muscles in her abdomen tensed, increasing the thrill she was already starting to feel inside. Emersyn let out a cry as her body gave over completely to him. Where she contracted, he expanded; where she floated, he remained a permanent rock, yet the two of them rotated like binary stars at the center of a galaxy. His fingers clamped against hers as they pushed each other off the edge and into oblivion, falling in ecstasy until they came crashing back down to earth.

She lay on his chest afterward, listening to his heartbeat. Gabe caressed her back, petting her like the cat she was, and she smiled with feline satisfaction. The fire had died down to embers at some point, but their body heat kept them warm. A thought erupted inside her, not one from her brain, but from her heart. Emersyn suppressed it at first, not wanting to risk ruining what the two of them had just shared. Their union had proven to her just how close the two of them were, and it was a beautiful thing to be admired delicately for as long as possible. But the knowledge inside her demanded to be out. "I love you, Gabe."

He gently pressed his hand to the back of her head and laid a kiss against her hair. "I know. I love you, too. I always have, Emersyn."

She turned her head so that her chin lay against his chest and she could look him in the eye. She smiled at him, thinking of what she'd seen when that telepathic link had been established. It connected them when they were in their animal forms to the other members of the L.A. unit, and that was important, but it was nothing compared to the deepened bond the two of them shared. Emersyn didn't know if she'd ever be able to get inside his head in the same way again, but she did know she didn't need to. She knew that when Gabe told her he loved her, he spoke an absolute truth that emanated from his very soul. He loved her in such a genuine way, one that she'd never thought possible, and it was a perfect reflection of her own feelings for him. "I know."

9

GABE STEPPED DOWN THE LADDER AND STOOD BACK TO CHECK HIS WORK. The house they'd chosen for headquarters was modern and clean, certainly not the type of place one would expect to go for a child's birthday party. But the brightly colored balloons and crepe paper that Emersyn had brought home were all up on the walls now as she wanted, and it was looking more like a home than an office space. She'd even given him a massive banner to put up declaring without a doubt that it was Lucas's first birthday.

Emersyn walked into the room, a smile spreading across her face. "Oh, Gabe! It's absolutely perfect! He's going to love it!"

"I'm sure he will," he assured her as he dropped a kiss on her cheek. "I think he's also really going to love having all his family here."

The blush of excitement that had bloomed in her cheeks quickly paled. "I hope he does, because I'm nervous as hell."

"There's no need. My mother is going to love you, and so are my sisters. I admit, Mom was a little irked that I'd never told her about you. She and I are pretty close, and she gave me a good lecture about leaving you behind. But then she got so wrapped up in the idea of having a grandson that she forgot all about it. I'm sure it's going to be the same once she gets here. She'll scoop up that baby and she won't give anyone else a second glance." In truth, Gabe was a little nervous about seeing his mother as well. He was excited, because he loved her and wanted to spend time with her, but he hadn't exactly told her about the Force. There would be some tricky navigation there as he showed off the large house and his new friends without giving too much away.

"Speaking of, don't you need to get to the airport?"

Gabe checked his watch and then kissed her again. A smattering of powdered sugar highlighted Emersyn's cheek, and he gently wiped it away with his tongue. He needed to leave, but for a moment, he wished he could just freeze time and stare at her. Emersyn was so beautiful, and on so many levels. Any man could look at her and see how gorgeous she was on the outside. He certainly hadn't forgotten it himself, but now he'd seen the rest and he found himself focusing more and more on how alluring she was inside. "I'll be back as soon as I can. Is there anything you need me to pick up while I'm out?"

"I don't think so." She ticked everything off on her fingers. "I've got to ice the cake but I've got that all ready. The punch is chilling in the fridge, and the table is all set up. I've had his presents wrapped for a week. Yeah, I think we're good." She gave him a breathless smile that made Gabe wish he had time to take her back upstairs for a few minutes before everyone showed up.

After fighting airport traffic and waiting on some rather slow baggage claim, Gabe arrived at headquarters with his mother and sisters in tow.

"Oh, my dear lord!" Mrs. Vinson pressed her hand to her chest as she took in the house. "Gabe, what am I missing? I didn't think your disability check would pay for a place like this."

It still startled him when anyone mentioned the shrapnel in his side. He hadn't been out of the military for very long, but his life had changed so much over the last few months. Gabe hardly even thought about what he was missing with the Delta Force, even though he'd been looking forward to what the rest of his career would've held for him. Now, the Force had filled in most of those gaps, and what he had with Emersyn and Lucas more than made up for the rest. "I told you I've got another job, Mom."

"Yes, but you still haven't told me what it is," she chastised as he helped her out of the passenger seat.

"He's some sort of secret agent," Hope teased, unfolding herself from the back of the car. "Like James Bond."

"Nah," Hannah argued. "It's probably something incredibly boring like a financial analyst or something."

Hope was closer than she realized, but Gabe just smiled. "It's somewhere in between. We can talk about that later. And I don't live here by myself. I share it with several others. The place is giant, though, so there's plenty of room." He brought them in the front door and started to show them around, but his mother cut him off.

"The rooms will always be here, sweetie. Let me get my hands on that baby!"

Gabe laughed and turned toward the stairs, but with perfect timing, Emersyn was already coming down with Lucas in her arms. Mrs. Vinson pressed her hands to her mouth as her eyes filled with tears. "Oh. Oh, my goodness. Beautiful. They're both absolutely beautiful." By the time Emersyn reached the bottom of the stairs, Gabe's mother had enfolded both her and Lucas in her arms.

Watching the tableau, Gabe felt a distinct sense of warmth pass through him as Emersyn hugged his mother back with ease and the two of them quickly began chatting about the baby. The conversation carried on into the living room, where he introduced his mate to his sisters. The rest of the Force and Melody joined them as the party started.

"The two of you seem to be getting along just fine," Gabe commented quietly in Emersyn's ear when he had a moment with her. It seemed that their time together was a rare and precious thing these days. There were plenty of errands to run with the Force as they worked to tame down the shifter gang activity in the area, and although it was going much better than it had in the beginning, it still took a lot of time to sit down and arrange all sorts of negotiations and contracts, not to mention simply listening to the people's problems so they would know best how to help. Any time they weren't busy with the Force, Emersyn was off at her clinic. He completely supported her in still doing the work she loved, but it made him miss her all the more.

She smiled at him and shrugged her shoulder, turning her head to look at Mrs. Vinson, sitting on the couch with Lucas in her lap. "We're mothers. I should've thought about that, since I've experienced it so many times at the clinic. You put two moms together in a room and they always have something to talk about. Of course, there's also the fact that your mom is so sweet and loving, and caring and open. You're very lucky."

"I am," he agreed, but not just because of his mother. There was so much more going on in his life. "And speaking of, there's something I want to talk to you about later."

She raised an eyebrow, and Gabe had the feeling she was going to demand that he tell her right away, but the party saved him. "I'm going in the kitchen to get the cake, if you'd organize everyone to start singing please."

"Of course." He swung Lucas into the highchair they'd set up in the living room on top of a large sheet of plastic. Amar turned down the lights as Emersyn entered the room with the cake, the candlelight glowing on her face and enhancing her enchanting features.

He realized as he was watching his friends and family sing to his son just how lucky he really was. He didn't know he even had a son until a few short weeks ago, and there he was celebrating his first birthday. Gabe was absolutely determined, no matter what, that he would be there for all the other birthdays, too. He had a lot of fathering to make up for, not just for Lucas, but for himself. He would do all the right things, even the things that were hard. At this early stage, he didn't even know exactly what all those things were, but he knew he was committed to doing them.

"Happy birthday to you!" The song finished. Gabe and Emersyn bent down, one on each side of Lucas, and blew out his candle for him. Emersyn quickly whisked the hot candle away and they stood back, watching as Lucas studied the cake in front of him. He reached out a pudgy, tentative finger and poked at the icing, bringing it back to his mouth and tasting it with uncertainty. His eyes lit up as he realized what he was actually eating. Lucas didn't hesitate then to grab a handful of the sweet treat with his fist and shove it in his mouth to the applause of everyone else in the room.

Gabe laughed, thrilled at seeing such delight on his son's face. Lucas noticed and offered his daddy a fistful of cake. He nibbled it out of his hand, never wanting this moment to end. The boy giggled in delight and began offering gobs of cake to everyone in attendance.

When everyone had cake—either from a plate of their own or from Lucas's offerings—and the mess had been cleaned up, it was time for presents. The baby sat on Emersyn's lap as she helped him peel back the brightly colored paper. Gabe put the bows on Lucas's head, eliciting more giggles. He watched as his son's excitement and energy wound further and further up. He hadn't understood exactly what was happening when Emersyn had carried him into the decorated room, but the further they got into the party, the more animated he became. Lucas clapped his hands, laughed, and wiggled delightedly, his eyes shining as he registered that all these people were gathered there for him.

The presents finished and Emersyn handed the baby over to Mrs. Vinson, who eagerly took him while Emersyn and Gabe's sisters went about picking up all the wrapping paper and pouring some punch. As his grandmother pressed a kiss to his forehead and Lucas's sugar-fueled enthusiasm reached its final peak, something changed in his eyes. Gabe had been about to help Hannah with the punch when he saw it, and he froze. He hadn't known Lucas long, but that look was something unmistakable. He grabbed Emersyn's arm as she passed by him with a bag full of wrapping paper and tipped his head toward Lucas.

She turned just in time to see it. Lucas was still just a tiny thing, but he had an alertness in his eyes as he sought out his parents. He gripped Mrs. Vinson's thumb, squeezing tightly and alerting her that something was amiss. Gabe and Emersyn slowly moved forward, wanting to comfort him, but not alarm him. The rest of the room fell silent as they realized something was happening.

"It's all right," Emersyn whispered, tears in her eyes. "You're okay. Just let it come." She made no move to take him away from Mrs. Vinson, knowing as Gabe did that it might stop the process.

It was painful to watch as Lucas as his tiny body began to writhe and shake. He wrinkled up his eyes, looking like he was going to cry, but the expression alternated with a smile. Gabe knew that feeling. It was such a wonderful thing sometimes to shed the human form and let out the animal out, releasing all the energy and tension of the world in a simple shift that allowed one to get in touch with their true selves. But it was also scary in certain ways. Gabe had been shifting for a long time, so it'd become second nature, but that didn't mean he'd forgotten the pain that could come along with bones cracking and distorting, organs that moved swiftly to accommodate the new body, the slight alteration in blood flow.

Lucas kicked out with one leg, and when it came to rest on Mrs. Vinson's lap, it was covered in dark fur. Gabe's heart leaped in his chest, but he waited, knowing that even though his son was finally showing signs of his shifter nature, a bit of fur wasn't enough to let them know exactly what he was inside.

The baby stared at his own leg in wonder for a moment before the change took over the rest of his body. He turned and buried his face in his grandmother's shoulder, and she cradled him gently as the boy's limbs thickened. His chubby baby body grew more barrel-like, showing a strength and musculature that his human side didn't quite possess, and his tiny little fingernails turned to little black blunt claws. His face changed rapidly, the adorable baby cheeks racing forward to create a long muzzle with a little dark nose on the end of it.

"He's a bear," Gabe breathed. It was the most glorious thing he'd ever seen in his entire life. His son was a bear.

"Just like you," Emersyn agreed, a catlike smile on her face.

"Haha! What a delightful little cub you are!" Mrs. Vinson enthused, snuggling Lucas close.

"I'm so relieved," Emersyn admitted. "All this time, I've been watching him for signs of a shift. I thought for sure we'd see an ear or a paw or maybe even a bit of fur, but not a full change all at once!"

Melody wrapped her friend in a hug. "I guess he was just saving it all up for the big day! Congratulations!" She let go of Emersyn to hug Gabe as well. In fact, everyone in the room was hugging and patting backs, charged with the good news.

Gabe scooped Lucas up in his arms, wondering at the thick coat of dark brown fur and the adorable little face. "You're one good-looking little man, either way."

Lucas's sudden shifting made the party last even longer than they'd originally planned, even though the baby's bear form didn't last for more than a few minutes. He'd hardly even noticed that the sun had set for all the joy that filled the room with light. "I've got to get you guys over to your hotel. It's getting late."

"I'll do it," Melody offered. "You two spend time with the birthday boy." She gave Emersyn a wink before heading out to help Mrs. Vinson into the car.

"What was that about?" Gabe walked up to Emersyn, who stood at the kitchen sink, washing out the last of the dishes. When they'd spent the evening out at the bonfire in the woods, they'd tossed around the idea of taking things slow. It'd been much harder than he'd ever imagined, and even now, he couldn't help putting his hands on her hips and sliding his arms around to embrace her from behind.

She leaned her head on his shoulder in a backward version of a hug before resuming her chore. "Oh, nothing."

"Is that so?" He rested his chin on her shoulder and inhaled her scent. The flowery fragrance of her perfume mingled perfectly with the natural essence of her skin, and it never failed to make his bear wake up and take notice.

"There's just something I wanted to talk to you about, but I wanted to wait until the moment was right." She rinsed a plate and set it in the drying rack.

"And is the moment right?" He'd teased her in almost the same way just an hour or two ago, and yet he found himself without any patience to know what it was. He kissed the side of her neck. "Lucas is upstairs asleep, so it seems to me we have plenty of moments."

Emersyn dried her hands and turned around in his arms, draping her hands on his neck. "Maybe so. But that doesn't mean any of them are the *right* moments. It's something kind of big, and we've already had quite a big event today."

"That's true, and I don't think you just mean our son turning one." Gabe smiled and rested his forehead against hers, still blown away by Lucas's remarkable transformation. "Can you believe it?"

"I can, given that he's your son and just as stubborn and determined as you are."

He lifted his head and looked into her eyes. There was so much love in his heart for her. Gabe knew that some of it was because his life had been completely changed by the ancient dragon ceremony that had not only enhanced their telepathic link, but given him a vivid look inside her mind and her life. It was hard to imagine having that happen with no change to someone's life. Even so, he knew he'd loved her even before that. "You're right. I can be stubborn and determined. Is it always a bad thing?"

"No," she said slowly, drawing out the word so that he knew she suspected there was more coming.

The moment might not be right for what she wanted to say, but he knew it was right for him. He couldn't wait any longer. "And if I said I didn't want to take things slowly between the two of us any longer because I simply can't stand the idea of having a wall between us when we don't have to, then would that be a bad thing?"

Emersyn tipped her head back. "I don't think so, but I'm certainly eager to hear more details."

"I love you, Em. I'm crazy about you. I thought it would be enough for a while that we would live in the same house and work together, but it's just wrong that we still go our own ways at the end of the night. I wanted to ask you if you'd consider moving in with me."

"No." Her answer was quick, but she was still smiling.

"Too fast?"

"No." Her smile broadened, showing her perfect teeth. "It doesn't make any sense to move into your suite since there's not a nursery like there is in mine. And I'm not sure I'd want to uproot Lucas again. I know it would be just down the hall a bit, but I think he likes his little room."

"Oh." Disappointment rushed through his body. The two of them had been doing so well together, and he'd genuinely thought she was going to say yes. He dropped his hands from her waist, not wanting to make her feel like he was rushing things. "I understand."

"But," she said with a grin, taking his hands and putting them back on her waist, "now seems like the right time to tell you what I wanted to say."

"Which is?" He was intrigued. Emersyn was always good at keeping things new between them.

"Believe it or not, I was actually going to ask you if you wanted to move in with me. The nursery is right there, and I've got a gorgeous view out the window."

He pulled her close, laughing at himself for thinking she could feel any other way than this. They'd been operating in perfect sync for the last couple of weeks. He pressed his lips to hers, enjoying her taste all over again as his hands skated across her back. "I happen to think it's the view inside your room that's the best."

She laughed and kissed him back. "So I can take that as a yes?"

"Without a doubt." He felt his body coming to life as her fingertips tickled the back of his neck and his tongue twirled with hers. Both the bear inside and the human he wore on the outside were utterly obsessed with this woman, and he would spend the rest of his life making sure she knew that. "Are you sure you can handle living with two bears instead of just one?"

Emersyn tipped her head and rolled her eyes toward the ceiling as though she were thinking. "Well, you're both pretty cute, so I think I can handle it. And what about you? This cat is pretty cranky in the morning before she gets her coffee."

"Then I'll make sure you have as much as you need stocked at all times." He locked his arms around her waist and lifted her off the ground, carrying her over his shoulder, out of the kitchen, and up the stairs. "For now, I think there's something we both need."

She laughed as she dangled over his back, pretending to pound him with your fists. "Put me down you big beast!"

Reaching her door, he flipped her back onto her feet but held onto her waist. "Nope. I'm never letting go of you again."

Emersyn reached behind her back for the doorknob, and he followed her into the room. The only thing that was really changing was the room he slept in. To some, that might look like they were still taking things slow, but Gabe knew it was so much more. It meant going to sleep with her in his arms. It meant waking up to see the morning sun shining on her curves. It meant being right there for Lucas if he woke up in the middle of the night and needed his parents.

It meant everything, and he had it all.

———

SAVED BY THE SOLDIER DRAGON

SPECIAL OPS SHIFTERS: L.A. FORCE

1

KATE STOOD ON A ROCKY OUTCROPPING, FEELING THE CLOSENESS OF HER vampire brothers and sisters around her as they crowded forward to see what their patriarch had in store for them. The brood had loyally followed Luca for centuries, but as they hiked far out on these lonely trails in the moonlight, they began to question his reasoning and motives. He'd remained silent until now.

Older than them all by hundreds of years—yet hardly looking a day over forty—Luca spread his arms wide at the scene below them. "Behold, my children. We've wandered the world and seen many things, but what lies before you is a veritable treasure trove of food and life."

Kate studied the sparkling ocean under the moonlight, where it nestled up next to the pale line of a curving beach and the city beyond it. There was no doubt the scene was beautiful, but she still didn't understand. Hunger boiled inside her, the relentless thirst for blood that could never be quenched. "Another new city." She licked her lips, wondering what delights waited innocently for them below.

"No, my dear. Not simply another new city." Luca gestured grandly with his hands, the streaks of white in his dark hair standing out in the pale light. "This is Los Angeles. It's the type of city that humans flock to, thinking their wildest dreams will come true. I suppose that's the case for some of them, but for us, it could change our lives completely. Not simply our dreams, but our reality."

"How?" Thomas demanded, daring to step to the very edge of the cliff and look down on the city with a threatening interest. His thick hair was black as pitch, darker than even the sky. Luca had sired him about a hundred years ago, which felt like yesterday to Kate. "We've been feeding on people everywhere we go, but this curse has its claws in us. Nothing is helping." He clenched his fists at his sides, no doubt just as angry and frustrated by the hunger that plagued them as the rest of them were. If only the New Orleans brood's matriarch hadn't been so territorial about her feeding grounds, Luca and his vamps would've still found sustenance from human blood. No one expected her spell to last this long.

Luca sighed as he turned back to his brood, steepling his fingers in front of him. "I'm well aware of what the curse has done to us: we feed, yet we still have thirst. I know. Not only that, I of all vampires remember when we could spend a week feeding on a small village before they ever realized what was happening, satisfying ourselves without any fear. There's no doubt the world has changed around us, and now, it is changing *us* as well. We've been faced with many obstacles, but we will endure, my children, just as we have for centuries."

"So, how will this place be any different?" Kate dared to ask. She was excited about living in a new place, and certainly one that looked as beautiful as this. "It looks as though there are plenty of people here, but we'll still only be able to feed for a certain amount of time before the rumors start to spread." Thanks to the internet, the world was far more interconnected than it'd been in the past, when they could have waited for word to pass from one villager to another before they had to leave.

Luca turned to Kate, lifting her chin with one finger, forcing her to look him in the eye. "You have so little trust in me after all these years? I suppose I need to remind you of who's been keeping you safe all this time," Luca said, his eyes darkening as they bored into Kate's, "of who gave you *eternal life.*"

"No." She turned away, guarding the scars on her neck where Luca had fed on her. As the curse had taken its toll, they'd each offered themselves to their patriarch to sustain his strength. But the pain of a bite from one of their own was excruciating for even a vampire. It'd been a relief when he'd left for a short time to find new hunting grounds, and she could only hope he was right about this new city.

"Good. Anyone else?" He looked at each of them in turn.

Kate kept her eyes focused on the city below them, knowing it was dangerous to challenge Luca. He was the oldest—and therefore, the strongest—and he'd managed to keep the brood safe for hundreds of years. If anyone knew what the next step was, it was him. He'd saved them from mortality, and he would save them from this curse.

Kate eyed Melissa and Kenneth, much younger vampires who'd only been with them for a few years. Since they were newly-turned, they'd been affected more than anyone else. At this point, they'd become so weak, they had to be carried around by the brood.

"As for exactly how this new place is going to help us, let me first take you to our new home." Luca held a triumphant finger in the air as he led them back down the path and into the coastal mountains. He could've flown, but the fact that the others couldn't kept him grounded. He moved with a speed that would look like little more than a blur to human eyes.

The world moved slowly for them, the night breeze barely shaking the leaves on the plants near the trail as they shot past with relative ease, considering their weakened state. A simple walk for a vampire was a marathon for a mortal, and it humored Kate to think of all the humans who'd likely huffed and puffed along that very trail in Topanga State Park.

Their leader brought them through hills and valleys until he stopped in front of a rock formation. It was shadowed from the moonlight, the small opening little more than a dark crevice. Other holes further up on the structure peered at the brood like suspicious eyes, wondering what they had planned.

"A cave?" Thomas remarked, shaking his head and sneering. "Luca, we've stayed in palaces and castles. Even an apartment would be better than *this*."

In one swift movement that was so fast, even Kate hardly saw it, Luca had Thomas pinned by the throat to the rock. "Insolence will *not* be tolerated," he hissed, only inches from Thomas's face. His eyes went black as his fingers dug into the younger vamp's flesh. "You will do as I ask because I never ask for anything that isn't for the good of our family. You understand this, and so, *you will do it*."

"I...understand," Thomas repeated slowly.

"Excellent." Luca gave him a fatherly but condescending pat on the cheek before stepping aside and leading the way through the mouth of the cave. He was tall and had to crouch to make it inside the small opening.

Kate followed. Her night vision was good, but it didn't quite penetrate the deeper shadows inside the cave. She moved slowly, pressing her hands to the cool rock while keeping her head down. When Luca had sparked a fire and lit a makeshift torch, she turned and helped the others bring Melissa and Kenneth inside.

Past the threshold of the opening, the stone floor smoothed out into a welcoming surface. The interior of the cave was far more extensive than it seemed from the outside, with a ceiling that reached high up beyond the light of the torch flames. The smaller holes Kate had noticed before provided little windows that made it cozy, but the fact remained that it was still a cave.

The brood settled in, setting their bags down near the wall and making a circle around their leader. Nastasya, almost as old as Luca and one of his first, spun in a slow circle with a critical eye and laughed as she lowered herself with a ballet dancer's grace to the floor next to Luca.

He arched an eyebrow in her direction but said nothing. He tolerated attitude from her more than anyone else, but she never actually stepped out of line. Kate knew Nastasya was just as loyal to Luca as the rest of them were, perhaps more so.

"Now, then. I know you're all wondering why we're here. It seems a rather unusual place for people like us to live, considering we're far more sophisticated than the mortals who've crammed themselves into the city. They have all the luxuries, and so should we. Right?" He looked around, watching both for agreement and any sign of rebellion. When no one spoke, he continued. "You can complain about our circumstances all you want, but you don't know what I've found here."

Kate leaned forward, desperate to hear. There had to be something extraordinary about this place if Luca was willing to live in such primitive conditions. He enjoyed a featherbed and running water just as much as anyone else.

"What first brought me to Los Angeles was the sheer amount of people. Gone are the days when we could focus on a random rural town. As we all know, humans have changed. Cell phones and the internet have altered the way they connect, and so, we must find ways to change with them. A sprawling metropolis with almost four million people is much easier for us to hide in than a village. It's merely a numbers game when you think about it. However," he continued, "there is something here in a much higher concentration than anywhere else in the world. Something powerful. And absolutely delicious."

"You're killing me," Nastasya said dramatically, touching the back of her hand to her forehead and draping herself on the stone floor. "I can't stand the suspense any longer, Luca! You've refused to tell us anything about your trip here while you left us behind in Vegas."

Luca smiled. "Once you find out, my dear, you'll be so eager to head down into the city, you won't be able to contain yourself."

"Please," she begged, still laying on the floor. Nastasya gripped his pant leg and pulled herself toward him. "Please tell me it's something that will rid us of this hex once and for all."

"Would I bring you here if I didn't have confidence in that? Now listen. I needed to feed while I was here. My plan was simply to find a human who'd made the mistake of wandering away from the crowd and get whatever I could. We all know that ever since this curse has hit us, even the healthiest flesh gives us minimal reward."

Several of the others moaned in agreement. They felt it every second of every day, and time dragged on like an eternity when one was destined to live forever.

"But this particular man that I found was different. He was stronger than any normal human, and I immediately knew he was anything but normal. His blood carried with it the strength and agility of an animal. I could sense a beast inside him, one that was part of him, yet not." Luca's eyes gleamed, but this time, with excitement and intrigue. "I believe it was a shapeshifter." He rose, full of energy as he spoke. "Imagine draining the blood from both a healthy human and a wild animal at the same time. It was the most remarkable meal I've ever had, and the most satisfying. I had far more energy afterward, and I hadn't felt that good in a long time."

Several of the vampires moaned, and Kate closed her eyes to savor the very thought of a buffet like that. Her body burned with the need that hadn't been sated in months. "Are you saying there are more of them?" she dared to ask.

Luca nodded, a smile stretching his face. "Oh, yes, my dear. So many. And if you go down to the city, you'll even *smell* them."

Thomas and Nastasya rose and prepared to leave, but Luca stayed them with a swipe of his hand through the air. "Not so fast! There's more you need to know before you dare to take your next meal. When I finished with the first, I immediately tracked down another. I had to understand what was happening and who they were. I found the next one, a woman, by her scent. I followed her out of a restaurant and to her car in a dark parking lot. She sensed me, and you all know that any normal human would never have known I was there. Instead of running, she turned and called out to me, warning that she would kill me. I remained hidden, waiting to see what she would do, and she transformed into a tiger right before my very eyes! They're animal shifters, my children, and they're far stronger than any other meal you've chased down in the past."

"We're ready for them," Nastasya urged.

He smiled. "Go and get your dinner."

The brood left as one, pausing only long enough to duck through the narrow cave opening that suddenly didn't bother them nearly as much. In her excitement, Kate grinned as she sped up to a flat-out run, covering the distance through the state forest. Even off the trail, taking the most direct route down to the city, she bounced from one rock to another and dodged low hanging branches in her urgency to get to the feast.

A trilling laugh sounded behind her. "I'll get all the shifters before you even get a chance to smell them!" Nastasya cat-called, moving swiftly past Kate and shooting off into the distance.

Kate laughed to herself. *This is going to be fun.*

She hardly gave herself a chance to slow down once she reached the bottom of the foothills and her feet crunched into sand. Kate sucked in a deep breath, taking in the scent of the ocean that lapped gently on the shore to her right. On the left, towering palm trees swayed gently in front of storefronts, houses, and restaurants. Bike rentals, head shops, bars, and even outdoor gyms filled the oceanfront. Even at night, there were people everywhere. She saw something different every time she blinked her eyes. The brood moved together, keeping in the darkness near the water as they blazed past, burning off their excitement so they could control themselves for the hunt.

Finally slowing down, Kate turned and looked behind her. She realized how far they'd come already, how much they'd skimmed straight past. The coastline seemed to stretch in both directions for all eternity, and she smiled. In all their travels with Luca, they'd never lived on a beach before. Castles in the mountains, mansions in the oldest towns of the world, and penthouses in the wealthiest cities, but never along a beach.

She paused as she passed a building, noticing the colossal reproduction of Van Gogh's *Starry Night* painted along the side of it. It tugged at her as she took a few steps closer.

"Hey, are you coming?" Thomas asked, stepping up next to her.

"Yeah, sure. This is just so beautiful." Kate moved further toward the light and population, realizing that as she did, there were paintings all around her. Every surface in the area seemed to be covered in some sort of artwork, whether it was the side of a building or a concrete bench. Someone had even covered the sidewalk with chalk drawings, though she couldn't see them from where she stood.

Luca was suddenly at her other side, drawing attention from the entire brood. "I should remind you to stay together, at least at first. We don't know what to expect from these shifters. I'm older and stronger, so not only was I capable of taking one down on my own, but I *need* one of my own. And don't forget to bring a little something back for Melissa and Kenneth. I hope this new blood will allow them to be able to hunt alongside you once again very soon."

Kate nodded as did the others. This was a chance at a good meal for them, yes, but it was also a mission for their entire brood to survive and carry on. She stepped back toward the group as they wandered into a bar.

"Oh, I can smell it!" Nastasya hissed, practically jumping up and down in place. "Luca was right. It's a different note from regular humans. Now, we just have to figure out which one it's coming from."

Once again, Kate was shocked at just how much there was to see and smell there. She even felt the vibration of the live music thumping through her blood as a band played live on a small stage in the corner. The song came to a crescendo and stopped, eliciting a whoop of encouragement from the gathered crowd.

The vampires lived so much of their lives in solitude. Sure, they had each other, but it was easy to feel isolated even among their own when they couldn't just walk through town on a sunny day. Kate had attacked travelers on dark roads in the woods, and she had dragged off the bodies of wayward college students who wandered too far from the streetlights, but they were always in hiding. This place felt alive, welcoming.

"Over here!" Nastasya's eager shout dragged Kate out of her reflections as the other vampiress grabbed her by the elbow and pulled her physically across the room. She stopped near the bar and pointed. "I think it's coming from him. Can you smell it? It's like a good steak, but with all the right seasonings and sides to make it a gourmet meal."

Kate concentrated, a difficult thing to do in this place, and sifted through the very human scents of most of the other patrons. She picked up the stony, cold smell of her fellow vampires and ignored it. There it was! The scent of blood, yes, but it was incredibly rich. It made her mouth water and her muscles tighten, a craving that was so strong, it was almost sexual as she inhaled. "Wow." Even before she got close to him, she could tell that he was a bear. Her mouth began to water in anticipation of the oily, nutritious taste.

"Let's go." Nastasya pulled her forward, but she didn't need to.

The scent was so powerful, so provocative that Kate couldn't resist it.

It was the scent of a warm summer day and verdant fields.

It was the scent of iron and sex and power, and it rose inside her, filling her with a savage yearning.

The only thing left to do was to devour him.

2

AMAR LANDED HEAVILY ON THE BACK DECK, EXHILARATED FROM HIS flight and wishing it could've lasted longer. Even a short trip was risky considering what a densely populated area Los Angeles was, but the wild hills behind the house made it a little easier. He allowed his body to melt back down into his human form. His shimmering obsidian scales rippled as they flipped over to reveal his warm, sepia-toned skin once again, and his spine compressed as he lost his tail and the length of his dragon body. As a man, he was still stronger than most. His time as a Special Forces Officer had assured that. Still, there was a powerful element to his inner beast that was hard to resist. He left his wings for last, spreading them out and giving them one last shake in the moonlight before he tucked them away into his back.

The expansive house looked like a typical southern California mansion to anyone else, but it served as the headquarters for the new L.A. unit of the Special Ops Shifter Force. It was not only their central office but their home, as the sizable bedroom suites were much like apartments. It was quiet now, with most of the members having already gone to bed, and he stepped into the kitchen to find a little something to eat before he did the same.

The lights were already on, and he found Garrison sitting at the kitchen table. The plate in front of him held several different kinds of deli meat, a sizzling pile of bacon, and two chicken legs. Amar didn't judge. The meal was fit for a dragon, which was exactly what Garrison was when he wasn't human. "Leave any for the rest of us?" he joked.

Garrison smiled. "With all the carnivores in this house, it would be crazy not to have plenty on hand."

Amar opened the fridge, found a smoked ham and carried the entire platter to the table. "But there will be fewer carnivores in here soon enough. I understand you're leaving tomorrow."

The other dragon swallowed, his face serious. "That was the plan."

"But?" Garrison had helped start the original Special Ops Shifter Force in D.C. and had come to the West Coast to get the new L.A. recruits settled. The other two members that'd come out with him had already left, and Garrison was set to follow suit, but Amar detected a hint of trouble in his voice.

"I happened to be monitoring the communications system tonight and got some information that makes me feel I should stay."

As the Alpha of the L.A. unit, Amar didn't know if he should be insulted. "I wouldn't worry about us. We had a bit of trouble with those biker gangs on that last mission, but that's only because the five of us were still new to each other." They'd had a bit of a rough start for a number of reasons, but Amar was still confident of their skills and experience.

Wiping bacon grease from his fingers, Garrison sat back and folded his arms across his chest. "It's not that. It's just something I don't think any of us has dealt with before, and it concerns me. We know shifters. We know how they act. We know what motivates them. We *are* them. But this is something wholly different."

"I promise you I'm on the edge of my seat," Amar said coolly. If Garrison wanted to drag this out, then so be it. He'd find out eventually. He'd lived a long time, and that had made him a patient man in most respects.

Garrison ran a hand through his deep black hair. "I got a report about vampires. And the fact that this report is coming from shifters has me infinitely concerned."

"The fact that we're talking about blood-sucking creatures of the night doesn't?" Amar challenged. "I like a good horror movie every now and then, but it seems to me that whoever reported this is letting their imagination get away with them." He dug into the smoked ham, savoring its salty flavor.

"That was my first instinct, too, but think about it. If you walked up to a human man on the street and told him you could shift into a dragon at will, he'd fucking laugh in your face. Yet here you are, as am I. There are other supernatural beings in this world, so maybe vampires aren't so far-fetched." He lifted his hand in the air, floating the idea for consideration.

Amar pursed his lips as he nodded. "That's a good point. I suppose a dragon shouldn't be so closed-minded. You don't have to stay, though. We'll get all the information downloaded and decide what to do about it." Amar liked Garrison and respected him, but he was also eager to be set free to run this group on his own.

"Are you sure? I'm only asking because this is such an odd situation. You might be dealing with all sorts of elements you wouldn't expect." He reached forward and snatched another strip of bacon, unable to resist the temptation.

Amar understood. The carnivorous side of him was impossible to repress, and anyone else in the house would be lucky if they got a chance at this ham. He also understood the uncertainty of the mission ahead, but that was something he craved. "You know, the missions I ran as an SFO were like that. Sure, we gathered what intelligence we could about a given region and its people, and we always had maps from the latest satellite imagery, but we never knew exactly what we were getting into. War zones change on an hourly basis, and so do people's loyalties when they're being pressed. As far as I know, I didn't encounter any vampires while I was there, but I learned to think on my feet well enough to handle it regardless."

Garrison was silent for a time as he considered this, and then a slow smile spread across his face. "You know what that tells me?"

Amar lifted his chin.

"That I chose the right man to lead this group. I'll get out of your hair tomorrow as long as you promise to call us if you need us."

"I can handle that, too," Amar laughed. He was eager to get started. "I still can't believe I'm here, you know?"

"Los Angeles?" Garrison said with a grin.

"No. The SOS Force. I knew I had to retire from Special Forces. No one was going to believe a man who'd already been serving as long as I had was still in good enough shape to keep going. It was time to gray myself around the temples a little and start pretending I was daydreaming about a rocking chair on a covered porch. Deep down, though, I knew there was no way I could just sit still and collect a retirement check. I needed something to keep me busy, and I was lucky enough that you found me." Amar still remembered the first time Garrison had approached him, a complete stranger coming to his house on the pretense of buying some old furniture Amar was selling on Craigslist. But Garrison already knew who—and what—he was, and he was soon shocking Amar with the news of the rest of the dragons in the world.

"You can blame the internet for that," the other dragon replied. "When my mate Maren and I started looking for other dragons, we didn't have much hope of finding them. We were the only ones we knew about, and even though we *wanted* to find more, I wasn't convinced we would. There was a rumor about your clan, though, that brought us to the Sahara and then to you. I think it was all very good timing on behalf of the universe, considering we needed a good recruit for this unit."

"We'd also thought ourselves to be the last of our kind. It's strange how people can manage to find each other, even in the expanse of this big world." The thought brought a wave of sadness, one that he was used to pushing aside whenever his past came up. He'd lived for centuries, and he'd seen more of the world and had more experiences than even most shifters could claim. Dragons lived an exceptionally long time, and he hadn't wasted it. *Katalin.* Her face rose in his mind's eye, young, innocent, and lovely, and he once again dashed the daydream against the rocks of reality and cleared his throat. "Anyway, I'm glad you did find me. I needed something to do, and now I have it. Let's get started on these vampires."

"Vampires?" A woman stepped into the room, her dark hair a bit rumpled. Emersyn was a stunning woman, even in her flannel pajama pants, and Amar knew her mate, Gabe, was a lucky man indeed. "I know it's late, boys, and I'm an internist, not a psychiatrist, but it sounds to me like you're starting to lose it." She crossed the room to the fridge.

"What are you doing up so late?" Amar asked. "Lucas isn't sick again, is he?"

Her one-year-old son whom she shared with Gabe was the center of attention at headquarters, and everyone was concerned when he'd fallen ill recently. Emersyn shook her head and smiled. "No, he's fine. I just couldn't sleep and thought I'd come down for a snack. It sounds like I'm missing all the fun. And the meat." She turned around and raised an eyebrow at the feast that was still spread over the counter before pulling out the ingredients for a turkey sandwich. "So, what's all this about vampires?"

Garrison got up to rinse the plate that had been holding all the bacon. "Well, I've gotten some reports about them in the area. I wouldn't normally believe it, except that—" He looked up as footsteps approached.

Raul walked in, carrying his laptop and wearing a faded Wolverine t-shirt. His eyes were glued to the screen, and the headphones over his ears kept him from hearing the rest of them, but he slowly looked up to find everyone staring at him. "Did I miss something? It's not morning already, is it?"

Amar laughed. Raul was the youngest of them, even though he was past thirty. He'd seen Raul's comic book collection on the shelf in his room, and he was often up at all hours of the night. Amar didn't know if he should attribute that to Raul's tendency to get lost on the internet or his wolf nature. "You haven't missed anything. We're just getting started, actually, and it sounds like we might just need to wake up the rest of the house and have an official meeting. I mean, why not do it in the middle of the night if we're talking about vampires anyway, right?"

Raul's dark eyes widened. "Did you just say *vampires*?"

"Yes, and I promise it's not a joke."

Gabe and Jude padded into the room and took a seat at the kitchen table.

"No, I know it isn't. Look." Raul jetted forward and set his laptop on the counter. "There's a shifter network online that I've been checking out. Pretty normal stuff, and they've even got it split up by area so shifters can connect with others nearby. The chat rooms for L.A. are massive."

"Don't tell me you're looking for a date," Emersyn teased.

He scowled at her but didn't answer her question directly. "Anyway, I figured I'd check out the underground scene and watch for any signs of people knowing we're here. Most people don't, but they do use this network to talk about things that concern them. This surfer says he and his pack have lost a handful of people."

Amar leaned forward, skimming through some of the information. "Missing how?"

"Well, the guy's being a bit vague about it. Everyone is, even though you have to be admitted into the chat rooms. Anyway, for the most part, their members are simply disappearing without a trace. They go to the beach or hang out at a bar, and then they're just never seen again. No word, no notes, nothing out of the ordinary at all. They just vanish."

Gabe rubbed his chin. "Like an abduction, almost."

"Yeah," Raul said with a bit of a snort, his dark eyes shadowed, "except for when they actually *do* find a body."

"Don't keep us in suspense," Jude said, rising and slowly shuffling toward the coffee pot. Apparently, he'd been the only one in the household who was actually getting any sleep before all this happened, and he was barely holding up his head.

"I've only seen one instance where they've actually found someone. He was in the valley of the foothills, and at first, his brothers thought it was someone else because he looked so different. He was white as a ghost and sucked dry, with puncture wounds all over his body."

"What did the punctures look like?" Emersyn demanded, her role as a doctor and her interest in anatomy quickly taking over. "Are there any pictures?"

"Here." Raul tapped the screen. "I've been messaging with the Alpha of a wolf clan privately. He doesn't really trust me, which I don't blame him for, but I did get him to share a few photos. They don't show the guy's face, but you can see everything else."

The doctor scowled at the screen, zooming in and moving around. "I've seen a lot of interesting things in the medical field, both in the service and in private practice. As strange as some of them are, they've always had some logical explanation. Unfortunately, I don't have one for this. It certainly does look as though he's been drained, and these bite marks appear to be consistent with the spacing of human canines." She shuddered as she took a step back.

"Sounds to me like you don't need any of the information I've gathered," Garrison said, folding his arms across his chest and grinning. "Raul, I have to congratulate you on finding all this."

"Eh, it's just a hobby, really. I've always been into this kind of stuff."

"The internet or vampires?" Gabe teased.

"Both," Raul admitted with a grin.

"Still, it's all pretty much the same information I had," Garrison said. "Now, the question is, what are we going to do about it?" He looked pointedly to Amar.

He rubbed his chin and smiled, glad to be put back into a position of authority—not because it gave him power, but because he enjoyed making decisions. There was something exciting about being given a certain set of information and then having to choose what to do with it. He'd done quite a bit of that in the military, and that was how he knew the job with the SOS Force was right for him. It was all the more intriguing considering they were meeting in the middle of the night to discuss immortal beings. "We have to start somewhere. Raul, see if you can arrange a meeting with the Alpha you've been talking to. Anywhere he wants to meet is fine with me; we want them to feel safe talking to us. We'll see what he has to say, and I wouldn't be surprised if there's other information he didn't share online."

"Can do." Raul turned the computer to face him once again and began typing.

"Other than that, I'd say we all need to get some sleep so we can get started on this as soon as possible tomorrow." Amar watched as the rest of the Force drifted out of the kitchen. Jude took his coffee with him, and Raul was still staring at his computer screen as he carried his laptop toward the stairs. Gabe and Emersyn held hands as they slipped back to bed. Amar felt for them, knowing that life had split them apart for what must've seemed like ages. He knew that familiar longing all too well, even though there was nothing he could do about it now.

"What about you, old fart?" Garrison teased as he got up to rinse the last of the dishes, knowing that both of them were centuries old. "Aren't you going to get some sleep?"

Amar shook his head and ran his hand along his dark hair. He'd been a fan of keeping it short even before his time in the military, and he'd have to trim it again soon. "There's no rest for the wicked, they say, nor for the curious. I think I'll be doing some research."

"Staying up all night to watch *Twilight?*" the other dragon asked with a smirk.

Amar had to laugh. He'd only known Garrison for a short time, but they'd developed a camaraderie that he enjoyed. He'd miss that once Garrison went back to D.C., but it'd also give him a better chance to fully step into his role as Alpha. "You know as well as I do that there's plenty of truth in fiction. All the legends that people pass down to their children have some basis in truth. That's how you found me, anyway."

"That's true. I suppose that means there's a real-life legend taking care of L.A. now, and I can safely head off to the Alps to find the Tatzelwurm."

"Tell him I said hello. Do you need a ride to the airport?"

Garrison shook his head. "No, I've got it covered. I'm leaving really early, so I don't plan to wake anyone up. Goodnight." He headed toward the guest room in the basement.

"Night." Amar stood in the silence of the kitchen for a long moment. He should have gone to bed. He, like the others, would need some rest if he was going to be a good leader for this first mission on their own. But the search for truth tugged at him, and he headed for the library.

————

"This doesn't exactly look like it belongs to a pack," Amar said the next night as he and Raul pulled up under a second-story balcony that formed the roof of a carport. The home was just like most of the others in the neighborhood, but most groups of shifters opted for sprawling mansions just like the one the SOS Force occupied. This was much smaller and simpler, cramped in next to the other similar houses on either side of it. Amar was starting to realize just how different each district in Los Angeles really was.

Raul shrugged. "It's by the beach, and I get the gist that they're really into the surfing scene. Anyway, this is the address he gave me."

"I have to say I'm surprised they gave you their home address, considering they don't know you. We could've met somewhere on the beach." Amar couldn't help the undercurrent of suspicion that flowed through his veins. It'd always been there, a part of himself as a dragon who'd been hunted over the centuries, but it'd been forged into something even more permanent by his time with Special Forces. No one should give their home address away to a stranger on the internet.

"I promised that we were here to help. Besides, we're about to walk into a house full of shifters. They could handle any normal strangers who might try to pull something off."

"As long as we're not vampires, anyway," Amar muttered. He'd ended up spending most of the night doing research, but it was a frustrating endeavor. Every myth about the creature changed from one tale to the next. There were a few consistencies, but there was never anything concrete enough for him to feel that he was prepared for what they were about to face. Amar knew this wasn't any different for his own kind, as dragons were just another myth, as far as most people were concerned.

The man who answered the door was exactly what Amar would've expected from someone who lived on the beach. His board shorts and tank top showed off his tanned skin, and the streaks in his hair continued the story of someone who spent a lot of time in the sun. "Come in," he said warmly. "My name's Zach. Have a seat." He brought them into a small living room, where several others were waiting. They watched him with a little more suspicion than their Alpha, but he couldn't blame them. If something was happening to their pack, they were taking a risk by trusting anyone. The setting sun beamed brightly through the wide windows and illuminated the room.

"Thank you. I'm Amar, and this is Raul. I appreciate you taking the time to meet with us." He took a seat, feeling all their eyes on them. They were the sort of group that would likely be laughing as they played in the sun and water, but the heavy sense of dread that had taken over them was palpable.

Zach shook their hands. "You're the one I was talking to online, right? My wolf brother?" He slapped an arm around Raul's shoulders and brought him into the room. "It's nice to meet you in person. You never know who you're talking to online, even in what's supposed to be a private group."

Raul seemed to enjoy the camaraderie, smiling as he sat down. "I understand. It's difficult in the world for people like us, both online and in real life."

"Do you have a pack around here?" Zach asked. One of the women on the other side of the room eyed Raul with interest.

Amar could understand Raul getting to know his fellow wolves, but he was ready to get down to business. He cleared his throat.

Raul got the message. "Of sorts. Why don't you tell us a little bit about what's going on?"

Zach looked at his hands, trying to ready himself, but another wolf with short, spiked hair spoke up. "Everyone is disappearing. We actually had two houses here near the beach that we occupied, but we're down to the point of consolidating into one. They've just up and gone."

"No witnesses? Has anyone been threatening you?" Amar asked.

The Alpha shook his head. "We keep everything pretty peaceful, and we get that in return. We hang out here, we go surfing, and we give the boardwalk shops plenty of business. I can't even remember the last time someone got into a fight."

"Interesting," Amar mused, leaning forward in his seat. "Is there any connection between the members who go missing, other than the fact that they're all from this pack?"

"I thought it was just the guys, at first," said the woman who'd been eyeing Raul. "But then my roommate disappeared. She went out to meet some friends and never came back. I checked with the people she was supposed to be hanging out with, and they said she never showed up."

"Tell me about some of the others," Amar urged, hoping to find something that would give him a clue. He'd latched onto this case, and he didn't want to let go of it until he'd torn it apart and examined every thread.

"It's basically the same story," Zach replied. "Jake went out to catch a late wave. Selina couldn't sleep and went for a walk. Matt said he had a hot date. Then they were all just gone."

"And the one whose body you found?" Amar pressed.

Most of the wolves averted their eyes then, turning away or looking down. Zach rubbed his neck nervously.

"I'm sorry," Amar added. "I know this can't be easy for you. But the more details we have, the more we can help."

"At this point, we're desperate for anything that might help," Zach admitted. "The one thing I don't completely understand is *how* you can help..." He trailed off and covered his eyes, running his hands down his face before slapping them back onto his lap.

Raul looked to Amar. The two of them had only been a clan for the last few weeks since the L.A. unit was formed and Garrison performed the sacred ceremony that united them all. They could speak to each other telepathically, but only when in animal form. Even so, Amar caught Raul's meaning easily. It was time to be honest. "We're from the Special Ops Shifter Force, a group of special forces veterans who've come together to assist shifters when no one else can."

Zach's eyes widened. "Are you shitting me?" He looked from Amar to Raul and back again. "I thought I just had a hold of one of those armchair detective guys. You know, the kind that watches too much *CSI*."

"Thanks a lot," Raul said with a snort.

The Alpha punched him playfully on the arm. "Hey, no offense, man. I mean, I've heard of the SOS Force, but I didn't know you guys were legit. Maybe just another online rumor."

"We're here and in the flesh," Amar said with a smile, "and we really do want to help."

"Okay." Zach pounded his fist into his hand a few times while looking at his pack mates. "Then I'll be honest with you. I think we're being hunted by vampires." He waited for the reaction.

Whatever he was expecting, he seemed relieved when Amar and Raul simply nodded. "We thought the same thing," Amar said.

"So you don't think we're crazy?" the girl asked.

"Not at all. It's an odd concept, and I can't say I've ever actually met a vampire, but right now, there isn't a better explanation. Tell me, are all of these abductions happening at night?"

Zach looked up at the ceiling and tapped out the cases on his fingers before looking at the girl. "Hailey, what about Morgan?"

Hailey's mouth tightened. "She said she was running to the corner store. It was eleven at night."

"Then yeah," Zach concluded. "All of them went missing at night."

"And the body that you sent me pictures of?" Raul asked, joining in on the investigation. "Do you still have it?"

Zach's face went solemn. "We took him out to one of the islands and buried him in a private spot."

"Did you call any authorities?"

"No way. Last thing we want is the cops buzzing around here."

There wasn't much information, certainly not enough for Amar to draw any major conclusions. Still, he wasn't about to give up on this pack. They needed the Force, and he would do everything he could to help them before they were gone entirely. "If you can get us the names of everyone who went missing, and maybe a photograph of each of them, that might help us. We can do a little research and see if we come up with anything. Unfortunately, I think a lot of this will rely on people making reports. If there are only shifters being affected, we're far less likely to get those." The thought was getting his head working on something, but it was an idea he'd have to wait to express until they got back to headquarters.

"Absolutely. Anything you need at all." Zach's shoulders relaxed, as though just knowing someone was on their side had made him feel better. "Hey, we were thinking about going out for a few beers. You guys want to join us?"

Amar was about to thank them and pass, but Raul instantly nodded. "Sure, that'd be great! We haven't been in L.A. very long, so maybe you can show us some of the good spots."

The wolves had been somber as they discussed their missing pack members, but they instantly brightened at the idea of going out for the night. They shot up off the furniture and flooded toward the door.

There was work to be done. Amar knew he needed to do more research, to comb the newspapers for any disappearances that might've been reported by humans, and maybe even make arrangements for Emersyn to exhume and examine the desiccated body. Right now, though, it was clear that the wolves wanted something different.

He followed them out the door and down the street. The sun had set during their meeting, quickly dunking the Venice Beach area into darkness. Amar watched the wolves, knowing he didn't fit in with the rest of them. Raul, though he was without a clan other than the Force, blended in easily with these guys. At heart, he was one of them, and they knew it. They likely smelled it on him instantly.

Watching the city around him, Amar thought of his clan back in the Sahara. They'd made their home near low mountains and an oasis. The African desert heat and the solitude were just what the dragons needed, and even today, humans rarely dared to go anywhere near their den. Amar had been glad to leave and explore the world when he'd been tired of the sand and loneliness. That was centuries ago now, and though he'd done many things with his life thus far, he was beginning to wonder if he would ever truly fit in anywhere. Even at home, the other dragons had thought he was crazy for wanting to get away, for leaving the safety of their flight and risking exposure. In most ways, he hadn't regretted it.

"Are you coming?" Raul's voice from up ahead broke his thoughts.

"Right behind you." Amar moved faster to catch up.

Raul lagged slightly behind the group to wait for him. "Are you all right?"

"Just deep in thought."

"Let it go," the wolf advised. "We might have all moved here for work, but no one's saying we can't party a little and enjoy ourselves. Besides, it can't hurt to get to know the local clans and packs better."

"That's true," Amar admitted, though he was sure his motives were different than Raul's. If they had time to observe this wolf pack, perhaps they would pick up on some clue that would point to the missing shifters.

"Not only that, but have you noticed how hot the women are here? *¡Mira!*" Raul gestured around him, focusing on a group of women in bikinis that strolled up the sidewalk on the other side of the street, even though it was well past dark. A few of them wiggled their fingers, making the wolf puff up his chest a little. "Seriously, man. Every single girl I've seen is smokin'."

"That's just because you want to see it," Amar replied quietly, with the wisdom of hundreds of years behind him.

Raul let out an impatient huff. "I don't know you all that well, yet, but you need to learn to let go and relax a little. Not everything has to be about business. You can't tell me you haven't noticed anyone since we've been in L.A."

Amar looked at him. Raul was so eager and excited. No doubt at least some of that was because he'd found some wolves there, people who were not only friendly, but whom he intrinsically meshed with. He had every right to feel enlivened by this experience, and Amar wasn't going to ruin it for him. "Maybe I just haven't seen the right one yet. Let's go see what we can find."

They followed the wolves into a bar that looked small and dull on the outside but was throbbing with life on the inside. The place was absolutely packed. Every seat at the bar was taken, and some patrons leaned in between the stools to signal the bartender. What tables were available had been taken up, and it was standing room only.

"This place is very popular with shifters," Zach said, shouting to be heard above the thumping music. There was no concern about being overheard. "Even the guys in the band are like us." He nodded toward the small stage in the back corner.

"I can tell." Amar could sense the animals inside the others. Most shifters could detect some sort of presence, even if they couldn't tell exactly what kind of beast they were dealing with. Amar highly doubted any of them were dragons, though.

"First round's on me!" Zach announced, throwing his hands up and stepping to the bar. He gave Amar a playful slap on the arm. "What'll you have?"

He opened his mouth to reply when something twisted deep inside him. It was like a writhing snake in his stomach, but Amar quickly realized it was something much more than that. His dragon was stir-ring inside him, suddenly awakened. Amar looked around the room for anything out of the ordinary that might've roused the beast. His eyes darted down the row of customers at the bar, but they all looked happily occupied with their drinks and their fellow shifters. He checked the tables and even focused on the band for a moment. Nothing seemed unusual at all. No one was acting strangely.

"Hey, you all right?" Raul asked.

Except for him, apparently. "Yeah. I'm fine."

"You look a little sick. If you don't like crowds, we can go some-where else," Zach offered.

The last thing Amar needed to do was make a bad impression on this pack. He forced a smile on his face. "I'm fine. Really. I'll have an IPA."

He accepted the pint glass Zach handed him a minute later, but he only took a perfunctory sip. Something was happening there. He could feel it.

More importantly, *his dragon* could feel it.

The sensation swirled inside him, crept through his bones, and seeped into his blood. Every cell of his body pulsated with it to the time of the music. The only thing that would fix it would be to shift, something he didn't dare to do, even in a bar full of people who wouldn't be shocked to see a man turn into a creature.

3

"CAN YOU BELIEVE THIS PLACE?" KATE LIFTED HER ARMS OVER HER HEAD and stretched her spine as they strolled down the beach, thrilled with the way the hunting had been there over the last few weeks. "I don't think I've felt better in centuries."

"It's fabulous. The hunting, the shops, the pier." Nastasya gestured behind them to the brilliant lights and sounds of the Santa Monica Pier. "I could sit on the Ferris wheel forever."

"Good thing you don't get sick from rides like humans do," Thomas said. "You shut the place down last night."

"Might as well live a little!" Nastasya teased.

"I'm just glad to feel like I'm living again," Melissa added. She walked arm-in-arm with Kenneth, a dreamy smile plastered on her face. "I can't thank you guys enough for doing what you did for us while we were so sick. I can tell I still have a long way to go, but this is so much better than having someone wait on me hand and foot."

Kenneth tightened his arm around hers. "We're very lucky," he agreed. "We'd never even have been able to walk again if it hadn't been for Luca's ingenious plan." He smiled at their leader.

Luca waved off Kenneth's praise, even though they all knew he loved it. "I'm simply doing what's best for all of us," he said graciously. "I'm glad you're enjoying yourselves, but I'm also glad to see my theory proven correct. Shifter blood is the magic cure for whatever ails you." The brood laughed.

Kate smiled, feeling as sated as a zoo animal, having its food pre-killed and thrown to it instead of having to put in the work for the hunt. They were still finding their own prey, but it felt like a luxury to simply sniff a few shifters out of the crowd and then catch them alone. Luca had been right: there were tons of them there. They could smell the animal blood almost everywhere they went.

"What's the matter with you?" she asked Thomas, who stared down at his feet as they walked, his dark eyes distant. "Aren't you feeling better?"

"Much, unfortunately," he muttered.

Kate slowed her steps, increasing the distance between the two of them and Luca. "What's unfortunate about that? I feel like I could run straight to the top of Mount Everest now, and before it took all my energy just to find one lousy meal." She still recalled the first victim they'd taken when they'd first arrived in L.A. Kate had used up most of her strength in that first run down the mountains and into the city, and by the time they'd cornered that bear shifter in the bar, she'd felt herself growing weaker by the minute. Even a partial drink of shifter blood had made a remarkable difference, though, bringing her back to life the way human blood hadn't been able to do for a long time.

"Sure. Me, too. But what happens now? I mean, will we ever be able to go back to feeding normally?" Thomas asked.

"I'm not sure why you'd want to." Kate couldn't stop the smile that spread over her face. She'd seen the humans who'd gotten high on cannabis while on the boardwalk, something the vampires couldn't do with any success. It left them happy and comfortable in their bodies, which was much the same way she felt. "Shifter blood is incredible stuff."

Thomas let out an impatient huff. "Yeah, but you're letting it go to your head. You know as well as I do that we can't stay in this area forever. What happens when people start to get suspicious around here and we need to go somewhere else? What if we can't find other shifters out there, or even not as many? Right now, we're living high on the hog, but that food source could run out at some point."

Kate looked out at the ocean and bit her lip. They'd only been there for a few weeks, and it was purely paradise for so many reasons.

She liked it, and they were doing so well that leaving had never occurred to her. "Maybe you should talk to Luca about it."

"No," Thomas said quickly. He was always moody, and now, more so than ever. "Luca always has his plans, and he doesn't want anyone else to intervene. I mean, he doesn't even let the rest of us hunt with him. He insists to do it on his own, keeping entire bodies for himself."

The underlying tension between Thomas and Luca had been building for quite some time, and it hadn't gone unnoticed. "He's looking out for us," she finally countered. "We don't have the experience he does, and he wants to keep us safe. Besides, it takes a lot of blood to keep someone as old as him going. He brought us here because he knew we had a chance of surviving with these shifters. You can't fault him for that."

"I can fault him for making us live in a cave like animals," he spat.

"If you have a problem with the way I run things, I suggest you tell me to my face." Luca was at Thomas's elbow, appearing there as if generated directly from the night.

Thomas's eyes widened for a minute before he turned a stony and insolent gaze to their leader.

"We were just talking," Kate babbled, worried both for herself and for Thomas. "He didn't mean any of that."

"Yes, I did," Thomas argued, putting his chin in the air. "You think that just because you're older than us, you know everything, Luca. But there are surely some things that even you haven't figured out, like how to find us a decent place to live. It isn't as though you can't come up with the money. I suppose you just get a kick out of seeing us curled up in the dirt so you can continue to walk all over us."

Kate clapped her hand to her mouth, wishing she could take those words and erase them from the air. Any of the vamps could get restless now and then, but they never spoke to Luca that way.

Their leader put a gentle hand on her arm. "Don't be so alarmed, my dear. Why don't you go off to hunt with the others? There are plenty of shifters out tonight. I can smell them already, can't you?"

As if he'd bade the wind to bring it to her, the deep, thick scent of shifter blood hit her nostrils. She inhaled deeply and closed her eyes. "What about you?"

Luca flicked a hand in the air. "I've already got plans for my meal. You should go on."

Kate hesitated for a moment.

"And I'm sure that Melissa and Kenneth could use your help. Poor dear things are doing much better than they were before, but they do still rely on the rest of us." Luca tipped his head slightly, giving her a disarming smile with his thin lips.

Kate smiled back. "Of course." She turned and ran down the beach, leaving Luca to speak with Thomas.

Nastasya strutted confidently away from the water and toward the string of buildings that faced it. "Can you believe the surfers here in Venice Beach?" she asked. "They're to die for. Strong and muscular, a little salty, oh!" She threw her head back. "I had one all to myself the other night. He was magnificent!"

A cry split the air behind them, something full of pain and fear, and a cold finger traced its way down Kate's spine as she realized just what it was. Thomas had crossed the line too many times, and he'd refused to back down. She urged Nastasya and the others on, not wanting to get caught up in Luca's wrath.

Nastasya's head turned to the side slightly as she listened, and a smile curled her lips. "Come with me, my lovelies, and I'll show you how it's done. Dinner's on me!"

Kate was grateful for the distraction of the hunt. It would've been too easy to worry about what had transpired between Luca and Thomas otherwise—and what it would mean for the rest of the brood. As soon as they entered the bar, the thumping music and the heady scent of shifters reminded her what they were there for. It was a night-club of some sort, with men and women openly grinding on each other on the dance floor.

Kate grinned as she and the others joined them. Melissa and Kenneth danced together, but she and Nastasya were there as single women, as far as anyone knew. Strange men had no hesitation in dancing right up next to them. She felt the heat of a man at her side and turned to him, moving her hips to the rhythm. He smiled at her, and as he moved closer, she inhaled deeply, sorting out his cologne and his blood. *Human. Young and strong, tempting on a certain level, but definitely not a shifter.* He grabbed her hips and turned her around, grinding against her backside. Kate detached herself from him, knowing he wasn't what she'd gone there for.

She made her way across the dance floor, feeling alive in a different way than feeding made her feel. Her life with Luca and the brood was often a lonely one, and it suppressed the sexual desire that had only been amplified when Luca had turned her. She licked her lips as she danced. This place was like a market for anything she could ever want. Kate could easily seduce a man for herself and use him for sex, food— or both.

Just like that, something changed inside her. All the energy and excitement that'd been coursing through her veins a moment ago had suddenly drained. The heady crush of the place was getting to her, so she headed toward the exit. She stumbled toward a door at the back and swung it shut behind her, cutting off some of the noise and leaving her in a short hallway. The restroom doors were nearby, but so was Nastasya.

"You're so goddamn sexy," Nastasya purred to a man she had pinned to the wall.

"Thanks, but I've got a girlfriend." His words were a protest, but he made no move to get away from her.

"And? That doesn't matter to me. I'm not looking for anything that'll last beyond tonight." She pressed her lean, athletic body against his, closing her eyes as she inhaled his scent. When she opened them again, her eyes were full and dark.

Kate moved past them toward the restroom so she wouldn't look suspicious, but she merely tucked herself in the shadow of a doorway and waited. Nastasya wouldn't likely need her help. Luca had warned them about the strength of these shifters, but none of them had been a problem so far. Kate knew nothing about how they worked, other than the fact that they could turn into animals and their blood tasted like heaven. Still, Nastasya had promised them a meal.

The man's eyes raked up and down Nastasya's trim body. "You, uh, you don't sound like you're from around here."

"I'm not. There's so much I don't know about your American customs. Perhaps you could teach me?" Nastasya thickened her Russian accent as she trailed a finger down his chest.

Kate stifled a giggle. Nastasya knew more about the world than this man could ever know.

"Yeah, baby. There's plenty I could teach you." He gripped her hips and pouted his lips slightly in what he surely thought was sexy. Kate thought it looked ridiculous.

"Then let's get out of here. There's a beautiful place down by the water, and I want to feel the tide wash over my naked skin."

That was enough to do the man in. He followed her eagerly back through the club and outside. Kate trailed them, catching the eye of Melissa and Kenneth on the way. They hung back just far enough so that their intended victim wouldn't realize anything was going on.

"I don't want to wait," Melissa hissed, her sharp teeth grazing her lower lip. "I've felt so good since this all started, and I can practically taste him already!"

"Hush," Kate warned, watching as Nastasya led the man down to the shore. The moon was bright, creating deep shadows under the fishing pier. She pulled him into the darkness, but Kate could still see what was happening. "We'll get our share. And soon enough, the two of you will be strong enough to do the hunting yourself."

Melissa clapped her hands in anticipation. "What do you think we should go for, honey? One of these surfer types Nastasya keeps talking about? Or something else?"

He wrapped an arm around her and pulled her close. "Anyone, as long as I get to sink my teeth into them next to you."

A strangled cry sounded from the beach. Kate shot forward, the others on her heels. By the time they reached Nastasya, she'd already sunk her teeth in for the first bite. Blood dripped down her chin and neck, looking black against her pale skin. "Dig in, my lovelies."

Kate threw herself down into the sand, feeling the delicious pressure of sinking her fangs into his flesh. Heat hit the back of her throat as the sweet elixir of life flowed into her body. The man was technically still alive, his beating heart thrusting the blood into her mouth. She ran her tongue along the line of jagged skin, savoring every drop.

"Holy shit," she said a few minutes later. The first bite had dried up. She could move elsewhere on the man's body to find another suitable spot, but she was too full even to consider it. She sat there on her knees in the sand, her body sagging with relief.

"Now, now, my dear. You know how we feel about anything holy." Luca stood over them, smiling at his joke. "I take it you had a nice feast?"

Kate looked up at him. "It was incredible," she gushed.

"Good. I'm glad. And you're all finding yourselves happy in our current situation, then?"

Something niggled at the back of Kate's mind. There was a reason he was asking them that. *Oh yes. Thomas.* He wasn't with Luca, which could have only meant their discussion didn't end well at all. A chill shot through her spine at the thought, but she knew questioning him would only make her his next target. "Of course."

The others all murmured their agreement as they lounged around the desiccated body.

"Good. I'll take this out to the woods for disposal, then. We can't be getting careless with cleaning up after ourselves like what happened last week. That's a sure way to get discovered and have to relocate once again."

The idea struck instant fear into Kate's heart. She scooted across the sand until she was clutching Luca's leg. "I don't want to leave," she begged. "I like the water, sand, and not having to worry about whether or not we'll find a nourishing meal." She ran her tongue against her lips, finding a stray drop of delectable blood on the corner of her mouth.

"And as long as you all listen to me and do as I say, then we won't have to leave." He brushed his hand through her hair and gently pushed her away. "Now, then. I'll take care of this, and I'll see the rest of you at home shortly." Luca easily hoisted the husk of a body over his shoulder and took off down the shore. His feet quickly accelerated him to a blur before he lifted off into the night sky and toward the hills.

"I hope I can fly like that someday," Kate sighed as she slowly got to her feet. She kicked some of the sand around, erasing the imprint of the man's body.

"Even I can't do it yet," Nastasya reminded her as she wiped the last of the blood from her chin and patted her hair back into place. "We'll all get there in time. Let's go."

The group made their way under the fishing pier and down the beach. They started off slow, having just finished their meal, but Kate could feel the energy moving through her body as they made their way up toward the boardwalk. It was like lava flowing through her veins and reaching out to all her cells, invigorating them with its heat and light. She felt it drift up into her head, and she experimentally stretched a bit to explore how sensational her body felt.

Then, in a flash so quick it nearly knocked her off her feet, that feeling was gone. It was taken over by that sick, swirling feeling that had bothered her when she was on the dance floor, only it was stronger this time. She was too hot, the warm feeling that was a pleasant rush only a moment ago suddenly too intense. She wanted to run down to the shore and plunge into the ocean, but she didn't have the energy. Her eyelids grew heavy, and she stumbled.

Nastasya caught her by the arm. "What's wrong?"

Melissa and Kenneth drew up next to her, concerned looks on their faces.

"I...I don't know." Kate leaned on the older vampiress as a shiver racked her bones. It was like her body didn't know what to do with itself. "Is anyone else feeling odd? Maybe there was something wrong with that guy." He'd tasted so good at the time, but the mere thought of it made her stomach swirl.

The others looked at each other. "We're fine," Nastasya said.

"I don't get it. Maybe I just need a second." Kate lowered herself onto the sand, both comforted and irritated by the grittiness against her body. She could feel every tiny granule grinding against her skin.

"Could it be some sort of reaction?" Melissa mused, putting a hand on Kate's shoulder. "Did you overfeed?"

"Oh, so now you think I'm hogging it? Is that it?" Kate snapped. She blinked, hearing the hatefulness in her voice. "I'm sorry, I didn't mean that. I'm just... I just... I don't know. I feel like I'm going to pass out."

Nastasya raised a slim brow. "I can't say I remember hearing of a vampire fainting before."

"Then tell me why my vision is all black around the edges," Kate countered. Something was having a substantial effect on her. It pulled and twisted and bent her from the very core of her body, and she didn't know how to stop it.

"We'll get you back to the nest," Kenneth volunteered. "Maybe Luca will know what to do."

They scooped her up out of the sand, their cold, immortal hands against her damp skin. To anyone else who passed by on the beach, they probably thought the trio was taking their drunk friend back home. Even so, Kate found that she didn't care how conspicuous they were. She just wanted to feel better.

Nastasya carried most of her weight, Melissa and Kenneth each taking a leg as they moved quickly along the beach and toward the foothills. Kate tried to analyze her body as she watched the stars pass by overhead. She pulled in steady breaths and blew them out again, knowing it wouldn't do any good. Kate was a vampire after all, and breathing for them was more about looks than any actual need for oxygen. Still, some instinct told her that was what she needed to do.

As they left the city behind and moved up into the hills, her body calmed down. Her stomach still swirled, but she no longer felt like she was going to pass out. "I can probably walk from here."

"No," Nastasya replied immediately, tightening her grip on Kate's arms. "I don't want to hear it from Luca if anything happens to you. He's already had an interesting night."

Kate spared a thought for Thomas and then let it go. She had other things to worry about. "Really. I'm doing a lot better."

"Luca will be the judge of that. We're almost there."

A few minutes later, they reached the cave. The group rearranged their grip to carry her inside, where Luca stood, alarmed by the situation.

"What's happened?" he demanded, rushing forward.

"We don't know. She got really dizzy and said she didn't feel good, so we carried her back here."

Luca's brows knitted together as he hovered over Kate. "That's strange. Nothing has made us feel ill until that damned curse came along. I wonder if it has something to do with that." His mouth was a grim line.

For the first time in ages, Kate was scared. Nothing ruffled Luca. Even when the curse had hit them and they were all quickly losing their energy with no help in sight, he was calm and determined. Whatever was happening with her had to be serious. "What do we do?"

He rubbed his chin. "You fed tonight, didn't you?"

"Yeah." Her stomach roiled once again at the thought, a betrayal of what a delicious meal it'd been.

"That's always the first step. So for now, you just need to rest. We'll see how you feel tomorrow." He patted her shoulder and moved off toward his corner of the cave.

Nastasya gave her one last look before doing the same, leaving Kate alone with her thoughts. She stared up at the rock ceiling above her, thinking. How long had she been a vampire? Five hundred years or so? She closed her eyes, trying to remember what it was like to be a human, hoping that might give her some clue as to what was wrong with her. Vampires didn't just get sick, or at least it wasn't anything they'd heard of until recently. Kate reached back in her mind.

Her oldest memory was of waking up with Luca over her, much the same way he had been just a moment ago when she was brought back to the cave. He'd smiled and touched her face, and he'd told her that everything was going to be all right. That was when she'd learned about the carriage accident and that he and his brood had rescued her, pulling her from the wreckage with life-threatening injuries. Luca had wanted to save her, and so he'd sired her with his bite.

She knew she was from Hungary, but that was it. There was nothing more, no hints or clues to lead her to any reasonable conclusion. Whatever was wrong with her wasn't going to be revealed that night, so she closed her eyes and tried to get some rest.

4

Amar moved from one side of the conference room to the other, examining a large map of Southern California he'd tacked to the wall. He frowned at it before making a mark in red along the coast to show the approximate place where Zach's wolf pack had found their deceased member. He used green to mark the places they'd said they frequented, and blue showed their home. After a moment's thought, he made another mark in blue since they'd mentioned they were originally split between two homes.

The light was changing in the rooms, streaming through the grand windows. Amar felt a jolt of excitement through his stomach, or perhaps it was simply the effect of not having slept. He refilled his coffee mug as he continued to work, checking the clock and wondering when the rest of the household would finally get up. He had information he needed to go over with them, and he didn't like having to wait.

Turning back to the table, he moved one sheet of paper aside and grabbed another one. He'd created several lists to keep his thoughts straight, each of them in a different color of pen. Flipping past the list of vampire characteristics, he added a few thoughts to the sheet that kept track of potential victims and motivations. After making a quick note, he moved to another one.

"Jeez, Amar. What the hell are you doing?" Raul rubbed his face as he stepped into the conference room. It'd originally been the dining room of the home, but most of them preferred to eat in the giant kitchen anyway.

"Just getting things prepared for our next stage of the mission. Have a seat. We'll get started as soon as everyone else is in here." Amar moved a stack of papers off a chair to make room for him.

"I was going to have some breakfast first. And some coffee. You might want to give us a second." He moved across the room toward the other doorway that led to the kitchen.

"I've been up all night doing this!" Amar protested. "Am I the only one who's taking this mission seriously?" He felt his dragon twist inside him, agitated and restless. "The D.C. unit chose me as Alpha for a reason, and I need the rest of you to fall in line."

"Whoa, calm down, man. What's going on here?" Gabe entered, looking to be in a similar state as Raul. He was at least dressed for the day, but he hadn't shaved yet. He looked from Amar to Raul with concern.

"Apparently, we've had a bit of a change in when our shift starts," Raul grumbled.

"We have work to do," Amar corrected, his voice grinding out of his throat. What he would give to just run straight out the back door, let his dragon free, and burn those damn parasites to ashes. It was a simple solution, but it was impossible to do when he didn't even know where the fucking things were hiding. There was also the possibility that they weren't vampires at all, but humans with some sort of fetish. Of course, that didn't explain how they'd managed to suck that one shifter completely dry, unless they had some sort of medical expertise he didn't anticipate. Even so, could they really have taken down a shifter? And how did they know that all of these disappearances were happening for the same reason? Maybe there was one 'vampire' death, and some sick psychopath had taken the rest of the missing shifters. There were plenty of those among the human population, and hell, even among the shifters themselves. These thoughts had been rico-cheting through his skull, and it'd been infuriating to wait to get them out.

"Don't worry, we'll get it all taken care of. We just need to get some breakfast in us. I'll go start some bacon and eggs. I'll make enough for everyone, and we can make it a breakfast meeting. Well, as long as you don't mind Lucas joining in so neither Emersyn nor I have to miss out." Gabe moved toward the kitchen.

Amar felt his resolve slipping away. He wanted them to be as psyched up about this as he was. He wanted their first mission on their own to not only be successful, but swift. He couldn't deny that Gabe and Emersyn needed to feed their child, though. If he was honest with himself, he couldn't deny that he was being a little unreasonable, too. "Yeah. Of course."

Half an hour later, the Force assembled in the conference room. Their plates were piled high with Gabe's efforts, and a highchair had been pulled up to the table between Gabe and Emersyn, where Lucas happily shoved fistfuls of scrambled eggs in his chubby little cheeks.

Jude was the last one in, and he let out a low whistle as he observed all the papers and maps. "What's all this? It looks like a library exploded in here."

"I've been busy," Amar said sharply.

"It might be easier to keep this all on a tablet or something," Jude noted as he picked up one of Amar's lists and skimmed it.

Yanking it back out of Jude's hand, Amar put it back where it went. "Call me old-fashioned."

Realizing he'd hit a sore spot, Jude sat down and picked up his fork. "Sorry. It just surprised me."

"It's fine." Amar turned to Lucas, smiling at the child and hoping he could focus on something sweet and innocent to calm the beast that was stirring inside him. His own breakfast sat in front of him on the table. It smelled delicious, but he wasn't even sure he could eat. He needed to focus all his energy on the task at hand. "As you all know, we're dealing with something very unusual here. Raul and I went out and met with a pack the other day. For the most part, we're simply talking about missing persons cases. These could be explained in many ways, so we need to find more clues. Raul, as a Communications Sergeant, you're our resident tech expert. Do you have any way to hack into the city's cameras?"

"I'll give it a shot," the wolf promised as he piled bacon and eggs on top of his toast to make a sandwich.

"Emersyn, I've had Zach—that's their Alpha—send me the exact coordinates for where they buried the body. How do you feel about doing an autopsy?"

She picked up Lucas's sippy cup and put it back on his highchair tray. "I can do that as long as they don't mind."

"They don't. I contacted Zach first thing this morning to ask him about it. They're not in love with the idea, but they understand it might lead us to some answers, so they want to go forward with it. I'll forward you both the coordinates of the grave and Zach's contact information. Some of the wolf pack may want to go with you, and they can help with the digging."

Emersyn gave a nod. "Works for me. I can take some time off at the clinic this week."

"Perfect." Amar was feeling the buzz of getting this all out of his system. He'd been frustrated at their lack of enthusiasm when they'd first gotten up, but Gabe had been right. They just needed a chance to wake up a little. "Now, our current focus needs to be on the vampire situation. I have plenty more I want to say on that in a moment. But talking with the wolves has brought up something else I think we need to address, not simply within our unit, but concerning shifters all over. We don't have a reliable way to spread news. If there have been any other disappearances from different clans, we don't know about them. Yes, there are the underground chat rooms that Raul has been frequenting, but I don't think it quite serves the purpose. We need something more concrete."

"What about an app? Something shifters could only have on their phones if they get a password from their local conclave," Raul suggested, his excitement beginning to build. "There could be an actual news side of it, and then more of a chat room and local discussion side."

"You'd have to find someone to run the news end of things," Jude added. "Otherwise, it's all just speculation. There has to be some way to verify the facts."

"Volunteers, possibly," Gabe mused. "Someone from each conclave, or chosen by each conclave to cover their jurisdiction. I like this."

"I think we'd need to do the app first. Security is going to be the biggest factor, but I can get with Hudson in the D.C. unit to make sure we cover all our bases." Raul snagged a clean sheet of paper and began making notes of his own.

Amar smiled as he watched them collaborate. Getting them motivated was exactly what he wanted. While a news app wouldn't be done on time to help them with their current mission, it could potentially be a part of future ones. Amar knew that other shifter infrastructure had slowly been rising to the surface over the years, including a shifter hospital in Dallas and a national registry system that had been developed by Hudson. They were heading in the right direction, even if they still lagged behind the humans. Of course, they had a lot more at stake.

"Wonderful. Just make sure we're not putting this ahead of the mission. We've got to find some way to nail down these vamps." He stabbed his finger on the table's surface for emphasis. "Does anyone have any ideas?"

"Sounds like most of the attacks are happening on the beach. Maybe we could just hang out at the bars and shops and see if we notice anything weird," Raul offered.

Amar pressed his lips together. "It's not a terrible idea, and it's better than nothing, but I'm concerned it's too passive. There are only five of us. Even if we split up, we couldn't possibly cover all the coastline between Santa Monica and Venice. And that's assuming all the disappearances are happening there. Maybe there are others further inland that we just don't know about yet."

Emersyn took one of Amar's lists and scanned it. "Any clues about vampires that could help us find them? I mean, I always thought they lived in dreary old castles in Transylvania, not the beach."

"Unfortunately, no." Amar scratched a hand through his hair. "That's the problem. There's very little to go off of here. I've been up all night, and I can't find a damn thing that'll help me." He slammed his fist on the table, but it did nothing to alleviate the frustration that was building up inside him.

"Easy man," Gabe said. "Like Garrison told us in the kitchen the other night, we're fighting something we've never faced before. It's going to be different than anything we've handled, both in military and civilian life."

"But this isn't *enough!*" Amar countered, slashing his hand through a pile of papers. They flew off the desk, scattering into the air. He turned toward the window, his arms crossed in front of his chest in an attempt to prevent his scales from emerging. He gritted his teeth, knowing he needed to get a hold of himself, but he couldn't.

"Come on, sweetling. Let's get you cleaned up and ready for the day," Emersyn said quietly to Lucas.

Amar heard the rest of them getting up to leave. Plates clattered as they were stacked together, and chairs squeaked as they were pulled out and then pushed back in. The sound of someone cleaning up drifted in from the kitchen. He closed his eyes against the beautiful scenery outside the window. Damn it. He'd been so excited to lead this group, but he was failing miserably.

A throat cleared behind him. "We'd like to talk to you for a minute, if you don't mind."

Amar turned, finding that Gabe and Raul were still in the room with him. Gabe leaned against the table, and Raul pulled out a chair. They exchanged a look before Gabe spoke again. "Is there something going on that you'd like to talk about? Something beyond just the mission? Because coming here to start up a new Force unit hasn't been an easy adjustment for any of us."

Amar swiped his tongue against the inside of his cheek, trying to decide whether or not to speak. Gabe wasn't wrong, but it was difficult to let it all out. "Look, I'm sorry that I've been losing my temper. I know that's not right, and I know I shouldn't have demanded that you assemble for a meeting when you've just barely gotten out of bed. It's just that I'd been up all night working on this, and I was getting impatient waiting for everyone else."

"If there's something we need to do to ease the pressure on you, we don't mind," Raul offered. "Just because you're our Alpha doesn't mean you have to take it all on your shoulders."

They were trying to help, and he knew that, but it still sounded like someone trying to take away a position that he knew he deserved. Moreover, it was a position he knew he could excel at if he could just get his head in the right place.

With a sigh, Amar sat. As he eased his body into a chair, he realized he'd been on his feet for hours. All night, maybe. He rested his elbows on the table and braced his temples in his hands. "The mission is fine. That's not the problem." He let out a dry laugh. "Actually, there are plenty of problems with it, but they're ones I know we can all handle. There's something else bothering me."

Gabe took a seat as well. "We're here for you, man."

"I know. And you—all of you—have been nothing short of amazing. There's plenty of talent and respect in this house, and I know there's a lot we can accomplish here. The problem doesn't have anything to do with our missions or the rest of you, though, so I don't think there's much you can do to help."

"But if there's something affecting you, it affects the rest of us," Raul pointed out quietly. "You could give us a shot."

"Okay, but I'm glad you're already sitting down because this isn't going to make a lot of sense." Amar wanted to be close to the rest of this clan. They were a motley crew of different shifters, most of whom had nothing in common before they joined the Force, aside from serving in the military. Thanks to Garrison, they had the telepathic link that would allow them to communicate in their animal forms, but there was more to it than that. They lived, worked, and ate together. They were family now.

"I assume you already know that dragons live for a very long time, hundreds or even thousands of years. I don't even know for sure myself, because there are so few of us left on the planet. Anyway, my flight had lived very peacefully in the Sahara, undisturbed by the growing civilizations all around the world. About six hundred years ago or so, I got the wild idea to get out and explore. I flew all over the place, living in quaint little towns and seeing the world. I loved it." Amar squeezed his eyes shut. The images of those days were still crystal clear in his mind, even though they'd happened so long ago.

"Eventually," he continued, "I wandered into Hungary, and just outside what's now known as Budapest, I met the most incredible woman. She was young and beautiful. Exotic and intriguing. She didn't want to talk to me at first. I thought she was just dismissing me as an outsider, but later, I'd learned she was just shy." He paused for a moment, remembering those first few times he'd seen her. Katalin's long dark hair was thick, slightly wavy, and even when she'd kept it held back in a braid, it was always trying to work its way loose. Her dark eyes and brilliant red lips made her physically attractive, but Amar soon came to find out there was so much more to her than her looks.

They spent an afternoon walking from her family's farm and into town, where she sold their meager wares. Eventually, Amar began showing up on the farm itself. Katalin shooed him away, not wanting to upset her father, but he couldn't bear to leave. Amar had felt the one thing that every shifter hears about when they're young that all the elders insist is true, yet that's impossible to believe until it happens. It was that feeling deep inside when his dragon recognized the one person he was meant to be with. It was fire and ice, torture and rhapsody.

"We were fated," he finally said, realizing he'd been so lost in his memories that he hadn't said anything for a bit. "I knew it, even though it was ridiculous. I mean, a creature that lives for hundreds of years can't possibly be with a mortal. Yet there was no mistaking it for me."

Katalin, human though she was, had believed him. Over the years, Amar had thought perhaps she just liked the romantic aspect of it, or maybe she went along with it because she thought of him as a ticket out of her simple life. Those were his darker thoughts, but at the time, he'd been thrilled. She loved him, and they would find a way to be together.

Amar forced himself to skip forward in time a little so he didn't bore his comrades with all the details of his historic love. "We were making plans and I left for a short while to get my affairs in order with my clan. When I returned, I couldn't find her anywhere. She was gone. I went to her farm and her parents were gone, too. The vegetables they'd grown were rotting on the vines. I asked around, desperate for some sort of answer. Those who were willing to talk to me simply said they didn't know. I thought maybe her parents had taken her and left because they didn't want her to be with me, but I never really knew. I searched all over for her for years. I searched myself, even, hoping to find some thread of that fated pull that would give me an indication of where she'd gone. But she was a mortal, and I knew after a while that it was time to give up. She couldn't possibly be alive anymore." He put his hands over his eyes and pressed, watching the kaleidoscope of colors that swirled in his vision.

"That's really tough," Gabe said quietly. "I'm sorry you had to go through that. I know what it means to find the one you're meant to be with only to lose her."

"I know you do." Amar's reply was hoarse with emotion. Gabe and Emersyn had been apart for a short time before the Force had accidentally brought them back together. Amar understood that pain, and it was one that hadn't gone away with time.

"I can't say I've felt that, myself." Raul scratched the back of his neck and looked out the window. "Is it really as strong as they say it is?"

"Yes," Amar and Gabe replied in unison.

Raul laughed. "All right, then. I guess I'll know when it hits me."

"You will," Amar said solemnly. "You'll know, yet you won't know if you want to jump for joy or get sick all over yourself."

"No offense, but that doesn't exactly sound like something I'd want to experience. Wouldn't it be easier to just be with someone else?"

It was Gabe's turn to laugh. "You can't. I mean, sure you can, physically. But it's not the same as that deep, emotional bond. The universe has determined that the two of you are meant to be together, and once you've experienced it, there's no easy way to live without it. Sorry, Amar."

"No. Don't apologize for the truth." Amar cut his hand through the air to rid it of Gabe's amends. "It's been very difficult. If you'd asked me about it just a few days ago, I would've told you that it was something I was learning to live with. I've kept myself very busy, wanting to have something to occupy my time. That was working well enough until yesterday." He hesitated. Amar hadn't wanted to tell them of his past, but now that it was out, it wasn't so bad. That still left current events, though.

"What, at the bar last night?" Raul had picked up on what was going on now. "You were fine for a bit, interested in the case and wanting to know more, and then you just sort of shut down."

"I had to, at least on the outside, because I definitely hadn't shut down on the inside." A wave of nausea crashed over him just in remembering it, or perhaps that was his lack of food. "I felt that same feeling again, as though Katalin was standing right next to me. It was so strong it damn near knocked me off my feet. I thought for sure I was wrong, but the more I think about it, the more I know I'm right."

Gabe pursed his lips and folded his hands on the table. "I've heard of there being more than one fated attraction for some. Do you think that could be it? Because we know that Katalin would have to be..." He spun his hand in the air to let them fill in the sentence for themselves.

"Dead, yes," Amar added. "I know that. But it wasn't just some random feeling. It was *her*. I could feel her in the very marrow of my bones. I looked all over the club, but I didn't see her. I don't know what's going on, and I don't know what to do to fix it."

"Wow," Raul breathed. "How could that even be possible?"

"I don't know, and that's part of what's driving me crazy," Amar admitted. "If it were feasible, I'd just focus all my free time on finding her, knowing she was still out there somewhere. It would be exciting more than anything else. But I know it's out of the question, which leaves me not knowing what to do about it at all." He let out another sigh. "So, there it is. I was once in love, and now those old feelings have come back from the dead to haunt me. And it's making me a complete asshole."

"It's not as simple as that," Gabe said with a smile. "Nothing, when it comes to women, is ever simple."

Raul shrugged. "Maybe not, but what do we do about it?"

"There isn't anything you can do." Amar felt confident in reiterating what he'd said earlier. "It was kind of you to listen to me, and it makes me feel a degree better. But it isn't as though we can just conjure her out of the afterlife and bring her here so that I won't be such a dick. I just have to find a new way to deal with it and put it aside."

"Maybe, but what if we can actually kill two birds with one stone?" Gabe tapped his chin as he thought. "We know there's something going on in this town, but we're having a hard time deciding how to proceed. The only idea that's been brought up—other than continuing mountains of research—is to hang out in the places where these disappearances are happening. That means hanging out in places where the surfers are, and at least one of those is the same place where you had that feeling."

"I see. So you're saying we go out to the boardwalk, hang out, and watch not only for anything that may lead us to the vamps, but also something more, like why I'm feeling this way." He frowned, not wanting any part of their mission to be about him.

Raul nodded. "One of the spots Zach mentioned was The Longboard Lounge. He said it's a spot where a lot of the local shifters go. We could start there."

Amar looked at them each in turn, seeing how much they believed in this plan. To him, it seemed loose and random. Percentage-wise, they weren't likely to get any real return out of it. Amar craved something more coordinated, a list of events that they could cross off as they were completed which would lead them to a final answer. It was a decent idea, but even he couldn't come up with anything better at the moment. "All right. We'll do it."

Raul and Gabe got up to leave, but Amar stopped them. "Could the two of you do me a favor?"

"Sure," Raul replied.

"Anything."

"As much as I appreciate you taking the time to talk to me, could we keep it between us? If the others ask, you can just tell them you called me out on being a jerk and I promised to fix it."

Gabe gave him an understanding smile. "No problem."

When they were gone, Amar began cleaning up the conference room, wondering if he would once again feel that way when they went out that night. Unfortunately, there was only one way to find out.

5

Kate opened her eyes and sucked in a breath, searching her mind. Everything felt normal as she experimentally stretched her arms and legs and wiggled her toes. She blinked as she grew more and more awakened, knowing there was something she was supposed to remember.

"How are you this morning?" Kenneth asked, coming over from the corner of the cave he and Melissa shared. "Doing better?"

Oh, right: the horrific feeling that had overwhelmed her. It'd practically knocked her knees out from under her, and if it hadn't been for the rest of her brood, she might very well have just lain there on the beach until the sun came up. Kate shivered at the idea. There were plenty of myths about how to kill vampires, and most of them weren't true. The sun, however, was a different case. "Yeah, I think so."

He stayed with her while she sat up. "Good. We were all worried about you."

"I appreciate it," she said honestly. "You guys are the best. What's the plan for today?"

Kenneth shrugged. "We've been waiting to decide until we checked in with you."

Kate glanced through the cave opening, seeing that it was fully dark. "I'm so sorry. I overslept. I didn't mean to keep you from anything."

"Nonsense." Luca was at her side, a cool hand touching her forehead as he smiled. "Right now, you are our priority, and it isn't as though the shifters go to bed with the sun. There's plenty of time in the night still."

"Maybe we should look for something further away from the beach," Nastasya suggested as she checked her reflection in an old hand mirror, making sure every hair was perfectly in place.

"Why?" Melissa asked, lacing up her boot. "The beach is lovely."

"Yes, but there could be some different—shall we say—flavors elsewhere," Nastasya smiled. "I'm quite certain I've tasted plenty of wolf over the past few weeks, and maybe a few bears, too. But I wonder just how many different kinds of shifters we can find."

Luca stood, holding out a hand to help Kate to her feet. "Just like the humans manage wild animal populations with their hunting seasons, we'll have to be careful not to overhunt these grounds. The good thing about L.A., though, is that it's brimming with food—and that food moves around a lot. Everyone makes their way out to the beach eventually. Let's go."

As they headed out through the woods and toward civilization, Kate realized how much better she was feeling. The shifter blood they'd been feeding on had done her some good, despite whatever those strange symptoms were the night before. She'd gained back almost all of her energy, and she was up for the hunt. Though she hadn't been sure about this move to L.A., Kate was finding herself in love with the area. Where else would they find wooded mountains, warm sandy beaches, and a bustling city all in one place?

"You children have fun," Luca said as they descended from the foothills. "I plan to do a little hunting on my own tonight. I think my hunger has only grown now that I've got a steady supply of shifter blood running through me."

The rest of the brood continued on, a small knot of friends going for a stroll along the boardwalk. "Just look at them," Nastasya purred as they passed Muscle Beach. "Those hard bodies are to die for." She paused, admiring the bodybuilders who were finishing their routines and wiping down the equipment for the night before they either went out or went home. "I think I know what I'm in the mood for."

"Suit yourself," Melissa said with a shrug, "but some of the ones who look like that have a weird taste to them. Steroids, supplements, protein shakes or something. Don't you remember the one we had last week?"

Nastasya flipped her hand in the air casually. "You can't let one bad apple spoil the bunch. The ones who work out like that have great blood flow, which makes feeding almost effortless."

"That's true. And I'm sure a decent amount of them are shifters. They always seem to be in great shape. I mean, everyone seems to be around these parts," Melissa joked. "But let's go to one of the clubs. It's more fun."

Nastasya gave one last, longing look at the muscled men and women as they moved past. "Fine, but I'm only agreeing because I think it's about time some of you younger ones start making some decisions for yourselves. You can't just expect me to be the leader every time Luca walks away."

"That's exactly what you want," Kate reminded her with a smile. "You like feeling as if you're second in command."

"I don't *feel* like I am," Nastasya corrected, "I *know* I am."

Kate shook her head and walked on, amused by the power struggle that regularly took place between Nastasya and her. One day, she would be just as old, and she hoped she would handle it with calmness and wisdom.

"Oh, check that place out!" Kenneth called. He and Melissa had wandered a little ahead of the other two, and he pointed at a packed nightclub. Guys in board shorts and women in bikinis wandered in and out through the throng of khakis and Hawaiian prints. The smell of salt was in the air, but so was the scent of shifters. The brilliant surf-board-shaped sign over the door proclaimed it as The Longboard Lounge.

"Works for me." Kate trotted toward them, joining them as they made their way to the door. "There's something about the surfers that's just delicious, like they've been marinated. Let's see what we can find."

"Fine." Nastasya slunk along behind them, pouting over not being the one to choose their hunting spot.

The place was packed to the rafters with shifters. Kate inhaled a deep breath through her nose and smiled as she moved through the crowd. A partial wall split the building into a bar and a dance floor, though the music could be heard throughout the place. Surfboards hung from the walls, one of which had a large shark bite taken out of it. The back of the building was mostly open, leading to an outdoor seating area. "This is gonna be great. I wonder why Luca didn't want to stay with us, though."

Nastasya made a noise of disgust that could barely be heard over the pumping music. "It's quite simple. He's stronger and older than all of us, and he needs a lot more blood to sustain himself. If he has to take an entire body for himself, then it only makes sense for him to hunt elsewhere. Besides, it also means he can hunt in whatever style he wants without any of us getting in the way."

"Right. Of course." Kate knew that, but she also had to wonder just what he did with all that time alone when the rest of them were always staying together. "Do you think... Do you think he might be trying to find someone else to bring into the brood? I mean, now that Thomas isn't with us anymore?"

Nastasya gave her a dark look, and her tight lips were enough to keep Kate from saying anything else. If the other woman knew anything, she sure as hell wasn't talking about it.

"I'm heading over to the bar. Want anything?"

"No, thanks."

Kate shrugged. "Okay. Let me know if you find anything." She moved around the edge of the dance floor and to the other side of the building. The alcohol they served there wouldn't do anything to her system, but having a drink in her hand would at least make her look like she belonged.

The bartender saw her walk up and smiled, setting down the glass he was drying. He examined her body with such intensity, Kate could practically feel his gaze. "Hey there, beautiful. What can I get for you?"

She slid easily onto the barstool made to look like a surfboard. "I'll take a gimlet, please."

"I'm sorry, what?" He leaned a little closer. "I don't think I've ever heard of that. Do you know how to make it?"

If vampires could blush, Kate knew she would be doing just that. Every now and then, she forgot just how long she'd been on this Earth compared to almost everyone else. "No, don't worry about it. Um..."

"How about I surprise you?" the bartender offered. "Something unusual, just like you."

She tipped her head at him, trying to get a lock on his scent without being too obvious. There were enough shifters in the place that it was difficult to differentiate one from the other. "Is that a compliment or an insult?" she asked innocently.

"A compliment, of course." He hardly broke his gaze with her, even as he grabbed a shaker and began pouring bottles into it with expert ease. "You have a bit of an accent. Where are you from?"

"A little bit of everywhere. My parents were from Hungary." Kate knew her accent had faded over the years, but she had to be careful not to give away too much information about herself. "What about you?" She studied his body, wondering if he would make a good meal. He was a bit on the skinny side, but at least he looked healthy.

"Right here on the beach," he said proudly as he passed a drink across the bar to her. The pale violet liquid was garnished with a tiny purple and yellow flower. "There you go. I've got to head down there, but let me know if you like it." He gave her one last smile before heading to the other end of the bar to take care of a group of college kids clambering for beers.

Kate took an experimental sip. It was good; delicious, in fact. She turned her stool slightly to watch the crowd. The bartender could be tasty, and his interest in her made him an easy target, but he was too prominent of a person. Everyone would notice if he suddenly went missing and cut off the patrons from drinking themselves silly.

She watched a couple at a small table near the wall, their heads bent close together as they talked and giggled. A pang hit her stomach as she wished she could have a relationship like that. Melissa and Kenneth were that way, constantly together and always enjoying each other's company. But they'd both been turned by Luca at the same time, and Kate hadn't had that chance. She chewed her lip, trying to tell herself she was doing just fine with the rest of her brood at her side.

Suddenly, that familiar horrible feeling washed over her, stronger than it'd been the night before. Kate managed to set her drink on the bar before she lost her grip on it. She inhaled through her nose and let the breath out slowly through her mouth. A deep vibration buzzed in her bones and made her blood dance. There was definitely something wrong with her, and now she was all alone.

"It's you."

She looked up to find a gorgeous, well-muscled man standing next to her. Kate furrowed her eyebrows, wondering how obvious it was that she felt like utter shit. "Do I know you?"

"You don't recognize me?" The man took his hand in hers, the deep umber of his skin a stark contrast to the pale pearl of her own.

Kate's insides were still roiling, angry, and insistent, though she didn't know what they were trying to tell her. She breathed heavily as she looked up from their hands and to his face again. His eyes were dark brown and glossy, earnest and solemn. He smelled heavily of shifter, and the scent only made her more light-headed than she already was. Somehow, it wasn't the same hunger that other shifters invoked in her. "I don't think so. Should I?"

His body was so close to hers now, and he lifted his free hand to gently touch her chin. "It's been hundreds of years, Katalin, but I certainly haven't forgotten you."

His touch sent a spark pulsing through her body. She jerked her hand out of his. "No one's called me by that name in..." Kate trailed off, knowing she couldn't say just how long it'd actually been. Whoever this man was, he knew her true name. She'd left it behind when she and the rest of the brood fled Europe over a hundred years ago, ready for a change and wanting something that blended in with American society. "Well, in a long time."

"I'm sure of that," he answered warmly. "It's been so long. I searched for you for ages, and I'd given up hope. It was the only thing that made sense. But now you're here. Tell me how."

Kate licked her lips. Could this man have possibly known her in another time? He didn't have the look of a vampire, and he certainly smelled like a shifter. Was there something about the shifters that Luca didn't know? "Maybe you've had too much to drink."

"I haven't had a drop, but we can certainly have a few rounds while we figure this out." He took her hand again and gently pulled her off the barstool.

As her feet hit the floor, she realized the woozy feeling had changed. The nausea had faded, which she was grateful for, and she now felt a snapping, electrical energy across the surface of her skin. Nothing was making sense, so she tried to focus on what she'd gone there for in the first place. She and the others were looking for a meal, and this strange, beautiful man could very well be it. The easiest thing to do was play along. "Okay. Let's go outside so we can at least hear each other talk. What did you say your name was?"

They stepped out onto the patio area, where the warm night air filtered the music into a gentle background. A privacy fence had been erected around the space, and tiny lights shaped like palm trees had been strung along it. These and a glowing fire pit made for an intimate atmosphere.

"I didn't, but I thought you would remember." He sat her down at a table in the corner, the same kind Kate had seen that other couple at just a few minutes ago. "I'm Amar."

"Amar," she breathed, rolling the name around on her tongue, but it wasn't familiar. She looked away from the soft, expectant look in his eyes. Kate had seen that look in other people, but it was never aimed at her before. "I actually go by Kate now. I'm sorry. Where exactly do we know each other from?" It was safer to prod him into giving information away rather than doing it herself. Her own truth was one that very few would accept.

He glanced around. "I'm not sure this is the right place to go into too many details. You could say that the two of us knew each other quite well. I'm surprised you don't remember me." His dark brows pulled down over his eyes, and the concern with which he looked at her shot straight to her heart. "What happened to you?"

Damn. It was easy to drain the blood out of the arrogant pricks they'd taken over the years. Kate enjoyed giving them a bit of punishment, and she knew the world as a whole was probably better off without them. Amar wasn't like that. Whoever this handsome stranger was, he definitely cared about her. The impossibility of it all was what threw her the most. "I was in an accident," she said slowly. Luca had described the horrific carriage accident to her a long time ago, but obviously, that wasn't the sort of thing that happened these days. Better to not be too specific. "I don't remember much from before that. Things are different for me now."

"I see." The troubled look on his face said that he didn't see at all. How could he? Even she didn't understand what was going on. "I think the two of us are going to need some time to figure all this out."

All Kate wanted to figure out was how to get him alone so she could make the initial bite and call in the rest of her brood. They were there for blood, and nonsensical chitchat wasn't going to get that for her. Flirtation was always a surefire way of getting these stupid men to do what she wanted, and the fresh air from the patio was making her feel better. Kate thought she might be up to it now. She smiled and touched the back of his hand. "Maybe if we go somewhere alone, we'll have a chance to do just that." Kate stood, keeping one hand on the table to steady herself. No matter how much she tried to play this out like he was just another victim, this man had some sort of intense hold over her.

Amar did the same, but he didn't give her a chance to leave. He wrapped his hand around hers and pulled her close, his other arm coming around her as he softly pressed his lips to hers.

What the fuck? Kate's initial instinct was to fight him off. She was the initiator, the one who chose where and when and how she touched someone. She had the power of a woman who'd lived for hundreds of years, and she sure as hell wasn't going to let some asshole get away with just planting one on her.

But she felt her resolve and body quickly melt under his touch. His lips were inviting, soft and warm, and Kate sank into them, kissing him in return. When Amar pulled back slightly from their liplock, she pushed forward to ensure it continued. A pleasant heat flooded her body and chased away the last of that strange feeling that'd been plaguing her. Her hands slid along his firm torso, fire coursing through her palms as they moved around to his muscular back.

Finally, he pulled away a bit, still holding onto her as he searched her eyes. "Does that mean you remember me after all?"

A syllable of laughter escaped her lips as she prepared herself to tell him she had no idea who the hell he was, but since he was a good kisser, she was going to let him stay around.

But just then, sparks bloomed at the back of her mind, stretching like fine threads of light over her brain as they took over. Images flashed in front of her eyes.

Amar against a pale blue sky.

Herself wearing a plain dress, the calluses on her hands scratching against the garment as she pulled it away from her skin.

A massive dark creature with scales and wings—who turned into Amar.

She blinked and once again saw Amar standing in front of her on The Longboard Lounge's patio, feeling as though she'd just traveled in time. "I...I..."

"Kate," he pleaded, "please tell me what's going on. Tell me how I'm holding you in my arms again after all these years."

"I don't know." The only thing she did understand was that some-how, this man was a part of her past. It was utterly impossible, but she knew it so deeply in her core, the knowledge had even driven her need for blood away. That realization put her in the present moment even more. This man was supposed to be her meal. If she didn't get him, then someone else might. "I have to go."

His hand was resting just above her elbow, and he was careful not to hurt her as he tightened his grip. "You can't. I can't possibly let you go now that I've found you again. I had this strange feeling last night, and now I know it was because you were so close."

She swallowed, his touch thrumming through her body and igniting her with a fire that her cold, immortal body hadn't known for centuries. "What kind of feelings?"

His smile made one corner of his mouth tweak up further than the other. It was disarming, endearing. "Again, I think that's one of those things we can't really talk about here. But let's just say my body knew you were around before I did."

Kate had plenty of odd feelings, too, but she also knew the grim fate this man would meet if she allowed him to stick around. "Then let's meet again tomorrow. Santa Monica Pier. Eight o'clock."

"Of course. Anything you say. Just promise me you'll be there, that you're not some vision I'm having."

She smiled, touched by his desperation and his apparent need for her. It shouldn't have affected her at all, but this wasn't just a typical guy thinking with the wrong head. If he were, he would've taken her up on her earlier offer to slip off. "I'll be there. Right now, I have to leave." Kate forced her hands to let go of him. She turned and stiffly walked away, weaving through the bar and out the front of the building. Kate kept walking, leaving the boardwalk behind and trudging through the sand until the tide washed around her shoes.

Whatever happened back there was pure nonsense. The man had drugged her somehow, or maybe he was in cahoots with the bartender. He couldn't have known her, nor could she have known him. But how did he know her true name? Maybe it was the peculiar sickness she'd been feeling, or some hallucination from the vestiges of the curse that'd been plaguing her brood. Theories rampaged through her head, shattering as she heard the near-silent footsteps of her comrades behind her.

"There you are," Melissa said, holding hands with Kenneth. "We saw you outside with that guy, and then you were gone."

"He looked delicious," Nastasya commented, running her tongue along her teeth. "Big, strong, and virile. I bet he would've been scrumptious. Why did you let him go?"

Kate opened her mouth to reply, but they wouldn't want to hear the truth. "I couldn't get him alone, and I knew I couldn't handle him myself," she lied. "I was going to find an excuse to get you guys, but then he had some emergency phone call and had to leave."

"Mmm," Nastasya said through pursed lips. "I thought you were better than that, Kate. It isn't like you to let your prey slip through your fingers."

"I'm just having an off night. I started getting that strange feeling again, and that's why I came out here. I thought maybe getting away from the crowd would help, and it has." The fresh air was wonderful, and she didn't feel either the swirling or the heat moving through her, but Kate couldn't explain how or why. "Anyway, I'm sure we can find someone else."

"Easy enough to say, but that doesn't feed us right now," Kenneth grumbled.

"I'm meeting him tomorrow night at the Santa Monica Pier," Kate replied automatically, wishing she could push the words back in her mouth as soon as she'd said them. She'd never had any reason to hide anything from the rest of her brood. Too late now, and so she might as well make this whole lie as good as possible. "He only got away for tonight, but I'll get him alone tomorrow and I'll send you a signal when I'm ready."

"Fair enough, I suppose. I'm still pissed at you, though," Nastasya sneered. "Come. Let's find Luca and see if he has anything for us."

They moved along the beach, and Kate wished she could transport herself to anywhere else in the world but there. She was desperate to know what was going on with this Amar guy, but that was impossible at the moment. The last thing she wanted to do was see the disappointment on Luca's face when he found out she'd let them all down. She didn't even feel like feeding. The rest of the night was going to drag by.

She cast a glance toward the boardwalk, wondering if Amar was still at The Longboard Lounge.

6

"HUDSON AND I TALKED FOR A LONG TIME ABOUT THE NEWS APP. HE agrees it's something that could really help shifters as a whole, but also the members of the SOS Force. He had no problem with me working up the basic ideas behind the app, and then his team will reinforce security measures to go along with it." Raul thumped the conference table eagerly. "I'm so stoked!"

"About the tech or finding vampires?" Gabe asked, clapping him on the back.

"Both!"

"I wouldn't be too excited about vampires if I were you," Emersyn remarked. Her son was with Melody, Emersyn's best friend who lived at headquarters to serve as their in-house daycare and the Force's bookkeeper. That left her free to open a laptop and show them what she'd put together. "That autopsy was disturbing. I'd hoped to find evidence that this was a college kid pulling a prank, if a deadly one. Maybe someone who was good at special effects or had a fetish. Unfortunately, the only thing I can conclude is that we're dealing with real blood suckers."

"Blood suckers?" Jude asked over his third cup of coffee. "As in, definitely more than one?"

Emersyn nodded. "Yes. The bite marks are all consistent with the spacing of human teeth, but it's obvious that several of them fed on this one body due to the slight size differences between each bite mark." She clicked through a slide show of the high-res photos she'd taken.

Amar looked up and then flicked his gaze away, his stomach churning. These photos were much more detailed than the ones Raul had first received from Zach over the internet. What disturbed him even more was the truth he suspected, one that he wished he could find some rational route around.

"I felt awful for the wolves," Gabe commented, having gone with Emersyn to do the autopsy. "They were very understanding and easy to work with, but it was clear they were really mourning both this guy and the ones who'd gone missing. I'd like to find an answer for them so they can get some closure, but it sounds like that's going to take some time while we continue to stake out the clubs. Anyone find anything interesting?"

Raul shrugged. "*Nada.*"

"Nothing for me, either. Just a typical night out at a bar," Jude agreed.

Amar frowned. He had gone with Raul and Jude to The Longboard Lounge to look for some evidence of these strange happenings, and they'd decided to split up. They hadn't seen him talking to Kate, nor had he told them the truth of what had happened between them. He was still processing it himself and wasn't certain what to do about it. "I think I might have a lead on one of them."

"Seriously?" Gabe said excitedly. "That's incredible! What happened?"

Amar sat stock-still, not wanting to make any nervous gestures that would give away how disturbed he was by all this. "I spoke with a woman for a while last night. She didn't say anything directly, but I have my suspicions that she may be one of them." He hated himself for saying it out loud, because he was admitting that his one true love, the woman he'd pined after for centuries, was the enemy.

Raul squinted and tipped his head as he looked at the side of Amar's neck. "I don't see any bite marks, at least."

Amar shot Raul a look that quieted the man, but he couldn't blame him for teasing him. Even though Raul and Gabe knew Amar had been searching for his mate, they didn't realize she was possibly an undead monster. "She had to leave, but we managed to make plans to meet up again tonight."

"Do you want someone to go with you?" Jude asked.

"No," Amar quickly replied. This was most certainly something he had to do alone. "I can handle it. The rest of you can split up between a couple of the other bars and see what you can find."

"If you're sure," Raul said hesitantly.

"I am." Amar stood, gathering the papers he'd brought in for the meeting but had hardly used. "We don't have much time until it gets dark. I'm going to get ready. I'll be at the Santa Monica Pier tonight. Be sure to let me know which bars the rest of you decide to go to." He turned and stormed from the room.

His mood hadn't improved when he arrived on the pier an hour or so later. The sun was sinking over the ocean, and there were people everywhere, gathering in knots along the railing or charging forward to get to the rides as quickly as possible. Amar envied their smiles and carefree laughter, that hopeful look in their eyes as couples paired off and strolled hand in hand down the boardwalk. They didn't have any worries in the world beyond paying a few bills or looking for a better job. *In some ways, it must be nice to be simple humans*, he thought.

Amar's boots thudded heavily on the boards as he made his way from the parking lot area toward the carnival-like atmosphere further down the pier. Booths and carts were set up, offering custom jewelry, fun photographs, and cheap souvenirs. He paused and leaned against the railing in the shadows between the decorative street lamps, watching the crowd and waiting.

He checked his watch, and half an hour later, he checked it again. There hadn't been any sign of Kate. Amar had positioned himself where he should be able to see almost everyone as they came and went on the pier, but there'd been no sign of her. His heart constricted as he thought once again about what Kate's story might be. If she were a vampire, and if Emersyn had confirmed that there were multiple creatures like them lurking on the beaches, then she was likely in some alliance with them. Was she one of the vile things draining shifters? He shuddered, having a hard time imagining the sweet, sexy farm girl he'd known so long ago doing such things.

But then his thoughts turned to the other vamps. What kind of situation did they have her in? Someone must've turned her, which meant someone fed on her. His fists curled on the railing behind him as he tried to control his sudden surge of anger. His dragon roused with it, ready to come bursting forth from his skin. If someone had hurt her, Amar knew deep within his bones that he would do whatever it took to exact his vengeance. Someone had taken Kate from his life and left him suffering for hundreds of years, and they had done god-knew-what to her. That wasn't a sin that could simply go unpunished.

Among all these churning feelings, Amar noticed one slightly different from the others. It was that same burning, twisting sensation inside as his dragon sensed her. Being near one's mate wasn't always comfortable, particularly when things were strained between the two of them. His body had calmed considerably once he'd pressed his lips to hers, but now that they'd spent the night apart, his body had reset itself. Amar glanced around the pier, knowing she couldn't be too far away. He saw only the typical crowd at first, until a slowly moving figure emerged from behind one of the restaurants.

She wore a lightweight hooded sweatshirt, the dark fabric pulled up over her head. Perhaps she thought it would make her less obvious, but it only made her stand out amongst the rest of the patrons who were wearing as little as possible. And of course, she wasn't hiding her beautiful face, which he couldn't stop looking at. It was the same face he'd fallen in love with so long ago. Her full, defined brows framed wide eyes that tipped up slightly at the outside corners. Her lush lips were a deep red, a shade or so darker than he remembered them. Her skin had always been on the lighter side, but she no longer had the healthy flush of pink in her cheeks that came from a day of work in the fields or a run down to the creek.

Pain wrenched his heart again as he thought of those halcyon days that'd been ripped away from him without warning. He straightened, letting her approach him. It was clear to Amar that she was feeling hesitant about this reunion, and her reluctance made his gut tighten.

She kept to the shadows as she made her way down the pier, her feet hardly making any noise until she stood in front of him. She kept her eyes focused on the ocean in the distance. "I'm sorry I'm late," she began. "I had..." She broke off, biting her lower lip.

"You always used to do that," he said softly.

"What?" She glanced at him sharply before looking away again.

"You'd bite your lower lip when you weren't certain of something." Amar thought about their kiss, wondering if her fangs were always present. Could she have bitten him right then if she'd wanted to?

"It's just that this isn't an easy thing for me to do," she said with finality, as though that vague statement should be enough of an explanation for the last five hundred years.

"Seeing me? Or getting away from whatever it is you have going on in your life?" He had his suspicions, but he wouldn't zero in on them just yet. His voice was already growing harsh with frustration, even though his dragon wanted nothing more than to scoop her up against his chest and protect her from the world.

"Both. I'm sorry, Amar. I still don't quite understand what's going on between the two of us. You say you know me, and that's just impossible. But after what happened last night, I want to find out more. I think I need to." Her lower lip started to tuck in again, and she stopped herself.

"I feel the same way, so at least we're starting on common ground." How strange it was to be with her, yet not be *with* her. They'd never argued about a thing back in Hungary, except perhaps when she'd worried about her parents' reaction to him. They had to dance around social rules, but at the heart of it, they'd always gotten along well. Their thoughts and emotions might not be lining up, but his body was certainly letting him know this was the same woman he'd lost so long ago. Every cell inside him yearned for her, and he gripped the railing behind him even harder to keep himself from doing anything stupid. "Where would you like to start?"

She flapped her hands uselessly. "I don't know. I feel like I don't know anything right now."

"Then I'll start." They weren't going to get anywhere like this, and he was ready for at least a few answers. Maybe he could coax them out of her by giving some of his own. "Shall we walk and talk?"

Kate nodded, and they started working their way down the pier.

"I don't suppose you remember who—or what—I actually am."

She looked out over the beach, watching the people below them. "A shifter," she said quietly. "When you don't look like this, you're a dragon."

He smiled. That would've been a hard thing to explain if she'd forgotten that part. "Yes. Because of that, I have a very long lifespan. I look like a human most of the time, but I live at least ten times as long. I left my family in the Sahara Desert a very long time ago and decided to travel the world. When I wandered into eastern Europe, I happened to meet you. Do you remember the day?"

This earned him another look from her, but she tore it away again just as quickly. "There's very little that I remember. A few things came back to me after we met last night, and when I woke up today, I felt as though I'd dreamed of them. That's silly though, because v—" She stopped herself midsentence, and her footsteps sped up a little.

Amar didn't push her. He had a good idea of what she'd almost said. "I came to one of the little markets on the outskirts of Budapest— I mean, what we call Budapest these days. I'd fed myself well on some of the livestock in the rural areas, but even a carnivore craves fruit and vegetables every now and then. I blame that on my human side. At any rate, I walked through the market and saw you. You didn't see me at first. You were busy helping another customer, but then your eyes turned to me, and I wanted to live in them forever."

She glanced up at him, and he knew it was no different now than it'd been back then. The woman he walked with wasn't the same, but the Kate he'd known was still inside her somewhere. He wanted to peel back the layers and find her. Then, Amar wouldn't need to remind her how good the two of them had been together. She would already know.

"What happened after that?"

Good. If she hadn't cut him off yet, then that had to be a good sign. He wanted to go through every single second they'd spent together, but it would take too long. "You were a bit shy at first, but soon enough, we started spending time together. I'd walk with you from the market to your farm, and I'd push your vegetable cart for you. At first, you tried to insist that you didn't need any help with it because you could do it on your own. I knew you could, but I wanted to help. Your father had been disabled after an incident with a horse, so you had most of the hard work to yourself. I could see it in your eyes, and I could also see the relief in them when you had your load lightened."

Right then, however, Kate's eyes were troubled as she paused to look at blown glass trinkets displayed at a kiosk. They all had 'Santa Monica Pier' emblazoned along the bottom of them. "It's a strange thing to think someone else knows more about you than you do yourself."

"You really don't remember any of this?" he asked, feeling frustrated.

"Don't judge me!" Kate snapped, coming to a stop and glaring up at him before she stormed down the boardwalk again. "You don't even know me."

"Not anymore, apparently, but at least I'm trying to!" Amar felt sand grinding against the boardwalk under his boots, and it was strikingly similar to the way this conversation felt. They had to slowly erode the outer surface that'd built up over the years to get to the heart of the matter. He could take a chainsaw to one of these boards and reveal the fresh, clean wood inside, but the damage would be too much to ever repair. "Do you want me to tell you the rest of what I know, or would you rather I wait for another time?"

Kate glanced over her shoulder, her eyebrows puckering together. She took another half-step away from him, increasing her physical distance as though it would keep him from explaining just how much she'd meant to him. "I don't know that there will *be* another time."

There had to be. He would make sure of it. Amar refused to go back to that incessant longing once again. He took her arm and pulled her close, keeping her body pressed against him as he held his face within inches of hers. "All right, then. We were growing closer as we spent more time together. You were concerned that your parents wouldn't like me, but once they saw that my intentions were genuine, they were accepting of me. Not the part about being a dragon. They never knew that."

"I imagine that would be hard for anyone to accept," she retorted as she yanked her arm out of his grip.

Amar resisted putting his arm around her or reaching out to hold her hand. That's what they might've done if they were still back in the Hungarian countryside, but everything was different now. The conflicting feelings inside him were hard to sort out. One moment, he wanted to kiss her, and the next, he wanted to scream at her stubbornness. "There are a lot of creatures who appear human, but aren't."

A smirk twisted Kate's face. "You're telling *me*."

"Well, I sure as hell wish you'd tell *me*." They moved past a few more booths, and Amar led her toward the Ferris wheel. It was as close as he was going to get to being alone with her.

"You seem to know so much already. Why should I have to tell you anything?"

Amar gritted his teeth together, his exasperation peaking. The world was a strange place, one where the ghost of his past was intermingling with new information that couldn't possibly be real. He grounded himself in the facts. No matter what else was happening, he knew what his truth was. "We'd started talking about our future together, so I had to take a short trip back to my homeland to tell my clan. When I returned to your farm one morning, planning to walk with you to the market like we always did, you didn't come out of the house. I waited by the barn for a while, because I didn't want to interrupt you if you were busy, but then I came up to the house. No one answered the door. You were gone, and so were your parents. I never saw you again until now."

"What happened to them?" she demanded as they joined the queue for the ride, her brazen façade melting a little. "My parents."

"Do you remember them?" he asked hopefully.

"No, but how could they have just disappeared? Or me?" Panic overtook her features, and Amar longed to soothe it away with his touch.

"I don't know. I walked around your village and asked everyone I could find, but no one had any idea. You were simply gone. I had a lot of different theories about it, but I never actually knew the truth."

Something flashed through her eyes. "I was told there was a terrible carriage accident."

"Your family didn't own a carriage," Amar couldn't help but point out.

Kate said nothing as they moved through the line.

"I looked for you for years, trying to think of all the places you could've gone. After a few decades, I realized there was no point. Either you were trying so hard to stay away from me that I was never going to find you, or you were dead. In fact, that last thought was a bit of a comfort to me."

"What?" She made a sound of disgust.

He shrugged. "At least if you were dead, I could have mourned you and tried to come to terms with it. I would've known you weren't avoiding me. But even after a hundred years, I hadn't moved on. Kate, I mourned for you. You meant everything to me." Amar stopped, feeling all that pain bubble to the surface once again. How could he possibly have his soulmate there, standing right in front of him, and still feel as if she were a stranger?

The ride operator waved them forward. The cars were generous ones, the kind that would hold quite a few people, and Amar was grateful when Kate decided to sit on the same side. She wasn't right next to him, but he didn't want to be any further from her than he had to be. Kate was angry and sullen, but he could deal with that as long as it gave him the chance to get to the bottom of this.

"It's not fair of you to do this to me," she said, folding her arms in front of her chest and looking out over the boardwalk.

The Pacific Wheel started up with a whir, lifting them into the air before stopping to accommodate the next set of passengers. "Do what?"

"To just show up in my life after all these years and act like I should just fall into your arms and proclaim my love for you. Is that how all shifters act? Like they're some sort of gods on Earth and that everyone should bow before them?" Her chin jutted out stubbornly.

He leaned in closer, so angry he didn't know what to do with himself. "How can you say that about me? You're the one who'd just somehow completely forgotten everything we shared. I guess I've waited five hundred years just to find out I don't mean shit to you. How pleasant."

"I never said you don't matter to me!" Kate was practically shouting now, though at least no one could hear them over the sound of the ride and the carnival atmosphere.

"How could I know? I'm trying here, but you're giving me nothing to go on." Amar focused hard on her eyes, wondering if he could've been wrong. Was this the Katalin he'd known? Could someone else have possibly made his body react this way? "I loved you, Kate. I've been in pain ever since the day you disappeared, and I'll be in pain for the rest of my life without you."

Her fists quickly snatched the front of his shirt, twisting the fabric as she pulled him close and pressed her lips to his.

Any animosity that'd been building up between the two of them instantly dissipated. Amar wrapped his arms around her and pulled her closer, deepening the kiss. In that moment, she wasn't a vampire or anything else, just his Katalin. His dragon let out a deep shudder of satisfaction, and Amar's hand curled possessively around her hip. When she pulled back and looked out over the ocean, it was difficult to let her go. "Change of heart?" he asked.

She kept her gaze out over the water, but at least she made no move to get away from him. "When we kissed at The Longboard Lounge last night, it triggered something. I honestly didn't recognize you at all before that, but it was like the kiss awakened something inside me."

"And what about this time? Did it do what you expected?" he asked. It would be a miracle if she suddenly remembered what they truly were to each other, and a welcome one. "I'm more than happy to try again."

She was silent for a long minute as they spun through the air. Her chestnut eyes were serious when she turned back to him. "I have to tell you something."

"I'm listening."

"Yes, but it's probably not something you want to hear."

She had a lover somewhere. Or she remembered him but didn't want to have anything to do with him.

"That carriage accident I told you about? Apparently, it was a bad one, and I wasn't going to survive. A man found me and whisked me away from the scene, and he saved me from death's door." Kate had avoided looking at Amar most of the time they'd been together, but now she stared straight into his soul. "That man was a vampire. And to keep me alive, he had to make me one, too. His name is Luca, and he's the leader of our brood."

"Is he... Are the two of you..." Amar choked on the words. He was a strong man, and he had no qualms about asking tough questions if they led him to the answers he needed. Somehow, it was different with her.

"No," she answered quickly. "It's not like that. He's like a father figure to us. Luca has been a vampire for a very long time, so he's quite powerful and knows how to keep us safe. I don't remember anything about my life as a human, or at least I didn't until I met you again. There are still a lot of blanks I need to fill in about that, but all this time, I've been roaming the world just like you have."

It was Amar's turn to look away. The dark waters of the ocean swirled to the west, breaking softly against the beach. What it hid in its depths was at least as complicated and mysterious as what he had going on with Kate. He wasn't the least bit surprised at what she'd told him. He'd already had his suspicions, but he loved her regardless. "I missed you so much. I feel horrible for having given up on you, but at the time, I had no idea that this—"

"Hush." She laid a cool finger on his lips and gave him a hint of a smile, the first positive look he'd seen on her face. "It's all a big mess, and neither of us is to blame."

"But what does it mean for us?" he dared to ask. "I still want to be with you."

"I need some time, Amar. There's a lot I have to figure out, and I can't just up and leave my brood." Though she'd opened up to him for a moment, that curtain quickly closed again, and Amar could tell she was hiding something. "For now, let's spend some time together and see where it leads."

"Then I'll have to settle for that." He pressed his forehead against hers. It made sense that she would hesitate a little at first. After all, that was exactly what she'd done as a human. She didn't have to be completely different just because she was a vampire.

The Ferris wheel settled to the ground and stopped, and Amar realized he hadn't even noticed its motion after they'd kissed. Kate was his whole world, and he had no qualms now about taking her hand as they stepped down from the car. He wound his fingers through hers as they moved further down the pier and headed down the steps that led to the beach.

"We're definitely not the average couple around here," she joked. "A vampire and a dragon."

"No," he agreed, "but I'm all right with that." Amar held her hand a little tighter as they moved further along the coast. It was beautiful there, even more so as they left the crowd behind. Much was unusual about his life, but none of it mattered if he had her at his side.

"I wonder if you might do me a favor." She glanced up at him and then looked away again, her bottom lip tucked under her teeth.

"Anything," he replied sincerely. He would fly to the moon and back if she asked.

"You're a shifter. A dragon. I know this, and I have a faint picture of it, but I'd like to see it again."

Amar smiled. His dragon was already reacting to her request, pushing further toward the surface. "And why would you want to see that, Katalin?" he teased.

She twisted her mouth into a smile she tried to repress. "I told you last night that no one's called me by that name in a long time."

"And I can't recall the last time someone asked me to shift into a dragon," he countered. "But for you, I'll do anything." They'd reached an area where the beach had turned rocky. The late hour and the fact that there weren't any bars or stores there made it feel remote, like they were standing on the very edge of the world. A lone car drove off in the distance, but the lack of street lights hid them from sight.

Amar pulled in a deep breath and finally let his dragon out. It had only been a few days since he'd shifted, given that he enjoyed a flight here and there when he could find the time, but it was different doing it for his mate. Her eyes shone in the moonlight as she watched his deep brown skin part in a million fissures, leaving tiny islands that slowly spun to show the onyx scales hiding beneath. She parted her lips in wonder as his wings erupted from his back, a massive span of black leather in the night that matched his powerful legs. Amar had always imagined that a transformation like this had to be an uncomfortable and even a horrifying thing for an outsider to watch, but Kate didn't flinch as his neck and spine lengthened and strengthened, his face breaking and reforming in the configuration of a dragon.

Instead, she stepped forward and touched his scaly jaw. "Absolutely beautiful."

"I happen to think the same about you." His voice was thick and raspy in this form, but Amar knew he was lucky to be the only shifter species capable of speech when in animal form.

She moved down his side, trailing her fingers down his scales as she went. "Did you ever show this to anyone but me? I mean, anyone who wasn't a shifter."

"No." It hadn't always been easy to hide this secret, especially in the military when he wanted to shift so he could blast the enemy with a forceful stream of fire. "Just you."

"I'm very fortunate, then." Kate touched the edge of his wing, sending a shiver of energy up his spine.

"We could fly for a little while if you'd like. Maybe up over the mountains." He inclined his chin toward the foothills that stretched up away behind them.

She quickly shook her head. "No. That would be too risky. Some other time, maybe."

Amar allowed himself to melt back to his human form. She was right. They were taking a bit of a risk just being out and about for a walk without showing off his reptilian side.

"You never did answer my question earlier, about the kiss," he reminded her as they walked along in the sand.

She bit her lower lip. "I saw an old man by a fireplace. He was holding a squash in his hand and nodding. That doesn't tell a lot, I know."

Amar smiled. "Sure it does. That was your father. His injury hurt unless he kept himself warm, so he was always by the fire. As far as the squash goes, he still wanted to be a part of the farm as much as possible. He'd always wanted you to show him what you'd pulled out of the field before you took it to the market."

"Wow." She shook her head and leaned a little closer to him. They'd made good progress down the beach already, leaving the bustling pier behind. Her feet seemed to float over the sand. "I don't suppose you'd be up for a few more memory jogs, would you?"

Unable to resist any longer, Amar planted his feet in the sand and wrapped his arms around her waist. His lips softly met hers again, and when he felt her respond, he claimed her mouth fully. Their tongues danced together, the textures colliding and contributing to his hunger for her. Amar's dragon stirred inside him, desperate to come out, but the feeling was different than what he'd experienced when they were still far apart. It was demanding and eager, but it was satisfied at knowing she was finally there in his arms. He felt a shiver on the back of his neck and knew that a few scales had made it through.

Amar pulled her down into the sand. Vampire or not, she was just as glorious as he remembered, and the decades that'd passed since their last meeting evaporated into the night sky. Her curvy body fit perfectly against his as he caressed her, his fingers having a mind of their own as they skimmed down the sides of her breasts, found the delicate dip of her waist, and explored her ample hips. Her hair fell around him in a gentle curtain as she kissed him. "I've missed you so much, Kate. After all these centuries, I can't believe you're here with me."

She trailed her lips along his jaw and down his neck, pulling his shirt aside. "I can't believe I couldn't remember any of this. Amar, you've done something to me."

"If a kiss has that kind of power," he said with a smile, "then imagine what else we could do to get your memories back." Amar gathered her hair with one hand at the nape of her neck so he could see her face. She was like a ghost of the past, something he never thought he would get back again. It was hard to believe she was even real, but he could see her, feel her, taste her.

Kate smiled, her face a delicate sculpture in the moonlight. "Let's find out if you're right." She stripped him of his clothes, working her mouth down his chest. It was clear that even if her mind had forgotten, her body still knew how to please him.

It took all his self-control to let her do as she wished. He'd been waiting for so long, the beast inside him wanted to throw her down in the sand and have his needs met that instant. His dragon thrashed inside him, arguing against any patience, but Amar sucked in a breath and forced it aside. There was no telling what the future would hold for them, so he wanted this to last as long as possible.

The cool air touched his skin, a sharp contrast to the dragon fire that had been building inside his body, threatening to rage out of control. As she cast her clothes onto the sand and pressed herself against him, her tongue traced along his skin, tasting him with agonizing slowness, and he brought his hands up to caress her shoulders and the back of her neck. He moved down to grip her backside, wondering just how long he could last.

"I'm remembering the two of us in a field in the foothills," she breathed against the side of his neck. "The sun on my skin, your hands on my hips." Kate kissed him again, a small moan escaping her lips.

"We'd sneak off on your way back home at the end of the day," he reminded her, closing his eyes in an attempt to control himself as she straddled his hips and slid against his shaft. "You were worried we'd get caught at first, but once things heated up between us, I could hardly get you to go home before dark."

"I didn't want my parents to worry," she gasped, grinding harder against him as a tear slid from the corner of her eye, "but being with you felt so good. It was like I'd been waiting for you all my life."

Amar raised his head and took her nipple into his mouth, caressing it with his tongue, loving it in every way he knew how. "We're meant to be together, Kate," he said softly. "A shifter knows when they've met the one they're fated to, and I knew it was you the instant I saw you."

She arched her back and tipped her head toward the sky, her eyes closed as the memories continued flooding back to her consciousness. "I didn't believe you when you told me that. I thought it was just a line so you could get me in bed. But you were so patient with me. You walked with me. You held my hand, but even for that, you waited."

He moved his attention to the other breast. "I didn't want to scare you away. I couldn't risk it. I needed you too badly. I loved you. And I still do."

"And you let things continue to build between us," she whispered, bending forward and lifting her hips. "You waited until I was ready." Lifting his throbbing member with her hand, she positioned him at her entrance and slowly sank her hips downward.

Stars burst in his vision, and they weren't the stars in the sky. Amar steeled his jaw, his hands clutching savagely to her hips as she moved with expertise against him. She rode him through all those years they'd missed together, grinding against him so that he was buried to the hilt. "I was happy to wait," he gasped. "You meant the world to me —the universe. I was devastated when you were gone. I never thought I'd get this chance again."

"Amar." His name was a whisper on her lips as she braced her hands on his shoulders, plunging against him and seeking out what she needed. "Amar!" She cried out her joy, the ecstasy thickened with tears that spilled down her cheeks and splashed against his chest.

Her crescendo urged on his own. Everything he'd been holding back came surging to the surface as he slammed himself against her, roaring his pleasure and pain as his entire body and soul fused with her.

Amar had his beloved Katalin once again.

His mate was finally back.

7
───────

Kate lay with her head on his chest. It felt so good just to be with him, to feel real again. Every time she touched him, more of her past came back to her. The effect had been tenfold when they made love, and she sorted through images of a distant childhood as she stared up at the stars.

"I can get you away from them," he told her. "You don't have to be with the brood anymore."

Kate pushed herself up on her elbows and turned to look at him, finding his eyes in the dim light. "That's not how it works. I *have to* stay with them."

"Why?" he challenged. "Don't you know I'd do anything to keep you safe?"

She sat up all the way now, hugging her knees to her chest and staring out over the ocean. "You know what I am, but you don't know everything. There's a reason we moved here, Amar, and it's because of people like you." Kate heard the shame in her own voice. She didn't want to have this conversation with him, and she'd hoped to put it off as long as possible, maybe even long enough not to have it at all.

"You're feeding on them. On *us*."

He made it sound so simple. It had been, until the last twenty-four hours. She hadn't remembered anything about her life before she'd been turned. There was the humanity that came with being a mortal, the kind of thing that kept most of them from doing such monstrous things.

She sniffed and wiped a tear from the corner of her eye. "We are, but it's because there's something wrong with us. Another brood cursed us, and once the spell took over, feeding on humans just wasn't cutting it anymore. Luca needs even more blood than the rest of us do to stay alive, and he had to resort to feeding on us just to keep up his strength."

"That bastard has been *feeding* on you?" Amar sat up, his fingers digging up angry fistfuls of sand. "It's bad enough he turned you, but now you tell me he's using your life force to sustain his own? I won't stand for it." Wisps of smoke escaped his nostrils in protest.

She turned and put a firm hand on his broad chest. "It *is* right, considering how much we need him. He was just using us to supplement whatever he could find in the wild, and as we made our way west, he happened to feed on a shifter. He could feel how much better it was for him, and when he found out there were so many shifters in L.A., he decided to move us here. We *need* shifter blood, Amar. It's no different than a human having to eat food to survive."

"Is that how you think of me and my kind? Nothing more than a future meal?" Amar shot to his feet and reached for his clothes. "If you could see the way the rest of the shifters are grieving for those they've lost, you might have a different opinion." He yanked on his pants and began walking back the way they'd come, the rest of his clothes in his hand.

"Hey! You're just going to leave?" She jogged after him, pulling on her sweatshirt. The spell of their romantic evening had been thoroughly broken now. They'd gotten past the easier truths and into the heavy ones. "You need to understand that this isn't straightforward." Kate stormed after him. "I mean, there's a lot we're both still unpacking here."

"When it comes to your past, yes. When it comes to who we each are and how we can make this work, yes. But what you're talking about is murder, and I can't help you if you're going to be so matter-of-fact about it. It was one thing if you didn't remember what it's like to be human before, but you do now. You know how it feels to see someone you love being hurt, considering the way you sobbed in my arms at all the pain and suffering your father had gone through after his accident. And that was quite some time after it'd even happened!" His chest heaved, and she swore she could've sensed his dragon trying to burst through once again.

That was hard to argue against, especially when the information felt both so new and so old. Kate knew exactly what he was talking about. She remembered the time when she'd broken down at seeing her father capable of little more than sitting in a chair by the fire and shuffling across the room a few times a day. "That might be true, but you can't really expect things to change overnight."

"And that means I can't expect you to make the right decision, either?" he contended. "Something is going to have to change around here, and if you're not willing to go along with me, I'll make it happen myself. We can't lose any more lives because of this. I could understand your lack of self-awareness before, but now, there's no room for excuses."

"Amar, don't try to pin me down to one side or the other. Just give me some time." She wanted to be with him. She knew in her body and soul that what he'd told her about being fated to each other was true. If things hadn't been so complicated when it came to Luca and the other vampires, it might have been an easy decision. "I can't just up and leave them. They've given me so much. We all depend on each other. And Luca would be furious—"

"Fuck Luca!" he growled. "Whoever that coward is, he's leading you down the wrong path. I know I can't force you to see that, but I can only hope you do before it's too late."

Kate swallowed. "What exactly does that mean?"

"Only time will tell. You have your secrets and your life, Kate, but so do I. It would kill me not to be with you, but I can't just ask the rest of the world to stop so that I get what I want." He rubbed his forehead in frustration, cursing under his breath as he looked out over the ocean.

"What does the rest of the world have to do with you and I being together?" she demanded.

He lifted one shoulder. "As you said, it's just not that simple. I'll be here for you if you decide you want something different for your life, but eventually, it'll be too late." Amar gave her the address of the house where he was staying. "I shouldn't be telling you this, but I will because I care about you. I'm not just a random shifter in town; I'm here because I'm part of an elite group of Special Forces soldiers who are also shifters. Right now, our mission is to track down the vampires who've been killing the locals and eliminate their threat. Whatever side of that battle you choose to be on is up to you." He turned and marched away through the sand.

She started to follow him through the sand, but she stopped. Kate watched him go, realizing that she may have just lost the only part of her past that still survived. She let her knees sink to the ground and covered her face. Only a few minutes ago, she had everything in the palm of her hands, but now it was gone.

No, that wasn't true. She'd only had the illusion of having every-thing. He'd tried to convince her she was still the same person she'd been hundreds of years ago, but she most definitely wasn't. He was just a ghost coming back to haunt her.

When his receding figure was out of sight, Kate fled down the beach back toward Santa Monica, hoping she wouldn't run into him anywhere. They'd covered a lot of ground on their walk, and it wasn't likely he was heading in the same direction as she made her way back to the pier.

"There you are!" Nastasya grabbed her by the arm and dug her fingernails in. Her thin brows were angry lines on her porcelain face. "We've been looking for you for hours. You were supposed to give us the signal when you were ready."

Shit. As stubbornly as Kate had argued on behalf of Luca and the brood to Amar, she'd nearly forgotten about them and what she'd promised. Fear flooded her body, and she realized just how hungry she'd become. "Uh, yeah. He stood me up."

"Then why didn't you come find us?" Melissa whined. "I'm starv-ing, and I thought we had an easy meal tonight."

"I'm sorry. He seemed really interested last night. I guess he was one of those guys who only wants what he can get right away. I'm sure we can find someone else." A finger of ice traced its way down her spine at the thought of her brood feeding on Amar, seeing the fear and confusion in his eyes. He was a dragon, something they hadn't experi-enced. How many of them were around there, anyway? If they found another shifter, would it be his friend or family member?

Kenneth snorted. "Look around. It's late enough that people are already starting to go home for the night. I don't want to have to settle for some strung-out junkie just before sunrise."

"We won't," Nastasya insisted before Kate could answer. "I'll find someone, and I'll make it a good one. Let's go." She strode away from the pier, which had mostly cleared off, and headed toward some of the late-night bars.

Kate went with them, unable to keep her focus on their mission. They all needed to eat. She could feel the urge in her system. It was a feeling that'd been more than welcome only a short time ago, something that let her know the excitement of the hunt was imminent. She would be rewarded by the trickle of hot, fresh blood down her throat and the way it fanned out through her system, bringing life to her undead body.

But she could only see Amar. At first, it was the anger and betrayal on his face. He truly believed what she was doing was wrong. *How could he not understand that I'd die if I didn't do this?* she thought. And it wouldn't be a quick death, either. It would be long and lingering, starting with the weakness and desiccation that had once overwhelmed Melissa and Kenneth. She'd have to rely on her brood for sustenance, and they were already pissed at her. Kate could easily imagine slowly turning to dust in a dark corner of their cave, dismissed forever.

Kate paid little attention as she watched Nastasya work her magic on some guy at the bar. She thought of Amar and the way he'd wanted to protect her. *And wait, does he honestly think I can't take care of myself?* she fumed silently. *I'm a centuries-old vampire, damn it. I've killed thousands of people over the years and I'm stronger than any human.* Luca had warned them against going one-on-one with a shifter, given how little they knew about them, but in her moment of anger and resentment, she thought she could do the job just fine. Let one of those bastards try to turn on her; she'd show him just how sharp her fangs could be.

"It's all right," Melissa said.

"What?" Kate blinked, bringing herself back to the current moment.

"You look really upset, but these things happen sometimes. Nastasya will find something for us. Remember when I had to take down my first? I did such a shitty job, and it was frustrating at the time, but everyone got over it. Well, except maybe me," she said with a little laugh.

"Yeah. You're right. Sometimes we just make mistakes," Kate admitted, though they weren't quite talking about the same thing. Her mistake had been ever listening to Amar, and she'd only made it worse by kissing him—and then a lot more. She'd been an absolute fool for a handsome face, and she'd let that stop her from doing what was most important.

"Look!" Melissa shrieked. "She's got him. That was easy. Looks like she's taking him out the back exit. We can go around through the alley and meet her there."

Kate followed the other two, her feet dragging. She was just hungry. It had nothing to do with her argument with Amar, and thankfully, he wasn't around so she wouldn't have to deal with his judgment. She just needed a nice long drink, and then everything would be back to normal.

But as they came around the corner and she saw Nastasya's teeth flash just before sinking into the man's neck, Kate didn't feel the usual rush of hunger and need wash over her. She dragged her body forward, practically forcing her teeth to protrude further out. A wave of sickness made it almost impossible to bite into the man's arm, tapping into the veins at his wrist, and when she tasted the tang of shifter, she didn't find it nearly as pleasant as it'd been only yesterday. Well aware that the others would notice if she didn't feed, Kate forced herself to at least take some of it. She cringed as the coppery taste flooded her mouth, trying to remind herself that she needed this blood to survive. No one could blame her for that, and the man was going to die whether she fed on him or not.

————

KATE WOKE WITH A JOLT, sitting up on her pallet and clutching her blanket to her chest, her breathing heavy as she tried to figure out where she was. She'd just been in a completely different country and time, walking behind a horse with long reins and watching as the metal edge of the plow dug deep into the fertile soil. Something was satisfying about seeing the dark, rich earth churning up, ready to accept the seeds she would drop in it the next day. It was getting late, and she should've gone in for dinner a long time ago, but it wasn't easy to run the farm by herself. Her father needed her to get this done, and they couldn't afford to hire a farmhand. They needed every spare coin they could save just to survive.

"What's the matter?" Luca asked from the other side of the cavern.

"Nothing, really," Kate said, coming back to her senses and remembering where she actually was. "I just..." She trailed off. "I'm just feeling a little off, I guess."

His dark brow furrowed. "That seems to be a reoccurring theme with you. I thought you'd gotten past that dizzy spell. Is it something else?"

It was absolutely something else. As more and more of her memories began flooding her consciousness, Kate couldn't simply tag along with the rest of the brood and pretend everything was peachy. She was scared, but she needed to start making some bold decisions; rationalizing was no longer an option. Still, Luca was waiting for an answer. "It might be."

"What about everyone else?" he asked, looking around at the others. They were rousing from their beds now that it was nearly dark, beginning to put on their clothes. "Is anyone suffering from strange symptoms?"

They all shook their heads, and Kate knew what he was thinking. He was worried the shifter blood hadn't subdued the curse. It wasn't an unreasonable thought. She wanted to tell him the truth so that he wouldn't worry, but how could she? She'd already let a shifter go free, one who the rest of the brood would've been more than happy to feed on.

"It's just me. I'll be all right," she insisted.

Luca's mouth tightened as he came to stand in front of her. "Perhaps you're not getting enough to eat. The four of you are sharing, and I think that's a good idea to keep you safe from these beasts. But maybe it's time to start taking down more than one per night. I don't want to risk any of you getting weak again."

Her guts retracted against her spine. Amar already knew they'd been feeding on his kind. What about the rest of the shifters? If the word was spreading, as it sounded, then they could run out of a food source quickly. "No, don't worry about me. I'm just a little under the weather. I think I'll stay here tonight." That would give her a chance to think things over without facing the conundrum of whether or not to feed.

"I don't like that idea," Luca argued. "You need to feed. If you don't, we risk you getting even weaker than you already are."

The few drops she'd had the previous night had been enough to sustain her for the time being. After all, they hadn't always been able to eat so consistently. She wouldn't curl up and die if she fasted a bit, but she'd need to figure something else out soon. "You're right. Can I just stay here for a few to rest? Then I'll be along soon."

His smile was a long line across his pale face. "If you're sure. You don't mind heading down into the city on your own?"

Kate did her best to return the look with the most genuine smile she could muster, even though she had very little reason to smile at the moment. "Yeah. I'd say I know my way by now."

"Very well, then. Just make sure you don't wait until it's too late. I don't want you to miss out." Luca turned to the others as they made their plans for the night's hunt.

Kate listened half-heartedly. She hadn't exactly meant to, but she'd given herself a chance to decide. Luca had approved of her staying there alone and coming down to the beach later, which meant she had the time to either rest up and get over this emotional chokehold she was in, or escape. Her throat tightened at the thought. Amar had promised he could get her away from the other vamps. She'd immediately rejected the idea at first, because it was impossible to imagine life without the rest of her brood.

But now that she'd spent time with Amar and their intimacy had brought back images of her life before her change, it was also impossible to imagine carrying on the way she had been.

She was killing people, taking their lives to fortify her own.

She was leaving behind grieving families who'd never know what happened to their loved ones, although they'd never get over the nightmares if they knew the truth.

That sick sensation washed over her yet again.

"What do you have a hankering for tonight?" Melissa asked her as they got ready to leave. "Maybe we can track down something that'll make you feel better."

Kate smiled. Humans brought each other chicken noodle soup when they were sick, and this was the vampire equivalent. "Anything is fine. Thanks."

"We'll be back at the Santa Monica Pier tonight," Luca said as they headed toward the cave's exit. "We might be able to find the shifter who got away from you, but there should be plenty of others there, too. Just join us when you're ready, dear." He gave her another smile as he left.

As soon as their light footsteps were out of earshot, Kate managed to relax a little. She pulled a deep breath through her nose and let it out of her mouth slowly. It wasn't fair that she should suddenly have her life turned completely upside down, but there was no going back now. And in order to go forward, she needed to decide. Waffling could be deadly, so she needed to make a choice and stick with it.

She rolled to her back and sat up, stretching her stiff body. The hollow feeling inside told her just how hungry she was from taking such a small meal the night before. She'd gotten used to eating well there. It wasn't like the old days when they traveled through Europe, making sure they left town after they'd taken only one or two lives because people would start talking. A big city like this didn't take nearly as much notice of only a few missing people, and the vampires were taking advantage of that.

They hadn't accounted for the shifters figuring it out, though, and Kate hadn't considered she'd be running into someone like Amar. Her heart wrenched as she thought of him and the look on his beautiful face when she'd told him she wouldn't go with him. He wanted to protect her; Kate understood that much. He wanted to make sure she was all right, and he knew she wasn't safe with the vamps. That was ridiculous, of course, because—

An image of Thomas floated into her vision. He'd stood up against the status quo, daring to question Luca. He'd pushed the man far enough that it'd cost him his life. What would happen to her when she finally admitted she could no longer draw shifter blood? Or even human blood? Would they just leave her to die? Would Luca kill her to make sure she didn't let their secret out into the shifter community? The patriarch didn't know what'd happened between Kate and Amar, but somehow, everything got back to him eventually.

"Damn it," she grunted as she shoved herself up from the floor of the cave. There was no getting around it. She had to go to Amar. She had to toss her pride aside and let him know that she needed help. She wasn't strong enough to get away from Luca, especially since part of her didn't want to. He'd meant a lot to her over the years; he'd kept them safe. A new lump formed in her throat as she folded her blanket and trudged toward the cave opening.

The stars burned brightly in the sky overhead as she moved down the trail. The moon was only a tiny sliver, but Kate could see the pale line of the path easily. Kate would get down to the beach and then duck in toward the city proper with the hopes of avoiding her brood.

She had no idea how to get to the address Amar had given her, but surely, someone would give her directions.

Kate paused just before she emerged from the trees, certain she'd heard something behind her, but all that came to her ears was the gentle rustling of leaves in the breeze.

As soon as she hit flat ground, she stepped up to a group of college girls and asked them for directions. One of them, her mouth full of popcorn, gave her an odd look. "Are you taking the bus or calling an Uber?"

"I'm walking." Kate could smell their blood. These were humans, not nearly as tempting as shifters. If she hadn't been so hungry, she might not have noticed their scent at all. As it was, she clamped her jaws together to keep her emerging fangs from showing.

Another girl, a blonde wearing a crop top and a navel ring, laughed. "That's gonna take hours! Are you crazy?"

"Look, could you please just tell me how to get there?" Kate was getting desperate. The longer she hung out on the beach, the more chance she stood of being seen by the rest of the brood.

"Take Colorado Ave up to Santa Monica Boulevard, I guess," said the third girl, pointing to the road that led straight off the pier. "That's at least a start. I'm not sure beyond that."

"Thanks." But Kate's stomach sank to her toes as she realized just how dangerous this was. She had no choice but to enter the night's hunting grounds. There might be another way, but this was the quickest, and she knew she had to get away from the brood as fast as possible if she had any chance of getting to Amar.

Tucking her hands in her pockets as she went down the street, she moved as briskly as she could manage without calling attention to herself. It was incredibly tempting just to pick up her pace, but there were still too many people on the sidewalks, and she had to balance the risk of being noticed against that of being found by the brood. She turned around several times, swearing she could feel eyes on her back, but she only saw the typical crowds. Sports and luxury cars rushed by on the street, and the lights illuminated the pristine sidewalks.

The skin on her back crawled as she entered an impressive neighborhood of modern homes. The sensation of being followed had grown as she went, but she was nearly there. The cells of her body surged, drawing her further forward as she sensed Amar's presence nearby. A smile spread across her face, no matter how much she wanted to be angry with him.

She was just stepping off the sidewalk to cross the street to the house that matched the address Amar had given her when Luca appeared at her shoulder. "Going somewhere, darling?"

A scream rose from deep inside her, but the look on Luca's face made it die before it ever reached her mouth. "Just, um, following up some leads I have on shifters." She took a step away from him.

His hand locked like a vise on her arm. "I don't think so. You wouldn't go this far on a hunch considering how ill you were feeling. Or is there something else you're not telling me?" His eyes narrowed into hers.

A strange light illuminated his eyes, shining brilliantly at her and demanding that she look at it. The last vestiges of resistance trailed away like smoke on the wind. Kate couldn't fight him. Her brain emptied of everything except the answer to Luca's question. "I know who I am now," she said slowly. "I have a life outside of the brood. I need to go to Amar." She tipped her head slightly as she watched the shifting luminescence in Luca's eyes.

"Who the fuck is Amar?" Luca demanded.

"I am."

Luca turned from her to find the source of the voice, breaking the spell so that Kate could do the same. Amar stood at the gateway just in front of the house, his shoulders wide, his fists curled at his sides.

"Let go of her," the dragon growled as his eyes flashed their reptilian form.

Instead, the vamp yanked her closer. "It seems you've been doing too good of a job getting close to your victims, Kate. It's too bad you didn't kill him when you had the chance. You would've been far more humane than I'll be."

Terror gripped her body as she imagined what Luca might try to do to him. "He's a shifter," she warned, hoping to persuade him, "and a much stronger one that we're used to dealing with."

"I know. I can smell the stink on him from here." Luca's fangs poked at his lower lip as he sniffed the air.

Suddenly, a flood of memories overtook her vision. She was no longer Kate on the streets of Los Angeles, but Katalin on a narrow farm road among rolling Hungarian foothills. It was late, with the sun dipping behind the mountains, and she was rushing to get back home.

She'd just turned into the end of the lane that led to their farm, practicing the apology she would give her parents for making them worry. Katalin had stayed at the market too long, hoping to sell the last of the potatoes she'd brought with her, and then she'd dallied with Amar. Oh, but it'd been impossible to resist! He was such a charmer.

Like lighting, a different man appeared on the road in front of her. He bared sharp fangs as he stopped her progress, his voice a hiss in the night. "You're a tender little piece of meat, aren't you?"

A woman stepped up next to him, tall and lithe and with a thick accent. She sneered as she raked her eyes over Katalin's body. "She's not very big. I'm not sure there's even enough blood inside her for a snack."

Fear gripped her, but Katalin had grown up learning the good sense of a farm girl. She didn't just cower to what scared her. Instead, she darted into the tree line near the lane, determined to get home and lock the doors.

The man's laugh echoed through the trees as they followed her. "But see how quick she is already, and how strong? She'll be a wonderful addition."

They'd captured her easily, taking her down with steely force, no matter how hard she fought. Luca's hands clamped on her shoulders as he took her down to the ground, the moist earth soaking her thin dress. Katalin could still feel the puncture of Luca's fangs as he bit into the delicate flesh on the side of her neck and the chill that eclipsed her body.

The woman whom she now knew to be Nastasya hissed nearby. "Let me have a little taste."

"We're keeping this one," Luca insisted, interrupting his drink to chastise her. "Even I can't go too far. We'll take her back to the castle so she can feed on one of our captives. But for now, I'm going to make this darling little creature forget all of this has ever happened, and then I'll do it again after she feeds. A complaisant brood is a happy brood, my dear."

As Katalin's pulse weakened, she was drawn by a transfixing light emanating from her attacker's eyes, and moments later, her mind went completely blank.

Everything she'd known about her life—and identity—had been erased.

Snapping back to reality, Kate's insides lurched as she now remembered how horrid that night had been. "You... made me do it," she stammered, holding one hand to her stomach. "You made me drink the blood of another with the promise of staying alive. If it weren't my only hope of ever seeing Amar again, I would have gladly died instead." She lifted her eyes, too exhausted and scared to be embarrassed. "And for centuries, you've had me believing a lie. How *could* you, Luca? I trusted you."

Amar was striding across the street, clearly not intimidated by the idea of facing the elder vampire alone. He had no idea how strong Luca was, and Kate wanted to stop him, but she didn't know how to. "Let her go. She stays with me."

"You think you can stop me?" Luca challenged.

Several more men appeared behind Amar. Kate knew by their thick scent that they were shifters, too, but they weren't dragons. Amar smelled of hot metal and brimstone, but the others emanated the redolence of thick fur and damp forests.

"I *know* I can," Amar confirmed.

Luca squeezed Kate's arm one last time before letting go so suddenly, she tumbled to the sidewalk. "Fine, but I won't let you vermin get away with this." He was gone in a flash.

Amar scooped her up, carrying her across the street and into the house. Kate tried to turn to him to tell him just how sorry she was, but her body was weakening.

"It's all right. You're safe now," he assured her just before everything went black.

8

"ALL RIGHT, MAN. I KNOW YOU'RE THE ALPHA, AND WE MIGHT NOT necessarily be privy to everything you do, but I think we need an explanation here," Gabe said as he held the front door open for Amar.

He was right, but it was difficult to know exactly where to start. Amar brushed past Gabe and the others. "Emersyn, I need you. She's not a shifter or a human, but do you think you can take a look at her and see what's wrong?"

"Of course. Bring her in here." The doctor swiftly led the way toward the room they'd converted into an exam room. She nodded toward the table as she washed her hands. "Is she injured?"

Amar was relieved at her professional stance. "Not that I know of, but there's no telling what might've happened to her since last night." His heart clenched in his chest. If only he'd brought her back there last night. Kate hadn't wanted that, and even as bound as the two of them were, he couldn't make her do anything she didn't want to. "I suppose I should explain."

"There's no need," Emersyn assured him as she began looking over her patient. "Just tell me if I need to worry about my own safety while I'm doing this."

"I don't think so."

The doctor raised a thin eyebrow. "Good enough, I suppose. You go on, and I'll see what I can do here."

"Thanks." Amar had been so grateful when he'd gotten this job, and right now, he was even more thankful for the team he was surrounded with. The years without Kate had made him a bit cold and distant, but he knew they would understand, no matter how crazy this was.

The men were waiting for him in the conference room. "That was a vampire you just carried in here, wasn't it?" Jude asked calmly over the rim of his mug.

Amar nodded, trying to figure out how to explain this.

"And she's your fated?" Raul questioned quietly.

"Yes." His shoulders sagged in relief. "I could feel her nearby. I should've told you as soon as I knew, but I wasn't sure how it was going to go. I'm still not sure of everything, and she's too weak to talk. I don't think the other vampire was joking, though. He's going to do whatever he can to get her back." This thought, among others, made him sick.

"I don't suppose there's any way you can turn them back, is there? I mean, at some point, they were humans," Gabe said.

"Whatever was human about them is likely gone forever," Raul replied.

"Then how do you explain Kate?" Amar questioned. "There's clearly some part of her that's coming back."

"That might be because she was already tied to you," Jude pointed out. "A fated bond is something much stronger than even typical familial ties."

"I agree with that," Raul said. "It's pure speculation, but in all the folklore we've found, there are no stories that have anyone converting back to their human form. If Kate has a chance, then that's great, but the rest of them will have to be taken care of."

Amar ran his hand over his face. "I'm not sure. Vampires or not, they're her people. It seems hypocritical just to kill them."

"We'll have to."

Amar swung his head around to see Kate enter the room on Emersyn's arm. "They're vicious, and they're deadly. Even if there's a trace of who they were, you'll never find it." She sat heavily in a free chair, her skin even paler than usual.

"I gave her an infusion of vitamins and protein, just on a hunch. Pretty much any carnivore responds well to that, so I figured it was worth a try. It helped, but..." Emersyn trailed off, frowning in worry over her patient.

"We can discuss that later," Kate said quickly. "Right now, the most important thing is that Luca has already sworn his vengeance. He knows I'm here, and even if he's pissed at me, he's going to do every-thing he can to bring me back to the brood. I'm sure he'll have the others with him, too." She tipped her head back and took a deep breath as though just speaking were a struggle.

Amar laid a hand on her shoulder, wishing he could do more.

"Tell his ass to come on over," Raul said with a bit too much enthu-siasm. "We can arm ourselves with garlic and holy water and—I don't know—ultraviolet lamps and take them down."

"This isn't a goddamn horror movie," Amar snapped. "We can stop relying on pop culture references at this point, I think." His dragon felt her proximity, a liquid heat that swirled pleasantly inside him, but it mixed with the urgency of doing something to save her. She looked like she was dying right before his eyes.

"You're right." Kate lifted her hand to cover his, pressing her shoulder up against her cheek so that she embraced him from the chair. "Not everything you've read or seen is accurate. We can't go out in the daylight; that much is true. But holy water and garlic won't hurt them—us—any more than they'd hurt you."

"A stake through the heart?" Raul asked, leaning forward in his chair.

"That would kill anyone. Even them," Kate replied.

"Can you tell us where they are?" Amar asked gently. "Is there someplace they stay during the day?" She was one of them, but in his mind, he'd already separated her from the rest. In whatever way was possible, she was different.

Kate nodded. "There's a cave in Topanga State Park. It doesn't look like much from the outside, but it's actually quite deep. In the furthest recesses, it's dark enough to keep them safe from the daylight."

"A cave?" Raul swallowed as he looked from Amar to Kate and back again. "So, do they, um, hang upside down while they sleep? Like in *The Lost Boys*? I love that movie!"

"Seriously? Do you have to be so immature about this?" Amar clenched his fists, wondering how he was going to handle the wolf.

But Kate gave a small smile as she shook her head. "No, and we don't turn into bats, either, but Luca can fly when he wants to. We usually sleep in beds, but since our current nest is a cave, we sleep on the ground."

"Is there anything stopping us from sneaking into the cave while they're asleep and staking them?" Jude asked.

Kate's mouth twisted, and Amar hurt for her. She was sitting there making plans for the death of the only family she's known for the last few centuries. The leeches needed to die—of that, he had no doubt—but that didn't mean this was easy for her. "The only problem I see is that they sleep in the darkest part of the cave, so you won't have the advantage of sunlight if they wake up before you get the job done." She turned her head to the side and rested her forehead on her fingertips.

"Why don't you let us get this figured out? You can come lay down in my room." Amar helped Kate out of the chair and brought her to the master suite, though he wished he was bringing her there for a different purpose.

"I'm sorry," Kate said as she changed into one of the old Army t-shirts he'd given her to sleep in. "I've caused so much trouble for you."

He yanked his eyes away from the soft curve of her breasts, inwardly telling his dragon to calm down. There would be time for all that later. Hopefully. "You don't have anything to be sorry for. We already knew we were up against vamps. You just helped bring it to a head more quickly. Really, that's a good thing."

"But I've led them to your home." She gestured to the room as she nestled under the covers, her dark hair spreading vividly over the white pillowcase. "They know where you're at, and they know how important shifter blood is for them. They'll do everything they can to destroy you."

Amar picked up her hand and kissed the back of it. "I'm not worried about them. Only you. Rest, and we'll get this figured out."

A knock came at the door. Amar glared at it, not wanting to be disturbed while he was with Kate, but he opened it.

Emersyn stood there, her face soberly professional. "I didn't want to say anything in front of the rest of them, but she's very weak right now. I gave her that infusion, but I don't know how long it'll last. She mentioned a curse, and I'm concerned for her health."

"What do you mean?" Amar looked from the doctor to his mate. Kate had mentioned the curse, but she'd seemed more than healthy when the two of them had tumbled in the sand together.

"She means," Kate said from the bed, "that I need to feed. I'm weak because I've hardly had any blood for the last few nights. I can't bear to do it now that I know the truth. All of these memories; all of the terrible things I've done as a vampire. I had my life ripped away from me simply because Luca thought I would make a nice addition to his family. He took me as one of his own, and he killed my parents. I just can't continue that cycle."

"You said shifter blood makes you stronger, right?" Amar felt his dragon raging inside him, angry all over again that Luca had done this to her.

Kate nodded feebly.

"Then, you've got it." Amar strode to the side of the bed.

"You mean yours?" Kate's dark eyes glimmered as she looked up at him. She shook her head, but her teeth were already showing their true nature. "I can't."

"You can. I give you my permission. Neck, wrist, whatever you want."

Emersyn cleared her throat. "If you're determined to do this, I could always get a needle and a bag."

"I don't think that's necessary." Amar looked once again to Kate. If someone had asked him a month ago if he'd be willing to let a vampire have a taste, the answer would've been an emphatic no. Everything was different now. "Go on now."

Kate tentatively pressed her lips to Amar's wrist and paused to look into the dragon's eyes. "Are you sure about this?" When he nodded, Kate's eyes flashed with hunger. "I promise I'll be careful," she whispered as she gently sank her fangs into his skin.

The doctor stayed only long enough to make sure everything was running smoothly and to remind Amar to see her afterward. It was a good thing she'd left because he was surprised by the way his body was responding. Seeing his mate there, laying amongst his sheets, looking up at him now and then as she raked her lips and tongue across his flesh, tasting the very essence of him, made him hard as hell. Yes, it was a risk if she couldn't control herself, and it would drain some of his energy, but none of that mattered as she savored the most intimate part of him. "Only you could make this arousing," he murmured with a slow smile.

Her lips parted from his skin as her tongue lapped a stray droplet on the corner of her mouth. "Is it too bold to tell you just how delicious you are?"

A shudder of excitement tingled through his body. He and his dragon were at war with each other, both turned on and shocked by this whole experience. That was one hell of a compliment, and it made him want to dive between her creamy thighs and take her right then. "Not at all."

After several minutes, she laid a kiss over his wound and gently pushed his arm back to him. "I should stop. I don't want to hurt you."

He stopped himself from asking if she was sure she had enough. The truth was that he'd let her bleed him completely dry if it would have helped her. His love for her was strong enough that he'd do anything, and right now, that included slaying a nest of vampires. "I'd better get back downstairs and help the others figure out our next step. Is there anything you need?"

Kate blinked at him with sleepy, satiated eyes. "Only you. Later."

"Definitely." He made sure the shades were pulled down over the wide glass doors that led to the private patio, grateful that his penchant for sleeping in a pitch-black room would keep her safe.

———

"This is the right location, according to the coordinates Kate pointed out on the map." Amar studied the cave entrance, which looked completely innocuous in the slant of evening sunlight. They'd spent most of the day planning and preparing, and there wasn't much daylight left. They didn't dare wait another night, giving the vamps the chance to come after them first. "We're going to have to make this one count."

"No kidding, especially since even Emersyn won't be able to stitch us up if these guys get to have their way with us," Gabe commented.

Amar glanced at his wrist. The doctor had cleaned it up just to be safe, but shifters healed quickly. The bitemark was already little more than two red pinpricks. "I'll have to tell her she has my utmost appreciation for staying behind with Kate."

The doctor's mate shrugged. "As much as she loves being part of the Force, you'd have a hard time parting her from a patient, vampire or not. Medicine is her true passion."

"We can chitchat about women later," Raul insisted. "Let's go!"

They stepped just inside the cave and paused to listen. Somehow, Amar imagined he'd heard some sort of noise, even if it was only the deep, even breathing of sleep. Pure silence hit his ears. In the last bit of daylight that filtered through the entrance, he signaled for the men to follow him.

Amar had excellent vision, far better than a human's and even better than most other shifters. The dragons had developed it over the years after all the time they'd lived in caves, but it soon grew too dark, even for him. He hated to do it, but he pointed his flashlight at the ceiling and turned it on the lowest setting. The resulting glow would've been dull in most environments, but in the depths of the cavern, it was a blaring light.

It revealed four bodies laid out on the floor, not stiff with their arms crossed in front of their chests like some movies portrayed, but merely slumbering. Amar's breath caught in his chest as he noticed a woman with long graceful limbs, a couple entwined in each other's arms, and a sharp-featured man who could only be Luca.

He was just about to signal the Force members to attack when Luca's eyes flashed open. He squinted against the light for only a fraction of a second before he was on his feet, racing directly at Amar. Armed and ready, Amar sliced the air with a stake. It whizzed past the vampire uselessly as the rest of the brood awoke.

"You know what to do!" Amar called out.

This damn vamp was quick, his limbs flying through the air in a blur as he attacked. Amar lashed out, and his bones rattled as he took the blows. It was like being charged by a stone statue, one that would drain the life force from him if it won. Amar knew what he needed to do.

A roar sounded behind him as Gabe shot forward in grizzly form, knocking the head vampire to the side, giving Amar the moment he needed. He sprang his dragon out into the world, his skin sizzling as his body became covered in scales, his wings brushing against the side of the cave. Most importantly, his teeth and claws were at the ready, along with the well of fire he kept deep inside him. He still held a stake curled in his ebony talons.

Thanks, I needed that, Amar told his comrades through their telepathic link.

A little help over here? It was Raul.

Amar swung his head around on his long neck to find the wolf engaged with the leggy woman. Her features were severe, yet beautiful as she danced around the shifter, swinging a dagger within inches of his ears and baring her fangs. "Do you have any idea just how delicious you are?" she laughed confidently with a thick Russian accent. "I can't wait to drain you dry, little puppy."

Raul was a competent fighter, but these vamps were a new enemy. The Russian had the advantage with her superhuman speed. Raul darted and dodged between her blows, but she was coming dangerously close.

Amar longed to get his claws into Luca, but Raul needed his help the most. He charged forward, holding back his fiery breath so as not to singe the wolf. The woman's eyes widened slightly when she saw the dragon coming for her, but then she narrowed them as she flashed her teeth. With a surge from his back feet, Amar sailed over Raul. He tumbled into the vampire, his weight knocking her backward. She cried out as her back scraped against the stone wall, but it wasn't enough to stop her. She kicked and thrashed beneath him, her teeth searching for any grasp she might get on the dragon. Amar pushed his hand forward, pinning her by the neck, and she whipped her head as she tried to get a bite on him. The knife flashed in his periphery, but teeth other than his own sank into her wrist. The vampiress dropped the weapon as her blood dripped from Raul's mouth. Readjusting the stake, Amar plunged it into her chest.

Time paused for a moment as Amar hoped they were right in thinking the stake would kill her. The vampire's eyes blazed a brilliant and terrifying black as she screamed. As scarlet foam gurgled from her wound, Amar yanked his hand back, watching her body convulse and then go still.

There was no time to wait for anything else to happen. Amar swung his great body around to find Luca and Gabe again, hoping he wasn't too late. His eyes landed on Jude, where another female vampire was already dead or nearly so at his feet. Her blood was an inky pool as it made a halo around her head and slowly soaked into the rock floor. A male vamp, the one she'd been sleeping next to, leaped onto the bear's back. Jude shook him off, flinging him against the wall, but the creature jumped back to his feet and went for Jude once again.

I've got this, Raul told his crew.

They'd hardly had a chance to use the telepathic link they'd established through ancient dragon magic when they'd first come together as a new unit of the SOS Force, but Amar was grateful for it right now. He let the wolf go to assist Jude.

Amar swung around, searching for Luca. There was no sign of the old vampire, and Amar's veins burned with the need to destroy him. Saliva dripped down his sharp teeth as he imagined snapping his jaws around the man's head, popping it free from his spine. There was no other sign of a struggle within the confines of the cave, so he reached out with his mind. Gabe was absent.

Just as Amar's heart constricted in fear, he heard a shout. "He's getting away!"

Amar darted toward the mouth of the cave. A gurgling hiss sounded as Raul and Jude finished off the other male, and then they were pounding on the rock behind him.

Gabe was just finishing his shift. Blood dripped down the remainder of dark fur that slowly disappeared from the backs of his arms as he shot through the cave opening.

Damn. Luca had been too much for Gabe, and he'd dared to head outside. Unfortunately, the cave mouth was just wide enough to allow a vampire through, but nowhere near large enough for a bear or a dragon.

I'll go. Raul had to duck his head and tuck in his tail. He was a much bigger wolf than the ones found in the wild, but he managed to wriggle his way to the outside world.

Amar cursed under his breath as he shifted into his human form. They were stronger and more capable as animals, so he hadn't anticipated any of the vampires getting away. He squinted against the fading light as he folded his wings into his back and regretfully retracted his claws, hoping like all hell that the vampire couldn't make it through even the smallest bit of sunlight.

He and the others stepped out in human form, listening and watching for any sign of the vampire, but they heard nothing.

"We should fan out and see what we can find," Amar commanded.

"Don't bother." Raul emerged from the woods, looking tired and pissed. "Those fuckers are fast. He's gone."

"I thought they couldn't handle the sunlight," Jude said.

The wolf lifted a shoulder. "Kate did say he was the strongest, and the sun is just about down."

"Shit." Amar knew he should've taken Luca down himself. It wasn't that the others weren't capable, but this was something he'd taken on his own shoulders. The asshole was out there, and now he knew where Kate was. "Let's head back and regroup."

9

KATE SAT IN THE KITCHEN. SHE'D SLEPT AS MUCH AS SHE COULD, AND even though Amar's bed was comfortable and smelled wonderfully like him, she could only rest for so long. She'd wanted to go with them. It only made sense, considering she knew more about the brood than anyone else. Amar had convinced her to stay behind, reminding her of the mental hold Luca'd had on her for ages. They now knew it took hardly more than a glance to bring others under his control, and the last thing any of them needed was Kate fighting on the wrong side.

Emersyn slipped in from the back deck, concern tracing lines across her face. "They're heading back."

Kate let out a breath. "Good. I was worried about them." She didn't like thinking about her family being dead. It was unfair that this was the only way to get away from them and live her own life, but even if they'd let her go, they would continue to kill.

"I'm afraid it's not time to stop worrying yet." Emersyn sat at the breakfast bar. "They took down three of them, but Luca got away."

A shiver of fear rippled along Kate's shoulders. "I should've known. He's too powerful."

"No. Don't think about it like that. They just need another shot at him. We're up against something new and unknown, but we'll get it figured out. They're on their way back right now; we'll rest up and discuss—"

"I'll do it." Emersyn was trying to comfort her. She was a kind woman, and someone Kate thought she could be friends with. But the doctor didn't understand what it was like to be a member of the undead. None of these shifters did.

"What?"

Already out of her chair, Kate went to the back door and looked out, noting it was fully dark. In one way, that meant it was safe for her to leave. In another, it meant it was more dangerous than ever. Luca would be out there. He might be fleeing to the next place, looking for some other concentration of shifters to feed on. Or he might be looking for her. Either way, she had to find him. "I'll take care of this myself."

"No, no, no." Emersyn shook her head emphatically. "You can't do that. You said yourself this guy is incredibly powerful. You can't possibly go after him alone. None of us should. Just give the guys a few minutes, and—"

"Sorry, but this is something I have to do." Kate slipped out the door. Emersyn rose from the table and came after her, but the vampire speed Kate had built up over the years was on her side. She was off through the backyard and heading toward the beach.

Kate's head was spinning as she hurtled down the streets, no longer caring if anyone happened to see her—she had a mission to complete. When Luca had turned Kate, he'd hypnotized her, wiping her memories and making her fit into the brood because she didn't know a life otherwise. Finding Amar brought her memories back, and she now realized all the unspeakable things she'd been coerced into doing over the years. It had felt like her own free will at the time, but Kate knew better now. If she didn't stop Luca, he would do it all over again. He would recruit a new brood, building them up to follow him without question, and once again begin taking countless lives to preserve his own.

She nearly turned her feet toward the cave, wondering if Luca would dare to go back to see the slaughter that was inevitably waiting for him there. No. He wasn't that sentimental. He'd only kept Kate and the others at his side because they served a purpose for him: they made him feel powerful. They looked to him for guidance, and he punished them when they didn't take it. He even fed off them.

And feeding was probably just what Luca needed to do if he'd just been through a battle with the shifters. Kate headed toward Santa

Monica Pier. There was a long stretch of shifter-laden beach to search, but it was at least a place to start. She jetted through the crowds, sorting through the scents of humans covered in sunscreen, shifters who'd recently been in their animal forms, and the saltiness of the ocean. She pushed past those who moved too slow, but she didn't see anyone moving nearly as fast as she was. Damn it! How was she supposed to do this? She moved in and out of buildings for hours, even her quick speed only aiding her so much. At this point, Luca could've already gone on to another city. The night was passing quickly, and the sun would be up before she knew it.

Trudging through the sand, Kate stopped. She was working too hard. She'd been able to find Amar through the bond they shared. As much as she hated to admit it, there had to be some sort of bond between her and the patriarch, too. They'd shared blood, and he'd burrowed his way into her mind. Kate closed her eyes and reached out.

There! She could feel him in her bloodstream. Now that she knew the truth about him, her instinct was to flee in the other direction. Instead, she turned and sped down the beach, hitting the foothills and charging into the woods. She knew she wasn't as strong or as fast as him. She might very well die, but at least she'd know she did everything possible.

"Luca!" she screamed as she spotted him, knowing he was too confident to back down from a challenge.

He stopped on the trail, turning to glare at her. "You've just scared off my prey, you little bitch."

Kate skidded to a stop before him. "Good. You've killed enough, Luca, and it's time to stop."

"And what about you?" he challenged as he strode forward, cocky as ever. "Do you think you can go on living the rest of your life without taking someone else's?"

She bit her lip. Kate didn't really know the answer, but it was something she'd have to figure out another time. "That's my problem now. Not yours."

Luca held out a hand, extending his slim fingers. "It doesn't have to be, Kate. Come back to me. I'll keep you safe. I'll take care of you. That lizard doesn't know what it's like to be one of us. He can't possibly understand you like I do."

She felt tempted by this logic until she noticed that familiar light set deep in his eyes. Kate shot her gaze down to his chest, understanding now that the light in his eyes was his way of hypnotizing and manipulating her. "What? You can't convince me with logic, so you have to coerce me?"

He sighed. "I don't know why everyone has to make things so difficult. Just like your parents. They could've just given themselves over to me. They already knew I was going to kill them. But no, they had to fight. Peasants are such a struggle."

Rage billowed through her body, and Kate shot forward like a javelin. She flung her fists into his chest with all her might. Amar's blood was in her veins now, and she felt its strength.

It wasn't enough for someone like Luca. He'd been around too long, and he'd had too many years to build up his defenses. He laughed as her blows landed with little effect. "Really, Kate? You think you can just give me the old left hook and take me down?"

Her brows drew down as her fists curled once again. "Fuck you!" She slammed him with an uppercut. Kate didn't know where she'd seen the move, but it was effective. Luca's head flipped back, and he staggered slightly. Not wanting to give him a chance to recover, she rammed her fists into the sides of his face, pummeling for every injustice she could think of. Her fangs dropped and her focus altered as she shifted into full vampire mode, but she refused to take him for his blood. She would starve to death before she let this asshole be the one to sustain her. Luca staggered further back until he was on the ground, her punches knocking his face to the left and right and back again.

She thought she was winning. She thought she had this. But his laughter broke through the blood that seeped from his gums. He reached up and caught her wrists easily. "You've let him get to you, Kate. You think I'm the bad guy, but he's the one who's made you think you're miserable in your life. You're not. You never had a single doubt about it until he came along."

"That's not true!" She pulled back, struggling to get her wrists free. She was trapped now.

"Oh, but it is." Luca bucked her weight off his legs with ease. He twisted around, still gripping her, and had her pinned to the ground in a fraction of a second. "It's so unfortunate you don't want to listen to me anymore, Kate. Now I have to kill you, just like Thomas. I don't think I'll be so quick about it this time." His eyes hazed over as he bared his teeth, his long fangs shining.

A burning sensation blazed across the top of her head. Kate's eyes widened as she realized the sun had begun its slow ascent. A small ray streamed across Luca's hair, turning each strand to ash that floated away in the gentle breeze. She smiled as the skin on his forehead crackled and flaked. She would die, too, but it would be worth it.

"Kate!" Amar's voice boomed through the woods. She didn't need to look to know he was in dragon form.

Luca looked to the side, spotting the shifter. He grinned, his fangs now long enough to poke against his lower lip. A few more ashes dulled his dark hair. "Did you come to join the party?"

"Let her go." Amar's footsteps vibrated through the earth as he approached.

Kate didn't dare take her eyes off Luca long enough to look for her mate. She kept her gaze on him as she forced her entire body to relax. She'd been pushing against her enemy, but that wasn't helping. He expected her to fight, and so she must do the opposite. As a vampire, she'd come to know her body quite well, and she had to prepare it for battle a different way.

Luca's head swiveled to look at her when he felt her go limp. His eyes narrowed.

"Stand up and fight me like a man!" Amar barked.

It was just the distraction she needed. Luca never anticipated the quick jerk of her leg that brought her knee up to her stomach, her muscles coiling like a spring before her foot shot out and landed square in his gut. Kate rocketed her assailant off of her, throwing him up into the air. He was just about to land on his feet when a massive flame engulfed his body. He screamed and twisted as he fell to the ground, but the blast of fire from Amar's throat was unstoppable now. It didn't end until the vampire was nothing more than a pile of ash.

Kate gasped as she sat up, the rising sun scalding her. Amar was at her side in a moment, wrapping her in the sable depths of his wings to protect her from the light. She leaned heavily into his scaled body, all her muscles collapsing with exhaustion. It'd taken everything she had to fight Luca, and now that it was all over, she wasn't sure she'd ever feel the same again. "How'd you find us?"

Amar pulled her in tightly so that the two of them were enclosed in the safety of his wings. "Luca got away from us at the cave. We went back to the house to regroup and figure out what to do. I was even going to ask you where you thought he might've gone, but then Emersyn told me you'd already left. I searched for you, and then I realized I knew exactly how to find you. The part of you that I'd lost has been brought back, and I just had to listen to my soul."

She let out a small laugh as she pressed her cheek against him, feeling the comfort of his heat. "When I showed up at your place, that's how I found you, too. What happens now?"

Her mate pulled in a deep breath and let it out slowly. "I've got a telepathic link to the others. They'll be arriving soon to help me get you back home now that the sun is up. We'll contact the packs that we know have been impacted, and we'll help them get the closure they need. Everything is going to be okay."

Kate nodded against him, knowing he was right.

10

——————

Amar rolled over and wrapped his arms around the warm body next to him in bed. The jet lag might've been miserable in any other circumstance. It'd been a hell of a long trip to Hungary, after all. They'd had to coordinate a few different red-eyes to make sure Kate didn't see the light of day. But he'd have gone through anything to give his mate this experience, and at least they had an excuse for staying in bed all day. "Hey there, gorgeous."

Her dark lashes fluttered and she scrunched her eyes shut as she buried her face against his chest. "No. Don't tell me it's time to get up yet."

"The sun is down, but I never said we had to get up." He ran a hand down her side, allowing his thumb to graze her breast.

"Oh?" she opened her eyes then and looked up at him mischievously. "Do you have other ideas?"

"I think I can come up with a few." His fingers moved down between her legs, massaging the heat that he found there. "The most important thing is that I'm with you, Katalin."

Her eyes fluttered once again, but this time with pleasure as she tipped her chin back and let out a low moan. "You know, I've been thinking it's time for me to take that name back. Kate's long gone now, anyway. What do you think?"

"I think that sounds perfect. I've always loved that name."

Her own hand covered his, encouraging him. "I'm pretty sure the locals already suspect me of being a witch or a vampire, but you're the one who's got me under a spell," she purred. She lifted her leg and bent it over his hip, giving him easier access.

He slipped his finger inside her slick warmth, his own body reacting to her pleasure and her obvious desire for him. "Do you mind?" he teased. "Being under my spell, that is?"

Katalin guided her palm down the V of his abs to his shaft, embracing him in long, firm strokes that she seemed to enjoy just as much as his caresses. "I think it's something I can handle. I mean, it isn't as though I'm not getting anything out of it."

"Is it enough?" Amar pressed his lips to hers before she could answer, his tongue darting into her mouth and exploring the variety of textures inside. Her tongue danced against his as he tasted her. There was so much to love about this woman. His inner dragon had never been more at peace than it had over the last few weeks as they'd gotten to know each other once again. She kissed him back, drinking him in as she pressed her body against his.

"Mmm, more than enough," she murmured when he finally pulled away. Katalin wrapped her leg tighter around him as she let out another moan, her hips bucking against him with fervent need.

He held her off just a little longer, enjoying her pleasant torture. He even added to it by taking the sweet pink bud of her nipple into his mouth. She was so unbelievably perfect, and he wanted to run his tongue over the entirety of her body. "You know, I never realized how horny vampires were. I think we've made love every night for a month straight."

She laughed, a beautiful sound like ancient bells, as she planted kisses along his chest. "I think you just bring it out in me. I can't resist you." Her eyes squeezed shut and her mouth opened, her entire body undulating as his fingers drove her desperation for him.

"Neither can I." His own body shuddered with need, and Amar rolled over to cover her.

Katalin might have remembered her time as a human, but it didn't slow down her lightning reflexes. She barred him with a quick flick of her wrists and used her legs to twist her own body around, effectively pinning him to the bed. "Not so fast," she cautioned with a grin. "I'm not done with you yet."

"I don't ever plan to be done with *you*." Amar had come to love the way she put him in check when she wanted to slow things down. She was a woman who was very much in control and knew what she wanted, and he was content to let her have it. Especially when she did things like this, spreading her warm thighs over his legs and taking him into her mouth. "I don't deserve you," he groaned.

She claimed him as her own, her breasts pressing tantalizingly against him as she worked, her tongue flicking over all the right places. Amar reached down and gathered her dark hair in his hands. He gripped it in his fist as he fought his dragon, which demanded control. He closed his eyes and pushed that inner beast back down, content to let this last as long as possible.

Katalin's fingers grazed greedily over his body, her own breathing coming faster as she worked on him. She sat up, replacing the warmth of her mouth with that of her core as she settled herself down onto him, burying him deeply and clenching her muscles to grip him. "How can you say you don't deserve me? You're the one who looked for me all those years. You're the one who fought for me, who was so determined to make me whole again." Her head tipped back and rolled to the side as she moved against him, a shiver of pleasure running through her body.

"Of course I would do all that," he said as he brushed his fingers down her ribs and around her back, pulling her down so that he could kiss her. "I mean, we have five hundred years of lovemaking to make up for."

Her fingers dug into his shoulders and she gritted her teeth as she contracted around him. His nerves fizzed with excitement at knowing she was getting what she needed from him. Katalin had always given him a rush of excitement that left him buzzing when she was human, and he'd realized that nothing had changed. There were so many ways they were meant to be together. As her legs wrapped around him and her hips ground in perfect timing with his, he knew it to the very depths of his soul.

Her fingernails ran against his scalp as her body shivered, inciting a riot within his own body in response. When Amar was with her like this, he was both man and dragon, yet neither, because there was no sensation quite like this he could compare it to. He was her and yet himself, two parts of one soul that were finally reunited. Tension built up inside him like a twisted rubber band, doubling over on itself. They held each other tightly, and he could feel it inside her, too. It was a wave of pleasure that they'd guided each other to, and they washed over the peak of it as they came for each other.

The two of them lay together for a while, a tangle of arms and legs as they tried to stay as close to each other as possible. Amar felt as though he could stay like that for the rest of eternity, but that would be a very long time for beings like them. Besides, there was something he wanted to do that night. "You up for a walk?"

"Oh, the pale woman and her lover out for another midnight stroll? Nothing like keeping up those rumors about me, right?" Katalin smiled up at him, clearly not affected by the gossip.

"Why not? They say people take vacations to make their own lives more interesting, but that doesn't mean we can't do the same for the people who live here." He rose from the bed, almost regretting it as the sheets pulled back and revealed that delicious body of hers. But no, there was something that had to be done. He'd thought about it too long not to do it now.

Twenty minutes later, they walked alone through the stone streets of the little village where they'd managed to rent a cottage. By day, it was a lively place full of people. Some of them were just as modern as what you'd find in any metropolitan area in the world, while others looked like an old photograph that had come back to life. Some of the little plaster-sided cottages still sported thatched roofs, and the crooked little fences between them only accentuated the quaintness of the town.

"Have you thought any more about what I said?" he asked, feeling far too big for this tiny village but enjoying it nonetheless.

Katalin gave a wistful sigh. "Yes, but I don't think I'm ready. I have no doubt that I could find my parents' old farm if I had the chance, but this trip has been too nice. I don't want to spoil it with all those old feelings. Besides, I'm working on starting a new chapter of my life."

"I understand." That was why, when Amar had booked their trip, he hadn't taken her directly back to the village where they'd met. It was enough to be back in the Cserhat Mountains, in a place that could remind them of their good times together without haunting them. "Anytime you decide you're ready, we'll come back."

"What, you mean to Hungary?" She glanced up at him, her face pale in the moonlight.

"Of course. We can come back here or go anywhere else you want to go. Katalin, if you wanted to live in Antarctica, I'd do it as long as I got to have you at my side."

"You're silly. And sweet." She planted a kiss on his jaw.

They reached the edge of town, where they would usually turn back, but Amar drew her on ahead. "The moon gives us plenty of light, and I wouldn't mind exploring a bit more. If that's all right with you, of course." If not, all his plans for the night would have to change.

Katalin glanced up at the trail that jutted off from the side of the road and into the mountains. "How about up there?"

"Exactly what I was thinking." The trail was steep and wooded, the interlocking branches blocking out most of the moon's light. "You know, the lady that works in the bakery would be horrified if she knew we were doing this. She warned me very thoroughly about traveling through the forest at night and the dangerous creatures who dwell here."

"Dangerous creatures like us?"

Amar smiled, finding plenty of humor in the truth. "In the flesh." The path narrowed even more as they climbed higher, rising above a sapphire lake. The trees were beginning to thin as they drew closer to the crest. "You know, it's a very strange thing to say, but I'm actually glad that you're a vampire. If you'd remained human, the two of us wouldn't have had nearly as much time together."

She rested her cheek against his arm. "I'm glad you can see an upside to that. And I'm also incredibly grateful to Drake and Sabrina. You've got excellent doctors on your team, you know that?"

"I do." Emersyn had consulted with Dr. Drake Sheridan of the D.C. unit and Dr. Sabrina Barrett in Dallas about his mate's need for shifter blood. Together, they'd created a substitute that kept her sustained without the need to tap anyone's veins, although Amar would do it for her in an instant if needed. "Here we are."

They'd reached the peak of the rolling mountain, where the village could be seen below as a dark smudge within the trees. "It feels like we're the only people in the world up here," she breathed.

"Which is perfect, because that's always how I feel when I'm with you." In one swift motion, Amar removed the ring from his pocket and knelt before her. "Katalin, will you marry me?"

"Oh, Amar." She pressed her hands to her face before wrapping them around his hand, tears in her eyes. "Of course."

"I love you." He slipped the sparkling ring on her finger with shaking hands and stood, pulling her in tight against him and kissing her deeply. He'd searched for her for centuries, and at one point, he'd given up hope of ever finding her again.

But now she was his. They belonged to each other, and he would never let her go again.

———

BONDED TO THE SOLDIER WOLF

SPECIAL OPS SHIFTERS: L.A. FORCE

1

RAUL LEANED BACK IN HIS DESK CHAIR AND LISTENED TO THE PHONE RING through his headset. This was the fifth time he'd tried to contact Lindsay, and he knew what was coming. There would be a pause as the call stopped ringing, and it would last just long enough that he'd think she picked up. But then it would just be her voicemail again, reminding him to leave a message as if he didn't already know how these things worked.

He was prepared this time. He was prepared to remind her that he hadn't left one of his favorite collections with her just because he liked her, or even as something to remember him by when he went overseas. Raul knew Lindsay was just as much of a comic book nerd as he was, and she'd keep them safe. They wouldn't get ruined by sand and travel as he hopped all over the world with the Green Berets, nor would they get sold at a yard sale for a quarter apiece simply because his mom wanted his room cleaned out.

"Hello?" came a breathless voice.

"Lindsay?" Raul sat back up. It'd been so long since he'd heard her voice that he couldn't be sure.

"Raul! Hey! I've been meaning to call you back. How's it going?"

He glanced at the empty place on his bookshelf. Granted, it was only vacant because when he'd moved into the Special Ops Shifter

Force's L.A. headquarters, he'd purposely left a spot for those comics, but still. "Um, it's fine. Everything's great. You?"

"If you were on the internet at all, you'd know!" Lindsay gushed. "I can't believe how well my YouTube channel has been doing. When I started it up, I figured it would just be a fun little side hustle. But it turns out people really like hearing about comics, movies, and gaming from a girl. I've even gotten sponsors, and I quit that awful job I had down at the diner. Life couldn't be better!"

"Sweet. I'm really happy for you." He was. Though Raul had technically dated Lindsay for a few years during his time in the service, he'd easily come to terms with the fact that they weren't meant to be together. She liked a lot of the same things he did, but it wasn't enough.

"Hey, do you remember that guy Shane who used to work downtown at the coffee shop?"

"Sure."

"We're getting married! And it's going to be more like a comic-con than a wedding. My mom's pissed, of course, because she wants me to walk down the aisle wearing a god awful wedding gown. Pfft! She clearly doesn't know me at all. And it's not as though I'm making her dress up. I just can't decide if I want to do a *Star Wars* theme, or maybe go with something like Joker and Harley Quinn. It's tough, but I'm so excited!" Lindsay paused for a moment to take a breath. "I'm sorry. Maybe I shouldn't be telling you all this."

"No, it's fine. Really. I'm happy for the two of you; you'll be great together. I was really just calling to see if you could mail me those comics I had you hold onto."

"Oh, yeah!" The sound of rustling overtook the phone line for a moment. "I've still got them all right here in the box. Just give me your address and I'll send them out tomorrow."

Raul rattled off the address.

"Wow, you're living in Los Angeles? What's going on? Are you some sort of movie star now? No. That's not it. You'd be a screenwriter before you'd actually want your face plastered on a Blu-ray cover."

He had to laugh a little at that. "No Hollywood stuff, just a different job that happened to fall in my lap. It's a good one, though, and the city's awesome."

"Raul? I know it shouldn't matter. I shouldn't even be asking you this, considering everything, but are there any hard feelings between us? I'd just like to think that we can be friends."

Raul smiled at the phone. Lindsay was a good person. He'd dated her because he'd thought they could create a solid bond over their common passions. Some of it, he could admit to himself now, was because he knew he was going into the Army and wanted a warm body to come home to. If he were honest with himself, though, there had never been a true spark between them. "Of course, we're friends. You don't know how good it was for me to have someone at home to write to about anything and everything—including bad movies that didn't do any justice to the book. I appreciate every time you wrote back, and I don't regret any of that."

"That's really great, Raul. You're such a good guy; I know you'll find the right person someday. Hey, I've got to go, but I'll get those comics out to you tomorrow. Thanks for calling."

He hung up, frowning at the phone. He didn't mind that Lindsay had moved on and was getting married, but why did she have to end the call by reminding him just how lonely he was? Raul had grown up hearing all about how shifters were different from humans because fate pulled them together into bonded pairs that couldn't be denied.

"It's so much more than attraction, *mi nieto*," his grandmother had reminded him when he'd first started dating as a teenager. "A woman might be beautiful, yes. But does she speak to your soul?"

Raul hadn't wanted to admit just how much his abuela's words had affected him, especially at such a young age. Immediately, Raul had wanted that for himself. He'd seen the soft looks his parents gave each other and the way his grandmother still pined for her late husband, and as a child, it'd merely been part of his pack's life. That simple conversation had changed the thought into so much more.

"Raul?" Amar called from the stairs. His footsteps were noiseless as he approached the bedroom door and knocked.

"Yeah?" Raul set his phone aside.

"When was the last time you checked on your app?" Amar asked as he entered the room. His eyes swept quickly over the electronics that filled most of the cramped shelves. "My phone has been blowing up for the last twenty minutes."

A small wave of guilt washed over Raul. He and Hudson Taylor from the D.C. unit developed the app as a way for shifters to communicate with each other without being outed. Raul had long ago found underground chatrooms where shifters spoke in code, but he and the rest of the Force knew just how important it was to get real information out to the shifter community. Still, he'd been too caught up in his own business to check the app that day.

"Then you might want to change your notification settings." Raul leaned forward and unlocked his computer screen, where he could see everything within the app from the back end. It wasn't the sleek, user-friendly interface that everyone else saw on their phones and tablets; just raw code, and he loved it. That was exactly what had inspired him to specialize in communications when he'd enlisted. "Just go into your settings menu."

Amar sighed and handed his phone to Raul. "You do it."

"Seriously?" Raul couldn't hide his smirk as he looked up at his Alpha. Amar was a formidable man, and when humans weren't looking, he was capable of shifting into a powerful dragon. He'd lived for centuries and survived wars and plagues, but the man sure hated a cell phone. "You can't tell me you don't know how to do this by now."

"I'm sure I could figure it out if I wanted to," he assured Raul, "but I don't. I won't deny how useful all this is to the Force and to the shifter community as a whole, but I get so tired of looking at a tiny screen."

"Here you go." Raul handed the phone back. "Now, let's see what people are posting about."

Raul had known, as soon as he'd decided to create this app, that there would be some interesting issues to tackle. First, they had to make sure it was a safe place for shifters to discuss what was happening around them. That meant giving the app a rather vague name—The Shift—that most people wouldn't pick up on. Those who downloaded the app were met with a screen asking for their credentials. They couldn't just make up a login name and password; instead, they had to have official credentials that were handed down from their local conclave. Hudson, who was also the CEO of Taylor Communications, had helped him work on all the security from the back end, ensuring enemies couldn't hack the app.

Perhaps even more importantly, Raul had known how dangerous it would be if this were treated purely as a social media platform, where anyone could say anything. The Force, conclaves, and clan leaders needed reputable sources so they'd be able to distinguish truth from speculation. They were still working on that part of it, but Raul had started the process by putting different badge types next to each user.

This also meant working with the conclave leaders and beefing up the national registry of shifters.

In short, it'd been a ton of work and had taken up a lot of time. But that didn't mean it wasn't worth it.

Raul questioned what was going on as soon as he started seeing the news feeds. "What's all this bullshit? There's no way we got hacked."

"If we did, then it was by someone with a lot of talent and a very active imagination. Personally, I wouldn't have gone with zombies."

Raul clicked on a video that'd been recently uploaded by a clan-designated reporter. It showed a woman sitting in a house by the beach, looking terrified. "I...I don't understand it," she stammered. "I'd heard about people who were dead suddenly showing up again. I wanted to just explain it away; maybe those folks were just missing their deceased loved ones. But then I saw it with my very own eyes! The old man down the street died of a heart attack last week and, I can't believe I'm saying this, but I saw him out on his lawn last night!"

"Weed *is* legal in California now," Amar commented under his breath.

"I ran back in the house and told my roommate," she continued. "She said I'd been sleepwalking and I'd just made the whole thing up, but when she looked out the window, she saw him, too! He was just standing there, staring at the roses he'd planted last year, but he was so real!"

"There are tons of stories like this, man," Raul said as he skimmed the reports. "It doesn't make any sense."

Amar grabbed a free chair and sat down. "I don't suppose it's much different than dealing with vampires."

Raul chuckled. Amar was a mythical creature on his own, and to humans, the rest of the shifter community would be, too. But the blood-sucking undead were new to all of them, and it'd made the situation even more complicated considering one of them turned out to be Amar's mate. "How is Katalin adjusting to life here, anyway? She seems like she's doing well, but she's also pretty quiet."

The Alpha tipped his head slightly to the side and smiled, a distant look in his dark eyes. "L.A. isn't ever going to be the perfect place for her, considering how sunny it is, but we get out at night as much as we can. And the shifter blood substitute Drake, Emersyn, and Sabrina concocted for her has made a huge difference in her lifestyle."

"And the wedding?" Raul had been thrilled for the couple when they'd announced their pending nuptials, though it also served as a painful reminder that he hadn't yet found his mate.

"All in due time. There's no rush, especially for the two of us."

Raul knew what he meant. Both Amar and Katalin had lived for several hundred years, so a few more months wasn't going to change anything.

He focused his attention back to the computer screen. He loved the supernatural and the concept that what people understood as reality wasn't always the extent of it. "Spooky shit like this is right up my alley. Let me dig around a bit, and I'll see what else I can find out."

"If you insist, but don't go doing anything crazy. I don't need you turning up as a zombie. I mean, no more of one than you already are in the morning." Laughing, Amar left the room.

There were plenty of possibilities, but Raul's intuition told him zombies weren't on the list.

His fingers flew over the keyboard as he quickly skimmed the other sightings that had been posted to the app. Most of them weren't from anyone with a badge. That didn't mean they were false reports, but he wanted the most reputable and reliable information possible.

One post in particular caught his eye.

"We at the L.A. Society for Spirits want to understand what's happening in our area. There have been far too many of these strange occurrences posted here and reported directly to us, so we know this isn't just a coincidence. The LASS will do everything it can to help understand why deceased shifters are suddenly being spotted all over the city, as shown in the video below. If you'd like to help, the LASS is currently recruiting new members."

The video below the post was one Raul had already seen, since it'd been shared several times. It showed a tall man breaking out the windows of a car parked on the street. Nothing would be all that unusual about the video or separate it from any other act of vandalism, except for the swirling mists that surrounded the man's figure. And Raul had seen several paranormal groups looking for recruits even before these incidents started happening, so nothing about that was strange.

What gave Raul pause was the profile picture of the woman who'd made the post.

It was a closeup that only showed part of her face, turned slightly away from the camera. Although it was a little blurry, as though she turned to run from something, it showed the angle of her eye and the delicate flush of her cheek. Her name—since The Shift didn't use screen handles—was Penelope Granger.

Raul blinked. He wasn't on the app to meet chicks. He'd created the damn thing to share information, and that was exactly what he was going to do. Firing off a quick message to the poster, he logged off the app and began looking up anything he could find about spirits rising from the dead. The Force had turned to mythology and legends to help them with their vampire problem, so there was no reason not to do the same now. Raul had learned, along with the rest of the Force, that there was often more truth in fiction than they'd realized.

Taking a break, he glanced out the window at the full moon. As a kid, Raul had loved the idea of being controlled by something else, of not having any excuse for being in his human form or his wolf form. Somehow, that had sounded more exciting than being able to change of his own volition. Aside from missions with the Force, when was the last time he'd shifted, anyway? Raul shut the curtains and went back to work.

It wasn't until he finally turned to go to bed around two a.m. that Raul pulled up The Shift on his phone and checked his messages.

We'll be at the Calvary Cemetery at midnight tomorrow night. You can meet us there.

2

PENNY SAT ON HER BED, RATTLING AWAY ON HER LAPTOP, WITH SEVERAL volumes about ghosts, cults, and ancient rituals scattered at her feet. She had so many things she needed to get done! Her job at the bookstore had always been fun as far as work went, but it was nothing compared to the hobbies she pursued on the side. She'd formed the Los Angeles Society for Spirits just after high school, and even though most of her family thought it was ridiculous, she knew the importance of what she was doing.

Her cell pinged. It was Ingrid. *Are you coming?*

"Shit!" Penny slammed her computer shut and tossed several books on the floor as she shot up from her bed. She stashed her laptop in her desk drawer and then tapped a quick message back to Ingrid. *Got caught up. Be there ASAP.*

She glanced at herself in the mirror as she grabbed her keys. Pressing a fingertip to her lips, she transferred the kiss to the little stamped charm on her bracelet. The letters "BFF" were hammered onto the surface, and it dangled next to tiny glass beads of yellow and light blue for each of their birthstones. The light blue one had a swirl of white in it, where Kayla's ashes had been incorporated into the glass.

"I miss you, girl. Every day."

Her phone rang as she charged through her apartment door, locked it behind her, and headed for the stairs. "I know, I know," she said when she answered. "I just completely lost track of time."

"Doing what?" her mother's voice replied.

Great. Penny rolled her eyes. She was already late, and now she had her mother to nag her the entire trip. "Just working on some things. Sorry, I thought you were Ingrid."

"It's nice to know you've got friends again, dear."

She couldn't stop another eye roll. Mrs. Granger had been talking to her like that for years. "I've always had friends, Mom."

"I know, but after Kayla—"

"Stop. I don't want to talk about that, not right now. Let's talk about you. What's up?" Penny stepped out onto the sidewalk. It was crammed with people as the time approached the dinner hour, and everyone was either heading home from work, heading into work for the evening shift, or trying to get somewhere to eat. Cars raced by in the open lanes and surged impatiently toward each other's bumpers as they waited for someone slow to turn. Fortunately, she didn't need to fight traffic since her destination was within walking distance.

"Mostly, I just called to remind you that we have a clan meeting tomorrow morning."

"I know, Mom."

"You say that, but you missed out on the last one. Your father is determined that you take over his position once he's ready to retire. This is important to him." She could hear the worry in her mother's voice.

Penny sighed. Most shifters probably thought the children of Alphas had it so easy. But Penny knew the reality of it. Her father constantly worried about the pack's finances because it took a lot of money to help ensure the prosperity and safety of so many people. Sure, they had a big house, but that was only because they shared it with half the pack. Someone was always there, no matter how much Penny just wanted to live like a normal family. With her mother's big heart, they were always taking in any stray wolf who happened to come along. And as for status? Her father's position didn't matter much when she was seen as the chubby weird girl who was into the occult.

"I know," Penny repeated, since she'd heard these words a million times over. "I'll be there. I just forgot what day it was last time. I've got things to do."

"I don't see how there's anything more important than family," Mrs. Granger countered. She was still speaking softly, as was her habit, but there was a bit more determination in her voice.

That was hard to argue with, although Penny wasn't sure she was up for everything that her parents and the pack expected of her. "We have lots of time, Mom. It's not like Dad's going to retire next week."

"He's not. You're right. You're also making my point for me. Your father isn't going to step back anytime soon, but I'm sure he'd like to at least know that when he *does* give up his position, he'll have someone reliable who'll take over for him. It might seem like a lot of time to you, but you have a lot more training to do."

Penny paused as she waited to cross the street and closed her eyes. So many times, she'd taken herself off to some fantasy world where she didn't have all these responsibilities resting on her shoulders. Her parents had practically come apart at the seams when they'd discovered she'd gotten her own apartment. It hadn't had anything to do with her not being old enough to live alone or having the money. No. It had all been about the pack and what was traditionally done. Her parents understood how important it was to them, but had they ever bothered to consider what she wanted?

"We can talk about this more tomorrow morning. Right now, I'm on my way to meet my friends for dinner." She moved quickly across the street. The flickering neon sign of the taco joint was within her sights.

"It's not that ridiculous ghost hunting thing again, is it?" Mrs. Granger gave an impatient sigh without waiting for an answer. "Penelope, I've told you before that you need to stop wasting your time. There are other things you could be doing that are much more important."

Gritting her teeth, Penny forced a smile onto her face. It wasn't real, but it would make her sound a lot nicer than she actually felt. "Mom, I've got to go. I'll see you tomorrow morning. I love you! Bye!" She hung up, feeling like an asshole, but also knowing there was no other way around it.

"There you are!" Ingrid called when she saw Penny walk in a minute later. She gestured from the booth that she and the LASS were taking up, even though there was no mistaking where her friends were in a place this small. There was also no mistaking Ingrid's brilliant red hair. "We went ahead and ordered loaded nachos for you."

"Thanks." Penny slid into the booth. Ingrid and Wendy were already seated on the other side, and Dylan had pulled up a chair to the end.

Penny was just about to tell him to scoot in so he'd be more comfortable when the empty space next to her was filled. She tried not to cringe against the wall as Tyler wrapped his arm around her. "There you are," he said, echoing Ingrid's words, but not exactly her senti-ment. "I guess you figured out that I saved a seat for you."

Keeping her eyes leveled at Ingrid, Penny sent her friend a why-the-fuck-didn't-you-warn-me glare. Granted, Penny already knew Tyler was going to be at the meeting. He was at *every* meeting, even when Penny conveniently forgot to tell him. After their break-up, they'd been trying to maintain some semblance of a platonic friend-ship, but Tyler wasn't very good at it.

"Hey," she finally said, turning to look at him. He was tall and lanky, a stature exaggerated by the way he leaned over the back of the booth. His eyes were rimmed in red, either because of the late hour, or whatever else he'd been up to lately. She'd really liked Tyler at one point. When they were both younger, their parents used to get together for inter-pack meetings. It was like a giant block party of nothing but wolf shifters, and it'd been a blast to see other pups like herself that weren't her cousins. But times changed, and so did their relationship.

"*Hey*?" We were a couple for how long, and all I get is a 'hey'?" Tyler turned to look at the others, thoroughly expecting them to agree with him.

"We're not doing this tonight. I've already had enough fucking drama for the day." Penny twisted the bracelet on her arm, once again thinking of Kayla. It'd been so long, but Penny knew Kayla would've been there for her, no matter what.

"Besides, we have a lot to discuss!" Ingrid chirped, excitement bright in her eyes. "I'm sure you all saw the same video I did, the one with the guy smashing the car?"

Dylan nodded sagely. His curly hair was wild as usual over his dark-framed glasses, and he leaned forward to put his elbows on the table. "Sure, but let's not get too eager. It's totally possible that someone faked that. You only have to click a few buttons with the right software to add that cheesy mist effect."

"Then how do you explain the rest of them? Like that woman who ran right out into traffic, screaming for help, and as soon as the car hit her, she was gone?" Ingrid snapped her fingers in the air for effect.

"There have been urban legends like that for decades," Dylan calmly countered.

Penny twitched her mouth to keep her smile at bay. Those two liked each other. There was no doubt in her mind, yet she knew that Ingrid and Dylan would each deny it. She was a believer, and he was a skeptic. They could never be compatible, right? Penny couldn't say anything about that for sure, but the tension between the two of them was always so thick.

Ingrid lifted her chin, but she also ran a self-conscious hand through her hair. "Who's to say those urban legends aren't based on something?"

"I see," Dylan said with another nod. "Next, you're going to tell me that you made out in a guy's car and found a hook hanging from the door handle."

"I...That's...No!" Ingrid spluttered. She sat back against the booth seat and folded her arms. "You know that's not what I mean."

"Okay, I think we can all agree that there aren't any hook-handed abductors lurking around the area," Penny said, trying to get things back on track before her father called and wanted to know why she'd upset her mother. "I think we can also agree that our best route is to take the information that we know is solid and pursue it. You all remember I mentioned we should go to the Calvary Cemetery tonight, right?"

They nodded their heads, except for Tyler. He was staring at his phone.

"That's where Victor Reyes is buried. It was easy enough to find his grave online, so it shouldn't be too hard to locate, even though the place is so big. That's where we start, and we start tonight." A surge of energy shot up from her stomach and touched the back of her tongue. She'd always been intrigued by spirits. These extraordinary tales that were circulating through the city were a little scary, but it was thrilling to think they might actually come face-to-face with a ghost.

"Why this particular one?" Wendy asked. She was sandwiched between Ingrid and Dylan, and she kept herself shrunk down into as small of a silhouette as possible. Wendy was a typical goth girl. She might have been in her twenties, but she still dyed her hair black and carefully applied a matching shade to her lips. It was a stark contrast to the pearlescent color of her skin, which was, of course, the point.

"We have more information about him than anyone else, and that means we can put a pretty solid ID on him. He was a known criminal when he passed away about a month ago, so there are mug shots to compare the video to." She'd spent far too long poring over the images, comparing things like the angle of the man's nose and the shape of his jaw. Penny knew she wasn't wrong.

"Hey, wait. Is this the guy in the liquor store video?" Tyler asked.

Dylan grunted. "Oh, I'm sorry. Are you actually paying attention for a change?" He and the other members of the society knew that Tyler wasn't there because of his passion for exploring the spiritual world.

"I pay *plenty* of attention, asshole," Tyler retorted, running one hand through his light brown hair and then carefully patting it back into place. "It's actually the rest of you who should be paying more attention. I'm going to take this group to the next level."

"Exactly what is the next level?" Penny asked, sure she wouldn't like the answer.

"The internet, obviously." He let out a short breath of laughter.

"We're already on the internet. I made a website and everything." Wendy's glare was openly disdainful.

"A website is nice, sure, but that's not where people really make their money. I'm talking about videos. Haven't you guys been on YouTube? There are guys that literally just walk around in abandoned houses, and they make a ton of money with ads and merch. There's no reason we couldn't do the same."

"Yes, there is," Penny instantly argued. "They're making those videos with the sole intent to make money. The Society for Spirits isn't like that. We need to *be* serious if we want to be taken seriously." She'd been laughed at plenty of times for her interest in the supernatural, and she wanted a world where it didn't have to be like that.

Tyler sighed. "If you say so, but we all know I'm right."

There was a collective sigh of dismissal among the group.

Penny wasn't going to let Tyler ruin this for her. "So, are we all on board to meet at Calvary Cemetery tonight at midnight?"

"Works for me," Wendy said.

"I'll be there with the equipment," Dylan volunteered.

"Yup!" came Ingrid's usual enthusiastic reply.

"Good. Just so you know, someone will be joining us." For some reason, this part made her nervous. Penny knew she should have been thrilled that a new person messaged her with interest in the group. The whole point of the LASS was not only to look for evidence of spirits, but to spread the word around. That wasn't going to happen if it was just the five of them. They needed more people. But she'd gotten a strange feeling in the pit of her stomach when she'd found the message from him.

"I hope this isn't one of those old farts who retired from teaching high school science and thinks he knows everything," Tyler cracked. "That's *not* what we need on our channel."

"No. This guy is from another group who's investigated these incidents, and I invited him along. I'm telling all of you this because this isn't a good time to be rude."

Ingrid sat up straight. "Hey! I'm not rude!"

"You're not necessarily the one I'm talking about," Penny replied.

"We'll do our best," Dylan promised. "But you know how it is. We've all spent our lives being the rejects. It's hard to believe that anyone would want to come hang out with us voluntarily unless they were punking us."

"Or what about the ones that rejected us from other groups? We've had a few of those," Wendy reminded them.

Penny sighed. "I know. But I have a distinct feeling that things will be different this time." Their orders arrived, and the friends dug into their cheap Mexican fare. There was so much more that Penny would've liked to discuss, but she couldn't keep her mind off their special guest for the evening.

She'd spent a lot of time on the internet. When it came to ghost hunting, there were simply more resources there than anywhere else. That meant she also exchanged plenty of messages with complete strangers, and they didn't bother her. But this time, something was different.

Her stomach swirled as she scooped up a pile of seasoned ground beef and cool sour cream with a tortilla chip. She had no idea who this guy was or exactly what about spirits intrigued him. The badge next to his name indicated that he was an authentic source of information, someone who could be trusted, but that wasn't the same as knowing a person. Penny couldn't even say why she'd invited him to one of their investigations in the first place. She'd sworn she wouldn't do that again after that incident with the retired high school teacher, and she'd make any newbies meet her first to talk.

Something was going to be completely different this time. She just knew it.

3

RAUL SLAMMED THE DOOR OF HIS TRUCK AND HEADED ACROSS THE street. This wasn't a part of town that was particularly active for night life, and he was grateful as he moved along the low fence. At first, it was chain link and barbed wire, which amused him, but it turned to cast iron further down. He easily hopped over.

The trees were dark silhouettes, shaking their branches in eternal torture as they loomed over the smaller shadows of the tombstones. Raul picked his way carefully without a flashlight, letting his naturally superior night vision guide him. He was a wolf shifter, after all, and if he couldn't see in dim light then what good was he?

Besides, it was easy to spot the group he was headed for. They had no qualms about turning on artificial lights, and they each carried one as though they were talismans against whatever bad spirits might have been lurking there. Even from a distance, he could see numerous other pieces of equipment lighting up the night. If the L.A. Society for Spirits was trying to keep themselves a secret, they were doing a shitty job of it. Raul grinned as he approached quietly, tempted to sneak up on them and hear their screams of terror when he jumped out from behind a lump of granite. No. He reminded himself he was there on business, and he needed to act like a professional, even if it wasn't quite as much fun.

The Special Ops Shifter Force needed the Los Angeles Society for Spirits on their side, after all. Raul was the closest thing the Force had when it came to a supernatural expert, but most of his knowledge had been gleaned from pop culture. Even he was a bit skeptical when it came to these supposed paranormal incidents that were happening in the city. Could anyone really reanimate after death? If so, why would they bother doing things like assaulting people on the street or breaking into a business? So much of this didn't make sense to him, and he hoped these ghost hunters could help clear up a few things. Either that, or he'd be heading straight down the rabbit hole of sensationalized reality TV. One good thing he could hold onto was the fact that he was dealing with other shifters, so he could be a bit more of himself.

"We're getting a big spike on the EMF reader. A huge one! Damn!"

"Does everyone have their cells off?"

Several assents came through the night air.

"Still, don't get excited about it." This voice was calm and like velvet, a little deep for a woman. It sent a shiver of pleasure rippling under Raul's skin and raised a few hairs along his hackles. He took a deep breath, once again reminding himself that he was there in a professional capacity. Whatever strange vibrations he'd been picking up were just the result of spending too much time online and getting crazy ideas stuck in his head.

"But look! It's steadily increasing! That's got to mean something."

"It doesn't mean anything until we can get baseline readings. We might have to come several nights in a row before we figure out what those actually are. And Ingrid, you know as well as I do that we have to check for any other sources that energy could be coming from. Are you sure all your phones are off?"

"It's probably me," Raul said as he approached, secretly pleased at the slight jump he got from several of the investigators. He pulled his cell from his pocket and turned it off. Given that it wasn't a typical cell and had been specially developed for the SOS Force, he wouldn't be surprised if it was messing with their equipment. "Sorry."

"Who are *you*?" A tall man stepped away from the grave they were surrounding and placed himself at the forefront of the group, blocking Raul's progress forward. He folded his arms across his chest and tipped his head back.

Most people wouldn't have been able to make out the man's features in the dark shadows of the cemetery, but Raul could. He could also detect the waves of anger and possession that rolled off him. This guy was the kind who liked to fight, and Raul had met plenty of others like him in the service. He stuck out his hand. "I'm Raul."

The man refused to shake his hand; he just stood there, waiting for the newcomer to be intimidated.

"I'm looking for Penelope."

A woman came around Tyler and shot him a scathing look before offering her hand to their guest. "Penny." She studied Raul with wide green eyes that slanted up at the corners. They were the same eyes that he'd noticed in her profile picture—that he'd stared at too long if he were honest with himself—and now they were looking right at him. She'd attempted to tame her wavy golden hair into a braid at the nape of her neck, and the strands that'd escaped were tucked behind her ears. With full lips and a pert nose, she was one of the most beautiful women Raul had ever seen.

As her hand wrapped around his, completing the gesture Raul had offered to her comrade, Raul thought he might explode from the inside out. Nuclear bombs were detonating throughout his body, sending a ringing buzz through his ears. After what felt like a small eternity, he realized that he was just standing there staring.

"I, uh, I'm Raul," he stammered, trying to get a hold of himself. He'd seen plenty of good-looking women before, and he'd never lost his cool that badly. There was just something about this voluptuous beauty that reached out and pulled his beating heart from his chest. The funny thing was, he wanted more. "We chatted online."

She gave him a small squeeze to end the handshake and offered a little smile that sent his blood racing through his veins. "Yes, I'm so glad you could make it. We've tried to reach out as much as possible to get some other folks interested in ghost hunting. It seems like these days no one's interested unless they're certain they'll find evidence, or that they'll become YouTube celebrities."

He thought he saw her give another look to the tall guy, who continued to stare straight down his nose at Raul.

The rest of them were watching him, too, but without the same open hostility. Could they tell that his wolf was going absolutely wild inside him? Was he acting like even more of an idiot than he felt he was? "Yeah, no, I'm just looking for a little information. You see, I'm with the SOS Force." Amar had given his express permission to tell them exactly who he was, given that they needed the Society for Spirits to work with them and serve as consultants on this mission. It still felt incredibly weird, and Raul felt a heat flush into his cheeks.

Penny's eyebrows shot up. "You're more than welcome to tag along while we do our investigation here, and then you and I can talk in more detail later." She turned back to the equipment set up around a fresh grave.

Raul noticed the doubtful looks exchanged among some of the other ghost hunters. They either didn't want him there because they didn't accept outsiders, or because he was on the Force, but tough shit. He ignored them and focused on the task at hand. "What do you have going on here?"

She shone her flashlight on the headstone. "This is the grave of Victor Reyes. He died last month, but there have been several sightings of him since then, including him supposedly robbing a liquor store. We're checking things out here first."

"I saw that video." Raul replayed it in his mind. "How do we know for sure that the dead guy and the robber are the same person?"

"A little bit of intuition, but I studied the video carefully and compared it to his mug shots. We'll have to stop talking for a bit now. We need to get these baseline readings, and we'll completely throw off the sensors." Penny and another man with dark curly hair finished setting up various pieces of equipment around the mound of lumpy dirt. "Dylan, do you have the camera ready?"

"All good."

Raul followed the lead of the other ghost hunters, taking several steps back from the grave and standing still. He watched and waited, but nothing happened. The lights on the various electronics didn't change. Nothing beeped. No ghostly mist arose from the grave to curse them.

"Okay, make sure we've got the temperature recorded this time." Penny was the first to move, making a circuit around the grave as she double-checked everything. "Anything on the camera, Dylan?"

"Just us chickens."

"Figures."

"You really think the dead are coming back to life? They don't seem to stumble around the way the movies portray." Once again, Raul suppressed a laugh. He had an embarrassingly large stash of *Night of* the *Living Dead* comics back at headquarters, but he'd never taken them that seriously.

Penny shot him a look. "Don't be ridiculous. You can't reanimate a body. This is just the spirit we're talking about. We're looking for evidence that it might've come up through the ground. Look here." She'd gone back around, bent over the grave, and leaned close to him as she pointed out small swirls in the earth.

His breath shortened in his lungs as the soft curve of her hip brushed against him, and his eyes immediately lost focus on the evidence she was trying to show him. Penny was affecting him in a way that made his inner wolf claw at the underside of his human form, demanding to be let out of its cage. He was nauseous and sweaty one moment and pleasantly dizzy the next. She was a force that affected him like the moon affects the tides, and the swirling waters that crashed inside him were proof of it.

"Are you all right?"

Raul blinked, realizing he hadn't even been paying attention. He looked to Penny, thinking she'd spoken to him. Instead, she was sitting on the damp grass and holding her head in her hand. One of the other team members, a girl with fiery red hair, was kneeling next to her.

"What happened? Are you all right?"

Penny glanced at Raul and away again. "I'm fine, Ingrid. I'm just a little dizzy."

But there had been something in that glance. It wasn't just embarrassment at feeling off in front of a stranger. As his heart pounded in his chest, Raul's mouth went dry, something he was grateful for as it kept him from saying anything stupid.

Something was affecting him and Penny, and he was damn sure it had nothing to do with ghosts. Was there any chance she could be... No. Right?

The guy who'd tried to intimidate Raul pushed past him to crouch on the other side of Penny. "You should take it easy. You know how sensitive you are to the supernatural."

"No, Tyler. I don't think it's that. I just... I'm fine. Okay?" Once again, Penny glanced past her friends and up at Raul with those emerald eyes of hers.

It was that look, that look right there, that told him he couldn't deny it. But why should he even want to? Penny was stunning, and it was clear from the way she ran the show with this group that she was a competent, intelligent woman. If anything, she was too good for him. No one had ever resonated with him like that, and he couldn't expect it of her. Raul clutched his fists against the denim of his jeans. Something was happening there. Ghosts? Fate? Both?

"Let's just get this done. We've got a job to do." Penny got to her feet, refusing help from either Ingrid or Tyler.

Raul cleared his throat. "Can you tell me a little about your equipment?"

"She doesn't have time to deal with you," Tyler retorted, once again stepping between Raul and Penny. "It's bad enough we have to keep under wraps due to the humans and government, but now we've just got the shifter version of G.I. Joe here."

"Stop it!" Penny hissed. She gestured for Raul to come a little closer, and she pointed to a small device that looked like a pop-up lantern. Instead of a single bright bulb or LED, it had rings of lights in different colors. "This is the EMF detector. As I'm sure you can guess, it detects electromagnetic frequencies. The stronger the frequency, the more it lights up."

"Does that indicate proof of a paranormal presence?" Raul had watched some of the ghost hunting shows on TV just to kill time, but he didn't put much stock in all the devices they carried around.

"No. None of this technically provides proof, but that's the problem. We don't yet know exactly how to prove that they're here or not. All we can do is take baseline readings in a given environment, compare them to any unusual anomalies, and then look for a rational way to explain those anomalies." Penny's arm grazed against his as she moved to check the screen on the camera.

His next question died in his throat as he concentrated on what that tiny bit of contact had done to him. Why was this so hard? He'd been on countless missions when he was with the Green Berets. Some might think his position as a Communications Sergeant kept him safely behind enemy lines, but that was never the case when it came to Special Forces. He'd constantly put himself in the line of danger, and he'd never had a problem with it. That'd been his job. This woman, by simply talking to him and showing him what she knew, was overwhelming.

He swallowed and remembered what he'd wanted to say. "So, you're basically telling me that you find ghosts by proving that they're not around?"

"Essentially. That's the best we can do for the time being and still do this whole ghost hunting idea any justice. It would be easy to claim that we're certain of paranormal activity based on a sudden change in temperature or a dog barking at empty space. But then we'd be looking past what could actually be causing these things and discrediting anyone who genuinely wants to find spirits. Even electronic voice phenomena isn't completely accurate, because people tend to hear what they want to hear." Penny had a clipboard in her hand now, and she scribbled some notes down.

"Hey, I like the EVP recorder," groused a girl leaning on the tombstone. She looked like a ghost herself with the pallor of her skin against the gloom of the cemetery. "We've gotten several answers from ghosts through that."

"This is Wendy, by the way," Penny said, gesturing toward the goth girl.

"What kind of answers?" Raul asked.

Wendy lifted her chin slightly and looked away, looking as though she might not be willing to answer him. "Whenever we do an investigation and we find anomalous readings, I usually ask several questions of the spirit. Sometimes they don't answer at all, but now and then, when we play the recording back, we hear some pretty clear words."

"Really? I'd be interested in what kind of experiments you've performed along those lines. I'd think the questions you ask and the environment in which you ask them could affect the outcome." He was speaking to Wendy, but he was incredibly aware of Penny.

"It doesn't matter," Wendy replied glumly. "Like Penny said, people hear what they want to hear. You could play back EVPs for a believer, and they'd hear a spirit answering questions. Play them back for a skeptic, and they'd find some other way to rationalize it."

"All right. So other than reading the equipment, what do you guys look for?" Raul wasn't sure if his unanticipated interest had something do to with genuine curiosity or his attraction to Penny.

She straightened and looked around, as though she expected the ghost to come strolling up the hill at any moment. "I'll note any phenomena. One theory is that cold spots or malfunctioning equipment could be caused by spirits taking up the energy in the environment as they try to manifest themselves. That works well with the laws of physics, but again, there isn't any proof. Sometimes it's a light that turns on by itself, a child who has conversations with a deceased relative, objects that move on their own, things like that."

Raul stuck around while they worked for a little while longer, trying to stay out of the way and still observe as much as possible. Other than Penny occasionally asking one of the other members about something or explaining a reading to Raul, nothing unusual happened. Dylan was packing the equipment back into specialized cases by one a.m.

Raul scratched the back of his head as he approached Penny. "I know it's late, but I'd still like to talk to you about some of this stuff if you have time." He felt like a teenager asking a girl to a dance, when really it was just business.

"Yeah, sure. I've got some questions for you, too. There's an all-night diner just a few blocks from here if that works for you. We could walk there." She aimed those viridescent eyes at him once again, and he noticed a flash of excitement in her gaze.

Fire blazed a trail from his heart to his groin, his pants suddenly feeling a bit too tight. Hell, he couldn't resist if he wanted to. Raul hardly noticed as she made sure the rest of the group was good with getting the last few things picked up. The warm breeze that floated around them as they made their way onto the street could just as easily have been an electrical storm brewing between them. It'd been something else to be in her presence when he'd arrived, but being alone with her intensified the effect.

Still, he couldn't exactly start this portion of the conversation by telling her how much he wanted her or how the rest of the world disappeared when he looked at her. "So, tell me what you know about this sudden wave of ghosts in L.A. Have you managed to gather any evidence?"

She shook her head. "Mostly, I'm still just collecting as much information as possible. It's difficult because every time I turn around, there's another video, another account. I don't know how I'm going to keep track of it all."

The city sent a glow of light up into the dark sky, making a halo of pale blue before the blackness of night took over. Several signs nearby competed with the light show, advertising a fortune teller and a convenience store. Raul stared at them absently as they walked, thinking about all the computing power he had back at headquarters. "I might be able to help with that. Creating a database and analyzing any commonalities between the instances could give us a real lead to follow."

"Us?" She looked at him, her full lips twisted into a smirk. "Are you really telling me the SOS Force wants to know about ghosts? Paranormal activity is the kind of thing most authority figures are quick to dismiss."

"We're not like most authority figures," he smiled back. "You'd be surprised by some of the things we deal with. And if these ghosts or whatever are affecting the lives of the shifters here, then we want to get involved." He certainly did, anyway. Amar was waiting to see what he'd report back after this encounter, and he'd decide for the Force as a whole after that.

"All right. If you're really serious, I'd be more than happy to let you help me crunch some numbers. We're lucky that we live in a time with so much advanced technology, particularly when it can help us so much. I'm afraid I just don't have the time or knowledge. Or the equipment," she admitted.

"I agree, and I have all of that." He was bragging. He knew it, but couldn't help it. "I was actually a Communications Sergeant with the Green Berets when I was in the service. My work was all about gadgets and making sure they worked, no matter the conditions. The Army has some pretty specialized tech, but the Force can certainly compete."

"I suppose we'll have to see what the computer data has to say about it, but I've got a theory."

"Which is?" Raul felt himself leaning toward her with the question, like a plant drawn to sunlight. He forced his feet flat and his spine straight.

"I've only seen information about these ghosts on The Shift. When it comes to new stories, there's often a lot of crossover between shifter and human sources. You know, like if there's an earthquake, then everyone will be talking about it. I discovered next to nothing about these apparitions on the human side of things. I find that a little too interesting."

"What do you think it means?" She could tell him it meant everyone in Southern California was going to have cheesecake for dessert the next night, and he'd listen raptly.

"I think it means that whoever or whatever is making these spirits walk the Earth, they're specifically targeting shifters. Every single ghost who could be identified was a shifter, from what I can tell. I can't explain that yet, but I do think it's something worth taking note of."

"Hmm." Raul turned away from her to give himself a moment to focus. "That should be a pretty easy thing to find out.

"If you really are serious about the Force working with us, then I think we could get to the bottom of this in no time. Here we are." She gestured to a squat, square building on the corner. LEDs had replaced the original neon sign that shouted "Curly's Diner" out the world, but from a distance, it would look as though the place had popped right out of the fifties. Large windows lined the front of the building, showing a long counter fronted in chrome and stools. Tables of a similar fashion marched in a row along the windows, and there were hardly any patrons inside.

His stomach growled as he held the door open for her and the scents of the place invaded his nostrils. Plenty of the restaurants in this part of the world touted vegan salads, hummus, and organic bean sprouts, but Curly's smelled of greasy burgers, fried chicken, and milkshakes. "I see no reason we can't collaborate. I might even have some connections that could get you some new equipment."

A waitress appeared at their table as soon as they seated themselves across from each other. She was an older woman, and she looked exhausted. "What can I get you folks?"

They ordered, and Penny's eyes snapped to his as soon as the waitress had turned to leave. "Why do we need new equipment? There's nothing wrong with what we're using."

He frantically shook his head, realizing how his statement had sounded. "No, that's not what I meant. You're the expert on that, and I'm not here to challenge you on it. I just meant I know some guys who're really into technology—and advanced technology, at that—who might be able to come up with something that actually could give you proof of the paranormal."

Penny's face pinched with skepticism. "I highly doubt that's possible."

"You don't know these guys. If it's feasible at all, they can do it." He drummed his fingers on his thighs, uncertain of what else to do with himself. He longed for those French fries to come along and help him keep occupied. And maybe if he had a burger in his mouth, he wouldn't say anything stupid.

"Well, you'd really have to talk to Dylan. He's the one who knows the most about our gadgets. I mean, I might have founded LASS, but that doesn't mean we don't all have our specialties."

"I see. So you're the leader of the group and the one who gathers all the information. Dylan is the technology guy. Wendy talks to the spirits. Ingrid is there for her energy. Tyler..." He trailed off as he tried to pin down the roles of the group. "Bodyguard?"

"Something like that, I guess. Sounds like you've got us all labeled pretty well, but I hope that also means you can see why we need to keep expanding. Everyone brings something different to the table, and the more people we have, the more we can do." She moved her hands as she spoke, showing just how much passion she had for this.

Raul could feel it rolling off of her in waves. It was more than just a hobby or a passing interest. It certainly wasn't about getting rich or famous. His gut told him there was more to the story. "Why did you found the LASS anyway?" he asked.

"Oh, you know, just..." She trailed off, her mouth slightly open as she looked at him. Penny blinked. "My best friend died when we were still in high school." Her pain was palpable to him.

"I'm really sorry."

She twisted a charm bracelet on her wrist. "Thanks. It was really tough at the time. Everything had been fine. We were on our way home from shopping for prom dresses, then this drunk driver came out of nowhere and t-boned us. She was gone instantly." Tears glistened against the verdant green of her irises.

Raul reached across the table and closed his hand over hers. Energy ricocheted between them, and it was so much more than just physical attraction. He could feel her grief and her heartache even more intensely now, and it only made him want to comfort her all the more. "Penny, I..." Raul wasn't sure what to say. No words could change her situation or make her feel better about it.

"No, it's okay." She moved her hand away from his to wipe tears from her face. "It's been a long time. In some sense, I know I should be over it and moving past it. My parents certainly think so. The funny thing is, when someone dies, people try to comfort those who are grieving by saying things like, 'Don't worry. You'll see them again someday,' or, 'She'll always be there in your heart.' They act like that person isn't really gone, and maybe that's why I got so attached to the idea of actually contacting her again."

"I see. So you founded the LASS with the hope of finding a way to talk to her." Raul longed to hold her hand again, but the moment was over. He desperately wished he could do something to make this better.

"Yes and no. I mean, I was always interested in the supernatural. Most people don't believe that folks like us exist, after all, so why can't there be something more? But yeah. Kayla's death made that idea even more important to me. I want to apologize to her and make sure she's okay. I'm so sorry." She gave an embarrassed smile as she snagged a paper napkin out of the dispenser to wipe her eyes and nose.

Raul smiled back, thinking how beautiful she was, even when she was crying. "Why should you apologize? It's not your fault that a drunk driver hit you guys."

"No, but I was the one driving. I can't help but think—every single day—what if I'd done something differently? What if I'd taken a different exit? What if I'd tried on one more dress or one less dress and we went through that intersection at a slightly different time? Maybe I could've reacted faster and saved her life." Another tear spilled over her lashes, and Penny quickly blotted it up.

"You can't blame yourself." Damn this table between them! He clenched his hand underneath it as he envisioned throwing it to the side and pulling her into his arms to console her.

"That's what everyone says, but I do anyway." She pulled in a staggering breath. "You know what's funny? Those prom dresses we were shopping for seemed like the most important thing in the world to me at the time. Like some pieces of fabric were going to change my life or something. It's ridiculous."

Raul swiped his teeth across his bottom lip. "I get that. I think that's pretty normal for teenagers. They're looking so hard for meaning that they'll find it in almost anything."

Penny nodded, dabbing one last time at her face as their food arrived and she thanked the waitress. "I'm sorry. I don't know why I'm telling you all this."

Raul did. And he had an idea that she might know, too, but he wasn't going to just say it. "It's okay. I don't mind, and it's good to know this isn't just something you do for amusement. If we're going to figure out what's going on with these ghosts, then I need to work with someone who's serious about it."

She rolled her eyes and laughed a little. "Some of the others think I'm a little too serious. I try not to let myself get caught up in a few flashing lights and immediately think we're in the presence of a spirit. I want to have some true, hard evidence before I make any claims."

"It's a good idea. People might be more likely to take you seriously. What's the next step in this particular investigation?"

They talked amicably for the next hour while they ate, and Raul felt the rest of the world melt away. There was no more Force and no more concern about what was happening in the city. It was just the two of them in this diner, and it could last forever as far as he was concerned.

"Oh, wow," she said when she glanced up at the clock on the wall. Her tears had dried and her eyes were clear again. "It's after three. As much as I'm enjoying our time together, I'd better get back home. I've got a pack meeting in the morning—I mean, in a few hours."

"Sure." Raul paid the bill to the waitress. "Do you need a ride?"

She paused for a moment, then a rosy blush spread over her cheeks. "Thanks, but my apartment isn't far from here."

They stepped out into the night, the sign for Curly's Diner casting alternating red and blue lights down onto them and illuminating Penny's golden hair. "Then, can I walk you home?"

Was that amusement in her eyes? It didn't matter since she nodded after a long moment. "That's nice of you, but I'm fine. I do it all the time."

Raul wasn't sure it was all that nice. He had no ill intentions, but he didn't want to be apart from her. He could feel her next to him as they walked down the street, mostly abandoned at this late hour, still entertaining the idea of them being the only two people in the world.

"It's really awesome that you're letting me work with you on this," he said as they passed a tattoo parlor. That was lame. Damn it! He knew how to talk to women. Penny, as he was finding out more and more every second, was different. He desperately wanted to say all the right things without giving her any reason to doubt him.

"And I appreciate you reaching out to me about it. I think it's going to work out well," she returned as she paused at an intersection, licking her lips ever so slightly. "This is where I turn off."

Raul's heart thundered in his chest. "Okay, then."

The sidewalk rippled. The buildings around them bowed out and then bent back in again. A shift happened somewhere in the universe, and it pushed the two of them together. When their lips met, Raul couldn't say who'd instigated it, but it didn't matter. Penny was warm and soft, and the barest space between her lips indicated there might be more to this in the future.

As she and Raul parted, her eyes opened slowly as if she were waking from a dream. "I'll talk to you later." A broad smile spread across her face.

"Sounds good." Raul watched her go, thinking how strange it was that his life could change that quickly.

4

PENNY'S ENTIRE BODY WAS BUZZING AS SHE HEADED DOWN THE SIDEWALK. She couldn't remember the last time she'd felt so good. The night air wrapped around her like a cloak as she glided down the street, the feel of Raul's lips against hers still warm and exciting.

Her phone rang in her back pocket, startling her out of her reverie. "Hey. Everything okay?"

"Yeah, I just wanted to make sure you're all right," Ingrid said. "I mean, we don't know that guy, and I'd feel like an ass if I didn't check in on you."

Penny smiled. Ingrid was always trying so hard to be a good friend. "That's really sweet of you. But I'm fine. We went to Curly's and had a bite to eat while we talked."

"Sounds to me like you had a *really* nice time," Ingrid said with a giggle.

"I didn't say that." But Penny couldn't stop smiling. Her cheeks were beginning to hurt.

"Your tone said it for you. Come on! Tell me all the lurid details."

Penny shook her head. She wished like crazy that Kayla could be there for this. It was the sort of thing they'd always dreamed and hoped about as girls. Just like any other shifter, they'd grown up hearing about how they'd someday find the person they were meant to be with. Penny knew that whatever she had going on with Raul wasn't purely physical, and she had to tell someone. "Okay, fine! But the details really aren't all that lurid."

"I still want to hear them!"

"Don't you think you should be in bed?" Penny pulled her key out of her pocket as she approached her building, thinking about how exhausted she'd be when she showed up for the pack meeting the next morning. Her mother would undoubtedly berate her about staying out all night, and her father would just give her that disappointed shake of his head. Penny didn't care, and she knew she'd never be able to fall asleep.

"Yeah, right! Now spill!"

"It was all very innocent," she began. "We just went down to Curly's and talked over a meal. But Ingrid, I swear I could feel something as soon as he showed up at the cemetery. It was like there was a freaking lightning storm happening between us! That's why I had to sit down for a bit. His presence just invaded my own. Wait—no, that sounds like a bad thing, but it wasn't! It was amazing!"

"That's so awesome!"

"I know," Penny admitted, even though she'd never really thought of herself as the mushy type. "I tried to dismiss it at first. You know I don't like to jump to conclusions. Raul is just so easy to be around, and before I knew it, I was practically telling him my entire life story. And you know what? He actually listened to me. He seemed to care. I... I can't believe I'm saying this, but I think we might be fated." It was such a crazy thing to admit out loud, but there. She'd said it. Now it was out there in the world, and she felt relieved.

Ingrid let out a wistful sigh. "You're so lucky."

"I want to agree with you, but I'm also not quite sure about all this."

"What?" Ingrid practically shrieked. "Why? It sounds like he's your knight in shining armor—or camo, I guess. Whatever the guys on the Force wear."

"He's not like anyone else I've ever met," she admitted. "It's just that after Tyler, I really wanted to spend time on my own. Not just six months or even a year, but a long time. I want to make sure that any relationship I get into is the right one, and that I'm doing it for the right reasons. I don't want to fool myself into thinking Raul is perfect just because I'm on the rebound."

"If you don't snap his fine ass up, someone else will," her friend cautioned.

She absently touched her lips with one hand, reliving that amazing kiss all over again. It wasn't the windswept, wild abandon that people write about in romance novels, but it didn't need to be. It was sweet and innocent and just perfect. "He kissed me," she admitted. "Or I kissed him. I don't know. I do know that I feel like a completely different person around him." Why was it so hard to describe something so wonderful? Maybe she needed to run off to the cemetery, shift, and howl at the moon for a while.

"And what about this whole SOS Force thing?" her friend asked. "You think that's legit?"

"I wasn't completely sure at first, but after talking to him for a while, yes. He told me all about his time in the service, working for the Force, and how they look out for greater L.A. as a whole. He couldn't give me too much detail, but everything about him was genuine." Her smile widened once again as she unlocked the main door to the building and headed up the stairs. Penny hadn't thought she'd get giddy over a soldier, but Raul just wasn't what she'd expect from a former Green Beret. He had dark, deep eyes that looked right into her soul and swept-back hair that she just wanted to bury her fingers in. "I can't wait to see him again."

"And when's that going to be?"

Penny rolled her eyes up to think when her gaze landed on a dark figure near her apartment door, just off the landing. Her heart swirled in her chest and her stomach dropped. "Soon. Listen, I'll have to call you back tomorrow."

"Oh, you're no fun! Okay, but keep me in the loop. And get some sleep!"

Penny hung up and put her phone in her pocket, her brows drawing together as she topped the stairs. "Tyler, what are you doing here?"

He leaned against her doorframe, obviously trying a little too hard to look cool as he studied his fingernails. "So, you're finally home from your *date*?"

She pressed her lips together. Her night with Raul had been nothing short of perfect, and this wasn't the way she'd wanted it to end. Thank goodness she hadn't taken him up on her offer to walk her home, or this could've been even more of a disaster. "You didn't answer my question."

Tyler detached himself from the wall and stepped forward, looming over her. "And you didn't answer mine."

"Last I checked, I don't have to. In case you don't remember, we're not dating anymore." She did her best to look fierce, but she knew she didn't pull it off very well. The short, curvy blonde could never be intimidating to a narcissistic prick like Tyler.

"And why is that?" Once again, his eyes looked slightly red around the edges. "You know, it was never my idea to break up, Penny. Something about you changed after Kayla died. For years, I did everything I could to stick by your side, but it was never good enough for you."

"As I recall, you were hardly there for me at all," she retorted. "Yeah, I was a little traumatized by the death of my best friend, but who wouldn't be? And then you decided to get all possessive and controlling. I don't have to put up with that shit."

"You need someone to watch out for you, Penny. You need someone to make sure you're not running off with strange guys in the middle of the night and staying out all hours."

Acutely aware of the fact that their voices were steadily rising and it was likely to wake her neighbors, Penny moved past him and unlocked her apartment door. "I'm not doing this. Good night, Tyler."

He stepped in right after her as though he owned the place. Penny turned and put her hand on the door, ready to slam it, but he'd come just far enough inside that there was no room. "You and I both know that there's a certain track you're supposed to be on in your life. You have a destiny to fulfill, and you can't just pretend as though it didn't happen." Tyler pushed the rest of the way inside and shut the door behind him.

Her jaw felt hard inside her skull as her eyes narrowed. "How dare you just march in here? I could call the cops on you for that!"

"As if they'd do anything! Besides, all I want to do is talk. You can't deny me that, can you? After everything we've been through? After how long we've known each other?" He was standing close to her again, doing that awful thing he did where he made her feel so small and insignificant.

Penny stepped away and tossed her key on the side table. Unbidden, Raul came to mind. She hardly knew him, but he didn't make her feel that way. He was taller than her, yes, but he walked next to her like they were equals. He was sweet and polite—and so damn hot. "There isn't anything to talk about. It doesn't matter how long we've known each other. Honestly, I'm not even sure what this conversation you're trying to have is all about."

"It could be about a lot of things." Tyler strode into the living room and plopped himself down on the couch, spreading his arm along the back of it. "It could be about you having a hard time dealing with loss."

She gave him a look, feeling her inner wolf getting more and more restless. She'd lose her deposit if she shifted forms and ripped his throat out right there on the carpet, but that was something that could be dealt with. "Don't pretend as though you care about that."

"You don't want to talk about Kayla? Fine. Then let's talk about how you're letting your entire pack down by failing to fulfill your duty to them." Tyler's hazel eyes held hers, challenging her.

"I see. So you think you can just waltz on in here and pretend that you're such a perfect son to your pack and your parents. Bully for you." She put her fist on her hip, pissed that he would dare bring this up. Again.

"Look. My dad's an Alpha. Your dad's an Alpha. Both your parents and mine know that we really felt something for each other. We had a connection. We can get that back if we just work on it a little more." He leaned forward, bracing his elbows on his knees and boring his eyes into hers.

Penny wanted to be sick. At one time, she'd let herself be convinced that there was some sort of destiny at play between herself and Tyler. After all, as he'd just pointed out again, they came from very similar backgrounds. She knew now, in the very deepest core of herself, that she and Tyler weren't meant to be. Penny had told him. She'd thought he understood, but clearly, there was more to be said.

"At one time, I would've agreed with you. I was attracted to you, and we had a good time together. Our parents were beyond thrilled at the idea of a match between us because it meant bringing our two packs together like some sort of medieval arranged marriage. I was content to go along with that because I didn't think I'd find anyone else." Penny remembered all those times when her mother had droned on and on about how she and Penny's father were meant to be together and that she just knew that Penny and Tyler were the same way. The Grangers had unapologetically continued to push her in that direction even after the breakup, certain that it was fate's design.

"Whoa. Hey." He stood up and came toward her, daring to trace her cheek with the back of his fingers. "What are you talking about? You know it wasn't like that. We weren't just the hanging onto each other for a lack of options."

She flinched as she took a step back, not wanting him to touch her. Not like that or in any other way. "I think I was. And you're right. Something did change inside me when Kayla died. It took a long time for it to really come out and manifest itself, but I know now that what we had was just a teenage love that we both grew out of."

He lifted his chin and straightened his shoulders, immediately dropping the kind-and-sensitive act. "You know now? I suppose that has something to do with that dick taking you to Curly's and seducing you?"

"It has absolutely—hold on." She put her finger in the air and moved toward him, poking him in the chest. "Did you follow us?"

"What choice did I have? You ran off with a complete stranger in the middle of the night! I had to make sure you were safe!"

A shiver like a trail of slime moved down Penny's back. She cursed herself for not keeping her senses open and noticing what was happening right away. She'd been so involved with and focused on Raul that the rest of the world had just slipped away as though it'd never existed. Now, it came crashing back down on her with full force. She snagged a pillow off the couch and whacked him with it. "You bastard!"

He put up a hand to fend off the blow, but it forced him to take a step toward the door. Penny continued her assault, using the slaps like punctuation. "You filthy, rotten, disgusting, creepy bastard! If you actually cared about my safety, you could've shown it in so many other ways! But no! Everything has to be about *you* and what *you* want. I'm sick of this shit, and I won't put up with it any longer!"

Tyler snagged her wrist and held it tight. "Stop, Penny! As usual, you're getting hysterical over nothing! It's as though you don't even remember how packs work! We look out for each other, and that's what I was doing for you. I'm just trying to build something between us that I know could be a great thing, and all you do is throw it in my face."

Penny reached around him and flung open the door. She pushed her face as far into his as it could go, feeling her sharp lupine teeth descend from her gums as she scowled up at him. "You listen, and you listen well, Tyler," she said in a low voice that wouldn't carry through the building. "You and I are *nothing*. I let you come to the society meetings because I thought you genuinely wanted to be friends, but you've made it quite clear that the only thing you care about is getting what you want. You're a selfish asshole, and I don't want to have anything to do with you. Now get the fuck out of my apartment and out of my life!" She pointed at the open doorway for emphasis.

"Penny..."

With every bit of strength and anger inside her, Penny put her hands on his chest and shoved. Tyler hadn't expected her to get physical with him, and he stumbled backward. His booted feet tripped over the fake ficus in the hallway, and he sprawled on his backside onto the worn carpet. When he pushed himself up with his hands, he looked dazed.

She gripped the doorway as she leaned out, still letting her teeth show. "Keep in mind that the only reason I'm not ripping your entrails from your body and slinging them from here to Long Beach is that I don't want to get in trouble with the landlord. Now *leave*." She slammed the door and shoved the bolt into place with shaking hands.

Penny sank to the floor, her body flooded with emotions and adrenaline. She closed her eyes and tuned in all her senses. So much of her life was spent on the everyday stuff that any average human would do, and she didn't let that she-wolf out often enough. Penny focused her hearing on the hallway, expecting Tyler to do something desperate. The only thing she heard was quiet shuffling as he picked himself off the floor and sauntered off down the stairs.

When she'd left Raul on the street corner, Penny didn't think she'd ever sleep that night. But that encounter with Tyler now had her heart racing for all the wrong reasons.

5

RAUL STEPPED INTO THE KITCHEN AND FOUND JUDE PACING THE FLOOR. He carried a giant mug of coffee in his hand, as usual, no matter what time of day, and had his cell pressed to his ear. "I know. It's not easy. Call me if you need anything else." He hung up and slipped his phone in his pocket.

"Everything okay?" Raul asked as he grabbed a bottle of water from the fridge.

Jude nodded. "It was just my brother, Reid. What's going on with you? Any creepy ghost news I should know about?"

With a laugh, Raul lifted a shoulder and let it fall. "Nothing concrete just yet. I went over everything from my meeting with the L.A. Society for Spirits with Amar. He agrees that it's something we can attack full force once we know more, but we need to gather more information before we make any big plans."

Well, he hadn't exactly told Amar *everything*. The Alpha would understand his feelings completely if Raul confessed he'd met his fated mate, but there was no point in spreading the rumor until there was something a little more truthful behind it. In that sense, it was just like this ghost hunting mission.

"Sounds right to me. I hopped on The Shift for a bit today and caught one of the videos. I've gotta say, I called bullshit on this whole thing at first, thinking it was just the latest online trend or challenge. If that's the case, then whoever's doing it is pretty damn good. I saw a guy dissipate into nothing but mist." He shook his head as he straightened his button-down shirt. Jude was always impeccably dressed.

"I know." Raul sat down at the long bar and rolled the water bottle between his palms. The chill of it felt good, but it did nothing to quell the fire that'd been burning inside his wolf ever since he'd left Penny. Last night, it was as if he'd seen all his energy and emotions flow outside his body to meet with hers. Once she was gone, he'd been left with a sinking, empty feeling that he didn't like.

"What's your deal, man?" Jude's words were almost sharp.

Raul snapped his head up. "Why?"

Jude tapped the counter, making Raul look down.

"¡Mierda!" The water bottle was nearly crushed in his hands. "I guess I was just somewhere else. I have this feeling that I should've stuck around to protect someone, and I didn't." Penny had sent him a text that morning to let him know she'd made all the arrangements for the next step of the investigation, so Raul knew she was fine. Still, it ate away at him. He got up and poured the remaining water into a glass.

"Trouble with your pack?"

"Nah. My pack is a very old one, originally from Mexico, and it's dwindled over the years. The few of us who remained migrated up here to L.A. in search of a better life for the pack."

Jude nodded as he refilled his mug at the coffee pot. "Do you ever think that the paradigm for shifters might be changing? That as we blend in more with human society, we're not as suited to living in clans and packs?" He stirred his coffee as he looked out the window.

Leave it to Jude to wax philosophical. Army Ranger or not, Raul always thought Jude should be working in an art museum or a university lecture hall instead of the SOS Force. "I don't think so. We listen to our intuition a lot more than humans do, from what I can tell. We know what pulls at us and we go with it. I think that includes our desire for pack life. Mine is small, and there were plenty of times growing up that I wished it were bigger, but I'd never leave it."

"You sound like you've been thinking about this quite a bit." Jude turned to him and raised one eyebrow.

"Just some personal stuff I've been thinking about lately. Nothing big." Great. Now he was lying to his comrades just to avoid admitting out loud what he knew he felt for Penny. There was nothing to be ashamed of. Amar had met his one-and-only, and the same could certainly be said for their other Force members, Gabe and Emersyn.

"Well, I'm here if you ever need to talk. What about your mission? Need any assistance?"

"Nah, I'm good." Raul couldn't possibly invite Jude along for this next step. It was difficult enough to be around Penny without feeling too self-conscious. He was sure the rest of the LASS had detected sparks between the two of them the other night, and someone as observant as Jude would know in an instant. "This is just a simple interview; it's nothing to worry about. Depending on where things go, though, I may need your help later. I'll give you a heads up."

"Anytime, as long as there's coffee." Jude clapped him on the arm and left the room.

Raul looked at the crushed water bottle still sitting on the counter. Just what kind of effect was Penny having on him?

He was still contemplating this an hour later when he drove to Penny's apartment. During the entire trip across town, he'd been thinking about what he should say, rehearsing conversations in his mind that may or may not ever happen. Everything had to be right. Everything had to be *perfect*. This was his one and only chance at experiencing true love. No pressure at all, right?

Penny was waiting on her front steps when he pulled up. Raul waved from the driver's seat, his stomach in a knot. At least she'd saved him from walking up to her place, knocking on the door, and feeling completely breathless when she answered it. But no. She still left him completely devoid of air as she hopped in the passenger side of his truck and shut the door behind her.

"Hey, you." A smile played on the peony pink of her lips.

Raul yanked his eyes away from them, no matter how much he wanted to lean over and claim those sweet lips of hers with his own again. They'd already kissed goodbye, but what exactly did that mean for them? Time to think about the mission. "So, you said Mrs. Reyes was all set to talk to us?"

Penny nodded and swiped a strand of her hair behind her ear. "She sounded a little confused about the whole thing, but she was more than happy to have the company. I don't know how much insight she'll be able to give us, but it's at least a start."

"Yeah. Definitely." Plus, it meant he got a chance to be with her again. Penny had been the only thing on Raul's mind ever since he'd met her. Even though that was just over a day ago, it felt like it'd been much longer. He felt the proximity of their bodies in the enclosed space of the truck's cab, and he tightened his grip on the wheel as he focused on driving.

He pulled out from the curb, noticing that a sleek black coupe pulled into the traffic just a few car lengths behind him. "Have the five of you figured anything out since I last saw you?"

She shook her head, sending that blonde hair spreading out along her shoulders. Raul's fingers tingled with the urge to touch it, to brush it back from her face and press his lips against—Damn it! He couldn't do his job like this!

"...just keep collecting and analyzing data," Penny was saying, oblivious to Raul's wild thoughts. "It's a slow process, but I think any legitimate science is going to be. You have to look at things from every angle and eliminate possibilities. If this apparition of Victor Reyes had only been seen by his mother or some other loved one, I wouldn't think anything of it. People see visions of their deceased loved ones all the time."

"So you're saying in those cases, they're just figments of their imaginations?" His wolf was once again scrabbling at the underside of his human form. How nice it would be to take Penny off into one of the parks that surrounded L.A., shift, and just run in the moonlight. He'd never seen her in her wolf form. They hadn't even discussed it, but he could tell in the deepest parts of himself that she was as he was.

"Yeah. You need so much more proof to consider something a paranormal event, and the mind is very powerful when it wants to be. That's a big part of the problem, actually, because we all see what we want to see. It's almost impossible to eliminate that completely." She was watching him with those eyes, shimmering green, excited, intriguing.

Raul sharpened his focus on the road. At any other time, he could get in touch with his animal side as a way to keep him on track. His wolf was always ready to focus, to work, to get things done. Those wild instincts were far more helpful in urban life than anyone would think. Penny's presence made everything different; a story he was starting to realize was only repeating itself over and over. "That's impressive."

"What?"

"That you're so aware of how your desires could influence your results if you let them, and that you're determined to find such cold, hard evidence that no one could argue against. I know we talked about it the other night, but I still think it's admirable." The black coupe was still following, far enough back that it could merely be a coincidence. Raul hung a right, threading his way toward the neighborhood in Northeast Los Angeles where Mrs. Reyes lived. The black coupe also turned right.

"I'm glad you appreciate it," she said with a little laugh. "The rest of the society gets impatient with me because every time we think we've had a breakthrough, I immediately dismiss it. Don't get me wrong. I get just as excited as they do, at least on the inside. I want to find this just as badly as they do, or maybe even more so. I just don't want to kid myself." She twisted that charm bracelet on her wrist once again.

"I've always been into the supernatural. I love movies and comic books, and I know most people dismiss it as entertainment. Given how much lore and mythology have been based on people like us, plus some other experiences I've had with the SOS Force, I have to wonder just how much is out there that we don't know about. There could be ghosts of some form wandering all around us, and we don't even know it."

"Of some form?" Penny twisted slightly in the seat to see him better.

The black coupe turned left as Raul turned left, an unnecessary turn that would take him the long way around to his destination. Raul didn't like being followed, but he did like having something that distracted him a little from Penny. "I did a little research on the subject once. It was quite some time ago, and I don't remember all the details, but the basic gist was that everything and everyone that's ever existed still does; they've just moved into a different vibration or frequency. It's a slightly different dimension that's intertwined with us, but we can't detect it. At least, not most of the time."

"Yes!" Her enthusiasm exploded into the vehicle and made him smile. "I've read some things along those lines, and I think it's such a fascinating idea. It really gives me hope for our project, and honestly, for seeing Kayla again, too."

He could feel his heart soften as she mentioned her best friend. Raul wanted to pull over, comfort her in his arms, and tell her everything he'd been feeling about her. He needed to tell her that she'd already been appearing in his dreams, but that it was the most pleasurable haunting he'd ever experienced. His wolf went right along with the idea, bristling at not being let out of its human cage. Raul was just teasing himself!

The black coupe made yet another turn behind him, so he forced those thoughts out of his mind. As he pulled up in front of Mrs. Reyes's house, he noted the coupe pulling in down at the corner. Interesting that someone else, at the exact same time, would be heading along almost the exact same route. Certainly, coincidences like that happened all the time, but Raul had reason to believe this wasn't just a coincidence. He kept his senses heightened as they got out of the truck.

The house was a tiny bungalow situated on a lot barely bigger than itself. The bright blue stucco siding was accented in black, with a low iron fence that served as a barrier around the graveled flower beds that surrounded the home. Someone had made sure every weed was plucked from those spaces, leaving only a lemon tree at one corner, a lavender bush at the other, and several yucca plants in between.

Raul swung open the screen door and knocked. The woman who answered was much older than Raul had been expecting, considering Victor Reyes had only been in his mid-twenties when he'd died. Her short hair was a steely gray cloud around her face, her golden skin tinged with pink at her cheeks. She smiled at them through her wire-frame glasses as she held the door open wide to welcome them in, her red skirt sweeping her bare feet. "Come in, come in! Get in out of the heat!"

"Mrs. Reyes, my name is Raul Castaneda, and this is Penny Granger. We really appreciate you taking some time to talk to us today." He couldn't help but smile as he walked into the small living room. Mrs. Reyes reminded him of his own abuela, as did the brilliant colors of her home.

"¡Siéntate, por favor!" Mrs. Reyes gestured at the couch as she closed the door behind them. "I hope you had a good drive. Sometimes the traffic just gets so bad. I don't get out very much anymore. Grocery delivery has certainly been a blessing for me, but I do miss just walking up and down the aisles and running into old friends sometimes."

Raul glanced at Penny as they sat on the couch, shooting her a look that asked if this woman knew what they were actually doing there. She returned with a shrug and a small smile.

"Mrs. Reyes, we don't want to take up too much of your time, but—"

"Oh, and where are my manners! I've got some fresh chocolate cookies for you and some lemonade. Do you like lemonade? Or would you prefer iced tea? It's so hot out." She folded her hands in front of her blouse and smiled at them expectantly.

"Um, iced tea would be fine. Thank you."

"Lemonade, please," Penny responded.

"Of course!" Despite her advanced age, Mrs. Reyes practically floated into the kitchen.

"Did you tell her why we were here?" Raul whispered. He had to lean close, wanting to speak softly enough that there was no chance the old woman could hear them in such a small house. The scent of Penny's perfume reminded him that even though he was on a mission and had to be professional, there were more feral urges constantly working under the surface.

"I told her about LASS and that we wanted to know more about her son. I didn't tell her you were with the Force, because I figured that was up to you, but everything else I explained over the phone. Like I said, I think she's just happy to have company. She'd probably treat us the same if we were selling vacuums."

Raul smiled. "My abuela would do the same thing, I think. She doesn't think anything bad of anyone."

Mrs. Reyes returned with a tray that she set before them on the coffee table, then carefully lowered herself into an armchair. "Do help yourself! There's plenty more where that came from. Did you already have lunch?"

"Oh, yes," Penny answered quickly. "We're fine, thank you. Mrs. Reyes, we'd like to talk to you about your son, Victor."

The smile on the old woman's face immediately sagged. "¡Ay! My poor sweet baby Victor. I'm afraid he's been gone for a month. I miss him so much."

"We're both so very sorry for your loss." Penny scooted forward on the couch and placed her fingers tenderly on the other woman's knee. "I know it can't be easy for you to talk about him, but we do have a few questions we'd like to ask if that's okay."

A short bark of laughter came through Mrs. Reyes's tears, and she quickly wiped her face with a lace handkerchief. "Actually, it's nice to have a chance to talk about him. As I said, I don't get out much these days. Victor was my entire life. I know what the media had to say about him when he passed away. They only wanted to talk about the mistakes he'd made. I know my Victor was not a perfect man, but I really couldn't blame him."

It was clear to Raul that they weren't going to get anywhere with Mrs. Reyes if they didn't play along. The poor woman was lonely and grieving, and for all they knew, this was the only chance she'd gotten to talk for a while. "Can you tell us a little more about him?"

She smiled sweetly at Raul, reaching to the end table for a framed picture. Mrs. Reyes held it in her hands, looking at it fondly as she spoke. "As you might've guessed, I'm not Victor's mother. He was my grandbaby. My daughter had him young. I knew she wasn't ready, but I told her what a delight she'd find in having a child of her own; I know I did. But it wasn't the same for Maria. She dropped Victor off one night, saying she had to work, but then she never came back. I got a note from her a few weeks later, telling me she knew I'd take great care of him because I'd always taken such good care of her, but that was it. We never saw her again. Victor loved me, and he seemed happy enough, but now and then, I'd catch him looking out the window, like he was staring off at the other side of the world. I always thought he was hoping to open the curtains and see his mother coming up the walk." Mrs. Reyes dabbed at her tears once again. "Oh, don't mind me. Go on! Eat your *galletas*."

Raul had nearly forgotten about them, and he obligingly picked one off the plate and took a bite. It was rich, sweet, and chocolatey, but it also had a hint of spice to it from chile powder. "These are so good! They remind me of home!"

The delight the comment brought to Mrs. Reyes was evident in her face as she beamed at him. "You two are a cute couple, you know."

Raul choked on his cookie.

Penny covered for him. "We're not a couple, Mrs. Reyes. We're just working together. For the moment. On this project."

Mrs. Reyes laughed. "Right. Sure. And I'm a Hollywood starlet. Now, really! Just look at the two of you! Him, so tall, dark, and handsome. You with all that long blonde hair and that curvy figure. You're just adorable!"

Recovering with a sip of iced tea, Raul cleared his throat. "We just recently started working together on this particular project, and I'm afraid it does involve Victor. I assume you've heard of the video of him that's resurfaced."

Mrs. Reyes looked from Raul to Penny and back again. "Is this about something he did? I already talked to the police. They showed up here every time he put himself on the wrong side of the law, and I told them the same thing every time. I'd left Victor's room open for him any time he needed it, but he was never here. He hadn't lived with me for over a year before he passed away, other than stopping in now and then and maybe spending the night. It's not nice to come snooping around for something else to charge him with, considering he's gone."

"No. We're not the police, and we're not interested in anything like that." Damn it. He'd wanted so badly for Mrs. Reyes to stop talking about what a good couple they made that he'd blundered right into the most sensitive part of the conversation. He took another sip of tea. "The video that I'm talking about shows Victor in a liquor store, but the strange part about it is that it was recorded less than a week ago. We're investigating some other paranormal activity in the area, and we're trying to eliminate some possibilities so we can figure out exactly what happened. Did Victor have any brothers or other family members that looked a lot like him?" Raul had already used the Force's massive computing power to determine that the man robbing the liquor store was unquestionably Victor Reyes, but this was a good starting point.

Mrs. Reyes shrugged. "He could have, but I wouldn't know it. He did look a lot like his mother, and if she had any other children, she never told me." She handed Raul the framed photo.

He took it and held it so that Penny could see it, too. Unlike the mug shots he and Penny had been studying, this was a photo of a young man in a suit jacket, smiling blandly at the camera.

"Have there been any strange happenings that you've experienced lately?" Penny asked gently.

The old woman's lower lip came out stubbornly as she tilted her head back. "You said you're paranormal investigators?"

"Yes, ma'am."

"So if I told you something a little strange, the kind of thing you normally can't tell people, you wouldn't think I'm crazy? You wouldn't try to put me in a home?"

Penny shook her head firmly. "I won't think you're crazy at all."

Mrs. Reyes hesitated for another moment before she nodded. "All right, then. I had a few of my church friends call and say they'd heard those rumors about a man who looked just like my Victor, running around the city and committing crimes. The poor boy is dead, and we should leave well enough alone! I went in my room one night and I prayed to God that he would heal my heart and let all this be laid to rest, once and for all. But then I went outside to take the trash out, and there stood Victor! Right in my driveway! I'm lucky I didn't have a heart attack because I was sure he'd come to tell me God had called me home!"

Penny was leaning forward again, fascinated and ready to dive into her area of expertise. "Did he say anything to you?"

"No." Mrs. Reyes pressed her lips together, suppressing tears. "No, honey. I think I said something to him, but I'm not even sure what. He just stood there and stared at me. He looked confused, and then he disappeared."

"I know it's difficult, but the more you can tell me about that night, the more we may be able to figure out."

Raul had to give Penny credit. He knew she was chomping at the bit to get to the nitty-gritty of this case, yet she was kind and sensitive. He couldn't think of a better person to be doing this.

"Well, let's see." Mrs. Reyes took a deep breath. "I was upset because I'd just talked to those ladies from church. That's how I explained it to myself. I was just seeing Victor because I wanted to. I can't think of anything else to say, really. He had this sort of fog around him, and I thought that was strange, but certainly no stranger than him just disappearing into thin air."

"When Victor was alive, was he into any spiritual practices? Was he a religious man?"

Something about Penny's question wasn't sitting right with Mrs. Reyes. She looked at her lap and rubbed her fingers together for a while as if she were deciding something. "Perhaps the easiest way to settle that is if you come with me." She pushed herself up from her chair and waved her hand over her shoulder as she headed down a short hallway.

Raul and Penny followed her to a bedroom, and she flicked on a light. "Victor moved out several times, so even when it seemed like it was permanent, I still kept his room just as he'd left it. Oh, now and then, I thought about fixing it up into a sewing room for myself, but I never quite had the heart to do it."

The room was crowded with furniture, and books and random objects cluttered up every surface. The walls that had at one point been baby blue were mostly painted over in black. The job had been a hasty one, leaving most of the trim work undone, so the original color still showed through. The décor, if it could be called that, looked like it'd been purchased from a head shop or carnival, depicting everything from the Satanic to the psychedelic.

"Did he say much about what he believed in?" Raul asked as he touched the spines of several books covering Wicca, medieval sorcery, black magic, and the ancient Aztecs.

Mrs. Reyes shook her head. "He didn't talk about it. Sometimes, I'd ask him what he was doing or what he was learning about, but all he told me was that I wouldn't like it. My Victor was a smart boy in many ways, but he wasn't really into books. When I finally saw him reading, I was excited for him. I hoped he was getting ready to go to college or something."

"And when he moved out, where did he go?" Penny asked.

Once again, the older woman's face grew solemn. "He didn't tell me that, either, just that he was joining a new clan. He wouldn't give me a name or an address; he just told me he was fine and that he'd call. I have a feeling they were all into this same stuff." She gestured with disgust around the room.

Raul felt a surge of energy in the pit of his stomach, and for a change, it had nothing to do with Penny. It was more about realizing the apparition they were looking into was part of something much more significant.

"This is interesting." Penny had picked up a piece of paper from a cluttered desk. "It's a map of Griffith Park, which is infamous for being paranormally active. And look, several places have been marked on it."

"Do you mind if we take this with us?" Raul asked.

Mrs. Reyes made that gesture of disgust again, flicking her fingers through the air as though she could rid herself of anything Victor might've done that she didn't approve of. "That's fine. It's nothing sentimental, and it isn't as though he'll be coming back to get it anytime soon."

"Thank you. We'll get out of your hair, but feel free to call us if there's anything else that comes up." Raul had no problem producing a rather vague business card that simply had his name and phone number and handing it to Mrs. Reyes. She was a sweet woman who touched his heartstrings.

"I'm sorry. I've been such a rude hostess," she said as she shut the bedroom door and they all regrouped in the living room. "Here, let me get you some cookies to go."

"You don't have to do that," Raul protested.

Mrs. Reyes gave him a sharp look, one he recognized from his own grandmother. "It'll only take a second."

By the time they were back out on the stoop, with Mrs. Reyes thanking them for stopping by and Raul holding a rather large container of cookies, Raul had nearly forgotten about their escort. But as he and Penny got in the truck, he noticed the black coupe pulling out once again.

"What a sweet woman," Penny mused with a little smile. "I feel so bad for her, though. She shouldn't have had to go through all that. I hope we can figure out whatever's happening with Victor and help her put her mind at ease."

"Yes, and speaking of minds at ease, how long did you plan to have your friend follow us?" He glanced in the rearview mirror. Raul had already formulated several ideas as to who was behind them, but the driver was growing bolder. He drove barely a car-length behind them, and Raul had seen enough of his features to be sure of his identity.

"What?" The quick snap of Penny's head hadn't been the reaction he was expecting. "Who's following us?"

"Tyler, I believe." Raul smiled a little as he worked his way out of the neighborhood and toward the highway. "Don't get me wrong. I completely understand. You don't really know me, and it's not necessarily the safest thing for a woman to get into a stranger's vehicle. I just thought you should know that I wouldn't have minded if you wanted to be more direct about something like that. You know, just invite him along."

She'd twisted herself around in the seat to look out the back windshield, and when she turned forward again, her face was twisted into a scowl. "That asshole! How long has he been following us?"

Raul's wolf raged at her reaction, making it difficult to keep his driving steady. "You mean you didn't ask him to do this? He's been trailing us the entire time, ever since I showed up at your place."

Penny let out a long sigh and folded her arms across her chest. "No, and I wish I could say I was surprised."

His throat tightened and his jaw muscles vibrated with tension. "Penny, is there something I should know about this guy?"

Her tongue roved over the inside of her cheek. "It's just the way he is, I guess. He and I dated for a long time. We haven't been together for a while, but I guess he's still a bit possessive." She slumped a little in the seat, either angry or embarrassed.

"Does he do this sort of thing a lot?" Raul moved onto the freeway, barely even aware of where he was going. The air in the cab was thick with tension, and he wanted to cut straight through it. That, or slam on the brakes and drag Tyler from his car.

"Not exactly, but things along these lines. I'm sure you coming around has only aggravated him more than usual." She pressed her hand to her forehead, her bracelet jangling. "Don't take that the wrong way. I'm not blaming you for his problem."

"No," he ground out. "I get it. But Penny, this isn't something you have to put up with. He has no right to treat you that way. I can fix this for you right now." Already, he could envision exactly what he'd do to the son of a bitch.

"No!" Her exclamation was practically a bark. "The best way to deal with Tyler is not to engage him. He's a bit of a nut, but just give him some time and he'll back off." Penny turned her head to look out the window, but Raul caught a look of something other than frustration. Worry?

"It doesn't have to involve you at all. I've got some resources I can—"

"I said no, okay?" Penny clenched her fists and pulled in a deep breath. "I appreciate it, Raul, but this isn't your problem."

Not his problem? Who was she kidding? Mrs. Reyes could see clear as day that the two of them belonged together. Raul could feel it every time he was around her, and even when he wasn't. How was the protection of his mate not his problem? He was just about to let all that loose when he remembered exactly who he was and why he was there. Penny had told him what she wanted, and he was representing the Force. Pushing his own will on a woman who didn't want it wasn't exactly something Amar would approve of, and Raul couldn't blame him.

"Fine." He gripped the steering wheel and fought his urge to smash the gas pedal to the floor. "I understand. Just please know that you can call me if you need me. For anything."

"Thank you."

The rest of the ride back to her place was mostly a quiet one, and they discussed nothing more personal than the next steps of the investigation. Raul watched his side-view mirror, waiting for Tyler to do something stupid. When Penny went up to the building without Raul in tow, however, the coupe zoomed off. Unfortunately, that did little to ease his mind.

6

————————

"Amar had something to attend to, so he didn't tell me a whole lot about what we're doing," Jude said from the driver's seat as he and Raul zoomed through the city. "It sounds like this ghost mystery you're working on is expanding."

"Unfortunately, yeah." Raul felt heavy as a stone as he sat in the passenger seat. He flicked through The Shift on his phone to distract himself, but it wasn't working. "It's all really weird, and I don't know exactly how it's going to come together yet. Part of the problem is that nothing sounds real."

Jude hit the brakes as they encountered rush hour traffic. "Looks like you've got plenty of time to fill me in."

"As I should've done earlier. I just wasn't expecting us to get a meeting with this clan so quickly." He rubbed a hand through his hair. It felt strange to talk to anyone other than Penny about this, but he'd already pissed her off to the point that the two of them were only exchanging polite texts that related strictly to the investigation. "Penny, the woman from the L.A. Society for Spirits that I've been working with, decided to start with Victor Reyes. He—or his spirit—was seen robbing a liquor store after he'd been dead and buried. She could easily identify him through all his mug shots, and I was able to confirm that identification using our own software. We talked to his grandmother, who says just before he died, he joined a clan that was all about the occult."

Jude rubbed his chin. "So he just randomly joined a clan? Without any family relations or anything?"

"That's what it sounds like. This guy's room was packed full of stuff that pointed to an obsession with the supernatural. Whatever he was getting into, my guess is that it landed him in bigger trouble than a felony charge."

"And do we have any idea what we should be expecting from this mysterious clan?" Jude nudged the car forward slightly, cool and patient, despite the crush of traffic around them and how slowly it was moving.

"Not really. They didn't seem too excited about us coming to meet with them, but I arranged it all under the guise of talking about the shifter registry and The Shift. I'd say we need to gather any information we can as fast as possible, just in case shit goes sideways." Something inside Raul was excited to be on what felt like a real mission again. Sure, he'd been doing his job when he'd gone to meet Penny in the cemetery and when they'd gone to talk to Mrs. Reyes, but he and Jude duping a clan into giving away information felt much more like his work with the military. It lacked some of the firepower and gadgetry that he enjoyed, but he could handle that.

"Simple enough. What kind of shifters are we dealing with?"

Raul shook his head. "That's one thing I hadn't been able to figure out. There's not a lot of information about this clan, and they don't seem to be under the jurisdiction of any of the conclaves. I could tell Victor and his grandmother were both bears, so I'm assuming that's what we'll be dealing with."

"And that's why I was chosen to join you?" Jude asked with a smile.

"Something like that, plus you're the only one available," Raul retorted. In a way, he was glad he was undertaking this step without Penny in tow. First, there was the potential that it could be dangerous work. She'd already made it quite clear that she didn't want him to protect her, no matter how badly his instincts demanded it. It was also nice to just head out with a comrade who knew how these things worked, allowing him to focus on the task at hand.

"I know you and I haven't exactly sat down and had a lot of heart-to-heart chats," Jude said slowly, "but I've got the feeling that there's something more going on here than just business." Traffic started moving again, but instead of gunning it like most of the other motorists, Jude just crept forward. His patience paid off, since brake lights illuminated before them only a second later.

Raul ran his tongue over his teeth. "I guess I haven't done a very good job of hiding that, have I?"

"Well," Jude said with a shrug, "it's not unusual for you to spend a bunch of time in your room or with your nose in a book, but I don't think I've seen you take as much interest in a mission as you have in this one. That, and there's that moony look in your eyes when you don't think anyone is watching."

"Seriously? Have I really been doing that?" Raul had been living completely in his own world, and it'd been entirely occupied by Penny. Other than their regular meetings, he couldn't recall much of any interaction with the rest of the Force members.

"Yeah, you have." Jude was a reserved guy, but he was grinning now. "Is this Penny a love interest of yours?"

Raul was used to being razzed about such things. Guys in the service talked plenty, although half of it was made up or exaggerated. Once again, Penny was different. "Something like that. I really felt something when we met. I don't want to say what I think it is, but she's changing my life. I can't do anything without thinking about her. On the two times I've gone out to discuss things with her, it's like I don't know how to function anymore. I hardly know her, yet I feel like I've known her my entire life. Of course, if I had known her my whole life, then why does she make me so fucking nervous?" He slammed one fist into his palm, frustrated with himself for having such a hard time controlling his feelings and what they did to him.

"It's okay. You don't have to say it out loud, because I know what you mean. I thought I felt something like that once, but other circumstances made me set it aside. It's not an easy thing. I sometimes wonder if humans get as messed up over a potential mate or family dynamics as we do." He inched forward again.

They were never going to get there, and Raul was letting the aggravation of it compound the irritation he was already feeling about Penny. "I need a break. I need to just get out into woods somewhere and run until my legs collapse under me."

"That's not a bad idea at all, and maybe you'll get a chance to do it at Griffith Park. I heard there was something about the area involved with all this, too?"

Raul nodded. "Victor Reyes had a map of the park with certain places marked on it. Penny said she was going to check it out while we talked to this clan. I tried to ask her to wait for me, but she doesn't want to let any stone go unturned that might get us some results. She did at least say she'd take someone else from the LASS with her, so that's something." He just had to hope it wasn't Tyler.

"I see your urge to keep her safe has surfaced," Jude said with a raised eyebrow, apparently more interested in Raul's personal drama than their upcoming meeting. "Have you told her how you feel?"

"No, and I don't plan to. At least not until all this is done with. I can't just sweep in there and tell her I want to work with her on this and then announce that I think we're destined for each other." His stomach was constantly flipping inside him, and he knew the only thing that really would make it better would be to either to have a good long shift, or to find time to be with Penny and make up for upsetting her.

Jude rubbed his jaw. "Just do yourself a favor and don't wait too long. You might regret that."

It sounded like there was more to that story, but Raul didn't want to pry. Traffic opened up and allowed Jude to accelerate to full speed, and he swept efficiently through the streams of cars, then off the highway and into a neighborhood.

"This...isn't exactly what I was expecting," Raul mused as he eyed the small houses and ratty yards. "Every other clan or pack we've visited has managed to get their hands on a little more revenue than this."

"Think we have the right address?" Jude asked as they glided past a house that'd caved in on itself.

"It's the best information I could find. Nothing to do but to go for it."

They soon parked in front of a house that was much bigger than its neighbors, but no better for the wear. Someone had ripped the roof off one wing and installed a foundation for a second floor that'd never been built. The siding was a combination of brick and stucco that was probably charming at one point, but now made it look like a cheap haunted house.

The effect was enhanced by the man who opened the door. He was tall and had the look of someone who'd been fit and healthy at one point, but had atrophied away to nothing but skin and bones. He eyed them both before raising his thin lip in a snarl. "What do you want?"

Raul put out his hand. "I'm Raul, and this is Jude. We're with the South Los Angeles conclave, and we're just here to talk to you about the new registry and news app." He smiled at the man, even though there was something about this situation that he found unsettling.

"Sure. Right." He didn't sound like he believed them, but he stepped back and opened the door wider. "Miguel said he was expecting you. On your left there." The goon pointed to an open doorway straight off the foyer.

Raul ignored the broken tiles on the floor and the cobwebs in the corner. What was far more interesting was the energy of the house. Several of the members were standing around, staring at them, and Raul immediately picked up that they weren't dealing with a bear clan, nor a wolf pack. It was a mutt mixture of both of those plus tigers, lions, and maybe a few coyotes. The energies were mixed and muddied. He pressed his tongue against the back of his teeth, feeling his wolf as it crouched into a defensive pose ready for action.

"Come in. Have a seat," said a serious looking man behind a desk that was just as battered as his face. Miguel was an older man, probably in his fifties, and the wrinkles that were starting to build up around his eyes and mouth accentuated the scars that crossed his face. Dark tattoos traced up his arms in the shape of some sort of tribal serpent.

Raul and Jude stepped in, and Raul was very aware that the man who'd let them in the house shut the office door behind them. He forced a smile once again. "I really appreciate you taking the time to meet with us. We won't keep you too long. We'd just heard there was a new clan in the area, and we want to make sure you're aware of all the upcoming infrastructure that's being put in place for shifters."

Miguel raised a thick eyebrow as he lit a cigarette and propped his feet on the desk. "Infrastructure? That's a fancy term for someone who dares to come into this *barrio*, man. But you can't fool me. There's no infrastructure for people like us."

"There hasn't been for a long time, but that's exactly what we'd like to change," Jude said smoothly. He certainly looked the part of a bureaucrat, and Raul knew he was the right partner for this mission, even if they weren't dealing with bears. "A lot of headway has already been made in other areas like Dallas, and we're trying to support as much of that as we can here. Did you know there are more shifters in L.A. County than anywhere else in the U.S. right now?"

"¡A poco!" Miguel replied coolly and laughed. "You think I give a fuck? I didn't start up this clan because I was interested in taking the census."

"Of course not, but there are advantages that come with having your members on the shifter registry. One of them is access to The Shift, a new app that's been developed only for shifters so that—"

"No, no, no." Miguel swung his feet down to the floor and leaned his elbows on the surface of the desk. "I don't think you understand. I don't care about your little roster sheet of shifters and your insurance salesman routine. The members that I've gathered here have their own lives to lead. Shifters don't need a bunch of government interference of their own just because they're jealous of what the humans have." His laugh was a grinding sound.

"As you may have noticed, there's been some strange activity for shifters lately." Jude continued as though Miguel hadn't said anything at all. "We feel the need to make sure everyone is protected, no matter what clan they're in or what conclave oversees them. This is our way of taking care of each other, regardless of clan finances, etcetera."

Miguel gestured at them with his cigarette, letting its ashes float down to the desk. "Look, the only reason I agreed to meet you was because I was curious about what you had to say. I don't trust you, and I don't have a reason to. You're lucky I don't tell my men to light your asses up. If you want to kid yourself by thinking some sort of organization is going to keep us all safe, then that's your business. I know better. I know it's all about control and money."

Raul ground his teeth together. He didn't take kindly to threats. Still, he knew the game they were playing. He and Jude were just innocent civil servants, not members of an elite force of veteran Special Ops soldiers. Miguel likely knew the SOS Force existed, but there was no point in waving it in front of his face and inviting him into a fight. They were heavily outnumbered.

"I'll just leave my card with you in case you change your mind," Raul said with a smile, standing up.

Jude opened the office door. The same men who'd been there as they'd come in the house were still waiting for them, leaning on walls or crouching on the stairs. They watched with haunted eyes as the two of them made their exit.

Raul kept his mouth shut until they were several blocks down the street. "That was interesting."

Jude nodded. "Was it just me, or did Miguel give away a lot more information than he intended to?"

"Agreed. That clan has zero funding, or else they wouldn't live in a pit like that. And based on their appearances, they either have drug problems or health issues. Did you notice every single one of them looked as though they'd gone without a meal for the past week?"

"They also looked like they wouldn't mind if *we* were the meal," Jude commented as he took a right. "It's obvious they haven't even been in that house for very long. There wasn't much furniture, and I didn't see anything in the way of wall hangings or anything else that would make it feel like a home."

Raul tapped his fingers on the door, looking out the window, but only seeing everything he'd observed at that house. "There's definitely something going on with them. It was like they'd just randomly assembled themselves into a ragtag, multi-species group."

"Miguel was a bear of some sort; no doubt about that. And I sensed a tiger in the man at the door, but yeah. Everyone was different, and they were all guys. That last part could've just been a show for our sake, but they're shady as fuck."

"I'd say the investigation is definitely heading in the right direction," Raul said. "I think this clan is going to lead us to something bigger."

"Do you need to go by Penny's place and tell her about it?" Jude had that teasing smile on his face again.

"You know, yeah. I do. Take the 710." Raul explained how to get to Penny's place. "If she's had a chance to check out the park, she might have some other information that could be important. She's a little irritated with me right now, but I think she'll be interested to know about our meeting."

"I see. So interested that it's worth more than a phone call or a text?" Jude goaded. "For the sake of efficiency and all that?"

Raul punched his comrade on the arm. "*Pendejo.* Shut up and drive."

"Call me whatever you want, man. You know I'm right."

Raul's wolf had already been restless that day due to the mission, but thoughts of being close to Penny again only made it worse. Sure, he could've sent her a text and let her know they had things to discuss, but what if she refused to see him? He wouldn't blame her, since he'd tried to encroach on her life more than he had any right to, but Raul wanted the chance to tell her face-to-face what an idiot he'd been.

By the time they reached her street, Raul had rehearsed numerous conversations in his head. Some of them ended with her slamming the door in his face, and others were variations on him being invited inside. He felt he was ready to handle any of them, and the most important part was that he got to see her.

The hope he'd been building inside himself was quickly dashed when he noticed a familiar form leaning against the wall near the front steps.

Jude gestured with his chin. "You need any help with that?"

"No." Raul unbuckled and grabbed the handle. "I can get this."

"Cool. You know where I am if you need me." Jude shifted into park and left the engine running.

Raul was used to living among humans, but more than once, he'd wished everyone was a shifter. That would mean it'd be easy to just morph into a wolf and get shit done. That would've been particularly helpful at the moment because lunging at Tyler's neck seemed like a good way to wipe that cocky look off the bastard's face. "What are you doing here?" he growled.

"I could ask you the same thing." Tyler slipped his cell in his pocket. Dark half-moons stood out under his eyes.

"None of your business, bro." He considered moving past Tyler and just heading into the building, but that would give the other man the advantage of being at his back. Jude could be out of the car in a flash, but this was his problem.

"Oh, but it *is*." Tyler detached himself from the wall and took half a step forward. "Everything was fine until you came sniffing around my girl, pretending you've got some sort of business here."

Raul felt all the tiny hairs along his back raise, threatening to be replaced by his dense coat. "I *do* have business here, on the authority of the Special Ops Shifter Force and all the local conclaves, not to mention Penny's. If you recall, she wanted me to work with her on this project." Granted, that was before he'd overstepped the line and done something to piss her off. He needed to talk to her and see why she was so offended by his offer to protect her from this dickhead.

"You and I both know you're hanging around for much more than an investigation. Penny is an important person, you know. Her father is an Alpha, and she'll be moving up to lead her clan within the next few years. The Society for Spirits is just something to help her pass the time for now, but she has much more important work to do. Important work that doesn't involve you." Tyler poked Raul in the chest.

Rage hit his system like a flood, thrumming through his veins. It demanded that he act, that he put this upstart pup in his place. "Penny can make her own decisions about me. She doesn't need you to do it for her."

"I'm well aware of what decisions she can make, which include keeping you at arm's length. Why do you think I'm here, Raul? Penny doesn't want to see you, and I'll do whatever it takes to respect her wishes." He moved slightly to his left so that he stood directly between Raul and the front doors of the building.

Raul knew that wasn't true. He'd irritated Penny. He'd said more than he should've and pushed too far too fast. It was only because he cared about her so much. She was a reasonable person, and once it was all right for him to talk to her in a personal sense, she'd come around and understand. "There's only one reason I'm not going to beat the holy living shit out of you right now," Raul rumbled, his voice mixing with a deep growl. He now felt fur sprouting across his shoulders.

"Why's that? Because you're a pussy?"

"Because unlike you, I *do* respect what Penny wants. I've also got a job to do, and I'm not going to risk it by doing something as unprofessional as painting these steps with your blood. Penny and I are going to work together, and we're going to get to the bottom of this problem. Once we do, you'd be wise to watch your back." Not giving Tyler a chance to reply, he spun on his heel and walked back to the car.

"Is that how you conduct your business?" Tyler taunted to his back. "Making idle threats? You're such a fucking poser! I know it, and Penny knows it, too!"

What Raul knew was that Tyler just wanted to drag him into a fight. Whether he knew Raul would be coming by or if he was just waiting for Penny, Raul couldn't say, but it was clear Tyler wanted the chance to prove his dominance. Raul had a good idea that wasn't going to impress Penny as much as Tyler wanted it to.

"I guess that went well enough," Jude commented when Raul got back in the car.

Raul grunted in response. "I'll just have to call her. We can head back to HQ and I'll see if I can dig up any information on Miguel and his strays." He brooded on the drive, worried that he'd made the wrong decision. It was the right thing to put his job in front of a potential relationship. He'd fulfilled Penny's request by sparing Tyler, but something still nagged at the back of his brain. Something wasn't right, and there were only so many things he could investigate at once.

"Wow. Can you believe it? It's just nuts!" Ingrid and Penny sat on Penny's living room floor, the information they'd gathered at Griffith Park scattered all around them in notebooks and on laptop screens. "I mean, I know what a reputation the place has. I've personally never been lucky enough to see any of the ghosts they say haunt it, and I haven't stumbled on any bodies, but still! This is just so intense."

Penny's ordinary motto of not getting excited was difficult to stick to this time. Although she hadn't been pleased when Raul asked her not to go to the park alone, she'd followed his advice. It wasn't always the best place, and the sheer numbers of murders and dumped bodies were enough to make her stop being so defensive. Was it really that bad that he wanted her to be safe? Did that really mean he was controlling or was he just a nice guy? Whatever. It didn't matter. She didn't want to think about Raul right now. She wanted to think about the way the sensors had practically set themselves on fire during their investigation.

"It really is," she admitted. "Not only did we see frequency readings off the charts, we'd already performed these tests in the park last year. That means we actually have something to compare them to. I still don't want to jump to any conclusions, but that's getting harder and harder to do."

"Not that I want to sound like Tyler," Dylan said from the couch, where he was rattling away on his laptop, "but I think we've got enough going on with these readings that we could make something out of this investigation if we wanted to. We've got more to go on than most of those shows you see on TV."

Penny smiled at him. For Dylan to start thinking about publicity, things had to be good. "We can talk about that when we go back to the park tonight. I want to catch this clan in the act and see what they're doing. Otherwise, there's not much to prove."

"How can you say that?" Ingrid squealed. "You saw those readings, but you also saw those bloody stones and the way the dirt was disturbed at some of those spots. Someone is *doing* something at Griffith Park, for sure."

"But doubters could argue that it's just kids trying to scare hikers with creepy setups," Penny argued. "I admit I had a major feeling of bad energy when we got close, even worse than when we went to Dead Man's Park. You know and I know that this is something big, but no one is going to listen to us unless we have some way to prove it." That was the constant problem when it came to ghost hunting.

"Well, I can't go tonight. I've got work," Ingrid said with disappointment.

"You?" Penny asked Dylan.

He shook his head. "No can do. I've got relatives coming into town on my mom's side. She'd kill me if I wasn't there to get my annual inquisition on why I don't do anything with my life. What about Tyler? I know he's not much help, but at least you wouldn't be alone."

"I think I'd prefer to be alone," Penny quipped.

"I know he's a bit over the top, but it's just because he's crazy about you," Dylan said, shutting his laptop and reaching for the case. "I'm not trying to say there's any justification for acting like a douche, just that he might have some reasoning for it in his mind. I've got to go. But I'll see you guys later."

"See ya."

When he'd let himself out, Ingrid turned to Penny with a smile that was a bit too big. "What about your new friend Raul? I'm sure he wouldn't mind hanging out with you in a remote area in the middle of the night."

"Well, maybe," Penny said with a shrug.

"Trouble in paradise? It sounded like you guys were really getting along after that night at the cemetery."

Penny sighed and began stacking up all her paperwork. "We were, but I think I was just caught up in the excitement of the night and starting an investigation that felt like it was really going somewhere. I mean, it had to be if it caught the attention of the SOS Force, right?"

Ingrid nodded, but she looked skeptical. "Sure."

"Well, and you know how it is when you suddenly start spending time with someone new. It's easy to get caught up in that. I should know better, though. I try not to kid myself into finding evidence of ghosts where there isn't any, and I shouldn't be any different when it comes to men."

"Even hotties who look at you with lava in their eyes?" Ingrid asked.

"Lava?"

Her friend laughed. "Yes, like he's melting from the inside out just thinking about you. Even in the cemetery, I knew there was something going on there."

"It was nothing. Besides, after we went to talk to Mrs. Reyes, I realized I was letting things get too personal between us. Raul started acting like it was his job to protect me, and he hardly even knows me." She'd often replayed the conversation between them in her head, and every single time, she'd sounded like a bitch. When she'd found out Tyler had been following them, the deepest part of herself had reacted with true fear. She couldn't blame Raul for offering to help, no matter his motivations.

"I see. So you told him to buzz off, and now he's not part of the investigation?" Ingrid helped put all the books they'd been studying back on the shelf and sat back down to put her shoes on.

"No, he is. Raul did a little work of his own while we were at the park, and he's asked to get together so we can go over stuff." Penny had read the text and left it that way without replying, feeling odd about her relationship—or whatever she should call it—with Raul. Was he genuinely interested in getting to the bottom of these odd incidents? Or was he just trying to find a way to get into her pants?

"You guys had enough chemistry going that first night that you told me you thought the two of you were fated. I've known you for a while, Penny, and even though I haven't been lucky enough to feel that sort of pull, I know you wouldn't say that if you didn't genuinely feel it. So you had a bit of a spat about something. Just give it time and be patient with him. He's a hell of a lot cuter than Tyler, anyway."

The two of them laughed over that, and Penny almost told Ingrid about her encounter with Tyler that same night. She decided to let it go, not wanting to dwell on something so negative. "You're right. And it's not as though I have to make any decisions about anything right this second. We've got a lot of work ahead of us, and that's what I need to focus on."

"Just keep me posted, so I can live vicariously through you until I find someone special of my own." Ingrid hugged her and let herself out.

After a quick text exchange, Raul agreed to meet Penny back at Griffith Park so she could show him what she'd discovered. She pulled her hair into a ponytail and then let it down again. Several shirt changes later, she was out the door.

As much as she'd tried to talk herself out of it, Penny felt butterflies shooting like fireworks through her stomach as soon as she pulled into the parking lot near the Greek Theatre and saw Raul. He was sitting on a low concrete wall that bordered the lot right next to where he'd parked his truck. His eyes met hers when he looked up from his phone, and he pocketed it as he approached her car. He waited patiently as she got out, keeping his distance until she slammed the door behind her. "Hey."

"Hey. It's quite a hike out to the places Victor had marked on his map." Penny felt like she could run straight up into the hills if it meant she could avoid this awkwardness.

"I'm up for it. That'll give us time to talk."

"Oh?" She felt her heart contract and her pulse quicken.

"As I said, one of my comrades and I visited that clan of Victor's." He fell in step beside her as they headed toward the bird sanctuary and the trails that traced all over the park. "I'm afraid they weren't too interested in talking to us, but we did our best."

"Any breakthroughs?" Penny was glad they had this investigation to work on. It was easier to talk about than whatever was happening between them.

Raul let out a light laugh that made her stomach clench. "It isn't as though they just invited us in and told us everything they'd been up to. I didn't want them to know why we were visiting them, so I didn't say anything about Victor or the undead. We just tried to ask some general questions that would be typical for any new clan, and the Alpha quickly dismissed us."

"That sucks. I was hoping for more, I guess." She kept her focus on the beautiful landscape that surrounded them. The setting sun angled beams of deep orange light through the scrubby flora.

"Don't check it off your list just yet. I know they're up to something. They're living in a run-down building, if you can even call it living. It's more like they're just squatting there, and they all look like they're starving. Everyone besides the Alpha had this haunted look in their eyes. Add the fact that they're a motley crew of every kind of shifter you can imagine, and it's hard not to think something's wrong."

Penny wished she'd gone with him and had seen these people in person. "You said they look like they're starving? That's...interesting."

"I'm listening."

"It's nothing I know for sure, just a hunch. But in any accounts I've found about people raising spirits, no matter what part of the world or what religion, there's always mention of the need to feed those spirits. They require a massive amount of energy to be brought back. In some European accounts, this was something along the lines of a crust of bread or other food. In the Americas, tribal cultures often tried to appease spirits through the sacrifice of a living being. I wonder if this clan has found a way to sap only some of the life out of a person or a group of people in order to bring these spirits back to life." Now Penny wished she'd left her hair up. It was hanging down in her face and sticking to the back of her neck, making it harder to think. Even so, just walking along the ridge line and talking with Raul was connecting some dots that she hadn't seen the lines between before.

"Oh, like tapping mana cards in *Magic: The Gathering*," Raul muttered.

"Hey, I used to play that game!" Penny looked up at Raul with a smile, surprised that a jacked, rugged soldier could ever be into such a thing, but happy to hear someone reference a part of her teenage life that she'd loved so much. She quickly looked away again when she saw the way he was looking at her. Ingrid was right. Lava. And it was working its way through her body.

"Sure. I told you I'm a nerd."

Penny smiled again but kept her eyes on anything but Raul. "Well, you're not wrong. There's got to be some sort of energy that would make these ghosts come back. It'd be hard to get away with human sacrifice without someone catching on. Just wait until you see some of the places we found. I'd say there was definitely something along those lines going on there."

"While obviously sacrifices would be a big problem, it's also an issue if they're putting the lives of their members in danger," Raul said, his face dark and serious as he easily lumbered up the trail next to her. "We need to be careful around these people."

They moved on through the park as the light turned from orange to blue to deep purple. Penny didn't see the tree root that stuck out along the trail until it snagged the toe of her shoe. A strong grip caught her elbow, effortlessly pulling her upright. Her cheeks burned as she looked up into Raul's concerned face.

"Are you all right?"

"Yeah, I'm fine." She straightened her shirt and tucked her hair behind her ear, blushing. His hand felt like a hot brand around her arm. "I just wasn't paying attention."

He stiffened, his eyes finding hers in the increasing darkness. "Did you hear that?"

She was too focused on Raul to have noticed, but she tuned her senses in. "Someone else is out here."

"Sounds like they're over there." He still held onto her as he listened.

"That's exactly where we're heading." The lack of distance between them had nearly made her forget why they were out there at all for a moment.

"We'll have to be quiet. How do you feel about shifting?"

Her body jolted at the notion. Penny had never shifted in front of someone she didn't know well, and even the rest of the LASS hadn't seen her wolf. But it would help ensure that they could truly be quiet as they moved through the park and that they'd be prepared to defend themselves if need be. Also, Raul wouldn't be able to hold onto her like that. She nodded.

"Good." He moved off the path and into the brush.

Penny paused just long enough to give him time to get a little ahead of her. She slipped into the trees and took a deep breath, letting it out slowly. Nothing happened. Glancing ahead to make sure Raul wasn't watching her, she tried again. This time, her human body melted away. She bent to the ground as her hands and feet became paws, and a bristling of hair snapped out of her skin all over her body.

Penny felt the customary tickle of her ears sliding up to the top of her skull, elongating, and sharpening to points.

As she became her true self, so too did she understand more of the truth of the area they were in. Though her senses were heightened even in human form, they were nothing compared to those of her wolf body. Penny's ears easily attuned both to the people further up along the ridge line, off the beaten path. She could hear their feet shuffling in the dirt and the rumbles of their voices. They were moving something heavy.

She also heard the gentler sound of Raul's four paws in the earth ahead of her, and she trotted to catch up. It was easier to be with him when they were like this, she quickly discovered. There wasn't the same pressure that came along with being human. They didn't need to explain themselves or worry about their behavior. They simply were there to observe, and at the moment, they were perfectly built for just that.

Penny was wondering how to tell him they were getting close when Raul stopped and took a sharp right. He stepped up behind a fallen log and sat, his thick tail whisking in the dirt. They weren't far from one of the ritual sites Penny had discovered earlier, and they had the perfect vantage point to watch the clan march through, carrying their torches high.

"Come along, my brothers! We, who have for so long been on the outskirts of shifter society here, will soon rule over them all! It takes but only the smallest offering from each of us. Your efforts here will pay off for years to come." The man at the head of the group was older than the rest of them, but he looked stronger. Thick, blocky tattoos snaked up and down his muscled arms, and he clearly had no problem ascending the trail. The other men, none of them older than thirty, were thin and frail. They seemed lucky to have made it this far, considering the way they were breathing and the large, wrapped object they were carrying.

It was set down with a solid thud on a flat stone when they came to the clearing. Penny assumed the Alpha was this Miguel that Raul had spoken of, and she watched as his glittering eyes observed his men spacing themselves with perfect uniformity around the stone. They clasped their hands and bowed their heads as Miguel chanted in a foreign tongue.

Raul's head pushed back on his shoulders, and his long tongue slid along his dark lips. His ears twitched and circled on his head. What-ever was being said, he didn't like it.

This wasn't the time, but Penny let her eyes linger. She took in the deep fur that ran down along his back, so dark that it blended in with the shadows. It faded to a deep gold that ran down his legs and along his belly, only a few shades lighter than his eyes. They were his wolf eyes, and though they were completely different than the ones she'd come to know, Penny could still tell that it was him inside.

A gasp came from the gathering, and she turned her attention back to the task at hand. The object the clan had laid on the stone had been unwrapped. The dead man lay stiffly stuffed into a suit, staring up at the sky. A mist swirled around him as Miguel continued to chant. He moved around the circle, slicing the wrists of each man, and their blood dripped down their fingers, running like dark syrup onto the stone. The haze eddied toward it as Miguel's chanting turned to a low drone in her ears.

The corpse didn't move, but the fog rose up from it and coalesced into a figure that looked exactly like it. The spirit turned to Miguel, looking confused.

"Go!" the Alpha commanded in English. "You died as a criminal, and now I give you the chance to continue living as one. Create your chaos!"

The spirit drifted off into the darkness, heading down the pathway toward the exit to the park.

When everything appeared to be over, Raul and Penny moved off through the woods. A few deeper shadows hid them as they retracted their thick coats and regained their limbs, and soon enough, they were once again two people, walking through the woods.

"That took a lot longer than it felt like," Raul said, glancing at his cell.

"What do you make of it?" She'd drawn a few conclusions, but they were selfish ones. Her mind had continuously turned to Kayla as she'd watched that spirit be called back from the next life through its former body. It didn't seem to be a very pleasant process for anyone, but Penny could see the potential for finally speaking to her old friend again.

"I'm actually a little angry that I didn't figure some of this out before." Raul was pacing in a small circle, gesturing with his hands. "Miguel had those distinct tattoos, and there was a book about Aztec culture in Victor's room. I couldn't understand all of what they were saying, but it was a dialect of the native tribes of this area. They were related to the Aztecs, as well as the other tribes along the coast and down into Mexico."

Penny was confused. "What are you saying?"

"You mentioned the European tradition of putting out food for spirits, and you linked it to human sacrifice here in the Americas. You were exactly right! I couldn't get every world—it's been too long since I've heard my abuela ramble on in the old tongue—but it's like Miguel and his makeshift clan have blended several tribal and spiritual customs in order to raise these spirits."

She was used to being the expert when it came to ghosts and rituals, but it was clear Raul was on the right track about this. "I'm afraid I don't know much about the Aztecs."

"It's incredible stuff, if you ever get into it. Just like many other cultures, they believed that death is just the next step, a way to move on to the next life. The spirits can go to one of the levels of either heaven or the underworld, but it can be called back to Earth when it's needed."

Her heart thundered in her chest. They'd figured out a way to bring spirits back from the dead. That meant Kayla could be out there, waiting for her to do the same. Penny tried to slow her racing brain and get back to her usual habit of remaining skeptical. "That means we know the general how, and we know a bit of the why. Miguel said something about ruling over shifter society. I don't see how ghosts are going to help him do it, though."

"That's all right. I plan to investigate this clan more thoroughly, and now with all the efforts of the Force, so we'll get it figured out."

They picked their way back, staying in the thickest parts of the brush looping widely around any path Miguel's clan might've taken just to be safe. The night was silent and cool around them, the stars brilliant in the sky. In a way, Penny wished she and Raul hadn't shifted earlier. It'd left her that much more in touch with her body, and as she moved along behind him through the woods, she couldn't help but pay attention. He seemed stiffer than usual, and when he turned his head to listen, she could see how his brows were drawn down and his jaw was set.

She cleared her throat. "Look, if you're upset by what we saw back there, don't worry about it too much. If Miguel could find a way to bring these spirits here, then we can find a way to send them back.

And at least, according to what we've seen so far, they're not able to stay for very long."

"I'm not upset," he replied, but there was a thread of tension in his voice.

"It would be understandable if you were. I can't say the LASS is very popular, but we've had a few guests tag along before. Seeing occurrences like these isn't something everyone can handle."

Raul stopped and turned to her. There wasn't much room between them and several young trees, the narrow trunks shooting hopefully toward the sky before branching out. "I can handle this. I'm not afraid of ghosts. I've seen a lot of shit in my lifetime already, and this is just another box to check off."

"Then what's wrong?" She lifted her hand, automatically reaching out to lay it on his chest. Penny realized what she was doing and started to pull it back, but Raul's fingers closed gently over her wrist.

He pressed her palm to his heart as he looked into her eyes. "I'm not worried about ghosts, Penny. I'm worried about you."

She was relieved to feel the booming cadence of his heartbeat under her palm because her own was pounding out of control. "Why should you be worried about me?"

He sucked in a deep breath that expanded his broad chest beneath her hand. "I stopped by your place yesterday."

"You did?" Just the thought of him showing up at her door was enough to send a surge of energy through her body. "I'm sorry. I wasn't home much yesterday."

"I wanted to talk to you about Miguel and his clan, but I also wanted to apologize. I can feel that there's something between us, and I pushed it too far. I don't ever want to do anything that makes you uncomfortable, and I'm sorry." His fingers gently massaged her skin.

Her wolf nudged her inside, demanding that she acknowledge not only how smokin' this man was, but how sweet. "It's all right. I think I was just thrown off by knowing Tyler was following us."

"And that's exactly why I'm upset. When I went by your place, Tyler was there. He was standing outside, and he told me in no uncertain terms that the two of you were together and that I needed to stay away from you."

Penny's hand curled into a fist against him. "We're not together, and we never will be again. That son of a bitch just wants to find a reason to pick a fight."

"Penny." His free hand came up to touch the side of her face, his thumb tracing softly along her jawline, then just below her lip before moving to cup the back of her head. "Penny, I'm absolutely crazy about you. I know in a way that I can feel but hardly explain that we're meant to be together. If you don't want me, then that's up to you. But I'm just so worried about you when it comes to Tyler. I couldn't live with myself if anything happened to you."

Tears burned at her eyes and threatened to spill over her lashes. She'd never experienced anything or anyone quite like this. "You care about me enough that you'd let me go? If that was what I wanted?"

"I would." More words lingered on those full lips of his. She could sense them as though he'd spoken them, but Raul wasn't like Tyler. He wasn't going to manipulate her by telling her how heartbroken he'd be or how he'd never get over her. Even if it were true, he wasn't going to say it.

"I don't want you to," she whispered, her lips and tongue alive with electricity.

He pulled her in, his lips soft against hers as he still held her hand against his chest. Penny parted her lips and dared to reach out, feeling a stream of bliss flow through her body as their tongues danced and explored. He pulled back, ending with a gentle kiss to her forehead.

"Raul," she said as he held her close in his thickly-tattooed muscular arms, "I think there's something I should tell you."

He moved, sliding his hand down her arm until it entwined with her fingers. Instead of answering, he led her through the woods, eventually coming upon a small clearing. It wasn't a typical lookout or picnic area, but just a circle of soft sand surrounded by trees. He guided her to sit on the ground next to him. "I'm listening."

There was nothing she wanted more than to ignore all the worry swirling inside her and just sit there with him, staring up at the stars all night. She owed him more than that, though. "I told you that Tyler and I used to date, but there's a little more to it than that."

"Okay." His gruff tone indicated that he didn't want to talk about Tyler anymore, but Penny knew she had to do this.

"It was sort of a childhood sweetheart thing, but it got more complicated than that. Both of our dads are Alphas of local wolf packs, pretty big ones. Once our parents figured out what was happening, they got all excited and decided he and I were mates. But I never felt drawn to him," she amended hastily, feeling Raul pull away emotionally more than physically. "I know that there's nothing between us. Tyler has held onto that notion, letting himself get all caught up in pack politics. In a way, I guess I have, too. I might've been more firm with Tyler if I wasn't worried about pissing off his pack and the drama of it getting back to mine."

"So, he gets to continue living his fantasy of being with you again someday?" Raul questioned.

"It's just a power trip," she replied, knowing that Tyler didn't think she was worth anything more than her bloodline. "He's got this notion of combining our two families into one, and then he'd be the Alpha of a super-pack. It's awful, really."

Raul had been studying her fingers, and when he looked up at her, their faces were merely inches apart. "What about your parents? Are they still expecting the two of you to make up and bond for good?"

She hated herself for dragging all this out in the open now. If she'd only told Raul earlier, when she'd first felt that cosmic tug toward him, this might have been much easier. "I'm not sure. I know they want me to be part of the leadership of our clan, but that doesn't mean I'm going to be with someone just to make other people happy. I know I'm meant for you and only you, Raul." The words flowed so easily off her tongue. She hadn't planned to say them, but she wouldn't take them back. They were real and true, and that was all that mattered.

"And I'm meant for you. I love you, Penny." Their lips met again then, but it was so much more than a kiss. All of their deepest feelings, everything they'd been holding back, radiated into each other. His arms wrapped around her as they eagerly tumbled to the sand below. Penny grazed her fingers through his hair as he buried his face in her neck, his teeth and lips exploring.

The feral side of her overcame everything else, and she pulled at the hem of his t-shirt with fervent need. His clothes had made no secret of his impressive body, but she needed to know it for herself. Stripping away the cotton material, her fingers explored everything she revealed, rippling along the muscles of his back and the strength of his spine. Raul pulled back only long enough to allow her to yank the shirt over his head before he claimed her mouth again, his tongue roving down her collarbone and into the vee of her neckline.

His palms were on fire as he slid them under her shirt, quickly heating everything he touched. His movements were firm and commanding, showing her how much he wanted her, yet Penny knew that he would stop at the slightest indication from her. That knowledge and power sent a thrill of sensuality through her body, and as he shimmied her jeans down over her luscious hips and groaned over what he'd discovered, she'd never felt more beautiful.

"You're incredible," he whispered as he pressed his lips gently to her navel. "I've wanted you so badly. Do you know how many times I've fantasized about you since we met?"

Her breath left her lungs as she explored him, her fingers cherishing every muscle of his abs as she reached for the waist of his jeans. He might be a gorgeous wolf inside, but right now, he was all man. Exposed in the moonlight, Penny expected him simply to take her. She wanted him desperately, her core surging in anticipation.

But Raul was more patient than she was. He smiled at her as he slowly pulled down one strap of her lace bra and then the other, caressing each of her nipples gently with his tongue. His fingers played with the waistband of her panties, teasing her. "Do you want this?"

"God, yes," she panted, stroking her fingers along his firm inner thighs and working upward until she held his rock-hard member in her hands.

Raul let out a groan, and he rubbed his thumb across her lips. "You make it hard for me to be a gentleman."

She bit her lip as she smiled up at him. "Raul, I've spent so much of my life being told what to do. I'm not going to do that anymore, not for anyone. This is all for me, and I want you so badly, I think I might die if I don't have you right now." Penny wrapped her legs around him to prove it, feeling the hard muscles of his thighs against hers.

Stripping her panties off, he sank into her slowly. When he'd buried himself to the hilt, a deep shuddering rose through him and exploded as a groan. "How can you feel so good?" he rumbled against her neck.

They'd hardly even started, yet she knew exactly what he meant. Being so close to him, intertwined, their arms and legs melding together, was exquisite. She closed her eyes to focus on the feeling, and her core tightened in response, pulling him in deeper.

"I want this to last," he growled as he slowly pulsed his hips against hers. "I want to have my way with you all night. I want to wake up with you like this." Raul was already filling her completely, but she felt him thicken inside her.

Penny gasped with pleasure as her body reacted to his. They were doing what any other couple would do, yet it was so much more. It wasn't simply their physical forms that were pleasuring each other. Their souls, forged together at the dawn of the universe and split apart by time, were converging. Her heart tripped along in step to his. "However long, we still have all night," she breathed. "I won't be done with you, Raul, not ever."

He pushed against her harder, their hips thrusting and receiving in perfect unison under the stars. Penny wrapped herself around him, wanting to know the feeling of every part of him. Raul had stepped into her life like a shadow that'd always been there, but had finally separated itself from the darkness to come into the light. He filled her body with a heat and hunger that she'd never known before. Now that she did, she never wanted to let go of it again.

"Penny," he murmured, "tell me what you want."

She arched her back and stretched her body underneath him, feeling their shared passion building. It glowed inside her like a universe being formed, burning brighter and brighter as it swirled and converged at her very core. "Just this," she breathed, uncertain now if she was still a part of her own body or his. "Please, just this. Oh god, I'm almost there."

He'd felt it too, she knew. Raul held her tighter and kissed her as they moved in time. As her ecstasy began to coil in her core, Penny held her breath, and every muscle in her body contracted for one long moment until she dropped over the edge of a vast cliff, falling along with Raul into a blissful state of peace.

It was nearly dawn by the time she made it back to her place. Penny had floated through town as she drove through the early morning traffic, unable to think of anything but Raul. True to his word, they'd stayed there in the park all night, cuddled together as they talked, taking breaks from their conversation to make love again. It was all so perfect. If it wasn't so early, she would have called Ingrid. Penny wanted to tell her that she'd been right that first night, they were fated. At some point, she'd have to call Dylan, at least. Not to brag about her night, of course, but because she'd missed several calls from him while she'd been with Raul.

Her body still buzzed with his touch and his kisses, enough that she dropped her keys as she tried to unlock the front door of the building. Penny bent to pick them up. When she straightened, darkness shrouded her vision. "Hey!"

Strong arms wrapped around her body, pinning her arms to her sides as rope wound around her wrists. She'd spent all night in a man's arms, but not those. Penny struggled against them. It was no use. Her feet swung out from beneath her, and she was being carried. She felt the coolness of leather upholstery and heard the slamming of a car door. Penny was just about to start wildly kicking her feet and thrashing her arms when something strong and pungent was pressed to the outside of the fabric covering her face. She reeled her head back, trying to get away, but there was no room. The early morning light that'd been seeping through the fibers slowly faded, and she was left in darkness.

8

AMAR TIPPED HIS CHAIR BACK, HIS DARK BROWS CREASING AS HE LOOKED at Raul. "You're sure about all this? No offense, Raul, but I know how your imagination likes to run away with you sometimes. When we heard about these odd appearances throughout town, I thought we were going to end up finding evidence of identity theft or someone who was good at special effects. Actual ghosts, though? That seems pretty far out there."

"This from a guy who's engaged to a vampire," Jude remarked quietly.

The Alpha snapped his head to the bear shifter, his eyes flashing gold. "You'd be wise not to talk shit about my mate."

Jude shook his head. "Dude, I'm not. I'm just saying that it wasn't all that long ago that none of us imagined we'd find actual vampires living right here in Los Angeles. When you take that into perspective, maybe a few phantoms aren't all that out of line."

"Fair enough," Amar admitted with a sigh, pinching the bridge of his nose. "Perhaps even we are susceptible to the human paradigm. You said this has something to do with an ancient tribal ritual?"

"Several of them, actually." Raul was exhausted. He'd been up all night with Penny, a thought that continually brought a smile to his face, and then he'd spent the morning refreshing himself on anything he'd ever known about this stuff. "The largest Native American tribe that lived in this area before colonization was the Tongva. They didn't do anything like what I saw at Griffith Park, but other tribes who were loosely related and spoke a similar dialect did. The Tongva had a few ritual curses they supposedly cast on the incoming settlers as revenge for taking their land."

"So, Griffith Park was built on an ancient burial ground?" Emersyn asked with amusement in her eyes.

"Considering the number of places around here that were built over more modern cemeteries, I wouldn't be surprised. Essentially, Miguel is blending several different techniques to raise these spirits. For the moment, they don't last long. I'm guessing he even has a bit of difficulty controlling them, considering that a few vandalism sprees aren't going to do much to help him take over the area. Still, he's done the biggest part of the work. The rest is just refining it." Raul leaned back and swiped a hand over his face. His eyes felt like they were full of sand from lack of sleep, but he would have done it all over again if given the choice. Spending the night with Penny had been the most magical experience of his life.

"Here." Jude slid a mug of coffee in front of Raul that matched his own. "You look like you need some of this high octane blend."

There was a hint of a question in Jude's eye, and Raul knew they'd be talking again later. "Thanks. I appreciate it."

"You mentioned something about a partial sacrifice?" Emersyn asked. As the Medical Sergeant in residence, it only made sense that this was the part she picked up on.

Raul nodded and described that aspect of it in more detail. "It's like they each offer a small part of themselves to give a spirit the energy it needs to come back. But everyone I saw at their clan's house looked like they didn't have much more to give."

She nodded, her mouth a hard line. "Depending on how many times they've tried this and how many members they have, this could be dangerous for them. I'll have to make sure I've got plenty of supplies on hand for whatever our next step is."

"I'd say the next step is as Raul suggested," Amar replied. "We bide our time while we gather some more information. While we know Miguel has evil intentions, he's technically not hurting anyone yet. The members who've joined his clan seem to be there of their own free will, and obviously, the dead bodies are already dead. I don't think a ghost can feel pain, can it?" He scratched the side of his face.

"I can't imagine it feels good to be dragged back to Earth against your will," Jude remarked.

"No, but even so, we need to know a bit more about what we're dealing with," Amar said. "We can start with a surveillance rotation, plotting out where they go and what they do. At some point, we may need to have someone infiltrate their ranks. It can't be Jude or Raul since they've already been seen, but Gabe or I could..."

Amar was still talking, but Raul felt his phone buzz in his pocket. He knew it was rude to interrupt a meeting, but he pulled it out anyway, hoping it was a text from Penny. Instead, he found a message from Dylan through The Shift. *I need to talk to you right away. Call me.* He'd typed in his number.

Raul had only met Dylan once, but he seemed like the most grounded person in the Society for Spirits other than Penny. He wasn't going to act like something was an emergency if it wasn't. "Excuse me for a second. I've got to take this." Stepping out onto the back patio, Raul dialed Dylan's number.

"Oh, thank god you called me back," Dylan said breathlessly when he answered the phone. "I was worried you wouldn't see my message or that I'd gotten the wrong person."

"You got me." A sour feeling ran through Raul's blood. He could hear the fear on the other end of the line. "What's going on?"

"It's Penny. I think. I mean, I shouldn't jump to conclusions. That's what she's always telling the rest of us, after all. Don't worry about all the lights and alarms until you know what they mean, you know?"

"Just tell me what's happening." Raul knew perfectly well that Penny was always trying to keep herself from getting her hopes up or getting excited, and he also had a good notion now that it was because she'd been burned one too many times. He clenched his free hand at his side, wishing Dylan would get to the point.

"Okay." Dylan pulled in several shaking breaths. "I was trying to reach Penny all night on her phone, and I couldn't. It's not like her not to answer, even if it's the middle of the night."

Raul felt all his muscles turn to mush in relief. He'd heard her phone buzzing in her pants several times the night before; she just hadn't been wearing them. Heat flooded Raul's cheeks as he tried to find a delicate way to explain why Penny had been so busy. "No big deal. See—"

"So then I went by her place this morning," Dylan charged on. "I knew it was early, but I had some equipment I needed to pick up from her. Her car was there, but I also saw Tyler's car screeching off down the road."

"Did you knock on her door?" Raul was already getting his keys, knowing he was going to have to start moving quickly.

"Yeah, but she didn't answer. Look, I'm sorry to bother you, but I'm worried about her. Tyler's been even nuttier than usual, and I just got a really bad feeling when I saw him leaving her place."

"You're not bothering me," Raul countered. "You did the right thing by calling. Just leave it to me, Dylan. I'll find her." He hung up and charged back into the conference room.

Everyone looked up, immediately alarmed by his stature and countenance.

"What is it?" Emersyn asked.

"Penny, who I've been working with." Raul's eyes shot to Jude's.

"Is she in trouble?" the bear asked.

"I think so. Her ex is part of her ghost hunting group. He confronted me about hanging around with her the other night, and he was seen peeling out at her apartment building. We don't know where Penny is." His heart clenched in his chest, recalling the memory of the way he felt the first time he shipped out.

Jude stood and came to his side. "This ex of hers, is there any chance he could be part of Miguel's misfit clan?"

Raul's eyes lifted to his as the connection slammed him in the forehead. "I didn't see it. It didn't make sense. That *cabrón* was too much of a blithering idiot, and I couldn't imagine him doing something like that. But Penny said he wants them to bond so he can be the Alpha of a massive pack, and he's been learning about ghost hunting from her. Fuck!"

"At least that means our enemies are all likely in one place," Amar offered. He nodded at the rest of the Force. "Sounds like we need to move our timeline up a little."

9

PENNY SWAM THROUGH AN OCEAN SO THICK, THE SUNLIGHT REFUSED TO penetrate its depths. Her body felt both heavy and weightless as she floated along, moved by the natural current no matter how much she struggled to guide herself with her arms and legs. Her brain sought some reasonable explanation for being there, but it came up with nothing. She searched again, but it was as though someone had filled her mind with fog.

"Penny."

She heard the voice. She didn't know whose it was, but she wanted to swim away. The current wouldn't let her.

"Penny," the voice intoned again.

"No!" she screamed, but no sound issued from her throat. The disembodied voice scared her much more than the water, and she fought harder as it dragged her upwards toward some dim source of light. It grew brighter and brighter, bursting through the water and yanking her out into the sun.

She opened her eyes. Trees swirled in her vision. "What the...?" Moving her mouth to speak was like taking a bite of dry sand.

"There she is," Tyler announced, his face swimming into view. "You were having one hell of a nap there."

Though she couldn't yet move her arms and legs, her body intrinsically shrank in on itself, wishing to get away from him. "What's going on? What did you do to me?" Her voice was still thick and cakey, but it was better.

He sat on the ground beside her, his legs bent and his arms wrapped around his knees. He looked like the casual, careless teen she'd met all those years ago, save for the deepening circles under his eyes. "What did *I* do to *you*?" he laughed. "Penny, this is something you brought entirely on yourself."

"What is?" Once again, she was trying not to jump to any conclusions. It was hard to believe, however, that Tyler could be up to any good.

He glanced over his shoulder and then back at her, hunger in his eyes. "You and I both know what we could've achieved together if you'd only cooperated."

"Tyler, it never would've worked. We're not meant to be together."

His hand closed around her throat so quickly, she'd hardly even caught it moving. "Don't you *dare* talk to me about what's meant to be!" he hissed, his face pressed into hers. "I had the chance to be one of the most powerful Alphas in the state, perhaps even the country. I knew what path we were headed down."

He was crushing her windpipe, and she couldn't argue against him.

"You want to talk about fate like it's some magic spell. Let me tell you, Penny, I know all about magic spells. They don't have anything to do with romance and feelings. It's about knowing what you want and taking it. Since you wouldn't give me what I want, I have no problem doing exactly that." He let go with a jerk of his hand.

Penny gasped for air, feeling like a fish out of water as she stared at him. "But...Tyler...What..."

"What am I going to do?" he asked mockingly. "I'm not going to make you mine in some sham ceremony, if that's what you're concerned about. I deserve much better than to have to put up with you nagging me for the rest of my life. It wasn't you I wanted anyway, but the power. I can have that. Now that I have Miguel on my side, I don't have to settle for just my clan and yours. I can have all of them."

Someone shouted nearby.

"Just a second," Tyler called back. He turned back to Penny. "The sun is going to set soon, and we'll be out of time before you know it. Tonight is the night we unleash panic and terror on the entire city. You only have two options."

Raul's handsome face floated in her mind's eye, but she knew he wasn't on Tyler's list. "What?" she croaked.

"You can help me. You can be part of our new clan, and with your experience and skill, you'll have no problem earning a good place. You'll assist us in our ghostly invasion of the city."

She shook her head, tears running down her temples and pooling in her ears. "No," she gasped. "I won't do that, Tyler, and you know it."

"That's fine," he replied, without a hint of rage for once. An odd smile tipped up the corners of his mouth, and she noticed how dull his eyes looked. "Then I'll kill you myself, and Miguel will drag your soul back to serve as our slave of chaos."

Terror ripped through her body. How could she make a choice like that? Her only hope was to stall him until she figured some way out of this. "I'll help," she finally said. "I'll help you."

"Good girl." Tyler hopped to his feet and grabbed her hands. "Let's go. You've got some training to do."

She allowed him to keep his arm around her once she was on her feet, but only because she knew she might fall over again otherwise. Penny blinked as she looked around. "We're at Griffith Park. At the old zoo." A cold finger traced down her spine. When the new zoo opened, this land had simply been incorporated into the park, and it still held many of the old habitats. She'd always found those abandoned cages and caves to be creepy, and being there with Tyler wasn't helping.

"Of course. As I'm sure you know by now, since you were so determined to figure out what was going on in the city, the ground here is even more sacred than a cemetery. We need a body or some other important object to locate a spirit, but we've found that the location is most important. The land here is incredible, filled with old curses and magic that dates back thousands of years. This is where we make our stand!" He gestured grandly as they moved up the crumbling asphalt path toward the enclosure that once held lions.

"If I'm going to help, then maybe you should give me a little more information," she said, looking around and desperately hoping for either someone who could help or a good way to escape. The old zoo was already flooded with members of Miguel's clan. They were dressed entirely in black, their thin frames moving slowly but surely as they carried bundles off a large truck. "How, exactly, are you planning to use ghosts to gain control of the local packs? It doesn't make sense."

"It makes perfect sense, Penny." He let out an exasperated sigh. "This is why you never got anywhere with the Society for Spirits.

You're too busy trying to look for the logical side of things and ways to apply science. But ghosts don't grow in a petri dish, Penny. There's so much more to the universe than we can see; we just have to open our eyes enough to let it in."

"Okay. You're right." That was always something Tyler liked to hear, even though he still wasn't making any sense. "You've obviously been doing a lot more research behind the scenes than I've given you credit for. Just explain to me what we're doing. I can't help if I don't understand it."

"No, I'm not going to make it that easy. You've always been the one in charge when it comes to the LASS, and I want to know what you think. You tell me first." He laughed as he guided her around a curve in the path.

"Um." She quickly flipped through all the footage she'd seen over the last couple of weeks. The ghosts were all shifters. They were creating havoc throughout LA, vandalizing cars and robbing stores. Sometimes, they simply scared the shit out of people. Miguel had said something about chaos when she and Raul had seen him successfully summon a spirit. "A ghost riot? Terrorizing the town and refusing to stop until you get what you want?" Penny could see how they could have some success with that. Ghosts couldn't be taken down by the police, or even the SOS Force.

"That was the first idea," Tyler admitted. He walked so casually down the old trail that he might've been talking about the weather or griping about taking a test. It was hard to see pieces of his former self come through, especially when she knew he'd changed at heart. "Then, we realized we were missing a great opportunity. I'll let Miguel tell you about it."

They reached the old lion enclosure. The fence in front of it had been torn down, and several picnic tables sat near the faux caves. The same man who'd led the ceremony the previous night sat in the mouth of one of them, glaring up at them.

"Miguel, this is Penny," Tyler said politely, giving a slight bow. "The one I told you about."

The older man scowled up at her. "Tyler tells me you know a lot about the other side."

She could pretend for Tyler, but not for Miguel. His energy was dark and she could feel it, even from several feet away. "I study it a lot, but I don't know what I'm capable of."

Miguel nodded at Tyler, who reluctantly let go of her arm and stepped back. "Sit," he commanded, pointing at the ground.

Penny gladly obliged. She still felt dizzy from whatever drugs Tyler had used on her, and the circumstances weren't helping.

"Here. You need to memorize this." Miguel shoved a piece of paper at her. The lines looked like complete gibberish.

"What is it?"

"An ancient tribal ritual. Just go by the pronunciation. You can see here that this is where you pause and collect the sacrifices. The men will know what you need from them. You can watch me for the first one, and then you'll be doing it on your own." Miguel tapped the paper to show her what he meant as calmly as if he was going over a grocery list. He handed her a small knife. "We're starting on those who were the youngest when they died, as they'll have the most power left in them."

Her stomach churned as she looked down at the stained blade, knowing exactly what it was for. "I don't know if I can do this."

Miguel snapped his fingers, making Tyler step forward again. "You said we had some sort of assurance for her cooperation."

"Of course." Tyler reached in the pocket of his black jeans and produced Penny's charm bracelet.

She gasped, dropping the knife and slapping her hand to her naked wrist. "How dare you! Give that back to me!"

"Oh, I don't think so. At least not until the time is right," he replied as he dangled it on one finger.

"Tyler," she hissed, "that's important to me."

He nodded. "I know. What was it you said? That Kayla's parents gave you a bit of her ashes so you could have them turned into a little glass charm?"

Penny felt all the blood drain from her face as her eyes focused on the little blue bead. "Yes," she whispered.

"Perfect. Then Miguel, here is your guarantee. Penny, Kayla will be the first spirit you'll raise. She and the other dead shifters from her pack will be held as hostages, along with the souls of many others. They'll do as we say until their clans give us control. The Alphas will be responsible for not only saving the lives of those walking the Earth, but the spirits of their dead." Tyler tossed the bracelet to Miguel.

Bile rose in Penny's throat. "I don't... I don't think..."

"Good. Don't think. Just do as you're told, unless you'd prefer to help our campaign in a more costly way." Miguel tucked her bracelet in his jacket pocket for safekeeping.

———

"CAN I HAVE SOME WATER, PLEASE?" Penny sat on the ground and put her head between her legs, trying not to pass out. She wanted to be stronger. Perhaps in some way she was, considering that her vision hadn't started to tunnel until after she'd watched Miguel perform the ritual. Now, saliva rushed along the sides of her tongue even as her throat went dry, and cold sweat stood out on her forehead and back.

Tyler sighed and sent someone off, who returned a short while later with a bottle of water. "Here."

"Thank you." The polite reply was automatic. Tyler didn't deserve her thanks, no matter what he did, not now. She unscrewed the top and took a sip. "There's got to be a better way. I mean, is it really worth it? Risking all these lives and souls just so you can be in charge?"

The back of his hand slammed into the side of her face, sending her reeling to the right. She caught herself on her elbow and looked up at him with shock.

"I've always wanted to do that." He straightened, looking satisfied with himself. "And you've always deserved it. This is what's happening, Penny. You can't talk me out of it or try to trick me into doing something different. I've thought long and hard about this. I've played a much more patient game than you probably ever thought me capable of, and it's about to pay off. Now let's get this over with."

She tightened her lips, wondering if she could actually do this. Penny could no longer doubt that Miguel's method worked, but was it truly just a matter of the right movements and words mixed with a little blood?

"Don't tell me I have to remind you how many times you've whined about not being able to talk to Kayla," Tyler mocked. He'd gotten her bracelet back from Miguel and spun it on his finger. "Every single day of our lives, it was Kayla this and Kayla that. 'Oh, how I wish I could just see her one more time and talk to her.' Well, your fucking wish is about to come true. You just need to quit being a little bitch about it and make it happen."

It was the middle of the night. Penny could hear other groups of shifters moving throughout the park and the horrific moans that denoted their successes. The spirits they raised found themselves not free to go do as they wanted, but bound to the whims of Miguel and his men. She closed her eyes and tried to drown out the sounds. How could she do this? How could she have let herself get caught up in this? If only she'd listened to Raul when he'd offered to protect her from Tyler. He had no idea just how right he was.

"We don't have all night," Tyler warned.

She looked up at him and nodded. "Fine."

He set Penny's bracelet on a low stone and stepped back, moving outside the circle but right behind her in case she tried anything stupid.

Penny gripped the paper Miguel had given her in both hands as she read aloud. She didn't understand any of the words, but she did her best as she focused on her pronunciation. This was Kayla. It was bad enough to bring anyone back who didn't want to be, but Penny had to do this right. She intoned the words, doing her best to follow the cadence she'd heard from Miguel. Though she had no idea what the words themselves meant, she did understand their intention: call this soul back to the mortal Earth. Bring it back and bind it to me.

The first part of the spell was over, and Penny knew it was time for the step she dreaded the most. Adjusting the grip of the knife in her hand, she reminded herself that this was Kayla. Her best friend. Kayla had always been there for her, and Penny had no doubt that the two of them would still feel the same way about each other if it hadn't been for that fateful night. She didn't want to help Miguel and Tyler, but this was her one chance to finally see Kayla again. Penny wasn't sure if she'd even get a chance to apologize, but she had to try. She had to do this right, for Kayla's sake.

The clan members stood as stiff as zombies around the stone and the bracelet. They held out their wrists, waiting for her with dead eyes.

Penny swallowed and stepped up to the first one on her right. She could still sense Tyler's eyes on her. Could she turn around and stab this knife straight through his heart? Maybe, if she were quick enough. But even if she killed Tyler, it wasn't going to stop this from happening. Miguel had recruited far more members than she could've imagined, luring them in by dangling power in front of their faces. That clearly wasn't paying off for them, but Penny wasn't sure they knew that. Judging by the emotionless looks on their faces, whatever had inspired them to join Miguel was no longer of any concern.

Her throat filled with bile as she pressed the tip of the knife to the first man's wrist. It was sharp, thank god, and it easily pierced the thin skin. Crimson oozed up from the tiny wound, which would soon join the legion of scars peppered all over the man's arm. Without waiting to watch him turn his wrist to pour the blood on the ground, Penny stepped to the next man.

As she raised the knife once again, a vision of Kayla clouded her eyes. Penny was back in high school, standing in the locker room. Kayla had been with her during first period, but Penny hadn't seen her during gym class. She suddenly appeared, looking sad as she rubbed her arm.

"There you are!" Penny had exclaimed, somewhat irritated that Kayla hadn't been there during class. "Coach Long let Destiny and Annabelle pick teams, again! So of course I ended up just standing there like an idiot until Destiny got stuck with me. This is so embarrassing, and I'm tired of doing it every day." She even remembered propping her foot up on the bench to tie her laces.

"Yeah, I'm sorry," Kayla had said quietly. "I was in the counselor's office."

Penny had been reaching into her locker for her bag, but she turned and dropped her arm. "Really? What'd you do?"

"No, I wasn't in trouble. You know Jenny Bledsoe? The one who wears those baggy hoodies all the time? She's in my math class, and I happened to see her arm when she reached up to fix her ponytail. She's been cutting herself." Kayla twisted her face.

"Oh. Wow." Penny hadn't known what to say. She'd heard of things like that happening, but she couldn't imagine anyone doing it. "Are you sure?"

Kayla had nodded. "She was covered in scars, Penny. It was so awful. I feel bad for telling on her, but I know she needs help. I just can't imagine anyone would want to do that to themselves, or maybe even kill themselves. I hope she'll be okay now."

Penny had wrapped Kayla in a hug. "I'm sure she will."

Blinking as she brought herself back to the present, Penny felt her tongue stick to the roof of her mouth as she made another cut. These men were surviving the injuries, just as Jenny Bledsoe had, but for how long? How many times could they do this before they, too, would be among those spirits being dragged back to Earth? With a tightening of her throat, Penny realized that was just another step in Miguel's plan.

If any members of his new clan perished, he'd simply use their souls instead of their bodies.

Determined to get through this and get it over with, Penny moved around the circle. She kept thoughts of Kayla close to her heart, as always, knowing that her best friend would understand why she was doing this awful thing. There had to be some way out of it, some way to change the future, some way to make it all okay again. Penny desperately wished she had her equipment with her, just in case it would tell her something about what was happening.

Finally, after slicing six wrists, Penny returned to her place in the circle and bent down to touch the bloody knife to her bracelet. This part of the ritual, at least, was in English. She suddenly realized that there might, in fact, be something she could do to change the outcome. "Come to me, spirit. Release the shackles of the afterlife that keep you from this realm and walk among the living once again." She cringed, waiting. Tyler hadn't noticed what she'd done.

The circle of the bracelet filled with blue light. It shimmered and bubbled, writhing within the confines of the metal until it shot upward in a column of luminescence. Suspended in the air, the blue light began to change. Penny had only witnessed the summoning that she and Raul had spotted the other night and the one that Miguel had made her watch earlier. There was something different about this one. Energy crackled in the air and flowed through her body as she watched the light coalesce into a familiar shape.

Kayla stood on the rock, the bracelet between her bare feet. Her dark hair flowed freely down past her shoulders, blowing in a wind that Penny couldn't feel. The spirit looked around with anger and confusion, and this only slightly dissipated when she spotted Penny. "What have you done?"

Penny took a step forward, feeling all the rest of the events happening at the park drop away as though they didn't exist. "Kayla, I'm so sorry. I didn't have a choice."

"Why would you do this to me?" Kayla wailed as she looked down at her body. "I've stayed close to you, so close that it's almost as though I've been here, but that wasn't good enough? Penny, how could you?"

"Holy shit," Tyler said behind her. Penny turned to look, seeing awe on his face. No, not awe. Fear. "Penny, what did you do?"

"I did as you asked," she ground out. It was one thing for Kayla to be angry, confused, and hurt. She didn't know what was happening.

But Tyler? "This was all your doing, so I don't know what your problem is."

"No, you messed it up! She's not supposed to be able to talk to you like that! You saw the way the others were. They just stood there and waited for directions!" He gestured wildly at Kayla, taking a slight step back.

The spirit turned to him. "I remember you, but you're not the same."

"Yeah, neither are you. But you're bound to my new clan now, and you have to do as I say. You need to come with me to your parents' house, and you'll stay bound until they convince your Alpha to surrender to us!" Tyler straightened his shoulders and thrust out his chest.

Kayla looked away from him and to Penny. "I'm not doing that."

"Nor should you," Penny agreed, feeling desperate. "He's part of a new clan that's using ancient rituals to try to take over the entire area. They're blackmailing shifters to give up control over their packs and clans by holding the spirits of their loved ones hostage."

"What the fuck did you do? This isn't how it's supposed to be!" Tyler's hard punch landed square in the middle of Penny's back, bringing her to her knees and knocking the breath from her lungs.

"Don't you touch her!" Kayla's scream was a keening wail in the night as she stepped down from the stone toward Tyler.

Penny focused on her friend's bare foot, so real that she could reach out and touch it. Air refused to come back into her body, and she gasped in desperation. But she also smiled as she turned her face to look at Tyler, the man whom she'd once loved who was now her enemy. "I brought her back, but I didn't bind her. She's free to do as she wishes."

"Shit!" Tyler's exclamation was cut off as Kayla hauled back and slammed him with her fist. Miguel might have been a crazy man, but the spells he'd created to summon these ghosts had worked well. They were capable of creating all the destruction and chaos he wanted, but Kayla had a mind of her own. She landed another wallop to Tyler's chest, not hurting him but putting him in his place. He stumbled backward into a tree, which he clutched for dear life as he watched the ghost with terror.

Kayla wasn't paying any more attention to him, though. She was watching the park around them. Her eyes were the same brilliant blue they'd always been, enhanced by that cobalt light of the other side that filled her now. "Something's happening."

"I know." Penny pressed a hand to her head. "The people Tyler is working with are raising spirits all over the place."

"No. Not just that. There's someone else."

Slowly sitting up, Penny glanced around. Much of the park was cut off from her vision by the hills and trees, but she could see the clan members shuffling along the pathways like zombies and the other spirits who'd been raised streaming toward the exits. All was exactly as she expected, until she heard a scream. A massive black dragon swooped down from the sky, fire blazing from its jaws. Penny's guts turned to water, but then she saw the two bears and the wolf that came charging into the park after it. A panther brought up the rear, her eyes watchful. "They've come to help us," she said with tears in her eyes, instantly recognizing the sleek wolf.

"And so will I," Kayla announced. "These souls have been bound, but only because they didn't understand what was happening. I might be able to change that." She strode off through the grass, no longer a dead teenage girl but a warrior.

Penny had been horrified when she'd awoken to this situation, but her heart now rose in her chest, filling with hope. Kayla and Raul were fighting for justice, and so would she. Already on all fours, she pulled in a deep breath. It was painful still, but the relief that came with transitioning to her wolf made it more than worth it. She felt the power in her muscles as they shifted and changed, accommodating to a form fit for four legs. The screams that surrounded her increased in volume as her ears swiveled to catch the sounds, and her sharp teeth ran with saliva. She dug her clawed feet into the ground as she turned, ready to fight Tyler.

But he was gone.

She swiveled her furry head from left to right, wondering where the hell that fucker went. Another fiery blast from the dragon illuminated the sky, highlighting the dark clouds that were slowly rolling in. The bears and Raul charged up a grassy hill, but Penny quickly lost sight of them among the crowd of other shifters who'd taken on their animal forms. Lions and tigers swarmed the old pathways. The roar of bears shook the trees as a pack of coyotes flanked them. Wolves crept in slowly from the shadows, creeping in ever closer to the SOS Force. Penny could hardly keep track of who was who, but there were so many animals that it looked as though the old zoo had reopened and run amok.

Barreling toward the fray, Penny was stopped when the lean body of a cougar pounced down onto the ground in front of her. He opened his mouth to let out a scream, showing off his brilliant white fangs and glowing yellow eyes. Penny felt her hackles raise. She'd trained with her father many times, but the enemy surrounded her. Her tail bristled as she circled the other beast, looking for its weak point. The cougar was well-muscled, and he looked as though he'd been incredibly fit at one point, but his stomach was tucked so high up into his ribs that he had to be from Miguel's group. The cat was ready to fight, but he wouldn't last long.

Penny swung her hind end around to get the right angle and attacked. Her teeth sank through thick fur, and she bit down harder to get through the rubbery feline skin. Blood burst into her mouth and streamed down her throat.

The big cat screamed in her ear as he tried for a counterattack. He swiped at Penny with his back claws, scraping the thin skin of her legs but doing no real damage.

Penny bit down harder, letting her lupine senses completely dominate as she ripped a hunk of flesh from the cougar's neck. She snarled as she spit fur from her tongue, ready to go again. But the defeated cat staggered away, its tail hanging limply along the ground behind it.

The evil clan was too focused on the center of the fight further up the hill, and no one had noticed her. Penny shot toward them, desperate to get to Raul. She could no longer see him among all the beasts who flooded the park, but the dragon was impossible to miss. She turned and darted up the hill. *Raul!* Her heart cried out for him.

I'm here. His telepathic reply was as clear in her head as if he'd stood next to her. *Get out of here while you can, Penny. There are too many of them.*

She gritted her teeth as she shoulder-checked a skinny coyote out of the way and sprinted by. *I'm not leaving! And please tell me the freaking dragon is with you!*

The sound that came through next might have been a slight laugh. *Yeah, definitely.*

We've got to get to Miguel. I think he's still raising spirits, and he's found the right spell to control them!

There was no reply. Penny waited, trying to be patient as her heart surged inside her ribcage. If he died because he'd gotten involved with her, if she lost yet another person who meant the absolute world to her, she'd never forgive herself.

I will, but please, Penny. Get out of here. Save yourself.

A running leap carried her straight over the head of a fox. *Hell, no. Something's happening.*

She ran faster, feeling her lungs burn. There! He stood with the other shifters he'd come in with, their backs against a rusty cage. Several of Miguel's guys surrounded them, toying with them as they crept in slowly.

Penny came up behind the enemy, charging faster and feeling all her senses converge as she focused on a ratty gray tail. She was keenly aware of Raul, watching her, sending her a message that told her to leave, but she couldn't. She wouldn't. Not when there was so much yet to fight for. Jumping into the air, she landed hard on a large tiger's back. It swirled to the right, throwing her off. Penny rolled to the ground, tucking her feet in so she could sprint as soon as gravity was done having its way with her. The tiger was on her in a heartbeat, its heavy toes flexing as it sank its claws into the soft skin of her underbelly.

The weight of the tiger was instantly gone as the orange beast went flying backward, with Raul on top of it. His low growl thundered inside him and rumbled through Penny's body as he snapped his jaws repeatedly at the big cat, dodging its teeth and sending its blood flying into the air. It fought much as the cougar had, but it didn't have the energy to take down the hulking wolf. Raul clamped his jaws over the tiger's throat and gnashed his razor-sharp teeth together, killing it instantly.

Penny knew there was no time to waste. She rolled over and got to her feet as she and Raul rejoined the others. *You said something was happening. What is it?*

Look over there. Raul gestured with his great head toward the old lion enclosure, where Penny had last seen Miguel. The man had shifted into his black bear. Several of his thugs were at his side, and Penny recognized the muted tones of Tyler's wolf. They were defending themselves not from any SOS Force members, but Kayla.

She stood before them, blue fire exploding like an aura around her. "This is the mortal who did this to you!" she cried to the other spirits gathered behind her. "This is the one who would control you to do his bidding, who brought you back into the pain of life from the other side, who would use you to gain power!" Kayla lifted a finger and pointed it straight at Miguel.

"Fuck off!" he spat back. "You're only here because you're bound to me. You must do as I say."

Kayla smiled as she shook her head. "You forget that you only tricked them into believing they were bound. A spirit cannot be tamed or bought or contained. You have no more control over us than what we're willing to give you, and we won't let you use us."

Miguel stood, lifting his chin and curling his fists at his sides. His dark eyes glittered in the night as he began chanting. Penny recognized the sounds of that ancient language he'd written down for her in his effort to make her abuse these poor souls. Her stomach trembled, but she took comfort in feeling her mate at her side.

Throwing back her head, Kayla curled her fingers around two massive balls of blue flame that formed in her hands. She screamed into the night as the spirits rushed forward. They were tired and angry, and that was all the fuel they needed as they attacked Miguel and his closest circle.

Penny and the Force stood at the ready to fend off the rest of the shifters. She expected them to attack, to defend their leader so they could claim the power they'd gone there for. She'd already tasted blood that night, and she was ready for more. But the array of beasts that had returned to the old zoo were slinking off into the night, melting into the shadows.

It was over even faster than it'd begun. Miguel and his men, including Tyler, lay dead in the mouth of the old caves, their blood dripping over the concrete and asphalt. Penny leaned against Raul, nuzzling her muzzle against his. *I've got to talk to Kayla.*

Go ahead, mi corazón. I'll wait for you. He retreated, but he only moved over by the picnic tables. If some of Miguel's fleeing minions decided to come back, he would be at her side in an instant.

Penny shifted back. Her human body was tired and sore from her efforts as a wolf, but that didn't matter as long as she got to talk to Kayla. She stretched her fingers as her claws returned to fingernails and stepped up to the ethereal being who'd led them to victory. "Kayla, I'm so sorry for bringing you back. I've wanted to see you for so long, but not like this."

Kayla turned to her, the brilliant blue light around her slowly beginning to fade. "It's all right. I'm glad I could help."

"I don't quite understand," Penny admitted. "I didn't do the binding part of the spell so you could have your own free will, but how were you strong enough to rally the rest of the ghosts?"

Kayla reached out and took Penny's hand, sending a bolt of energy up Penny's arm. "Because of you. I've been dead for years, but you've always kept me close to your heart. You've spoken to me every day, and it's kept a connection open between us. I think it also has something to do with how young I was when I passed. There was still a lot of potential left in me, and I guess I was saving it for something good." She smiled, an apparition, but still the same old Kayla.

Penny felt a tear spill onto her cheek. She let it fall, knowing there would be plenty of others behind it. "I have to tell you something."

"I don't have much time." Kayla brought up her other hand, and she and Penny intertwined their fingers. "I've used up most of my energy already."

"It's okay. I've been rehearsing this for a long time, just in case I ever found a way to talk to you." Tears streamed down her cheeks like a hot flood now. "I'm so sorry about what happened that night. I was driving, and it was all my fault. I would do anything to go back in time and change things so that I could have you with me again. I hope you can forgive me for what I've done."

"Forgive you?" Kayla pulled Penny forward and wrapped her arms around her. "There's nothing to forgive. It wasn't your fault. It was just an accident. There's a reason I died that night. Maybe it was so I could be here to help you, or maybe it was something else, but either way, I've come to terms with it."

"I just miss you so much." Penny buried her face in Kayla's shoulder, wishing she could hold onto her forever.

"I miss you, too, but I'm always here with you. You'll see me again. Not in this form, but I'm around. Just watch for me." Kayla pulled back, holding Penny at arm's length. The azure flame around her was completely gone now, and she looked pale and drawn. "I've got to go, Penny. But please don't blame yourself. Everything is all right now."

Penny nodded, lifting her hands to clear the tears from her eyes. When she opened them again, Kayla was gone. Only a swirling mist remained. Penny fell to her knees, bawling so hard, her stomach hurt. Warm arms wrapped around her, and she leaned back into Raul. He held her and let her cry.

10

_____

"I HAVE TO ADMIT, THIS ISN'T AT ALL WHAT I EXPECTED WHEN WE WERE called to work on a house in Beverly Hills," Penny admitted as she and the rest of the LASS packed up their equipment. "I was envisioning something modern, with nothing but floor to ceiling windows and state-of-the-art technology."

"I'm glad it's like this," Ingrid said, carefully zipping up a bag and admiring a fireplace surround that they'd been told was hundreds of years old and imported from France. "It's the perfect setting for one of those old whodunnit mysteries."

Wendy sneered at the photographs of all the celebrities and politicians who'd supposedly stayed there or rubbed elbows at parties. "Not exactly my cup of tea, personally."

"Not exactly active, either," Dylan grumbled as he helped load the equipment onto a small cart. They'd needed so many monitors, cameras, and frequency detectors that they hadn't been able to haul everything in with backpacks alone. Besides, this looked more professional.

"Well?" Tammy Jones, the poor realtor who'd been trying to sell the place for months, came trotting into the room in her cream pantsuit. "Did you find anything?"

Raul glanced at Penny. It'd been two months since the incident in the old zoo at Griffith Park. It'd completely drained her, both physically and emotionally. Raul had stayed by her side as much as possible, hoping the trauma hadn't been too much for her. Even though she seemed all right now, he always watched her for any sign that she needed a break.

Penny smiled at the realtor. "Actually, yes. It seems that there's quite a bit of activity in the den and the kitchen."

"Shit." Tammy wrung her hands together. "I was hoping you'd say the complete opposite. Despite how gorgeous this place is, I'm afraid it hasn't been an easy sell, and I think it's the ghosts. If you hadn't found any signs of activity, I was going to add that to the listing. Is there any way you can get rid of it?"

Penny bit her lower lip. "It's more like *them* than *it*. And no, I can't get rid of them for you. It's not as though we're talking about rats or roaches. These were people at some point. The best I can do is try to find a way to communicate with them and see if there's any way we can help them pass on to the next life."

"Could you? Could you really do that?" Tammy's eyes widened under her helmet of perfectly coiffed platinum hair.

"Before you get out your checkbook, you have to understand that there's absolutely no guarantee. All I can do is try." Penny smiled, looking a little nervous.

"That's fine. That's absolutely fine. You just tell me when you need to be here, and I'll make sure to let you in. No, actually, I think I can get you a key and the passcode to the gate. I'm not sure I want to be here myself."

When they'd carried everything out to their vehicles and said goodbye to the other ghost hunters, Raul affectionately put an arm across the back of the seat and around Penny's shoulders as they headed back to Force HQ. "I'm proud of you."

"Why's that?"

He glanced at her as they paused at the end of the driveway, her face illuminated by streetlights. "I know things haven't exactly been easy on you lately, but I can see the sudden boost of interest in the paranormal has been good for you. You've turned your passion into a business."

"Not on purpose," she corrected him. "It turns out a lot of people were just waiting for someone to come along and work on their ghost problems. I tell them they can donate whatever they'd like."

"And they do," he reminded her, "generously. I know you needed some time to work through your grief with Kayla, but now you're out almost every night."

"That's not because of LASS and it's growing popularity."

"No?" He maneuvered his truck through the sparse traffic of the early morning hours.

"It's you. You've been there for me, and I don't want to miss out on a single moment with you. Even when you hardly knew me, you were there for me. You're pretty incredible, Raul." She aimed those gorgeous green eyes at him, flashing in the night.

He felt that deep need stir inside him, the one he couldn't seem to avoid even they were talking about something as bland as what to have for lunch. If he was around her, he needed her. "I have some pretty great inspiration."

They pulled into the garage of the large home that served as headquarters for the Force, where Penny had been staying with Raul. The equipment was safe in the truck for the moment as they slipped upstairs to their room.

"I'm going to take a shower," Penny said as she pulled off her shoes and set them in the closet. "Wanna join me?"

"You always know how to make me an offer I can't refuse." Raul pulled her into his arms and kissed her hungrily, knowing without question that she was his. They couldn't keep their arms and lips off each other as they moved through the bedroom, shedding shoes and shirts as they made their way to the bathroom. His hands roved over her body, taking in every curve and feeling his wolf howl his pleasure.

Penny pulled back and smiled at him before turning on the massive shower head. He watched the tempting roundness of her backside as she bent to adjust the temperature and wondered just how long he'd be able to last.

He stepped in after her and took the bottle of shampoo from her hands. "Let me." He slowly massaged the lather into her damp hair, taking down the shower head to rinse it away. Raul dragged his tongue along the curve of her neck and shoulder before taking her loofah and bath gel from the shelf.

"You don't have to do that," she said.

"I want to." Raul worked the soapy scrubber over her neck and shoulders, down her back, and over her ass. "Turn around."

"Raul!" she giggled.

The way her wet hair clung to her body made Raul's cock spring to attention. "I like to take care of you," he murmured as he soaped up each breast and worked his way down to the juncture of her thighs. "You're a strong woman, Penny, and you're going to be the Alpha of your pack someday, but there are still a few things I can do for you." He was on his knees now, relishing in the lather over her thighs.

She touched his jaw, her emerald eyes soft as they roved over his face. "You do a lot for me, Raul. So much more, I think, than I do for you."

"Not true. You're the part of me I've been missing for so long, and I never thought I'd find you." He began to softly caress the sensitive pearl between her legs with his mouth. "I'm so glad I did," he added, flicking his tongue with a little more pressure. They'd spent their nights together for the last couple of months. At first, he simply held her, knowing she was hurting inside. But then she turned to him, needing him a different way that he was happy to oblige. Now, Raul felt as though he lived his days and nights just waiting for the next time he got to touch her, to kiss her, to hold her against his body and feel their wolves come to life inside them.

"Oh, god." She closed her eyes and pressed her hand to the shower wall. "Raul, you're going to make me wake up the rest of the house."

That only drove him on further as he explored her, his thumbs skimming along the insides of her thighs. He could taste her excitement, and it was driving him wild. Just as she was on the brink, he kissed his way up the curve of her stomach, slowly bringing himself back to his feet as he thoroughly toured each of her full breasts with his tongue, spiraling in toward her nipple. He slid his arm around her lower back to support her, feeling her falling against him.

Penny reached for him, her nails scraping against the muscles of his back as she propped her foot on the side of the tub and moved her back against the wall. She moaned as she guided his throbbing hardness inside, her grip letting him know that she wanted him just as badly as he wanted her.

Raul closed his eyes as he buried his face in her neck. He really had been waiting for this woman all his life. She both completed and complemented him, keeping him in check when he went too far, yet driving him to be the person he was always meant to be. Raul wanted to take all her pain and heartache and make it disappear, because he could handle it as long as he knew she was there for him when it was all over.

He opened his eyes in time to see her tip her head to the side, her eyes closed and her lashes on her cheeks, her mouth open in ultimate pleasure as the water splashed down on her. She was beautiful, not just in body, but in spirit. Her hips moved in perfect timing with his, an ancient dance that only two fated souls could do together. Raul smoothed his hands once again over those hips of hers, unable to get enough. A flood opened up inside him, one he wasn't ready for but couldn't stop. He pressed himself harder against her as he felt his girth increase and every cell in his body thrust in her direction. He crushed his mouth to hers as he gave the final push and emptied himself into her.

But Penny's nails dug into his hips and ass, keeping him pressed to her body. "I'm not done with you yet," she whispered as she ground against him. Her nipples were hard against his chest despite the warmth of the water. "Knowing you get off on me really turns me on."

Raul was more than happy to oblige as her slick heat worked against him, her body tensing as she crested that wave and rode it down, her hands hard against him, demanding him, needing him. Penny's groan of pleasure against his neck made him smile. "Me, too."

———

THEY WOKE up early the next morning, dressing in a rush before dashing down to the kitchen for a quick breakfast. Raul could barely choke down his bagel, washing it down with too much coffee.

"Are you all right?" Penny asked from the other side of the bar as she sliced an avocado.

"I think my wolf is playing jump rope in my stomach," he replied. "I guess I'm a little nervous."

Penny came around the bar and ran a gentle hand down his cheek and up through his hair. "You're cute."

"What?"

"It's cute seeing a big strong guy like you, one who fights all the world's greatest assholes for a living, so nervous about meeting my family." Those green eyes of hers sparkled up at him.

"I can't help it. I know how important you are to them, and I want them to be happy with your choice." Raul knew that in some ways, he had a lot to offer as her mate, but when it came to facing her parents, he wasn't sure it was enough.

"You worry too much. You and I know we're fated to be together. That's enough. I also happen to know that as soon as they see how sweet and perfect and protective you are, they'll be thrilled."

He didn't bother trying to make small talk on the way to her parents' place. Raul was busy rehearsing conversations in his mind, hoping he would say and do all the right things. Penny could tell him it was all going to be fine, but he knew how important this was. It would only create more tension in her life if her family didn't accept him, an outsider from a small pack they'd probably never heard of. So much had gotten better for her lately, and he didn't want to be the one to ruin it.

"Mom? Dad? We're here." Penny led him through the front door and into the living room.

Mr. and Mrs. Granger were seated on a large couch, but they rose as soon as the couple entered the room. Their gaze fell instantly to Raul.

"This is Raul Castaneda," Penny said, making the introductions. "Raul, these are my parents, Bonnie and Dan Granger."

His stomach clenched, but then he saw the looks in their eyes. They were just as nervous and hopeful as he was. Everyone in the room wanted the best for Penny, whatever that might be. Raul smiled and held out his hand. "It's nice to meet you."

Dan smiled as he took Raul's hand. "You, too. We've heard a lot about you."

As they moved through drinks in the living room and dinner in the dining room, Raul felt more and more at home. The Grangers were welcoming, polite, and accepting. Dan listened with interest as Raul told him of his time in the Army and his work with the SOS Force. Bonnie mostly only made small talk, but Raul caught a glimpse of a wink and a nod meant only for her daughter across the dinner table.

"Well? What do you think?" Penny asked Raul later in the evening when the two of them stepped out the back door to have a moment alone.

"Me? I'm more concerned about what they think. Your parents are great. They make me want to go home and see my family." There was something about a comfortable family meal that made him crave that sense of connection.

"You don't have anything to worry about." She took his hand in hers and led him to a wooden bench under the trees. "They definitely like you."

"That's good, because I couldn't stay away from you even if they didn't." He smiled as he kissed her. "I love you, Penny. You mean the world to me."

"I love you, too." She looked up at him, her thumb grazing his cheek, but then she suddenly jerked her head to the side. "Do you see that?"

Raul looked to the back edge of the groomed part of the lawn, just before it turned to woods. A brilliant blue ball of light floated steadily just in front of the trees. It bobbed twice in the air before it rocketed up into the sky and disappeared among the stars. "Kayla?" he asked quietly.

"I think so. And I think she approved of you, too." As she kissed him, all was right in the universe.

———

FORBIDDEN MATE FOR THE SOLDIER BEAR

SPECIAL OPS SHIFTERS: L.A. FORCE

1

JUDE SUTTON OPENED THE FRONT DOOR OF THE SPECIAL OPS SHIFTER Force's headquarters, a sprawling Los Angeles house that he'd come to call home over the last few months. He was getting comfortable there, but that day, he wasn't sure how to feel about what was waiting for him outside.

As soon as he saw his brother Reid standing at the entrance, any doubt vanished from his mind. A short beard had grown out around Reid's boyish smile, and his dark hair brushed against his forehead. He was the same Reid that Jude had always known, and there was something comforting about having family nearby. "Come on in, man! I'll introduce you to everyone. Is this all you brought?" Jude indicated the small, rolling suitcase resting at Reid's feet.

"You know how I am. Always on the run, and I don't need much," his brother replied with a shrug.

"Yeah, I know." Jude was smiling, but that was exactly why he had some reservations about bringing Reid onto the Force in the first place. They were an elite group of special ops soldiers who also happened to be shifters, and they used their skills to help diffuse disputes among local clans. After all, most shifter issues couldn't be brought to the police.

Jude also knew that even though Reid was usually content to flap in the breeze, the Force would be a great place for him. "You showed up at the perfect time, you know. Everyone is here, but we won't start on anything official until tomorrow."

Reid rubbed a hand through his beard uncertainly. "Look, there are some things I need to talk to you about first."

"Just get your ass in here. We'll have plenty of time to talk. I promise." Jude didn't want to talk, because he had a good feeling of what Reid was going to say. He didn't want to be chained down. There was too much of the world to see, and too many things to do. Sure, L.A. was a busy place, but he'd tire of it eventually.

They stepped into the kitchen, where everyone had finished eating dinner and was cleaning up. "Hey, everyone. This is my brother, Reid. Reid, this is Gabe, Emersyn, and their son Lucas. Emersyn is our medical specialist, so you can see her when you have the sniffles. Melody, here, is our bookkeeper and takes care of Lucas."

Emersyn was busy getting Lucas cleaned up from his dinner, but she waved and smiled. Gabe strode forward to shake the newcomer's hand. "Nice to have you on board."

"Amar, here, is the Alpha of our group, and this is his mate, Katalin." Jude made a mental note as he introduced this particular couple that he'd have to let Reid know that Katalin was a vampire. She wasn't going to drink his blood or anything, but it was certainly something to be explained. The fact that vampires even existed had been unknown to them until recently.

Amar held Reid's hand firmly. "If your brother is any example, you'll be a great fit here."

Jude gestured at the couple sitting at the end of the breakfast bar, their legs and arms entwined around each other as they enjoyed a piece of cake together. "Raul, when he's not busy making googly eyes, is our tech guy. This is his mate, Penny."

"It's nice to meet all of you," Reid said.

"I won't harass you with all the specifics of our operating procedures tonight," Amar assured him with a glint in his eye. "We've got plenty of time for that tomorrow."

Reid was uneasy. He didn't need to say it; Jude could sense it. The two of them had been so close growing up that they practically thought like twins at times. Jude poured himself a large mug of coffee despite the late hour and gestured at the doorway. "I'll give you a tour of the house."

"What's up?" he asked as they crossed through the open floor plan of the massive living space. "I thought you were interested in becoming part of the Force, but there's obviously something bothering you."

Reid pressed his tongue inside his cheek. "I want to talk, Jude, but not here. Let's get out and go for a run or something."

Jude set his mug down. "Fine by me. Even working with shifters, I don't seem to ever get enough time in my bear form." They stepped out onto the back deck and skirted the pool, then Jude took a deep breath and let his human form go. His bear was always eager to get out, and there was something about the pain of shifting that Jude found pleasurable. He didn't mind the stretching of his face as it extended into a muzzle, or the pulling of his scalp as his ears lifted to the top of his head. The deep ache that came from the elongation of his spine and the shift in his joints only let him know that he was free. Then there was the tingle of every hair exploding from his human skin, and he was his natural state once again.

Is this safe here? Reid had also morphed, his bear still that same dark color that Jude remembered. His legs and underbelly were nearly black. Being family, they could speak to each other telepathically.

Absolutely. No one can see through these hedges, and we can slip out this way toward the national parks. There's a shitload of them around here. Jude eagerly led the way down the path and out into the wilderness. The sun had just set, and as lights came on all over the city, they escaped to the darkness. His muscles burned as he ran, letting out all the steam that had built inside his human form as he'd dealt with work and decisions and worry. In these moments, he could simply be himself.

They paused at the top of a rocky outcropping, where the stars were just beginning to wink to life overhead. Jude couldn't quite smile in this form, but he still had the same sensation inside. *You don't know how good it is to see you again. You're going to love it here.*

Yeah. Reid stepped out to the very edge of the bluff and looked down over the darkening carpet of trees below them. His inky coloring made him blend in remarkably well with the surrounding landscape. *What exactly is the policy on joining the Force?*

Jude felt his nerves stirring inside him. That was a feeling he'd often known when he was young, and it was only by keeping himself cool and calm that he'd been able to make it as far in life as he had. He wasn't going to let his concerns for Reid change that. *What do you mean?*

I know you pulled some strings to get me here, and I really appreciate it, but—

Don't do this to me, Jude interrupted, his own voice gritty in his head. *You were the one who called me. You were the one looking for the next step in life. Don't come all the way out here just to fucking bail.*

Reid was quiet for a while as he looked up at the stars. *You've still got that weird birthmark on your chest, huh?*

Jude turned away, letting out a huff of exasperation. While his bear was covered in typical light brown fur, a shade that closely matched his human hair, he bore the swirling lines of a helix in silver on his chest. It'd been one thing that Reid always liked to tease him about, even when they were younger. *Get to the point.*

I just don't want to make any life-changing decisions. I'm not sure what the future holds for me right now. If being recruited by the Force means staying with them for the rest of my life, then I can't do it.

Rubbing his shoulder against a tree, Jude thought about this for a moment. Reid had always been the wild one, the unreliable one. He'd gotten the two of them in more trouble than Jude could even remember at the moment. It figured that he'd want to know he had a way out, and it irritated Jude. *The Force has been one of the best things to ever happen to me. You know how tough it was for us growing up. I never had a good sense of family, but I craved it. The Army gave me some of that, but the Force has given me even more. I haven't regretted it for a second.*

So the dude in the Spiderman t-shirt is your brother now instead? Reid teased.

Raul may act like a teenager sometimes, Jude admitted, *but he's a stand-up guy. They all are. And the Force really does function like a clan. We have a strong Alpha in Amar, and we work well together.*

Reid shook his head, the movement shivering down his neck and back. *I'm not trying to knock what you have going on here.*

It certainly didn't seem that way to Jude, but he wasn't interested in starting an argument. With a deep breath, he let himself fall back into his human form. Some things were easier to talk about outside his head. He sat and let his legs dangle over the cliff. "You've just got me worried."

Reid, also back on two feet, settled down next to him. "You don't have to worry about me, Jude. I'm not a scared little kid anymore. I'm a grown man, and I've seen combat just like you have."

"Easy enough for you to say. You were younger when it all

happened, and you probably don't remember it the way I do." Jude looked off to the right, the images of those days as a child flashing unwillingly before his eyes. It was one of those things he'd tried to talk himself out of remembering, telling himself that it didn't really matter because it'd happened so many years ago. But it never worked.

"I remember," Reid countered. "I remember being at the Hoffmans that night, and that Mom said she and Dad would be back as soon as she could. And then they weren't. You certainly wanted to handle things, though."

Jude pressed his lips together. "I was trying really hard to be strong for you. I mean, you were my little brother. I can look back on it now and see that I was being completely ridiculous, telling Mrs. Hoffman that if she'd just give us a ride back to our house, I'd make sure you put on your pj's, brushed your teeth, and went to bed." He smiled a little at the simplicity of it; that at that moment, those little daily things were what mattered, even though they'd just been orphaned.

"I have no doubt you would've, too, no matter how much I tried to fight you on it. You've always been like that, Jude. I think you've been responsible ever since you were born." Reid's face twisted into a smile as he recalled their childhood.

Jude sighed. "You're right. Sometimes I wish I could let go of that, but I can't. I still find myself looking for the right way to do things, as if there's ever only one. I've got make all the right choices, ones that will still be right years down the road. I can't say it's been an entirely bad thing, though. It did land me with the Force, and I meant what I said about how good they've been for me."

"Right. Your family," Reid nodded. "I get it. We were dropped off with babysitters that ended up becoming our adoptive parents, and there's no denying that affected us. You've coped by trying to find a place to fit in, and I've mostly coped by trying to make sure I'm left out. There's no perfect way."

"No," Jude said with a frown, "but I do think the Force is the best option for you. You won't have to look for a job or even a place to live. You know you'll be with other shifters, so that means fewer worries about keeping your truth a secret. There's no better option."

Reid raised an eyebrow. "You're not even going to bribe me with the L.A. nightlife or how hot California chicks are?"

Jude elbowed him. "I have no doubt you'll figure that part out on your own."

"It wouldn't matter, because it wouldn't work anyway. I've met my mate."

Blinking out into the darkness but not seeing it, Jude wondered if he'd heard his brother correctly. He swung his head over to see Reid grinning at him. It wasn't the mischievous smirk he was used to, but something completely different. Jude couldn't remember seeing Reid look like that since he told him he was joining the service. "Are you serious?"

"Yeah. Never expected it. In fact, when our unit was sent to Thailand for some cross-training, I just saw it as a chance to see some new places. But then I met Mali, and my entire life changed. I've always heard people talking about meeting their fated, but I didn't think it would happen to me. It's incredible."

"Wow." Jude was genuinely happy for his brother. He'd felt that fated pull before, too, and it'd been just as remarkable as everyone said it would be, except he couldn't do anything about it. A pang of jealousy stabbed through his heart as he extended his hand to shake Reid's. "Congrats."

"Thanks, man. I actually brought her back to the States with me. That's why I'm concerned about committing to the Force. I'm not just making decisions for myself anymore, you know?"

"I get it. You should've just told me."

Reid shrugged. "Sure, but just blowing into L.A. and announcing that the rest of my life is being mapped out isn't really me. Come to think of it, settling down with a mate isn't really me, either. I don't know. I just thought it was better to say it in person."

"Yeah. Of course." Jude bit his lip, thinking about Annie. How long had it been since he'd seen her? Did she even remember him? There wasn't much reason for her to. It was yet another time in his life that Jude wished he could completely forget. God, it would've made things so much easier.

"I realize it wouldn't necessarily be up to you, but if I *did* decide to stay, would it be an issue for Mali to stay, too?" Reid's look changed from that innocent, 'I-hope-you're-happy-for-me' look to one of grave concern.

It made Jude realize that Reid was so much more of a man than the last time he'd seen him. Jude had worried when Reid joined up, just a fresh-faced kid who was determined to change the world. Apparently, the world had changed Reid, and only for the better. "Probably not.

You saw that most of the members already have their mates here. We're all shifters, and we know how important it is."

"What about you? Haven't you found anyone to settle down with?" Reid asked. "I'm sure the girls out here are just falling all over you and your strong-and-silent-type routine."

Jude felt his brows lowering. It was just the way he was, and whether people liked it or not, that was their problem. But these thoughts were making his anger simmer just under the surface of his skin, vibrating down to his bear, daring it to come back out again. Getting into an argument with Reid wasn't a good way to make his brother stay, nor would it help his own mood. "No. Not really."

"Well, you never know. Like I said, I never imagined I'd meet Mali. I'll tell you the whole story sometime. And I can't wait for you to meet her. I think you'd really like her."

"I'm sure I would."

Reid pushed himself up from their perch on the cliffside and then paused. "You sure you're okay?"

"Yeah."

"I mean, I know we haven't been around each other much lately, but I do still like to think I know you better than anyone else in the world. If something's up, you can tell me. In fact, I really hope you do. I don't want you sitting here telling me it's no problem for Mali to be around, and then find out it is."

"No," Jude replied quickly, realizing he'd given Reid the entirely wrong idea. "That's not a problem at all. Of course, we'd have to talk to Amar out of courtesy, but I'm sure it'll be fine. I've just got a lot of shit on my mind right now."

"Okay. Well, you know where I'm at if there's anything you want to talk about." Reid hesitated a moment and then spoke again. "I should be getting back to the hotel and talking to Mali."

"Right. You go on, then. I think I'm going to stay out here for a little while."

Reid looked like he wanted to argue with him, but the two brothers had always been pretty good about letting the other live his own life. When Reid had been young and particularly wild, he'd always counted on Jude to pick him up if things got out of hand. Jude knew that Reid would listen when his mind was heavy and he needed to unload a little. Their lives hadn't been perfect, but their relationship was about as good as it got.

Reid turned to leave, shifted back onto four feet, and lumbered off into the darkness. Jude leaned back and tipped his gaze to the sky, automatically focusing on Ursa Major. His mother had told him so many years ago that it was the first great bear, and the stars that composed it represented the spirit of all the bear shifters who'd ever existed. Ursa Minor nearby was just as important, depicting all the young bear shifters who were still figuring out who they were.

Jude knew, as a rational adult, that the constellations didn't really mean anything. They could be helpful for navigation or telling time, or even for locating a comet that happened to be coming nearby, but they were just random arrangements of stars. He still enjoyed looking at them and thinking of all the ancestors who'd come before him, even if he didn't know who they were. Somehow, people were always looking for guidance from the stars, even though it wasn't going to get them anywhere.

The chill of the night had seeped in around Jude without him noticing. Without his bear fur, it was starting to sink into his flesh. He got to his feet, cast one last glance at the sky, and turned for home.

Home. That was a term he'd struggled with. For most, home was the place where you grew up, where you went when the rest of the world had turned against you, where your parents were still waiting with open arms. For him, home had been many places across the globe. It'd been the Hoffmans' home, which they'd generously opened up to the boys. It'd been a small dorm room with little more than a bed and a bookshelf, and it'd been a tent that floated through the sands of the Middle East at the whim of his commanding officer. The house the Force had chosen as their L.A. headquarters was home now, but how long would that last? Would things change for him? Did Reid have a point about making permanent decisions? Jude shook his head. He didn't really want to know. He just wanted to be sure his brother was taken care of, and everything after that would fall into place.

2

ANNIE MARTINEZ STEPPED INTO THE KITCHEN OF HER CLAN'S CLUBHOUSE, the place she'd called home for her entire life. It was a sizable kitchen, one that was more than capable of handling the steady influx and outflow of members as they came and went. It was always a place where the other bears could go when they needed a place to stay, whether they were waiting for the paperwork on a new place or because they were out of a job. The Martinez clan would always take care of their own.

But when she checked the large marker board next to the fridge, Annie frowned. "Jordan?"

No response.

She strode through the kitchen and poked her head into the living room.

Austin was slumped on the couch, his latest guitar in his hands, but he looked up and smiled when he saw her. "Hey, cutie. What's up?"

Annie inwardly rolled her eyes. She'd been ignoring Austin for years, yet he kept spouting off these ridiculous and degrading names as though they were going to impress her eventually. "I'm looking for Jordan. Have you seen him?"

Austin shrugged as he plucked out a few notes. "I think he's upstairs packing. Why don't you come over here and I'll play you a song?"

"Uh, thanks, but I've got things to do." She turned for the door.

"It'll be a good one, I promise."

Steeling her spine, Annie turned back around. "I appreciate the offer, but it's not really my thing."

His bright blue eyes never left her as he stood up and set his guitar on a floor stand. Austin advanced toward her, stopping when he was only inches away. He reached up and ran a finger along her jawline, his lips softening. "Annie, I don't think anyone in this clan really understands you."

Her gut contracted. "Why do you say that?" Austin was just not her type. He'd played in tons of metal bands, and his style fit the stereotype: jailhouse tats, under-shaved hair that was longer on top, and a ring through his eyebrow. He might have been hot to some women, but Annie knew how rotten he was at his core. She'd known him forever, and she wasn't interested.

"Come on. You're constantly making sure everyone else has what they need, whether you're making up a bed for someone who comes in off the street in the middle of the night or helping Jordan get a Christmas present for whoever his girlfriend of the month is. Who takes care of you?"

Ah, so that was it. Just some old bit, recycling a pickup line that had probably worked on some bimbo in his past. Austin was right that others didn't understand her, but that wasn't why. "I've got things to do, Austin." She turned on her heel and headed for the stairs.

By the time she got to the second level, Austin had plugged his guitar into his amp and was thrashing away. Sighing, Annie passed her own room and headed toward her brother's. The door was open a crack, and she knocked on it lightly before pushing it the rest of the way open.

Jordan looked over his shoulder and smiled. "Hey, little sis. What's up?"

Annie frowned at the clothes strewn all over the bed and spilling out of the closet. "I thought you were packing for your next trip. You don't even have your suitcase out."

"Yeah, I do. It's over there. Somewhere." He gestured at a cluttered corner of the room.

"Okay, then why does it look like a damn Goodwill tornado in here?" she challenged, picking up a silk shirt and deepening her frown as she studied the wrinkles. "I thought you were supposed to be some Hollywood hotshot actor. How are you going to go out in *this?*"

Her brother snatched the shirt out of her hand, crumpled it into a ball, and chucked it into a duffle bag. "Us *Hollywood hotshots* usually have lovely assistants that unpack everything and steam it. I don't have to worry about any of that bullshit. You should know that by now."

They'd barely started the conversation, and Annie was already feeling tired. She didn't like to see things done improperly, and an Alpha ought to feel the same way. But Jordan didn't seem to care. "I do know that, but I still think it sucks for you to take advantage of them. Those poor production assistants probably don't get paid nearly enough to have to put up with your ass."

He let out a bark of a laugh. "Annie, you forget who I am! They're scrambling to come to my hotel room."

"I want to talk, Jordan. The last thing I need is another arrogant dick around this house." Annie shoved a pile of ties aside and sat on the corner of the bed.

"Austin after you again?" he asked as he moved to his dresser and hunted down a comb. "You know, you might want to give him a chance."

"Why?" This wasn't the first time he'd said it.

Giving up on the comb, Jordan moved a pile of books off a chair, turned it around, and sat in it backward. "Come on, Annie. At least just think about it. Agree to go on just one date with him and see how it is."

Annie's lips puckered sourly at the thought. "Oh, I'm sure it'd be *great*. He'd take me out to some dive bar where some asshole would spill beer all over me, and then we'd have a romantic time in the back alley while he tried to put his hand up my shirt."

Jordan rolled his eyes. "He's not that bad, Annie. I wouldn't even consider him as a possibility for you if I thought otherwise."

"He might not be as bad as I like to imagine, but that doesn't mean he's good, either. The two of us have nothing in common, and I don't feel that..." She trailed off. Annie knew what she was supposed to feel when she found the one person who was right for her, but only because she'd heard others talk about it. She'd thought she felt it once, but she'd been deeply mistaken.

"Not everything has to be permanent, Annie. A dinner together doesn't mean you're signing up for the rest of your life. I just think you could benefit from getting out a little. You spend too much time running around the clubhouse, trying to make sure every tiny thing is taken care of. That can't be good for you."

She planted a fist into the mattress. "Someone has to do it! Did you see the marker board by the fridge? I made it very clear that everyone can simply write down what they want from the store. If we're low on bread, just write it on the board. It's not hard, yet no one will do it."

"It's not that big of a deal. Just buy bread." Jordan noticed a pair of khakis draped across his desk, picked them up, and tossed them at the duffle bag he'd thrown the silk shirt in. The pants hit the side and fell to the floor, and he made no move to pick them up.

"You really don't understand, do you? I never know what I need to get from the store. I'm the only one who pays attention to what bills need to be paid. The house would've been sold for taxes if it weren't for me. Everyone just treats this place like it's some frat house they can trash whenever they want to and not clean up after themselves. It's like I'm the only person who cares about this clan!" She hated it when she got angry. That shaking feeling was too similar to the way she felt when she was nervous about something. It also stirred up her inner bear, which only made her even angrier.

"Hey, I care!" Jordan countered, swiping a hand through the air. "How do you think you're able to pay all the bills? That money comes from the jobs that I do, whether it's an action film or some hosting gig or whatever my agent tells me to do. I'm gone all the time, and it's for you guys."

"Yeah, that's right. Go ahead and play the martyr, Jordan. You sacrifice so much when you have to drive to the studio or fly to some exotic location just so the cameras can focus on your pretty face while you get pampered by half-naked women. Give me fucking a break!" She flopped back on the bed, wondering if her life had just been one big nonsensical dream she'd never wake up from.

A crumpled t-shirt landed on her face. "If you're going to cry about it, then just come with me. I'm heading to Vegas this time. You could have a lot of fun."

Annie chucked the t-shirt back at him. "Right, and just leave everyone here to fend for themselves. They might be grown shifters, but they sure as hell don't know how to manage the clan on their own." She took a deep breath, realizing she was getting far too angry.

"Jordan, I came up here because I was frustrated with the house, but there's something I really need to talk to you about."

He rolled his desk chair a little closer, looking worried. "What is it?"

She sat up and folded her legs underneath her. "Jordan, you're the Alpha of our clan. I know you have this great acting career, but it's not fair that you're always off shooting on location. An Alpha should be home leading his clan more than anywhere else."

His shoulders sagged and he shoved himself up from his chair, tossing several more random items in his bag. "You know, you tease me about playing the martyr, but what about you? The only thing I ever hear is that you don't think I'm doing enough for the clan, yet I don't hear anyone else complaining."

"Like they're going to complain right to your face when they're thrilled just to be able to say they know you," she mumbled. Annie had seen her brother's face grace the covers of far too many magazines, and it wasn't special to her anymore. "I just think the responsible thing to do is to stay home and take care of the members."

He cracked a short, derisive laugh. "I wish you could see just how funny this is."

"What?"

"Annie, don't you remember what things were like when we were younger? Back when Uncle Jack was still the Alpha and you weren't so concerned about the job I was doing? You were always gone. You were out looking for trouble at all hours of the day and night, and I was constantly worried about you. When I did catch up with you and tried to say something, you'd just toss some hateful words at me and leave again. You sure didn't want me taking care of you, yet you come to me now and say I'm not taking care of everyone else." His handsome face had transformed from that of a carefree actor to a pissed off Alpha.

It only angered Annie even more. "I was a kid, Jordan. I was just old enough to get myself into trouble, but still young enough not to want any guidance. Not from you or our parents or anyone else. You can't still be holding that over my head."

But Jordan was on a roll. He picked up a pen and tapped it against his other hand thoughtfully. "What's even more ironic is that you don't want to have anything to do with Austin, yet he's exactly the type of guy you would've gone out with back in the day just to piss me off."

"If you think Austin is so fucking great, then why would you say he's the kind of guy you'd be pissed to see me with? You can't just pick and choose what works better for you on any given day, Jordan. I know they let you do that when you're on the set. If you want bagels, then they dump all the doughnuts in the trash and get them for you. Real life, the kind the rest of us lives, doesn't work that way."

"I live a very *real life*, thank you very much." Jordan was packing in earnest now. He still wasn't folding any of his clothes or paying much attention to what he was bringing with him, but the bag was filling up quickly. "I think you're the one who needs a reality check."

Annie let out a puff of air, willing to let that one go if she could just make her point. "Jordan, things are different now. You're not just some kid who knows he'll have to take over someday. You *are* the leader of this clan. The very livelihood of everyone in it depends on you. I'm happy to help in any way I can, but it shouldn't feel as though I'm the only one working toward that goal."

"Fine. When I get back from Vegas, I'll sit everyone down and remind them to put the groceries on the marker board. Does that suit you?" He zipped the duffel sharply.

"I think you should quit your acting career. I know you enjoy all the money and fame, but the exposure is too risky for people like us."

Jordan had started to pick up his bag, but now he slammed it back down on the bed. "What? What are you talking about?"

"Everywhere you go, people are trying to take your picture. It's only a matter of time before you do the wrong thing in the wrong place and someone figures out you're a shifter. That'll hurt everyone. You, me, our clan, every other shifter group in the world. It's a huge secret to keep." She pleaded with him with her eyes, mentally begging him to understand.

"Like you'd know anything about keeping that a secret, considering you've never shifted in your life." Jordan snatched the bag and turned for the door.

Annie felt a pit hollow out in her stomach as tears blurred her eyes. She could take the ridicule from anyone else, but not him. Jordan had never insulted her like that, not even when they were kids. She clamped her teeth together, trying to find some response.

"I'm sorry." Jordan dropped the bag once again, this time by the door, and came to sit with her on the bed. "That was a low blow. I shouldn't have said that."

"It's fine," she lied. "Besides, you're just making my point for me."

"What do you mean?"

"I'm not a *real* shifter, and—"

"Yes, you are," he interrupted.

Annie gave him a sharp look, one she'd developed when they were younger and her hardheaded brother wouldn't stop arguing with her just because he was so determined to be right. "No, I'm not. I know there's a bear inside me because I can feel it, but I've never seen it. There's nothing I can do to bring it out. I'm technically in charge when you're gone, but no one respects me. I might as well just be some human servant the rest of you keep around because you feel sorry for me. I can't keep doing this, Jordan."

He was silent for a moment, thinking. Jordan had always been like that. At times, it absolutely infuriated Annie when she felt like he was taking up everyone else's time while he mulled over a situation. He was impulsive in most aspects of his life, so it was difficult for her to understand what made him occasionally decide to slow down.

"I know it's been tough on you not to be able to shift," he finally said. "I saw it as we were growing up, and all the other kids would shift and run off to play in the woods. I know that made you feel left out. But I think there's another side of this situation you could focus on instead."

Annie looked up at him curiously. "What's that?"

"You think you're stuck in your human form, but it just means you have a different way of looking at the world than the rest of us. Don't look at me like that! It's not necessarily a bad thing. Maybe there's a strength to your human side that the rest of us don't see because we're too fixated on our bears. I'm not saying I know what that is, exactly, but I will say you're far more organized and focused."

She rolled her eyes. "Oh, how exciting."

"It's not a bad thing, especially because it means you do such a good job of helping me run this place. I couldn't do it without you, Annie."

"That's all well and good for you to say, but you don't see what it's like when you're gone. If I've got you standing behind me, the rest of the members are willing to listen. As soon as you leave, I might as well be speaking gibberish. You have no idea how little respect they have for me." She could hear the poutiness in her own voice and she hated it, but she was being truthful. The other members didn't seem to care at all about what she said or did, or even that she was the Alpha's sister and technically in charge when Jordan was gone.

He let out a huff of a sigh. "Annie, think about it. If you were so low in their eyes, would someone like Austin be so interested in you? He's a prominent member of our clan, shifts any time he wants to, yet he's never said a single thing about you not being able to. I don't think it matters as much to everyone else as it does to you."

Jordan had a point, and Annie felt it drive home straight to her heart. "Maybe. I'll think on that one. But even if everything you say is true, I think something's going on among our members."

"Like?"

"Most of it is just a feeling, but there are things I notice, too. They stop talking as soon as I walk in the room. Or a few of the men head off and reconvene without saying anything to the rest of us, even when I've got something scheduled for that day." It wasn't anything concrete, but it was something she'd been worried about for a few months. There was a ripple of tension somewhere in the clan, but she couldn't put her finger on it.

"I think you're paranoid."

"I am not! I might not be the Alpha, and I might not be as in touch with my bear as the rest of you are, but that doesn't mean I'm wrong!" Damn it! They'd been heading on a decent track with the conversation, but once again, he had to blow her off. It was always like that with Jordan, and Annie suspected it was because he just didn't want to deal with any problems that might stop him from going to Vegas.

"Okay, okay. I'm sorry. I'll look into it as soon as I get back from my trip, okay? This part of the shoot shouldn't take more than a couple of days, as long as it all goes as planned. Then we can sit down and discuss this in depth. As it is, I'm going to be late for my flight." He patted her on the leg and stood. "You'll do just fine while I'm gone. I promise."

Annie pressed her lips together to stop herself from saying something she might regret. Jordan was good at getting under her skin, but he was still her big brother and she loved him. "Do you need a ride to the airport?"

"Nah. The producer is sending someone to pick me up."

When he'd left, Annie made her way back down to the kitchen. Austin's music was still blaring from the other room, but at least that meant he was busy.

The fridge door shut, revealing a slim woman with her auburn hair pulled up into a ponytail. She smiled at Annie. "Hey! I just updated the grocery list for you. It looks like we're out of pretty much everything."

Annie shrugged. "That's what happens when you live with a bunch of hungry beasts. Here, if you check the fridge and pantry, I'll write everything on the board." She picked up a marker, glad that there was at least one person in the clan who listened to her.

"Definitely meat of all kinds," Michelle said as she peeked into the freezer. "It's like a wasteland in here, and I heard a few of the guys talking about having a barbecue this weekend."

"Of course," Annie muttered under her breath as she scribbled on the board.

"I wouldn't worry about it," Michelle said, immediately picking up on her friend's irritation. "I mean, there are a lot of guys in this clan, and of course they're all bears. They pretty much live to eat."

"I know, but I just had a big conversation with Jordan about how this clan is run and how frustrated I am with all of it. You know, all that stuff we've talked about. I guess I was hoping that if I sat down with him and hashed it all out, he'd finally listen. But no, I'm stuck with everything the same as it's ever been."

"Ice cream," Michelle said as she shut the freezer. "Definitely lots of ice cream. And I know you're frustrated with Jordan, but it could always be worse. We've heard of those other clans where their Alphas and other high-standing members decide to take over territory that doesn't belong to them or use their members for other financial gains. Jordan's arrogant and self-centered, but I don't think he'd let things get too far out of hand."

"You're just saying that because you think he's cute," Annie teased.

Michelle was more than willing to own up to it. "Sure, but I do still think it could be far worse."

"Maybe, I'm just so frustrated. I feel like I'm spinning my wheels, like I used up all my potential when I was young on running around and trying to find new ways to irritate my elders. Now what? I just sit around and make grocery lists and harp at everyone for not picking up their socks? It's not exactly a glamorous life."

"Flour. We're getting a little low on sugar, but I think we're fine for now. Tea. All the good chips are gone." Michelle had her head in the big pantry cabinet, sifting through what was left. She emerged with two bars of dark chocolate and handed one to Annie. "You need this. And a man."

"Not that argument again," Annie said as she rolled her eyes, but she took the candy bar and tore it open. "Jordan was yet again telling me I should go out with Austin."

Michelle had her lips pursed and her eyes raised.

"Don't."

"But it could be good for you! You have to admit he's kind of cute, and who wouldn't want to date a musician?"

Annie leaned on the counter. "Someone who prefers peace and quiet."

"I think there's more to it than that," Michelle noted.

"You're right." Annie had been thinking about it a lot, and it was time to say it out loud. After all, Michelle was someone she knew she could trust implicitly. "Austin isn't completely terrible, in the same way that Jordan isn't a completely terrible Alpha. But you know just as well as I do that I'm supposed to feel something. I'm supposed to get that feeling inside that makes me practically unable to control myself. I don't have that with Austin at all, and I don't know if I ever will. I've never met another shifter who can't shift, so I'm in completely unknown territory. I thought I felt it that one time with Jude, but he obviously didn't feel anything, and it's supposed to be mutual." She tore off another hunk of chocolate, wishing it made her feel better.

"Oh, yeah. That's the guy who used to hang out with your brother, right?"

Jude hadn't been in their clan, he'd only come around to visit now and then. Annie remembered him well; how couldn't she? "Yeah. I swore there was something there. I was so excited because I wasn't sure I'd ever feel it. Jude hardly even looked at me, though, so I must have been mistaken."

Michelle frowned and pulled her close. "Don't get too down on yourself. I think we shifters put way too much pressure on ourselves to find our mates. It's a lot to think about, especially when you consider that the right person for you could be on the other side of the world. And then there's the whole debate on if there's only one person, or if there are more."

Annie sighed, exhausted from so much thinking and feeling. "Yeah, I know. And I know I'm hard on myself. I just feel like I really need to be doing the right thing, especially with Jordan being Alpha."

"I think you're more concerned about it than the rest of us are. Come on. I'll throw some shoes on, and we can go grocery shopping together."

"Thanks." Annie smiled at her friend. There were a lot of things in her life that she'd like to change, but at least she had one person who seemed to understand.

JUDE REFILLED HIS COFFEE MUG AND CHECKED THE TIME. REID WAS supposed to call back soon, after he'd had a chance to discuss a few things with Mali, and this wasn't the time to be a flake. Sure, his brother had faced some hard times since leaving the military, and every soldier who suddenly found himself without the brotherhood of the Army needed time to adapt. He'd known men who'd roamed the country without a plan for a full year, just trying to find something that called to them as much as the service had. Hell, he'd considered doing that himself when he'd been honorably discharged. Jude didn't want to see that happen to Reid. He knew the Special Ops Shifter Force could be a great home for him, and he was eager to serve alongside his true blood brother.

His cell vibrated against the counter, and Jude picked it up, expecting to see Reid's number. The top of the screen flashed an indicator saying the call was being imported from his old line, the one he kept before he had an exclusive phone created for the Force by Hudson Taylor in the D.C. unit. It wasn't a number he recognized, but he answered anyway. If it was a telemarketer, then maybe he could have a little fun. "Yeah?"

"Jude?"

The skin along his spine rippled at the sound of her voice. No, that couldn't be right. It'd been years since he'd heard from her, and she had no reason to call him. He cleared his throat. "Uh, yes?"

"It's Annie. Jordan's sister?"

"Hi." He leaned his free hand on the counter, blinking. "It's, um, been a long time."

"I know, and I'm really sorry to bother you. I wasn't even sure if you were stateside right now." Her voice was desperate.

Jude's mind instantly flashed back to one of the last times he'd been around Annie, when he'd come home on leave and visited his best friend, Jordan.

JUDE SAT on the sofa in the living room, quietly relieved to be back in civilization instead of sleeping in a sandy tent. It wouldn't last long, and he'd be back overseas before he knew it, but he'd earned his break. Jordan, his best friend since grade school, seemed more than happy to host him. That is, until his little sister had walked in at midnight.

"Annie!" Jordan shot up off the couch, his fists curled as he marched toward his sister. "I've been trying to get a hold of you for hours. Where have you been?"

"My phone died, okay?" She was tiny compared to her older brother, all big eyes and waves of dark brown hair. She flashed a look around Jordan at Jude, and her jaw tightened. "I'm fine."

"Were you out with that Dakota guy again?"

Annie tried to move past Jordan to the kitchen, but he wouldn't let her. "What's it to you?"

"The guy's an asshole, that's what."

"Kind of like you're being right now?" She slipped past him through the doorway and glanced once again at Jude. "Sorry to interrupt your visit. I just need to grab my jacket."

"Of course." Moving out of the way so that she could retrieve the garment from the back of the couch, Jude felt something surge inside him. Whatever was happening there was none of his business. As the future Alpha of his clan, it was up to Jordan to take care of his family. Even so, Jude was overcome with the urge to sweep her up into his arms and fix whatever was bothering her.

"You don't need your jacket," Jordan barked. "It's late, and you need to be in bed. We've got a meeting in the morning."

"I don't care. It's not like anyone cares about what I have to say,

anyway." Annie shoved past her brother and left once again, slamming the door behind her.

Jordan plopped back down on the couch and took a swig of his beer. "She kills me, man. I worry about her. This asshole Dakota that she's dating isn't any good for her."

Jude was still staring out the door Annie had gone through, feeling as though his heart had gone through it, too. Annie had always been a pretty girl, but something was different. He grabbed his beer to drench the desert that now occupied his throat. "How old is she now?"

"Eighteen, but that doesn't mean she can just do whatever she wants. The clan comes first, you know?"

Jordan rambled on about responsibility and how important it was for shifters to stick together, but Jude wasn't listening. He was thinking about Annie, and how strange it'd felt to be around her. She wasn't just Jordan's little sister anymore. Never before had she evoked that strange, swirling feeling in Jude's gut that made him want to shift just to get past it.

"...kick the ass of any guy who tries to take advantage of her."

That part caught his attention. "Right. Of course." This was Jordan's younger sister, not just some random hot little piece of ass. That was difficult territory to navigate.

"Are you there?"

"Uh, yeah. Sorry. I'm here." He hardly even knew what to say. Why would she suddenly call him after all this time? "How have you been?"

"Not good, actually." Her voice was thick, as though she was trying not to cry. "I know this is a really slim chance, but have you spoken to Jordan lately?"

Jude ran a hand through his hair and then quickly put it back in place, even though she obviously couldn't see him. Hell, his hand was shaking. "Can't say that I have. He seems to be pretty busy now that he's a Hollywood big shot. We've only managed to hang out a couple of times in the last few years."

"Damn. Okay."

"What's going on?" Jude realized Annie wasn't just calling to catch up on old times.

Annie sighed. "Jordan's missing. He was supposed to be back in town after shooting a movie on location. His flight landed yesterday, but he never called to have me pick him up at the airport. Sometimes he just catches a cab or someone from the studio gives him a ride, but I haven't even gotten a text. No one has seen or heard from him, but the rest of the clan thinks I'm just overreacting. I don't know where he is, and I don't know what to do."

"I'll help you." His reply came automatically, without even thinking about it.

A heavy pause sounded over the line, but when Annie spoke again, it was with disbelief. "You will?"

There was no doubt in his mind. "Absolutely." Jude was already grabbing his keys and heading out toward the garage. "I assume you guys are still here in L.A.?"

"Here? You mean, you're in the city, too? I guess I just assumed you were somewhere else, with your military career and everything."

As he started up his sedan and pulled out of the garage, Jude had one thing on his mind, and his inner bear echoed it: *get to Annie as fast as you fucking can.* "I'm actually discharged now, and my current job has me back in the area. I assume you guys still have the same clubhouse?"

"Yep."

"I can be there in about twenty minutes, depending on traffic. I'll be right over." He swung out onto the street, hardly paying attention to the other cars on the road.

"Thanks. Drive safe."

Jude hung up. The logical part of his mind, the one that focused on missions, wondered if he were doing the right thing. After all, Annie hadn't actually asked for help, only if Jude had seen Jordan. He was pulling himself away from any other Force business that might need attention, as well as his brother.

But those gut feelings that he was always trying to tamp down came bubbling to the surface. He'd just been thinking about Annie a few nights ago when he'd been out with Reid. How strange was it for her to be calling him now? Pure coincidence? And that urgency in her voice. It pulled something out from the very center of himself, a place where he'd stuffed so much of his life into the tiniest, densest ball possible to keep it hidden from his day-to-day life.

Jude slammed the steering wheel, frustrated at himself for not being able to look at this logically. He'd known Annie when she was younger, but when he'd come home on leave and had the chance to visit Jordan, his bear took notice of her in an entirely different way. It didn't mean it was actually that fated pull that he'd been waiting so long for. She was blazing hot, and he was just a young horny guy who hadn't hooked up in a while. There didn't have to be any more to it than that, nor did there have to be any more to their present situation than the fact that she needed help, and he could give it. Jude had one hell of a set of resources at his disposal, after all.

Parking in a side alley, Jude stepped around to the front of the house. Built over a hundred years ago, the Martinez clan house was just as Jude remembered it. A portico jutted out to cover a brick porch. He and Jordan used to climb out the second-story window and hang out on the roof of that portico all the time, dreaming about girls and what they'd do with the rest of their lives. Just to the right was a towering banana tree that took up the entire strip of yard on that side of the walkway.

Jude stepped up to the door, feeling energy move and curl inside his veins as he rang the doorbell. He was just there on business. Helping other shifters was what he did for a living now. If someone called them for help, regardless of whether the Force members knew them or not, they'd help. A nagging voice in the back of his head reminded him that he hadn't even run this past Amar, but he let it go.

Annie answered the door herself, and the second she did, Jude knew he was in trouble. She was no longer a whip of a girl that was his best friend's little sister. Her dark hair and eyes spoke of the Puerto Rican ancestry that Jordan had mentioned at some point. Glazed in a light red, her full lips were in a firm line that said she was all about business, just like the fist on her curved hip.

Somehow, she seemed just as surprised as he did, standing there blinking at him for a moment before she said anything. "That was faster than I expected. Come on in."

Jude followed her into the living room. The furniture had changed since the last time he'd been there, but the house still had the same feeling to it. The thick wood trim and floral wallpaper recalled a time when Hollywood was only in the first stages of being known for the film industry. It was probably old and oppressive to some, but Jude had always found the homeyness of it to be comforting.

"Let's go out here. I don't want to talk inside." Annie led him straight through the house and out the back door, stepping into a gazebo near a large shade tree.

Jude hesitated as he followed her. He felt his bear pounding at the underside of his skin, demanding to claim what he'd been denied for so long. He felt a prickle on the back of his neck as it gained ground, threatening for his other form to come thrusting to the surface. Jude willed the beast back to the best of his ability and sat across from her, as far away as possible without being rude.

"I'm sorry if I jumped the gun on coming out here," he said. "It just sounded like this was a serious situation."

Annie leaned forward and opened a mini-fridge embedded into a serving table in the center of the gazebo. It was hard not to look at her body, studying the luscious way she'd filled out. Even something as simple as the way her dark lashes lay as she looked down into the fridge was driving him absolutely wild. Jude wanted to jump up from his seat and pull her onto his lap. He could easily envision the startled look in those dark chocolate eyes, and his mind quickly changed it to one of intrigue as she let him protect her from whatever the world was throwing at her. No! This was Jordan's sister. There were a million reasons why he couldn't do this. The cold bottle of lemonade she put in his hand only went a short way toward cooling the fire roaring inside him.

"It is a serious situation," Annie said as she sat back down and used her free hand to swipe her thick hair away from her neck against the heat. "It's made all the more serious by the fact that no one around here will listen to me about it."

"Just tell me everything that's happening, and we'll figure it out from there." If he could focus on the details of her crisis, then maybe he could distract himself.

She leaned forward, bracing her elbows on her knees, and took a deep breath. "Jordan was heading to Las Vegas to shoot part of a movie. It was only supposed to take a couple of days. He hasn't come home or called, and he's not answering his phone. I tried talking to the airline to see if he was on his flight, but with all the privacy laws these days, they wouldn't tell me a thing. Same with the hotel where he was staying. I don't have the number of anyone who was involved in the production of the movie." Annie flapped her hands in the air in frustration. "I don't know what else to do."

"It sounds like you've certainly given it a good start. You mentioned that the rest of the clan wasn't worried?"

She made a face he didn't know how to interpret, but the corners of her mouth turned down in disgust. "Everyone thinks I'm just getting upset over nothing. They think Jordan just stayed in Vegas so he could have a little fun. I'm not saying that's impossible, but it's really weird for him to not contact me. Besides, he told me he'd help me out with something when he got back." For a moment, Jude saw a flash of the little girl Annie used to be. The last time he'd seen her, she was an irreverent teenager. But he'd also known her before that, when she was still young and vulnerable.

It made him feel sorry for her, especially since she seemed to be tackling this alone. "Has he done that other times? Stay on location after he's done shooting, I mean."

Annie shook her head. "Most of the time, he doesn't have much of a chance. His career has really taken off, but I'm sure you know that. He's actually at the point of turning down roles because he doesn't have the time."

Jude's mind was working through several ideas, and he was grateful for it. He needed a logical procession of steps to keep himself from wondering if Annie's hair was as soft as it looked. "If you can give me his flight number, I might be able to get the information the airline wouldn't give you. I have a few connections."

Annie closed her eyes as her brows drew together, and when she opened them again, she looked like she was going to cry. "I'd really appreciate that, Jude, but I didn't mean for you to get dragged into this. I was just desperately trying to find some way of getting a hold of Jordan, and I thought of you."

Did she have any idea what she did to him by saying she'd been thinking about him? Blood rushed straight to his groin. "Annie, it's fine. This is actually what I do now."

She tipped her head. "Find missing people? Are you a private investigator or something?"

"In a certain way, I suppose you could say that. I'm actually with the Special Ops Shifter Force." He hadn't asked for clearance to tell her about the Force, and he might pay for that later. They tried to keep themselves as secretive as possible. Like any other shifter, the wrong information with the wrong person could spell serious trouble. Jude knew he could trust Annie, though.

Her head pushed back on her neck. "Seriously? I'd heard rumors about that, but I wasn't sure it was real."

"We're real, all right. All of us served as special ops. We're here specifically for people like you in circumstances like this. I've got some great coworkers who can help us find the information from the hotel and the flight, or even if he rented a car. There's a lot we can do." A reassuring smile spread across his face. "I'm sure we can figure out what's going on."

A tear spilled over her lashes and down onto her cheek. As she rose from the bench and crossed the gazebo, she threw her arms around Jude. "Thank you so much! You have no idea how hard this has been on me, and I've felt so alone."

He instinctively wrapped his arms around her, his bear thrashing inside him at being so close. In that moment, the world could've stopped turning and he wouldn't have noticed. She was sexy as hell, but it was so much more than that. Jude swore he felt her bear responding to his, bonding as two souls that had been split apart when the universe was made and then forced to seek each other out to be reunited once again. He was once again overwhelmed with the urge to carry her away and make everything better, no matter what it took.

When she pulled away to sit next to him, Jude felt cold despite the heat of the day. "I really can't thank you enough for this, Jude. Jordan and I don't always get along, but he's my brother. I'm concerned about him, and I can't help but be worried about what would happen to the clan if he didn't return."

"It'll be all right, Annie." He would make sure of it. He could do a lot more than the average guy, and he'd push himself even further than that if it meant making Annie happy.

"What's going on here?"

Jude turned at the new voice. A man stood at the entrance to the gazebo, his pale blue eyes flicking back and forth between Jude and Annie. The newcomer wore a t-shirt with the sleeves cut off to reveal the tattoos that snaked all up and down his arms, and he didn't look pleased. Jude silently cursed himself for being so caught up in Annie that he hadn't even heard the man approach.

"Austin, this is Jude. He's an old friend of mine. Jude, this is Austin. He's one of our clan members."

Austin extended a hand to shake Jude's, being sure to clamp down with a tight grip. "Nice to meet you."

Jude raised an eyebrow, well aware that he was being challenged. He stopped himself from placing his body between Austin and Annie, knowing that would only escalate things. "You, too."

"Annie, you need any help here?" Austin asked pointedly.

Jude felt his jaw harden. There was clearly something happening between the two of them, and Austin didn't want Jude to be there. Was he hiding something, or was it merely his interest in Annie? Jude knew he had no claim over her. Even if she were feeling the same as he was, she was the sister of an Alpha. She had prominent blood and was second-in-command over this clan. She was also his best friend's sister, and Jude was just an orphan who had nothing to offer her. Still, he was choking on the idea of this Austin character being anywhere near Annie, or even part of the same clan.

"Everything is fine. We're just visiting," Annie replied, her eyes practically shooting lasers at Austin.

His brows lowered and he squared his shoulders, looking ready to fight, but Austin gave her a curt nod. "All right, but I'll be right inside watching. Just yell if you need me." He marched away.

Jude scratched the side of his nose, wondering how he could've forgotten. Annie had always loved bad boys like that douche, the kind who would probably be just as likely to hit her as kiss her. He didn't like it, but he had to remember that this wasn't his territory. "I take it he's your boyfriend?"

Annie's mouth tightened as her eyes widened. "Austin? Not a freaking chance!"

"He certainly seemed interested." Jude once again wrapped a shroud of calm, quiet solitude around himself. Without it, it was too easy to fly off the handle and lose his temper.

She snorted as she stood to retrieve her bottle of lemonade from where she'd left it on the other side of the gazebo. "Oh, sure. He's interested, but I don't think he's *genuinely* interested in me."

Jude kept his gaze on her eyes and the cut of her cheekbones. "Why wouldn't he be?"

Annie didn't seem to notice the implied meaning behind his question. "Austin looks like the kind of guy who wouldn't be interested in anything more than a music career in a metal band, but I think he's power-hungry. Jordan is an Alpha and a Hollywood star, and Austin just wants to kiss his ass. I'm not sure how he thinks that's going to work by doing it through me, but I'm not a psychologist." Her face soured as she glanced toward the house.

Resisting the urge to turn around and see if Austin was watching them through the window, Jude returned the conversation to his original reason for being there. "As far as Jordan goes, email me all the information you have and I'll see what I can find. I may have to fly out to Vegas myself if we don't find any other leads to pursue."

"I'm going with you," Annie said instantly. "If Jordan is out there, I want to be the first person to tell him just how pissed I am at him."

The two of them flying off to Vegas together? Once again, Jude felt his body and his mind wandering to places where they didn't belong. "We don't know what's really going on. It could be dangerous."

"I don't care. Jude, I've been spending too long sitting here worrying about everything. Jordan himself called me out for being too invested in the day-to-day running of the house instead of thinking on a bigger scale. I don't want to admit it, but he's right. I need to get out a little more, and I'm plenty capable." She paced back and forth as she spoke, flinging her hands through the air as though she were casting aside any doubts that Jordan or the others had about her.

Jude nodded. "All right. Give me a day to see what I can come up with, and then I'll call you." He stood and turned to go, ready to get out of there. There were too many uncertainties. Could he really believe Annie when she said she wasn't involved with Austin? If Austin was interested in her only as a means to finding power, then why was he so suspicious of Jude? Could it be at all possible that Annie might care for him the same way he cared for her? It would be much easier if he could distance himself from her and focus on the intelligence aspect of finding Jordan.

"Jude." She said his name as he stepped out of the gazebo onto the grass.

Her voice sent a shudder of excitement through his body, and he reminded his bear that he only wanted her because he couldn't have her. "Yeah?"

"Thank you."

He turned to see genuine appreciation in her eyes, and it cut straight to his heart. He'd seen that look before, when he'd served overseas and had helped liberate towns from oppressive leaders. That was the look of the people who needed help, the ones who needed it so badly, they'd do almost anything to get it. Many times, Jude never knew what ended up happening to those people he'd helped. He hoped he'd get to know the rest of Annie's story, at least. "No problem."

He headed back to the house, dialing Raul's number on the way.

4

"LADIES AND GENTLEMEN, PLEASE FASTEN YOUR SEATBELTS AND PUT UP your trays as we prepare for landing at McCarran International Airport in Las Vegas."

Annie did as the flight attendant asked, feeling cramped and stiff despite the short flight from L.A. Jude had argued a second time against her coming with him to search for Jordan, but she'd insisted. To Annie, any amount of danger and intrigue didn't matter to her. She just wanted to find her brother, chew him up one side and down the other for making her worry, and get back home.

Now that they were actually on their way, she was starting to regret it. Though she'd sat next to Jude during the flight, her body surging toward him the entire time, he'd hardly said a word. She'd tried to start conversations with him about the weather or the view, and they always fizzled out after a few exchanges.

It was incredibly frustrating. Annie hadn't expected to feel what she did for Jude when he showed up at her home. When she'd opened the door, she was shocked to find every cell of her body reacting to his presence. He was older now, and he'd matured into a gorgeous, hard-bodied soldier. With his pale brown hair hanging over his forehead and those mesmerizing green eyes, she'd wanted to throw herself over the threshold at him.

He'd come on business, though. He'd come to help his childhood best friend. If the way Jude was acting was anything to go by, Annie didn't have anything to do with it.

She stood and stretched as they waited for their turn to deboard, watching the back of Jude's neck. His brawny frame towered over her, and Annie couldn't help but wonder if other women on the flight had noticed him. The flight attendant who'd smiled so sweetly at him when she'd brought his crackers and a tiny cup of soda had certainly let her gaze linger for a little too long.

"So, what's the plan?" Annie asked as they filtered through the airport toward the luggage carousel. "You said Jordan wasn't on his flight or in his hotel, and you were able to find out that he hadn't rented a car anywhere, but is there anything you did find?"

He glanced at her before quickly reverting his gaze to the spinning rack of suitcases, reaching forward to snag both his and hers in one quick movement. "We really shouldn't talk about it here."

Annie tightened her lips. He didn't seem to want to talk at all, which was going to make this a very long trip, no matter how quickly they were able to find Jordan. "I understand, but it's not like anyone else here is paying attention to us." The airport was busy as passengers darted back and forth to catch their planes or move on to their final destinations, and no one had even given them a second glance.

Jude gave her that look again. "Annie, I realize it might look that way. We need to be as cautious as possible. Let's get settled into our hotel and get a feel for the area. Then we'll talk."

"Fine." Annie kept her mouth clamped tightly shut as she and Jude caught a cab from the airport, thinking about the situation she'd gotten herself into. First, she was in a horrible position with the rest of the clan. Austin had questioned her thoroughly when she'd explained she was leaving, and something had kept Annie from telling him that she was taking a trip with Jude. Annie had never thought she'd be the kind of person who'd lie to her clan members. After all, her job and her life were all about taking care of them. But given the way Austin had reacted to Jude's presence when he'd come to the house, and that no one but her seemed interested in finding out why Jordan hadn't come home, Annie made up a story about visiting a friend who wasn't doing well. Austin had been left in charge, believing she was in Oregon.

Then, there was the problem with Jude. She'd called him in a desperate attempt to see if he'd heard from Jordan, and then he'd shown up. Annie hadn't expected that. Now she was stuck working alongside a man she could hardly resist, and it was making her angry. She was mad at herself for feeling this way about him, and frustrated with him for obviously not wanting to have anything to do with her. Hell, Jude hadn't even wanted her to go to Vegas to search for her own brother. Once again, Annie was just the tagalong that no one wanted.

She squinted out the window at the brilliant sunshine that illuminated the hotels, restaurants, and 24-hour wedding chapels that dotted the city. It might have been a decent place for some folks to visit, but right now, she just wished everything was back to normal.

The cab pulled up in front of the Bellagio, and Annie tried not to look astonished as she got out of the vehicle and gazed up at the tall building while the fountains erupted behind her. She'd known that Vegas would be glamorous, and her brother's career gave him the chance to stay at all sorts of impressive places, but Annie had never been to any of them with him. "This is where he was staying?"

"That's what my sources tell me," Jude replied with his usual solemn manner as he pulled their suitcases out of the trunk and nodded toward the revolving doors.

Annie didn't want him to know just how overwhelmed she was as she took in the expansive lobby with its marble floor and art glass fixed to the ceiling. Every single thing, from the door handles to the light fixtures to the little sign in a flower bed, looked to be top-of-the-line. It made Annie realize just what a sheltered life she'd been living, and it bothered her. If her brother was a big star, and if she was second-in-command of a Hollywood clan, then why did she live such a simple life? It was yet another way that she was different from everyone else around her, and it only made her more irritable as she waited for Jude to check in for them.

The elevator ride to their floor was just as silent as their flight had been. Annie folded her arms in front of her chest, wondering just how long she could handle it. She opened her mouth to ask him what she'd done to anger him when the elevator dinged and let them off on their floor.

"Here's your room," Jude said as he handed her a keycard. "I'm right here, and there's a door adjoining the two. I thought that would be the safest option, just in case." His mouth twitched slightly as he turned on his heel and went to his room. He paused at his door without looking back at her. "Let's take an hour to settle in, and then we can get started."

The luxury that waited for Annie on the other side of the door was fabulous, but she hardly cared as she flopped down on the bed and pulled her cell out of her pocket to call Michelle.

"Hey! How was your flight?"

"Tense, just like everything else." Annie had told Michelle the truth about her trip, and it was nice to have someone to vent to. "I must have done something wrong, but I have no idea what. Jude will barely talk to me. He hardly even looks at me! And I'm not even worried about it being in a romantic way at this point. It's just so obvious that he's avoiding me."

"Don't overanalyze it. Some people don't travel well. From the tone of your voice, it sounds like you're one of them."

Annie scowled at the ceiling. "Maybe, but everything seemed fine when he came to the house. Something changed, and I can't help but wonder if Jordan told him at some point that I can't shift."

Michelle sighed. "Even if he did, it's not like Jude is going to hate you for that. And Jordan would have to have told him a long time ago, since you don't know where he is right now. Just calm down and at least try to enjoy yourself while you're there."

"Easier said than done." Annie's next scowl was directed at the door that joined their two rooms. "It's going to be really awkward."

"What if Jude just doesn't know how to act because he's never had a civilian on a mission with him?" Michelle suggested.

It was reasonable. In fact, it made far more sense than any of the wild thoughts that'd been zinging through Annie's mind. Her body was out of control, craving him, wishing she could do something spontaneous like throw her arms around him the way she had in the gazebo again. Annie's father had always said the most reasonable explanation was usually the right one. "Yeah. You could be right. How's everything going at the house?"

"Oh, fine. Austin is taking advantage of the fact that you put him in charge, but only with dumb guy stuff like starting a poker tournament or a pool party. Harmless, really."

"He doesn't have any access to the finances or anything, so there's only so much he can do." Annie frowned, wishing she'd had a better choice than Austin. Michelle certainly would've been a good one, but she didn't rank high enough to be put in charge without others throwing a fit. "Just take care, and make sure you let me know if you run into any trouble."

"Of course."

After hanging up, Annie pushed herself off the bed and forced herself to unpack, take a shower, and get dressed. She felt a little better, trying to remind herself that it didn't matter if she liked Jude or not. She could be professional, as he was. This wasn't about her or him or anything else. It was about Jordan. Still, she stood in front of the big mirror in the bathroom, trying to decide which shirt she should wear. Something black with a little glitz of sequins at the bottom? Something more casual? The sun was falling quickly, but Annie had no idea what the rest of the evening held for her.

She was forced to make a decision when Jude knocked on the door between their rooms.

"Damn it," she muttered as she threw on the black shirt and crossed the room to let him in.

He didn't actually have to duck to get through the door, but the way he carried his head made it seem as though he had. Why did he have to be so goddamn irresistible? Why did she have the urge to press her head against his chest and listen to his heartbeat? Annie could feel her bear protesting beneath the surface of her skin, angry and frustrated at its continued denial of freedom. She shook it off, reminding herself that she'd already decided to be professional, but it wasn't working very well.

This was only made harder by the fact that Jude had dressed in fitted jeans that hugged his ass just right. He'd paired them with a pale green button-down which enhanced the color of his eyes.

His eyes swept down her body and quickly snapped back up to her face. "I hope I gave you enough time."

She put a hand to her face, worried for a moment that she'd forgotten to put on makeup or brush her hair. Annie realized she was just thinking too hard about a simple statement yet again. "Yeah. Of course. I wasn't sure what to wear since I didn't know what we were doing."

His mouth twitched in the closest thing she'd seen resembling a smile since they'd left L.A. "It's perfectly fine. I'd like to get a feel for the area and just spend some time here before making too many inquiries about Jordan."

Annie frowned. "Isn't that a waste of time? I thought we'd be sneaking into the kitchens or questioning the staff." As soon as she said it, Annie realized how dumb that sounded. This wasn't a movie, and Jude was supposed to know what he was doing.

"You can keep any torture devices you brought along stowed away for the moment," he said, humor in his voice. "I know it sounds like a waste, but I'm thinking of this whole city as enemy territory right now. There's plenty of recon I can do in terms of satellite images and databases, but it's important to know the feel of a place, too. If you're paying attention, you can get a feel for what illicit things might happen in a place that seems completely tame."

"Oh." Annie turned away from him and busied herself with taking her shoes out of the closet. "I didn't know that. I guess that means you think something bad really did happen to Jordan?"

"I'm trying not to speculate and just go with facts. All records of him fizzle out shortly after he checked out of the hotel. Annie?"

She was still kneeling in front of the closet, trying to keep the tears that burned the backs of her eyes from spilling down her cheeks. "It's fine. I'm fine. I'm sorry. I just got a little emotional there for a second."

His hand was so warm as his palm smoothed across her shoulder, she thought it might burn her up from the inside out. "This is why I wasn't sure about you coming along with me."

"Are you sure?" she retorted, shaking off his hand and standing. "I figured it was just because you didn't want Jordan's annoying little sister dogging your footsteps and getting in the way."

"Hey." She'd tried to step away from him, but his grip was firm as he pulled her close and bent his head to look her in the eyes. "It's not like that at all. You have to remember that I've been in this business for a long time now. I know how difficult it is for someone to get involved when they think the life of their loved one might be at stake. This isn't going to be easy. I can tell you've got a lot of fire in you. If you think you can use it, then come with me. If you don't think you're up for it, then stay here, relax, get a massage if you want to, and know that I have this handled."

All of her breath left her body. Jude was standing in front of her, promising to take care of her. His words had turned into a lightning bolt that struck her right in the center of her heart. Instead of killing her, it brought her to life and sent a tingling sensation through her core, radiating out to her limbs.

It was only that tiny nagging thought of Jordan that brought her back to reality. "I'll come with you," she finally said, her throat dry. "I want to be involved in this, and I'd like to think I can be."

"Just promise me that if at any point it doesn't work out for you, you'll come back here. I can even arrange security for you if need be. I just don't want anything to happen to you, Annie." His soft eyes lingered on her face for a long moment before he strode to the window. "There's a lot in this city, and the heavy tourism is going to make it a little harder. I've got someone working with advanced facial recognition technology that can be applied to almost all the cameras in the city. That, I think, is going to be our easiest route, but while we wait, we just need to do as much observation as possible."

"Okay." He made it all sound so easy. "I'm not sure how two people are supposed to do that. There are hundreds of thousands of people living here, not to mention the millions of tourists." Annie had done a bit of research before she'd left, but it hadn't truly prepared her for what she was getting into.

"Just trust that I have this as well covered as possible. It might feel like it's only the two of us, but it isn't. Do you trust me, Annie?"

Damn those eyes! Jude could be asking her to believe the moon was made of cheese and she'd have to say yes. She really did trust him, though. There were so few people in the world who believed in her, and Jude seemed to be one of them. "Yes."

"Good. Then let's get started."

A short time later, they were across the street, surging upward in a glass-walled elevator. Despite herself, Annie felt a smile playing across her lips.

"What is it?"

"What?" The small crowd of people meant the two of them were crushed together in the small space. Annie was aware enough of Jude even when they were in an open space, but now she could feel the heat that radiated from his body. His scent invaded her senses, making her wonder what it would feel like to run her hands over the smooth planes of his bare chest.

"That big smile on your face," he said, his breath tickling her ear.

She lifted one shoulder and let it fall. "When we decided to take this trip, I thought it would be a little different than this. I knew this replica of the Eiffel Tower was here, but I didn't think we'd be going up in it."

He glanced through the glass at the structure that passed by as they rose ever higher. "Things aren't always what we expect."

Annie had the distinct feeling that he was talking about much more than this tourist trap. She felt him put his hand on her lower back as they stepped out of the elevator at the top and reminded herself that Jude was just being a gentleman. When they found Jordan, he'd want to know that Annie was safe and taken care of, after all.

They stepped out onto the viewing platform. The railing was caged all around to keep tourists from doing anything stupid, but even before they stepped up to it, Annie could feel the warm breeze washing through her hair. A couple in the corner stood with their cheeks pressed together as they looked out over the city. Nearby, a man was down on one knee with a ring box in his hand and a hopeful look on his face as he gazed up at the woman he wanted to marry.

Jude cleared his throat uncomfortably as he guided Annie around to the other side of the tower. The sun was sinking quickly behind the mountains in the distance, creating a deep blue bowl overhead that capped the lights of Vegas as they glowed to life. The fountains in front of their hotel flipped and thrashed as they went through their routine.

Annie curled her fingers around the grate, glad it was there.

"I know it doesn't seem like much in the way of our mission," Jude said, his body pressed close to hers as they kept as far away from the rest of the visitors as possible. "It's just one of those gut things."

"And what does your gut tell you about Jordan?" She almost didn't want to ask. It was too easy to get lost in the romance of their location. This was where people went to do the things they couldn't bring themselves to do in their regular lives, whether it was gambling or getting married or even just relaxing. If she let it, this could be her chance to show Jordan and everyone else in the clan that she was more than capable of being a leader. That was more important than anything, so why did she yearn for him to throw her over his shoulder and carry her back to his room?

"That he's all right, but that he needs our help," he replied quietly. "Jordan and I haven't had a lot of time together over the last few years. We've both been very busy, but I know what sort of guy he is. He can get lost in things like show business, just like anyone else could, but he's got a good head on his shoulders and good instincts. I don't think he'd get himself into any trouble on purpose."

Annie's face pinched as she thought about her brother. "What kind of trouble do you think he's in?"

"There are too many questions and far too few answers," he said cryptically.

She could agree with that, though, not just about Jordan, but about herself and even Jude. "And it seems we only keep finding those questions."

"That's not surprising. It's going to feel that way until this is all over with." He smiled at her when she looked up at him in confusion. "You get used to it eventually. You hungry?"

Coming back down the Eiffel Tower and moving through the strip, the crowds pressed in close around them. Everything was brilliant lights and signs and people shouting, and Annie felt overwhelmed by the crush of it all. She narrowed her focus on the center of Jude's muscular back as he threaded through the tourists, but there was too much to see. She was constantly craning her head to see the lights or one of the many street performers. A man posed as a statue in various positions, and another dressed as Elvis created quick spray paint art on small canvases that he pawned to passersby. Several superhero characters promised a photo for a few bucks, and musicians and magicians were dotted along between them. Annie paused to watch one of them pull card after card out of a rabbit's ear when she felt a warm hand slip into hers. She started to jerk it away when she realized it was Jude.

"I thought I lost you for a minute," he said, sincerity radiating from his eyes.

"Sorry. I just got distracted."

"That's all right. We're going to have to cut our little recon mission short, anyway. I just got word that someone matching Jordan's description was seen out on the west edge of town." Jude tugged on her hand as they headed back to their hotel.

She fell into step beside him, not sure if she should feel hopeful, angry, or elated.

5

___

JUDE TENSED HIS HANDS ON THE WHEEL OF THEIR RENTAL CAR. "AREN'T you going to eat that?" he asked, nodding his head toward the In-N-Out Burger bag in her lap.

"I don't know that I can. I'm too nervous." Annie bit her lip. Her arms were folded over her chest as she looked out the window.

He could understand that. When he'd gotten the call from his Force comrade, Raul, Jude had hardly wanted to believe it. Why would Jordan not only suddenly refuse to come home, but settle down in a rental out on the edge of town? If Jordan were going to settle down in Vegas, he'd want someplace right in the middle of the downtown hubbub. He was just that kind of guy, or else he'd never have made it as an actor.

Jude was also concerned about having Annie with him. God, it'd been nearly impossible to control himself already, and they'd hardly even started! The plane ride had been excruciating, feeling her right there next to him. He'd booked their hotel rooms right next to each other for safety's sake, but he also knew that meant she was right next door. Even as he'd stowed away his suitcase and heard the water running in his suite, he'd imagined the soapy lather sliding over her breasts and down her thighs. It was the kind of thing a teenage boy should be fantasizing about, not him.

And then there'd been that ridiculous trip to the top of the Eiffel

Tower. Jude hadn't been lying when he'd told her it was the beginning of their surveillance to help them get a feel for the area. He
really did want to see it all in one big view. It was just like climbing a
tree or heading up to the roof of a building to see the lay of the land
and how people flowed through it. But he also found himself wanting
to be in a place like that with a woman like her. No, not *like* her. Her.
Just Annie.

Did she have any idea what she did to his bear? He'd seen the fire
and passion in her eyes when she'd insisted on coming on this trip.
Some of it, he knew, was some sort of desperation to prove something.
Some of it was likely out of concern for her brother. At its heart,
though, Jude knew that Annie was more than most people could see.
She wasn't just the head of a clan who worried for her members. Still,
all of her fine qualities might not mean squat if they ended up having
to actually face an enemy. Jude had to keep her safe for Jordan's sake.
He could only hope that their lead brought them straight to the man,
and then it would all be over. Jude could wash his hands of the whole
situation and go on pretending there was nothing between the two of
them.

"All right," he said as they pulled up in front of a house in a very
modern, angular design that seemed to be popular in the area. "I don't
have a whole lot of information. I only know that he was seen here. He
might be here, he might not. I don't know if anyone else is inside, so
basically, we have to be ready to fight."

"Fight? It's my brother," Annie reasoned. "If he's gone off on some
bender or is having an early midlife crisis, it's not like I'm going to
hogtie him and throw him in the trunk. I just want to know that he's
okay."

Jude pinched the bridge of his nose. Annie was a smart girl, but
that was her problem. She was trying to be reasonable in a situation
that might not be reasonable at all. "You work with shifters every day.
You know that our animal sides keep us from doing things the same
way normal humans would. All I'm saying is that we have to be
prepared for the worst."

She shot him that look again, the one that said she didn't like being
told what to do, but she nodded. "All right."

It didn't make Jude feel any better as he stepped out of the car and
walked up to the door. His eyes roved over every aspect of the building
he could see, wanting to be one step ahead of any ambush that might

happen. It all seemed quiet as he walked onto the porch and knocked on the door.

The man who answered looked remarkably like Jordan. He had the same dark, wavy hair, steely blue eyes, and square jaw that had become so famous on the silver screen. Even though it'd been a while since Jude had seen Jordan, though, he knew this wasn't him.

Annie had noticed as well. "You're not my brother," she accused.

The man looked back and forth between them before he stepped back and swung the door shut. Jude's hand shot out, crunching against the wood to stop him, and he shoved harder, pushing it open.

"Shit!" The man let go of the door and darted toward the back of the house.

Jude instantly went after him. He was in his human form on the outside, but his bear instincts had taken over. He barreled into the house, hearing the door slam back and shiver on its hinges. The man knocked a lamp off an end table, but Jude easily cleared it as he charged into the kitchen. The back door was just within reach, but the man who wasn't Jordan had locked it. He was fiddling with the latch when Jude snagged him by the back of the shirt and yanked him backward. Not-Jordan flung his arms out to catch himself, landing a glancing blow to Jude's jaw. He was trying to pull Jude down to the floor with him when Annie stormed up and stomped her heel into the man's crotch.

"Ah!" Not-Jordan squeaked, immediately stopping any efforts to get away or gain an advantage. "What the fuck! You didn't have to do that!"

"You didn't have to run away," she pointed out.

Jude gave her a quick, appraising look before pointing at an extension cord hanging near the garage door. "Hand me that." It didn't take long to tie him up in a chair while Annie went back into the living room to shut the front door.

Pulling a chair up so that he sat in front of the man, Jude took a moment to calm himself. Adrenaline was still pumping through his system, and his body was fighting him as to what form he should be in. His bear wanted to come out and swat this asshole around a little, but Jude knew that he needed to be calm and collected.

"Who the fuck are you?" Clearly, Annie didn't feel the same way. She was bent forward, her face only an inch from their captive's. "Obviously, something's going on here, or you wouldn't have tried to bolt like that."

The man curled away from her, probably not wanting to get his package smashed a second time. "Hey, I don't know who you two are or what you're doing here. What do you expect me to do?"

"Annie." Jude pressed his tongue against his teeth, waiting for her to turn around and look at him. She didn't, but she did back off. She came to stand next to Jude, one hand on her hip and one foot tapping impatiently against the cheap linoleum.

Jude leaned forward. "Now that you're finally willing to listen to us, I'll tell you that we're here looking for Jordan Martinez. I find it odd that you look so much like him."

"Yeah, well, I'm his stunt double, Evan Boyer. But I haven't seen Jordan for a couple of days."

"You sure went down quickly for a stunt man," Annie commented.

"That's because they don't try to demolish my dick when I'm on set," Evan replied with a sneer.

"I'm sorry about that," Jude replied, not giving Annie a chance. He had a good feeling she wasn't sorry at all, but they needed to get any information they could out of this guy. "We might've gotten a little carried away. We're here because Jordan hasn't been seen or heard from in the last several days. We were notified that someone fitting his description was seen here, and it turns out to be you. Perhaps you have some insight as to where Jordan is."

A bead of sweat stood out on Evan's face. "What are you, the police or something?"

Jude smiled. "Something like that."

"Well, I don't have to say anything. I don't know who you are or what you want, or why the hell you think I have anything to do with it. I suggest you untie me right now unless you want to find your asses in jail. I have a lot of connections, you know!" Evan struggled against the extension cord.

Annie jumped forward, ready to go at him again, but Jude grabbed her by the waist and held her back. She struggled against him, her backside twisting and turning against his front, and damn it if he didn't like it. He smiled at Evan over her shoulder. "Talk, or I let her do what she wants. I don't have to tell you she's a little pissed right now."

She was either playing into the scene or was genuinely angry, but Annie lurched forward to swing at Evan, just missing his face.

"Fine! Fine! Jesus, nothing scarier than a crazy bitch."

"I'll fucking gut you if you speak to her that way again," Jude warned.

"God! All right. Sorry." Evan glanced at the back door, probably wondering if he had any chance of escaping, then deciding he didn't.

Jude held onto Annie with just one arm now, not quite trusting her enough to let her go completely. She wasn't being rational, and he couldn't blame her, but he didn't want to squander this opportunity. "Tell me about the last time you saw Jordan."

"I was out here to shoot a few scenes for the movie. It was an action film, so of course, there were plenty of shots for his stunt double. They've been hiring me for every flick he does because I look so much like him. It's great that I get steady work, but it sucks for him to get all the glory, you know?"

"Go on."

Evan glanced up at Annie again, who had calmed down with Jude's arm around her. "You sure you've got her?"

He could feel her vibrating in his arms, ready to attack. Jude smiled. "For the moment. You might want to hurry up."

"Okay. Well." Evan swallowed. "I figured that if something tragic happened to Jordan, like he got in a car accident or fell off a cliff or something, I could pretty easily slip in to take over his career. They'd ask me to finish shooting the movie in his place since we're practically twins, and it would spin off from there. They'd have the looks *and* the stunt man all rolled into one."

"You murdered my brother?" Annie screeched, struggling toward Evan once again. "I'm going to kill you!"

"No! I didn't!"

Jude stood, put both his arms around her, and swung her to the side. "Keep it up," he whispered in her ear. This was working. He pretended to legitimately struggle against keeping Annie in check, and even though she was much stronger than she looked, he had a good handle on her.

"I didn't kill him! I was going to, but I didn't get the chance! I told him we'd go out for some beers and a night on the town when we were done shooting, and I slipped him a few pills. He passed out just like I planned, but when he woke up, he turned into a bear! It scared the fuck out of me, but I still had him tied up. I thought maybe I could use him in a completely different way and make a shit ton of money off blackmail or selling him to some freak show, but these other guys showed up and paid me for him."

"Who?" Jude demanded.

"I don't know. They didn't even use their first names, but they didn't seem surprised at all that the dude had turned into a fucking bear. It was the weirdest thing, but it was easy money and I wasn't going to turn it down."

"Where did they take him?"

"I don't know. They didn't tell me a thing. They just handed me a bag of cash, loaded Jordan up like some circus animal, and left."

Annie was fighting against Jude in earnest now, truly ready to rip this man to shreds. "I suggest you tell me everything you know," Jude warned.

"It was a big blonde guy in a black Jeep. A pretty new one. That's all I know. Jesus Christ, she's going to kill me!"

Annie had managed to slip Jude's grip slightly, snarling as she lunged toward Evan.

"Not if I can help it!" boomed a loud voice from the kitchen doorway.

All three of them turned to see a large man. His head was shaved, and his muscles rippled under his fitted t-shirt as he came into the room. "What the fuck is going on here? Evan, is this some twisted sex game or something?"

"Keith! Thank God! These crazy fuckers broke in and tied me up! I think they were trying to rob us." Evan wriggled in his chair, making it thump against the floor.

"I don't think so." Keith moved into the room and reached forward with one meaty hand to wrap it around Jude's neck.

Jude smiled at the mountain of a man. Evan was lying, but Jude had an advantage. He let his human form fall away, and by the time Keith grabbed him, he was clutching the throat of a bear.

"What the fuck?" Keith scrambled back to reveal another man who'd come in. This one wasn't as big as Keith, but the way he dodged out of the way made Jude think he was yet another stunt double. Great.

"They're some sort of bear freaks! Just like Jordan!" Evan screeched. He was bouncing in earnest in his chair now, trying to get to the door.

Jude let go of Annie. She went after Evan, issuing a swift kick to his chest that sent him sprawling backward on the floor. She darted past Keith and slammed her fist into the jaw of the second man.

Focusing on Keith, Jude rushed forward on four legs. His roar filled the room and echoed off the ceiling as his teeth clamped down on the big man's arm. He tasted of salt and grime, but Jude didn't let that stop him. He bit down hard, yanking his head to the side to increase the size of the wound. Blood filled Jude's mouth as Keith's scream overtook his own. A yank brought him down to the floor. Jude's claws sank into his flesh as he trampled him to get to Annie.

She'd made the other man bleed profusely from his nose, but he'd managed to get his hand into her hair. He yanked her head backward. "You stupid little bitch!" he screamed, pulling his fist back as he prepared to land a punch.

Jude was already possessed with the spirit of his bear, but his sight went red with rage. Nothing could stop him as he slammed his body into the other man's. Annie's hair fell from his hands as Jude ripped into his torso, keeping his promise. The body went limp beneath his paws, but Jude didn't care. Something even deeper than his inner animal had been activated, the part of him that wanted to protect Annie at all costs. He'd gone completely wild.

"Jude! Jude!" Her hand was on his shoulder.

He pulled back, seeing just what he'd done. Jude turned away as he shifted, lumbering back into the kitchen as he slowly morphed into walking upright once again. He turned on the kitchen faucet, washing his hands and splashing his face. "Are you all right?" he asked hoarsely.

"Yeah, I'm fine. Just a little banged up, but I'll be okay. What about you?"

Drying his hands on his jeans, he turned to look at Annie. The skin around her eye was discolored. "You're going to have a shiner."

"Whatever. What do we do about *them*?" She gestured with her head to the two remaining men.

"Nothing. Come on." He took her by the arm as they went out the front door and into the night air. It felt too cold on his bare skin. "They were in on it with Evan. From what he said, they knew about Jordan. I'll call in what information I have to my headquarters so the search can continue. For now, this is a dead end."

Annie was quiet as they headed back toward downtown. She combed her fingers through her tangled hair and fidgeted uncomfortably in her seat, tucking her hands between her knees and then against her sides. She said nothing.

"I know it probably doesn't seem like it, but that was a start toward finding Jordan. I'll get the vehicle tracked down, and we'll find him."

"Okay," was her only response.

He wasn't good at this. He'd turned into something completely undomesticated back there, a bear who had no sense of morality or when to stop. "If you're bothered that I killed that guy, just know that he deserved it. He was going to kill us if he had the chance."

"It's fine."

Jude was on autopilot as he drove, paying almost no attention to traffic or signs, but knowing he was heading in the right direction. He wanted to make this better for Annie. "You know, you were pretty savage back there. I'm impressed at how well you did against those assholes."

"I did grow up with a brother and all the other guys in our clan," she reminded him quietly. "Things were usually a little wild."

"Yeah. I guess that's true." Jude hadn't thought of that. He and Reid had wrestled plenty of times, and even though the Hoffmans' had brought them into their clan, it wasn't the same. "You're pretty lucky."

She didn't respond.

He was messing this up completely. Jude wanted to help. He'd run to her rescue without even talking to Amar. The rest of the Force was well aware of the situation and helping him out remotely, but maybe it would've been better if he'd asked Gabe or Raul to go in his place. They would've been far more impartial, and they wouldn't have felt obligated to bring Annie along. "Look, I know you're upset. Whether it's because you're worried about Jordan or that you're upset with me, we can talk about it. I know you can't be happy. You didn't even shift during that fight back there."

Annie turned to him, the streetlights flashing intermittently on her face. She opened her mouth to speak and slammed it shut again, turning away toward the passenger window.

Jude's teeth gritted together so hard it made his jaw hurt, but he didn't care. Annie was in emotional pain, worried her brother would never come home again. Maybe she was pissed at Jude for his violence, but that wasn't something he could get around. He'd killed before—both in combat and while serving with the Force—and he'd probably have to do it again.

He was infatuated with a woman who could never possibly love him back. She had the clan life and a sense of belonging that he would never understand, and Jordan—wherever he was—would kill him in an instant if he acted on what he felt. He'd put himself in a completely impossible situation.

She was still quiet as they went up to their rooms. Jude hesitated in the hall just long enough to hear her bolt the door behind her before he went into his own, wanting to make sure she was safe. He showered, letting the hot water wash over him in the hopes that it could rinse away all his feelings, but it only made things worse.

With a towel wrapped around his waist, he made sure the door that joined their rooms was unlocked. He couldn't keep fantasizing that she might suddenly come to him, revealing that she, too, had been turned on as he'd held her back in Evan's kitchen.

That she felt all the same turmoil inside that he'd been suffering from.

That she knew she wanted to be with him forever.

That they'd been cut from the same cloth when the universe had whirled to life.

He just wanted her to be safe. That was his duty at this point, no matter what had happened to Jordan.

He dialed Raul. "Apparently, the facial recognition software doesn't account for stunt doubles."

"*Mierda.* Are you serious?"

Jude swiped a hand down his face, still feeling tired and dirty even though he'd showered. "Yeah. Things have only gotten more complicated. I've got a vehicle you can look for, though. It'll be a pain since I don't have a plate number, but it was at that same house within the past week."

"I can do it," the wolf promised.

"I know. I'm just not sure I can."

Raul let out a snort. "You've gotten yourself in over your head with this girl, haven't you?"

"Is it that obvious?" Jude rolled his eyes toward that damn shared door once again.

"I knew it had to be something big if it could pull you away from L.A. right as your brother got into town."

Shit. He'd hardly spared a thought for Reid ever since Annie had called. "Is everything all right?"

"Oh, sure. We've just been spending some time with him, letting him know how we do things. There isn't much happening down here at the moment, so that makes it a little easier. Don't worry about any of it."

"Thanks. Let me know as soon as you find out about this Jeep. We'll follow it. If we haven't heard anything from you by the morning, we'll just head back to L.A. It's probably a good idea to get Annie back home."

"Sounds good."

They hung up, and Jude went to the window of his room. There was a certain kind of beauty in the hectic energy of the city, though he usually preferred more rural settings. Even so, it was hard to appreciate it when he knew Annie was so upset with him.

6

ANNIE STOOD RIGHT IN FRONT OF THE DOOR THAT LED TO JUDE'S ROOM. She reached for the knob, but then she dropped her hand before she managed to turn it. Instead, she tried to explore the hotel room. It was luxurious and by far the most beautiful place she'd ever stayed. It should have been exciting, but there was too much on her mind for her to enjoy it.

Where was Jordan? Was he still out there somewhere in Vegas? Who had come to literally buy him from Evan? It was the most convoluted thing she could've fathomed. What if it was someone from the government? What would this mean for their clan and the rest of the shifters in the world?

She sank down on the bed and braced her forehead on her palm, staring at her phone and trying to decide if she should call Michelle or not. Annie needed someone to talk to. She had to get some of this off her mind, but no one could give her answers. Even Jude could only do so much, and he'd assured her he would find Jordan.

Jude. Annie glanced up at that door once more, knowing he was just on the other side of it. She'd been horribly rude to him. He'd misread her, thinking she was angry with him.

She pressed her lips together as she thought. *Does he deserve to know the truth? Would he even care?* She felt so much for him, and yet it was obvious those feelings weren't mutual. He was putting himself in harm's way to help her, though. The least she owed him was an explanation.

The day had been long enough, but Annie summoned the last ounce of courage she had in her body and stood. She knocked on the door.

He answered so quickly, the breeze from opening the door played with his wet hair. His eyes were wide, his lips slightly parted, and his chest incredibly bare. He wore nothing but a pair of athletic shorts, which showed the impressive muscle he'd built during his time in the service. A fine dusting of hair graced his chest, growing thicker as it trailed toward the waistband of his shorts. She knew she shouldn't look at him this way, but she couldn't help it.

"Is everything all right?" he asked.

"Um, yeah. I just wanted to talk to you for a minute."

He stood there for the longest second in all eternity before he stepped back and held the door open wide. "Come in."

His room was a mirror image of hers, and it shouldn't have embarrassed her to see the large bed in the back corner. Still, she could think of much more entertaining ways for the two of them to use up their time in Vegas than just waiting around. His body, fresh and clean and smelling of soap; those arms wrapped strongly around her like they'd been when he'd tried to keep her from decapitating Evan... No. This was serious.

He snagged a t-shirt from the closet and pulled it over his head as he moved toward the seating area and gestured her toward an armchair. "What's on your mind? Need anything to drink?"

"No, thanks." She sank into the chair, glad that she didn't have to stand for this. She hadn't told anyone beyond her immediate family and clan members. She hadn't even wanted *them* to know; it was just too embarrassing. But anyone who was going to spend a lot of time with her needed to know the truth. Folks didn't expect people in wheelchairs to walk down a set of stairs, and other shifters shouldn't expect her to suddenly turn into an animal.

"Not even coffee?" He picked up the carafe from the machine in the kitchenette and poured himself a mugful.

"It's kind of late for that, isn't it?" She smiled, glad for the distraction, but knowing it was only prolonging the inevitable.

"Not when you drink as much of it as I do. I haven't had nearly enough in the past twenty-four hours, so I figured this was a good time to do a little catching up." He sat down, their chairs separated by a small, round table. His brow wrinkled in concern. "I'm sure you want to know what's next. I've called in all the details I can, including the vehicle description and everything Evan told us. We'll find him."

"But—"

"No, we will." He held up his hand to keep her from arguing, even though she hadn't intended to argue with him at all. "Annie, I've been on extraction missions in foreign countries where we have far fewer resources. Whatever Evan intended, and whoever these other guys are who have him, they're not going to get away with it. They don't seem to realize that not only are they dealing with a Hollywood star whose face would be recognized almost anywhere, but a guy who has the SOS Force at his back."

"I know, and I believe you." Annie sensed that he needed to hear that, although she didn't understand why. Jude was strong and capable, and the reassurance of someone like her shouldn't matter. She cleared her throat. "There's actually something else I wanted to talk to you about."

"All right." Jude waved his hand for her to go on as he took a sip from his mug.

Could she do this? He might not be romantically interested in her, but overall, Jude was a good guy. He'd asked her to trust him. "You noticed earlier that I didn't shift when we were fighting off Evan's men," she began. "I know that wasn't exactly the normal thing for people like us."

"It's okay," he said softly, leaning forward and torturing her with his proximity and his kindness. "I know this has been a very stressful situation."

"Let me finish, please. I know that wasn't exactly normal, but neither am I. I...I can't shift." The words hung in the air between them. Annie couldn't take them back, but she wondered how well he'd respond to them.

"You can't?"

"Nope."

He took another long, slow sip of coffee. "Have you ever been able to shift, or is it just right now?"

Annie knew what he meant. Sometimes, if a shifter was very ill or very stressed, it made that basic function extremely difficult. "I've never been in any form other than the one you see right now."

His eyes flicked down her body and back to her face. "Why?"

She lifted a shoulder. "I really don't know. Mom and Dad were always kind about it, but I could tell they were upset. I'm not like all the other shifters, and I'm sure it was a big disappointment for them, especially because of our Alpha bloodline. There aren't a lot of doctors who can help with this sort of thing, but the few specialists they took me to didn't really have any answers. They said it just happens sometimes." Now that she'd popped the cork, it was all coming out in a flood. "I'm really sorry. I should've told you earlier. I was coming out here with the intention of helping you with this mission, but I'm not the kind of help you were expecting."

Jude's face twitched as emotions flashed over it. "There's nothing to apologize for, Annie. I'm glad you were able to tell me. I'm sure this hasn't been easy for you."

She let out a short laugh that brought a few tears with it, and she blinked them away as quickly as possible. "To say the least. This was exactly why I was so worried about Jordan being gone all the time and leaving me in charge. It's an honor, but it doesn't do me much good when they don't think of me as one of them."

"The clan members give you trouble over this?" His fingers were entwined in front of him, his knuckles white. Perhaps this revelation was bothering him more than he was letting on.

"Some of them, yes. It's made me worry a lot about the future leadership of the clan. I don't want anyone to question Jordan just because his sister is a weirdo. He promised me we'd figure some things out when he got back, and now I don't know if he'll ever *be* back. I don't know what's going to happen to me or all the people I care about." The patterned carpet blurred in front of her eyes as the tears came in a flood.

"It's all right." Jude was at her side, his arm wrapped warmly around her, his fingers tracing over her bare skin just below her shirt sleeve. "That's a lot to think about. I'm really sorry you're having to go through all that."

His words only brought her more pain. Annie knew he was just saying those things because he felt like he had to. As much as she wanted to lean into his embrace and tell him her other secret, she knew it could never happen. It was right of her to tell him the truth about never shifting, but explaining her feelings would only complicate things.

Jude got up and came back a moment later with a box of tissues. "Would it be all right if I asked you a few more questions?"

"Sure." What did she have to lose, after all? Jude knew what only a handful of other people did.

"I don't know how it feels for you, but I can feel my bear inside. When I'm in my human form, it's like there's an animal living just under the surface of my skin. Is it the same for you?"

"Yes." It sure as hell was, and that damn bear had been going berserk every time Jude was around. It still wouldn't calm down, even though she'd already told herself she wasn't going to do anything about her feelings for Jude.

"Do you know if there are others like you?"

Annie flooded one tissue and snagged a second one. "It was implied, back when I was a kid and my parents took me to those specialists. They said it was rare, though."

"I see. And I suppose that means you don't know if anyone ever manages to get past this."

"I mean, I'm twenty-five years old and I've never been able to do it. What could possibly change now?" Her face was swelling from all the crying. She could feel it, and she knew that meant it was also turning some interesting shades of purple and red. Great.

"It was just a thought. I don't know what the procedure is like for something like this." He had his hand on her back now, running it smoothly up and down her spine. "We've got a few excellent doctors on the Force who might be able to help: one in D.C., and one in L.A. I understand there's another shifter doctor affiliated with our Dallas unit, too. Maybe she knows something about it."

Annie shook her head. "Maybe. I don't know. I'm not sure I could handle getting hopeful and going through a bunch of tests just to get let down again." She easily remembered all those late-night conversations she'd heard when she'd snuck out of her bedroom as a kid, with her mother crying and her father murmuring reassurances. Eventually, Jordan had been brought in on those meetings, too. They were talking about her, how she was different, and what it would mean for their family for the future. She hated it.

"What if the two of us worked on it? Together?"

Swiping a tissue across her eyes, she finally looked up at him. "What?"

"It's going to be difficult for us to know what to do next about

Jordan until I get more information from headquarters. We could spend all night visiting the casinos, hoping we happen to bump into him, but the chance of that happening is slim to none. Instead, we could see if there's anything we can do to find that bear inside you."

It was a sweet offer, but she didn't think it was going to do any good. "Jude, that's kind of you. But I've tried about a million times. Jordan used to take me out into the woods, telling me he'd find a way to make it work for me. He'd get all excited with this plan for me to perfect my shifting without telling anyone and then have me suddenly drop into full bear mode at the dinner table as a way of telling our parents. Obviously, that never worked. My parents tried, too, as well as a few other senior clan members they trusted. It just isn't going to happen."

He nodded and sat back in his chair, sipping his coffee. "I understand. I'm sure you've tried a lot of different things, but I want to help in any way I can. You're obviously unhappy, and I want to make it better."

Annie couldn't understand why he'd care so much, but he was the only option she had at the moment. He'd gone out of his way for her, and if he truly wanted to do this, then she could give a little. "All right. What do you want to do?"

Jude set his mug aside and stood up with far more ease and energy than a man who'd had a day like theirs should've had. "Get a good pair of shoes on. We'll go out to Red Rock Canyon."

"What?" Despite how hard she'd been crying, she wanted to laugh now. "Can't we just close the curtains and try it here?"

He gave her a look that was gentle but also said he meant business. Jude was good at that. "I'm personally not interested in drawing any more attention to ourselves than we might already have with our activities at Evan's place. This could get loud and possibly destructive, and that would be hard to explain."

Annie's cheeks colored, thinking of just what their hotel neighbors might think if they were in there roaring and thrashing about. "I guess that's true."

"Personally, I've also found it to be helpful to be out in the middle of nowhere. We live in a world full of humanity, but that makes it hard to tap into that wild side of ourselves. It's at least worth a try."

Jordan had already tried getting her into the outdoors for this, but that had been a long time ago. "All right. I'll be back in a second."

She went back through the doorway to her room and found a pair of sneakers. She was exhausted from all the emotions she'd already gone through that day, and she could feel it in her bones. Despite her best intentions to keep herself at bay, she was happy to have an excuse to spend more time with Jude, and they were soon on their way back out to the edge of the city.

He parked the car in the deepest shadows just off the road and headed into the park with eagerness in his step. "Tell me what methods you've tried before."

She skirted the scrubby bushes and followed him into the rocky outcropping that took up the area. "Oh, lots of things. Meditating. Spending time with others in their bear forms. Wearing talismans that were supposed to have the spirit of the bear inside them. Getting drunk."

"Really?"

"That last one was Jordan's idea," she said with a smile. "He thought I just didn't know how to relax. He wasn't totally wrong about that, but the only thing I got out of it was a hangover."

"Other than drinking, those were probably all good methods. I can't say that I know the perfect solution, but I imagine this is sort of like teaching someone to walk after they've been in a bad accident. We don't know how to teach something so intrinsic."

"That makes me feel a lot better." She was grateful for the darkness so Jude couldn't see her scowl. This was a stupid idea. She was already embarrassed, and she hadn't even tried yet.

"I just mean that it makes it difficult. Would you be able to tell someone how to blink?"

"No, I don't suppose I would." Annie blinked, acutely aware of the motion now that he'd brought it up, but still unable to describe it.

"Humans have physical therapists who've gone through a lot of training to know how to help someone learn to walk a second time. We don't have anything like that in the shifter world that I know of; I'll have to talk to our resident doc, Emersyn, about it sometime. Anyway, I guess I'll just start by trying to explain everything I do when I shift."

"Okay." It seemed incredibly intimate for him to tell her such a thing, especially since it wasn't something she shared.

They moved further into the park before he finally came to a stop in a small valley created by the rocks. It shut off the lights from the city, making the stars overhead sparkle brilliantly in the deep black sky. "I guess the first thing I do is reach down inside and get in touch with my bear. It's always there, and sometimes it's closer to the surface than usual. Sometimes I can hardly keep it at bay. But it's like I'm telling this other thing that lives inside of me that it's allowed to come out. Over the years, I've been able to do this with just a deep breath."

Annie pulled air into her lungs and closed her eyes, envisioning the beast she knew was inside her. It responded, confused, but it didn't exactly come bursting forth. "Okay. What else?"

"The bear and I are the same being, yet we're not. It's like I'm not only giving it permission to come out, but assuring it I won't be hurt if it does. My human part just goes to the inside, like they trade places."

"That makes sense." Annie imagined what that must feel like, a human curled up inside a great bear. She'd fantasized about it plenty of times, but that had never made it happen before. "What's next?"

"Well..." He trailed off. "Shit. This is harder than I thought. I'm sorry. I just never thought about it in this depth before."

"Don't worry about it, Jude. I appreciate it, but I don't want to waste any more of your time than I already have." Annie turned to go back the way they'd come.

"You don't get to give up that easily. I'll shift first, and I'll pay more attention. Then we can try it for you." He let go of her arm.

Annie watched as he filled his lungs with air. Jude made no other special movements that she could see, but as he exhaled, his human form began to fall away. Fur exploded over his body. His arms and legs grew thicker as he bent forth and stretched his fingers into paws and claws. Even in the darkness, he was a magnificent beast. She hesitantly stepped forward.

Jude watched her, his green eyes now dark but welcoming, like a deep emerald velvet. Anyone who didn't know the truth about him would think he was just a wild beast, but in those eyes, she could see he was something completely different. Though she'd grown up surrounded by bears, he wasn't like the others. She reached out and touched the top of his head, gently at first, hesitantly, wondering if this was really okay. Jude tipped his muzzle up, encouraging her. She stroked his ears and down his neck, in awe of that strange pattern in the fur covering his chest. As much as she appreciated his beauty from a human standpoint, she longed to see what he was like as a fellow bear.

He seemed to know this, and he nudged his big black nose against her side. Annie nodded, hoping beyond all hope that she could do this. So many times in her life, she'd been left behind because she couldn't be what her genes told her she should be. This was one thing she didn't want to miss out on.

Stepping back to give herself a little space, Annie got in touch with her inner bear. *It's all right to come out. You've been hiding for so long, and I know you want to be free. You won't hurt me. We'll just change places for a little while.* Annie sucked in a deep breath and let it out.

Nothing happened. Though she mentally commanded her body to change, it refused to do so. There were no twisting bones or relocating organs, and she had no more hair than she'd woken up with that morning. She was just a human. Annie sighed.

A cold nose on her thigh startled her, but it was just Jude. He watched her in earnest, commanding her with his silence to try again. Somehow, it was easier to try when he wasn't in his human form, like she wasn't being watched as closely. He'd already shifted in front of her, letting her see that strange in-between configuration that some shifters didn't like to share with others. That was one way in which he'd opened up to her. Annie found herself constantly owing him, but never in a way that felt like a burden.

She nodded. Jude had told her about taking one deep breath, but maybe she just wasn't strong enough to do it that way. Annie sucked in air, visualizing it as the bear side of herself coming in. Every outward breath was her human side leaving, and the more she breathed, the more ursine she should become.

Ideally. After standing there for what felt like an hour, she was still human. "I'm sorry."

Jude turned away from her as he shed his bear form. It looked so easy for him to command his body as his shaggy brown coat receded into his skin and his face folded and flattened into the one she was familiar with. "Don't be sorry. It's not like I expected it to happen right away, and you shouldn't either."

Annie balled her fists at her sides. She'd already cried enough for the day, yet she felt tears prickling her eyes once again. "Maybe this wasn't the best time for me to bring this up. I've got too much on my mind."

"That's completely understandable. Don't give up on yourself just yet, though. Shifting is a big thing. Maybe we need to look at it like eating an elephant."

"Huh?" She looked up at him, silhouetted against the stars. Jude was so perfect. He'd served the country and now served his fellow shifters, and he carried it all out while looking like he belonged on the cover of GQ.

He smiled. "It's a big project, and you have to do it one bite at a time. Come over here and sit." Jude brought her to a large boulder.

She sat next to him, surprised when he took her arm in his hand and turned it over to reveal her inner wrist. His fingers were warm and gentle, but she could sense that inner strength in him.

"We think of shifting as the entire body all at once, but it isn't always like that. I've had times when I didn't want to shift, but I was getting so riled up about something that part of me started to change. Say, for instance, suddenly having a lot more hair on the back of my neck."

Annie laughed. "That could be inconvenient in a business meeting."

"You're telling me! Try this. Focus just on this part of your body, this thinner skin right here. Imagine what it would feel like to have your fur come straight through the skin. That's what it feels like. It isn't as though it regrows every time; it just forces its way through."

She kept her eyes on her arm, not daring to look up at his face when they were so close to each other. She wanted him so badly. He was sexy, yes, but it was so much more than that. He wanted to help her find Jordan, and he wanted to fix a problem she'd had her entire life. It was a far bigger task than one man could possibly handle, yet he wasn't ready to give up on her. He was the perfect man, and that only made her all the sadder for not being able to have him.

"What about the skin?" she asked quietly. "Does it just stay in the same spot?"

"It seems to. It grows and changes when your whole body shifts, but that's nothing you'll notice if you work on just this part. Concentrate on each hair and what it must feel like. Don't worry about anything else."

It was easier said than done, but she tried. She envisioned a humiliating amount of hair suddenly erupting from her skin, each hair tickling as it poked its way through.

But once again, nothing happened.

7

"LET'S TAKE A BREAK." THE STARS PROVIDED ENOUGH LIGHT FOR JUDE TO see the exhaustion in Annie's eyes. Her shoulders sagged, and she no longer wanted to stand up as she attempted the transformation, but that emotional drain was the worst part to witness.

"I really wanted to make this happen," she said pitifully, sitting down with a thump on a nearby rock. She bent forward and rested her forehead on her knees. "It seemed like a good backup plan, something that would help me run the clan if we can't find Jordan. I don't think it's ever going to happen."

"Come here." Using his foot to move a few rocks aside and even out the ground, Jude waved her over. "You're wiped out."

Annie pulled herself up and staggered over without protest. He thought she might just say they should go back to the hotel and get some rest, but Jude doubted either one of them would be able to sleep. "I'll rest, but I don't think it's going to help."

Jude laid down next to her. "You're just as stubborn as your brother, you know that?"

He heard her smirk more than he saw it. "So I've been told. What kind of stubbornness do you know in him?"

"Are there multiple kinds of stubborn? I wasn't aware that they could be categorized." He was smiling, too, so worn out from the past twenty-four hours that he wasn't sure if even he could shift at the moment.

"Oh, sure. There's the kind of stubborn he was when we were little kids, and he insisted he should be allowed to live in the woods by himself and hunt for his own meals."

"Seriously? Mr. Hollywood Hotshot wanted to do that?" Jude hadn't known Jordan until they were in their early teens, when childhood fantasies had been replaced by dreams of girls and fast cars.

"Yup. He even ran away once because he said the walls of the house were suffocating him. I guess Jordan was just super in touch with his bear then. I didn't understand at the time. I was happy to sleep in my bed instead of out on the ground."

"And now?" Jude was incredibly comfortable despite the hardness of the earth beneath them.

Apparently, Annie felt the same way. "With everything going on in my life, it's kind of nice to just *be*. I don't get a lot of chances to do that."

"I'm sure it's difficult being in charge of everyone like you are." He couldn't truly understand her clan life. Jude had been adopted into a clan, but wasn't the same. Jude, Reid, and the Hoffmans didn't live in the clubhouse or have much to do with the day-to-day operations of the members.

"When they let me be. Jude, I really appreciate you bringing me out here and helping me with this. You didn't have to."

Yes, he did, but he wasn't going to say it out loud. He had to do it not because he had some sort of obligation to her that she might be offended by, but because he knew there was a deep connection between them. He had to do it because he wanted to do it, because he wanted her to have every possible chance at happiness. He wanted everything for her that she didn't have, and all that she deserved. "It's no problem."

"Can I ask you something, though? About your bear?"

"Sure." He liked just laying there with her, staring up at the stars, pretending they were the only two people in the universe. Jude would talk all night long if it meant they didn't have to go back to reality.

"When you shifted, I saw a mark on your chest. This silvery little swirl. What is that? I'm sorry if it's something I shouldn't be asking. I've just never seen anything like it before."

If it was anyone else, Jude might've been embarrassed. But it was

Annie, and it was different. "I don't know. Some sort of birthmark, I guess, because I've always had it."

She rolled up onto her elbow so that she was looking down at him, outlined by the stars. "Is it...Is it there when you're in this form?" Her finger swayed, vaguely pointing at his chest.

Jude's gut contracted against his spine, excited that she might even remotely be thinking about his body. "No, it's not." he replied quietly. "Annie?"

"Yes?"

This was a mistake. He knew it even before he said it, but she'd opened up to him and told him something that no shifter would willingly admit to another. She'd made herself vulnerable, and it was time for him to do the same. "I know it was tough for you to tell me about not being able to shift. You were carrying that around and felt like I had the right to know."

She looked away toward their feet, embarrassed again. "I'm sorry if it bothers you."

"No, Annie." He sat up, pulling her with him and taking her hands in his. "What I'm saying is that there's something I've been carrying around, too. I don't know if I should tell you or not, because I don't know what consequences it'll bring, but I will if you'll let me."

She looked up at him, excitement and intrigue in her eyes. "Of course you can."

Jude swallowed. Jordan would kill him once they found him. He might be grateful to Jude for taking care of his sister, but this was crossing the line. Still, they were in the middle of nowhere, and there could be no repercussions from anyone but her right now. "Annie, I'm crazy about you. Every time I'm around you, I can feel something change inside me. It's like my bear goes absolutely wild with the urge to be with you, but it isn't just physical. I'm in love with every part of you, your body and your soul."

She squinted at him with disbelief. "You are?"

"Yes, and I know it's not right for me to say this. I know you're from an Alpha bloodline and Jordan is my best friend, but I can't deny the way I feel about you anymore. What you do to me is what all the other shifters talk about. You give me that innate, deep-rooted sensation that I've finally met the person I'm supposed to be with. Annie, I don't want this to scare you or make you feel like you have some sort of obligation toward me. I just want you to know that I love you."

Annie was as still as a statue, her face illuminated by the stars as she stared at him, her lips slightly parted in a look of wonder. "I feel the same way about you. I love you, too, Jude." Her voice was thick with tears, but they weren't the same tears she'd cried over Jordan or over her frustration with her body. "I always just thought of you as my brother's friend, and I thought you were cute, but for the longest time, it didn't go any deeper than that. Then it was like everything changed in the matter of a second, one of those times that you were on leave from the Army and hanging out at our house. I didn't think that could be possible, that I'd suddenly feel something I hadn't felt before. Not being able to shift made me doubt myself even more. If I couldn't become who I was supposed to be, then how could I actually be feeling that? Was it even fair of me to feel that way toward you when I couldn't shift?"

"I don't care about any of that. I've known shifters who've found their mates in people who aren't shifters at all."

"So..." She trailed off, her breath coming heavily and heaving her chest as she watched him, waiting.

Jude lifted a hand and skimmed it along her jawline, pressing his lips to hers. He closed his eyes and let himself fall into it, pushing away all the worry. He'd had concerns about what his feelings for her would mean in the real world, and so did she, but the real world could wait.

Her lips were soft and warm, inviting him in. She opened her mouth and deepened the kiss in a way far more intimate than he'd imagined it could be. Annie explored his mouth, showing him her hunger and desire for him.

His bear was in utter bliss as Jude grabbed her by the waist and pulled her onto his lap. Annie's legs wrapped around him easily, a small whimper of desperation for him escaping her lips as she ran her hands down his back and skimmed them under the hem of his shirt, igniting all his pulse points in glorious energy.

For a moment, he let his guilt wash over him. "Annie," he breathed as he moved his mouth along her jaw and down the delicate curve of her neck. "You don't have to." But God, did he want her to. He crushed his arm around her waist, holding her tightly against him and never wanting to let go.

"I *want* to," she whispered back, pulling his shirt over his head. "I've wanted you for so long, Jude."

His desire was a burning fire that blazed through the marrow of his bones, buzzing in his blood. He slowly stripped her clothing away, wanting to touch every inch of her. From the bend of her elbow and the hard roundness of her knee to the curve of her hips and the swell of her breasts, every part of her was enticing. The anticipation of what would come next left him tingling down to the tips of his toes.

"I want *you*," he said as he dragged his tongue along her shoulder and moved the strap of her bra aside, knowing what he needed. He laid her down on the sandy ground, stripping her bra and panties off so that she lay naked before him. Not vulnerable, but glorious. Jude grazed the tan line that ran from her shoulder to the top of her breast and then further, teasing her nipple with his tongue as she tangled one hand in his hair.

Her other hand was free, and it roved over his shoulder and down his arm, her fingertips exploring the curves and valleys of his muscles. She moved further down, spreading her fingers across his abdomen and down between his legs, touching, lingering. Jude's body had already been ready to go, but she elicited a low moan from him as she curled her fingers around his eager shaft.

"Fuck," he grunted, trying so hard to control himself. That'd been the game ever since he'd jumped in his car and gone to meet her at her house. She made him not want to control himself at all, to act like the wild beast he'd been suppressing for so long.

She caressed his shoulder with her lips, moving up his neck and to his ear, where she swept the tip of her tongue against his lobe. Her right hand continued its play between his legs, stroking, exploring, asking.

"Annie." Jude lowered himself into her, scooping his arms around her back and holding her against him, savoring the moment. They were joined physically, but he knew this was far more than that. She was warm and soft around him and underneath him, and Jude didn't want it ever to end.

As much as this was feeding their souls, their bodies had demands that had to be met. Her hips thrust against him as they moved in perfect rhythm. She was heaven and earth, right there in his arms.

Annie pressed her hips upward and arched her back, compressing herself against him. He could feel her body shivering from the inside out, which only drove him to work harder. He thrust faster, hoping to stave himself off as long as possible.

Her legs wrapped around him, pulling him tighter against her, and a moan of pleasure escaped her lips. Gripping his shoulders with her hands as she moved against him, she threw her head back and cried out into the night. Her ecstasy echoed against the rocks that surrounded them and up into the stars as her body constricted in ripples of pleasure.

Jude followed quickly in her footsteps, thrilled to see such contentment playing across her features. He held her tightly as he came, his entire body focusing on their connection before he let go. He worried he might crush her in his grip as everything he'd felt for her, everything he'd been pressing down inside himself, came shooting to the surface.

She lay next to him, peeking up shyly over his shoulder. "I had no idea. About how you felt, I mean."

"Am I that mysterious?"

"Yeah," she replied instantly. "If you've actually been feeling the way you say you have, then you're an expert at hiding it."

He leaned over and kissed her. "It sure as hell hasn't been easy."

Annie moved her head up onto his chest. "I think we both needed this. I know we have a lot to go back to and a lot of work ahead of us, but I'm glad we were able to get away from it all for a bit."

Jude laughed. "Do you know how crazy people would think we are? We're right here next to one of the top destinations in the country and have top-notch hotel rooms, but we're laying out here on the ground in the middle of nowhere. It's better like this, or at least I think it is." He was enjoying the shared warmth of their bodies, the feeling of being naked under the sky, the euphoria of being with Annie, and finally getting the chance to tell her the truth.

"I think so, too." She settled in more closely at his side. "Do you ever look up at the stars and wonder how many other shifters are doing the same thing at the same time? I know it sounds stupid, like something out of a movie, but I've always thought there was a certain kind of magic to them."

"Absolutely." He put his arm around her, wanting to just hold onto her forever. Annie was like a drug he couldn't get enough of, and it was an addiction he was enjoying. "My mom died when I was really young, but she always used to talk to me about the stars. She said that Ursa Major was the first great bear and that it represented all the bear shifters in the world. It was like a celestial representation of us, someone we could always look up to even when we didn't have another bear around."

"That sounds a lot more romantic than just calling it the Big Dipper." Annie looked up with him, her hair falling over his chest and tickling his throat.

He liked it, though. "Ursa Minor is up there for all the bears who don't quite know who they are or what their destiny is yet. It was always one of my favorite constellations to find as a kid. I felt like I was seeing myself up there in the stars." Jude looked back to Ursa Major, thinking about his mother. She'd said the stars that made up the pattern represented all the bear shifters who'd ever lived. He knew now, as an adult, that it'd all been metaphorical, but he couldn't help but wonder if she'd been watching over him all these years.

"No one ever told me that," Annie said, sounding wistful. "Everything was about meetings and business and checking the books. My parents had a very corporate view of the clan. I thought Jordan would handle things a little differently. He does, but it's still not the way I'd run the ship."

"And what would you do?" He leaned his head to the side, pressing his cheek against her scalp.

"It doesn't really matter," she hedged.

"Sure it does."

Annie moved her head to look up at him. "You give me too much credit, Jude."

"Then maybe you should take it."

"All right. If I were to run the clan, I'd want it to be a bit of the casual side that Jordan likes and a bit of the more organized side that my parents preferred. I've spent too much time trying to make up for Jordan's lack of management, and maybe that's part of what made everyone resent me so much." She frowned, laying her head back down on his chest.

He stroked her hair. It felt so intimate, even considering what they'd just done. Jude noted that his bear was quiet and content. Every time he'd been near her, it'd gone crazy. They were as close as possible now, but it'd finally gotten what it needed. "I doubt they resent you."

Annie was quiet as she looked up at the stars. "I resented myself. I was angry at myself for not being what everyone else expected me to be, but I can see now that those expectations were probably all from me, too. I've spent so much time being acutely aware of how different I am and paying such close attention to it, that I don't give anyone else a chance to be close to me."

"I know how difficult family relations are." He was proud of her for making such a breakthrough, but he knew the same thing wouldn't come for him. Jude was an orphan. There was no one to make up with. He and Reid had a good relationship, and Annie was the only other person who mattered.

Her body had been still, but Annie suddenly shoved up off his chest and was scrambling to her feet.

"What's wrong?" He listened, tapping into his animal's senses. All was quiet around them.

"Nothing. I want to try again." She stood before him, naked and glorious, grinning from ear to ear.

"Annie, you don't have to do that."

But she was giggling now. "Yes, I do. Jude, you make me feel more alive than I've ever felt before. So many times, I've tried to get closer with my bear, trying to get it to come out and play for a while. I couldn't do it, but there's something about being out here with you in the way that we are that just feels different."

Before he could offer any advice, Annie had sucked in a deep breath that thrust her breasts forward. She tipped her head back into the starlight, and her shoulders sagged. Jude got to his feet, worried something had gone wrong. She fell forward, bracing herself on all fours as her back lengthened, muscles and fur blooming all over her body. Her beautiful face molded and changed into that of a bear. He watched in fascination as her ears rounded over and moved up to the top of her head.

"You're beautiful," he said as he approached her, admiring the flecks of gold and black in her fur. "This is the part of you I was able to see even when you couldn't show it to the rest of the world."

She looked up at him with her ursine eyes, which were the same rich color as her human ones. Annie nudged his hip with her cold nose.

He smiled, knowing what she wanted. "Yeah. Let's do this." Jude stepped back and shifted, molding and forming into his own version of what Annie had now become. As good as it'd felt to be human with her, being in their true forms together was remarkable. There was a certain connection that simply wasn't there when they stood on two feet.

Jude noticed an odd vibration coming from her. *Are you all right?*

Yeah. It's a little scary, and I'm not used to it yet, but I finally know who I am. Annie turned her nose toward her left flank and then her right, trying to see the entirety of herself. *I'm glad you're here with me.*

Me, too. The two of them ambled off into the night, leaving their clothes in a pile behind them, picking up speed as they ran through the canyons and used them as their playground.

8

L.A. SEEMED TOO FAMILIAR AS ANNIE AND JUDE PULLED AWAY FROM THE airport. While their trip to Vegas wasn't intended to be a vacation at all, she'd liked being somewhere different with him. It was nice to get away from everything she'd known before. If she hadn't, she might never have found the other side of herself.

Of course, coming back to L.A. also meant having to face the awful fact that Jordan was still missing. "When do you think you'll hear back about that vehicle?"

Jude kept his eyes on the road. "It just depends. There's no certain timeline, but I'm sure they'll find it. I'll go to headquarters and help with the search."

"If we need to go back to Vegas, I'd be happy to join you," she said with a smile. Their night under the stars had been absolutely sublime. Annie couldn't have asked for anything more spontaneous and romantic, and she'd been reliving it the entire plane ride back. Her body was still tingling with all the energy, both from her time with Jude and from finally being able to shift. She'd tapped into a part of herself that'd always been there but refused to come to the surface, and she knew she'd never be the same again.

"We'll just have to see what happens," he replied noncommittally. "It might be too dangerous."

Annie sank into the passenger seat. Jude had gone back to that quiet, stoic façade he'd put up before they'd gone out to Red Rock Canyon. Somehow, she imagined it would be different between the two of them now, but she'd been wrong. "Is everything okay? I mean, between us?"

His jaw tightened, and her stomach sank. Something was definitely not okay.

"Please, Jude. Just talk to me."

He flicked on the turn signal but still wouldn't look at her. "I've been thinking a lot about what happened between us. I was being honest when I told you what I'd been feeling for you, and I'm glad that we both got that off our chests. But I still don't feel right about betraying Jordan."

"He's not going to care." Annie believed that, but she could see the little fantasy world she'd so quickly built up around herself and Jude crumbling to pieces. They'd had a magical night, running through the canyons and bluffs, being themselves and being together. They hadn't come back to retrieve their clothes until dawn, and when they'd gone to the hotel, they'd tumbled into his bed.

"You say that. Annie, I know you're a pretty realistic person, but things are different between guys. I saw the way Jordan was always trying to keep you away from the wrong guys, and how much he worried about you." His knuckles turned white on the steering wheel.

"That doesn't mean you!" Annie felt anger rising in her system at the notion, bringing back those same old feelings of frustration and defeat. She couldn't possibly have come this far, only to have the one person who truly understood her turn around and let it all go.

"It does. Trust me, Annie. I know it does. When we find Jordan, if he finds out what happened between us, he'll never speak to me again. I can handle that, but I don't want to ruin any relationship the two of you have. Family is more important than anything."

"No, it's not!" Her voice filled the car. She could hear that shrill quality that always came through when she got frustrated with her clan when they refused to do what was best for them. Everything she'd longed and hoped for was being yanked out from under her. "You can't possibly sit there and tell me that a fated connection, something so deep and special that you can only share it with it one other person in the entire world, is more important than anything else!"

He glanced at her and then back at the road, bracing one elbow on the door and propping his head on his hand. "You don't understand."

"Then make me," she growled. "Don't sit there and talk to me like you know so much more than I do just because you've been able to shift your entire life, and I've only been able to do it for a day."

"It's not about that. Damn it." Jude sighed. "I don't want Jordan to think I took advantage of you when you were vulnerable, nor do I want you to look back on the situation and think the same thing. That's not all of it, though."

"You might as well tell me, then, because all my patience went out the window about half a mile back." Annie put her tongue between her teeth and bit down just hard enough to keep herself from crying again. This emotional roller coaster was more than she could handle.

"Annie, you come from a prominent bloodline of Alphas. Your clan has been handed down from one generation to the next for as far back as anyone can remember. If shifters had royalty, you'd be part of it."

She'd never thought about it like that, but she still didn't see how it was relevant. "Your point?"

"I have absolutely no business being with you. I was lucky enough to get adopted into a clan when my parents passed away, but I was always on the outskirts. I've been the black sheep my entire life. If you're going to be with someone, it needs to be somebody who deserves that position."

Annie's mouth fell open as she tried to wrap her head around what he was saying. "Are you seriously telling me you don't deserve me?"

"Don't bother telling me it's not true. You might not see it right now, but in time you will, and you'll be glad that I backed out of this before it was too late." He turned into the driveway in front of the Martinez clan's clubhouse.

"I can't fucking believe you, Jude," Annie said bitterly, feeling betrayed. "I opened up to you. I told you everything that I'd been going through, and you seemed to understand. I guess you just used that to get what you wanted out of me." She unfastened her seatbelt and let the buckle fly back, knocking into the post. When she got out of the car, she slammed the door behind her. All the violence in the world wasn't going to make her feel any better about this.

Jude got out of the car as well, moving carefully and wearing that same neutral look on his face. He reached for the trunk, but she slapped his hand away.

"I can get it myself, thank you very much." Somehow, her suitcase had grown far heavier in the two days since she'd left L.A. Her anger fueled her strength, however, and she whipped it out and onto the sidewalk.

"Annie, I understand if you're mad. I just want you to recognize where I'm coming from." He stood there by the trunk like he was waiting for her to change her mind and say it was all fine.

"Oh, don't worry. I understand *completely*." Annie stepped up close to him, not because she wanted to be near him, but because she didn't want to risk anyone overhearing what she had to say. "You've had a little time to think about it, and you don't want to put up with the embarrassment of being with me. I might be able to shift now, but I'm still not as worthy as someone who's been able to do it all along. I don't fit in with your Special Ops Shifter Force bros and all the superhero shit you do. And you know what? That's absolutely fine with me, Jude." She turned on her heel and marched up the walkway.

"Annie! It's not like that!"

She ignored him, and by the time she was letting herself in the side door, she heard him getting back into his car. Part of her was upset that he didn't follow her and try to argue his case anymore. She wanted to argue with him. She wanted to yell and scream and punch him in his stupid, perfectly-chiseled face. But there wouldn't be a chance to do that. After all, he wasn't arguing in favor of them being together. Jude didn't want to have anything to do with her.

The only thing she wanted to do was get up to her room and collapse into bed, but as she turned for the hall, she nearly ran into Austin.

"Hey! There you are! How was Oregon?"

"What?" she snapped, not wanting to deal with him.

"You said you went to Oregon to visit your sick friend or something," he reminded her.

The hallway was too close. Annie thought she might suffocate if they stood there much longer, and she didn't really give a shit what Austin or anyone else thought of her. The universe had let her down. "Yeah, well, I lied. I went to Vegas to look for Jordan." She pushed past him.

Austin followed her into the living room. "Whoa, hold on. Did you find him?"

Annie stopped and sighed, her breath hot in her mouth. This was one of the many aspects of returning to real life that she hadn't been anticipating. Until they found Jordan, she was still in charge. She'd spoken to Jude about dumb ideas like balancing the way she ran the place, but with the way she felt right now, she just didn't give a shit. "Why would you care? I came to you when he didn't come back from his shoot, and you told me he was probably just hanging out with some showgirls. I was the only person in this damn house who wanted to make sure he was all right."

"I'm sorry about that." Austin took her suitcase from her hand and put it in the corner. "Sit down. You look really upset."

The last thing she wanted was for a man like him to patronize her. Even as upset as she was with Jude, she wasn't going to just fall into his arms. That was probably what he was hoping for; he was always trying to find a way to get under her skin. The fact remained, however, that Austin was one of the most senior members of their clan. Just like the Martinezes, his family had been around for generations. If anyone deserved to know, it was him. Still. "Is Michelle around?"

He shook his head. "She went to the store and out to run some errands. She knew you were coming back today, and she didn't want you to be upset if things hadn't been handled around here." He smiled at her.

Annie turned away from him, not wanting to see anyone give her that look. His smile wasn't anything genuine anyway. It was just another way he was kissing her ass. She sank down onto the sofa. "An old friend of mine said he'd help me find Jordan. We went to Las Vegas, since that was the last place he'd been seen. We didn't find him, but someone thought they saw him. It turned out to be his stunt double."

"Oh. So, is he really missing, then?" Austin sat down too close to her, but she had no room to scoot away.

"That seems to be the case. The worst part is that this stunt double was a human, and his plan was to take over Jordan's career. He found out about Jordan being a shifter, and he ended up selling him to some other guys. I'm just waiting for a little more information so I can figure out what to do next." Annie stood, feeling claustrophobic, and went to the window. She craved the wide-open space she and Jude had found out in Red Rock Canyon, though she didn't want to share it with him or anyone else.

Austin followed her. "Information? Is this that guy that was with you out in the gazebo? I don't know anything about him, Annie, but you shouldn't trust him with clan information. That could be dangerous."

She gripped the windowsill, thinking about how wonderful it'd felt to let her claws free. "He's not dangerous." Not physically. And Jude wouldn't do anything to betray Jordan. That could be counted as a point in his favor if he hadn't used it as an excuse to stomp all over her heart.

"What kind of information are you waiting on? Maybe it's something I can help with."

Annie shook her head. Austin could probably hold his own in a bar room brawl, but he didn't have the same resources that Jude did. It wasn't like they could just drop in a few of the local hotspots and hope to find Jordan sitting at the bar somewhere. "The stunt double gave us a description of the vehicle, and it's being tracked down."

"What kind of vehicle?"

She felt her shoulders tense with irritation. Annie didn't need an inquisition like this right now. It would've been better to wait until she could gather everyone together and tell them all at once. "It's just a black Jeep, okay?"

Her eyes lifted as she said it, resting on a black Jeep parked in the driveway. She'd been so furious with Evan that she'd hardly even heard the description of her brother's captors, but now she could remember it as though the stuntman was whispering it in her ear at that moment. *A big blonde guy with a black Jeep.* Surely not...

She turned, finding that Austin had closed in on her. He put his hands on either side of the window frame, pinning her against the glass. "You really shouldn't stick your nose where it doesn't belong, Annie."

Panic flooded her system. "What the hell are you doing, Austin?"

"What I should've done a long time ago." In one swift movement, he snatched her wrists and twisted her arms around behind her back. Austin pulled her close so that he spoke right in her ear. "I thought I could do it the nice way, Annie. I was going to convince you that the two of us were meant to be together. After all, no one else would want a reject like you. It was supposed to be easy. You had to be stubborn, though."

Annie swallowed. "I don't understand. You're mad at me because I wouldn't go out with you?"

He shook her arms, making her head wobble painfully on her

neck. "No, you stupid bitch! I never really wanted you, I was just sick and tired of seeing you and your incompetent brother lead this clan without a clue. Jordan didn't give a shit what happened because he was too caught up in his career, and you had so little of a life, you cared too much about what happened. I'd make a far better Alpha, and if I have to jump in and take the position, then so be it."

Rage and fear mixed nauseatingly in her stomach. "Austin, we can talk about this. Just let me go. If you want to have some hand in the administration of the clan, that can be done."

His laugh was sharp enough to crack through the room. "I was going to marry you and wait at least a year before I offed Jordan and took over for myself. I mean, we all know no one would tolerate you in the position, but my bond with you would solidify me as the Alpha. I'm not playing the long game anymore."

Fine. She'd tried to play nice and get him to talk. It pissed Annie off to no end that she'd been right about Austin, yet no one had listened to her, but her complaints would have to wait. "Just tell me what you did with Jordan."

"Oh, you'll get to find out for yourself." Austin shoved her forward, back down the hall, and to the basement door. "You're lucky we didn't run into each other out in Vegas. I must have left right before you showed up at Evan's place. I figured your trip to Oregon would be the perfect time for me to head over to Nevada and pick up my prize." He opened the door.

Annie resisted, struggling against his grip. She let out a scream, one even louder than the one Jude had elicited from her back in the park, but just as primal.

Austin yanked hard, making her slam her head on the doorjamb. "Might as well keep your mouth shut, bitch. Anyone who's not on my side was sent out of the house for the night. No one who can hear you will be willing to help you." He dragged her down the stairs after him.

"What are you going to do with me?" she panted. Annie remembered Jude taking note of the fact that she hadn't shifted in the fight she'd helped him with. She dug down deep inside herself, hoping to find her bear and bring it out again. Her head spun from the blow, making it difficult to concentrate. No, it was best to wait. Let him think she was weak. He'd already made mention of 'what she was.'

"That remains to be seen. I think I'll play with you for a bit, and then I'll kill you. The only thing keeping me from doing it right now is coming up with a good cover story as to why both you and your brother disappeared. It shouldn't take much to convince the other members to elect me as their new Alpha. They already know I deserve it." Austin hauled her across the room, where one of his goons was waiting for her.

Annie looked up at Austin's accomplice. It was Mike, another man she'd known her entire life. He'd always hung out with Austin, but she'd never guessed he would be in on a scheme like this. "Mike, you don't have to do this. You don't have to do what he says."

But Mike smirked down at her. "I'm going to be his beta, so yeah, I do." He held her arms in place, crushing her biceps in his enormous hands as Austin fastened metal zip ties over her wrists.

"You'll be easy to dispatch when I get the chance later tonight since you're nothing but a weakling anyway, but there's nothing like a little precaution," Austin explained as he yanked them tight. "Even if you could shift, these would only cut off your circulation as soon as you became a bear."

He opened the door to a storage closet in the far corner of the basement and flicked on the light. Annie gasped as she saw a familiar figure already lying on the concrete floor. "Jordan!"

"You guys can have a little time to catch up before I get rid of you," Austin said. He shoved Annie into the room and slammed the door behind her.

Her knees hit the concrete, abrading through her thin jeans, and the metal strips bit into her wrists. Her heart was running solely on fear and adrenaline, and Annie scooted forward until she was next to her brother's crumpled form. "Jordan? Are you all right?"

"Oh, Annie. Oh, god. He got you, too. I'm so sorry. I'm so sorry for everything. I should've believed you."

With her hands bound uselessly behind her back, Annie bent forward and laid her head on his arm. "Yes, you should've, but I can berate you about that later. What is all this?"

Jordan struggled to sit up, using the wall behind him for leverage. He had a gash above his eye that was slowly seeping blood, and his facial hair had grown out into a thick stubble. "I'm still trying to figure it out. It started with my goddamn stunt double."

"I know about Evan," she offered. "When you didn't come home from Vegas, I started making phone calls. Austin wasn't concerned about your whereabouts, but now I know why. Anyway, I called Jude. He was going to help me find you."

"Jude?" Jordan whipped his head around to look at her. "Well, that was a pretty good choice."

"It turned out to be, even though I had no clue about this SOS Force stuff at the time. He and I went to Vegas to find you, and we found Evan instead. He told us about his plot to take over your career, but I'm afraid I didn't know until just now that it was Austin who'd come after you."

Jordan nodded. "Yeah. I called the clubhouse when I checked out, and I told Austin I was going out with Evan. My guess is that he figured it'd be easier to take me out in a strange place instead of the living room, but it didn't quite work out the way he planned."

"I wonder what's stopping him from killing us." Annie looked at the door. She'd heard Austin lock it behind him. Was he still on the other side of it, or had he gone upstairs? What had he done with the rest of the clan?

"It's a show for him," Jordan grunted, wriggling against his restraints. "He can't just slaughter us and take over. There are plenty of members who are content to just follow whomever the official Alpha is, but they're not going to stand for outright murder. Austin's trying to figure out his story."

"Which will be easy for him to do now that he's got us both down here. He told me he sent away everyone who wasn't in on his plan, too." Unwillingly, Annie wished Jude was there with them. That serene demeanor of his could be really useful right now.

"I'm sorry, Annie. You need to know that I'm really, really sorry. I'm sorry for being such a shitty Alpha. I'm sorry for not realizing how much you care about the clan. And I'm incredibly sorry for blowing you off when you said something was wrong. You know this clan better than anyone, and I should've listened to you." He turned to her, his handsome face twisted by grief.

"You're not a shitty Alpha," she said, feeling sorry both for him and herself. "We just have different ways of running the show, and it was difficult for us to make them both work."

"No. *I'm* difficult. And selfish. And look where it's gotten us." He bent his head to look over his shoulder at his bindings, which were the same as hers. "There's nothing I can do to get us out of this. I can't shift unless I want to lose circulation in my paws, and you can't possibly fight them on your own."

Annie bit her lip. She'd imagined giving Jordan the good news when they had a moment to themselves, maybe over dinner. There was no better time than now, especially since she didn't know how long they'd live. "Jordan, I have to tell you something. I can shift now."

His brows wrinkled together. "You can?"

Her cheeks heated, despite their current situation. "Yeah. It was something that happened while I was... with Jude."

A trickle of blood seeped from the corner of Jordan's mouth as he smiled. "Is there something between you and Jude?"

"Yeah. Well, I mean, there was. He told me everything he'd been feeling for me, and I'd been feeling it, too. Jordan, I wasn't sure if I would ever feel that. Even when I did, I doubted it. I didn't think I was good enough. I was so excited about it, but Jude doesn't want to have anything to do with me anymore."

"What did he do to you?" Jordan squirmed to straighten up, the smile on his face quickly turning to a scowl. "I'll kill him."

"That's exactly what he's afraid of. He said he didn't want to be with me because it would make you angry, and he refused to betray you. Then he rattled off some stuff about being an orphan and not belonging to a clan in the same way that I do and something about bloodlines, that he's not good enough for me. I don't know. I think it was just an excuse because I'm not like everyone else." She looked down at her lap, feeling ashamed all over again.

"It's probably not an excuse," Jordan replied quietly. "Jude and his brother were orphaned when they were really young, but I guess he told you that. He's been hung up on it ever since, because he doesn't believe he actually belongs anywhere. He told me on one of his visits home from the Army that he loved the brotherhood of it. There were times when his service was miserable, but he liked knowing he was a part of something. Knowing him, I wouldn't be surprised at all if he thinks he's not good enough for you."

"Really?"

Jordan nodded. "He's spent a lot of time distancing himself from anything that might make him happy, because he's too worried about it breaking his heart again. And he was always working so hard to be strong for Reid. Even as a kid, I could see how much he was hurting.

When we get out of here, Annie, I'll sit down with him and have a long talk."

"So, you wouldn't be upset if he and I were together? I mean, not that I need your permission, but he seems to think we do." A small ball of excitement built up in her stomach, even though she didn't want to get her hopes up.

"Never." He leaned against her, the closest he could get to hugging her at the moment. "Annie, I know I've been protective of you. I've worried about you, and you shouldn't have had to feel the need to push back against me all the time. I want you to be safe and happy, but I'd never deny you of your fated destiny. If Jude is your one true mate, then so be it. At least it's someone I know and trust. Not like Austin. And I'm sorry about that whole thing."

"Don't worry about it. I don't blame you. You just wanted the best for me, and Austin pulled the wool over both our eyes." She hoped she'd get the chance to see just what it was like to dig her claws into his flesh before this was all over with.

"I wanted you to be happy, but that wasn't the only reason I was so weird about you finding someone." Jordan snuck a look at her from the corner of his eye. "When I took over the clan, Mom and Dad and some of our older relatives sat down with me. I figured it was just going to be one of those long boring talks about how important it was to be the Alpha, how it might be hard at first, and all that. There was some of that, but they also said there would be some very important shifters to come from our bloodline. I don't understand all of it, but they said there was this prophecy about one of our mates carrying the mark of the helix. Jude has it, doesn't he?"

Annie's mind was suddenly filled with the image of that silvery, swirly mark on Jude's chest. "Yeah."

"I thought so. It's been a long time since he and I were both in our bear forms together, and I hadn't even thought about that mark until I was told about this. I just kind of dismissed it, but it sounds to me like the two of you really are meant to be together."

"Wow." Annie already knew what she felt in her heart and soul for Jude. There was little that could convince her otherwise, and even his denial of how good they could be together wouldn't have kept them apart for long. She'd let her temper and heartache get the best of her.

"I'm happy for you, but I just hope you get the chance to tell him. I don't know what we're going to do." Jordan tipped his head back against the wall, mussing that hair that'd been the subject of countless articles in men's magazines.

"I'll tell you what we're going to do. We're going to shift and get the hell out of here." Annie had a true purpose in her life now. She had to get back to Jude, and if that meant going through Austin and the assholes who chose to follow him, then so be it.

"That's not going to work. I already told you. These things will cut right into my flesh if I shift, and they'll be far too tight."

"They will, but it's not like anything bad will happen immediately. Austin used these on you with the thought that you'd be down here by yourself. Bear teeth are pretty damn strong, so if I shift, I can tear enough of the metal to get you free. Then you can do the same for me. We'll tackle the door together." Now that she had a plan in mind, she couldn't wait to see it come to fruition.

"Shouldn't I be the one to shift first?" Jordan asked. "It's going to hurt."

Annie grinned at her big brother. "I'm smaller than you, so it won't hurt me as badly. Besides, I do all my own stunts." She turned away from him and closed her eyes, thinking about Jude and that night under the stars. Annie promised herself they'd find a chance to relive that night if she got out of this. She tapped into that feeling of wildness and freedom that came with her bear, happy to see it rise to the surface with much more ease this time. She moaned as her bear emerged and found itself in the same shackled position as her human, the ties cutting painfully into her. Annie knew she could do this.

9

Jude went straight to the coffee pot as soon as he got back to headquarters. There was something comforting about listening to the grinder decimating the beans and the pot steaming and bubbling away. It filled the kitchen with his favorite scent in the world—other than Annie.

Damn it. There'd be no getting away from her. He could tell her they would stay away from each other, and he could keep his distance from her as much as possible while they searched for Jordan, but she would always be there in the back of his mind and the depths of his heart. Their distance over the passing years had made his wonderment about her subside, but now that his beast had claimed her, there was no turning back.

To make matters worse, he felt like a complete asshole for letting her down the way he had. Annie needed him. Logically, though, Jude knew it'd been the right decision. The hard ones usually didn't feel good.

"There he is, finally back from his little Sin City trip! How'd it go, bro?"

Jude had just pulled a mug down from the cabinet, but he turned to find Reid standing just behind him. A woman was at his side, short and diminutive with skin like porcelain. Her ebony hair was streaked with traces of auburn, and her dark eyes had a look to them that said she'd be glad to kick ass and take names if she needed to. Jude liked her instantly. "You must be Mali. I'm sorry you got stuck with the likes of my brother."

She smiled sweetly up at Reid and laughed. "If it's my burden, then I'm willing to bear it."

"Hey!" Reid protested, but he planted a kiss on her neck. "Mali, this is my brother, Jude. Jude, this is Mali."

"Since you're here, can I assume you've decided to stay on with the Force?" Jude filled his mug to the brim and sipped some of the hot, bitter liquid from the top. Perfection.

"I tried to call you about that, actually, but you haven't been answering your phone," Reid pointed out.

"Oh, right. Sorry." Jude had seen a missed call, but he'd been too preoccupied with Annie to worry about it. His brother would always be there, and Annie... well, Annie was a different story altogether. "I've been a little preoccupied with my mission."

"Does that mean it went well, or did it go to shit?"

"Before I start answering your questions, you need to answer mine. Are you staying?" Jude took another sip, using the motion to hide the fact that he was holding his breath.

"Yeah." Reid gave another lovey-dovey look to Mali. "It's going to be the best for both of us here. Besides, you won't have any excuses to bail on our wedding."

"Congratulations, guys." Jude shook each of their hands. Not all destined mates chose to take that extra step, but he was truly happy for Reid. "That's great news."

"Thank you. Now that you know it's official, tell me about Vegas."

Jude glanced at Mali. He had no doubts about her, considering she and Reid were meant to be together, but some things could only be discussed among brothers.

Fortunately, she seemed to get the hint. "I have a little more unpacking to do, if you gentlemen will excuse me."

Reid watched her backside as she glided from the kitchen. "She's something else, man. I can't believe how lucky I am. It's the sort of thing that makes me wish everyone would find their mates."

"I don't know. What if you find the one, but it's impossible for the two of you to be together? Surely, that has to happen now and then." Jude frowned down into his cup, finding no solace in the dark brew.

"Okay, sounds like you have plenty to talk about. I think I'll make myself comfortable." Reid turned for the fridge, pulled out a cold cut and cheese platter, and sat down at the bar with it. "I'm all ears."

"Do yourself a favor and keep Mali out of any missions you might go on," Jude advised. "No offense to her, she seems like a great girl. But it makes things so much more complicated. It's enough to think about keeping yourself and the other Force members safe while accomplishing your task. Women just add a whole new layer of trouble."

"Jude," Reid warned, "you're beating around the bush. It's not going to have any leaves left on it by the time you're done."

"Okay. What really happened, if I were to write up a report about it, is that Jordan's stunt double drugged and kidnapped him in order to take over his career. Someone else came in and bought Jordan off of him, and we have no idea who it was or why they would do such a thing. They knew he was a shifter, though, so there's definitely something crazy going on."

"That's fucking wild," Reid admitted, sandwiching a piece of cheese between two hunks of salami. "What's the redacted part?"

"Having Annie next to me on the plane, in the car, in the hotel room next to mine, and fighting alongside me. I know I felt something for her a long time ago, but enough time had gone by that I thought I must have been wrong. I was determined to remain professional, but then she opened up to me and told me one of her deepest, darkest secrets. And I repaid the favor by blabbing about how I felt about her." Just retelling it made him feel a little nuts.

Reid squinted painfully. "And she didn't feel the same way?"

"She did, actually! She told me she was feeling the exact same thing. We hooked up under the stars, Reid, and it was the most incredible thing I'd ever experienced in my goddamn life!" Jude slammed his fist down onto the countertop.

"I know you pretty well, Jude, but this isn't making sense. What exactly is the problem?"

Sinking onto one of the barstools, Jude leaned his elbows heavily on the counter. "She's Jordan's sister. I can't possibly be with her. It would ruin everything between my best friend and me."

Reid raised an eyebrow. "Dude, you sound like me before I met Mali."

"What does that mean?"

"You know exactly what it means." Reid punched him gently in the arm. "I didn't want to be tied down, and I would've made any excuse not to be. I would've made up some story that sounded good enough inside my head, but once I said it out loud, everyone would know it was complete shit."

"It's not shit," Jude argued. "There's a lot going on for the two of us. Besides, Annie is second-in-command of her clan right now. If we don't find Jordan, she's going to become Alpha. It wouldn't make any sense for her to be dealing with all that, and for me to be working with the Force. We'd never see each other. What?"

Reid was leveling the most serious look Jude had ever seen on his face. "That's pretty much the same things. It's just another way to justify what you're doing, even though it's completely wrong."

"Like you'd know," Jude sneered, feeling bitter at the world.

"Go ahead and be mad at me if it makes you feel better, Jude. I'm not worried about it, because I know eventually, you're going to figure out how you're sabotaging yourself. Just do me a favor and think about this: it's one thing to screw yourself over if you're the only one who's going to suffer. It's completely different if it affects someone else." Reid covered the plate and got up to put it back in the fridge.

"I'm not screwing anyone. If anything, I'm making the decision that's best for everyone, even if it's not best for me. I'd say that's pretty generous." Jude knew he was making himself miserable, but Annie would have a better chance of happiness with someone else. In the back of his mind, he was also holding onto the idea that Annie was too good for him. Reid wouldn't want to hear that, but it was true.

"Oh, you're such a friggin' martyr," Reid cracked. "Who says it's up to you, anyway? I mean, when Mali and I met, it was a completely mutual thing."

"You've known her for how long? And you're already acting like you're the expert on fated mates," Jude derided. "I don't need Professor Reid to lecture me on the ways of the heart."

"I think you do. You're hiding behind your excuses, and you're acting as though this is all up to you. Annie is a grown woman, and she can decide for herself. Hell, the universe has already told you how things are supposed to be. Who are you to argue?"

Jude's lips tightened. He had no retort for that. Reid was right. "Fine. I'll give you a point for that one. But even so, how am I supposed to get around the Jordan problem? He was always so concerned about who Annie ended up with."

"Since you don't even know where he is, I wouldn't worry about it for now. Drive over there, scoop her into your arms, and tell her you can't live without her. Spend all day in bed together, banging from sunrise to sunset, and then decide if you really care about what Jordan says." Reid softly stared through the living room toward the staircase, no doubt thinking of Mali.

"You're right, but you're also love drunk. I don't know. Maybe she and I should sit down and talk it over, but not right now. I've got to find Jordan first. Everything else has to wait."

"Fair enough," Reid conceded. "In the meantime, I think I might take my own suggestion." He moved toward the stairs.

Just then, Raul came in from the conference room. "Jude! I'm glad you're here. I was just about to call you. I found some intel on the Jeep."

"Awesome. Where do I need to go?" He was more than ready to run back to Vegas or anywhere else as long as it kept him far away from Annie.

"About twenty minutes away," Raul said solemnly. "Just knowing it was a black Jeep wasn't much to go on, but I was able to tap into enough surveillance cameras that I found the one that'd been at Evan Boyer's house. A few more tries and I got a plate number, but you're not going to like where I traced it back to."

"Just tell me," Jude urged. "Jordan's probably in serious danger."

Raul sighed and set his laptop on the counter. "Right here. It's Annie's clubhouse. The Jeep belongs to a guy named Austin Reed."

"Shit." Jude easily remembered the guy who'd come out to the gazebo to confront them when he'd gone to visit Annie. "This was an inside job. I thought because the stunt double was involved—who's not a shifter, by the way—that it was something entirely human."

"At least you don't have to worry about the word getting out about us," Reid pointed out, having stuck around to find out what was going on instead of following Mali upstairs.

"Except that I just dropped Annie off at that exact address," Jude replied. "I've got to go."

Reid nodded. "I'm coming with you."

"I'll round up the others, and we'll be on your heels," Raul promised, shutting his laptop with a click and heading off into the house.

"HERE WE GO." Jude pulled to a halt once again in front of Annie's house. "We've got to do this right, Reid. I don't know how many clan members are working against the Martinezes, or even if Annie is still here." A wave of nausea washed over him as he imagined all the harm that could've befallen her in the short time since he'd dropped her off.

"It'll be all right," Reid assured him, smiling slightly. "I'm glad to be on my first official Force mission with my brother, and I can't think of a better way of welcoming Annie to the family than by rescuing her."

Jude glanced at his brother. "You have to take this seriously," he warned. "This isn't just some stupid mission where you can act like a hotshot and not worry about the consequences."

"The only reason I'm not going to take that as an insult is because I would've done something just like that only a few years ago. Despite what my military records might say, things are different now." He got out and shut the door behind him. "I'm on this."

Checking his phone, Jude nodded. "I've got the confirmation from Raul. They're heading in through the back, so we've got the place covered. Let's go."

He strode up to the door as though he were just coming back to return an item Annie had left behind. In fact, that was the exact excuse Jude had cooked up as they'd prepared to leave the house, and he was ready with it when a man answered the door with a scowl.

"What do you want?"

"I'd like to see Annie, please," Jude said with a pleasant smile.

"Who are you?"

"Just a friend. She accidentally left her jacket in my car, and I'd like to return it." The jacket he had draped over his elbow was actually Emersyn's, and it'd been conveniently on a hook near the door.

"I'll take it to her," the man offered. He had shaved his head, which revealed a thick, ropy scar that wound back from his forehead and around his ear.

Jude had to wonder what kind of accident would make a wound like that. "I'd rather deliver it to her myself, actually." Without waiting for an invitation, Jude pushed past the man and into the living room.

"You can't just come in here!" he protested, but now Reid and Jude were both in the room. "Just leave the jacket and go."

"I wouldn't want to put the burden on you," Jude explained, still keeping that calm demeanor as he surveyed the room. There was no evidence of a struggle in there, but Annie's suitcase stood in the corner.

Knowing what a stickler she was for checking every box and tying up every loose end, Jude doubted she'd have come home and just left it there.

"Fine. Have it your way." The man slammed the door behind them and swaggered up to Jude, his fists curled at his sides, and swung a meaty hand at Jude's head.

Jude easily dodged it. "There's no need for violence. Just fetch Annie for me, please."

The bald guy swung again, lower this time.

Jude swerved backward. "I can tell that you're either a little hard of hearing or a little slow. I'm not here to fight. I'm just here to see Annie."

Reid snickered, bringing the bald man's attention.

"Oh, yeah? You think this is funny, asshole?" Growling, he went for Reid.

It was just the distraction Jude needed, and he saw the glint of mischief in his brother's eyes. Reid had this. Jude headed through the doorway and into the kitchen. No one was there, and he continued into the hallway just as a door opened to his left.

"Dominic! What's going on up here? I told you to answer the door and get rid of whoever it was!" Because of the direction the door opened, the man didn't see Jude right away. But as soon as he slammed it behind him, Jude recognized Austin.

"*You*," the blonde man said, narrowing his eyes. "What the hell do you want?"

"I'm here to talk to Annie, and I'm tired of repeating myself." Jude assessed his opponent. Austin was a big guy with plenty of muscles, but he didn't have the look of a trained fighter. Behind him, Jude could hear choking sounds coming from the man who must have been Dominic.

Austin nodded. "I see. You come sniffing around here once or twice and think you have some sort of right to her. Well, Annie told me she never wants to see you again."

"I want to hear it straight from her mouth," Jude challenged.

"No," Austin thundered. "In fact, she's chosen me as her mate, which gives me the authority to speak for her."

Jude knew it wasn't true. Annie didn't want to have anything to do with this thug, but the very idea of it sent a fire of rage and jealousy through his blood. "I want to hear it from *her*," he hissed.

"Intruders!" Austin shouted before charging down the hall toward Jude.

Jude was ready, and he blocked the first blow. It reverberated in his bones, but already he had that urge to protect Annie. He shoved Austin back with his elbow, knocking him against the wall. Before he could gain his balance, Jude snagged the front of his shirt and slammed him into the wall once again. "Tell me where she is, right now!"

"Fuck off!" Austin kicked out with one foot, bending Jude's knee backward.

Pain flooded his vision with swirling colors, but it reached deep inside him and pulled out his best weapon. His knee popped back into place as his leg thickened and shortened, the effect rippling up his back and tickling the underside of his scalp as he shifted into his bear form.

Austin had done the same, and now there were two bears in the hallway with very little room to maneuver. There was no place to go but forward, and his ursine mouth didn't allow Jude to ask any further questions. He attacked, shoving the other bear backward as he bared his teeth and slashed his paws through the air. The two of them tumbled through the narrow space, spilling out into a conference room.

Jude roared his rage and anger, finding that same fury inside him back at that little house on the outskirts of Vegas. Annie was in trouble, and he would stop at nothing to save her.

Austin had the advantage of knowing the room, and he thrust Jude toward the table. He caught himself as he crashed into a rolling chair that sped off across the room, knowing the full weight of Austin's attack was coming swiftly on his heels. The other bear fought with no style, but he was strong.

Jude felt the edge of the table making a hard line against his back as Austin roared in his face, and he swiped his claws toward the other beast. The house had erupted with crashing and shouting, and Jude knew the rest of the SOS Force had arrived. A second, deep black bear showed up through the door of the conference room, but Jude didn't recognize him. Now it was two against one.

Driving his paw forward with all his might, Jude sank his claws into Austin's side. The bear moaned in agony, his hot breath a cloud in Jude's face. With his claws still in the other man's flesh, Jude shoved him hard to the side. He needed to use all the inertia he could get, and he charged down the line of chairs until he slammed Austin's giant head into the flat-screen television mounted on the wall. Blood spurted through Austin's fur, and he sank to the floor.

Jude could already feel the other bear coming after him. He didn't have much time. Just as he turned, a wolf crashed through the window, who Jude instantly recognized as Raul.

I've got this one. Raul bared his teeth as he bounced off a chair and leapt onto the table, crashing down onto the back of the darker bear's neck. *Find Annie.*

How's everyone else? Jude sent the message out to the rest of the Force, not knowing who had shifted yet. Through ancient dragon magic, they shared a telepathic link that was typically reserved only for mates or those in a true clan, not one that'd been pieced together like the Force.

Reid, who hadn't yet been inducted into the Force with their official ceremony, still had a brotherly bond with Jude that allowed him to speak. *There are a lot of these bastards. I just took out two in the living room, but I think more are coming.*

I just came in through the kitchen door. It was Gabe, which meant there were now three Force members who were there fighting as bears. *Emersyn is at her clinic, and Amar is out on recon. No dragons or panthers for us today.*

I'm glad you're here. I'm heading downstairs. Though Jude didn't like to pin himself into any sort of corner, there had to be some reason Austin was in the basement earlier.

I've got your six, Reid replied.

It would've been handy to be in his human form to navigate the door handle, but Jude didn't want to waste time. He crashed against it with his shoulder, splintering the area near the latch. One more hard ram and it was off its hinges, hanging sadly through the opening to the stairwell.

Jude charged down, immediately confronted by two more of Austin's men in bear form. Like him, they weren't trained fighters. They lunged forward, both attacking at once and hardly giving each other enough room to swing their arms. As they came straight for Jude, he picked the one on the left and charged as well. His teeth sank into the thick flesh of the bear's neck. Jude clamped down harder, ignoring the blows that were hitting his back.

I've got him! Reid called out.

The other bear was no longer hitting Jude, and a heavy crash sounded as the two bears went tumbling away into the corner.

Blood filled his mouth, and he let go just long enough to get another good hold. His would-be attacker bellowed in pain as he flailed uselessly at Jude's back. One claw made it through Jude's thick fur, and he felt the burn of blood as it welled to the surface. Jude wasn't playing around. He clenched his teeth as hard as a vice and yanked his head to the right, ripping out the other bear's throat. His enemy fell to the floor, twitching.

"Very good," a familiar human voice said.

Jude turned to see Austin coming down the stairs. Blood ran down the side of his head, the wound mostly closed due to the inherent healing powers of shifters. He grinned as he staggered off the bottom step, puffing out his chest, full of just as much arrogance as ever. He clapped slowly as he came to stand in front of Jude. "What's the matter? You can't face me like a man?"

Jude knew better than to fall for that. He would be vulnerable while in the middle of his shift, and he wasn't going to give Austin the least bit of an advantage. It stopped Jude from saying all the things he wanted to the asshole, and that was the only thing that tempted him.

Austin glared at him, his anger simmering clearly just under the surface. "You and your friends can come and fight, but you'll never win. There are far more clan members here who want me to be their Alpha, and we'll get our way. You might as well tuck your stumpy little tail between your legs and head on back to wherever the hell you came from, because you're on *my* territory now."

Just then, a door on the side of the room crashed open. Two bears charged through it. Jude instantly recognized Jordan, with his dark coat and broad shoulders. Annie was next to him, the gold flecks in her fur sparkling brilliantly despite the poor lighting. Brother and sister attacked in unison, taking Austin down forever.

10

ANNIE SLOWLY STOOD, TRYING TO REGAIN HER BALANCE AFTER SHIFTING so quickly back into her human form. Everything had happened so fast, and it was going to take some time before she could catch up to the rest of them.

But seeing Jude just across the room was all the motivation she needed. Annie swiped a self-conscious hand through her hair as she stumbled to him and pulled him into a kiss. It was pure instinct. She didn't know if he'd push her away, but she was rewarded with the warm embrace of his arms around her back, pulling her in tightly as he deepened the kiss.

"I'm so glad you're here," she whispered against his lips, still clinging tightly to him.

"Of course I am," he said. His eyes skidded to the side and his cheeks reddened. "Um, your brother's here, too."

"I'm afraid you're the only one who cares about that," Jordan said, clapping his old friend on the shoulder. "Annie and I had some quality time together stuck in that closet, and she told me about your concerns."

Now it was Annie's turn to have her cheeks redden. She didn't want Jude to think she was talking about him behind his back. Most of the time, Annie didn't worry too much about what people thought about her. Like everything else with Jude, this was different. "I didn't know if we'd ever get out of there."

"It's all right," Jude said, pulling back a little and squeezing her hand. "There's no point in keeping it a secret."

"Especially for such a dumb reason," Jordan said playfully. "Dude, I couldn't possibly be mad at finding out the two of you are mates. You're one of the people I trust the most in the world."

Jude was the one who needed convincing, but hearing Annie's brother say this to him still made her feel better. That didn't take care of all their problems, though. "Jude, if there's some other reason you don't want to be with me, then please just tell me now." Her lungs froze in her chest as she gazed into those deep green eyes of his.

"Hold up," Jordan interrupted. "There might be more that the two of you need to hash out later, but I've got something I need to tell you, Jude."

Jude glanced at Annie and then back at his friend, hearing the serious tone in Jordan's voice. "What is it?"

The actor stuffed his hands in his pockets. "When this clan was handed down to me, I was told that someone in our bloodline would be fated to a bear who bore the mark of the helix. I didn't know anything about that when we were younger, but now, there's no doubt in my mind that it's you."

"The mark of the—" Jude touched his chest. "Oh. What does that mean?"

"Beats me," Jordan replied honestly. "We can talk about it later. I'm going to go make sure the rest of the house is secured. It's going to be interesting to sort out who's who. I never expected my own clan to revolt against me."

"I've got a man up there. I'm coming with you." Jude took Annie's hand and headed for the stairs. "I have to tell you, I was pretty impressed to see you take Austin down like that."

Her cheeks flushed again, but for a different reason this time. "What can I say? I learned from the best."

"You definitely didn't learn that from me," Jude argued, keeping her at his side as they made their way upstairs. "That was all right there inside you. I just helped you find it."

She knew she should've been happy. They'd found Jordan and took down Austin. They still had a few things to take care of, but everything was going to be okay. Still, Annie didn't know where she truly stood with Jude. He'd come to her rescue, but that didn't mean anything. "Jude, if we need to find time to talk about it later, then we can, but I really want to know where we stand." She didn't like thinking they were just going to go on with their lives without getting down to an answer.

He paused as they reached the upstairs hallway. "The truth is, I've been a complete idiot. I guess I was afraid that if I let myself love you, it was going to fall apart just like everything else in my life. I'm absolutely crazy about you, and if you can forgive me for being such a jackass, then I want to be with you for the rest of our lives."

Heat flooded her body as he held her close. "I do forgive you, but only if you can forgive me."

"You? What am I supposed to forgive you for?" Jude took her hand once again as they headed toward the living room.

"I know I'm not perfect. I can be too uptight, and sometimes I take things more seriously than they need to be." It was something she'd started thinking a lot about since that magical night in Red Rock Canyon, and it was something she wanted to change.

"I think I can handle that," Jude replied. "Besides, if it weren't for you taking things so seriously, none of this would've turned out the way it did."

———

A FIRE CRACKLED in the center of the clearing. Annie walked through the dark trees, keeping her eyes focused on the light ahead of them. "Are you sure this is what you want to do?"

Jordan walked along beside her, his head held high. "There's not a doubt in my mind."

That was great, but there were still plenty of doubts in *her* mind. "You were the one who was chosen for the position," she countered. "I don't know if it's a good idea to mess that up. When I came to you about problems within the clan, I never meant that you should step down as Alpha."

"I don't see it as stepping down," Jordan said. "I'm not just quitting because I have other things I want to do. I'm doing my job as Alpha by making sure that the clan is taken care of by the best person for the job. That's you, Annie. It always has been, and I'm pissed at myself for not seeing it before now."

"I didn't do anything."

"You did." Jordan stopped and took her by the shoulders, turning her so that she faced him. His face had been shaven clean, and the wounds he'd endured had healed over nicely. He'd informed his producer that he was ill and had to take a short hiatus from shooting, but he'd be back on the set within a few days. "You knew something was wrong, and you came to me. When that didn't work, you went to someone else who could help. If it weren't for you and Jude, I'd be dead right now. The rest of our clan would either be dead or wish they were. Annie, you've always taken better care of this family than I have. You deserve this, and everyone knows it. It might've been my idea to do this, but everyone else agreed."

She nodded, glad to know everyone was on board. "I guess let's get this part over with, then."

A drum sounded, cueing Jordan to enter the clearing. Annie stood back and watched as he marched to the fire in the center, bending to take a blazing torch from the pile of wood. He held it high over his head.

"The clan recognizes the Alpha, he who watches over us all," intoned the elderly voice of their Uncle Glen.

The gathering of bears murmured their assent, and another drumbeat sounded.

Annie pulled in a breath and followed her brother's path. She kept her eyes focused on him as she entered the circle, keenly aware of the rest of the clan's eyes on her. Their number had been pared down significantly now that Austin and his cohorts had been removed. Even so, plenty had come out to see this unprecedented event.

"The clan recognizes the beta," Uncle Glen announced.

Coming up next to Jordan, Annie stopped and stood with her shoulder nearly rubbing his arm. Her stomach roiled inside her, but then she caught a glimpse of Jude standing just outside the edge of the firelight. He smiled at her, and once again, she knew everything was going to be all right.

Jordan held the torch high. "I've been your Alpha for five years now," he said. "I thank the clan for everything it has done for me, but I recognize that I haven't done enough for it. For *you*. We are a gathering of some of the greatest bear shifters to exist, and you deserve the very best. This is why, with your permission, I pass this torch and the position of Alpha to my sister, Annie Martinez." He lowered the flaming piece of wood and held it in front of her.

Annie swallowed. The procedure was simple enough. There was no reason for it not to go well. Jordan had assured her that this was what everyone wanted, including him. Even if there were some bears among their ranks who still weren't certain about her, they wouldn't dare go against what he wanted. Would they?

She took the torch, the wood rough on her hands, and the fire warm on her face. She stared into the flame for a moment before hoisting it as high over her head as possible. The gathered shifters erupted with cheers and applause, showing her their approval.

It was Uncle Glen's turn again. "We recognize and welcome our new Alpha!" he announced, eliciting even more accolades from the crowd.

Annie waited patiently for the noise to die down. "Thank you. I will guide the clan for my entire life, and I will listen to the guidance of my elders." She placed the torch back on the fire to represent her oneness with the clan.

After more applause, the ceremony turned to a bonfire party. Food and drinks were brought out, and everyone took the chance to catch up with each other.

Jude handed her a glass of wine. "You were spectacular."

"If you say so. That was actually a little embarrassing." She didn't like having all those eyes on her, though she knew it wouldn't be the last time. Everyone would be watching her first actions as Alpha.

"At least it's over. I'm hoping that means the two of us can find a little time to be alone together." He raised one eyebrow, the fire reflecting in his gaze.

Someone cleared their throat, and Annie turned to find Uncle Glen standing nearby. "I wanted a chance to speak with you."

Jude stepped back. "I'll be over here with Jordan."

"No, I want to talk to you, too," Glen corrected. "I understand you carry the sign of the helix."

A troubled look passed over Jude's face, but he quickly cleared it away. "Yes. Jordan and I were just discussing that last week."

Glen put a hand on Jude's shoulder. "I want to apologize to you. I didn't realize any of this until Jordan told me about it, and if I had, I would have told you a long time ago. You might not remember me, but I was around sometimes when you used to come to the clubhouse."

"What is it?"

"Jude, I know you were orphaned when you were very young. What you might not realize is that the symbol on your chest is a sign of very prominent lineage from a very old clan, one that was unfortunately decimated the night that your parents were killed."

Annie watched the exchange with interest, though she felt for Jude. It couldn't be easy for him to bring all those memories to the surface.

"I never knew much about that night," he replied honestly. "We were young, and the Hoffmans never wanted to talk about it."

Uncle Glen nodded. "That's understandable. It was tragic. You see, your original clan was at war with another that was trying to take over their territory. They lost their final battle that night, but you and your brother were lucky enough to have been at the Hoffmans'. Our clan, your parents' clan, and the Hoffmans' had all been friendly with each other for a long time, which is why I know anything about this at all."

Jude glanced down at the ground. "I see. At least they died nobly, fighting for what they believed in. Our foster parents just told us it was an accident."

Annie slipped her hand into his. She didn't want this night to be marred by such terrible news, but it needed to be out there.

"I'm sure they were just trying to protect you," Glen replied. "Your father was the Alpha of his clan. He had that same mark on his chest, as it only ever showed on the first-born. You are a descendent of great nobility, Jude. Do with that what you will, but know that we're delighted to have you as part of our family." He clapped Jude on the shoulder once again, gave them a nod, and moved off to mingle.

"Are you all right?" Annie asked. Jude was always so stoic on the outside. It made him hard to read, but she was working on it.

He turned to her and smiled. "Actually, yeah."

"I would've thought you'd be upset hearing all that."

He put an arm around her and pulled her close. "No. I miss my parents, but that's a very old wound. It's not going to go away, but it can't really get worse. Knowing they were fighting for something they believed in makes me proud. If I'm honest, I can't say it hurts to know the truth about where they stood in their clan and what that patch of fur means. Now I know I'm good enough for you." He kissed her on the forehead.

Annie leaned into his embrace. "What are you talking about? You've always been good enough for me."

"You can say that, but now I know it." He trailed his kisses down her nose and to her mouth, ignoring the large number of people who'd gathered there for the ceremony. "So, Alpha Annie, what are you doing after this?"

"You, if I'm lucky," she teased.

They joined the festivities, eating and drinking and celebrating with the clan. The two of them ended up slipping away and heading back to the clubhouse while the fire was still burning brightly.

"I don't want you to miss out on any of the ceremony," Jude said as they headed inside. "I know this is a special night for you."

"Then you can help me make it extra special," she replied, grabbing his hand and leading him up the stairs to her room. The ceremony in the woods and the clan's acceptance of her had brought out something inside her, and Jude brought out even more. She felt every cell of her body tingling with life, and she didn't want to waste it.

Jude grinned. "I think I can help you with that." He shut the door behind him and grabbed her by the waist, yanking her into his arms and pressing his mouth against hers. He was already hard against her, which only made Annie all the more eager for him.

She kissed him back, scrunching her hands through his thick hair and down his neck. Her body surged toward him, hungry for all she knew he could give her. She felt her need for him in the very marrow of her bones as she pulled off his shirt and tossed it aside, pressing herself against his bare skin.

Jude growled softly as he scraped his teeth across the side of her neck. His big hands moved under her shirt, his thumbs brushing her pert nipples through the satin material of her bra. She lifted her shirt over her head to assist him, feeling her core tighten as he brushed his lips over the tips of each mound.

"How long is it going to be before anyone else gets back here?" has asked as he unbuttoned her jeans and sank his fingertips down between the denim and her thighs, touching the entire length of each leg as he removed them. "There are so many things I want to do to you tonight."

"I'm sure we'll have time for at least some of them, and then you can save the rest for tomorrow, and the night after that, and the night after that." Annie was down to her bra and panties now, and she was eager for him to catch up. She stripped away the rest of his clothing so that his hardness brushed against the thin layer of fabric that still separated them from each other.

He was absolutely gorgeous in either form he was in, but at the moment, Annie found herself particularly appreciative of this one. His broad chest and chiseled abs were just the beginning. The way he held her, the way they fit together at their most intimate moments when their souls reached outside their bodies to touch one another was the most attractive thing she could imagine. "I want you to know how much I appreciate you," she said as she dropped to her knees in front of him.

"You don't have to do that to let me know—oh." Jude's head thumped against the wall as it rolled back, and his hands tangled in her hair.

"I want to," she murmured, kissing and licking down the length of him. "Besides, it turns me on."

"If you insist," he panted, his hands hardening into fists as he tried to control himself.

Annie had felt a tremor of electricity starting at her core as they'd come into the room, and now it cascaded into waves of excitement that drove her on as she pleasured him. Hearing his moans and knowing how much he was enjoying it made her want to do this all night.

His knees were shaking by the time she finally pulled back. She took his hand and brought him to the bed, thinking they would get down to business.

But Jude had a different idea. He grabbed her by the waist, his strength fanning the fire of her infatuation as he flipped her onto her back. He mounted the bed so that he was on top of her, bracing himself on all fours and grinning down at her. "You can't possibly think you can be so good to me and not get anything in return."

He kissed his way down her neck, along her collarbone, and down the delicate skin of her side. He clung to her tightly as his tongue made slow, lazy circles around each nipple, sucking each one of them into the hot wetness of his mouth and leaving them cold and longing when he was done. His lips worked down the plateau of her stomach, and he surprised her by skipping down to her inner thigh and making his way down her legs.

Jude's hands took over the work by the time he reached her legs, and he massaged his way back up her body. His fingers were warm and knowing, finding even the tiniest of aches in her body and working them out slowly, never rushing. He was so patient, even though she lay spread out and ready before him.

"Turn over," he murmured.

She did as she was told, not wanting this incredible feeling to stop. It felt physically good to have his fingers brush her hair aside, rubbing her shoulders and moving further down her back, but there was so much more to it than that. Jude cared for her. He wasn't just there to get what he needed and go. He appreciated her like no other man in her life ever had, and she felt it in the way he squeezed and rubbed her.

"Did I put you to sleep?" he asked as he pressed his palms into her backside.

"No, but I think I've melted inside," she said with a smile.

"Turn over again. I think I missed a spot." Jude moved further down the bed between her legs, flicking his tongue against her sensitive bud. He was hot and wet against her, and after that impromptu massage, Annie had no choice but to relax into the feeling. His tongue worked against her, twirling against her soft, aching flesh until her thighs were quaking and her hips bucked against him. Pressing two thick fingers inside her, he rhythmically pressed against her G-spot, and within seconds, her inner walls began to contract, every muscle rippling in perfect synchronization as she reached her peak.

But he didn't stop there. Jude pulled her to the edge of the bed and took her from behind, his cock sliding into her as his hands gripped her hips. As his right hand slipped between her legs, his fingertips began massaging slick circles over her clit.

"I want you to come as many times as possible," he said, bringing his left hand up to cup her breast as he dragged his tongue along her back.

She couldn't resist the magic he worked on her, and Annie was grateful there was no one else in the house as she screamed her pleasure twice more. Annie turned over beneath him, once again rejoicing in the way he filled her. She wrapped her legs around him as his hips thrust against hers, and before she knew it, she was being pushed over that edge yet again as Jude buried his face in her shoulder and growled with his release.

Annie fought to catch her breath as they lay next to each other, too hot to bother getting under the covers. "I'm glad we did this tonight."

"You don't think you're missing out on anything happening in the woods?" Jude tucked her against his side and held her tightly.

"There's nothing I'd rather do than this. Besides, if we get our own place like we talked about, then this could be our only chance to have fun in this room." She snuggled in against him, feeling how calm her bear was inside. Never in her life had it been so much at peace.

He kissed her forehead. "I think that'll be a good idea. I actually saw a place online that I think might work. We can go look at it tomorrow if you want."

"Grab your phone and show me the pictures. Maybe we could drive by it tonight." Until they'd started talking about it, Annie hadn't realized just how much she'd wanted a change, and getting out of that house she'd been living in her entire life was the perfect start.

"Nope." He sank further down into the mattress.

"No? But I'm excited about it."

He grinned as he tangled his legs with hers. "So am I, but I've got other plans for tonight."

Her protests were drowned as he kissed her, and Annie realized he was right.

Everything else could wait.

———

BRIDE FOR THE SOLDIER BEAR

SPECIAL OPS SHIFTERS: L.A. FORCE

1

"I JUST CAN'T GET OVER THIS DRESS," ANNIE GUSHED AS SHE HELPED fasten all the tiny buttons that went up the back of it. "The embroidery alone is exquisite, and the way it drapes on you is just beautiful. It's a shame that we wait until our wedding days to wear such pretty things."

Mali smiled in the long mirror. So much had already gone into this day, and she wanted to look perfect. She knew that perfection had different definitions for different people, but she'd never been more excited in her life. She was about to marry her one true mate. "I thought it was a bit too expensive, but Reid insisted."

"He didn't see you in it, did he?" asked a horrified Mrs. Hoffman from where she sat perched on the corner of the bed. Mali was quickly learning that despite being a shifter and raising two rowdy boys, Reid and Jude Sutton, she was still an old-fashioned woman.

"No, I just told him how gorgeous it was, and he insisted that I go ahead and get it. He's been like that ever since we arrived in the States." Mali looked down at the way the fluttery, gauzy sleeves of the wedding gown draped to her elbows. She could feel the way the neckline dipped in the back, and the silk underskirt was pure heaven against her legs. The dress was spectacular, and she hoped it was a sign of how promising the future would be for them.

"I don't think you have anything to worry about," Annie said with a smile, smoothing the fabric and making sure she didn't miss a button.

Her fiancé had told her all about the Special Ops Shifter Force when she'd agreed to leave Thailand with him. She knew that it was an elite force of veteran special ops soldiers who were also shifters, and that they spent their time protecting and serving the shifter community. He'd explained just how many shifters there were in the U.S., even though the human population had no clue of their existence, and that the Force was always trying to ensure peace among the various clans. Reid's particular unit covered Los Angeles and its surrounding area, but there was also a unit in Washington, D.C., and another in Dallas.

What he hadn't told her was just how incredible the mates of the other soldiers were. Even though Annie was the closest thing Mali would have to a sister-in-law, Emersyn, Katalin, and Penny had welcomed her so warmly that she was quickly settling in to life in California. They were all there that day, surrounding her with love and giving helpful tips. She'd never expected to have an instant family waiting for her on the other side of the world.

"I'm sure you're right," Mali finally replied. "Still, I feel a little woozy."

Emersyn had been styling Penny's hair, but she set down her comb and came to press her hand against Mali's forehead. As the resident physician, who spent her time both with shifters and inner-city humans, she was the expert on these matters. "I'm sure you're just nervous. That's pretty normal for a woman on her wedding day. Still, nerves can do a number on you. Sip some water, remember to breathe, and make sure you don't lock your knees. I have some meds that would help if you'd like them."

Mali shook her head. "Thanks, but I'm good. I want to be fully present today. I don't want to miss a thing." She smiled, reminding herself that the dizziness and nervous energy she felt was pure excitement about making her love known before a large group of people. She and Reid were fated to each other, and the bond their inner bears had made was permanent, but it was extra special to celebrate it with everyone else.

"How did the two of you meet, anyway?" Katalin asked. The vampiress was centuries old and had heard every story there ever was to tell, but she loved hearing Mali talk about her homeland. Katalin and her mate, Amar, liked to travel when they got a chance to get away from the Force.

"It was random, really," Mali admitted. "The kind of thing I never expected to happen. Since we're from two completely different parts of the world, we're lucky we met at all."

"I know the feeling," Katalin replied with a smile as she handed Mali her earrings. She was living in Hungary when Amar happened to come through on his travels.

"It's common for the U.S. military to cross-train with Thai soldiers, and Reid was in my country with his unit. One day, a friend of mine suggested we go out to the field where they were training and check out the hotties. I had plenty of work to do, but I would've worried about Lamai if I'd let her go on her own." Mali smiled a little to herself. She and Lamai had always been good friends, even though they were polar opposites. While Mali was concerned about getting her education and finding a decent job, Lamai wanted to blow off all her responsibilities and have fun. In fact, if Mali had gotten in trouble growing up, it was usually because Lamai had roped her into doing something stupid. "My friend always had this notion that she'd meet some wealthy American and run off with him."

"Are things really like that over there?" Penny asked. "I mean, we've heard stories like that, but I didn't know if they were true."

Mali's mind momentarily flashed to the destiny that might've been waiting for her if she hadn't found Reid. "You could say that things aren't always ideal, and many people are looking for a better way of life."

"I'm sorry. I shouldn't have asked," Penny mumbled.

"No, it's fine. I mean, that was why Lamai and I were there in the first place. She always got excited when she happened to meet a tourist or anyone who might give her insight into a different life. We shifted into our animal forms so that we wouldn't be so obvious. I didn't expect any of the soldiers to be shifters, so I thought we'd go unnoticed." It hadn't been that long ago, but Mali's life had changed so much since then. She still remembered the thick dew that rubbed onto her coat that one fateful morning as she moved through the tree line with Lamai, trying to get a glimpse of the foreign soldiers.

"Are there a lot of shifters back home?" Katalin asked.

"Yeah, they're just split apart more than they are over here," Mali explained. "While some live in the cities, a lot of us live rural lives. We're not with other shifters very often, and they're not talked about.

I've just gone most of my life treating everyone else as human unless I pick up on an animal scent."

"That's certainly the safer route," Emersyn agreed as she pinned Penny's blonde locks into place.

Mali bent her head forward so Katalin could fasten the back of her necklace. "Lamai and I were in the trees on the edge of the field, just watching. I was getting a little bored, to be honest, but then one of the soldiers started coming our way. He broke right out of formation and started marching through the field, coming right at us. Someone yelled at him, but he just waved them off. It was Reid, and he'd sensed me. I could feel him, too, especially as he got closer, but I was scared and ran off. He told me later he got in trouble for wandering off toward the trees." She laughed a little at the memory. To think she'd turned tail and bounded away from someone so important to her. Truth be told, Mali had sensed there was something about him from the moment he'd broken formation, but it was so unexpected that she hadn't known what else to do.

"That sounds just like my Reid," Mrs. Hoffman admitted. She had been Reid and Jude's foster mother after their parents passed away, and though she looked like a conservative woman with her outdated bouffant and floral dress, she accepted Reid for who he was. "He was always the kind to wander off when he was a boy, too."

"At first, I thought I couldn't possibly be right about him. His effect on me was so incredibly strong, like a drug, and I'd never felt anything like it before. I tried to ignore it; I had my family and our rice farm to consider. But I couldn't sleep that night, so I slipped out and went back to that same tree line. Reid was there, and we spent the entire night together. The next thing I knew, I was packing my bags to come here." Her cheeks flushed as she thought about that night. Reid had been a foreigner and a soldier, the type of man she wasn't supposed to trust. But the way their souls connected told her nothing else mattered.

Mali hadn't expected to find him there. She'd thought she was crazy for even thinking of going back, though Lamai would've been proud of her for doing it. Mali had wandered along the path, knowing every little crook and turn like the back of her hand. When he'd appeared out of the darkness, she couldn't run away a second time. Her inner sun bear had demanded to come out, yet she'd managed to keep it wrangled. She'd wanted to know exactly who this man was and why he was there.

They'd talked for hours, slowly moving closer and closer together as the stars swirled in the sky. By the time they were close enough to touch, any doubt about him had been erased from her mind.

This was her mate.

The One.

The person a shifter could spend her entire life trying to find.

And he was *right there*.

"How romantic," Emersyn swooned as she finished styling Penny's hair. "You could write a book about it. Actually, you might find a lot to write about if you were so inclined. I'm sure a lot over here is different from what you've been used to. Many would enjoy your perspective."

Mali nodded. The women had already taken her shopping and out to eat several times, showing her the sites around Los Angeles and doing everything they could to make sure she didn't have much trouble acclimating to her new home. It was nice that she and Reid were staying in the SOS Force headquarters; she never needed to look for long if she needed someone. Even with such an excellent support network around her, it was easy to feel a little lost now and then. "It really is different here. It's funny, actually, because it's a lot like the way it's portrayed on TV. I was almost expecting to come here and find that everything in L.A. was just one big backdrop that they rolled up at the end of the night." She hadn't been sure if she would enjoy a large city like this, but thanks to everyone around her, Mali was starting to fall in love with the area.

"You know, you and Reid don't have to stay right here in the heart of the city," Mrs. Hoffman advised. "Sam and I have moved out to the country, and it's awfully nice. We'd be more than happy for the two of you to come and live in the guest house for a while. You know, have a little time to yourselves while you get to know each other. That's important in making a relationship work, and it doesn't hurt to have a few acres of land where you can get out and be yourself."

Once again, Mali felt her heart overflow with warmth and love. In the first few days of getting to know Reid, she'd only been concerned with how they'd felt about each other. As time passed and she realized she'd have to meet his entire clan, she'd come to worry about how well she'd be accepted. Mr. and Mrs. Hoffman had welcomed her with open arms as soon as Reid introduced her, and the rest of their clan had been just as inviting. The two of them had spent tons of time visiting relatives and friends, and that didn't even include the small family that the SOS Force itself comprised. "That's very kind of you. We've discussed staying here for now so he can be close to work. I'll let him know, though." It was tempting to have more opportunities for shifting safely. That was difficult in the city.

Mrs. Hoffman leaned forward and patted her knee. "No pressure, dear. Just always know that it's an option for you."

Mali patted the back of her future mother-in-law's hand. "I really do appreciate it. Everyone has been so kind to me, and I know I'm going to love it here. I only wish my family had been able to come."

"I'm sure that can't be easy for you, but perhaps we can get them out here for a visit sometime soon. Now then, have you heard about our tradition of something old, something new, something borrowed, something blue?"

"Yes, I believe so." Mali thought maybe one of the other women had mentioned something about it, but she hadn't given it another thought. The blood drained from her face as she realized she might have already messed up her first American tradition. "I didn't do anything about it, though."

"No, no," Mrs. Hoffman said. "Most of the time, it's the people around you—the people who love you—who help you take care of that. I've got something old for you." She withdrew two hairpins from her purse. "These have been passed down through my family for a few generations. I'd like you to have them."

"Are you sure?" Mali asked as she gingerly took the pins. Each one had a blue crystal at the end, surrounded by a tiny cluster of diamonds. They were absolutely beautiful, and Mali wasn't sure she was a true enough part of the family yet to accept such a gift.

"I wouldn't have offered if I wasn't," Mrs. Hoffman assured her. She stood up and pushed them each into Mali's carefully coifed here. "There, now. You've got something old and blue in these, so that's two."

"Your dress counts as something new," Emersyn pointed out.

"I was hoping you'd borrow my bracelet," Annie said, slipping a pearl cuff from her wrist. "It would go perfectly with your dress."

"You're all going to make me ruin my makeup," Mali gulped as she put it on. She'd known this day would be special because she'd be marrying Reid, but now, there were so many more reasons.

A knock sounded on the door. Annie opened it and smiled up at her mate, Jude. As Reid's brother, he'd welcomed Mali just as everyone else had, and she knew she and the quiet bear could be good friends. "We're all ready, and it's time," he said.

Mali's stomach swirled, not because of the vow she was about to make, but because she knew everyone would be watching. "I'm usually not a nervous person," she said shakily as she stood and braced her palms on the makeup vanity.

"Don't let a few wedding day jitters get in your way," Mrs. Hoffman encouraged.

She and the other women filed out the door while Jude waited for her just outside the room. Mali thought of him as the tamer version of his brother, a man who was far more reserved in his speech and actions. There was still that same inherent wildness in him that was in all shifters, and she could sense it, but it felt completely different.

He smiled at her once again. "You look fantastic. Reid is going to flip when he sees you."

"Thank you. And thank you for agreeing to walk me down the aisle. I don't have anyone else here to give me away." Mali swallowed the tightness that built in her throat every time she thought about her family. They'd refused to come to America, knowing they had other responsibilities at home. Once she'd known the date of the wedding, she'd tried to reach out to them. They hadn't responded, and Mali knew that deep down, they must've been unhappy about the match she'd made.

Jude offered her his elbow and squeezed her hand gently when she tucked her arm through it. "I think there are actually quite a few men who would've been honored to give you away. Our foster father, for one, or any of the men on the SOS Force. Don't tell them you know, but they were all secretly hoping to be chosen."

"I hope I didn't offend anyone."

Jude paused at the bottom of the stairs and looked at her, his face solemn. "Mali, you strike me as the kind of woman who can be incredibly tough, someone who doesn't mind stepping on a few toes to make things happen. The very first time I met you, I saw a look in your eyes that said you'd gladly kick ass and take names if need be. I know you want to fit in with everyone here, but don't think for a second that you have to grovel. Everyone loves you."

She smiled and let out a little laugh. "My parents always used to complain about how stubborn I was and that I didn't always like to follow tradition. It was one thing back home, but I don't want to mess up now that I'm here."

"It's not as though Reid is going to put you on a plane and send you back," he assured her. "In fact, I've never heard him speak about anyone as he does of you. I'm much more worried that *you're* happy with *him*."

"I am," she said, feeling more confident about that than anything else. "I definitely am."

"Then let's go get you married."

Mali and Jude walked through the main area of the Force head-quarters until they reached the retractable wall that faced the back-yard. The music started up right on time as Jude slowly escorted her down the aisle lined by white folding chairs. Large bunches of white and pink peonies had been set out on the side tables, and a gentle breeze stirred up some of their petals. These swirled through the sunset sky, contrasting the deep green carpet of grass under her feet, and made Mali feel like she was in a dream. Nothing this breathtaking could've actually been real.

And the most fantastic part of it was yet to come. Reid was standing there, waiting for her. Mali had always thought he looked handsome, no matter what he was wearing, and she'd seen him in everything from his Army uniform to his birthday suit. But in a tuxedo? Wow. The best accessory of all was the warmth and love she saw in his eyes as she slowly made her way to him.

As much as she wanted to keep her focus on Reid, it was impos-sible not to see everyone else who was there to support them. Amar, the Alpha of the L.A. Force, stood as the officiant, his eyes gleeful. Emersyn, Katalin, Penny, and Annie were her bridesmaids, while Gabe, Raul, Jude, and Jordan, a longtime family friend and Annie's brother, stood on the groom's side. It was all so perfect. She couldn't remember a time in her life when she felt happier.

At the end of the aisle, Jude slipped Mali's arm out of his and offered her hand to Reid. He gave them each a wink before moving off to the side with the other men.

"You look beautiful," Reid said, his eyes glistening.

"I feel like I'm going to shift," she admitted. The emotions were just so much to deal with, and she'd always felt that her inner sun bear was a safe place to retreat to, no matter what else was happening in the world.

"We only have a human marriage license, not one for bears," Amar noted in his deep voice. "Let's hold off on that part, shall we?" This earned a chuckle from those standing closest to them who'd managed to hear it.

"Are we ready?" he asked.

Mali nodded as she looked up into Reid's eyes. She'd never been more ready for anything in her entire life.

2

REID HARDLY HEARD THE WORDS THAT AMAR INTONED. THEY'D GONE over them a million times, both in deciding exactly how the ceremony should go and in rehearsal. He'd heard the words in his head as he'd helped organize all the white chairs into rows, and he'd been murmuring them to himself as he hung paper lanterns from the tops of the fence posts and strung them out across the yard. They'd echoed in his mind the night before the wedding as he'd stood outside and watched the sun sink, noting the exact time of day and the lighting it provided to make sure everything—down to the tiniest detail—would be right for this wedding.

But now, as he looked into his bride's eyes and felt her soul link with his, Reid knew that none of it really mattered at all. They'd found each other, and they were going to be together forever. He knew this in the same way he knew the sun would rise the next morning and that gravity would continue to keep his feet on the ground. It wasn't a doubt or a question or even a hope. It was a fact.

"As the leader of our clan, as someone approved by both parties, and as someone who loves these two people so very much, I now pronounce you man and wife. You'd damn well better kiss that bride!"

Reid easily pulled Mali into his arms. Her gauzy white dress made her look ethereal, like a fairy he could never catch, but she was real as he pressed his lips against hers. In a moment of instinctive hunger, he was tempted to heave her over his shoulder, carry her off, and put a cub in her belly. The resounding applause from the gathered crowd made him pull back, and he cradled her delicate face in his hands as he looked into her eyes. "I will love you, honor you, and protect you for the rest of eternity," he promised. "No matter what."

Her dark eyes blinked up at him. "Kiss me again before I start crying."

He happily obliged as Amar boomed, "Mr. and Mrs. Reid Sutton, everyone!"

Another round of cheers went through the crowd, and Reid took her hand as they headed down the aisle. The photographer pulled them off to the side while the rest of the Force moved quickly to rearrange the backyard into a reception area. Long tables with white linens were brought out, with candles and centerpieces placed promptly by the women. It made him feel good to know that his friends and family not only approved of his marriage, but were willing to do so much to help. The only longing left was in knowing they had quite a bit of socializing to do before he could get Mrs. Sutton alone.

"I sure hope these pictures turn out good," he said as he posed behind Mali, his arms around her waist and her bouquet in her hands.

"The samples the photographer showed us were great," she said just before putting on a smile for the camera.

"I just want them to be worth it if it means not spending this time with you the way I want to." He pressed himself against her back, his hardness swelling against her.

She laughed as she leaned into him. "Oh?" she asked innocently. "And what exactly is it you'd rather be doing?"

"Put it this way. By the end of the night, all of L.A. will have heard you screaming my name," he whispered against her ear as the photographer called over the rest of the wedding party to pose.

"We'll have plenty of time to test that theory soon enough," she promised.

But after the photos, there were toasts from everyone Reid had ever known, the cake cutting, the bouquet toss, and what felt like a million other little ceremonies.

"Do you regret doing it like this?" he asked when the music finally cued up for their first dance and he could have her fully in his arms. They'd debated on how to have this wedding. Some shifters got married in the traditional human way, but plenty of others opted for a simple exchange of vows in the middle of the wilderness.

"Not for a second," she promised him. "You?"

"No. It's beautiful, and the only thing I really want is for you to be happy."

Her smile had the warmth of the sun, though it had sunk behind the horizon hours ago. The paper lanterns had been lit, illuminating tables of their loved ones around them and deepening the shadows in the corners of the large yard. "I *am* happy. Everyone back home talks about America as though it's the most amazing place to be, and that anything can happen here. I admit I didn't really believe it. I thought it was just a delusion people were teasing themselves with, making them feel like there was a chance of things getting better. It turns out the rumors are true. I can't imagine not being here and spending this day with you."

"Funny, though. With all this pomp and circumstance, I haven't been able to spend much time with you. That's not going to change anytime soon, either. We're obligated to dance with some of the other guests, and I've got lots of relatives I have to visit with." Reid hadn't always thought of himself as someone his adoptive family would be proud of. Now that he'd served in the Special Forces and brought home a stunning bride, he felt he finally had some bragging rights. But his bear was driving him wild in knowing that Mali was officially his, and he wanted a chance to do something about it.

"They say the waiting makes it all the better in the end," she said as the song died out.

Jude cut in and took Mali off in his arms, while Reid began the traditional dance with his mother.

"You've really turned yourself around," Mrs. Hoffman said, reaching up to pat him on the cheek. "You even cut your hair! This girl really has changed you, hasn't she?"

Reid felt his cheeks flush. "Yeah, you could say that."

"Oh, sweetheart." She stepped back a little and looked him over. "You're a far cry from that little boy I came to know all those years ago. I admit I always felt sorry for you after your parents passed. You and Jude deserved more than that, and I did my best to give it to you, but I know it isn't the same as a real mother's love."

"Don't say that." Perhaps it was the mushy way Mali made him feel inside, which had quickly eroded the tough-guy exterior he'd always put forth, but in that moment, Reid realized just how much his foster mother meant to him. It'd hurt when their parents had dropped them off at the Hoffmans' and never returned. Until recently, Jude and Reid hadn't understood that their entire clan had been wiped out in a war with another clan. Knowing the truth hadn't changed the way he felt about his foster family, who'd done everything they could to give them the best life possible. "You *are* my real mother."

"Oh, honey." Mrs. Hoffman pulled him close and rested her tearstained cheek against his chest. "You don't know how much that means to me."

Fortunately, Reid was spared from having to bawl his eyes out in front of everyone by the flow of the reception. He danced and visited and toasted until his feet screamed at him from his dress shoes. Another part of his body ached, but in a very different way. He scanned the crowd for Mali, but he didn't see her.

"Hey, have you seen Mali?" he asked Emersyn as she finished filling a plate for her son Lucas at the buffet. The boy was old enough to walk around steadily on his own two feet now, and he eagerly reached for the food his mother held.

"Hang on, baby. Let's get you to a table first. I think Mali went inside the house to change."

Reid raised an eyebrow. "I'll go see if she needs a hand." He stepped out of the backyard, leaving behind the lanterns, tablecloths, and the chinking of champagne glasses for the relative peace of the house. He spotted a familiar figure in the kitchen, and he stepped up quietly behind her before wrapping his arms around her waist and pulling her in tightly. "Hello there, Mrs. Sutton."

Mali giggled as she put down her glass and leaned back into him. "Unhand me, you monster! I just got married, and I haven't even had the chance to share my husband's bed with him yet." She tipped up her face to kiss him.

"I certainly wouldn't want to mess that up. I happen to know your groom, and he's rather eager to get his life started with you." Reid turned her around in his arms and kissed her neck. "You smell amazing."

"We should get back outside," she said even as she tipped her head to the side to expose her throat. "It is our party, after all. Everyone's here to see us."

After pressing his lips against the warmth of hers once again, Reid pulled back and looked down at her. She was beautiful, both inside and out. Anyone could claim they'd met by sheer chance, but Reid knew better. The universe had brought them together, just as they were meant to be. "I can't believe we were able to fit so many of our friends and family in that backyard."

"Not all of them," she said with a frown. "I wish my family would've been able to come over from Thailand."

Reid pressed his forehead against hers, knowing how difficult it had been for her to come to the U.S. and start anew. "We'll find a way to get them here, and then we can get married all over again."

She gave him a playful smack on the arm. "You don't mean that."

"Yes, I do. I'll marry you as many times as I need to." Getting in a monkey suit and dealing with a hundred of his closest friends wasn't exactly his idea of a relaxing time, but he'd do anything she asked of him.

She thanked him with a deep kiss, and her eyes were suggestive when she pulled back. "I'm going to get my things and go to the hotel."

"Okay. Let me just say goodbye and I'll be right behind you." Reid knew the pleasure of lying next to her in bed, their naked bodies sharing their heat, but there was something even more exciting about doing that on their wedding night. They already belonged to each other in the deepest parts of themselves, something he'd known on that first night he'd spent with her in the woods. The wedding gave it extra meaning as they made their love known publicly.

"No." She put a finger on his chest, stopping him with the lightest touch. "I have a little surprise planned for you. Stay here and enjoy your family a little longer. You'll know where to find me."

He watched her head off to the bedroom they'd be sharing at the SOS Force headquarters, wondering if he should've insisted that they spend their wedding night there. Reid didn't want to wait any longer than he had to. Still, it would be nice not to worry about everyone else around them listening as they consummated their marriage.

A hand clamped down on his shoulder. It was Jude. "Congratulations, little brother. It was a beautiful ceremony."

"I couldn't agree more, but I think I'm ready for it to be over with."

"And disappoint all the people out there?" Jude gestured toward the back of the house, where the retractable wall had been pulled back to make the party space flow easily between the house and the yard. The night was divine, and everyone was enjoying it under the stars.

"I've got more important things to take care of," Reid replied with a smirk. "You'd know more about that if you put a ring on Annie's finger."

"Hey, now. We've only just recently gotten together. She's had to spend almost her whole life being responsible and doing what everyone else wants. I'd like to give her some time." Jude put his hands in his pockets and looked down at the floor.

Reid couldn't remember ever seeing his brother look so shy. Quiet and reserved, yes, but always busy watching the rest of the world around him. "Annie's had a good effect on you. I'm glad you found her."

"Me, too. She's really something else, and it sounds like she and Mali are getting along well. The four of us should go out together sometime. You know, once you two get past the honeymoon stage and you can tear your eyes away from each other long enough to know what's going on around you," Jude joked.

"Yeah, yeah. Like you're not just as lovesick." Reid had seen the way his brother mooned over Annie.

Jude ignored the comment and changed the subject back to the newlyweds. "I noticed Mom gave Mali the hairpins," he said with a grin.

"Really?" Reid knew that was big. It meant that everything his foster parents had said was genuine, and they really had accepted Mali into the family. "Neither Mali nor Mom told me that."

"They've both been a little distracted tonight," Jude advised.

"Right. I'm going to make the rounds, and then I'm taking off."

But of course, everyone wanted to chat with him. They wanted to see the bride again. They wanted to know what their plans were for married life and if they could expect any cubs soon. Reid had to extract himself from his foster parents, who reminded him time and again how much he meant to them and that they could come stay at their place any time they wanted to.

After receiving several more congratulations and making excuses for Mali's absence, Reid trotted out to the garage and headed across town. He hadn't been in L.A. very long, having just joined the Force, but already, he knew he was going to like it. There was always something happening, and now he had Mali to help him explore the city. Reid let out a contented sigh as he thought about how much his life had changed. He never thought he'd settle down, and now, he was happy to do so. Mali had made a huge difference in his life.

To save time, he and Mali had checked into their hotel earlier in the day. Reid hadn't wanted to waste time after the ceremony, and he was glad he had the keycard in his pocket as he took the elevator upstairs. Reid wasn't about to deny her the joy of a honeymoon, and they had a trip planned for New York City after they'd rested from their nuptials. If he had it his way, they wouldn't get out of bed for the rest of the weekend. Considering she'd said she had a surprise for him, she was probably thinking the same. What kind of surprise would it be?

The first surprise was in finding the hotel room door shut, but not latched. He pushed it open warily, glancing down the hall to see if she'd stepped out to get some ice. "Mali?"

The overhead lights had been turned off, the room illuminated only by the candles that had been lit on every surface surrounding the massive bed. A tray of chocolate-covered strawberries sat next to an ice bucket and a bottle of champagne. She'd gone all out, and Reid couldn't say he minded being romanced a little.

"Mali?" He moved through the suite, wondering where she'd gone. When he pushed the bathroom door open, he saw her suitcase on the floor. It'd fallen over, her clothes spilling out onto the shining marble. Reid's heart raced. She'd been there, but now she was gone. It wasn't like her to leave a mess, even when she was in a hurry.

As he straightened, he noticed a smear of blood on the corner of the bathroom sink. Reid's bear went wild inside him. The instinct to protect his mate was a strong one, and something had definitely happened to her. He rushed back out of the bathroom to search the room for more clues, pulling his phone out of his pocket as he did so.

"Jude, I need your help. Mali's missing."

3

MALI STRUGGLED TO BREATHE AS THE BLACKNESS SURROUNDED HER. SHE felt dizzy and disoriented, her body hurting down to the very marrow of her bones, and she fought the urge to vomit. She didn't want to wake up, because it sounded like far too much effort, but whatever drug had been injected into her body was starting to wear off, and she couldn't seem to stop her eyes from cracking open.

She gasped, immediately regretting it because of the way it burned her lungs. Mali's brain fought to reconcile her current surroundings with where she was actually supposed to be. Her mind tunneled backward, upheaving all the darkness that was clouding it, until she found herself at her wedding. *Yes.* And of course, Reid was there. But then she'd left for the hotel. It all grew blurry again after that.

Her mouth was so dry, her tongue felt as though it were made of fleece. She squinted into the darkness as she rubbed her wrists. They were sore to the touch, which didn't make any sense. "Hello?"

"Ah, she's awake," a female voice said in the dark.

Mali didn't recognize it, and fear shot through her bloodstream. She tried to summon her sun bear to the surface, to keep it on deck just in case she needed it, but the beast was hiding deep down inside her.

"I know what you're doing," the woman continued. "I don't have to be able to see all that well to know. It's what everyone does when they first get here."

Taking a deep breath, Mali took stock of herself. She'd never been completely unable to bring about the beast inside her. More often than not, she was fighting against it. Even though she hurt all over and desperately wanted to know what was happening, the most important thing she could focus on in that moment was that she was okay. Sore, shaken, and confused, but okay. "Who's they?"

The voice responded with a derisive laugh. "*They* are you, and everyone else like you, which includes me."

Arai wa? In her native Thai, her addled mind wondered what the hell was going on, and this didn't make it any clearer. *This bitch seriously wants to speak in riddles right now?* Mali didn't even know if the person she was talking to was a friend or an enemy, but she had no choice but to play along. "All right. Then who are *you*?"

"Don't you know? I'm the same as you." The source of the voice moved a little until a woman's face appeared in a pale blue shaft of moonlight, her dark hair a wavy tangle of darkness. She looked as though she could've been from a similar part of the world as Mali.

"Look, whoever you are, and whatever you want, I'd much rather you just tell me. I feel like shit, and I don't understand what the fuck's happening." Mali pushed herself up into a seated position, finding a cold metal wall behind her back.

"Me? Oh hell, honey. I don't want anything. I mean, I'm sure I did at some time. There's really no point in it now because life's not about what I want. It's about what other people want from *me*. I've learned that over the last few years, and you will, too. It's about the almighty dollar. And power. There's always power involved."

Mali's head was pounding now. "I must really be out of it. None of this is making sense. Could you just tell me what happened?"

"I don't know. I wasn't there, but I could guess."

"Maybe you could start by telling me who you are." Mali's brain was so muddled, she wondered if this woman was someone she was supposed to know and had simply forgotten. Her brain hammered against the inside of her skull as she rolled her shoulders in an attempt to work the soreness out of them, but it was too painful.

"Keiko," was her simple reply.

"Mali."

"Pretty. I'm guessing your animal belongs to some sort of exotic shifter species, something unusual that people don't see every day. They don't need any wolves or black bears here. There are plenty of those in the world." Keiko rolled her hand in the air as though what she was saying were obvious.

"I guess you could say that." She'd already given her name, but she didn't need to advertise anything else about herself, not until she knew what was happening. Mali's eyes were beginning to adjust to the dim light. Most of the room was still shrouded in darkness, but she got the impression there were other sleeping forms around them.

"No surprise. Like I said, that's what they want. They need something unusual, or else they don't make enough money for it to be worth all the effort. Now, as to what happened to you, I'm going to say you were just going on about your life, thinking everything was peachy. You never imagined that anyone would try to use you or kidnap you, so you were pretty damn surprised when a group of men showed up and tried to take you away. You look like the kind who fought back, which would explain all those cuts and bruises all over you. These assholes don't take no for an answer, if you get my drift. They probably had a little help with some sort of tranquilizer, so that's why you feel like shit. That, and they like to cut corners, so it was probably some cheap street stuff. Keep that in mind for next time. It's easier to just go along with them. It hurts a lot less." Keiko let out another laugh and ran a hand through her hair. "Usually."

"Why would someone do such a thing?" Mali asked. She twisted to look at her arm, where a large gash intersected her bicep. A memory swam up somewhere from the back of her mind. She'd fallen against a bathroom vanity and sliced it on the sharp corner. But the bathroom in that memory wasn't a familiar one.

"Don't try too hard to wrap your brain around this, girl. It's not going to help. It'll never make sense."

"*You* sure as hell don't," Mali snapped. Her voice sounded far too loud, and the way it echoed told her that the rest of the walls were made of metal as well. "If you're going to talk to me, I'd appreciate it if you'd just cut to the chase and explain what's going on."

"Why should I?" Keiko retorted, her indifferent tone suddenly cross. "No one told me how it all worked. I had to figure it all out myself."

"Fine. Then I'll do the same." Mali turned away from the one face she could see in the darkness. She could use someone to fill her in on what exactly had happened, but in the meantime, she could fend for herself.

She could also hope that Reid was trying to save her from this unknown hell. She closed her eyes and concentrated on his face. As foggy as Mali's mind was, she could still recall Reid in the finest detail. It wasn't just his sweet brown eyes or his sexy hair or that boyish smile. It was the little mole on the side of his neck. It was the way he smelled when he was freshly out of the shower. It was the way his stubble rubbed against her cheek.

What was far more important in the moment was the fact that Reid wasn't just a typical husband. He was part of the Special Ops Shifter Force, and Mali had to hope that would mean he'd be bringing her home soon.

"Fine."

Keiko's sudden word startled Mali into opening her eyes again.

"I'll tell you."

Mali didn't reply. Whoever this woman was, she apparently liked to play head games. But Mali wasn't up for her bullshit.

"You've been kidnapped, but that much you already know, I'm sure. You're being trafficked. It might be for sex, sport, or even just cleaning someone's house. They'll sell you off to the highest bidder, and to them, it doesn't matter what you get used for. This time, I believe we're the property of a trafficking ring that operates under a man named Dean Bryant. There are others, though." Keiko scooted a little closer, the moonlight shining brightly on her eyes.

Mali blinked, trying to take this all in. Her heart retracted in her chest as she tried to find some flaw in Keiko's explanation. She wanted this to be some mistake, some nightmare she would wake up from. But the cold, dark room around her was very real, and everything her new acquaintance had said fit in with their surroundings. "Someone's going to find us. All these people can't just go missing without someone taking notice. It doesn't make sense."

"Maybe not, but that's the truth of it anyway. I can't even count how many times I've been bought and sold at this point. I don't bother trying, either, because it's not going to make things any better." Keiko's cheeks were sunken in, and with her wide eyes, it gave her a haunted look. Mali couldn't tell if the haggard quality of her features was a trick of the moonlight or the result of years of mistreatment.

"That's horrible," she whispered. "We've got to get out of here."

"You think I haven't tried before?" Keiko shook her head. "There are too many guards, and they know what'll happen to them if they let someone slip through."

"But—"

"I wasn't kidding about what I said before. The best thing you can do is cooperate. You'll sell for a lot more if you aren't bruised up and if your buyer doesn't think you'll be a problem."

Mali was appalled at her sense of logic. "Cooperate? Just so they can make a *profit* off me? That's fucking ridiculous!"

Keiko tried to shush her. "You probably think so now. The whole idea is new to you. Trust me, though, you'd much rather go to some rich executive with a fetish than a low-level drug lord who just wants to pass you around to gain favor with his other lowlifes."

"But that's not right," Mali urged. "No one has the right to do this to us!" The moonlight was shifting, moving up along the wall as the moon sank toward the horizon. Mali didn't want to be left in the dark, but then she realized it was nearly dawn. The slit of a window at the top of the wall would be letting much more light in soon. Unfortunately, this wasn't a situation where seeing the sun rise was going to make things any better.

"Try telling them that," Keiko said. "They can do whatever they want. They have us, and they have the power to keep us here. Look, I know it seems a little scary right now, and I'm sure I didn't help with that. There are times when it's really not so bad."

Mali couldn't believe that for a second. She'd only just arrived in America a couple of months ago, coming to a place where everything seemed so promising. This was the country where she could achieve anything she put her mind to. While Mali hadn't yet known what that was, she'd been ready to find out.

How could this be the same place where people were abducted and sold? How could the same folks who cherished life, liberty, and the pursuit of happiness also turn a blind eye to such a horrid thing? Even more disturbing, how could one of the victims actually be okay with it?

"Don't look at me like that," Keiko warned. "You don't know me or my situation."

"Well, care to fill me in?" Mali challenged. She hadn't decided if she liked Keiko or not, but so far, she was the only friend she had.

Keiko sighed. "If you insist. I guess you could say I was made for this type of life. I'd been in and out of foster programs the entire time I was growing up. Some kids were lucky enough to get adopted, but that happens less and less as you get older. You see, some people sign up to be foster parents not because they have big hearts, but because they want that paycheck that comes from the state. Anyway, by the time I turned eighteen and aged out of the system, no one was interested in me anymore. This guy saw me sitting by myself in the back corner of a café, not able to afford anything to eat, and he told me if I went with him, I wouldn't have to worry about that again."

Mali's heart broke. How many people like Keiko had been through something similar? It was horrible to think that things like that happened in the States when she thought she'd left it all behind in Thailand. It wasn't quite the same situation, but still. "Shit. I'm really sorry to hear that."

"Don't be sorry," Keiko said with another of those breathy laughs she liked to let out. "It was my fault for going with the guy in the first place. But hey, I was hungry, and I had no choice."

Mali liked to think anyone had a choice if they looked hard enough, but she'd seen plenty of girls in her own country who'd ended up in similar situations. "And this man sold you?"

"Yep, and then on and on and on. I've been arm candy in Vegas casinos, treated to designer dresses and fine food as long as I'm willing to do whatever a man says in the hotel room later that night. I've been chained up in a damp basement and everything in between. I've come to learn that you just wait it out until the next roll of the dice. If you know how to pull your mind out of your body, you don't really even have to be present for the bad stuff."

"Haven't you ever tried to fight back? To get away from it all and make a life for yourself?" Mali asked. The room was growing lighter now, and the forms around her were beginning to get clearer. Most of them were women, and some of them looked fairly young. Her stomach was cringing against her spine out of fear, hunger, and disgust.

"That's easy to say, but words won't get you anywhere." Keiko trailed a hand through her dark hair again. "What prospects do I have? I've never worked an honest day in my goddamn life. Everyone would just see me as a drug addict or a loser, or find some other way to blame me for what happened. Maybe they're right, but either way, I'm stuck."

"I don't believe that," Mali said fiercely. A fire was beginning to grow inside her. Sun bears were naturally quiet and shy, but that wild animal force was present in all shifters. She hated that she was a part of this, but even more, she hated that so many others had already been. It wasn't anything new, and it was incredibly wrong. "There's got to be something you can do. We can get out of here, and we can go to the police."

But Keiko simply shook her head. "There's no point, sweetheart. They don't think we're any better than the men who do this to us. And you, you've got an accent. You're foreign. That means you'll just get deported, and they won't even bother counting you as a statistic."

"But I'm married to an American."

"Heh. You think that matters?" Keiko laughed. "Here, you don't have an identity anymore. You're *no one*. Do you honestly think you can stand up against the man in charge of this whole operation and accuse him in public? Your silence tells me everything I need to know. You're no better than the rest of us. You just want to go home and go to bed, but I'm telling you that's never going to happen again."

"No, fuck that. There's got to be something we can do." The room had lightened enough now that she could count about ten other people crammed into the room with them. There was a toilet in the corner, but it didn't even have a seat, let alone a curtain around it for privacy. The place looked like some sort of prison cell, but Mali had a feeling that even prisoners had it better than this.

A woman was looking at them from across the room with sleepy eyes. Her coloring made Mali think she might be a Latina, and her accent proved it when she spoke. "Keiko is right. There's not much you can do. Unless you have a gun, I suppose, or you find some way to avoid the drugs and rip their faces off. I've tried that one. It didn't go well."

"Drugs?"

"They'll keep you sedated enough that you can't shift until you've been sold and you're someone else's problem. Not that it matters, but my name is Alejandra."

"It's...nice to meet you," Mali replied. "I'm Mali." She needed Reid. She'd settle for any member of the SOS Force to come bursting through the metal door at one end of the room and proclaim them all saved. That was what the Force did after all, wasn't it? They helped people in the shifter community who didn't fall under the jurisdiction of the human government, and if this room of people didn't fit that description, she sure as hell didn't know what did.

"I know. I heard the two of you chattering for the last hour, with no concern that the rest of us might need our sleep," Alejandra replied.

"Sorry," Mali muttered, feeling somewhat chastised. The very least someone could ask for was a decent night's sleep when something like this was happening.

"What are you?"

"I'm sorry?" Mali was still focusing on Keiko's story and wondering what Alejandra's might be, and for a moment, she didn't understand the question. Even when she did, she suddenly felt protective of her other form. Someone had already injured and kidnapped her human self, and there was no reason for that to extend to her sun bear. "Oh. Well, it doesn't really matter."

"Sure it does," Keiko countered. "My Japanese heritage doesn't pay off well for me. I'm an Iriomote cat. We're extremely rare and beautiful, which has made me quite the target. If you were something big and monstrous like a buffalo shifter, then at least you'd just be sold for physical labor. Not that I'm saying that's okay, but in some cases it might be better than the shit I've been through." She stood and stretched.

Mali was astounded that she could act so casual about all of this. She had to get out of there before she became as desensitized to it as the others were. "What about you?" she asked Alejandra.

The other woman grinned. "I guess I'm in the same boat as Keiko since I'm an ocelot shifter. I try to console myself that it's better they want me in live form instead of for my fur. Now, what are you?"

Mali swallowed. She didn't really know these people, but she had no one else to trust. "A sun bear."

"Ah, that explains it, then," Keiko said as she stretched forward, touching her hands to the ground and thrusting her hips up in the air. "You're rare, indeed. It'll be interesting to see what someone buys you for. You might be someone's personal escort, or you might be performing in the circus." Keiko laughed, but Mali didn't find anything funny about it.

"No, someone will keep her in their private collection," Alejandra said. "I've seen how long sun bears' tongues are, so I'm sure they'll use you for all kinds of sick things."

"You know, I've actually heard of another sun bear somewhere in the system recently," Keiko mused.

Mali briefly wondered if it could be anyone she knew. Even in Thailand, a sun bear clan was highly unusual. Could her sister have somehow been caught up in this mess? She shoved the thought away, not willing to think Tasanee should have to suffer this way. It was bad enough that Mali had left her behind.

"You'll go for a really high price, that's for sure," Alejandra added, jarring Mali out of her troubled thoughts. "I know it might not seem like it, but you should feel lucky."

Mali was just about to ask her what that meant when she heard other noises in the building. The light had increased quite a bit at this point, and she could tell that the walls that surrounded their room were constructed inside a much larger building with a high metal ceiling. It looked like some sort of warehouse. "What is this place, anyway?"

"Just a holding pen for us until Bryant and his men decide what they're going to do with us," Keiko answered. "There are probably at least a dozen rooms just like this in this building."

Now that she could see it all by the light of day, Mali couldn't let herself deny the reality of her situation. She wanted to come up with some sort of escape plan, but she didn't know enough. It didn't help that her stomach rolled and boiled with hunger and nausea, and her muscles were still so sore that she could hardly move.

The steel door burst open, admitting a man just about as large as the doorway. His bulging eyes were intersected by a scar that ran down the length of his face, and he balled his fists at his sides as he scanned the room. "I suggest you all stay perfectly still if you want any chance of getting breakfast," he growled.

He stalked into the room, and Mali saw there was another man behind him. This one was far thinner with a large nose, but he looked just as mean. The slimmer man moved around the perimeter of the room, pausing at each prisoner for a moment before pronouncing their animal form and moving on to the next one.

"Ocelot," he accurately said when he passed by Alejandra. "Blackbuck. Manatee. Tapir. Antelope." He paused at Keiko and squinted at her. "Iriomote cat. Very rare."

Mali pulled her knees against her chest and wrapped her arms around them. Some shifters were better than others about sensing whether someone had an animal inside them or not, but never had she seen someone who could do *this*. Even having spent all night in the same room with them, she'd never have guessed Keiko or Alejandra's other forms if they hadn't told her. Whoever this man was, she couldn't possibly hide from him. Even so, she hoped her hibernating sun bear stayed huddled inside. Maybe if Mali wasn't worth anything, they'd let her go.

The skinny man stopped in front of her, his shoes nearly touching hers. He put his hands on his hips and smiled, but it didn't look like he was amused. He glanced over his shoulder at his burly comrade and then back at her. "Yep. That's it. A sun bear. What are the odds?" He let out a snort of a laugh before moving the rest of the way around the room, rattling off more animals. Mali realized then that the other guy was making a note of their shifter forms.

When they had finished their rounds, the larger man stepped up to her and held out a meaty hand. "You're coming with me, dollface."

Mali swallowed as she glanced at Keiko, though she knew what the other woman's advice would be. *Don't struggle, and it won't be so bad.* Mali wasn't sure she could believe that from the look of these men, but like her new acquaintances, she didn't feel she had a choice.

She tried to push herself to her feet on her own, but whatever they'd given her that night hadn't worn off just yet. All the strength had left her muscles, and she wound up having to put her fingers inside his fleshy palm. A shiver of disgust ran down her arm to her spine as he easily pulled her up off the floor and brought her outside the room. When the skinny guy joined them, he slammed the door.

Mali jumped. The beastly man had her by the elbow now, holding on just tightly enough that if she tried to escape, he could easily squeeze his fist and break a bone or two. The trio marched down a hall with similar doors on either side of it, and she hated to imagine that there were dozens more just like her who were trapped behind them. Eventually, after going through several sets of locked doors, they emerged into the daylight.

Without a word, the men sat her in the back of a van. She felt as much as she heard the locks falling into place as they took off down the road.

4

——————

REID PACED, HIS FISTS CURLED AT HIS SIDES AS HE FOUGHT TO CONTROL his inner bear. He knew his mate was in trouble; there was no mistaking it. He had to find her and protect her. Unfortunately, he still had no idea what he needed to protect her *from*.

"Reid, you should sit down. Maybe have something to eat." Jude approached him, trying to put a hand on his shoulder, but Reid shrugged his brother off.

"As if I could fucking relax or eat right now!" he growled. "Do you have any idea what I'm going through?" He felt a sharp pain under his fingernails as his claws threatened to shoot through. He wanted to fight. He wanted to lash out with all the rage and pain that'd been building inside him ever since he'd found out Mali was missing. His bear demanded vengeance, and Reid was determined to exact it as soon as he got the chance.

"I do, actually," Jude replied in that annoyingly calm manner he always seemed to have. He sat down on one of the couches and casually took a sip of coffee.

Reid shook his head before turning around and pacing the other direction. The spacious house that served as the headquarters of the SOS Force had an open floor plan, yet he still felt as though he were trapped in a cage. The retractable walls that'd made the house such a great party space during the wedding had been closed once again, adding to his claustrophobic feelings. "I highly doubt it. I have no idea where Mali is or what happened to her. I need to get out there and find her." He pounded a fist into his thigh.

Jude raised an eyebrow. "I'd suggest shifting and going out for a run in the woods, but I'm not sure I could trust you not to slaughter some random jogger right now."

"Would you blame me?" Reid roared. "Someone out there has done something to her. Jude, I don't even know if she's dead or alive, for fuck's sake! I'd gladly destroy anyone who stands in my way of getting to her. And *you* might be at the top of that list right now, with your fair-trade, organic coffee and blasé fucking attitude, like you think everything is just going to work out because it always does. I don't see how anyone who drinks as much caffeine as you can possibly just sit there and be so chill at a time like this!" His voice was echoing in the space created by the tall ceilings.

With a sigh, Jude set his coffee on the side table. He rubbed his forehead with the back of his thumb and leaned forward. "I'm more than happy to set all your insults aside, considering the situation. You have to remember, Reid, that things don't work the same way they do in the military."

"Clearly not, or else we'd already be out there getting her back. Fuck it. I'm just going to go." He stormed off toward the garage, tired of waiting around.

"Reid."

He paused, though he hated himself for it. Jude was his older brother. He'd always been the calm and rational one, and it'd always driven Reid crazy. When they'd grown up and gone their separate ways, Reid thought he'd be happy to get rid of Jude for a while. After all, he didn't need someone always looking over his shoulder and tut-tutting everything he did. Still, Jude was the only blood relative he had left. He needed Jude far more than he wanted to admit.

"What?" he snapped without turning around.

"If you're that determined to go look for Mali, then I'm not going to pretend that I can stop you. I do ask that you give me five minutes before you go."

Reid whirled. "Five minutes? Do you have any idea what could happen in five minutes? Hell, if I'd have shown up at the hotel five minutes earlier than I did, maybe we wouldn't be in this situation!"

Heat flushed his cheeks as he unwillingly imagined walking in on the abduction and killing the bastard with his bare hands.

"Five minutes," Jude repeated.

Reid let out an angry huff, but he walked back over to the living room area. "Fine, but I'm counting."

"I have no doubt of that." As though he were trying his damnedest to be an asshole, Jude picked up his coffee and took another slow sip. "What I was trying to say is that the SOS Force isn't like the military. You think it is because we were all involved with the Armed Forces. We're soldiers inside, just like we're animals. But the part you're not letting yourself think about is the intelligence. You were briefed before you went on a mission, but you didn't always see the amount of data and processing that went into each situation before it was acted upon. The higher-ups knew what they needed from you long before you did."

"What's your point?" Reid asked impatiently.

"Simply that you have to be a witness to part of the process now that you didn't have to before. Believe me, I know it's frustrating. Our assignments are far more personal than they were for us back then. We're dealing with people just like us who live in our very neighborhoods. What's worse is that sometimes we're out there trying to rescue those we love." Jude leaned back, his bright blue eyes watching Reid as though he expected some sort of revelation after this idle chatter that wasn't doing anything to help.

"I really don't have time for this shit."

"I know, Reid. Don't forget that Annie and I were working together on the same mission, and then she was kidnapped. I've been in your shoes, and I don't envy that position. But please, just let things happen. If you go out there right now, you're liable to go off half-cocked, compromising both the entire Force and any chance you might have of rescuing Mali. You need us right now. We're doing everything we can to find out where she is and what's happened."

Reid wanted to argue with him. His very nature was telling him to do so. There was nothing more important than finding Mali, but Jude's logic rang true. Reid could head out into a city of millions of people and try to find her, or he could be a little patient and at least have a way to zero in on a possible starting point. "Fine, but I guess that means you're going to have to put up with me in the meantime."

Jude smiled. "I always have, man. Amar spent most of the night as his dragon, flying high over the city. Gabe is still working with the hotel and its nearby businesses to see if he can find any witnesses. Raul might look like he's doing nothing more than sitting behind a screen eating Cheetos, but I have no doubt that he's working his hardest. Perhaps you and I can go over the details of last night. We might find a clue we can pursue."

Finally consigning himself to a chair, Reid realized just how tired he was. His muscles burned from all his pacing, and his eyes were so tired, they felt like they were going to dry up and roll back in his head. He hadn't even changed out of his clothes from the wedding. He was living a nightmare that was hell on Earth, and there was nothing he could do at the moment to get out of it. An image of Mali was burned onto the backs of his eyelids, but he couldn't make her appear in real life.

"We can try," he finally said gruffly, "but I don't think it's going to help. We've already been over this."

"Maybe there's something we missed," Jude encouraged. "I know you're tired, but just tell me everything."

"Okay." Reid pulled in a deep breath. He didn't want to live through this again. Still, he'd go through any amount of torture imaginable to bring his mate back. "I got to the hotel—"

"Anything unusual happening in the parking lot?"

Reid was caught off-guard by the question, particularly since Jude was always so patient. He pulled his mind back to that moment, trying to remember. "A car might have been leaving, but I can't be sure."

"All right. Then what?"

"I already had my keycard, so I went straight up to the hotel room. Before you ask, no, I didn't see anything unusual in the lobby. The first odd thing was that the door was open. I thought maybe she'd stepped out for ice..." Reid trailed off as he lived through that scene once again. It would've been so perfect—if only she'd still been there. But there was the suitcase on the floor, the blood on the bathroom counter... Even the blue crystal hairpins that his mother had given Mali had been left behind. She wouldn't have just walked off and left those. There was no way this had been voluntary.

Reid heard the sound of someone clearing his throat. He opened his eyes and turned to see Raul standing only a few feet away, watching them with excitement and concern on his face. "You guys have a second?"

"Of course," Jude answered.

Raul was hardly ever without some sort of device in his hand. He held up his laptop, the keyboard folded around to the back so that it formed a tablet. "Um, I hate to say this, but I may have found a lead on The Shift."

Reid had heard of the news app. Raul had teamed up with Taylor Communications to create a secure central hub for news and chatrooms accessible only to shifters. They needed a verification code to gain access, so humans couldn't simply stumble across it. "And?"

"And I'm sorry that an app I helped create could be involved in something like this." He tapped the screen a few times so that it was mirrored on the wall-mounted television. "Clans and other organizations have the opportunity to set up private chatrooms within The Shift. The idea behind this was that people could communicate with only a select group of shifters to set up meetings and whatever without it being public to everyone else on the app. This one caught my eye, and I had to do a little hacking to get into it." He tapped the screen again, pulling up far more information than Reid's tired mind could take in all at once.

"From what I can tell," Raul continued, "this is a trafficking ring. The whole thing is based entirely around shifters, whether we're talking about the buyers, sellers, or the victims."

"You've got to be shitting me." Reid had racked his brain all night, trying to come up with someone who'd be interested in Mali. She held no government secrets, and she didn't have any enemies that he knew of. Something like this hadn't even crossed his mind.

"I'm afraid not," Amar confirmed as he strode in the room. He still carried the brimstone scent of being in his dragon form recently. "Raul showed it all to me. It sounds like this is a very powerful group of people led by a man named Dean Bryant. He's a real asshole, even outside of trafficking."

Raul glanced from his Alpha to the screen, pulling up a listing of all the 'merchandise' that was available. "We're not talking about typical shifter breeds. You can see here they've listed ocelots, whales, manatees, blackbucks, an Iriomote cat, and..." He hesitated as he looked at Raul. "A sun bear."

"Let's go." Brushing aside the exhaustion that he'd finally acknowledged, Reid jumped to his feet. "Where is this place?"

"Hold on." Amar moved forward, taking up the center of the room.

He naturally carried an air of authority around him, which made him the perfect choice as their leader. "In most of our other missions, we've dealt with small-scale organizations that only have so much influence over a given area. This Bryant guy is different. From what I can tell, he's curated his clan, much like we have here. They're from all different walks of life and are comprised of numerous species. He's a bear himself, but he uses his clan as his employment roster."

Once again, Reid wanted to argue. He could easily picture himself standing up and telling Amar that none of that really mattered since they'd all be dead as soon as he got a hold of them. But that same animal instinct that made him want to go flying off the handle was also telling him that he needed to do as his Alpha requested. "What do we know about them?" he asked roughly.

"We don't have detailed information on all of them," Raul answered. "The most important one other than Bryant is probably a guy they call The Hound. Apparently, he can tell what kind of shifter someone is simply by being near them. It might be by scent, although I can't say even my sniffer is that good."

"That would make him quite the asset for someone dealing in trafficking rare species," Jude added. "All he'd have to do is get near someone in a busy restaurant or a crowded store to know what they were."

Reid swallowed. He'd taken Mali all over Los Angeles so she could get to know it better, and Emersyn and the other women had done the same. "It could've happened anywhere," he gasped, suddenly feeling just how vulnerable they all were as long as there was someone like that around. "Shopping, making arrangements for the wedding. Hell, he could've even sniffed her out when she got to the hotel if he was hanging out in the lobby. I never should've let her go."

"Don't do that to yourself," Amar warned. "We can't take the blame for the crimes others commit. If we did, we'd be flogging ourselves until we're dead. The better option is to make a solid plan for invading this hell hole. Raul?"

The Communications Sergeant nodded. "From what it looks like, Bryant hosts a big party for all the most affluent shifters he knows. On the outside, it looks like nothing more than an exclusive social gathering, but that's where he auctions off the men and women he's abducted. They can either bid for time with these exotic breed shifters, or they can buy them outright. Bryant is flexible as long as he's getting paid well."

Reid felt sick, his bear roaring to wrap its jaws around Bryant's neck, tearing his head from his lifeless body. Mali had told him about the abundant sex trade in Thailand. It wasn't an uncommon path for young women who often felt they didn't have any better options. Even though she and her family shunned it, their opinion wasn't going to change the reality of it happening all around them. He'd thought he'd gotten her away from any chance of that in the States, where everyone was free to pursue the careers they wanted to. Reid was starting to understand that the American Dream wasn't all that it seemed.

"Can we infiltrate?" Jude asked.

Amar nodded. "Possibly. Raul thinks he can hack his way into getting an invitation for one of us."

"Me," Reid said instantly. "I'm going."

"I don't think that's a good idea," his brother replied predictably. "You're too involved in the situation, and you're likely to give yourself away."

"Actually," Amar interrupted before their discussion could carry on any further, "it probably *should* be Reid. We're still trying to sort out all the members of Bryant's organization. If there's a chance any of them have seen us before, they may know that we're part of the SOS Force. I don't think they'd wait around to see if we were going to blow the whistle on them or not. Reid's just started here, and only a few people in the area know him."

"We can still keep it as secure as possible, even if you're in there alone," Raul said, setting down his computer and fishing in his pocket. "I've been working a lot with Taylor Communications. You won't believe the technology they have access to. Check this out."

Raul withdrew a small plastic box from his pocket. He opened the lid, but nothing appeared to be inside. "You see it?"

"No," Reid admitted, unsure if he cared. He didn't need gadgets and plans, he needed to get to Mali. All this planning and plotting was driving his grizzly crazy. When he was still in the Army, he'd been surprisingly good at following directions, given his wild past. He could be patient if his commanding officer wanted to explain things in too much detail or made him wait to get started until the time was right because he was getting paid either way. This wasn't like that, not at all.

"That's the whole point," Raul replied with a grin. "It's the smallest transceiver he's been able to make yet. It can be implanted along the jawline, just in front of the ear. You'll be able to hear us and we'll be able to hear you, but without having to be in our animal forms. And if Bryant has the kind of security that I imagine a man like him must, then you don't have to worry about passing through a metal detector. It can't pick it up."

Reid frowned at the box. "How far away can the rest of you be?"

Raul tipped his head from side to side. "*Ay*, that's the one pitfall. We'll still have to be in the same building. We can handle that, though."

"I don't want you guys to have to put your lives in danger," Reid said, his throat tight with anticipation. "If something happens to me, it's no real loss. But L.A. needs the SOS Force."

"And they'll still have it when we all come back in one piece," Jude assured him. "You don't get to be the Lone Ranger on this one."

"Agreed," Amar said with a nod. "We don't know just how many people we'll have to fight to get to her and the other captives. The party is tomorrow night. We'll work on our plans for getting into the building, and Raul will get you an invitation. You just need to have that tux dry cleaned. Oh, and you'll need a mask. Everyone shows up in disguise." Amar smiled, and he and Raul left the room.

Fuck. Reid bent forward and put his head between his knees. His eyes were closed, and he watched the colors that swirled on the backs of his lids as if they could give him some sort of answers. But no. There was no real answer to this problem. Nothing was guaranteed, and even with the plan they'd formulated, he was still going to have to wait.

"You all right?"

It figured that Jude would be there, playing the role of the older brother. Reid knew he could appreciate it in some other moment, but not this one. "Of course not, shithead."

The sofa creaked slightly as Jude rose. "We're going to get her, Reid. It might not be easy. We might make one hell of a mess. But at the end of it all, we're going to get Mali back."

Reid lifted his head and looked up into Jude's eyes. It was easy for him to see his sibling as cold and distant because that was the way he acted most of the time. It was as if nothing affected him and he just floated through life, waiting for the next phase of it to come along.

But now, he saw the passion that burned behind those icy blue eyes. Jude cared for Mali, not in the same way Reid did, but with a good amount of intensity. When he said they would be getting Mali back, he meant it.

Reid nodded. "I know we will."

5

———

THE RIDE IN THE WINDOWLESS VAN HAD BEEN ROUGH AND BUMPY, AND ITS driver had little care for a passenger who didn't have the luxury of either a seat or a seat belt. She'd braced herself against the walls and the floor, her sore muscles and joints arguing with her. The trip made her nauseous, and Mali had the fleeting thought that vomiting all over the floor might be a nice—if very small—method of revenge against her captors, but she couldn't quite bring herself to do it.

The van suddenly slowed, and the turns it took were smoother. Fear quickened in her veins. Mali had no idea if this meant things were about to get better or infinitely worse. Her heart thudded in her ears as the engine shut off, and a moment later, the door slid open. She squinted, expecting sunlight, but they were in the dark, cool interior of a garage.

"Let's go," the big man said.

Having little other choice, and with Keiko's advice still ringing in the back of her mind, Mali scooted to the doorway and stepped down. She walked alongside the big man, the skinny guy just behind them, as they passed two long rows of vehicles. Whoever owned this place had a lot of money; there were classic, collectible, and sports cars parked everywhere. Most of them she couldn't even name, but they certainly weren't just for going back and forth to work.

After unlocking and heading through a steel door, Mali blinked to see that they were standing in an incredibly elegant house. She tried not to gape as she was led through a sizable kitchen, all done in white with commercial-grade appliances, and into an extended sunroom. The interior wall was covered in flagstone, and an active fountain gurgled happily at the center of the room. The tiled floors were covered here and there with expensive rugs, and the ceiling vaulted up toward skylights. The windows that occupied almost one complete wall of the room peeked out onto manicured gardens, stone statues, and a pool. The sage green paint on the wood trim might've given it a cozy feeling if she hadn't been so terrified.

"Ah, there she is." A man had been seated on a long couch, but he rose as she entered. Apparently, these guys were all tall. He wasn't nearly as broad as the massive man standing right next to her, but he could easily overpower her. With his dark brown hair combed back, green eyes, and a thin-lipped smirk, he looked like a handsome villain from a Hollywood movie.

The other men moved out of his way as he walked a slow circle around her, and Mali could feel his eyes trace every curve of her body. Even though she was still wearing the sundress she'd put on after changing out of her wedding gown, the process made her feel completely naked.

"And this is the one?" He wasn't talking to her. He was talking about her, like a piece of meat for sale.

"Absolutely," the skinny man replied. "There's no mistaking the scent of a sun bear. Sometimes the cat species are hard to define, but not this one. Nothing like grizzly or polar, that's for sure."

"Another fantastic job by The Hound," he said approvingly.

Her cheeks heated, and she glared at the new man. "Who are you, and why am I here?" Mali had heard the horrible things from the other women back at that warehouse or whatever it was, but she wanted the information directly from the source.

The man laughed. "I'm Dean Bryant, if you really want to know. Perhaps you've heard of me?"

Mali raised an eyebrow. "Perhaps you can go fuck yourself," she spat.

Dean flicked his long fingers at the other two men. "Could you boys leave us for a moment, please?"

Her original captors stalked out of the room, leaving Mali and

Dean alone. She wasn't sure she liked the situation any better. Dean looked unassuming, but he didn't feel that way.

"Please, have a seat." He gestured to a cushioned wicker chair.

She sat, not because she wanted to be obedient, but because she was exhausted. Mali kept her eyes on him as he resumed his seat on the couch.

"What's your name?" he asked, his fingers steepled under his chin.

"Mali." There was no point in lying.

"Mali," he repeated. "That's a lovely name. Rolls off the tongue and easy to remember. Your face is going to be easy to remember, too. That's going to get you a lot of work, and my employees who remain conscientious are well rewarded. They get to stay here with me and have bedroom suites all to themselves, plus all the food and clothing they could need. Netflix, too, if you're interested." He laughed at his tasteless joke.

She simply stared at him. Questions were building on her tongue, but Dean was already making it quite clear that he only revealed things on his own terms.

"You've got a great body, but I don't like the way you're looking at me," he warned. "I suppose I should tell you what's expected of you while you're here. You'll have a room assigned to you, and after you've settled in, you'll have free reign of the house and grounds. A rather high wall surrounds the entire property, and I do keep security guards around the clock. You have to stay here and do as I say, and there will be a price to pay if you don't." He smiled as though it were all very simple and ordinary.

Mali swallowed. "What kind of work am I supposed to be doing?" She had a feeling she didn't really want the answer to this question, but she was tired of wondering.

"Are you aware," Dean asked slowly, "of just how much money people will pay to spend a little time with someone as rare as you?"

Far in the back of her mind, Mali had hoped that Keiko and Alejandra were wrong. Even once she'd arrived there, she'd held onto a vague dream that it would all be a big misunderstanding and she'd be allowed to go home. She let those hopes go, flying off like birds over the pristine garden outside. "I suppose I'm not."

Dean chuckled. "You're a little reserved, but there's some spunk in there. It's going to make you even more popular than your animal form. I'll tell you what. I don't usually give anyone an explanation of what I'm doing. I don't feel that I owe it to them, considering you and the people like you are simply the tools of my trade. But I like you, and I think you could be a wonderful asset. Let's talk shop, shall we?" He stood and went to a sidebar, where he poured two glasses of whiskey.

Mali took the drink he handed her. She wasn't much of a drinker, and the scent of it was overpowering, but she didn't want to give him any more of the upper hand than he already had by showing him her vulnerabilities.

He sat once again. "I specialize in shifter species facing extinction, the kind you can't find just anywhere. Sometimes—most of the time, really—they're sold. There are buyers from all over the world who come to me. The ones who are not as rare or who are harder to control get auctioned off to the highest bidder."

She'd taken a sip of the whiskey, which burned her throat and brought tears to her eyes, though she did her best not to let him see. "So, you sell them off like animals?"

"That's what they are, aren't they? Cats, dogs, deer, lizards or whatever? They're a commodity. Humans are, too, but I don't deal with them. I like the thrill of tracking down—shall we say—a limited edition?" He gestured with his glass to one wall, where a silvery leather wing draped from the floor to the ceiling.

Mali hadn't noticed it at first, as it nearly blended in with the gray flagstone. She realized, with her guts turning to water, that it had once been attached to a dragon. She'd only ever met one dragon in her lifetime, and that was Amar. If Dean could take down someone as formidable as him, then he was a powerful man indeed. "And the ones you don't sell?"

"Oh, I still make plenty of money off them. You'll be sold at auction, but the buyers only get to have an evening with you. You take them back to your room and make them happy, whatever that might mean. As long as you do, you get the privilege of staying here."

"I see."

"I'm glad you do. As long as we have an understanding, then you don't have a thing to worry about. In fact, there are plenty of shifters who'd be glad to have the privilege of staying here with me. Their fates could be much worse."

Mali thought of Keiko, who'd been bought and sold like a used car. She would probably look at this as quite the opportunity, as sick as it was. Her stomach hollowed out around her sip of whiskey as she realized just how good this was for anyone working in the sex trade. It was vile and degrading, being made to work merely for the exchange of housing and meals, no matter how nice they were. No one should live like this, no matter what the circumstances were.

Though the sunroom was quiet, other than the gentle gurgling of the fountain, Mali knew she and Dean were not alone. He was a rich and powerful man, and he likely had plenty of security all over the place. She would have to bide her time, but she wasn't sure how patient she could be. "I understand."

"Wonderful. There will be a rather lavish party here tomorrow night. The guests will all be wearing disguises to protect their identities, and I expect you to be dressed to the nines. Hugo will show you to your room, where you'll find everything you need. Dinner tonight is at eight."

The door to the sunroom opened right on time. Hugo—which she now knew as the name of the giant man who'd escorted her to the house—was waiting for her. Mali followed him obediently, but she was thinking about Reid. He'd told her many times about the work he'd done with the Special Forces and how it required the best observational skills. She took note of the layout of the house, including all the doors and windows. She watched for security cameras, and even though she knew they must be there, she didn't see them. Whoever this guy was, he had all the money in the world to hide what he was up to.

"Here you are," Hugo said as he stopped at an open door on the second floor. "Stay here until dinner. You'll be given more instructions later."

Mali stepped inside. An elegant sitting area with a timbered ceiling held comfortable furniture upholstered in floral fabrics. These were clustered around a low coffee table, which held a large vase of long-stemmed red roses and faced a fireplace with a flatscreen television on the wall above it. A wide doorway led to a canopied bed on the right side.

She turned around to find that the door had already closed behind her. Mali tried the knob, but it was locked. She pressed her ear to the door, wondering if Hugo was standing outside, or if he'd left her to her own devices. The door was thick, heavy wood, so she couldn't tell.

"Fine," she muttered to herself as she explored the room, looking at the locks on the windows and the French doors. "We'll play it your way, but only for so long."

———

SHE COULDN'T APPRECIATE the fineness of her accommodations, but Mali took advantage of them as much as possible. She found the large bathroom attached to her suite outfitted with every kind of shampoo, lotion, and makeup she could ever possibly want. She felt guilty as she washed the dirt, blood, sweat, and tears off her body, leaving her torn and ruined sundress in the trash can and donning a sleeveless burgundy number. Whoever had set up the room must have taken her measurements while she was unconscious, because everything in the massive walk-in closet looked like it would fit her. Mali passed up a pair of black stilettos and picked up some flats instead, just in case there was a chance to run.

A knock sounded on her door just before eight, and Hugo stepped in without waiting to see if she was decent or not. "It's time to go down for dinner," he growled.

Mali nodded as she followed him. She hated the luxury she was surrounded with, knowing it was all bought with the shame and tears of countless women. She hated to think that some might even have counted themselves lucky to be there, women like Keiko. As horrible as her life had already been, Keiko would likely have been thrilled. Mali secretly hoped she wasn't the only one selected for the 'honor' of dining with Mr. Bryant.

The dining room that Hugo led her to quickly proved she most certainly wasn't the only one there. A gaggle of women had gathered around a sidebar, where The Sniffer passed out drinks with a creepy smile. Everyone was outfitted in a similar fashion as Mali, in dresses that flattered their figures and complexions, and they all seemed far more comfortable than she did.

One of them noticed her standing in the doorway. She elbowed a woman next to her and gestured with her head, and the next thing Mali knew, they were all looking.

"Come on over and get a drink," said a woman in deep blue. She had wavy blonde hair that fell past her shoulders, and her legs were so long, she looked like she belonged in a swimsuit commercial. Her smile was dazzlingly white as she held up her glass. "It's one of the best things about the day."

Mali's stomach turned. She hadn't eaten anything since the wedding, and at this point, she wasn't even sure how long ago that was. Time was passing in such a strange way, sometimes moving far too quickly, yet at other times, hardly moving at all. The scent of food drifted from the kitchen, making her mouth water but also triggering her gag reflex. "No, thank you. I don't think I could drink anything right now."

"Ah, I get it." The blonde detached herself from the rest of the group and sauntered over. She was bold enough to lay a hand on Mali's arm as though the two of them had been friends for years. "You're new, right? It all takes a little getting used to. Just do yourself a favor and make sure you do everything you can to pamper yourself. Eat every time a meal is served, even if you're not hungry. Drink lots of water. We can exercise in the garden on nice days, and there's a gym downstairs. Take a long hot bubble bath. Just try to enjoy yourself as much as possible." She gave another one of those blinding smiles.

Mali's eyes shifted to The Sniffer, who was quite occupied at the bar. Hugo was heading through the swinging door into the kitchen, and the chatter of the other women was enough to hide her own quiet voice. "How can you say that? Dean explained what I'm supposed to do here. It's horrible!" It took all her self-control not to stomp her foot in indignation.

The smile immediately faded from her face. "Look, we all feel that way, but there's nothing you can do about it. If you're here, then you're here to stay. It's a lot better than what some of the others get. Just smile and play nice. It'll go better for all of us."

"What do you mean?" Mali asked with a scowl. She felt so stupid. Everyone around her acted as though they knew what was going on, like it was customary to be forcibly recruited into a job like this. It wasn't normal, and it shouldn't be.

The other woman's jaw tightened, and she led Mali by the arm to the French doors on the other side of the room. These, like the ones in the sunroom, looked out over the garden. Mali could see a little more from there, where winding paths curled around stone statues and carefully curated flower beds were in full bloom. "I mean that if we all stay on our best behavior, things are better. Dean might be a snake, but he does know a lot about the finer things in life. If you do what you're supposed to do and keep him and his clients happy, and you don't make any trouble for security, then you can get almost anything you want. Did you see the woman in the red dress?"

Mali turned a little more toward her companion so that she could see the group. The woman she spoke of was easy to pick out in brilliant scarlet with her dark hair twisted up on the back of her head. "Yes."

"That's Rita. She's been here for a long time, and she's brought in a ton of money. Dean gives her anything she asks for. She even has a little chihuahua he lets her keep in her room, and she can go out into the garden to walk him any time of day or night. If she wants a dress or some jewelry, she gets it. We're like racehorses here, and we're treated like queens as long as we bring in that moolah." The tightness that showed around the blonde woman's eyes told Mali that she wasn't as comfortable there as she portrayed herself to be.

"What's your name?" Mali asked suddenly. She wasn't going to get out of there alone. She'd need help. This woman—and the others like her—knew this place far better than Mali did. They could be the help she needed.

"Libby," she replied with a smile. "You?"

"Mali."

"That's a beautiful name."

The compliment meant much more coming from someone other than Dean, but it didn't still the urgency in her heart. She had to get back to Reid. There was no telling how far she'd been whisked away after being knocked out at the hotel. Her mate was a smart, capable man, but as much as she hoped he was on his way, she wasn't going to just sit around and wait to be rescued. "Thank you. Libby, have you ever thought about trying to get out of here? I mean, there are quite a few of us. A dozen, maybe. They couldn't stop all of us if everyone ran for it at the same time. And with someone like Rita, who has such freedom over the grounds—"

"No." Libby's voice was firm, and any hint of a smile had been completely erased from her face. "No, and don't you dare say another word about it."

Mali was taken aback. "But you can't like being here!"

"Of course not! You should see some of the men who come through this place, wanting a little time with us. Just because a man is rich doesn't mean he's attractive or kind. But I don't have to worry about having a roof over my head or paying bills, and I wouldn't get to dress like this if I were back on the streets, now would I?" Libby put her chin in the air, daring Mali to say otherwise.

Mali could see what was happening. Libby had been in this position long enough that she'd convinced herself it was a good one. She'd probably had a rough life, and by comparison, she wasn't going to find anything better than this. Someone who'd been starving and poor yesterday would feel as though they'd hit the jackpot if they got to live there. Libby hadn't told Mali anything about her past except for that barest hint, but it was enough. "No. I suppose you're right."

Relief washed over Libby's blue eyes. "Thank you. I see you eyeballing Rita, and I wouldn't advise talking to her about this, either. She'd rat you out in a second, and it would only earn her more favor with Dean."

Even if Libby wasn't willing to help her organize an escape, it sounded as though she was willing to be more of a friend than Mali had in anyone else at the moment. "I won't. Thank you."

Diminutive maids from the kitchen scurried in an out with multiple courses for their meal, starting with delicate organic vegetables and building to a fantastic salmon entrée. It all tasted bitter in Mali's mouth, but she ate anyway. She'd need her strength.

After the meal, everyone broke up. Mali watched them leave the table, unsure of what to do with herself. Some of the women went upstairs, presumably to their rooms. Others went into the common rooms of the mansion to play pool or watch movies. As she was trying to decide who she should attempt to speak to next, Dean slid into the chair next to her.

"Mali, my newest asset," he said, the sparkle in his eye no doubt brought on by the whiskey she could smell on his breath. "How has your first evening here been?"

"Fine, thank you." It wasn't fine. Not a damn bit of this was fine.

"Good." He stretched the word out long and low, like a trainer trying to soothe a horse. "Since you're so new, I ask that you go ahead and retire to your room. You'll need your rest for tomorrow's party. I'm sure the other women will help you get ready if you need it. You're going to do fantastically, but if you're concerned about whether or not your skills are up to par, I could always put you through a quick test." Dean arched one eyebrow suggestively.

Mali's dinner threatened to come back up. "I'm—I'm a bit tired, actually." She didn't know how to reject a man who held her life in his hands, but there it was.

Surprisingly, he smiled. "A cunning woman. Just polite enough not to make a man angry, but still trying to exact her own limitations. Yes, you're going to do just fine. Hugo, please take Mali to her room."

When she was back upstairs and Hugo had shut and locked the door firmly behind her, Mali threw herself onto the bed. She curled into a ball, not caring about getting the damn dress wrinkled. Reid floated in her mind. She desperately wanted to reach out to him. According to Keiko, they'd given her a drug when she'd been abducted that had kept her sun bear at bay. She needed that animal side of herself to communicate with her mate telepathically, to give her a chance to at least tell him that she was all right. But as she summoned it, pleading with it to come to the surface for only a moment, she knew that Dean had succeeded in keeping her subdued. Maybe he'd drugged the whiskey she'd had in the sunroom, or maybe it was something he'd put in the food, but either way, he wasn't going to let her animal side out until it suited him.

Left as nothing more than a human for the moment, hot tears burned the backs of Mali's eyes and flooded out onto the bedspread. It picked up the pigment of her eyeliner—which had made her feel like such a traitor to apply—making an inky gray circle where her tears puddled. Mali hadn't known how much she needed her mate until they'd met, and now, she could never be whole without him.

Allowing herself a moment to fantasize, Mali imagined him bursting in through the French doors as the great grizzly that he was, slicing his claws through anyone who stood in his way so that he might take his mate back to safety. It was the kind of thing women dreamed of when they wanted a romantic fantasy. For Mali, knowing it probably wouldn't happen only broke her heart even more.

"Oh, Reid," she whispered through the tightness of her throat. "I want to talk to you. I want to run my hands through that hair of yours and tell you that you need a comb. I want to see you give me that sarcastic smile when you're making jokes. Most of all, I want you to hold me in your arms and tell me everything's going to be all right, because right now, I don't think it will be." She cried harder, the sobs racking her chest. "I know you'll do what you can to find me. I just don't know if it's possible."

Her illusion of being saved by Reid turned sour as she imagined herself becoming just like Rita, being pulled along by Dean Bryant's schemes and doing whatever was necessary to make the best possible life for herself. No matter how many luxuries she added to this idea, it was still the worst fate she could imagine.

"No." She sat up, wiped her tears with the back of her hand, and looked around at the room as though it were the enemy. She wasn't just going to sit around and wait to be rescued. If the party Dean had mentioned was tomorrow, she didn't have much time. She had to get away from there.

Mali marched to the closet, kicking off the flats and leaving the dress as a puddle of burgundy fabric in the corner. She flipped through the racks of finery and dug through the drawers until she found a pair of gray flannel lounge pants and a comfortable t-shirt. No doubt this was meant for sleeping when there was no one around to see her, but it was the best she had for the moment. Donning her new clothes and summoning all the courage she had left, Mali looked around the room. She needed a plan.

Everything seemed like a bad idea, with too many possibilities for failure. If she hurled a chair through the window, it would surely bring all of Dean's men running. There was no way for her to pick the locks unless she had her sharp sun bear claws to help her, but of course, that wasn't an option. She could wait until morning and hope that she'd have a chance to escape from a different area, but every tick of the mantel clock brought her closer and closer to that damn party. She had to do something before that.

Settling on a plan that had to be good enough for the moment, Mali pulled a red rose from the vase on the coffee table. Holding the stem carefully so that it wouldn't prick her fingers, she bit the head of it off. It tasted horrible, but Mali gnashed it between her teeth. Saliva built in her mouth, but she let it flow, mixing with the red pigments from the rose petals. Carefully tucking the thorny stem back in amongst the others where it couldn't be seen, Mali went to the door.

"Hugo?" she called, knocking on the wood. "I don't feel good." Red-tinged saliva dripped down her chin and onto the front of her light gray shirt.

"That's what they all say on the first night," came his gruff reply.

"No, really." She thunked her hand against the door and slid down toward the floor, kicking out with her foot to knock the lamp from a nearby table. The crash had its intended result, as Hugo flung open the door and sent her tumbling.

"What the hell is going on?" the man barked.

Mali lay weakly on the floor, letting a little more of the dark liquid run out of her mouth to make a crimson puddle. She clutched at her stomach and chest, moaning as she drew her knees up. "It hurts. Please. It hurts so bad."

Hugo stood over her for a long moment. Her eyes were closed, but the shadow of him was impossible to miss. He nudged her knee with his foot. "Come on. Get on your feet. I've been through plenty, and I know better than to believe you. Get up and go to bed, or I'll take you to Dean."

The only movement Mali made was to writhe some more, gritting her teeth to show just how much pain she was in. "Please," she begged again. "Just make it stop." She coughed into her hand, letting it fall back onto the floor palm-up so he could see the redness smeared across it.

"Oh. Shit." His mammoth hands grabbed her on each side of her ribs and lifted her off the floor. "All right. I'll have Dean call the doctor." He set her on her feet and kept one arm around her, moving her toward the stairs. He stopped as he put one hand on the rail. "Actually, maybe I should just leave you in your room."

"No, please don't. I don't want to die alone." Mali leaned against his chest as she convulsed with another coughing fit, this time letting a glob of chewed-up rose petal shoot out of her mouth and mar the white front of his shirt.

"Fuck! She's coughing up blood clots! Dean!" Hugo picked her up and carried her swiftly down the stairs. At the bottom, he set her in a nearby chair and shot off through the house. "Dean! You've gotta call someone!"

This was the opportunity she'd been looking for. As soon as Hugo was through the doorway, Mali was on her feet. She was in one of the multiple living areas of the home. They all looked alike to her at this point, but Mali knew at least one of them had to have an unlocked door. She tried several of the French doors along one wall in vain, finding the handles firmly in place on each of them.

"This way," came the deep rumble of Hugo's voice.

There were too many rooms, and she hadn't yet memorized the floor plan, but Mali took off. She heard cursing and yelling, and every vibration of sound made the back of her neck prickle as though someone was about to snatch her up. She skirted away from the media room and into the study.

There was a massive oak desk at the center of the room with papers scattered across it. A tumbler of whiskey sat abandoned on the smooth surface. No doubt this was the room Dean had occupied just before Hugo called him, and she'd managed to circle through the house and avoid them. Hope rose in her chest as she reached for the patio door's handle and turned it.

Mali darted out, quietly closing the door behind her so they wouldn't know what direction she'd gone. Her heart was pounding too hard in her chest, but it pumped much-needed adrenaline through her body. Wiping the back of her hand across her mouth to mop up the rest of what the rose had left behind, Mali took off across the gardens.

It was dark, and the only outdoor lights were right near the house itself. Mali didn't have her animal vision to help her, but the pale stones of pathways and steps gave her some semblance of the layout. The taste of that awful rose still clung to her tongue, but it'd worked well enough to get her outside.

Mali moved quickly and carefully, hoping her eyes would at least adjust somewhat to the dark. She tripped over a paver stone and stumbled into a bush, but she continued to move. If she just kept going, eventually, she'd find the wall that Dean had mentioned. After that, well, she'd figure it out.

The night air was cool against her skin as she skirted around a tree. Voices sounded from the house, an unintelligible shout. They'd probably figured out she'd made it outside, though Mali could hope they at least didn't know what door she'd used. The skin on her back prickled, as she knew they were looking for her, possibly even following her, but she resisted looking over her shoulder. That would only ruin what little night-vision her eyes had built up in the last couple of minutes.

Descending several stone steps, Mali found herself in an open space where the ground was graveled in pale stone. One tree stood at the center, sheltering a wrought iron table and chairs, but it would only make her stand out to anyone who was looking for her. She darted over to the left to skirt around it.

And smacked right into fabric and flesh.

Something abrasive wrapped around Mali's ankles as an animal yipped and barked, and a tiny mouth sank into the flesh just below her knee. Mali smacked it away, and the chain around her ankles only tightened.

"I have her! She's here!" Rita called. She moved quickly in the dark as she unclipped her dog from the leash that was serving as a rather effective binding and yanked it into a tight knot. "I hope you're ready to pay for what you've done," she snarled at her captive.

"Please, just let me go," Mali gasped. The pain around her legs was intensifying as the circulation to her feet was cut off. She pulled at the leash with her fingers, but it was useless. It was wound too tightly around her, and she was too weak from everything that'd already happened. "I don't want to be here. If you do, that's your business, but I just want to go home to my mate."

Even in the dim light, Mali could see something flash in Rita's eyes. It was gone as quickly as it came, and she once again only looked at Mali with a spark of hatred. "They're already coming. Can't you hear them? You have to take your punishment for this so the rest of us don't have to. I'm not going to be the one who suffers Dean's anger."

Hugo and another man were on her in a minute. The leash was unwound, and Rita walked off to fetch her dog without another word. A brilliant light exploded in Mali's face as someone held a flashlight pointed at her.

"You're a very clever little thing," Dean's voice said from behind the light. "I'll give you credit for your attempt, as it never hurts to exercise the strength of my security force. That's mostly because you are truly rare indeed, and I know there's a lot of money to be made from you. Be warned, however, that if you pull anything like this again, I'll have you slaughtered in a second. I won't waste my time more than once, and you can't fool me with false complacence. Hugo, do it."

Mali twisted and turned in the brute's grip, wondering what 'it' was, but she soon felt a small stab in her arm. She could feel the injection burning in her bloodstream as it forced her sun bear even further toward the center of herself, making sure it wouldn't even have the thought of coming out for a while.

"Good night, Mali." Dean's voice echoed in her head as the dark garden turned completely black.

6

"ARE YOU SURE THIS IS THE RIGHT KIND OF DISGUISE?" REID ASKED. HE pulled off the mask that Melody had just handed him and studied it. With its narrow chin, sculpted cheeks, and high brows, it looked like some sort of vaudeville devil. "I'd be much happier in camo."

Melody, who served not only as the daycare provider for Gabe and Emersyn's young son, but also the Force's bookkeeper, urged him to put it back on again. "Trust me, you'll stick out like a sore thumb if you go in there looking like a soldier. These people are expecting someone elite, the kind of man who's so powerful, he can go to an illegal party like this and not worry about the consequences."

"Does it have to cover my whole face?" he asked. "There's no way Mali is going to recognize me."

Cocking out one hip and balling her fist on it, Melody gave him a look over her glasses. "That's the whole point, genius. If she thinks you're there in the same room with her, she might give the whole operation away. She's not a trained soldier like you are. The only thing this mask leaves exposed is your jawline, which is essential for the communication implant to work. I still need to fix your eyes, though." Melody gestured for him to take off the mask once again, and she began working him over with a black eyeliner pencil.

"You're pretty damn thorough," Reid said grouchily, fully resenting the idea of having to wear any sort of makeup. He wanted nothing more than to get into this mansion Raul had found and get Mali back. He'd forced himself to get some sleep so that he'd be as prepared as possible, but all the preparations were driving him crazy.

"I did a lot of theater when I was in college. I don't mind getting a chance to exercise those skills a little." She handed him a mirror. "Here. Put the mask on, and tell me if you see yourself or some other random guy."

Reid did as he was told, pulling back a little in surprise when he studied his reflection. "Damn. Okay. You really know what you're doing."

"Unless Mali can recognize your throat, I don't think we have anything to worry about. And the tux was returned by the dry cleaner in decent condition? No pit stains or anything?"

"Looks good to me." He still thought he looked absolutely ridiculous, and he sure as hell hoped he wouldn't be the only one showing up dressed this way. If they suspected him before he even got to the party, they'd be starting right back at square one. That wasn't acceptable when it came to rescuing Mali.

"Good. I think the guys are ready for you, so I'll leave you in their capable hands." She paused, studying his face. "Even through this disguise, I can tell you're worried. I can't pretend to imagine exactly how it must feel to know your mate is in danger, but I can tell you that the Force is on it. I've seen them do some incredible stuff, and they wouldn't be doing any of this if they didn't think it was going to be successful."

Not for the first time, Reid was touched by how considerate everyone there at the Force was. Most of them—Melody excluded—were hardened soldiers, yet they all understood just how much Mali meant to him. "Thanks. You said Emersyn is going to be standing by? In case Mali has any injuries?"

A wrinkle of concern passed over Melody's brow, but it disappeared quickly and she nodded. "The doctor is in."

"Reid?" Jude poked his head in the room. He grinned when he saw his brother. "Looks like Melody is wasting company money on frivolous costumes again."

"Shut up." Reid stood and followed his brother out to the garage, where he ducked into the back of a limousine. Emersyn was already there, ready to go with her medical bag. Gabe was seated in the front, posing as the driver. Raul had his laptop open, as always.

It took Reid a moment to realize that Amar was the other man in the back of the limo. "Did Melody do some work on you, too?" Reid asked.

The Alpha grinned. "She insisted. I have to admit I was a bit skeptical at first when she came after me with a rubber nose and a big palette of makeup, but I think she's right. No one is going to know it's me, at least not at first glance. I should be able to secure a spot with the rest of the staff while you're in the party. Raul will be monitoring your comm from out here, and Gabe and Emersyn will be standing by."

"It looks like there's a large parking area off to the side of the house where I can park this boat while we wait," Gabe noted, pulling the limo out of the garage and onto the street.

"Let's do another test on your comm really quick," Raul enthused. He clicked a button on his computer, inciting a strange noise that filtered straight into Reid's ear. It cleared quickly, and when the tech genius sent a signal, Reid heard it perfectly. "All right. Good enough for now. Let's just hope there aren't too many walls between us once you get in there. It's too new to know much about it yet, but it's our best bet for a high-security operation like this."

Reid nodded. He thought of Mali and wondered how she was doing. What kind of conditions were they keeping her in? What might they have already done to her? If anything had happened to her...

"Reid." Jude's voice was a low grumble in his ear. "She's all right."

"Hmm?"

"I can tell by the look in your eyes that you're fearing the worst. Raul and Amar have done a lot of research on this operation. If Mali is at this party, then she's one of the lucky ones. They wouldn't bring her here and put her on the auction block if they'd done anything..." He trailed off, not wanting to state the alternative out loud.

"You know, I've been on a lot of crazy missions. I've jumped out of choppers into every kind of situation imaginable. If someone had asked me six months ago how it would be to go on a mission that involved rescuing my mate, I would've laughed it off and said it was no problem. After all, even before I met Mali, I knew what a strong urge there would be to protect the one I was fated to be with. I wouldn't have thought it would be this difficult."

Jude looked down at his lap. Even in the passing glow of streetlights, Reid could see the distant look in his eyes. "I really do understand, Reid. I can't promise that it'll be easy, but we'll get you and Mali through this."

"Yeah. Thanks." Jude's words only did so much to make him feel better. What he needed was to hold Mali in his arms. He craved her warmth, her scent, and the intriguing way her sun bear reached out and touched his very soul, not only stirring his grizzly, but encouraging him to be a better man than he'd ever been.

Somehow, he didn't feel any closer to his objective when the limo pulled into the curved motor court of their destination. Gabe did his duty as chauffeur, stepping out of the car to let his passenger out. He gave Reid a nod that would've looked like a sign of respect to his boss to anyone else, but Reid knew it was his way of wishing him good luck on the mission.

He approached the double doorway of the mansion, noting the other men who were entering. Reid would have to tell Melody when he got back to headquarters that she'd been correct, as they were all dressed similarly. Oddly enough, a few of them already had women on their arms. Reid had to wonder just what kind of world he was walking into.

"Your invitation please, sir," said a man at the door. He was gigantic and looked ridiculous in his tuxedo, and he wasn't wearing a mask. Reid noted the scar that split his face but said nothing as he held out his phone to display the bar code Raul had rigged up for him. The bouncer scanned it with his device, waited for a moment as he looked at the screen, and then nodded. "Thank you, Mr. Chancellor. Drinks are being served in the sunroom. I see you're a first-time guest, so please feel free to ask the staff if you need anything at all."

"Thank you." Reid went inside, not having a clue as to how he was supposed to get to the sunroom or anywhere else. That part was fine with him. He could spend time wandering around, and if he looked a little lost, that was far better than being overconfident.

"You in?" Raul asked in his ear.

"I am." Reid kept his voice low and quiet, not wanting to make it obvious that he was wearing a wire.

"Good. I can hear you loud and clear. So far, so good."

He first found himself in a large living room with leather couches, hardwood floors, and a high ceiling. Men and women lounged with their drinks, but they paid little attention to him. Reid scanned the faces of the women in particular. Anyone who wasn't wearing a mask was probably the staff Scarface had referred to. What did that mean for the women?

He approached a blonde who had just finished a conversation in the back corner of the room. "Excuse me."

"No excuses needed for a handsome guy like yourself," she purred. Her deep blue eyes only met his for a moment, though she gave him a dazzling smile.

It unnerved Reid. There was no doubt in his mind that this woman was being used. Why else would she be so subservient as to not look him in the eye? He cleared his throat. "I was told there were drinks in the sunroom?"

"Of course. I can take you there if you'd like. My name is Libby, by the way." She strolled through the next doorway without waiting for his answer.

"It's nice to meet you. I don't suppose I could ask you how all of this works, could I? I mean, I just want to make sure I'm in the right place at the right time, if you know what I mean."

Libby let out a tinkling laugh as she skimmed her fingertips over his shoulder. "Of course! You wouldn't want to miss the main event. An announcement will be made, but the bidding starts at midnight in the library, just over there." She pointed through a doorway to a room full of bookshelves. "If you buy any merchandise outright, then you can take it home and do as you wish with it. Most of the items going on the auction block tonight are purely for the evening, so you'll be escorted to a room."

Though she was giving him exactly the information he wanted, Reid felt his skin getting hot under the mask. The women were being treated as nothing more than objects. Sure, he might not always have been a perfect gentleman in his lifetime, but it was appalling to think about, nevertheless. "Thank you," he ground out, trying not to let his façade slip. "I also hope I can thank you for your discretion on this conversation."

"Oh, sweetheart." Libby signaled to the man behind the bar for two drinks. They were produced quickly, and she handed him one without asking what he wanted. "I'm the ultimate in discretion. It doesn't matter what your needs are or how you want to satisfy them, because I'll never tell. I can promise you one hell of a night if you manage to win a little time with me." She jutted out one hip clad in blue silk and rubbed it suggestively against his.

"I just might do that," he said for lack of anything better to say. This woman had told him quite a bit, but Reid knew he couldn't expect her to just spew out a bunch of information about Mali if he asked. "Thank you very much for your time."

"No problem, big boy." Libby moved on to croon at someone else.

Reid wandered through the house, trying to act as normal as possible as he sipped his wine and nibbled at the buffet. As much as he'd hated it at first, he was grateful for the mask. It made him feel less obvious, like he had something to hide behind while he observed the battleground.

"How's it going in there?" Raul asked in his ear. "I haven't heard anything interesting for a while."

Reid stepped into a nearby bathroom, knowing it was probably the safest place. He shut and locked the door behind him and even checked behind the shower curtain. No one was there, but there was no doubt this Dean Bryant had some sort of surveillance all over the place. He took his phone out of his pocket and pretended to make a call while he spoke to Raul. "It's been quiet. I know Mali is here somewhere. I can sense her, but it's faint."

"I've got a drone with night vision hovering over the house. If anyone leaves, I'll know it."

Reid closed his eyes, wondering if Raul had any idea just how reassuring that was. He'd thought of different things that could go wrong, including the possibility that Mali could find a way to escape and dash off before he had a chance to rescue her. If they missed each other, it could spell disaster for everyone. Still, there was something else that was bothering him. "The women are working the floor, offering drinks and help. I haven't seen Mali at all. What if she's not the sun bear that was listed?"

"I don't think it's very likely," Raul answered. "They're super rare. I will say that the more I've dug into the situation, the more I'm finding. There are at least two holding warehouses, which is where I believe they sort the victims out and decide what they want to do with them. It's possible that she hasn't been brought to the house yet, but that would mean there's another sun bear on the market. Statistically, the chances are very good that it's her."

"All right." Reid checked his watch, feeling his stomach curl with anticipation as it ticked closer to midnight. "This would be a lot more fun if we did it a different way, you know."

"I know. Hang in there. Find your mate, and then we'll get you home. Amar made it into the kitchen, so you've got backup right inside the house."

"Sounds good. Over and out." Reid knew that Raul would be able to hear him regardless, but the old habit was hard to break.

Everyone was drifting toward the library when he emerged from the bathroom, getting ready for the big event of the night. Reid noticed that the unmasked women who'd been working the floor like car sales-people only a few minutes earlier had disappeared. He followed the mass into the library, where several rows of chairs had been set up facing the mantel. While he waited, Reid couldn't help but notice how ironic it was to sell off sex slaves in a library. Then he noticed that this room, unlike the others he'd seen around the house, had almost no windows. The one large window behind him was fully covered with a thick red curtain. That had to be the key. Dean wouldn't chance anyone spying through the windows and seeing what he was really doing.

A slim man stepped up onto the raised hearth and everyone quieted down—except Reid's bear, who wanted nothing more than to tear this asshole's limbs from his body, one by one. The host smiled amicably, and standing there in his tux, he looked more like a man ready to accept a company award for perfect attendance than the kingpin of a shifter sex trafficking ring. The only difference was the mask he wore, which was far less concealing than what his guests sported. It was of a simple Venetian masquerade style that only covered his eyes. "Ladies and gentlemen, thank you so much for coming tonight. These parties simply wouldn't be as exciting without you."

He went on to explain the workings of the auction. "All of you should be able to check the information on your invitation to find details about each item number. If you win an item, payment is expected immediately in our counting room." Dean Bryant gestured to a small room off to the side. "Whatever you do win, I encourage you to enjoy your purchase right away."

A few whoops of laughter rose from the audience.

"Again, thank you all so very much for being here, and I hope you have a wonderful time. Let's get started!"

Reid steeled his jaw and sat glued to his chair as he watched woman after woman being paraded out to the hearth. As soon as he'd found out Mali was in this prick's hands, he'd expected to see terrified women in shackles and rags. But from what he'd seen that night, it was nothing like that. These women pranced onto the hearth like spokesmodels, smiling and flirting and waving their fingers at anyone who bid on them. As they tossed their hair, showing off glittering rings and shining necklaces, it gave Reid less and less hope of actually seeing Mali there.

After a set of redheaded twins was auctioned off for the evening, the host paused dramatically. "Ladies, gentlemen, I have a very special treat for you tonight. You'll know what I mean if you've read the description for lot number 457. She's brand new to our stage, but I promise she's far more feisty than she looks." He waved to his left.

Through a side door came Mali. She wasn't being dragged to the auction block, nor was she drugged into a stupor. She watched her feet as she walked across the floor and onto the hearth, stepping carefully so as not to twist an ankle in her stiletto heels. Her glimmering pink gown smoothed over her curves and set off the depths of her hair. She stepped up next to Dean and turned to face the audience, her arms down at her sides as she stared straight over their heads.

Reid sucked in a breath and crushed his fingers into a fist inside his pocket. That was his mate up there, being sold off like a Cadillac at a car auction. His bear roared inside him as thick hairs prickled the underside of his skin, threatening to burst through the surface and bring teeth and claws along for the ride. He was heavily tempted for a moment. It wouldn't take long to scoop her up, crash through a window, and barrel off through the night.

No. Everyone else there was probably a shifter as well, and Dean had incredible security. The only reason the Force managed to get in was due to their specific skills. He had to wait, and he had to bid.

"Let's start the bid at a thousand for the evening," Dean invited.

Several men raised their hands, Reid included. Unlike a traditional auction where everyone had numbered paddles, Dean relied on two goons who stood at the front of the room and watched the action.

"Do I have two thousand? How about five? At that price, I'm tempted to put a bid in myself."

Several more hands went up.

"Bro, you've got plenty of bargaining room," Raul said in Reid's ear. "Melody's going to have one hell of a time balancing the books this month!"

The Force had plenty of revenue, no matter what happened, but Reid knew he would've given everything he had and more to get his mate out of this hellhole. He kept his hand raised as the bids continued to rise.

"You just can't wait to get a piece of that hot sun bear ass, huh," commented the man seated next to Reid. He wore a mask that was composed of two faces, one looking to the left and one to the right. Only one of his eyes lined up with each face, making it difficult to know where to look. "Can't say I blame you, but if she's new, she's gonna be a handful."

Reid knew what was happening. This man thought he could talk Reid out of bidding.

"Do I hear eight thousand?" Dean called.

Reid wasn't about to give up. "Maybe I *like* a handful."

"You say that, but have you ever had Rita?" Two-Face gave a low whistle. "Man, she's naughty! She's up for anything, and I do mean anything. I tried to buy her outright, but Dean said he wouldn't let her go."

Reid's bear was thrashing inside him. Nothing could stand in the way of him getting to Mali. Not money, not some sleaze bag who wanted her for himself, and when it came down to it, not even Dean and his men. He'd fight until there wasn't a breath left in his lungs, and it would be sweet to crush the breath right out of this asshole next to him. "If you know what's good for you, you'll shut the fuck up."

Two-Face recoiled slightly. "Hey man, I'm just trying to help you out."

"What part of *shut the fuck up* don't you understand?" Reid jabbed his face forward, giving a clue as to what he might do if this douche didn't follow his advice.

"Gentlemen," said a low voice at Reid's elbow. "Let's keep things civil, or no one will get a chance to bid." It was one of Dean's goons.

Reid nodded and faced the front once again. He was pissed at himself and the world, and the rage inside him was almost impossible to contain. The bids continued to tick up, but the hands in the audience slowly went down.

"Sold," Dean finally proclaimed as he pointed straight at Reid. "Twenty thousand for the evening. Congratulations, sir."

As he'd seen the other winning bidders do, Reid headed into the counting room. He had to wonder how many thugs Dean managed to employ since he hadn't seen this one yet. Pulling twenty thousand dollars from his coat and handing it over as though it were nothing more than pocket change, he turned to leave the room and found Mali standing there waiting for him.

She didn't meet his eyes, her shoulders slumping as she stared at the wall. She clutched a small evening purse, her nails digging into the sequins. Reid's heart broke as he resisted the urge to reach out, take her by the arm, make her look at him, and tell her she was safe.

But Scarface was standing on the other side of Mali, and he grinned at Reid. "I'll take you to your room for the evening, sir."

As eager as Reid was to be alone with Mali, he didn't dare argue. If she recognized his voice and gave any inkling of it, it could put them both in some very hot water. Instead, he followed the goon and Mali through several first-floor rooms and up the stairs.

Despite the situation, Reid found himself studying Mali's backside as she climbed the stairs ahead of him. The way her body moved was irresistible. It was one of the many things that'd drawn him to her in the first place, along with the softness of her skin and the way her ebony hair fell like silk around her shoulders.

He shook his head. This wasn't the time. They'd reached the top of the stairs, where a long hallway had identical doors running down each side of it. The thug stopped at one of them and turned to Mali as he drew a syringe out of his suit jacket. He must have caught the tension this immediately aroused in Reid because he shook his head and laughed. "Oh, don't be one of those guys who tries to play the knight in shining armor. And if you're worried about whether or not she'll still be able to give you a good time, I'm just making sure she will. You see, Dean wasn't kidding when he said this one was feisty. We've had to keep her shifter form at bay until the auction." He stabbed the needle into Mali's arm, quickly thumbing the plunger and sending who-knew-what into her bloodstream. He shook her other arm until she looked him in the eye. "You remember what Dean said, now."

She nodded and opened the door to the room.

The anxiety that'd been building in Reid's system had come to a peak, but he still had to wait. The door was shut behind them and probably locked, but Reid wouldn't have been surprised if the guard was standing just on the other side to make sure everything went smoothly. He reached up behind his head, preparing to take off the mask, but as he turned to Mali, searing pain ripped through his jaw. His vision reddened as he stumbled backward, falling over an ottoman.

Mali had partially shifted and was standing over him, the strong, curved claws of her sun bear dripping with his blood. "Don't you fucking touch me," she said in a shaking whisper. "I don't care who you are or how much money you paid. I don't even care that I'll die if I don't give you what you want. I know who my mate is, and that's the only man I'll ever be with." She swung her claws back, ready to rake him again.

"Mali! Don't!" Moving with speed fueled by adrenaline, Reid whipped off his mask.

Her face was twisted with rage and hatred, but it fell away first from her mouth and then her eyes as she stared at him in disbelief. Several heavy breaths racked her shoulders as tears welled in her eyes. When she finally spoke, her voice was thick with emotion. "Reid? Is it really you?"

"In the flesh. I mean, what's left of it." He let out a nervous laugh as he pushed himself up from the floor and folded her into his arms, his grizzly releasing a sigh of contentment. They might have been in enemy territory, but as long as they were together, everything was all right. "I'm so glad you're okay."

"*You're* not." She pulled back, examining the lacerations along his jaw.

Just having her now-human fingers touch his flesh to examine the wound made his blood vessels tremble. "I'd like to just play that off and say it's only a scratch, but I think you've actually managed to knock my communicator out." Reid waited a moment, knowing he'd get a confirmation from Raul in his ear if the transceiver was still working, but he heard nothing. "I guess I'll have to send him a text."

Mali had found a handkerchief in a drawer, and she pressed it to his jaw as she looked up into his face with those soulful dark eyes of hers. "After finding you when we lived so far apart in the world, I knew I couldn't possibly go on like this. Not like the other women do. I meant what I said, Reid. I'd rather die."

Her words rang his heart like a bell. "God I love you, Mrs. Sutton." He bent his head and fell toward her lips. She smelled of the wrong kind of perfume, but his animal instinct let him sort out her natural scent and relish in it. Reid clutched her hips and ass desperately, pulling her hard against him and feeling that it still wasn't close enough. "I thought I'd lost you. You don't know how crazy it drove me trying to find you." He kissed her again, fully this time, his tongue roving into her mouth. The bear inside him groaned with powerful need as it reunited with Mali's ursine soul.

She was feeling it, too, her hips thrusting against him with urgency. "Reid," her voice trembled. "Reid." Mali didn't ask, but she didn't need to.

He swept her off her feet and into his arms, moving toward the bed as their tongues danced, getting to know each other once again. Reid's instincts were driving him to the one place he'd wanted to be for the last two days, the one place he'd worried he'd never be again, and he groaned with relief as he laid Mali on the bedspread and she put her arms around him.

"I missed you," she said as she shoved his tux jacket back and tore at the buttons of his shirt. "I wanted to reach out to you so badly, but they kept my bear drugged, and—"

Reid silenced her with another kiss. "Not now, Mali. We can talk all about that later. Everything's okay." He couldn't be sure if he was telling her or himself, but it was true either way. His hand skimmed up her thigh, running under the pink dress to find her panties. Keeping one hand on her ass, he found the zipper on the side of the dress and pulled it down, revealing the curved side of one breast. Yanking the sparkling fabric aside, he sucked her into his mouth.

Mali let out a gasp that turned into a low moan as her head fell back on the covers. She raked her fingers through his hair, shimmying his pants down with her feet. Her hand roved down his abdomen and further until she claimed him, stroking the soft skin of his hard cock with need.

Reid burned for her, feeling his muscles quiver with weakness at finally being so close to her. He might be a man who could fight any enemy, but he was weak when it came to Mali. Her grip on him had drained all the blood from his head. He stripped the dress the rest of the way off of her lithe body, running his lips and tongue along her jawline, down her neck, around each nipple, and across the smooth plane of her stomach, then dove his head between her legs, relishing the taste of her.

"Reid!" she gasped as his enthusiasm built and he sucked at the petals of her flesh. She clasped her legs around his neck and shoulders. Mali's hands cradled her breasts as she writhed on the bed. "I'm not going to be able to stay quiet if you keep doing that," she panted.

Though that might've been her way of telling him to stop, it only drove Reid further. Let her scream. Let her cry out so loudly in her pleasure that the whole house could hear them and the guards would come running. Mali was his. Nothing else in the universe mattered. He slid his hot, eager tongue into the deepest part of her core, bringing it back out to tease her center of pleasure until her thighs quivered around him.

Mali's fingers dug into the bed linens, twisting them up around the two of them like a shroud as his name left her lips over and over again. Her hips bucked against him, demanding more, and Reid was more than happy to give it. All thoughts of his mission and what he was probably supposed to be doing right now had gone straight out the window as his inner bear demanded that he provide his mate everything she needed and more.

When he couldn't bear it any longer, Reid moved up the bed so that his mouth was by her ear. "Ride me," he told her, knowing she loved being on top.

But Mali grabbed his shoulders and shook her head. "No, not this time. I want you to take me."

No matter what he thought about it, his body and bear both agreed. He was already throbbing against her, and it took only the barest movement to sink into her heated depths. Reid rolled his eyes back in his head.

"Are you all right?"

Reid swallowed, knowing that as soon as he began moving again, he wouldn't be able to control himself. As it was, it was difficult enough just to remain human as the honey of her arousal soaked them both. "There's nothing that turns me on more than hearing you get off. Other than *feeling* it."

She teased him with a swivel of her hips. "I never said I was done with you, you know."

With a roar, Reid buried his face in her shoulder as he thrust against her, feeling her velvety walls stroke down his length. Mali spread her legs wider, beckoning him further inside her, and the feeling of her smooth calf along his backside was enough to drive him crazy. Reid's body was alight. Every nerve was singing with rapture as he got to know his mate all over again. He tried to hold back, wanting the moment to last as long as possible. It had always been good with Mali, but this was something else.

Mali's nails dug into his back as a whimper of satisfaction escaped her throat, and when Reid felt her convulse around him, he could no longer hold onto that last thread of control. He drained all of his life into her, feeling the pulse and release of tension all over his body as he exploded.

Even when they had no more to give, they lay in bed together and held each other. Reid knew, without the slightest shadow of a doubt, that he would never let go of her again.

7

MALI CLOSED HER EYES. WITH REID'S WARM WEIGHT ABOVE HER, nothing bad could ever happen again. She stroked her fingers through his hair, allowing herself the simple pleasure of seeing it spring back into place every time she let go.

"That was intense," he murmured against her neck. His entire body had gone limp.

Mali smiled. "You're an absolute beast, and I love you for it." The pleasure Reid had brought to her body had made her mind erase the mansion and the horrible people that surrounded them, but it was impossible to keep reality at bay forever. To think that she might've been forced to do that with someone else, someone she didn't love, someone who would use her...

"What is it?" Reid lifted his head, his brow wrinkling as he reached up and wiped a tear from the corner of her eye. "I didn't hurt you, did I?"

She couldn't help but smile at him. For a burly guy who didn't like to follow the rules, he was one hell of a gentleman. "No. Not at all. I just fell back to Earth, and it occurred to me that we're going to have to get out of here somehow."

"Don't you worry about that." Reid pushed himself off the mattress, dropping a kiss on her breast before he sat up all the way and began looking for his pants. The wound on his face had stopped bleeding, but it stood out against his jaw as he dug out his cell and started firing off messages as fast as his fingers would move.

Mali got out of bed, too, throwing on the dreaded pink dress. She couldn't stop the smile that played at her lips as she zipped it back up. "I put this on tonight because I was told to. I already made some trouble for Dean, and once they got me back into my room, he made it quite clear that he'd slaughter me if I didn't do what I was told. He wanted to keep me here because he knew he could make a lot of money off of me, but I wasn't worth it if they couldn't count on me to behave myself."

He tipped his head as he studied her, his humor reflected on her face. "And what's so funny about that?"

"I knew I couldn't behave for long, but I wanted to keep my own skin for as long as I could. I thought I'd be sold to some stranger tonight, and I was prepared to take him hostage and use him to get out of here. If I'd have known you would be the one to buy me, I might've been a little more excited about it."

Reid set his phone on the bed as he tugged his clothes back on. "I haven't known you all that long, not compared to how long I want to know you, but you always see the humor in things, even when the world is going to shit."

She shrugged casually, knowing she hadn't handled her captivity as bravely as she would've liked to imagine. "I do my best, but it's a lot easier when you're at my side."

"We're about to get a real test here in a second. Gabe, Raul, Jude, and Emersyn are waiting outside in the limo. Amar is downstairs somewhere. They're going to create a couple of distractions for us, and we're going to get you out of here."

Mali's heart soared, knowing this nightmare was about to be over. "I'm ready. What do I need to do?"

Reid eyed the stilettos she'd been wearing at the auction as he put his mask back on, which only sported a smear of dried blood from the claw marks. "Put on some shoes you can run in and stick by me. Some of this will just be off the cuff."

When they were dressed, they went to the door. Surprisingly enough, it wasn't locked. "They were probably too worried about your safety," Mali joked as they stepped out into the hall.

Hugo was watching over the second floor, and he strode forward as soon as he saw them emerge. "Is there something I can help you with?" He addressed Reid directly.

"We're just going downstairs to get something to eat," he explained simply, taking a few steps toward the stairs.

Mali hung on his arm like the obedient escort she was supposed to be, smiling and giggling.

Hugo eyed her warily before addressing Reid once again. "I can have some food brought to your room."

"No, thanks. I'd prefer to get it myself." He put his arm firmly around Mali's waist and walked away.

The guard caught up with them easily despite his size. "You can leave if you'd like, sir, but the girl must stay in her room."

Mali knew they'd only get so far before someone got suspicious, but she hadn't thought it would've happened so quickly. She felt Reid's hold on her tighten even more at the mention of these people keeping her prisoner. "The girl stays with *me*." He hauled back and landed a solid punch to Hugo's jaw.

Reid had lost control, and Mali stepped to the side to give him room as he shifted. Claws burst from his fingers as his hands widened and flattened. He fell forward to all fours, his back stretching and twisting to accommodate his new body as hair mushroomed from his skin. It was deep brown, nearly sable on his legs and belly. Black lips encased his sharp teeth as he let out a furious roar, and he moved his lumbering body between Mali and the guard.

Even as she stood behind him in human form, Mali could feel his bear inciting her own. Nausea rose in her throat. The drugs they'd given her to keep her bear at bay had been reversed by that last injection after the auction, but it made the whole experience feel new again as her animal side took over. Those same impressive claws that she'd raked Reid's face with split her skin. Her ears moved back and up as they changed shape, and the sound of the brawl breaking out in front of her changed along with their position. The golden collar of fur around her neck was a stark contrast to the deep charcoal brown of the rest of her body, but one she had always secretly loved. The remarkably long tongue of a sun bear scraped over her sharp teeth, and though she was small, she was prepared to fight with everything she had.

But Hugo had changed, too. Where the brute once stood, a tiger now occupied the hallway. He still bore the same scar over his eye, and he was ready to fight for the rules of the house. He swatted his razor-sharp paws toward Reid, hissing and spitting as his tail swished from side to side. Shouts arose from other parts of the house, but the two beastly males had no clue as they sparred.

Reid dodged a blow from the tiger, but he didn't see the one that followed it. Hugo shoved forward and pinned him against the wall, his white teeth preparing to sink into bear flesh. Reid tucked his head and shoved his attacker, knocking the cat backward. He pursued the fight, barreling forward as he swiped and bit, slashing the brilliant fur and staining the carpet with blood. One final push sent the cat through the railing, tumbling toward the first floor.

Let's go! As Mali's mate, Reid's mind was telepathically connected to hers when they were both in their animal forms. *Sounds like the others have already gotten started.*

Mali sprinted after him, perking up her ears. Something was happening down in the front entryway. It must have been Gabe and Raul, because she swore she could hear the roar of a bear alongside the howl of a wolf. As she and Reid made their way down the stairs, several patrons and staff came streaming past them from the direction of the kitchen.

Reaching the bottom landing, she saw a brilliant ball of fire burst through the kitchen doorway. The doorway itself exploded into pieces as a massive black dragon shoved through it. The Hound was bold enough to come forward with a gun, but Amar made him regret it with another stream of flames.

Mali and Reid fought their way through the chaos that had built on the first floor. She moved in his wake as they shoved aside patrons and slashed at guards, the crush of shifter bodies making things confusing. The air smelled of blood and smoke. Mali knew Reid was conversing with the rest of the Force. They were his clan, so he could mentally communicate with them the same way he did with her, but she was out of the loop. She could rely only on what she heard and saw, which was made even more confusing by the crush of rare animals that blended in with bears, cougars, tigers, and wolves.

Help! A voice called out inside her head. *Mali, if you're there, help me!*

Stunned, Mali paused for a moment. She barely dodged a tiger who came racing toward the kitchen as she tried to reply to that familiar voice. *Tasanee? Is that you?* She reached out for it, but the voice was gone just in time for Mali to notice a lynx come barreling down the stairs. It dashed into the dining room and back out again to avoid the flames leaking in from the kitchen. Skittering away from Amar's leathery wings and deadly claws, it raced through the rooms, desperately seeking a way out.

Mali couldn't speak to it the way she could with Reid, yet she knew in her heart that it was Libby. The blonde had been confident in herself the night they'd met, but Mali had seen the fear in her eyes when Libby had told her not to make trouble. She'd been through a lot already, and even though she'd tried to play off her position at Dean's as being good for her, Mali knew better. Now she was scared and running for her life, afraid she'd burn in the flames.

Not able to stand idly by and let this happen, Mali broke away from the main knot of fighting and headed for the back exit that led out toward a glimmering swimming pool. The doors, like most of the others, were locked, but she wasn't going to let that stop her. Every door in the house except the front was made of glass. Mali's sun bear wasn't nearly as big as Reid's grizzly, but he was currently fighting a rather mangy-looking wolf.

Tucking her shoulder in, she shoved herself at the door. The glass shuddered in its frame, but it didn't break. Anger and frustration burned inside her. She'd only been trapped like a zoo animal for a couple of days, and already she knew it'd scarred her very soul. She could only imagine what a longer imprisonment had done to Libby and the others like her. Mali looked over her shoulder, seeing the lynx panting as she paced the floor. No, it wasn't that Mali could imagine Libby's inner turmoil. She could see it clear as day on her face.

It fueled Mali's energy, and she pounded against the door again. The glass cracked, giving her more hope as she continued her efforts until the door shattered and fell out onto the concrete. The inertia carried Mali's body forward, the broken glass slicing through her skin as she stumbled outside.

The effort wasn't in vain. Mali turned to see Libby's lynx form leap through the new opening. She paused long enough to look over her shoulder at the sun bear, and Mali saw gratitude in her feline eyes before she dodged around the pool, leapt over a concrete urn full of greenery, and was gone.

Mali! Reid's voice thundered in her head.

I'm over here! Squeezing back in through the broken door, Mali saw Reid standing in the middle of the living room, swiveling his giant head from side to side as he looked for her. He'd sustained several injuries, just like she had. His fur was already dark, but now it was blackened even further by rivulets of blood, and several tigers and a wolf lay at his feet. Dragon fire rippled across the ceiling, licking at the second floor and threatening to bring the whole place down as several guards still in their human form tried to battle the blaze.

It's time to go. Reid turned for the front exit. A wolf and two bears joined him, and when they emerged from the house, she spotted the shadow of a black dragon swooping overhead.

Mali followed the others, grateful for the four legs of her bear form since she didn't know the way in the dark. Her only experience with the grounds had been that one attempt at escape, and she thought that might've been on the other side of the house.

A limo materialized out of the shadows. Emersyn jumped out of the driver's seat and yanked open the back door. "Any injuries?"

The group quickly returned to their human forms to accommodate the car. Mali pulled in a deep breath and let it out as a sigh as she let her sun bear melt back into her body. Since coming to America, she'd spent much of her time in human form, simply because she was always going out and seeing the sights. She hadn't realized how much she'd missed her sun bear until Dean's men had drugged her.

She shivered as the thick fur retracted, leaving only smooth skin. It pinched and pulled as her face returned to the visage she was used to seeing in the mirror, and the lack of animal-enhanced vision and hearing made her feel as though she'd just submerged her head underwater.

Mali dove into the back of the limo and Reid pulled her onto the seat next to him, looking her over. "This gash on her is healing up, so I think we're all right. Amar might need you, though." He gestured to their Alpha. Most shifters healed quickly when they came back into their human forms, but the majority of Dean's guards had gone after Amar because of his size and formidable fire. He clutched his side as blood spilled through his fingers.

"I've got him," Emersyn said, moving in close with her medical bag.

"I'll drive. Gotta admit I'm starting to like it." Gabe hopped into the driver's seat and the limo took off into the night.

Mali knew there was work ahead of them, but for the moment, she nestled into the crook of Reid's arm. As she watched the city lights flash by, her thoughts drifted to her sister, hoping she was safe.

THE SUN WAS COMING UP, AND REID HAD NEVER BEEN SO GRATEFUL TO see it. The sky over Los Angeles was tinged in blues, purples, and golds, and the clouds were highlighted in pink. The last two days had been pure hell. They were home now and Mali was safe and sound, but not even the hot water of the shower could completely wash away the emotions he was struggling with.

Reid turned toward the shower head and let the jets stream over his face, rubbing his hands over his skin before turning off the water. Scrubbing a towel through his hair and wrapping it around his waist, he stepped out of the bathroom. It was time to talk.

When they'd first come back, Mali had insisted for Reid to be the first one to clean up. Reid expected to find her conked out cold from her misadventure, but the bed was still made. He tugged on a pair of sweats and a t-shirt, thinking perhaps she'd gone downstairs.

The scent of breakfast drifted through headquarters. Jude, predictably, was refilling the coffee pot. Melody was minding the griddle, scooping up blueberry pancakes, fluffy scrambled eggs, juicy sausage links, and crispy bacon as fast as the Force could down them. She laughed as Emersyn scolded Amar.

"Listen, that wound is pretty deep. The best thing you can do for yourself—for the entire team, if that makes any difference—is to just lie down for a while." She hovered over the Alpha, her eyes darting nervously to the bandage on his side.

Amar, shirtless, glanced down at his ribcage. "Looks like you got it all wrapped up to me, doc. I'm a dragon; I'll be fine before you know it. And I'm hungry."

Emersyn's face tightened, and she pursed her lips around an argument. "Fine. But don't come crying to me when the pain is killing you later. I shouldn't need to remind you that I've seen plenty of soldiers wanting to play tough in my day, and it hardly ever pays off." The golden eyes of her inner pantheress flashed as she stormed over to get her own breakfast.

Reid joined her as he poured a glass of juice. "Is Mali down here somewhere? I know you said you wanted to check everyone out." The doctor had been quite insistent that everyone who'd been on the mission needed to be examined after returning from Dean Bryant's place. She didn't want anyone to leave so much as a splinter in their foot if something could be done about it.

She raised an eyebrow. "I haven't. I thought she was still with you."

A stab of fear ripped through his heart. Surely something couldn't have happened in the short time he was in the shower.

But Jude stepped up behind him, gesturing to the back door with his coffee mug. "I saw her step outside a little while ago."

"Thanks." Reid left his juice on the counter and jogged outside, needing to know that his mate was all right. She'd been through a lot in the last forty-eight hours. Reid had seen prisoners of war who were never quite the same again, and it was only through a lot of love and support that they managed to live normal lives. He'd hoped that Mali wasn't struggling that much, but he wouldn't risk it for anything.

The morning air was fresh and clean, and the first rays of the sun illuminated the natural auburn highlights in Mali's dark hair as she stood at the back corner of the yard. She'd changed out of that ridiculous dress—one that could only remind Reid of Dean—and put on plaid pajama bottoms and a white tank top. As Reid approached, he noticed the last bit of fur on the backs of her arms receding into her skin.

"What are you doing out here by yourself?" he asked gently. He was more interested in knowing why she'd shifted, but she would tell him if she felt comfortable.

Mali turned, and though she smiled at him, her eyes were haunted.

"I have a lot weighing on my mind, and I'm trying to decide what to do about it."

Reid pulled her into his arms, wishing there was something he could do to make all her concerns go away. "There's nothing too pressing. We've got you home, and that's the most important thing. Why don't you come inside and have some breakfast? Everyone else is in there." When she hesitated, he added, "Don't worry if you don't want to talk about what happened. You can when you're ready."

Her lips pressed together as her eyes wandered over the paper lanterns that were still strung across the yard from their wedding, which felt as though it'd happened a year ago at this point. Eventually, her gaze wandered up to meet his face. "I don't think I'm hungry yet."

Reid took her by the hand and brought her to a patio table, but Mali was too tense to relax into the oversized chair. "Have you seen Emersyn yet? She's got Amar all fixed up, and I think she's itching to get her hands on someone else. She could make sure there isn't any glass still buried in your shoulder, and maybe she could give you something to help you let go of all this."

But Mali shook her head. "No. There's a lot I need to talk to you about, Reid. I'm just not sure how I'm going to do it."

His stomach growled, but he ignored it and put his hand over hers. "I'm listening. Just talk."

She pulled in a deep breath. "When I left Thailand, I was excited to come to a country that promised such a good life. I hardly thought about what I might be doing by leaving my family behind."

Reid's eyes narrowed slightly as he tried to figure out where this was going. Mali had talked about her family a lot, but never with such sadness. "You can't feel bad about that. No one expects their kids to live at home forever."

Mali shook her head. "Maybe not here, but the culture is different there. The daughter of the family is responsible for the financial well-being of her parents. If they need anything, she must take care of them. It's not always easy to find a good job, so sometimes, daughters end up working in the sex industry."

Reid was glad he hadn't had a chance to eat anything, because he could tell this conversation was going to give him a stomachache. It had already killed him to think of anyone who had to turn to such things to make a living. Even though there were plenty of soldiers who'd paid for sex when they spent time overseas, that was something he'd never participated in. "You did mention something about that."

Mali turned her face toward the rising sun, her dark eyes distant. "It's bad, Reid. The worst part is that it's socially acceptable. In some areas, the parents actually expect their daughters to become prostitutes, and they're so proud of her if she does that they throw a big party with all their friends and neighbors."

"You're kidding." It was an automatic response, but he knew Mali wouldn't joke about something like this.

"And if there's not a daughter, some parents will even pressure their sons into dressing as women and force them into the industry, too. Some Thai parents push this agenda in the same way that American parents push their children to go off to college and become doctors and lawyers."

Reid stared at his hands, folded between his thighs. When he'd spent time over there, he'd known that he could get anything he wanted in certain districts. He just hadn't realized how much they normalized it. "I had no idea."

"I tried to ignore it, honestly. That might not be the right answer, but what can one person do? When I left, I worried for my sister Tasanee because I knew she'd feel the burden of our family on her shoulders. I brushed it off because I knew my parents weren't like the others. They didn't approve of selling your body, and I knew even if they got desperate, they'd never encourage her to do such a thing." Mali sucked in a deep breath, and when she let it out, a tear trickled down her cheek, bright and sparkling in the sunrise. "But now I'm concerned that Tasanee might not have escaped that fate, regardless. You see, when Dean's men first captured me, I talked to some of the other women. Among all the other horrors they told me, there was also rumor of another sun bear in captivity. I know there aren't very many of us, but if Tasanee is in Thailand, then she couldn't be here, right?"

"Right." Reid rubbed the back of his neck, wishing the world was a different place.

"The drugs kept my sun bear suppressed, and I had my hands full with getting myself freed, so I didn't think about it for a bit. But when we were fighting our way out of there, I heard Tasanee in my head. Her sun bear had always been stronger than mine, and she was begging me for help. She was only there for the briefest moment, but something was very wrong." The first tear dripped off her jawline, a second one already forming in its wake.

Putting a hand over hers, Reid nodded. "And so you came out here to shift and see if you could get a hold of her again." The familial tie between the sisters would have given them the same telepathic link as the one shared by mates and clans. Its greatest flaw was that it only worked when both parties were in their animal forms.

"Yeah. She told me she's been behaving herself, so her captors aren't drugging her anymore to keep her in check. Reid, I feel so horrible. While I've been out here exploring the city, my sister told me she and my parents were captured by some locals hoping to cash in on them. Now Dean's trafficking cell has a hold of my family. I bet Tasanee will be used the same way they were going to use me, and my parents will probably be sold to collectors or for labor." Her face collapsed, and she turned her hand over to squeeze his.

"I understand, Mali. Come on." He stood up, pulling her gently out of the chair.

"I don't want breakfast," she protested.

"Oh, you're going to have some breakfast," he countered. "No matter what other hell is happening in the world, you have to eat. I learned that in the Army. But we've got to brief the rest of the Force on this. No matter what, we're going to get your family out of there."

Mali looked up at him in disbelief. "Really?"

"Of course. My main priority was getting you out of that place, but I already knew I'd have to find Dean next. I was under no illusion that this was over, Mali, but knowing your family is involved means we've got to get right back on it."

———

THE FORCE HAD MOVED BACK into the converted dining room that was now their conference room, and Mali had finished explaining everything she knew. Reid hated for her to be constantly reliving her grief and frustration, but hearing it from her firsthand was the best way to formulate a plan.

Raul had begun typing on his laptop from the moment she started speaking. It looked as though he wasn't paying any attention, but Reid knew better. By the time she was finished, he was projecting his screen onto the television. "Unfortunately, everything you've just related to us matches up perfectly with some of the other information that I've found. I haven't been able to stop looking this guy up since we found out about him, and it turns out he's no small-time operator. We all know about the mansion, which is probably burned to the ground at this point. There's also the warehouse that Mali was held in, where he sorts out his latest victims and decides what he's going to do with them. There's another warehouse on the other side of town, too."

Reid shook his head. Mali had not only told the group about her family being taken from Thailand, she'd also explained everything she'd gone through from the moment of her capture up to her rescue. She'd understood its importance—both to the mission and rescuing the others—so she'd pushed through and got it off her chest. In a way, Reid wished he'd never had to hear it. "To say that was hard to hear is an understatement, and knowing how many more people might be affected is just sickening. We have to end this guy once and for all."

Amar, having finally put a shirt on, leaned back in his chair and folded his arms across his chest, anger apparent on his face. "One hundred percent." He nodded at Raul to continue.

"I've managed to use satellite imagery and local cameras to monitor the comings and goings at each of the warehouses. The one we believe Mali was in seems to get visits from all over the place. But the other warehouse seems to get most of its traffic from the airport and the docs. If I had to take a guess, I'd say this is where they bring in anyone they've smuggled from overseas."

Jude, with his ever-present mug of joe, stared into its depths. "As far as the overseas portion of things, do we think Dean is arranging all that himself and sending his own people into other countries? Or is he buying people off some other organization?"

Emersyn sat forward, her elbows on the table. "I'm no expert in intelligence, but I have done a lot of medical charity work around the world. In much the same way that African tribes were the ones to capture and sell slaves to the colonists, there are plenty of syndicates who work the same way in other parts of the world. Dean would have to be incredibly powerful to have resources and control that far away, so I'd venture a guess that he's buying what someone else has already stolen."

Raul nodded. "I have to say I agree. There wasn't much I could find on Dean when it came to international records, other than a few vacations. While those were probably not innocent trips, judging by his character, it's not the kind of paper trail you'd expect to see for someone who's doing a lot of business overseas. But I was able to confirm that Dean is in possession of a family of sun bears. He's got them listed as inventory, just like he'd posted for the auction party."

"Forgive me for asking," Gabe interrupted, "but how can someone be dumb enough to post all this on the internet? Don't get me wrong. I'm glad the information is out there for us to find, but doesn't he think someone else will find it, too?"

Raul shrugged. "He might think he's safe using a private, encoded chatroom on The Shift app, but anything can be cracked with the right strokes on a keyboard. I'm a pretty decent hacker, so any info they thought was protected really isn't."

"All right." Reid slapped his palms on the table. He was tired, and there was nothing he wanted more than to take Mali up to their room and sleep the day away. He didn't want to think about human trafficking again for the rest of his life, but none of that was realistic. They had work to do. "What's our plan?"

It was a relatively simple one, and Raul's intel and satellite imagery made it all the easier to sort out. With his special ops background, Reid had a fairly good idea of what they'd do, even before they discussed it.

"All right," Amar said with a clap of his hands. "I think that about wraps it up. We're not leaving until nightfall, so I suggest everyone gets all the food and rest they need beforehand."

Reid stood and held his hand out to Mali, watching her carefully. "What do you think?" he asked quietly a few minutes later when he shut the bedroom door behind them.

Mali sat on the edge of the bed to strip off her clothes. "I feel like I'm living in a nightmare. These sorts of things aren't supposed to happen."

Reid crossed the room to pull the curtains over the window, blocking out most of the light so they'd be able to get some sleep. It was what they both desperately needed. "I know, baby. It'll be over with soon enough. I'll make sure of it."

Standing up, Mali pulled back the covers. She stopped, staring down at the crisp white sheets. "Do you really think we'll find them?"

"I have every confidence in the members of the Force. They're skilled, and they're determined. In the short time that I've been with them, I've seen them fight for complete strangers. We'll all do the same for your family."

She allowed him a small smile, but it wasn't the same joyous look he was used to seeing on her face. He settled in next to her, pulling her close so that her back was against his chest. He wrapped his arm around her petite frame and held her as he closed his eyes, wanting to make it all okay for her again. Mali was warm and soft against him, but he agonized over the tension he sensed in her bones and muscles. Reid knew it would remain there until Mali's family was safe, and he was determined to make that happen.

9

MALI THREW HER ARMS AROUND HER PARENTS AND HER SISTER, FEELING A deep love fill her. Though it'd only been a few months since she'd seen them, it had felt like an eternity.

But there was still one task to take care of.

Mali turned to find Dean Bryant standing there, waiting for her, his smile mocking. She'd hated him from the first moment she'd set eyes on him back in his mansion, but that hatred had only mushroomed as she came to know him better.

"You," she growled. "This is where it ends."

Dean threw his head back and laughed. "Right. Just like you were going to escape, and just like you thought you'd defeated me last time. Good luck."

"I won't need it." She charged forward, shifting into her sun bear form on the fly. Mali knew she wasn't the most ferocious beast on the face of the planet, but she didn't have to be a deadly carnivore in the wild. Dean was defenseless as she jumped up at the last moment, her teeth crushing his throat, blood running into her mouth.

"Mali? Mali, are you with me?"

Mali snapped to, blinking. "I'm sorry. I was doing some visualization techniques, and I guess I dozed off a little."

Reid, behind the wheel, put his hand on her leg. "You sure you're up for this?"

"Yeah," she replied instantly. "There's not a single doubt in my mind."

"All right. How about you two?"

"I'm beyond ready for this," Amar enthused, slamming one fist into his palm and getting pumped. "I'm going to fry every single one of those bastards."

"Just be careful that you don't burn the place down until we've had the chance to get everyone out," Katalin warned with a smile. "You tend to get a little overeager when you're in your dragon, and I'm sure the social justice aspect of things is only going to make it worse."

He raised an eyebrow at her. "You don't really think I'm going to go in there and ask them over for a barbecue, do you?"

Katalin laughed, snuggling closer to him on the bench seat.

"I do appreciate you and the others coming," Mali said to Katalin. "I wish we knew how many guards are actually at this facility, so we'd know exactly what we're getting into, but I'd like to think that having ten of us will help."

Katalin reached forward and patted her arm. "It can't hurt, especially when half of us are enraged women." Once Emersyn had spread word to Katalin, Penny, and Annie, the other women had immediately insisted they join the mission. They'd been so insistent that not a single member of the Force tried to deny them the chance to help. Penny had even arranged for all the vans for the mission, the empty space in the back of each of them representing their hope that they'd soon be filled with the rescued victims.

Amar looked at his phone. "I just got a message from Raul. We'll be closing in on the warehouse at approximately the same time, so unless someone runs into a late-night traffic jam, we're on schedule."

Mali tried to relax in her seat, knowing there was nothing she could do just yet. She had to wait. She was waiting to see if they could get past the guards at the warehouse. She was waiting to see if her parents and sister were there. Most of all, she was waiting for this to be over with. There would still be some work to do even once she was with her family again. Amar had told her they'd be raiding the warehouse she'd been kept in as well, and that they wouldn't stop until everyone was free.

"We're here," Reid announced as he pulled off into an industrial area. Their target building was a couple of blocks away, but they wouldn't be bringing their vehicles up close until they were ready to load them with their rescues.

Reid parked in the deep shadow of a squat brick building that smelled of petroleum. The four of them slipped out of the van and quietly shut the doors behind them. Mali's senses were heightened as they picked their way across the parking lot, hearing every crunch against the broken asphalt. The dark shape of an owl detached itself from the roof of a factory, and the movement caught Mali's eye, even though the owl's wings were silent.

Amar held up a hand when they could see the warehouse, and he turned to Reid and nodded. They were too close for speech now, but they'd talked enough about the plan that none was needed.

Mali knew what she had to do. She felt self-conscious about shifting in front of Amar and Katalin, even though Amar himself was a dragon and Katalin had been living amongst the shifters for quite some time. There was no time for shyness since there were lives on the line. Mali felt the changes begin in the center of her body even before they appeared on the outside, as her organs began to shift and make way for the sun bear it was becoming. It was easier without those mysterious drugs in her system, easy enough to make it feel completely natural. Her lengthy claws scraped the ground as she dropped to all fours, and she immediately reached out for Tasanee in her mind.

Nothing.

Reid had shifted as well, and his grizzly stood solidly next to her. His dark form blended in perfectly with the shadows, and only the glitter of his eyes would be visible if someone happened to stray through the area and look in the right direction.

As a vamp, only Katalin remained the same. Mali had been concerned for her when she'd found out she was coming on the mission, but Reid explained what a strong and skilled fighter she'd become throughout the centuries. She'd started her life as a human, but she had little fear of death considering her near immortality. Her vividly pale skin was far easier to see in the darkness, but the trio wouldn't need to remain hidden for very long.

Do you think the others have gotten here? Mali asked Reid, concerned that if the slightest thing went wrong, they might lose their best chance. If they couldn't get inside, Dean and his men would be alerted to what was happening and might take precautions to keep a raid from happening.

Reid paused for a moment before answering. *They are. Jude and Annie are on one side, Gabe and Emersyn on another, and Penny and Raul are just coming up to the back. We've got the whole place covered.*

They watched as Amar approached the warehouse, a plain metal building with a single door and an overhead garage door on one side. Though Mali couldn't see them from this angle, she knew there was at least one door on each of the other walls. Amar approached that single door on the front, but he didn't get to it before a man emerged. It wasn't anyone Mali recognized, but he slammed the door behind him as he glared at Amar. He held a pistol in one hand, pointing it steadily. "Who the hell are you?"

Amar put his hands out to either side to show he was unarmed. "That doesn't really matter. I'm just here to make a deal with you."

"Yeah? I'm not here to make deals. You either have business here, or I shoot you. That's how it works."

Mali could tell Amar was grinning just from the sound of his voice. Reid had told her the Alpha enjoyed confrontation, especially with those who deserved a little vengeance. "No, the way it works is like this: You let me in the building to get all those innocent people out, and I'll let you live. If you don't, you die."

"Fuck off," the guard grumbled. He raised the pistol slightly, but he was too slow for Amar.

He darted forward, smacking the gun out of the man's hand. Hitting the asphalt, it skidded off toward the corner of the building. When the guard retreated inside, Amar didn't follow him. Instead, he gave him time to call his boss while he shifted.

Mali's eyes widened. She'd seen several shifter forms in transition before, but never a dragon. Hell, up until recently, she didn't know they existed. He took a wide stance to keep his balance as scales erupted all over his body and deep onyx wings sprouted from his shoulder blades. His neck elongated as his head and face stretched into the massive form of a reptile, and his teeth snapped together eagerly as he dropped to all fours and shoved his way into the building. Several shouts of alarm sounded from inside.

That's our cue! Reid announced.

Mali, Reid, and Katalin ran forward. Amar had already begun the work of decimating the guards at the front of the building, but there were still plenty of them. It was late, and they'd been lounging around as they awaited orders. Reid put his head down and barreled into a large man with bright red hair, slamming him against a wall. Mali followed behind him, snapping her jaws and clawing.

Katalin quickly proved what a good fighter she was as a blonde man with a long beard approached her with a grin. "You're a pretty little thing. I think we could make good use of you around here." He made a swipe at her through the air, missing by a mile as she ducked with superhuman speed. Katalin slammed her fist into his crotch, nailing him with a powerful uppercut when he doubled over, and an arc of blood flew from his nose as she sent him flying backward.

Someone grabbed Mali from behind, his human arms wrapping around her middle as he transformed into a cougar, his claws digging into her skin. Mali twisted in his grip. She'd known coming in that she'd be an easy target considering her size, but she wasn't about to let anyone think it was a disadvantage. Mali let her legs drop out from under her, ignoring the searing pain along her abdomen as she rolled to her side and raked her claws into his belly. The cat howled in pain and surprise, caught even further off guard when Reid's mouth closed on the back of his head. He shook his head sharply, snapping the cougar's neck.

Amar was in the corner, tearing apart the last of a guard. Katalin was still dancing in a circle with the blonde man, but she smiled even as a sheen of sweat glittered on her brow. "We're good here. You guys go on ahead."

Mali was more than ready. She'd had her first taste of the fight, and she wanted more. She searched for her parents in her mind, wondering if there was any chance they were in their sun bear forms. She couldn't find them, which caused a clench of worry in her gut, but she charged forward into the main area of the warehouse.

It was eerily similar to the one she'd been put in. Walls had been erected that were tall enough to keep the occupants inside, but they didn't reach the vaulted ceiling. Narrow windows up near the ceiling allowed the glow of moonlight. The guard room had been lit, but the hall that was created by the prison cells on either side was pitch black.

Mali used the climbing skills of her sun bear and scaled a wall, leaving clouds of drywall dust in her wake as she reached the top. Her sensitive ears picked up the chaos being created by the other teams as they broke into the sides and back of the building. She caught a dark shadow moving in their direction, but it wasn't one she recognized. *We've got company heading our way.*

Got 'im, Reid confirmed. She soon heard her mate's deep growl as he quickly dealt with the problem.

While wild sun bears spent a lot of time foraging and sleeping in trees, Mali didn't usually have to use her arboreal skills. Even so, they were strong as she made her way along the walls. *We need some light in here,* she grumbled. *I can tell there are people in here, but I don't know where my family is.*

Don't worry. You'll find them. We won't leave until we do. Another crash sounded in his wake as he dispatched yet another of Dean's men.

Mali reached out with her mind. She was tempted to shift back into her human form, wanting her voice so she could call out. As she considered this, several heavy thuds sounded below her. Looking down, Mali noticed Jude shoving his shoulder against one of the steel doors. He and Annie had gotten past the guards that had stood in their way, and the two bears were trying to bust through. It was obvious to Mali, even being so new to the Force's way of operating, that it wasn't going the way they were expecting. *What's wrong?*

Reid was just below her, inspecting the doors himself. *These things are overbuilt to keep the prisoners in, and we probably won't be able to get them open unless we find the keys. Looks like they swing out into the hall-way, too, which is only going to make it more difficult.*

Maybe Amar can get them open or tear down these walls. The dragon was by far the strongest and most terrifying of the group, but Mali didn't know how far his skills extended.

I'll ask him.

Just then, a roar and an enormous burst of fire exploded from the guard room.

Panic bloomed in Mali's chest. *What's going on?*

The backup we were expecting the guards to call for has arrived. Even in her head, Reid's voice was sober.

So much for not burning the place down. The only benefit of the fire that had started in the front corner of the building was that it shed a little light into the dark rooms. Mali glanced down to see the terrified faces in the room below her, but none of them were familiar. She wanted to tell them not to worry, that they were going to get out of there just fine, but until they could get the doors open, she wasn't sure what she could do.

Mali moved to the next room, but the light from the fire hadn't reached that far. The room below her was nothing but a black cube. Mali was just about to move to the next one when the wall shuddered wildly beneath her. Everyone who wasn't directly fighting a guard was now trying to get through the doors. They needed Amar in the front, where he could handle the heat and tackle incoming thugs more efficiently than anyone else, which left the rest of them to start the rescues.

But the others didn't realize just how much they were shaking the walls. Mali held on, digging her claws in as much as possible, but there wasn't enough purchase to keep her from tumbling into the darkness.

The ground came up to meet her with a hard thump, and all the air left her lungs. She heard nothing for a long moment, and when her ears began working again, the sound came rushing to her all at once. Her breaths rasped in her lungs as voices murmured urgently around her. Mali swallowed, cringing at the pain in her side. All around her was blackness, and she couldn't tell if it was because of the darkness or if she'd hit her head too hard. The answer came to her when a twisted flower of fire reached across the ceiling, bringing light to the cavity she'd just fallen into.

"Mali?" someone said in her ear.

"That couldn't possibly be her, silly girl," a gruff voice responded. "Mali is out living the good life."

Even as she desperately fought for her body to cooperate with her, Mali felt something different growing inside her. It was hope. Excitement. Love. She knew those voices.

"It's her, Niran. Even in her bear form, I'd know my girl anywhere." A cool hand wrapped around Mali's paw. "What are you doing here?"

Any thoughts Mali had of shifting back to human were out the window. As much as she wanted to tell her parents and sister everything, she was too overwhelmed with emotion. Part of it was concern for getting out of there, but even that was buried by the love and relief she felt at being near her family again. She was content to lay there for a moment with her mother's head on her shoulder, inhaling her scent and knowing they were together again.

"I don't understand," Tasanee said. She'd been the first to speak and to recognize Mali.

"I don't either," her father replied. "The real question is whether this is a good or a bad thing."

His comment and the growing fire overhead made Mali realize the urgency of their situation. She rolled over, escaping the embrace of her mother. Adrenaline flooded through her system as she stood on all fours and rammed her shoulder into the door. It had been one thing to break a glass door in Dean's mansion, but this heavy lock didn't want to budge. Mali wasn't going to let some piece of metal keep her from getting what she and the others had worked so hard for. She was small for a bear, but she put every ounce of weight and muscle behind the next blows. The door shivered in its frame once, twice, and then slammed open.

Katalin had just come racing down the hall in time to see Mali stumble out. "The fire's getting worse. We've got to go. Let's get outside!" She dashed toward the other end of the building.

Mali grunted at her family and gestured with her head, urging them to follow her friend. She still had work to do. She watched her parents and sister go, the fire making shadows jump on their faces before she turned for the next door.

Dean was standing there in front of her. The fire blazed behind him, roaring as it ate through the cheap building materials. The smoke was getting thick, yet he looked as though he wasn't bothered by it at all. "Mali, is it? I can't say I'm surprised to see you're involved in this raid. You were so determined to get away, and once you finally did, you decided you had to get everyone else out, too. You can try all you want, but I promise you'll never stop me."

Mali! Where are you? I think I just saw Dean in here somewhere.

So much had happened in the last few minutes that she'd gotten separated from Reid. *I know. I'm standing right in front of the shitbag.*

There was no response for a moment, and though Mali had never known emotions could be shared through the telepathic link, she could feel her mate's anxiety.

Where are you? I'm coming.

It's all right, she replied. *I've got this.*

No!

Dean's smile widened as he closed in on her. "What are you going to do, you cute little teddy bear? Cuddle me to death?" He was a quick shifter. The light brown hair was soon blazing orange striped with deep black, matching the flames that danced around them. His feline body was thick and heavy, far bigger than she'd expected based on his human form. The flames were a brilliant red in his eyes. He barely even crouched before diving at her, his sharp white fangs dripping with saliva and his claws hungering for her flesh.

Mali tucked down and rolled back, raising her best weapons. The force of Dean's jump was enough, just as she was hoping it would be. Cat skin was tough, but her claws punctured him just below the sternum. With all the outrage and frustration and fear that she had in her body, Mali pulled forward against the momentum of his jump. She barely felt his heavy paws coming down around her ears as she saw the deep red line that split his belly open.

His energy changed, and Dean let out a strangled cry as he fell to the ground. Mali's claws were incredibly long and thick, and they'd pierced him deeply. She looked away, not interested in seeing the cascade of blood, nor the guts that tried to follow in its wake. Mali turned to the back of the building, away from the flames and toward the arms of her mate.

10

"THIS PLACE IS ABSOLUTELY INCREDIBLE," NATCHA SAID AS SHE LOOKED
lovingly at Mali. "You didn't have to go to all this trouble just to have a
second wedding for us, sweetheart. We would've been more than
happy to see you stand up together in the living room and hold
hands."

"I know, but we wanted to make it special. It *is* special because
you're here." Mali had spent the last three weeks visiting with her
parents and sister, but even still, every time Mali looked in their eyes,
she felt a surge of love and happiness. As much as she wished they
could stay, she knew they had the rice farm to get back to.

"Still, this is quite the place." Niran put his hands on his hips as he
turned to look out at the ocean.

A rocky outcropping formed a long, slender point where waves
crashed against the rocks below. Reid had managed to find a private
beach they could rent that was far more than just sun and sand, and
Mali loved how different it was. A tent had been set up further back
from the water where Mali could get ready, and a tangle of woods hid
the parking lot and the road from view. It felt as though they were on
the very edge of the world, and she wouldn't have it any other way.

"Are you doing well?" she asked on impulse, ever worried about
how her family was adjusting to L.A. Mali had been lucky enough to
have such a great support system when she'd arrived. She hadn't

expected to have anyone but Reid, yet she'd come to rely on the Force and everyone associated with it heavily. She already thought of Gabe, Raul, Amar, and Jude as her brothers and their mates as her sisters. Still, the traumatic way in which her family had come to America wasn't the best start.

Her father pulled her into his arms and hugged her tightly. "You don't need to worry about us, dear. Your friends have been very generous, too. You'll have to tell them to stop that." He smiled down at her.

Mali laughed. "They're wonderful people, and I know they care about you." So many nights, she and Reid had stayed up late talking. Mali would tell him all her worries, and if there was anything he couldn't fix right away, he promised to find a way around it.

"You need to know how proud we are of you," her mother said quietly. "Mali, you've told us about what you went through, and we know what you did to save us. I won't thank you because I know you'll tell me not to, but I'm so delighted to see what a strong young woman you've become." Natcha folded her arms around Mali as well, and then Tasanee had joined them. The four of them stood there like that for the longest time, and Mali let out a peaceful sigh as she soaked up all that love.

"You have guests arriving," Tasanee said.

Voices and footsteps could be heard just outside the tent. Mali looked up to see that Keiko, Alejandra, and Libby had shown up. Her family let her go, and she wrapped her newest friends in her arms. "I'm so happy to see you! I know you've been busy, and I wasn't sure if you would make it!"

"Are you kidding?" Keiko asked with a smile. "You've only helped us completely turn our lives around. The very least we could do is show up when we're invited."

"Are you doing okay?" Mali looked at each of them, seeing how much they'd changed in the short time they'd been out of the trafficking world. Because of Emersyn's medical work in the inner city, she had connections for getting the victims back home or on their feet again. By the time the Force had gone back to raid the warehouse where Mali had been kept, there were dozens of men and women who needed help. It was more than the Force could handle alone, though they'd certainly contributed a lot.

Alejandra squeezed her arm. "This is your day, so you shouldn't be worried about us, but we're doing great. Keiko and I are sharing an apartment, and I plan on going back to school. In the meantime, I've picked up a waitressing job."

"What about you?" Mali was most concerned about Keiko. The poor woman had been trafficked so many times, she hardly knew what normal life was, and Mali didn't want her to feel that she had to return to that world just to keep a roof over her head.

Her new friend smiled. "I'm actually working at a little stationery store. I wasn't sure I'd like it, but I'm really coming to love the quiet. Here, I brought you a gift." She held out a small pink bag with handles.

"You didn't have to do that!" Mali peeked inside, finding a beautiful journal with orchids on the cover and a fountain pen. It was completely different from all the other gifts she and Reid had received for their nuptials, and she absolutely loved it. "It's gorgeous! Thank you so much."

"I thought..." Keiko hesitated for a moment, glancing off to the side and losing much of the confidence she normally had. When she spoke again, it all came out like a flood of water. "It's just that Emersyn got me in to see this counselor. I was scared and didn't even want to go at first, and when I did, it was tough to talk to her. She had me start journaling, and it's been really helpful. There's just something so therapeutic about getting it all out on paper, and if it's something that really bothers me, I can just rip the page out, light a match to it, and watch it burn away. I just wanted to pass that along in case it could help you at all."

"Oh, Keiko." Mali pulled her friend close once again. She'd done nothing but hug everyone that day, and her emotions were threatening to overwhelm her. It touched her heart to know that Keiko was on her way to healing, which was what she wanted for all of those poor victims. "Thank you again. I had actually been thinking about doing some writing, so this will be perfect."

Keiko and Alejandra moved off to take a seat, and Libby had a moment with Mali. "I never got a chance to thank you for what you did," the blonde said quietly.

"You don't have to thank me."

"Yes, I do. And I also need to apologize to you. From the very moment you arrived at Dean's, you were looking for a way out. You knew what was happening was wrong, and if you would've had help from the other women and me, things could've been different. I should've helped you, and I never should've told you to just put your head down and deal with it. I'm so sorry, and I don't deserve all the help you and your friends have given me." Tears glimmered in her deep blue eyes.

Mali shook her head. "Yes, you do. You were a victim, and you'd been trained to keep yourself under Dean's thumb. He's gone, so that's not going to happen again, but there are others out there who are still doing it. It happens to humans, too."

Some of Libby's normal certitude had returned as she cocked an eyebrow. "Sounds like you're about to become a warrior for social justice."

"I've been thinking about it a lot. I might write. I'm sure I'll do some volunteering at the shelters. Maybe there will be more, but I'm not sure yet." It had weighed heavily on her mind for the last few weeks, and Mali knew she wanted to make a difference. Her path wasn't completely certain, but she knew she'd figure it out. Reid had already told her he supported her one hundred percent.

"Good for you. If there's anything I can do to help, just let me know." Libby ducked out of the tent as Emersyn and Annie came in.

"I think we're all good to go," Emersyn said with a smile. "You don't seem nearly as nervous this time."

"No," Mali admitted. "I guess there's something to be said for already having been through it once." She put the gift from Keiko in a safe place, eager to put it to good use later, and stepped outside.

Everything was ready for her, just as it had been back at SOS headquarters. An archway of foliage and tiny solar lights had been erected out at the very end of the point, with chairs and more solar lights making a pathway toward it. The sun had just set, illuminating the sky in a beautiful palette.

"Ready?" Her father tucked her hand in the crook of his elbow and patted it several times, and Mali could hear the music starting up.

"I am."

"I know I already told you this when you were getting ready to leave home, but I really do approve of this match," Niran said.

"I'm so glad," Mali smiled. "I assumed you didn't, since I never heard back from you when I'd tried reaching out about our wedding date. I hadn't realized you'd been taken away from the farm, though."

"You know we would've been thrilled to be there," Niran reassured her. "Mali, your fated bond is obviously nothing that requires my approval, of course. I know that, and so do you. Still, I think it's important for a daughter to know that her parents are pleased with her mate. You're a smart, strong woman, and I can't wait to see what you do next with your life."

"Thank you so much, Daddy. I love you." She dabbed at one eye with a lace-edged handkerchief.

They stepped out onto the rough ground. As much as Mali had enjoyed the first ceremony, she instantly knew this was the one she was going to remember as a little old woman surrounded by her grandchildren. There was something magic in the air. Maybe it came from knowing that her family was there with her, safe and sound. It could be that she was starting on a whole new path with her life. Most likely, it was because everything she wanted was all coming together at the same moment. Her entire world was coalescing that night, and it felt amazing.

Reid was waiting for her, eager to take her hand again. He was so handsome, casual in his khakis and a white button-down with short sleeves that showed off his muscular arms. The sea breeze played with his hair, and Mali's heart lifted even higher in her chest. Even once she got a hold of that lovely journal and pen from Keiko, Mali knew it would be difficult to find the right words to describe just how she felt about him.

"Take care of her," Niran said to Reid with a wink. "I know you will."

Mali, her hand tucked in Reid's, lay her head on his shoulder as they went through their vows, so secure in her love that she was thrilled to be doing this with him once again. The ceremony itself went by quickly, followed by a small potluck picnic and dancing under the stars.

Reid's eyes were soft as he looked down at her. "Has the evening been to your liking, my love?"

"My cheeks are sore from smiling, my stomach is sore from laughing, my feet are sore from dancing, and my heart is full of so much love, I think it might burst. I think that means yes." She pulled back a little from her husband so she could see the stars glimmering in the sky out over the ocean. "Reid, I never imagined life could be this good."

His brow creased with worry for a moment. "Even after...everything?"

He didn't need to say it for Mali to know what he meant. It was impossible to forget about Dean and all the horrible things he'd done, even though he and most of his men were dead. "Sometimes we have to go through something bad to see just how good things are. I was already happy with you and with my life, but now I know there's so much more waiting for me. I'm excited to see where our future takes us."

Reid pulled her in tight and bent his head to kiss his bride, enticing her to open her mouth by teasing her with the tip of his tongue. As her lips slowly parted for him, he deepened the kiss, leaving a burning deep in the marrow of her bones. Raking his mouth over the curve of her jaw and up to her ear, he paused to whisper in her ear. "Want to get out of here for a while?"

Mali nuzzled her forehead against his cheek. "And leave all these people who've come just to see us?"

He nodded without hesitation. "Absolutely. No one could deny a couple of freshly married lovers, could they? I mean, we didn't exactly get that honeymoon we were planning."

"True." Mali lifted her head long enough to look around, noticing that the guests were dancing, eating, and visiting. The party was still fresh and promised to last long into the night. "Where do you suppose we go when we're out here in the middle of nowhere?"

Reid tipped his head toward the woods. "I've got an idea or two." Breaking their embrace, Reid led her by the hand away from the beach. They slipped into the shadows of the trees, deepened by the fact that the sun had completely sunk past the horizon.

"This reminds me of when we first met," she said as another wave of excitement tingled over her skin. "I don't know that I'll ever look at trees the same way."

"We've got all night to explore them." Reid let go of her hand. It was dark, but with the intuitive knowledge of a mate, she felt his shift coming. He was already a well-muscled man, but his body expanded as he let his bear take over. His hair was so dark in the gloom of the woods that it appeared to be completely black, making him a creature of the night.

Mali followed suit, once again allowing the animal that lived inside her to come forth. She'd needed her sun bear a lot lately, and it was nice to simply bring it out for nothing more than a night run with her mate. They took off as soon as her four feet hit the ground, darting around trees, dashing up hills, and skidding down the other side of them. They ran until their hearts and lungs burned with the effort, feeling the wind through their fur and the ground hitting hard beneath their feet. Their path took them up through the woods and back down toward the coast, emerging on a rocky shore similar to the one they'd left behind with the other partygoers.

Is this where you take all your dates? Mali teased as they came to a stop at the edge of a tide pool. The moonlight glimmered in the shallow water, her face a dark reflection as she peered down.

Only the ones I want to be with forever.

She turned to look at him. Reid stood on the shoreline as well, his face lifted as his snout sniffed the breeze. He was beautiful in any form he took, but it was a beauty that—just like her love for him—she couldn't quite explain.

I'm going to write a story about us. Even in her head, she could blurt things out, and though Mali hadn't meant to say it, she didn't care. Reid would understand. He always did.

His big head turned in her direction. Even as a formidable grizzly, he could have a gentle look in his eyes. *I can't wait to read it.* That was it. No questions, no asking her how she was going to do it. She'd said what she wanted to do, and he supported it.

Mali loved the freedom of her sun bear form, but she let it go. By the time she walked over to Reid, he was on two legs as well. He took both of her hands in his, one side of his mouth quirking up more than the other.

"What is it?" She'd seen that mischievous look.

He tipped his head to the side. "Let's go check out that grotto over there."

Mali looked, seeing a cave that had been worn into the side of a small cliff by centuries of splashing water. As they stepped inside, she couldn't help but laugh a little. "Maybe I'll have to put this in my book. It does have a rather fantastical quality to it, doesn't it?"

He traced his thumb down the side of her face. "Yes. Just like you." Reid pulled her into a kiss once again. She felt how ready his human body was for her, but she also felt the rapture of his bear. Her own bear felt the same, and the next thing she knew, she was tugging at his shirt, fumbling to get the buttons unfastened. Reid pulled back only long enough to let her slide it off his shoulders. He stepped out of his shoes as he opened his fly, and Mali slipped her fingers inside his waistband to explore his rippled abdomen and his firm backside.

Mali had worn a simple white sundress for the ceremony this time, not wanting to ruin her expensive gown, and she was glad for it as Reid impatiently lifted it over her head and tossed it aside. She heard the whisper of it landing somewhere nearby, but she instantly forgot it as his warm body pressed against hers. The rest of the world had evaporated until it was just the two of them in this seaside cave, making love as though it was their first time.

Lifting her off her feet, Reid carried her a few steps to the cave wall. Erosion made it a smooth curve against her back as she wrapped her legs around him and Reid slipped inside the heated wetness of her core. He pressed himself inside her, burying himself deeply as her moans carried through the cave. His hardness throbbed with excitement as he kept himself still within her. Mali could feel the raw muscle of his arms and legs as he held her against the wall. Dipping his head to drop kisses across her forehead, Reid continued down her nose and across each of her cheeks. He slipped his tongue into her mouth, and the low groan that escaped his throat told Mali just how turned on he was.

Mali wished they could stay like that forever. Reid fit inside her like a puzzle piece, and their souls were custom cut for each other in the same way. She could feel him quivering inside her, enticing her inch by inch toward the ecstasy she knew would be coming. He was always a thorough lover, and her excitement sparked like electricity through her body. Mali arched her back and pushed her hips forward, intensifying their connection.

Reid growled in anticipation as he lowered her to the damp sand beneath them, and she kept her legs twined around his body, never wanting to let go of him in any sense of the word. She clung to him, planting kisses along the hard lines of his shoulder and up his neck. He turned to take her kiss against his lips as he dug his hands down into the soft sand to grab her hips.

Mali gasped as his arousal sank in to the hilt, but she clutched at his hips when he tried to pull back. "No," she whispered with a playful smile. "I want all of you, and don't you dare think of giving me any less."

"Wouldn't dream of it," he replied with a wink. Reid thrust against her, the movement of their hips making a divot in the sand as they drove each other further and further toward the edge.

Like the white-capped waves that were crashing on the shore only a few yards away, Mali felt her body building momentum, cresting higher and higher. Every molecule of her body danced, and the moment she peaked, she let out her primal hunger for him as a wail that shook the cavern around them.

Reid planted his fists in the sand on either side of her shoulders, throwing his head back and joining her with a cry of his own as his body responded to hers. His muscles rippled, contracting and releasing, as he let himself go.

For a moment, the roaring surf and her body were one and the same, and she slowly slipped back to reality as she opened her eyes. Mali realized she'd been scratching all up and down his back in the throes of their passion. "I didn't hurt you, did I?"

He pecked her forehead with his lips. "Never." Reid pushed himself up, and when he reached down to help Mali to her feet, he started laughing.

"What is it?"

He brushed the sand from her backside. "I think everyone is going to have a good idea of what we've been doing when we get back. It's in your hair and everything."

Mali eyed the breakers on the rocky shore. "Then let's go wash it all off. I'll race you." She took off before she'd even finished her sentence, her bare feet confident as she hopped over a sharp rock and sprang out into the ocean.

The water was deep there, and Mali let herself fall into its cool depths for a moment before kicking her way to the surface just in time to see Reid make some waves of his own. He easily swam over to her, and there was something erotic about feeling his naked body against hers underwater.

Mali clung to his shoulders as she lazily kicked her feet. "I love you, Reid."

"I love you, too. You're the best thing that ever happened to me, Mali. I'm so glad I have you back." He kissed her again, but the passion was different this time. It wasn't the pure, raw, sexual desire he had for her, but the ardor of love, devotion, and destiny.

As they swirled together in the waves, Mali realized she could see the lights from the party down the shore. She could've stayed out there in the ocean with him forever, but they had obligations to return to. "I don't suppose being soaking wet is really any better than being covered in sand, is it?" The crush of the ocean was driving the air out of her lungs, and she realized just how tired she was.

Reid began swimming for the shore. "Maybe not, but I really don't care. If everyone thinks we had sex on the beach, the only thing they can be is jealous."

They found their clothes and got dressed, taking the long way back to the party on two feet. Mali twined her fingers through his. "I don't think I'll ever stop wondering how I got to be so lucky."

"You've got it all wrong," Reid corrected. "I'm the one who's lucky."

She squeezed his fingers. "Nope, it's me."

He nodded, grinning. "All right. Then whoever makes it back to the party first is the luckiest one. Keep in mind, you only beat me to the ocean because you cheated and got a head start. There's no way you're going to win this."

Mali raised an eyebrow. "Oh, you think so? You're on."

They took off. Mali was fast, but Reid was faster. She didn't mind. As she sprinted behind him, Mali got to watch the way his strong legs propelled him forward. She alone was witness to the way his hair blew back in the breeze he created and that wicked smile on his face when he turned to look over his shoulder.

Reid might have been the one to get back to the party first, but Mali knew without any doubt that she was the lucky one.

———

FERAL SOLDIER WOLF

SPECIAL OPS SHIFTERS: L.A. FORCE

1

GABE SMILED AS HE WATCHED HIS SON TODDLE ALONG THE BRICK walkway along the Cabrillo Marina in San Pedro, just as excited about seeing all the ships as he had been earlier in the day when they'd first arrived.

"Up, Daddy! Up!" Lucas turned to his father and flung his hands in the air, curling and releasing his fingers for emphasis. Ever since he'd started talking, he hadn't stopped, and his enthusiasm was boundless.

Although he'd already hoisted his son up on his shoulders numerous times that day, and even though doing it once more made some of the shrapnel embedded in his body shift uncomfortably, Gabe happily obliged. Lucas and Emersyn were everything to him. "Need a better view, huh?"

"You'd think he would've gotten enough after Dana and Brian let us take a tour of their yacht," Emersyn said with a fond smile. "I think he's hooked."

Feeling his son's sturdy grip in his hair, Gabe winced. "I have to agree. It's beautiful." He'd never been much of a seaside man, but the view of all the ships docked in the marina, their many masts slowly rising and falling like a floating forest, was captivating. They'd seen everything from the newest, top-of-the-line cruisers to the most battered and sea-worn trawler, and every single one of them was majestic in its own way.

Emersyn checked her watch. "We'd better be heading back. I've got a few more things to do before a busy day at the clinic tomorrow."

"Boat, Daddy! Big ships!" Lucas slapped his hands gleefully on his father's head, unaware of how uncomfortable it was.

Gabe didn't mind. "I know, buddy. There are lots of big boats and ships here. But we've got to get going. Wave bye-bye to the boats." He lifted his own hand to demonstrate.

"Bye-bye, boats! Bye-bye, ships! Bye-bye, ocean!" Lucas called out as they headed back toward the car.

"This was a great idea," Emersyn said as she fell into step alongside her mate. "I think he'll be talking about it until we agree to bring him back, though."

"Bye-bye, birdies! Bye-bye, cars! Bye-bye, trees!"

Gabe's heart had already been overflowing with joy, yet more and more poured out of it. He'd never realized he could be this happy. At one time, he'd measured his success by the salary he brought in. Now he knew there was so much more. "That's all right. We'll go to the zoo next weekend, and then we'll get to hear about the animals instead of the boats."

"Bye-bye, clouds! Bye-bye, man!"

It was as Lucas called out this last farewell that Gabe's gaze fell on a man sitting alongside the walkway. There were any number of drifters in and around Los Angeles due to the nice weather, and he was used to seeing them set up in long rows along beach walls. This man had propped himself up in the shade of a palm tree, a duffel bag at his side as he rested his forearms on his knees and gazed out over the water. Gabe's attention was first caught by the fact that the homeless man wasn't begging for money. He started to turn away when he realized the features under the man's long hair and beard were familiar.

"Kent?"

Dark blue eyes lifted to meet his, and the hardness in them faded as he recognized Gabe. "Hey, man. They always say it's a small world, but I never believe them."

Gabe couldn't even begin to calculate the odds. He lifted Lucas down from his shoulders and held out his hand as he made the introductions. "Kent, this is my mate, Emersyn, and our son, Lucas. This is Kent, who served on the Delta Force with me. He saved my ass more than once."

"Daddy!" Lucas said with a pout. "Bad word!"

"You're right, buddy. Sorry. Kent did save my life, though." There was a deep contrast between the meticulous soldier he'd once known and this transient in front of him. Gabe needed to get to the bottom of the situation, but it wasn't exactly a family event. He gave Emersyn a meaningful glance. "Why don't you two head home. I'll take an Uber later and catch up with you."

"Hey, don't change your plans on my account," Kent started to argue.

"It's fine," Emersyn assured him with a smile. "Lucas and I are ready to go get ice cream, anyway. Aren't we?"

The boy immediately forgot about boats and began yammering about ice cream as he strode hand-in-hand with his mother down the walkway.

Gabe turned back to his old friend. "What are you up to these days?" It was a far more meaningful question than it would've been if they'd bumped into each other at a cocktail party or the grocery store. Kent was obviously on the down-and-out, and Gabe had a feeling the man's whole life was stuffed into that duffel bag.

Kent rose to his feet, a hint of the man he'd once been still obvious despite his tattered appearance. "Not much. I just hopped off a fishing boat. You can get hired pretty easily when you just want a ride from one place to another. Working under the table isn't as bad as everyone wants to make it out to be."

"I understand. Listen, there's this great place I'm staying with a few other buddies from work. Have you heard of the Special Ops Shifter Force?" The elite outfit that both he and Emersyn belonged to consisted entirely of special ops veterans. They'd kept it a secret for as long as possible, but word spread fast among the shifter community, and Gabe knew he could trust Kent implicitly.

"Yeah, I think so." Understanding made those dark blue eyes change a little. "No shit. Are you one of them?"

"I am. I just got lucky, really. But we've got a big house that we use as our headquarters, and it's not all that far from here. Why don't you come home with me for a bit and get a shower and a good meal while we catch up." It was difficult to address the situation Kent must have been in directly, but Gabe couldn't simply leave him there.

Kent shook his head. "I can't do that, man. I wouldn't want to impose."

"It's no imposition," Gabe insisted. Emersyn worked a lot with the low-income community, with both humans and shifters alike, and she was rubbing off on him. He hated to see anyone go without. "At least let me buy you a cup of coffee. I haven't seen you in years, and I think I spotted a café a few streets back."

His old buddy looked like he was about to turn him down again, but after a moment of hesitation, he nodded. "Lead the way."

———

KENT PULLED the door to the coffee shop open, the scent of strong espresso and baked goods floating through the air. There was an underlying scent of something that had burned, though, putting an acrid odor in the mix. The place had a distinctly old-world feel with its timbered ceilings and tiled floors. Several glass cases that doubled as counters were trimmed in wood, though they held remarkably few pastries. He rubbed a hand over his beard as he and Gabe approached the cash register. "I'm not sure they'll want a dirtbag like me in here."

Gabe sat down across from him and flicked his hand through the air. "Who are they to give a shit about what you look like if you're a paying customer? Besides, you don't look that bad."

Kent knew he wasn't technically a paying customer, since Gabe was the one who'd offered to pony up. At least his clothes weren't as bad as what he'd seen on some of the others in a similar position, drifting along until they found their next chance at work. "Do you know what's good here?"

His old Army buddy shrugged. "Can't say I've ever been in here before, man. I think I could use some strong coffee, though."

"Yeah." Kent skimmed the bakery case, feeling his stomach rumble angrily at the very thought of food. "What do you think of..." He trailed off and jerked his head as a new scent hit him. Kent having an inner wolf meant he had an exceptional sense of smell, so he immediately began sorting them out, trying to pinpoint what it was. Among the aroma of ground espresso beans, the buttery scent of flaky pastry, and the sweet fragrance of frosting was something altogether different and intoxicating. He felt his eyes dilate with it, and saliva dripped from his emerging fangs. Despite the effect it was having on him, Kent had no idea what it was. The full moon was approaching, something he had to be constantly aware of because it always made him a little off. Maybe that was it.

A woman emerged from the kitchen, wiping her hands on her apron, and she smiled at them as she approached. Her chestnut hair was pulled up into a bun at the crown of her head, but Kent could see the natural highlights streaking through it. Her green eyes were strikingly pale by comparison to her dark hair and olive skin, and the way her apron strained against her curves was tantalizing. Kent realized his gaze was lingering too long on the nametag pinned to her chest. Alessia.

"What can I get for you guys?" she asked sweetly.

Fortunately, Gabe answered, since the entire English language had just officially left Kent's mind. "A couple of large coffees. I'm afraid I'm not familiar with some of the pastries you have here. What's good?" He gestured at the desolate case.

Alessia slid open the door on the back and pulled out a tray of fat, round blobs covered in sugar that sagged on one side. "The bomboloni are usually pretty popular. They're basically filled donuts, and I have them in Nutella or cream right now." She bit her lip as her smile faded a little. "They are a bit greasy on the bottom, though. I also have some sfogliatelle, but the pastry came out a little too crunchy."

"We'll take a couple of each," Gabe said with a nod as he pulled out his wallet.

Kent had hardly even taken note of what they were about to eat. Something about this woman was all-consuming. He pulled in a deep breath, thinking she might be the source of that heady scent. The one thing he could tell, though, was that she wasn't a shifter. She was sexy as hell, and the way she'd pronounced the names of the Italian pastries made him want to watch her tongue as she spoke. But she was absolutely human. Maybe he just needed to sit down.

"I'll bring your drinks right out to you," Alessia said as she handed Gabe his receipt and the plates of pastries.

The two men took up a booth on the side of the room, and Kent found himself facing the counter. "I do appreciate this, but you didn't have to do it." It was hard to keep his composure when everything inside him was going so wild. He felt embarrassed at explaining his hardships to Gabe, he was horrifically hungry, and that woman was so alluring, his wolf was frantically pawing to get out. He couldn't even begin to imagine the sort of chaos he'd cause if he turned into a massive wolf right in the middle of the place and jumped over the counter.

"I'm more than happy to do it. Why don't you tell me a little more about what's been going on since we saw each other last?" Gabe picked up the cone-shaped pastry and bit into it. The resulting loud crunch that echoed in Kent's ears confirmed that Alessia hadn't been exaggerating.

He plucked a bombolone off the plate, wanting to avoid the subject at hand. There was just too much to tell, and he wasn't even sure where he wanted to start. Kent had been staying away from anyone even vaguely associated with the military for the past year, and if he hadn't been so close to Gabe when they were both on the Delta Force, he'd never have even agreed to have coffee together.

"What about you?" Kent asked as he took a bite of the doughnut, finding it to be not as greasy as Alessia had warned, but sickeningly sweet. "It looks like you've achieved a lot."

Gabe raised an eyebrow, looking like he was going to argue, but then he nodded. He launched into his story, but Kent wasn't completely listening.

He couldn't keep his mind—or his eyes—off Alessia.

She was back behind the counter now, fiddling with the huge contraption that was somehow required for coffee these days. Kent would've preferred a simple black brew from an old-fashioned Mr. Coffee, but he was far more intrigued by the waitress than the machine. She began pouring a bag of beans into a grinder, frowned into the bag, and went searching for another one. Once she found it, Alessia struggled to open it and eventually resorted to scissors. Every move she made suggested she was brand new to the business. Her hands shook, she dropped things, and with his finely-tuned hearing, Kent could detect her cussing to herself.

As Gabe wrapped up a summary of his life since the military, it was no surprise that what Alessia brought them smelled awful.

"Is there anything else I can get you?" she asked.

You. Kent shook off the thought, knowing his wolf was trying hard to get the best of him. "I think we're fine. Thanks," he replied tersely. He didn't miss the slight lift of her eyebrow as she headed back behind the counter.

"You sure you're all right?" Gabe asked.

"Yeah. I've just been spending too much time around sailors." He lifted the cup Alessia had brought and took a sip, but he nearly gagged. "Shit! This tastes like rocket fuel."

"It can't be that bad." Gabe tried it for himself, his eyes widening with shock. "Damn. They served better stuff in the mess tents."

It was true, but Kent was once again distracted by Alessia as she worked behind the counter. She stood with a tray of cookies on top of the glass display cabinet, a bag of icing in her hand. The tip of her tongue stuck out just far enough to touch the corner of her lips as she carefully squeezed the bag. Alessia was just a random human, but he found himself focusing intently on the way her fingers worked.

The glistening of her pink tongue.

The plump curve of her ass as she bent over the counter.

He chugged back the horrid coffee just to snap himself back to reality. "I've gotta get out of here, man. My wolf is a little wild these days. Thanks again for the coffee, though." He stood, leaving the shredded remains of the misfit pastries on the table, and headed for the door.

"Hold up." Gabe caught up with him on the sidewalk. "The café was a bust, but the offer to come back to my place still stands. Think of it as a favor to me."

Something inside Kent, perhaps the same part of him that'd gone so berserk over Alessia, was quickly retreating. "I don't know. You said you share the place with the rest of the Force, and I really don't want to impose."

"It's not a problem. See it as a repayment for one of the many times you saved my ass. You can have a shower, a meal or two, and even spend the night. Hell, Emersyn's a doctor, if you need any sort of medical attention." Gabe's eyes were earnest as they steadily watched him.

Kent wanted to resist, just as he did any other time someone offered him a handout. They never came without strings attached. A meal or a bed was always accompanied by some sort of sermon or medical study. Homeless life wasn't easy, and it seemed there were few ways of getting out of it with any semblance of dignity.

At least, when it came to Gabe, he knew there wouldn't be any demands in return. This was his friend, someone who'd served with him, a brother in arms. They'd fought the enemy together as they'd sworn to do, and nothing said their bond ended just because they were no longer in the service. "All right."

As they made their way down the street and Gabe summoned an

Uber on his phone, Kent couldn't take his mind off of that human female at the coffee shop.

2

"Miss? *Miss*?" a demanding voice called from the counter.

Alessia slammed the oven shut, realizing too late that the impact probably didn't do any favors for the pastries inside, and forced a smile on her face as she headed out of the kitchen. It was the same customer who'd already complained several times that afternoon, and she looked like she had another objection on deck. "Yes, ma'am?" Alessia asked pleasantly.

"I ordered an iced latte, and the one you gave me is hot." The customer slid the cup across the counter with her finger.

"I can fix that for you right away."

"No, I just want my money back," the woman insisted. "Every single thing you've given us has had something wrong with it. The pastries are either too hard or too soft, and one of them was under-baked. Do you realize I could report you to the health department for that?"

"I'm sorry." Alessia knew the customer was always right, but unfortunately, she actually was. "I'll just need your card again."

Heaving a sigh, the woman whipped her debit card out of her purse and handed it over, rolling her eyes a little. "This used to be a great place, you know. I used to come here all the time with my girl-friends and my kids. I told everyone about it. I guess things went downhill when you changed owners, huh? It's just not *authentic* anymore."

Alessia's cheeks burned. The pasticceria was just as authentic as it had ever been, if it was the heritage of the owner that determined it. Her grandparents had come to L.A. from Italy when they were young, and her mother had married a man of Italian descent. Alessia had her mother's dark hair and pale eyes, but she'd failed to inherit any of the kitchen skills that'd been passed down among the Russos for generations. "I guess you can just go to Olive Garden if you're not happy," she snipped as she handed the woman back her card.

"You won't be getting any more of *my* business! And just wait until you see my Yelp review!" The woman yanked her card back and left before she even had it stuffed in her purse. She nearly collided with another woman on her way inside, and Alessia caught another snide remark before the customer had made it completely outside.

"Damn, what'd you say to her?" Robyn asked as she walked up to the counter. Robyn worked at an insurance agency down the street and made regular visits for coffee and goodies. Alessia always knew she could count on her friend for constructive criticism, and she loved seeing all the vintage dresses Robyn always wore.

"I was honest with her. I don't think my nonna would approve of that as a marketing skill," Alessia commented.

"Do I smell something burning?" Robyn asked.

"Shit!" Alessia raced back into the kitchen, yanked the tray out of the oven, and dropped it with a clatter on top of the stove. "Another batch ruined," she muttered as she shoved the swinging door and returned to the counter. "I don't know why I haven't given up yet."

"Because you like to torture yourself," Robyn answered as she adjusted her cat-eye glasses on the bridge of her nose. "And you know your grandparents are counting on you. I mean, you did say the place would've ended up going under if nobody had stepped up to run it."

"I know. Apparently, it takes a lot more than being a Russo to make that happen." She glanced at the wall, where a framed picture of her grandparents when they'd first arrived in Los Angeles hung. They'd retired, ready for an easy life, and she envied them for that.

"What about the rest of your family?" Robyn asked as Alessia handed over her usual caramel cappuccino. "Can't they come in and help? Or maybe you could hire someone."

Alessia shook her head as she wiped down the counter. "My

parents are gone, but you know that. My sisters are both married and have kids, and they said a long time ago that they were too busy to have anything to do with the family business. I wouldn't dare hire someone, because even a barista from a chain store would do better than me. It would be too embarrassing."

"I really think you're being too hard on yourself," Robyn insisted. "Besides, work isn't everything. I mean, if my life were nothing but selling insurance, I think I'd go insane."

"Yeah, I saw the pic you posted last weekend of you and that hottie. Unlike me, you actually have a personal life." She thought about the guy who'd been in earlier. He was rough and rugged, looking like he'd just returned to civilization after spending six months in the woods, but he'd set her core on fire the moment he and his friend had walked into the shop. Alessia didn't think burly men who hardly did more than grunt were her thing, but he'd kept popping into her mind as she went to bed that night.

Robin rolled the coffee on her tongue. "A bit too sweet this time, but the coffee flavor is great. Hey, online dating is where it's at, girl. There's no better way to meet men. I'd much rather go out *knowing* I'm going to meet up with someone than just taking a chance. They're certainly not all winners, but it's a great way to check them off the list."

Alessia shook her head. "Been there, done that. The last guy I met online wouldn't stop talking about serial killers. He was creepy as hell, and he tried to kiss me, even though it was obvious there was zero chemistry between the two of us." She shuddered just remembering that night.

"Like I said, they're not all winners," Robyn said with a smile as she stuffed a couple of bucks into the tip jar. "You'll find the right one when you least expect it. That's what I keep telling myself, anyway. Good luck. I've got to get back to the office before my boss realizes he doesn't know how to use the copy machine." She lifted a hand as she left, her bracelets jangling.

Alessia sighed as she went about her work. Robyn's advice wasn't horrible. Alessia did everything at Russo's, from sweeping up the crumbs and taking out the trash to running the cash register. Those were simple enough tasks, but the food prep part just wasn't coming to her.

She went into the kitchen and started whipping up a new batch of bomboloni, hoping she'd figure out some magical trick that would make them work this time. As she gathered her ingredients and prepared her workspace, her mind drifted back to that hot customer again. There was no doubt about her attraction to him. Her hands didn't shake like that when she made coffee for other customers. He looked like a hardened criminal, but one with a heart of gold, a rogue that could sweep a woman off her feet and melt her panties with one smoldering look. Grabbing the rolling pin, Alessia sighed, allowing herself to imagine how those strong, roughed-up hands would feel roving over her body.

A sound from the dining floor snapped her out of her reverie. Alessia dusted her floury hands on her apron and headed to the front, prepared to tell whomever it was that they were out of everything for the day and to come back tomorrow.

The man at the counter was familiar. Alessia had seen him in the pasticceria before, and she'd never had a good feeling about him. He wore his dark hair swept back and just a little too long so that it curled over carelessly at the ends, and he had that arrogant confidence that always irritated her.

"Can I help you?" She didn't really want to. Whatever she managed to serve him would inevitably get thrown back in her face anyway. This guy was dressed to the nines in his designer pants and button-down shirt, and he looked like the sort who expected only the best.

"I hope so," he said with a smile. "Nice place you've got here. I've been admiring it for quite some time."

"Well, I can whip up any of the drinks on the menu pretty quickly, but I'm a little short on the baked goods at the moment." The simple fact that a customer had come in and interrupted her baking process made her feel all the more discouraged about her current attempt.

"No, no," he said with a smile. "I mean the place itself. The building. I'd like to buy it."

Alessia stared at him for a second. There wasn't a sign in the window, and she'd never even entertained the idea of selling. "I'm sorry. It's not for sale."

"My apologies. I should've introduced myself. I'm Marco Cipriani. Perhaps you've heard of me." He held out his hand to shake hers.

She couldn't help but notice the wolfish quality of his smile as she accepted his handshake. Alessia figured he was just another real estate douchebag, thinking he could knock the building down to build slummy apartments. He looked the type, and now he was acting like it. "I'm Alessia. It's nice to meet you, but really, the building isn't for sale."

"Alessia." He drew out the sounds in her name, rolling it on his tongue like he was tasting it. "That's a beautiful name."

"Look, I've got things to do. Unless you're going to order..." She trailed off, hoping he'd get the hint.

Marco laughed. "Alessia, the only thing you need to do is accept the generous offer I'm trying to make. I know how difficult the real estate market can be. When it's a buyer's market or a seller's market, it never seems to be timed with your needs. But you won't have to worry about that again, nor the hefty taxes I'm sure you pay on this place."

"What part of 'I'm not selling' don't you understand? Now, if you'll excuse me." Alessia turned toward the kitchen door. The cash register was locked, but there was hardly anything in it anyway if this jerk really wanted to help himself.

"I don't think *you* understand," he said as he snagged her arm just above the elbow. "Everything is for sale if the price is right, and it's time for us to sit down and talk numbers."

His grip was a gentle one, his fingertips playing softly against her skin, and it sent shivers running up and down her spine. She sensed the strength in those fingers, knowing they could close quickly on her arm if he decided to do so. At that moment, Alessia wished Robyn had chosen to come to Russo's just a few minutes later so she wouldn't have been there alone.

"What *it's time for* is for you to get the fuck out of here," she spat, yanking her arm quickly and stepping backward where she would be out of his reach. "I've told you several times already, and I shouldn't have to say it again. What kind of asshole are you, anyway? Coming in here and acting like you can just buy my business like this? Leave, or I'm calling the police!"

If only her cell phone wasn't sitting on a shelf in the kitchen. She'd stopped carrying it last month after too many close calls of nearly dropping it in the giant stand mixer, and she doubted she could get to it quickly enough.

"I'm sorry. You're right." Marco put his hands in the air, palms out, and bowed his head slightly. "I've been so rude."

Just as she began to relax, thinking he was going to leave, Marco sprang into action. He leaped over the counter with the quick ease of a wild animal. His eyes stayed focused straight on hers like a laser, making Alessia feel like a rabbit about to become his prey. She backed away, but there was no place to go. He had her cornered against the coffee machine, and the only way to get out from behind the counter was to get past him.

Flinging her arms behind her to search for some possible weapon, Alessia's grip landed on a tiny plastic spoon used for measuring scoops of coffee. *Fuck!* She flung it toward him uselessly and turned to find something else, but Marco was too quick.

He snagged her by the wrists and twisted her arms behind her back, wrenching them painfully together as he gripped both of her wrists in one hand. Alessia's back arched against the agony, but that only gave him even more advantage as he brought his other arm around her neck. His inner elbow squeezed against her windpipe.

It all happened so fast, yet somehow, she still managed to have time for regret as his tight grip slowed the flow of air into her lungs. Why hadn't she ever taken that self-defense course that'd been available last fall? Why hadn't she hired someone else to work with her so she wouldn't have been alone? Why had she been the only one in her family who'd been willing to take on the burden of Russo's when she was so utterly incapable of running the place?

Alessia kicked and stomped, hoping her heel would happen to land in the right spot and cripple her assaulter the way she'd seen on TV. Marco was strong, though, far stronger than what his lean figure suggested. He was moving her now, and they were heading toward the side door.

She twisted and writhed, demanding that her muscles find a way to move. This was the kind of thing that happened to people in other parts of the city. It was the kind of thing she'd heard about on the news, gave half a thought for how terrible it was, and moved on.

But now she was the victim.

"Stop," he hissed in her ear as he paused just inside the kitchen. "You already showed me you didn't want to sell me the shop and do things the easy way. You would've been much better off, but now we're going to do things the hard way. If you can't work with me, then I'll make it happen."

Fear overtook her completely. Her stomach roiled, and every nerve was on fire. Her muscles hardly even responded to her demands now, and they burned with the efforts she'd made earlier. Alessia's eyes rolled as she looked through the kitchen, praying for something that would've helped her, but there was nothing she could do. This beast of a man had her, and she couldn't even yank her wrists out of his grip long enough to grab a knife.

Marco hustled her out the side door and into the alley. A slick black car was waiting there, the engine already running, and Alessia realized just how far ahead Cipriani had planned. Marco's thick-fingered hand came down on the back of her scalp as he bent her down and shoved her into the backseat, sliding in immediately after her and slamming the door. A man in the front seat tossed him a length of rope.

Marco's hand was quick and invasive as it dove into the pocket of Alessia's apron. She tried to squirm away from him, but he only pulled harder on her wrists. His other hand closed on her keys. "Lock the place up, Dante. Get a sign on the window saying that Russo's will be shut down for a week. Make sure you turn off the oven, too. I've got to attend to the financial aspect of our new business." As Dante got out of the passenger seat and went into Russo's, Marco kept his grip tight on Alessia, and the car pulled out onto the street without him.

"You're a snake," Alessia sneered as she squirmed as far away from Marco as she could. Her heart was thundering. Marco was a predator, and she was sure he could hear it. Well, that didn't matter anymore. There was no time left for pretending. "You think I'm going to sell the business to you just because you pull some dumb stunt like this? You're gonna go away for a long time."

Both Marco and the driver burst out laughing. "Did you hear that, Enzo? She thinks I'm going to the big house!"

"That's a good one," the driver agreed with a smile. "I didn't know you caught yourself a funny girl, Marco. Maybe she can stick around for a while and entertain the rest of us."

Marco's eyes raked up and down her full figure as he studied her. "Maybe. She's a little feisty, so it'll depend on how well she behaves herself."

"Fuck off!" Alessia cried. She heard the shakiness in her voice and hated herself for it. She didn't want to be scared, but there was no telling what this guy might do to her.

His eyes grew serious as he pushed his face closer to hers. "You don't like the situation you've found yourself in? Maybe you should've cooperated with me when I asked nicely. Or maybe I should've just whacked you on the spot and not given you a chance to argue. Do either of those sound any better?"

She didn't respond, turning away from him instead. The heavily tinted windows cast a deep sepia tone over the neighborhood she'd known and loved for so long, as though it were something of the past that she would never see again.

3

KENT STEPPED OUT OF THE SHOWER AND GRABBED THE TOWEL OFF THE rack. Everything in this place was nice, even the bath linens. He broke a little further inside at knowing just how different his life had turned out from Gabe's. It wasn't that he was jealous. It was yet another example of how his wolf had royally screwed everything up for him.

He shook off those dark thoughts, focusing instead on how good it felt just to be clean again. He'd spent the last couple of months hopping from one boat to another, and he hadn't been sure the smell of fish and salt would ever come off. His hair and skin felt completely refreshed as he dried off, cleaned up the edges of his beard, and put on the clothes Gabe had lent him, but inside, he knew he didn't deserve to be there.

As he stepped out of the bathroom, the scent of cooking drifted up the stairs. Kent followed it, using his senses to easily find the kitchen in this massive house. Gabe stood in front of the industrial-sized stove, and he turned when he heard his old comrade coming.

"Hey, you're looking pretty good! Are you hungry?"

"Always, but you know that." Kent eyed the steaks on the griddle. "With a big house like this, I would've thought you'd have a cook and a maid."

Gabe shook his head and smiled. "Nah, we all just pitch in. Besides, when we're out on missions or have a busy week, we might not eat at regular times. The only technical employee we have is Melody, who doubles as both a bookkeeper and a babysitter. She's great. You'll probably meet her later, but I thought it would be good if it was just us guys tonight. Grab that bowl there for me and we'll head outside."

Kent felt like a fish out of water in this huge house, but the effect was only magnified when he followed Gabe through a wall that retracted to make a doorway between the living area and the patio. Four other men were already seated at a table, and they looked up as soon as Gabe and Kent joined them. Kent felt their eyes assessing him, wondering what his deal was.

"Guys, this is Kent. He served with me in the Delta Force, and you can thank him for the fact that my hide is still mostly intact. Kent, this is our Alpha, Amar."

Amar rose to shake his hand, his dark eyes studious. "Nice to meet you."

"You, too. Thanks for having me." It all felt so forced, not like the camaraderie that Gabe had bragged about, but then again, Kent knew he was throwing a wrench in the works. He sensed something different about Amar, but he couldn't put his finger on it.

"Raul, here, is our technology and communications specialist. He's the guy for anything that has to do with buttons or screens. Jude and Reid are brothers."

Kent made the rounds, shaking hands with each of them before settling down. "I hope I'm not interrupting any of your plans." He glanced up at the moon, noting it wasn't quite full, but it was getting dangerously close. He could blame that for his feelings of unease, perhaps, but he'd been living with the instability of his wolf for so long, he was beginning to wonder if it was the moon's fault or his own.

"Not at all," Amar said kindly. "Gabe tells us you're in need of a job, and he thinks you'll be good for the Force."

Kent focused on his steak. With the heavy traffic, it'd taken almost an hour to get to Force headquarters from the San Pedro area, and Gabe had spent much of that time regaling Kent with tales of what the Force had already achieved in the short time it'd been established. This wasn't just some veterans' club, but a serious regiment of men who were determined to continue their work as soldiers. "I'm not here to beg for any favors."

"Are you kidding?" Gabe said as he passed the salad bowl. "You'd be a great addition. Do you remember when those insurgents had captured a bunch of innocent civilians in Fallujah? It was one hell of a mission, and it felt like it lasted forever, but we got it done. And it was all thanks to you."

"That was a long time ago." Kent stabbed his fork into a bite of steak, realizing more with every passing second that he never should've taken Gabe up on his offer. He'd always liked Gabe, and not just because they were serving together. Gabe was young and determined, but he was also a good person at heart and a great soldier. Kent had allowed himself to get excited about catching up, but they should've just left it at coffee. Gabe had moved on to bigger and better things, including a family and a place where he belonged. Kent knew he'd never have that.

"Don't be so humble," Gabe said as he clapped his friend on the shoulder. "You were a badass."

Amar had been observing the entire exchange. "Kent, maybe you could tell us a little about yourself. Why did you leave the service?"

It wasn't necessarily a loaded question. All of these men had already separated from the military. Gabe had been injured, his body peppered with shrapnel, and he assumed the rest of them had similar stories. It was an interview in its own way, Kent was sure. There was no better time than now to get this over with. "I was dishonorably discharged."

The silence that fell over the table was heavy.

Jude, who perhaps was even more reserved than Amar, sat back and took a sip of coffee. "Would you care to tell us what happened?"

"Yes." It was time to get it off his chest. Kent had been carrying this load for the longest time. It wasn't the type of thing a civilian would understand, and it wasn't something he was proud of. Who better to tell than veteran special ops shifters like himself? "I went AWOL, but not on purpose. My wolf has feral tendencies, particularly during the full moon. When I was younger, that was always when I'd act out or get in trouble, and it's only gotten worse with age. If the moon is full, my wolf completely takes over."

"Meaning you're unable to shift back into your human form?" Raul asked. Gabe had already told Kent that Raul was a wolf as well, so he was the one most likely to understand. Yet he didn't.

"Meaning that I have no idea what happens during that time," Kent explained. He set down his fork and sat back, stroking his beard. "It's sort of like getting blackout drunk and not remembering what you did. I was on base one night, and the next thing I knew, I woke up naked in the desert. I later found out that three full days had passed, and no one had any idea where I'd gone or what I'd done. Hell, I might still be wandering around out there if I hadn't stumbled onto a road. A Humvee went by, full of men from my unit. They recognized me and brought me back."

"And then you were court-martialed," Reid filled in.

Kent nodded slowly. "It's not like I could've told them about my wolf, you know? I had a psych evaluation and they didn't find anything, so military prison was an interesting experience, to say the least. Now, I'm left with a DD, and I'm worse off than a convicted felon. No one wants to hire me. I can't get housing. No veteran benefits or any other government assistance. I can't even vote."

Gabe shook his head. "I'm really sorry, man. I had no idea. I would've done something to help a long time ago if I knew—"

"No," Kent countered. "There isn't anything you or anyone else can do. I spent some time feeling sorry for myself, feeling that it wasn't fair because I hadn't chosen to leave my unit. But I've come to accept that this is just the way I am inside, and unfortunately, it's dictated how the rest of the world will see me on the outside."

A phone rang loudly, breaking the heavy tone that had settled over the table. Raul stood up. "Excuse me. I've got to take this." He headed into the house.

"I know that medical help isn't anything most shifters think about," Gabe said, "but Emersyn is a top-notch doctor. We actually know of another doc in Dallas who knows a lot about shifter medicine, and the Alpha of the D.C. Force is an M.D., too. It's something that the SOS Force as a whole has been working on. Maybe there's something that can be done to help you bring this under control."

Kent pulled in a deep breath. "That's good to know, and I'm not saying I'll turn it down, but I think it's happening because I haven't found my mate yet. I'm forty years old, and it's only getting worse as time goes on."

The other men nodded. "We all know how that feels," Jude said. "Many of us have only just recently found ours, and I think I can safely speak for all of us when I say it changes a man. It's like a deep itch that you can't scratch on your own."

"But for me, it's turned into a disease," Kent added. He was somewhat relieved that they were all so understanding. And even though none of them had gone through the exact same experience, they didn't give him a hard time.

"I still think you should try working with us for a while," Gabe replied. "I don't like the idea of you being out on the street."

Kent didn't need to look at the Alpha to know what Amar was thinking. "I can't sugar-coat this. I'm too much of a risk, man. It sounds like a great opportunity, but I'm not going to put you or the rest of the Force on the spot."

Gabe wasn't going to give up that easily, which was typical of him if Kent's memory served him right. "I'm sure being jobless and homeless hasn't done any favors for your wolf. Maybe if you spent some time here with the Force, things would get better. And I can go with you on all missions. I'll take full responsibility."

Amar pursed his lips as he thought, and then he looked at Kent. "You technically aren't allowed to serve again, but the SOS Force isn't the military. It's a possibility."

Raul returned just then. "That was a call from a woman named Filomena down in the San Pedro area. She just saw a bakery owner being kidnapped by a local wolf who's supposedly been trying to take over the neighborhood for decades."

"Interesting," Reid commented. "Sounds like we're going to have a fun weekend."

"Actually, it's a little more interesting than you realize," Raul said, still holding his phone in his hand. "The woman he kidnapped is a human."

Something else was said after that as the Force members discussed their next actions, but Kent hardly heard them over his thoughts. *A bakery? In San Pedro? A human? Woman? Could it possibly be...?* He felt his hackles raise down his back, an itchy sensation as a long line of fur sprouted from his spine and rubbed against the inside of his shirt. *Mine,* his inner wolf demanded. He shouldn't be feeling this way, no matter what his batshit wolf had to say about it. There were probably plenty of human women who ran bakeries, right? And the chances of them getting caught up with shifters, well, it was possible. Humans and shifters worked and lived alongside each other all the time, usually without any idea.

"This would be a great chance for Kent to get his feet wet." Gabe mentioning his name brought Kent back to the present moment to see a familiar light in his old friend's eyes. "We were on the Delta Force together, and this is just the type of situation we were trained to handle. I'll be there every step of the way."

Amar sat silently for a long moment, steepling his long, umber-toned fingers in thought. "It wouldn't be the first time we took a chance on someone new," he finally said. "Gabe, if you're truly willing to make sure this goes down the way it should, then I trust you to do that. I think the question now is whether or not Kent actually wants the chance." His dark eyes met Kent's.

He'd already said at least two or three times that he didn't deserve to be there or have a position on the Force. He'd told Gabe that he didn't want any handouts. Yet he heard himself answering the complete opposite as if someone else were using his mouth like a puppet. "I'm in."

Those two words sent Raul shooting up out of his seat again. "I'll need to get you a phone. Ours aren't exactly like the regular cell phones you see on the street. Well, I'll explain it all to you later. I'll be right back." He jogged out of the room.

Jude drained his coffee mug, and a small smile played on his lips. "You're in for a treat. Raul hasn't had the chance to train anyone on a new gadget since Reid joined us. You'll know more than you ever wanted to by the end of the night."

Amar checked his watch. "I'll give you all an hour to make whatever arrangements you need to, and then we'll meet in the conference room. If a human is involved, as this Filomena says, we have to act fast and be extra careful." He shot Gabe a serious look as he took his plate into the kitchen. "No room for mistakes."

Reid followed the other two, and then Kent and Gabe were left alone at the table. Kent turned to his friend, wondering if he could genuinely hold up his end of the bargain. Gabe vouching for him like that implied that Kent would do his absolute best not to fuck this up. No doubt his human side could do that, but what about his wolf?

"I want you to know how much I appreciate this. *All* of this," he added, to include the house, the shower, and the meal. "I just don't want to let you down."

"You won't," Gabe said firmly. "You never have before."

"You've got a lot more confidence in me than I do." Kent realized there was still some steak on his plate, and he began cutting it up. His wolf nudged him to just pick the damn thing up and rip into it with his teeth, but he had to at least pretend to be civilized.

"I've learned a lot since I've been with the Force," Gabe said, tipping his head back to look up at the sky. "I thought everything had to be a certain way, or it would've all been wrong. I thought there was only one clear path for me, and I had no choice but to take it. When that mortar hit and left me full of shrapnel, I didn't know what the hell I was going to do with myself. It was like that path and everything around it had been wiped from the face of the Earth, and I didn't know how to continue. The Force made all the difference."

"And your mate and son?" Kent pressed, not quite willing to let himself believe that joining the Force would fix all his problems. He, like any other shifter, had longed for a mate to share his life with. He'd yet to find her, and that was only harder with his current situation. "You can't tell me they didn't make up some of that difference."

"They did," Gabe admitted. "Absolutely, they did. But I don't think I'd have them if it weren't for the rest of the guys. We all know how to keep each other in check, and I think there's a lot to be said for being around people who understand. You'll see how it is." He stood and picked up his plate. "Need any more to eat?"

He probably could've eaten the whole damn cow. "I'm fine. I just want to sit out here for a bit."

"Okay. See you in an hour." Gabe went in the house, probably to rinse his plate, check-in with Emersyn, and kiss their son on the forehead. What a picturesque life.

Kent chewed slowly as he finished his meal. The little things could make a huge difference sometimes. A meal. A hot shower. A warm bed. They made a person feel more human, and in a good way that even a shifter could appreciate. It was no wonder Gabe was so domesticated. Kent just didn't know if he could possibly be the same.

4

It seemed like a lifetime since Kent had been on any sort of mission. Everything he'd done with the Delta Force and with Gabe felt almost as though it'd happened to someone else. Even so, he found himself studying every detail of the Russo residence as he and Gabe pulled up in front of it that night.

It was dark, but the streetlight and the warm glow of the porch lights revealed an older home with stucco siding and a tiled roof. The arched entry to the porch was echoed in the arched door, giving it an Old-World feel. While architectural details were nice, Kent found himself also noting the placement of the other homes nearby, how the light fell, and where someone could easily hide as they prepared for an ambush.

"You doing okay?" Gabe asked as he put the car in park and turned off the ignition. "I knew I wanted you to be on the Force, but I wasn't expecting a mission for you so quickly."

"Doesn't bother me," Kent replied honestly, still studying the place. "I don't like sitting around with nothing to do, and I've had too much of that lately. Let's go see what we can find out."

Before they'd made it halfway up the sidewalk, the front door opened, and an older woman hustled out. She clattered down the steps and raced up to meet them. With her silver hair and dark eyes, Kent thought she must have been Mrs. Russo until she grabbed his hand and introduced herself. "Thank you so much for coming. I'm Filomena. I'm the one who called you. Oh, that poor girl! I do hope there's something you can do to help her."

"I'm sure we can," Gabe assured her.

"Good, good. I've been friends with the Russos for a long time, you know. My deli is right across the street from their pasticceria. The Ciprianis have been sniffing around that neighborhood for a long time, trying to gain control over the whole thing. I just thought of them as an annoyance until I saw them drag poor Alessia off." She wrung her hands in front of her.

Alessia. If there'd been any doubt that the same human woman who'd caught his attention just the day before was the victim, Filomena's words erased it. He wanted to get onto the case as soon as possible. "We should get inside and discuss this."

"Yes, of course!" Filomena took Kent by the hand and led him up toward the porch, fussing the entire time. "Oh, I'm so worried. I'm just glad I happened to look out the window at the right time and see it happen. I left my nephew in charge of the deli and shifted into my eagle-owl. I was able to follow them, so I can give you directions. I was exhausted by the time I got back, but it was more than worth it. I only wish I could've done something to get her to safety."

"Don't worry, ma'am," Gabe said as they approached the front door. "We've been trained for these situations, and we'll do everything we can to make sure she's safely returned."

Filomena nodded and opened the door to reveal a cozy living room. A fireplace rested at one end of the room, though nothing was burning in it. The ceiling could've used a new coat of paint, and there were worn spots on the hardwood floors, but overall, it looked like just the sort of comfortable place that grandparents would live in. Mr. and Mrs. Russo sat in two armchairs, their hands clasped together, and they rose to greet their visitors.

"Meet the Russos, Mateo and Isabella. They're Alessia's grandparents," Filomena said, making the introductions. "I'll go make some coffee." She flitted off into the kitchen.

"I'm Gabe, and this is Kent. We want to help your granddaughter, but we need as much information as possible to help make that happen. I know some of this might be painful for you to talk about, but any details you can think of will help."

Kent realized in that moment just how much Gabe had changed.

Though he'd never been a rude man, he'd always been pretty blunt. Now he almost sounded like a grief counselor or a customer service rep, although Kent supposed in a way he was.

"There's no mystery behind what happened here," Mateo said with a flick of his hand toward two chairs as their guests sat down. "Those Cipriani bastards have been sniffing around the neighborhood forever. They're greedy and selfish, and they figure they can extort as much money as possible out of the locals if they have all the control."

"Sit down, Mateo," Isabella chided softly.

"How can I sit at a time like this?" he asked, gesturing wildly. "I spent my whole life building up that pasticceria. We both did. Marco's father wouldn't stop pursuing us, desperate to get a hold of that place. He came in every month, then every week, then every day. Finally, I was ready for him. I sent a bullet flying, and I was unlucky enough to have missed his head by an inch. It scared him off for a while, but that son of his has a whole different tactic. *Il figlio di puttana bastardo!*"

Isabella gave her husband a look, but she didn't chastise him for cursing. "I'm afraid we were foolish enough to think we were in the clear by the time we retired and left Alessia in charge of the bakery. The Ciprianis hadn't harassed us for the longest time, and we thought they'd given up. You must know we never imagined they'd do something like this or... or we never..." She broke off sobbing, and Mateo handed her a handkerchief from his pocket.

"You see what this *diavolo* does to my family?" Mateo raged.

"Please, don't take his anger or my sadness to be directed at you in any way," Isabella pleaded between sniffles. "We just love our Alessia so much, and that's exactly why we were so pleased to hear that Filomena called you. This isn't a job for the police, as you know. We need people like you."

Kent and Gabe exchanged a look. As far as Kent knew, the age-old habit of keeping their shifter identities a secret was still going fairly strong, with a few exceptions. He wasn't going to be the one to out them. "What do you mean, people like us?"

Isabella gave a small laugh. "What, you think that after running a business in this district for the past sixty years, we wouldn't know about shifters? We are simple people who just wanted to build our lives here in America, but we're not so simple that we don't pay attention. We're practically the only humans left in the neighborhood."

Mateo nodded. "We've managed to befriend quite a few of our

neighbors, and for the most part, it's never bothered us. Except the Ciprianis. Those wolves are an exception to the rule."

"I guess that means we don't need to worry about that part of things, then," Kent commented.

"Oh, no," Isabella warned just as Filomena came back in with a tray. "Alessia doesn't know."

Even Gabe had been caught off-guard, and he cleared his throat to buy himself a moment. "I don't understand."

The two older folks looked at each other and then down at the floor. "We never told her," Mateo said. "Her parents passed away rather young, and Alessia always needed us the most. She became our baby, essentially. At first, we just wanted to protect her. A child can't keep a secret like that, so we didn't give her the burden. As she got older, we thought she might figure it out as we did."

"I think we justified it because it's easier not knowing sometimes," Isabella added as she accepted a cup of coffee from Filomena. "She had enough on her mind. Besides, most humans have no idea. It doesn't affect them at all."

"Do you think Marco would have told her?" Gabe asked.

Filomena answered that one, and rather sharply. "I doubt it, at least not until it's the last card he has to play. He uses his human form for the most part. A human will quickly shoot a wolf who comes prowling through the neighborhood, but another person is a different matter."

"Your secret is safe with us," Mr. Russo assured them, "but we're very worried about Alessia. She's probably terrified as it is. I can't imagine what it would be like for her if she found out now."

Kent couldn't help himself. He imagined the temptress from the bakery being held captive by some dirtbag, and it set his insides on fire. *Mine.* His wolf's demand echoed in his head as he threatened to take over, simmering just beneath the surface. His gums ached where his sharp teeth forced their way through, but he reined himself in before he could make a complete disaster of this meeting. He sucked in a deep breath, reminding his wolf that he had to keep his shit together. This was his only chance with the Force. If he fucked up now, he'd be right back out on the street. "Have the Ciprianis gotten in contact with you?"

"Yes," Isabella said with a nod. "We were told we have to give them the pasticceria, or he'll kill Alessia." She choked on the last words, bringing her husband's handkerchief up to cover her face.

Mateo ran a hand down his wife's back. "I don't know what we're going to do. We obviously can't let any harm come to our granddaughter, but how can we let them get away with taking our business? Even if we were only dealing with humans, I'm not sure the police could help us. It isn't as though the place makes us any real money at this point, but it's part of our family."

"We've seen a lot of bad pack politics that involve just these sorts of things," Gabe said. "Let us negotiate for Alessia's release. That's the first and most important step. After that, we can worry about the bakery."

The Russos looked a little doubtful, but Mateo picked up a small notebook from a side table. He held it out, and when Kent took it, he saw a phone number scrawled in shaky handwriting. "Marco Cipriani said to call him when we've made our decision."

Kent rant his thumb over the pencil markings. It struck him just how innocent the Russos were, and how unfair it was for them to get caught up in something like pack politics. Gabe had seen situations like this during his time with the Special Ops Shifter Force, but Kent knew it was also something they'd experienced a lot with the Delta Force. Someone always wanted the upper hand and was willing to do anything to get it. That meant killing, kidnapping, blackmailing, anything. What would the Russos have done if Filomena hadn't contacted the SOS Force? What would have happened if the SOS Force didn't even exist? He started to think his hope for a place to belong might be a little more realistic, but first, he needed to prove that he deserved it.

Kent looked at Gabe, conveying his thoughts without saying a word. Gabe had explained to him that the Force itself was like a clan, and through an ancient ritual, they were able to communicate telepathically while in animal form. Kent hadn't even come close to being fully accepted into the group, but the amount of time he'd spent serving with Gabe overseas worked in a similar way. They were on the same wavelength, and they both knew what needed to happen and who needed to do it. After getting the slightest nod from Gabe, Kent stood. "I'll just step into the kitchen and make the call if you don't mind."

The Russos looked both startled and grateful. "Yes, of course. Anything you need at all."

His wolf writhed inside him as he stepped into the next room, not wanting to have those kind elderly folks listen in. There was no telling exactly how this would go, after all. The kitchen cabinets looked to be original to the home, the white paint on them just the latest in many layers and colors. It was a welcoming room just like the rest of the house seemed to be, and Kent could easily imagine the family meals that had been cooked there with so much love. Had Alessia been a part of those?

No! He chided himself as he pulled his newly assigned cell out of his pocket and forced himself to concentrate on the job at hand. It didn't—couldn't—matter how he felt about Alessia. There wasn't time to contemplate why he felt such a raw desire for her when she was merely a human. This wasn't the right time to consider those pale green eyes of hers or to envision the tears welling up in them as she suffered at the hand of some asshole.

His throat tight, he listened to the other end of the line ring once, then twice.

"This is Marco," came a smooth voice from the other end.

"I'm calling to negotiate the release of Alessia Russo." Kent had been worried about how this mission would go down. Gabe had vouched for him, which was a risky gamble on his part. But Kent could already tell that it wouldn't be that hard to slip into his old habits. He kept his voice even, calm, and professional. There couldn't be any possibility of angering the man before he got a chance to get to Alessia.

Marco let a moment of silence elapse before he spoke again. "Is that so? You don't sound like the folks I talked to on the phone."

Marco was leery of him, which Kent fully expected. "No, but they've contracted me to get things taken care of. I'll be the one who finalizes the transfer of Alessia and the Russos' property." He wasn't about to toss out threats or say that Marco would never get a hold of the bakery. Though this phone call was a small step, it was still vital that he didn't piss the man off during their hostage negotiation. If Marco really wanted to, he could kill Alessia and still find a way to get what he wanted.

Marco let out a short laugh. "All right. If you say so. I'll meet you tomorrow night." He rattled off an address.

Kent didn't need to write it down to memorize it. That was where

Alessia was, and now the address was permanently burned into his mind. Why did he feel so strongly about this human when he hardly even knew her? "We don't have to wait until tomorrow. I know it's late, but I'm sure you wouldn't mind getting this over with."

Marco laughed again. It was a dry sound that grated straight down Kent's spine. "I'm sure you wouldn't, but I'm not going to let the Russos off that easily. My family has been trying to work with them for a long time, and they should've come to an agreement earlier. I'm done playing nice. I'll see you tomorrow night." The line went dead.

The only thing that stopped Kent from slamming his fist into one of the nearby cabinets was the fact that they belonged to the Russos, who were already suffering enough. His wolf was begging to get out, to thrash and tear at something, to taste blood between his teeth and on his tongue. Kent curled his hand into a fist and bit his knuckle, trying to get control over himself.

"Everything all right?" Gabe asked from the doorway.

Kent released the tension that had been building up in his shoulders. How easy it was to slip into those ways that had ruined his life, but it was up to him to fight against it. "Yeah, as good as it can be. Marco won't meet me until tomorrow, but at least that gives us some time for a little recon."

"And probably some rest," Gabe suggested. "Come on. We'll let them know what's happening, and I'll see who's available to come work security here in the meantime. I don't think we should leave the Russos completely unguarded."

"I agree, considering the way the guy was talking on the phone. His grudge against them goes way back. While I don't have any doubts that I can safely get their granddaughter home, I can tell you already that I don't trust this guy." The Russos had referred to the Ciprianis as wolves. In an ideal world, any wolf shifter should have something in common with another. Kent knew that wasn't going to be the case this time.

5

ALESSIA'S STOMACH ROILED AND RUMBLED. MARCO HAD ORDERED HIS goons to bring her food a few times, but she'd refused to touch any of it. She didn't trust him as far as she could throw him, and she wouldn't put it past him to poison her. A man who would go to such extremes just to buy a failing bakery had to be a little off.

That obviously hadn't kept him from making a ton of money, considering the place he'd brought her to. After Marco had shoved her in the car and bound her hands, he'd found something to cover her face with. Alessia had no idea what part of town they were in. Time was passing differently for her as she feared for her life every second. She'd been shocked when Marco had whipped the cloth off her face and she'd found herself in a basement. People in movies who got kidnapped were always bound up in damp, filthy, rat-infested holes. There, though, she was surrounded by thick, luxurious carpeting, quality furniture, and even a flatscreen television.

Enzo, the one who'd been driving, was her current babysitter. He sat on a leather sofa, flicking through the TV channels with a bored expression on his face. Every now and then, he glanced over at her, but for the most part, she was being ignored.

Good. That was better than having to deal with Marco himself. She didn't like the dangerous glimmer in his dark eyes. Alessia understood she was being held hostage, and as soon as her grandparents signed

Russo's over to him, she'd be set free. At least, that was what Marco said, but Alessia didn't believe him.

She squirmed against the zip ties that kept her held tightly in her chair. "Can you let me up? I've got to pee."

Enzo rolled his head to the side to give her a grumpy look. "How can that be? You haven't had anything to eat or drink."

Damn it! He had her on that one, though Alessia hadn't expected Enzo to think that much. It was obvious that Marco was the one who ran the show, and the rest of them were there for their brawn, not their brains.

Any further thoughts of escape left her mind when she heard footsteps on the stairs that she'd come to dread. Marco appeared a moment later, looking impatient. "I hope you're ready, Alessia."

"For?" Did she even want to know?

"Someone's coming soon to collect you. I hope he was smart enough to bring the deed for your little bakery." Marco's smile extended too far toward his jawline, as though he was hoping he'd get the chance both to kill her and get the pasticceria.

"Don't hurt my grandfather," she pleaded. Alessia sounded weak, but she was too tired to care. She just wanted to get this over with. "He's an old man."

Marco let out a bark of laughter. "Oh, that may be, but he's resourceful enough that he's found someone else to come in his place."

"What?" Alessia's mind searched for someone who would fill that position. One of her brothers-in-law? She didn't think they'd be the type to get involved. "Who?"

"I didn't exactly ask for all the details," Marco retorted. "All that matters to me is getting what I want, and making sure anyone who's in my way gets swiftly out of it."

The doorbell rang, echoing through the house. Marco swatted Enzo on the shoulder. "Go get that. I'll be up in a second with our bargaining chip in tow."

With a sigh, Enzo turned off the TV and stood. "Sure thing, Boss." He slowly stomped up the stairs, obviously not nearly as interested in the matter at hand as Marco was.

Marco took a folding knife from his pocket and flicked it open. He strode confidently toward Alessia, and she flinched as he leaned down. She felt the chill of the blade against her skin and then the sudden release of pressure as the knife cut the zip tie from her wrist.

He laughed, and his proximity to her ear made it repulsive. "I suggest you behave yourself during this meeting. There are only two ways it can turn out. I'm sure you won't like one of them, but I'm absolutely certain you'll hate the other."

Alessia's blood ran cold. She was convinced this man would kill her if it meant he could get what he wanted. Anyone who would kidnap someone just to get his way couldn't possibly be stable. It was for that reason that Alessia took the hand he extended to help her up, even though the mere thought of touching him made her skin crawl. What other horrid things had this Marco character done? How many other people had he manipulated? Her only hope was that this meeting he spoke of meant she was about to go home. She didn't want to think about what might happen if it didn't go well.

They stepped out of the basement and through a hallway before Marco guided her to a lavishly appointed office. Top-of-the-line furniture in solid wood with a deep, polished surface decorated every wall. With the leatherbound books on the built-in bookshelves, coffered ceiling, and even a small stone fireplace in the corner, Alessia felt as though she'd been transported to another time. The view of the city through a large window was the only thing that reminded her of where she was.

Marco pointed at one of the armchairs to the left of the desk. "Sit, and behave yourself. Understand that keeping you tied up was merely a way of making it a little easier for my men to watch you, but you have no chance of getting out of this house alive if you try to do something stupid."

Alessia nodded. She did understand, but she instinctively kept looking for a way out of there. There had to be some door left unguarded, right? She chided herself for even speculating. She was a helpless woman in a hopeless situation, and the only chance she had was whomever her grandparents had sent to deal with this.

Enzo entered with another man in tow. He glanced at his boss, who dismissed him with a flick of a hand. The door shut quietly behind him, leaving the three of them in the office together.

The newcomer's eyes shot to hers and then steadied on Marco, as though she wasn't even there, but Alessia instantly felt a flood of adrenaline. She recognized that face. She knew she'd seen those dark blue eyes before, eyes that skimmed over everything and took in the tiniest of details. There was a look in them that she'd noticed before, a depth that she couldn't explain. And those lips had most definitely been on her mind, at least until she'd gotten tangled up with Marco. They were full lips that immediately hinted at sarcasm before a word was even spoken, though the hard line they were set in suggested he was ready to be serious. This was, without a doubt, the hot, scruffy guy that had shown up in the bakery.

The newcomer extended a hand to Marco. "Pleased to meet you. My name is Kent."

And then there was the voice. Alessia trembled in her chair, trying to understand what the hell was going on. Who was this guy, and why had he come to Russo's just a few hours before she'd been taken hostage? Was he some sort of government agent? Was he spying on her? Was he part of the whole scheme to get the pasticceria from her grandparents?

Marco shook Kent's hand, but he kept his chin lifted defiantly in the air. "You can come in here acting like a real estate agent, Kent, but I'm not interested in bargaining. I've already made my demands quite clear."

"I understand. My concern is simply that I hear everything directly from you. Mistakes can be made when you go off of secondhand information." Kent sat on the other side of the room without being asked, crossing one foot over his knee and looking as casual as if he were sitting down at a family reunion. "Why don't you tell me a bit about what's going on?"

"It's very simple: I get Russo's, and you get the girl. I don't get Russo's, and the girl gets whacked." Marco smacked his palm on the back of Alessia's chair for emphasis.

It was a mere vibration that rattled through the chair, but it made her jump anyway. Alessia's face flushed as she glanced across the room at Kent. He still wasn't looking at her. Why did she want him to so badly?

"I understand. Could you tell me a little more about why you want the bakery? That might help me work with the Russos and come up with an amount we can all agree on." He smiled at his host.

"We're not talking about money anymore. I made an offer, and it was refused. The deed for the girl, and that's it."

"I'm sure it's been very frustrating for you, trying to make this happen," Kent said calmly as he picked at the hem of his pants. "The world is kind of a crazy place these days. The real estate market is never where you want it to be, and that makes it a lot more difficult to achieve your goals."

A small sigh escaped Marco's lips, but then he took an aggressive step forward. "Who the hell are you, anyway? You'd better not be some pig, or both of you are dead."

Kent put both his hands in the air, his fingers spread wide, and he was still smiling. "I've got no badge, and you're welcome to search me for one. Your boy there already made sure I wasn't carrying. I'm not here for anything like that. In fact, you had me pinned from the start. I'm just a real estate agent."

Marco laughed. "You've gotta be shitting me. Those old farts put their granddaughter's life in the hands of a Realtor?" He laughed a little harder as he slapped the chair again. "Your family is more pathetic than I thought, Russo."

Her face burned once again. Why the hell should she be embarrassed? Who were her grandparents supposed to call in a situation like this? Well, the police would've been a good start. Alessia studied Kent again, feeling that there was some sort of truth that he wasn't showing. He had to be more than a real estate agent. Even if he was a cop, that didn't explain why he'd been in her pasticceria and why he was there now. Just a coincidence? It didn't feel like it.

"Back to the matter at hand," Kent said, ignoring Marco's humor. "What were your previous business dealings with the Russos like?"

"That's not relevant," Marco growled. "The bastards have been holding out on my family for years. They've refused to cooperate, and the old man even tried to gun down my father. I'm done playing nice."

"You're done. I get it. I just want to help you get this over with as quickly as possible. I think that would be best for everyone, don't you?" He gave the slightest glance toward Alessia.

"Do you have the deed?" Marco demanded, suddenly getting even more agitated. "The only thing that's going to make this happen any faster is if you stop yapping and hand me the right piece of paper."

Despite Marco's anger, Kent stayed utterly calm. "The Russos have it all prepared for you. You're a savvy businessman, and you understand how these things work. In order for the paperwork to be legal, it has to be signed in front of a Notary Public. I'm happy to escort you there so we can get this wrapped up." Kent stood, ready to go.

"I'm not that stupid." Marco charged forward, his shoulders set and his fingers curled. Anger rolled off him in waves as he snagged the front of Kent's shirt. "I don't know what it is about you, but I don't trust you. Whatever you're trying to pull won't work. I'm going to get that building, and I don't need some jamook like you to step in and pretend you're making it happen. I've watched my father run our family, always trying to work out negotiations, and while it may have gotten us a good start, I know this is the time to be ruthless."

Kent made no move to extract Marco's fingers from the front of his shirt. "I get it. You've got a lot to live up to, and it seems like there's nothing you can do to really make it happen. At least not fast enough to keep your father happy. Some dads are tough acts to follow."

Marco's shoulders slumped and he let go of Kent. He remained right in front of him as he dragged a hand through his hair, ruining the comb marks and clutching a handful of it at the end. "Fuck it. I never should've bothered with all this song and dance." He turned toward Alessia.

She automatically recoiled in her chair, her muscles contracting. Alessia knew she should be doing something to save herself, but she was cornered. Marco stood between her and the door, and even if she ran from the office, she would never get out of the house. The other men had already proven they would do whatever their boss asked, and she'd be dead before she ever made it outside.

Kent reacted quickly. He bolted forward, wrapping his hands around Marco's waist as he barreled his head into his back. His foot shot out in front of Marco's, and the two men went tumbling to the floor. Marco swept behind him with his fist, briefly making contact with his attacker's head, but Kent dodged it skillfully, almost as though he'd known it was coming. The tendons in his neck bulged as he strained against his opponent, and his eyes flashed a silvery blue as he fought. Kent's legs wrapped around Marco's as he pinned the other man's shoulder to the floor. Kent's elbow was a sharp angle in the air as he drew his arm back, his fist landing square in Marco's face, and then Cipriani went limp.

"Come on." Kent jumped up from the floor and reached for Alessia's hand. "We don't have a lot of time before he wakes up, and I have a feeling he's going to be a little cranky."

Alessia's mouth was agape, too shocked to react.

Kent snagged her hand and pulled her up from the chair. He still held her fingers tightly as he unlocked and slid open the window, yanking the screen aside.

"Are you high? We're not going to jump out the window!" she shrieked, still trying to wrap her brain around reality. It was all just some horrible nightmare, and it still wasn't over.

"There's a roof down there, and there's a car waiting for us. We don't have time to discuss this." Kent let go of her hand, but only so he could scoop her up in his arms. He quickly sat on the windowsill, swung his legs over, and leaped out into the night.

She was too scared to scream as they dropped through space. She knew she was going to die. Alessia felt his heavily muscled arms tighten around her as he landed with a thump, his rough hand sliding against her thigh as he stood her on her feet.

"You good?" he asked gruffly.

Her lungs didn't want to cooperate. In fact, her entire body felt numb, but her brain was going completely wild. "I...guess so?"

"Good. We've got to keep moving. His goons will be onto us any minute." Kent grabbed her hand again, not giving her a chance to argue, and took off running across the roof.

She stumbled after him, glad that the darkness hid the ground below so she couldn't focus on just how high up they might have been. Alessia concentrated instead on the heat of his hand against hers.

He stopped suddenly and reached for her. "One more jump."

"I can do it myself," she protested, taking a step backward. Her foot slipped a little on the rooftop, and another bolt of adrenaline stabbed through her heart.

Kent's head cocked slightly as he gave her a lopsided smile. "We're not going to risk it, Princess. Let's go." In one quick movement, he'd swept her off her feet and into the air once more.

They landed hard, and the grass was cool and wet under Alessia's feet when he set her down. Alessia's lungs burned as she took off after him, the shadows of trees tricking her eyes and making her lift her feet too high to avoid tripping. She felt as though she was hardly running at all, being pulled along like a kite behind Kent as they hurtled through the night. Something dark and shiny emerged from the darkness, and Alessia heard the metallic sound of a car door. No overhead light came on as he shoved her inside and slid in after her. Alessia's chest tightened as she remembered Marco doing something very similar. "Who the hell are you, anyway?"

Someone was in the front seat, and the car shot into motion. It cruised quietly around the corner before its headlights came on.

Kent smiled. "I'm the real estate agent, remember?"

Damn, he was handsome. She looked sharply away, not wanting to let that influence her at all. If she'd merely jumped out of the frying pan and into the fire, she wanted to know. "Who are you *really*?" she demanded. "I'm not dumb enough to think a real estate agent moonlights as some sort of action hero. Tell me who you are, right now. I've already been through enough shit." She was in no position to demand anything, considering he'd probably just saved her life. Still, it had all been too much.

He put a gentle hand on her shoulder. "I'm Kent, and this is my associate, Gabe." He gestured to the front seat, where the driver waved. "We were hired by your grandparents to get you out of there. You're safe now; we're not here to harm you. We can either take you back to your place or to your grandparents' if you'd rather not spend the night by yourself."

Shadows slid over his face as they drove through the city. Kent's eyes were such a dark blue, like the depths of the ocean. And Alessia felt herself falling straight into them. *What was that he'd said about not being alone?* The car pulled to a stop at a light, jerking her back to reality. "I, um, I'd rather just go to the bakery. I want to make sure everything is all right. I don't know what Cipriani and his men might've done to it."

"Fair enough," Kent said with a nod. He leaned back, pulled a cell phone out of his pocket, and dialed. "In the meantime, call your grandparents. They've been worried sick, and I'm sure they'd rather hear the good news straight from you."

Alessia took the phone, frowning at it for a moment before she put it up to her ear. It was rugged looking, and it wasn't a model she'd seen before.

"Hello?"

Her grandmother's shaking voice made Alessia stop wondering where this Kent guy shopped for mobile devices. "Nonna! It's me! Is everything okay? Are you guys all right?" She realized with a shock that she'd been so concerned for her own life that she had no idea what may have happened to them.

"We're fine, *Gattina*! What about you? Are you injured?"

"No." Shocked, exhausted, and wildly curious, but not injured. "I'm safe. I think Marco was about to do something crazy, but Kent stopped him." Alessia paused. She realized she probably shouldn't have told her grandmother that, because there was no reason to make the poor woman fret more than she already had. It also made her think a little more about the details of her rescue. She turned away from Kent and toward the window, pressing the phone up close to her ear. "Who are these guys, anyway?"

"Just some old friends of the family," Nonna said.

Alessia had always trusted her grandparents, but she had to wonder about this. They were getting older, after all, and it would have been easy for someone to take advantage of them. If Kent was going to charge them some exorbitant fee and hold it over their heads, they were no better off than they'd been in the first place. "Whatever this cost, I'll do everything to help."

"No, no, no. There's nothing like that to worry about." Nonna's voice was firm, the tone she took when she would accept no arguments. She didn't use it often, but when she did, there was usually an old family recipe involved. Alessia knew she meant business. "The only thing you do need to worry about is keeping yourself safe. Watch out for Cipriani or any of his men. They're not the kind to take no for an answer."

"Okay." Alessia swallowed. There was much more happening than she understood, but it was obvious she wasn't going to uncover everything that night. She reminded her grandmother of how much she loved her and got off the phone, promising herself that they'd sit down and have a long talk soon.

"Here we are," Gabe said from the front seat.

Alessia never thought she'd be so glad to see Russo's. The lights had been shut off, and the building hulked moodily in the dim streetlight, but it was intact. She was vaguely aware of the two men getting out of the car to follow her inside, but she didn't argue. They'd already done this much for her, and if they wanted to make sure the building was clear, then it wouldn't hurt anything.

She found her spare key tucked behind a loose brick and let herself in through the side door, trying not to remember the way Marco had dragged her out of it only the day before. She flicked on the lights over the counter, leaving the dining area in semi-darkness. It was enough light to see by without making anyone think the place was open for business. Everything was as she'd left it, including the items she'd dragged off the counter, except someone had turned off the stove. "It's okay," she said as she leaned on the counter and breathed a sigh of relief. "Everything is all right, and I appreciate all you've done."

"It's our pleasure. Just let us know where to take you, and we'll let you get some rest," Gabe said. He stood next to Kent, both of them scanning the place.

Alessia lost her words for a moment as she realized that she recognized Gabe as well. He'd been in the bakery with Kent. It was a coincidence for one of them to have been a patron, but both? "Um, no that's okay. I just want to stay here."

"I'm not sure that's a good idea," Kent replied.

"My phone is here," Alessia replied, suddenly feeling incredibly stubborn as she ducked her head into the kitchen and retrieved it from the shelf. "My car is outside. I'll be fine. I just want to get some baking done so I can get a head start for tomorrow."

"Then I'll stay here with you." Kent said it with such authority, as though it wasn't a suggestion, but a statement of fact. He lifted his dark eyebrow ever so slightly when Alessia looked at him, daring her to challenge him. "I don't have anything better to do."

Gabe hesitated, but he nodded. "All right. I've got to get home to Lucas. I promised Emersyn a night out with the girls if we wrapped up on time. Just call me if you need anything." He ducked out the side door.

"Hand me your phone." Kent held out his hand expectantly.

Alessia didn't know what sort of narcissistic complex made this guy think he could just tell her what to do, yet she handed him her phone without arguing. "Is this a habit of yours? Running around and rescuing damsels in distress?"

"Not exactly." He set his phone on the counter next to hers and swiped at the screens of both. "You could say I'm testing the waters, trying to see if it's a habit I want to get into."

"And?" The man was merely standing next to her, leaning against the granite, yet she couldn't take her eyes off him. Maybe it was because he'd just saved her from certain death, but she didn't think a man had ever looked so wildly appealing.

"Here." He handed her phone back. "You've got my number now."

"How did you do that? The screen was locked." She frowned up at him, even though he was smiling.

"There's an app for everything."

"Is there an app for getting rid of a big brute lurking around my bakery so he doesn't bug me while I work? Or am I stuck with you?" Flustered both at the ease with which he'd hacked her phone and his proximity, she turned away and began straightening the coffee area.

"You're stuck with me."

Alessia gathered several cups and spoons, swept past Kent, and carried them into the kitchen. She was determined to slow both her breathing and her heartbeat, and the mundane task of washing dishes was at least one place to start.

6

KENT WATCHED THE KITCHEN DOOR SWING SHUT BEHIND HER. RAUL HAD been so eager to show Kent all the inner workings and latest upgrades to the Force phones, and because he'd been determined to make a good impression, Kent had listened. That had come in handy in making sure that Alessia had his number in her phone, so there wouldn't be any excuse for her not to call him if she needed help in the future. But would she? And why was he so determined to stay there with her? She was just a human. She was just some woman he'd run into a couple of times. It was no more interesting of a coincidence than running into Gabe on the street.

At least, that was what he told himself as he followed her into the kitchen. She was bent over a sink, scrubbing like her life depended on it.

"You know, the last twenty-four hours must have been hard on you. Most people aren't put in a hostage situation, and when they are, they don't go right back to work." He walked up slowly behind her.

"I suppose something like that can make chores seem exciting again." She sighed and braced her wet hands on the edge of the sink. "No, that's a lie. I just want the familiar. I grew up here, you know. Practically right here in this kitchen. I sat right over there and did my homework while my Nonna baked. I worked here after school once I was old enough."

"Sounds nice," he replied honestly. "It doesn't surprise me at all, though. Your grandparents seem like good people, the kind who care a lot about their family."

She stiffened for a moment before she continued washing. "I'm afraid you have the advantage. I don't know anything about you, and I highly doubt that you know anything about *real estate*."

Kent leaned against the wall near the sink and crossed his arms in front of his chest. "I know a little about a lot of things, but you're right. I'm not a real estate agent."

"So?" she pressed as she slammed a cup down onto a drying rack. "What *are* you, then? You work for the FBI or something?"

Even in the short time he'd been with the Force, Kent already knew the drill. He couldn't just tell Alessia the truth. There was nothing he wanted to do more, although he couldn't explain why. She had some sort of hold over him, something that made him go absolutely crazy. He had no business being alone with her that night. The moon was too full, just like her lips.

Her breasts.

Her hips.

His wolf had been responsible for him blurting out that he would stay there with her, though his human side knew he couldn't trust himself. Still, he didn't regret it.

"Well?"

Kent had lost himself in thought just looking at her. "It's a private security company," he said quickly.

"I see. So how much do my grandparents owe you? I mean, something like that can't be cheap. I imagine that's normally a service that only the rich can afford." She turned away from him toward a cabinet, but not before he saw her brows knit together in concern.

"It's not like that at all, actually." Hell. This woman—this very *human* woman, he reminded himself—didn't even know about shifters.

She gave him a look over her shoulder. "Right. Whatever you say. I know you can't be completely normal, not with that jacked-up phone you have." Alessia reached up for a canister of flour, the hem of her shirt lifting and exposing the small of her back as she stretched upward.

Kent felt his wolf stirring again. For a second, he hated Gabe for even suggesting that he be on the Force. He wouldn't be able to control himself, and Gabe would be the one to pay for it. He gripped the side of the sink, squeezing tightly in an attempt to keep his lupine half at bay. He needed a distraction. "So, what are you making?"

Alessia shook her head and sighed. Her hair was tousled from her adventure, but it framed her soft features beautifully. "Just some turnovers. They're not what people expect from a pasticceria, but they're something I know I can actually make."

"Didn't your grandmother teach you everything?" From his time with the Russos and with Alessia, he'd understood that she'd grown up there, eventually taking over the business. It didn't make sense that her baking skills were a little lacking.

Alessia let out a laugh. "She tried, poor thing. I'm afraid I didn't inherit that natural knack for cooking that every other Italian seems to have."

Damn, just the way she moved as she measured out ingredients caught his eye, and he watched her like a predator from a few feet away. The flick of a wrist, the curl of a finger around a measuring cup, the way her ass wiggled slightly as she sprinkled flour. *Mine*, his wolf growled. He was hungry for her, hungry in a way that he knew was dangerous. His throat was tight as he spoke again. "Maybe you could tell me a little about it. I don't know jack about baking."

Another laugh escaped from her lips. "Sure, I can tell you about what I've learned over the years."

"Such as?" He pushed away from the wall and took a step forward. His wolf obviously wanted to be closer to her. Maybe if he gave it a taste of what it wanted, it would be satiated enough to let him think rationally.

"Such as, you always measure vanilla in teaspoons, not cups. Oh, you should've seen Nonna's face when I made that batch of brownies! She thought she was giving me something easy to start with, and she just about died." Alessia laughed again as she began mixing the pile of ingredients.

Kent felt the beast simmering just under his skin as he watched her move. He'd never realized just how sensual it was to watch a woman work with dough, kneading and pulling it, massaging it with her fingers.

"Definitely make sure you don't mix up baking powder and baking soda. They're not the same thing." She looked up, realizing he was standing right next to her.

Kent thought about backing away. He knew he was too close. He knew he shouldn't have even been there. But he felt a deep, insatiable need inside, something feral, hungry, and inexplicable. He was supposed to be there to protect her, but who would protect her from *him?*

She smiled uncertainly. "You probably know all this, though, don't you?"

"No," he answered gruffly, reaching out to tuck a stray strand of hair behind her ear. That small touch sent a bolt of electricity through his arm, and he bit his lip to keep it from running away with him. "I want to know more. I want to know all about you, Alessia."

She dusted her hands on a kitchen towel and then flicked him with it gently. "Come on. You don't really mean that."

The comment caught him off-guard, and it pushed his wolf back down for just a moment. "Why wouldn't I?"

Alessia sighed. "I don't know much about you, Kent, but it's obvious you live an adventurous life. On a good day, I'm just lucky to keep this place running. It's like we're from two completely different worlds."

You don't know the half of it. "I don't think that has to stop us from getting to know each other a little better."

Her shoulders sagged as she sighed, staring down at the ball of dough she'd formed on the butcher block. "Kent, it's so strange. I know you were in here before. Both you and Gabe, actually. It all seemed normal at the time, but I couldn't stop thinking about you after you left. Then, of all the crazy things, you showed up to save me from Cipriani? I just can't help thinking that..." She trailed off, her eyes lifting to meet his.

Kent saw something in her eyes, something he'd been feeling ever since he'd shown up at Marco's place and discovered that the captured baker was, indeed, the same woman who'd been on his mind. It had seemed impossible to him, and now he knew she'd been wondering the same thing. That wonder mixed with desire and filled her eyes, turning them to deep green pools of unknown depths. He was hardly aware of what his own body was doing as the two of them moved closer, pushed by fate more than anything else, until his lips were pressed against hers. *Yes,* his wolf confirmed from inside him. This was it. This was what he needed.

Kent tensed in a moment of shock, wondering what the hell he was doing, but then he gave in. He relented everything he'd been feeling for the last twenty-four hours, those feelings that had only escalated when he'd gone to Marco's and had seen her there. He cupped her jaw in his hand, pulling back just enough so that his lips brushed against hers as he whispered, "It drove me crazy to see you there at Marco's. I wanted nothing more than to get you out of there and..." Kent trailed off as his throat tightened once again, knowing he was about to do something stupid. He would've ripped Marco limb from limb if that was what it took to save her. *Anything.*

If Alessia thought it was stupid, then she was no more able to control herself than he was. She pushed up onto her tiptoes to press her mouth against his once again, and when her lips parted, she welcomed his tongue as it dove inside. Her breasts pushed against his chest, needful, demanding, wanting. Alessia's hands explored his solid body, skimming his chest and his arms and the back of his neck, and when the fabric of his shirt bunched up against her palm, she swatted it aside impatiently. Her breath came in short gasps that he could feel inside her chest, as if the very air was getting in the way of what she wanted.

Kent knew and understood that impatience, as he felt it in himself. He wanted her with a blind passion that drove him from within, and he willingly gave in to it. Now, there was no stopping him.

He wrapped his arm around her waist and thrust her up against the nearby wall. Her hands flew up, startled, but she relaxed again as he nibbled the tip of one flour-coated finger. He worked his way up her arm, his mouth caressing her skin as his hands slipped from her hips and up to unbutton her thin denim blouse, flicking it aside impatiently to expose the delicate, lacey cups of her bra. Kent felt ravenous as he dipped his head to run his lips across the exposed mounds, inhaling the scent of her skin and knowing he'd never have enough. His wolf was still there, demanding and insistent, but as long as he fed it by staying close to Alessia, he knew he could keep it at bay. He dragged his teeth ever so gently over the smooth surface of her skin, losing himself in the taste of her.

As if she knew just what she was doing to him, Alessia's floured fingertips played along the sides of his head and into his hair. Her chest heaved against him as she gasped her pleasure, and he felt her hair falling around them both as she tossed her head back. Alessia yanked the sides of his shirt, and he broke off his kisses just long enough to let her pull it over his head.

Kent knew they were both driven to make this happen. They needed it, and even though it was probably for different reasons, that was enough for him. He dipped his fingers into the waistband of her floral leggings, savoring the slow appearance of her flesh as he dragged them down over her curves. Her black lace panties matched her bra, and what control he thought he had started to slip.

She pulled and tugged at his pants, and their desperation culminated as soon as they were free from the confines of their clothing. Kent took her, pressing her up against the wall as he buried his eager member inside her. Alessia moaned, but her arms and legs clung to him. Her hips moved in time to his as their fevered lust turned from looks and longing to a tangle of arms and legs that couldn't be split apart. She clung to him as though she would fall off the very surface of the Earth without him.

It was wild and foolish and exactly what he shouldn't have been doing, but no amount of reason or logic would've fit in his brain any longer. He felt the gentle slap of her breasts against him as he moved, the deep heat of her core surrounding him, and that was all that mattered. His wolf felt it, too, and it stood poised and ready as Alessia undulated against him.

"Kent!" she breathed. "God, yes! Kent!"

"Alessia." He managed only to choke out her name as the full force of his ardor built and broke. His muscles trembled as he came, and he buried his fingers in the flesh of her backside as he fought the feral animal inside him. He thought he'd been winning, but the wolf was simply biding its time. He felt his fangs drop from his gums, and he knew that if he let Alessia look him in the eye, she'd see his true self. He ducked his head against her shoulder.

"Are you all right?" she asked breathlessly.

"Definitely." Being with her had satisfied his human side, but his wolf still clamored inside him. His chest heaved as he fought to keep the rest of his wolf from surfacing. There was no telling what it would do or how she would react. His knees were weak with the effort, and he let himself sink in front of her, dropping kisses the entire way. "I just can't get enough of you."

It was true, but it was a poor ruse. His mouth skimmed her abdomen, so she couldn't see the wolf that was anxious to come out, but her tantalizing scent and taste were overwhelming. As he moved lower, the sweet delicacy was too much to resist. *Mark. Now.* Before he could think, his fangs obediently sank into the thin skin of her inner thigh.

Alessia yelped, the sound filling the kitchen. Kent yanked his head back, horrified to see the droplets of blood that welled up from the wound. His wolf, as insistent as it'd been up until now, retreated, along with his fangs. "I'm so sorry, Alessia," he whispered. "I'm so sorry."

"That was kinda hot." She grabbed his hands from her thighs and pulled him up. "Don't be sorry. It was amazing. All of it."

She was smiling, but Kent knew that was only because she didn't understand the true implications of what had just happened. They were two consenting adults, and the sex had been great, but...

"Hey, get that sad puppy dog look off your face. You're going to ruin the most mind-bending night of sex I've had in years," she giggled.

He pulled her into his arms and held her, resting his chin on top of her head. She had no idea what this meant, but he sure as hell did.

He'd been a beast, literally.

His wolf had marked her.

And ready or not, her life was about to change forever.

ALESSIA WATCHED KENT CAREFULLY AS SHE BUTTONED HER SHIRT. HE was acting differently; she was sure of it. Though she wouldn't call herself the most experienced woman on the planet, she knew most men puffed their chests a little after sex, even if they hadn't been that good. Kent had been *great*, so it seemed odd that he'd retreated into himself. "With moves like those, you're going to make it hard for me to get any work done around here," she joked.

Kent glanced at the abandoned dough on the counter before he retrieved his shoe from across the room. "Yeah. Sorry about that."

She bit her lip. She'd never had sex like that in her whole life. It'd been intense, better than she could have ever imagined, but there was also a deep passion to it, like magic. Maybe he'd felt it, too, and it'd scared him. "Listen, Kent. If you're concerned about what all this means—you know, between the two of us—don't worry about it. I had a great time, but I'm not here to rope you into anything."

He shook his head as he put his shoe on, anguish clear on his face. "It's not that, Alessia. I'm just really sorry."

"About the bite?" She laughed, something that was so much easier to do when he was around. Sometimes it was because he made her nervous, but most of the time, it was because he brought new feelings bubbling to the surface. Kent made her feel completely different, and she liked it. "I meant it when I said it was okay. Yeah, it hurt a little, but it was kind of a turn-on. I'm not sure I've ever gotten a man so riled up before."

"I'm glad you think so, but I'm still sorry."

She pressed her lips together, wondering where to go from there. Kent had swooped in and saved the day, defeating a guy who would've readily killed them both, but all of a sudden, he was acting like something had gone horribly wrong. "Are you wanting to get home or something? My car is here, and I could drive you." She reached up on the wall for her key ring.

"No." His fingers closed around her wrist tightly. They loosened as he brought her hand back down. "No," he repeated, more gently this time. "I want to stay here with you for a little while if it's all right."

"Of course. I can make us some coffee." Their tryst had been hot and satisfying, and she wanted a drink that felt that way, too. Maybe it would put both of them back to rights. She chattered idly to fill the empty air between them as they stepped out to the counter. "You know, I remember being one of the first kids in my class to start drinking coffee all the time. I wasn't one of the cool kids, but that part about me was. The other girls were so jealous. They didn't know that Nonna would only let me have decaf, and I sure as hell wasn't going to tell anyone."

"Is this what you've always wanted to do with your life? Run the bakery?"

She smiled simply to have him participating in the conversation. It felt a lot more normal, and she hadn't liked the tension between them a moment ago. "Well, yes and no. I had all sorts of ideas about being an actress or a singer or any number of things, but the pasticceria is in my blood."

He made a face.

She ignored it as she poured the grounds into the pot and turned it on. "I always hoped I'd be much better at it. Fortunately, I took plenty of business classes. At least the financial side of the place doesn't escape me. It's just that...oh." She touched the back of her hand to her forehead.

"What's wrong?" he was at her side in an instant, his hand cupping her elbow.

"Oh, it's nothing." Alessia forced a smile. She liked Kent, certainly enough to hook up with him in the back of the bakery, but being sick in front of someone was completely different. "I'm just a little dizzy."

"Let's sit you down." He gently pulled her over toward the dining area.

"I'm okay, really," she said as she sat. "I'm just a little woozy. You know, come to think of it, I haven't had anything to eat since before I left here the other day."

"They didn't even feed you?" Kent cursed under his breath. "What can I get you?"

After she directed him to the fridge in the back, Alessia braced her forehead on her fingers and put her elbows on the table. It was more than just hunger, she was sure. Her skin was hot, even as the center of her froze over. She gritted her teeth as she fought off a chill, but the ever-watchful Kent didn't miss a thing as he returned.

He slid a plate with a thick mortadella sandwich in front of her, along with a bottle of Coke. "I think we need to talk."

"I don't really want to right now." She glanced down at the sandwich. Aside from her under-leavened ciabatta roll, there was nothing wrong with it. She loved the salty, savory taste of mortadella, and she probably really did need to eat, but for some reason, it looked entirely unappealing. Her stomach swirled inside her, but not in a way she recognized as typical nausea.

"I'm sorry, but we do." Kent sat across from her, and the seriousness in those cerulean eyes scared her a little. It scared her even more as he continued to speak. "There are some things about me that you don't know."

She plucked at the provolone cheese poking out of her sandwich. "That doesn't surprise me," she said casually, even though she immediately began imagining all sorts of awful things. Was Kent part of the mob? Did he have some sort of disease? Was he wanted by the federal government?

"Have you heard of shifters?"

Alessia slowly lifted her eyes up to him. "Um, what?"

"Shifters. People who can turn into an animal at any given time. Some are bears, some are lions or tigers. Well...I'm a wolf."

Something bubbled up inside her, and the next thing Alessia knew, she was laughing. "Oh, come on! It's sweet of you to distract me while I don't feel good, but that's a bit much."

He licked his lips and leaned forward. "I'm not making this up. I'm a wolf shifter, and there are quite a few more shifters around here than you probably realize. Marco is one, too."

"So." She swallowed. The words weren't coming, but she tried again. "So, um, do you just split your time with the wolf fifty-fifty?"

"No, it's a little different than that. I can shift any time I want to, but it's harder for me to control during a full moon."

Unbidden, the memory of Kent fighting Marco swam up in Alessia's mind. She'd seen his eyes change completely, and they'd certainly looked like something wild. "There's no such thing. If that were true, everyone would know about it. No one can keep a secret these days, especially one as crazy as *that*."

"Shifters can," he replied quietly. "We have been for a long time. We're not supposed to tell anyone who doesn't share the same secret, but now, you're too deeply involved not to know."

"Kent, this isn't funny anymore. As stupid as this is, you're scaring the hell out of me. I've had enough of that for a lifetime after what I just went through. If this is your idea of a joke, then maybe you should just go home and let me worry about what happens here." Tears welled up behind her eyes. Though she hadn't exactly been heroic during her captivity, Alessia had been braver than she imagined she would've been in such a circumstance. Now that it was all over and she could feel just how tired and overwrought she was, it was too hard to keep up appearances.

"I swear, Alessia. I'm not fucking around. I'm a shifter. So is Gabe. So is Marco. So are most of the people in this neighborhood. I can even make you a list of shifter celebrities if you want."

She pursed her lips. "Right. I'm sure they put that right at the top of their resumes."

"It's real, Alessia, and you're involved now. I bit you. I...marked you. I shouldn't have done it, but I couldn't control myself. Hell, I haven't been able to control myself since the moment I met you. But there's a chance that you may become part wolf now." He put his hand over the top of hers where it lay on the table.

Alessia yanked it back. "If what you say about shifters is true, how can I become one from just a little bite? That's like something out of a comic book. It can't possibly work that way."

"It does, or at least it can. I haven't experienced it before, but it's what I was told a long time ago. Still, I think it's important to get you somewhere you can be observed and taken care of. I've got some friends who can help." He stood and reached for her hand.

Alessia didn't take the offering, though she wished she had as she got up and found that she was dizzy all over again. Even so, she stubbornly folded her arms in front of her chest. "Exactly how would you explain what happened? That you just randomly decided to bite my inner thigh, and now it's time to put me in a cage and watch me for stray hairs?"

"I have a feeling they'll understand. All of my coworkers are shifters, and they know the territory that comes with being one." He sighed and looked away, his hand braced on the back of his neck.

"There's something you're not telling me." She didn't know how, but she knew it with a certainty she felt inside her bones.

She thought he might argue against that, but he slowly nodded. "It's the least believable part of the story, actually."

"Um, less believable than the idea that you can turn into Cujo at the drop of a hat?"

"Kind of." Kent rubbed his forehead. "Every shifter is destined to be with someone. For us, it's not really about dating around and finding someone we can stand to be with long-term. It's about finding our one true mate, the person we're fated to spend our lives with. Usually, it's another shifter, but on rare occasions..." His eyes watched her, solid and steady, those deep blue orbs keeping her from slapping him and walking out the door.

"Are you saying... *I'm* that person?"

"So it seems."

Her head was spinning. This was just too much. "I...I think I need to sit back down before I pass out."

Just as her knees began to wobble, Kent scooped her up in his arms and held her close to his chest.

"I'm going to take you to see my coworkers, okay?"

"Fine. It's not like I can explain this to the nurses at the walk-in clinic."

Kent got Alessia situated in the passenger seat of her car. The night was cool, and Alessia had pulled a jacket from the backseat. She felt like absolute shit, worse than the last time she had the flu, but still, she demanded answers from Kent. He'd explained that he worked with other shifters on the SOS Force and that he'd come to save her because of his job with them, but she still couldn't quite wrap her mind around it. It was like a fog had rolled in, moving slowly enough that she didn't notice it until it was too late to do anything about it. "Prove it to me," she finally said.

"What?" He glanced at her from the driver's seat.

"Prove it to me. You say you can turn into a wolf whenever you want to. Well, I haven't seen any fur growing on you yet. And don't argue with me about some other ridiculous rule. You've already told me what you think you are, so there's no point in trying to hide it now."

Kent gestured at the early morning traffic in the glow of the rising sun. "We're not exactly alone, Alessia. I don't know how well my wolf could drive, but if it did, it would make for some very interesting head-lines. The kind that would cost me my job if I still have one."

She frowned at him. A wolf who cared about a job? Now that was crazy. "How long have you been with this Force, anyway?"

His frown wasn't an answer, but a reaction to his thoughts. "I just started. Rescuing you was my first mission, but I did a lot of hostage work when I was in the service."

Alessia slumped in her seat. She was sure she had a fever. Exhausted and emotionally drained, Alessia was aware that made her vulnerable. Still, for some reason, she was actually starting to believe this man. Why would he lie to her about such a ridiculous thing? A scheme like that could only last for so long before someone found out the truth, no matter how much they wanted to believe it. "All right."

"All right, what?"

"All right, I believe you. About the shifter thing, I mean. It's insane, and I might regret it later, but I believe you." She turned and looked out the window, admiring the view as though she were seeing it for the first time. Everything was a little crisper and clearer, like it was in high definition.

"Hold my hand." He kept his left hand on the wheel and stretched his right one out to her.

"I see. I'm the one who just found out I'm surrounded by ferocious beasts, but you're the one who needs his hand held." She took it anyway, wanting the warmth and comfort of him. It was irresistible when it was so close, and she could've used a little comforting herself.

"Good. Now watch my arm. I shouldn't be doing this at all, but here goes."

Alessia did as she was told, watching his skin and waiting for something explosive to happen. He'd already expressed the notion that he didn't know how well he could drive while in his wolf form. The fact that she worried about it told her everything she needed to know, though it was strange to stare at his arm so long and expectantly. She watched the smattering of dark hair on the back of his wrist and was just about to give up when she saw something change.

She jumped as a tuft of hair cropped up on the inside of his forearm, a perfect little forest of dark gray fur. Kent flipped his wrist over and did the same on the other side, this time, the hair a little coarser and thicker.

"See?" he asked, sounding more relieved than satisfied.

Alessia hadn't managed to take her eyes off of him, her mouth gaping. She was waiting for more, perhaps even wanting it. She wanted to see how this all worked and what happened. It simply wasn't fair to make her wait. "You can do that all over your body?" she asked quietly.

"And more. I actually *become* a wolf," he said quietly, glad he'd been able to get through to her.

Alessia had been so desperate not to believe him, yet the irrefutable proof was in front of her. If what he'd said about being a shifter was true, then that meant everything else was, too. "Oh, shit."

"I know. We'll get it sorted out."

Her mind was reeling by the time they pulled up at a huge house just as the sun was edging up over the horizon. Kent seated her in the massive living room and told her to wait while he got the others, and before Alessia knew it, she was surrounded by a small crowd, most of them in their pajamas.

A woman in a fuzzy pink bathrobe elbowed her way through. "Everyone can go back to bed. This is a medical issue, so I'll handle it." She gave a grumpy glare to the others, who shot curious looks at Alessia, but they did as they were told. "I'm Emersyn."

"Alessia. I'm sorry for all this commotion so early in the morning. We don't have to be here. I'm sure I'll be fine."

Kent, standing at her shoulder, stiffened.

Emersyn gave no hint of noticing, but she shook her head and sat down on the ottoman in front of Alessia. She took her pulse with one cool hand. "Kent gave me the short version. I think it's best if you're with other shifters right now. No one at a human hospital is going to know what to think. They'd probably just give you antibiotics and send you home."

"Would that work?" Alessia asked hopefully.

"No." Emersyn's reply came quickly as she leaned forward and checked Alessia's eyes. "The truth is that there's really not much we can do but wait. Marking a mate is a very antiquated practice these days. It probably hasn't happened in centuries, so we don't have any reliable medical evidence to work with. A transmission of saliva directly into the blood is bound to have effects, but I can't guarantee what they'll be."

"Won't she become one of us?" Kent asked. He hovered nervously behind Alessia's chair.

"That's possible. There's not a school for shifter physicians, so I've done a lot of my own research to supplement what I know. Some stories have been passed down of people becoming halflings if they get only a small amount of saliva in their bloodstream."

"And what does that mean?" Alessia didn't know this woman, but she liked her. She felt she could trust her, shifter or not.

"It means you would only have a partial shift from time to time, never becoming a full wolf, and you'd likely have very little control over it."

The last of her hope was shattered with that statement. "That's even worse."

Kent's hand squeezed her shoulder gently. "It'll be okay, Alessia. I know it's all been a big shock, but we'll get through this. You can stay right here at HQ."

Emersyn nodded. "Yes, that would be a good idea. If you do shift, you'll have people nearby who can help you through the process. For us, it's sort of like learning how to walk."

"No. I don't want to do that." Alessia stood and turned around, looking for the door. "I'm tired. This is nuts, and I just want to go home. I have a business to run!"

Kent trotted after her as she headed toward the entryway. "You can't just leave. It's dangerous out there. If you're a halfling, any other wolves in the area are going to smell you from a mile away."

"I don't care. Let them come. They'll be pretty damn disappointed when all they find is me! I just want to go home, Kent." She gripped the doorknob tightly, wishing it could root her back in some sort of reality that made sense. Alessia knew it was all real, yet she was waiting to wake up from this nightmare.

"Fine. Then I'll go with you. This is all my fault, anyway."

She pressed a hand to his chest to stop him from coming any closer. Alessia could feel the heat over his pounding heartbeat. Not too long ago, she would've been thrilled just to be touching him. Now she was furious with herself for ever trusting a man just because he'd disguised himself as a knight in shining armor. "No. I'm going by myself. No matter what happens to me now, whether I wake up as a full-blown wolf in the morning or I have to start wearing hats to cover my fuzzy new ears, my life is royally fucked." She stormed out and slammed the door behind her, heading off into the morning and whatever her new life would bring her.

8

"KENT."

Gabe appeared in the doorway to Kent's room at Force HQ, a room that he'd already thought of as temporary, but he worried it was about to be even more so. "Hey."

"What the hell?" Gabe stepped inside, his face disappointed, and his shoulders sagging. "Tell me what happened. All of it. There wasn't much time this morning, since we were more concerned about Alessia."

Kent sat on the edge of the bed. He should've been exhausted. Between the rescue mission and his time with Alessia, he hadn't slept all night. Their tryst now felt as though it'd taken place a week ago, even though it'd been less than a day. "To be honest with you, I'm still trying to figure it out myself. There's a lot to think about, and I want to have it all straight before I meet with Amar." The Alpha had made it quite clear that there would be an official discussion about this incident, and Kent couldn't blame him.

"Yeah." Gabe sat down next to his old friend and scratched his chin. "He was pleased with how well the operation had gone, but he's pretty pissed that you bungled it so quickly and so badly. He didn't tell me what he plans to do yet."

"I'm sorry," Kent said sincerely. "I'm sorry to you, especially. You put your faith in me to be a part of this team. I really thought it was the new start I needed, and if I've fucked that up for myself, then that's one thing. But messing up your life is unforgivable."

"Kent, you and I have been through a lot over the years. I forgive you. I'm sure Amar will have my ass, but don't worry too much about my position here. Just tell me what happened."

He owed him that much, but Kent was still trying to sort it out in his head. "I believe she's my mate," he said solemnly.

Gabe nodded. "I gathered that much. I couldn't imagine you'd do something like that otherwise."

Kent launched himself off the bed and resumed the pacing that'd taken him through most of the day. "But it doesn't make sense, man. She's a human. Plain and simple, nothing more. I was going crazy for her even while we were trying to eat those awful pastries in her shop. I don't know why she would trigger me like that if she didn't have an animal inside her to respond to mine."

"I couldn't even begin to explain that to you, other than to tell you to look around," Gabe replied. "The rest of us certainly haven't ended up with mates who are exactly like us. Hell, Amar and Katalin met when she was still a human, and even after she became a vampire, they still managed to make it work. Crazier things have happened."

"I suppose so." Kent wanted to take comfort in Gabe's words, but it was hard. He knew he'd failed his best friend, the Force, and the woman who was supposed to be his mate. "I told you about how unpredictable my wolf had been and how that got me kicked out of the Delta Force. Hell, that was what made me leave my pack for the service in the first place. I was always pissing someone off."

"Is that what this is?" Gabe questioned, tipping his head to the side. "Your wolf freaked out?"

Kent laughed, not because it was funny, but because it was just so damn hard to explain. "Yes and no. It was hard enough being *near* her, but when we started messing around, there was definitely a feral side of me that took over. I didn't mean to mark her, but at that moment, I was fully under its control. There was nothing I could do to resist it. But since it's happened, my wolf's been a lot less erratic than usual, considering the phase of the moon right now. I should be taking off through the hills and disappearing for a while, but instead, all I can do is sit and wonder how I'm ever going to get Alessia to forgive me."

"Shit. That's a tough one," Gabe agreed.

"Yeah. Now we have to see if everyone else around here is as sympathetic as *you*. I hate to admit it, but I really need this job. I need everyone here. A shifter on his own isn't worth much."

Later that evening, Amar called the official meeting just before dinner. He sat solemnly at the head of the conference table, his dark eyes sweeping around the room, waiting patiently for everyone to settle before he spoke. "I think we all know why we're here. Kent, we'd like a full debriefing."

Kent nodded. He'd known this would be the first step. He'd been through that and much worse back when he'd been court-martialed. It'd helped that he'd already had a chance to unload some of the heavier, emotional stuff with Gabe, so he dove right in.

He began by explaining how he'd already run into Alessia at Russo's and how she'd made him feel. The others listened quietly, but no one rolled their eyes or snickered. It was easier to explain the smaller details of the mission itself, especially since all of that had gone the way they'd expected. The Force had made sure a few contingency plans were in place, depending on how Marco reacted, and Kent had followed the program. Even when his story came around to Alessia and what he'd done, he noted that the other Force members were patient. It was still embarrassing and aggravating that he'd put himself through this once again, but at least this time, he was dealing with fellow shifters.

Amar nodded to Emersyn. "Do we have any updated information on the human?"

She shook her head. "I'm afraid not, but I think it would be a good idea to check on her every couple of days. I'm happy to do that myself."

Kent balled his fists under the table. He should've been the one dealing with Alessia, medical issue, or not. Still, he understood. He'd already bared his teeth. Now, he had to submit with his tail tucked between his legs for a little while.

"Very well. Not too soon, seeing as how I don't want to scare her off. She knows about us, and it's quite possible she could become one of us. I'd rather she feel she can come here if she needs any kind of support. Gabe, you said her family was receptive to the shifter concept?"

"Definitely," he confirmed. "Their friend who called us is an eagle-owl, and the Russos explained they'd known about us for a long time."

"Good." Amar cleared his throat and looked down at the table.

Kent felt himself pitching forward in his seat as he waited for the gavel to come down. He wouldn't blame the Force a single bit if they kicked him out. He'd acted poorly, and even though he could've put this on his wolf, he was still the one who'd bitten an innocent woman.

"There's no doubt that the actions taken by Kent showed poor judgment and control," Amar finally said. "A woman who previously had no idea that shifters exist now not only knows of us, but may very well become a shifter herself. The fact that she refuses to stay here at HQ makes her an even further risk to our entire community. We don't know her well enough to guess who she might tell and whether or not they would believe her. Then there's the fact that she and her family are already in danger because of the Ciprianis."

Kent hung his head as he listened. It all made so much sense, but where was that logic when he'd found himself in Alessia's arms? Whatever the case, he couldn't go back in time and change that.

"That being said," Amar continued, "I think we all understand exactly what it's like when we meet our mates. We aren't fully in control, no matter how much we might want to believe we are. I'm not trying to embarrass you, Kent, but you said you thought your wolf had been acting out because you hadn't met your mate."

Kent swallowed and nodded. This wasn't exactly going in the direction he'd expected. "It's a theory, anyway. So far, it seems to be proving true."

That seemed to be enough for Amar. "My recommendation is that you continue with your probationary period with the Force until the next full moon. If you can get a hold of yourself and we don't have any further incidents, then we don't have anything to worry about. If you can't, then you're gone. Anyone else have a different idea?"

No one spoke up.

"Good. Kent, I suggest you take tomorrow off. See if there's anything else that needs to be straightened out before you get involved with another mission. Clear?" Amar's gaze brooked no argument.

"Crystal."

The Force was dismissed, and the others in the house joined in for dinner. Kent obliged himself to eat with the rest of the group, even though he wanted nothing more than to crawl in a hole and pretend none of this had ever happened. He understood that people were a lot like animals in certain ways, and sharing a meal created a bond. He would've been a fool to miss out on that just because he felt like an idiot. They'd accepted him, and they'd given him a much better chance at turning his life around than anyone else had given him since his dishonorable discharge. This was his new family, whether he liked it or not.

The next day, he found it much harder to take the day off than he'd expected. Not all that long ago, Kent would've been thrilled at the prospect of laying around all day, watching reruns, taking a long bath, and stuffing his face. Instead, he was restless and agitated. Kent couldn't stop thinking about Alessia, finding that there could be very little joy in anything else if she were still angry with him.

When the house had become unbearable, Kent decided to take a walk. He strode quickly down the sidewalk, hardly paying attention to his surroundings. That wasn't like him, and he knew it. He'd been highly trained, and good observation skills were vital to making any mission a success. Whether it was noticing a bribe being slipped between hands or a person being treated poorly, the tiniest details could often change an entire operation. Right now, though, Kent didn't give two shits about what kind of flowers were growing at the house across the street or who nearly ran him over with their scooter. The only thing on his mind was Alessia.

When he'd been walking for an hour and had finally stopped to get his bearings, Kent suddenly realized what he was doing. He'd thought he'd been rambling idly, just needing to get out and move his feet, but he'd ended up heading almost due south. Straight toward San Pedro.

Straight toward Alessia.

His instincts had taken over when he hadn't been paying attention, and his wolf was just like a lost dog heading home.

The bus station was nearby. Kent figured he'd already gone this far, and there was no point in trying to fight it. He wanted her. He *needed* her. It didn't mean he had to do anything crazy. Amar and the others hadn't even asked him to stay away from Alessia, although they certainly would've been within their rights if they had. They only wanted him to stay in line. Kent knew that he'd be a lot more likely to do that if he could just see that she was all right.

Remembering Filomena from the deli across the street, he headed into the bookstore next door.

"Can I help you?" asked an old woman from behind the counter. The place smelled of musty paper and strong coffee.

"No, thanks. Just browsing." Kent moved through the shelves until he'd managed to position himself near the big window at the front of the store. He picked up a book, but he didn't even look at the title before flipping it open. The only thing he was truly interested in was across the street at Russo's.

The 'Open' sign was on and flashing. Alessia hadn't mentioned anything about other employees or family members who helped out, so he could only assume she was the one running the place. That was good. If she was able to work, at least she was all right. Kent watched patrons come and go, thinking he'd caught a glimpse of Alessia's dark hair in the windows at one point.

When the bookstore closed, he stepped out onto the sidewalk. The air smelled of salt from the nearby ocean, car emissions...

And Cipriani wolves.

It was a scent Kent couldn't possibly mistake after having been in their den to rescue Alessia, and he didn't like picking it up now. Those bastards were close by. He'd felt like a creep for watching over her pasticceria from a distance, but now he knew he'd done the right thing. He would be there when Marco and his gang showed back up, and he would show them no mercy.

Even though he could smell them like a pack of filthy dogs roaming through the neighborhood, Kent caught no visual signs of them as he lounged on a bench, pretended to browse at a nearby hardware store, and took a long walk around the block. It was getting dark, and the scent had faded.

The lights inside the bakery allowed Kent to see in as he leaned against a lamppost. She was sweeping the floor, and he swore he spotted a small smile on her lips, despite the mundane task. Was she thinking about him? Did she have any idea that he was nearby, longing for her? He liked to think so, but in his heart, he knew it wasn't true. She had his number, and his phone had been silent.

The lights went off one by one, and Alessia emerged from the side door. She got in her car, and Kent straightened as she pulled out onto the main road. He didn't want to leave her. Even just being near her the way he had been for the last few hours had been strangely comforting to his wolf. It was the instinct of knowing his mate was protected, and he didn't want that feeling to go away. As the car pulled off into the distance, Kent felt as though a rubber band was being stretched between the two of them, growing thinner and weaker the longer it pulled. The only options were for it to yank the two of them back together or to snap in half. As he headed for the bus station, he wasn't sure which it would be.

9

"Hey! I'm glad you stopped by," Alessia said warmly as she wiped down a table.

Robyn put one hand on the hip of her green corduroy jumper. "Like I was going to stay away, considering what you've just been through. I feel bad that I couldn't come by earlier. It's been kind of a hectic day at the office."

"Eh, no problem. I'm fine. I'm just glad it's over with." Alessia moved with ease behind the counter. It was almost closing time, and she'd had a fantastic day. Everything in the bakery had been running so smoothly, and she loved it.

"How could you possibly be all right?" Robyn argued. She had her hair swept up into a curled ponytail that day, looking like she'd stepped right out of the sixties. "I'm not even sure you should be at work."

Alessia glanced around the shop to make sure there weren't any customers around. The afternoon hours were always a bit slow, except for a few folks who stopped in for an after-lunch coffee, and the dining room was empty at the moment. "Actually, I'm really glad I'm here. I feel amazing! It's like this experience has given me a new lust for life. I've got more focus, energy, and motivation, and it's showing. I even overheard a conversation between a couple of women who come in here all the time. They were talking about how much the pastries have improved this week, and they were wondering if Nonna herself had come back to work! How great is that?"

"Wow. If getting held hostage is that good for you, then I guess every woman should put it on their bucket list," Robyn joked. "Even your skin is glowing. I'd call it denial, otherwise."

As Alessia handed Robyn a caramel cappuccino, she remembered what Kent had said about shifters being everywhere. Was Robyn one of them? Would she have any way of knowing? She'd been friends with Robyn for a long time, but she'd never thought of either her or herself as anything but 'normal.' Alessia clamped her lips around her questions and went back to work, preparing things for the next day so her morning would be a breeze.

"I think I just needed a swift kick in the ass, you know? Something to make me realize my life is worth more than I've been giving it credit for." She smiled, determined not to let even the smallest bit of doubt creep in. It really had been a good day, better than she'd had in a long time.

"Okay. Just promise me you'll call if you need anything. I'm here for you."

"I will, thanks. Have a great night!" Alessia felt warm and pleasant as she finished closing the bakery. She wiped down a table where she'd overheard a conversation about whether or not a couple would go for fertility treatments. It was a private matter, spoken in low voices that she wasn't supposed to hear, just like she wasn't supposed to have heard the other women talking about how great the pastries were. It was just one element that made Alessia wonder, but it was hard to forget.

Boxing up a few leftover pistachio cannoli, Alessia headed to her grandparents' place for dinner. She noticed everything looked brighter and more vivid. The trees were a deeper green, the sky a more lucid blue. The cracks in the streets and the bricks in the buildings all stood out in sharp relief. Tightening her hands on the steering wheel, Alessia wished she was still at work. At least when she was running the one-woman show that was Russo's, she could get her mind off her impending change.

It also kept her mind off of Kent. It wasn't just his bite and its consequences that she wanted to forget. Damn him for doing this to her! Even if he and the other shifters were wrong in their suspicions and Alessia wouldn't experience any real change, she'd always wonder about it. She felt like a lab rat who'd been exposed to some strange new disease, and everyone was just sitting around waiting to see if she died, exploded, or turned into some mutant superhero.

Alessia pulled up in front of her grandparents' place. She smiled as she carried the pink box to the door and let herself inside. It'd been too long since she'd just slowed down and had a family dinner, and the normalcy of it was exactly what she needed.

"Alessia! My sweetheart! *Fragolina!*" Nonna came out of the kitchen with her arms open wide, dragging the scent of her famous Bolognese sauce along with her. She wrapped Alessia in a warm hug before pulling back and scowling up at her granddaughter. "Why didn't you come to see us sooner? We've been worried sick about you, you know."

"I know, Nonna. I'm sorry. I've just been busy, and I think I needed a little time to myself. Here, I brought you a few things."

Nonna was a sweet woman, but she was also brutally honest. She lifted a brow at the pastry box. "Will I be pleased?"

"I think so," Alessia said with a smile. "They're still not as good as yours, but I'm improving."

"We'll have them after we eat. Come on. Let's sit."

Alessia joined her grandparents at the dining table. She loved being there, as she'd come to think of the place as home quite some time ago. Her grandparents' house had always been the one constant in her life. Whether her parents had passed away, she'd had a fight with one of her sisters, or she'd struggled with a relationship, everything there was the same.

The conversation centered on the meal and the weather for the first few minutes, but it inevitably turned to the most recent excitement in their lives. "Alessia," her nonno said quietly as he set his fork down, "are you all right? What you went through with the Ciprianis couldn't have been easy."

She might as well get it over with. She couldn't blame them for wanting to know. Alessia sopped up a bit of the Bolognese on her plate with a chunk of bread. "It really wasn't that bad, at least in retrospect. They tried to feed me, although I refused the food. I was tied up, but the chair was comfortable, and there was a TV on. It was a lot better than what I would've imagined for a hostage situation."

Nonna leaned over and patted her arm with a crooked hand. "My dear, just because things could be worse doesn't mean they're good."

Licking her lips, Alessia nodded. "I know, but it's over now. There's no point in dwelling on it." She didn't miss the look her grandparents exchanged. "What? What is it?"

Mateo's fingers flicked idly against the tablecloth. "The Ciprianis want the pasticceria very badly. They've tried to get it from us before."

"They have?" Alessia had been blotting at her mouth with her napkin, but now she flopped it on the table. "Why didn't you say anything?"

"It was a long time ago," Isabella said. "Marco's father was in charge of their little street gang back then, and he thought we would be easy targets. He thought he could get what he wanted out of us because we were older."

"Ha! Not so easy for him with a bullet zinging past his skull!" Nonno laughed as he slapped the table. "I took care of him!"

"Only for a little while," Isabella reminded her husband. "We worry that they won't be satisfied. Marco is dead, but his family is very determined."

"He died?" Alessia mused. She scratched her arm as she contemplated that night. Kent had been fighting with his bare hands. Was he that much stronger because he was a wolf? Was it something he'd learned in the military? She had so many questions, but Kent was the last person she wanted to think about.

"That's what we understand," her grandfather replied. "You hear things in the neighborhood. Is there something wrong with your arm?"

"No, I don't think so." Alessia glanced down. The spot she'd been scratching had grown red, but she couldn't see any reason for it to itch so badly. "Maybe it's just dry skin."

"I have some lotion for that," Nonna said, putting her finger in the air as she got up from the table. "I'll be right back."

"You don't have to do that," Alessia countered.

But her grandmother was already disappearing through the doorway.

"She worries about you a lot," Mateo said quietly, leaning forward over the table. "She wouldn't admit it, because she wouldn't want the others to get upset, but you've always been her favorite."

"That's not true." Alessia smiled at the thought, but she frowned again as she curled her fingers to keep from scratching that spot. It was on the inside of her forearm, a long stripe that just felt strange. It was itching and burning, like something was crawling around on the underside of it.

"Did you get into something at work?" Nonno got up and came around the table to look. "Maybe an allergic reaction to something?"

"I don't think so. I've been working with those same ingredients for years. Ah!" Alessia stomped her foot on the floor as the itching turned to outright pain. Her skin tightened and spasmed, and she was sure it was about to light itself on fire, considering how hot it felt. She reached out with one cautious fingertip and found that it wasn't just hot on the inside, it was hot to the touch. And sensitive.

"This...I don't like this," Mateo said. He patted his pants pockets and then looked around the dining room. "Where's my phone? We should see a doctor."

Feeling sick and dizzy, Alessia slid from her chair to the floor. She clutched her arm, unable to fathom this sudden, intense pain. What had she done to it?

The answer came as a single hair shot through the surface of her skin. It was followed by a second, and then another. Alessia heard odd, strangled noises and realized they were coming from her throat as she watched the gray-brown, shaggy hairs burst forth.

Her grandfather was back at her side, his cell dangling in his hand as he looked. "Now *that* is not an allergic reaction I've seen before."

Nonna had rejoined them, the bottle of lotion in her hand, but she nearly dropped it in a bowl of tagliatelle as she bent to examine her granddaughter. "*Dio!* What's happening? What did that wolf do to you?"

Alessia swallowed and tried to get control over her lungs. It'd happened so fast, and even though she knew the answer, she still had a hard time arriving at it. She'd heard everything that'd happened in the bakery that day. When she'd baked, she'd done it by instinct as she smelled and tasted her way to more delicious pastries. She'd wanted to deny it, but the proof was now right there on her arm. "He, um, he bit me."

"What?!" Mateo exploded. "It's a good thing he's dead, or I'd kill him myself!" He slammed his fist against the table as he let out an unintelligible string of Italian.

"No, Nonno. Not Marco. Kent." Her face heated when she spoke his name. She hadn't planned on telling anyone what'd happened between herself and Kent, not even Robyn.

Her grandfather helped her back up into her chair. "I see."

Alessia ran her hand down the thick line of fur that now graced her inner arm. It was softer and much more luxurious than she would've imagined. She was just about to explain to them that Kent was a shifter when she realized what'd already been said. "Hold on. You asked what that wolf did to me."

Another look between them. "Sweetheart, we've known about shifters for a long time. They're all over this neighborhood. In fact, we're some of the very few humans who are here."

She'd heard something similar from Kent, although he'd given her so much information that she simply hadn't retained it all. There was too much to understand. "You have? Why didn't you tell me? Didn't you think I needed to know?"

Her grandmother shook her head. "No. It's a huge burden, and you have enough going on in your life. We wanted to protect you. With people like the Ciprianis around, it's easy to believe that all shifters are bad. They're really not. There are plenty of good ones, including Filomena and that Kent who saved you."

"Filomena?" Alessia thought her world had been shaken when Kent had spilled the beans, but discovering that shifters had been right under her nose her entire life was even more disturbing. "It's like the entire world is playing a prank on me."

"I'd say it's just trying to change you," Mateo said. He pointed at her arm. "Do you know what's happening with this? Is this supposed to happen?"

Alessia opened her mouth, prepared to explain what Emersyn had said about potentially turning into either a fully-fledged wolf shifter or a halfling, but she realized that wasn't what her grandfather had meant. She looked down at her furry arm, not knowing if this were part of the process or what it might mean. "I'm not sure. It sounded like it was pretty much a wait-and-see situation."

"Not doing you much good if the people seeing it don't have a clue about it," Isabella advised. "You should get a hold of that Kent. He seemed like a nice young man. He'll know what to do."

"You don't understand! I told you he's the one who bit me!" Alessia cried. She didn't want to explain exactly how that had happened, but her grandparents were understanding enough that they didn't ask.

"He can still help," Mateo said softly. "He's a shifter, and we're just a couple of old humans."

"What about Filomena?" Alessia asked desperately. "You said she's a shifter. Maybe I can talk to her."

Isabella shook her head. "You could, but Filomena had to leave town for a family wedding. Besides, she's an eagle-owl. It might be different."

Alessia let out a long sigh. She didn't want to have to deal with any of this, but it was obvious that she couldn't avoid it any longer. "I'll think about it, okay?"

"Sure. In the meantime, you should eat." Nonna made urgent gestures toward Alessia's plate.

The meat in Nonna's Ragù alla Bolognese smelled divine, and as Alessia picked up her fork, she realized she was able to sense every other ingredient in the thick sauce. *Tomato, celery, carrot, onion... basil, garlic, parsley...red wine, olive oil, cream...salt, black pepper...the little pinch of sugar Nonna always adds*. It was an intriguing experience, but it wasn't normal.

Alessia polished off her meal, knowing that her grandparents were right. She had to get a hold of Kent.

10

KENT STARED AT THE MESSAGE, DARING TO THINK IT WAS REAL. HE'D been desperately hoping for some sort of communication from her. She'd been so angry with him that night, yet when he'd seen her at her café, she'd seemed perfectly fine. It comforted him to know she wasn't writhing in pain somewhere alone and that Marco's gang hadn't returned for her, but he still wanted nothing more than to be with his mate.

Meet me at Point Fermin Park tomorrow night, she'd texted him.

I'll be there.

Kent reread the text exchange several times. He hadn't dreamed it. He wasn't just letting his fantasies get to him. This was real.

He allowed himself to imagine what that meeting might be like. Kent could easily picture Alessia in a gauzy pink dress that looked warm against her olive skin, rushing past the lighthouse and into his arms as she told him how much she needed him. She was a shifter now, and she wasn't willing to live in this world unless she could be with him.

"Fucking idiot."

"What'd you call me?"

Kent jerked his head up from his phone and found Jude standing behind him in the kitchen. "Sorry, man. Not you. I was talking to myself."

"Sounds like the conversation of a man in love," Jude remarked as he went to the coffee pot.

With a sigh, Kent looked for the right words. The Force already agreed to let him stay on a little longer, but Kent still felt as though he owed something to the rest of them. "It's hard to explain," he began.

Jude put up one hand to stop him. "Yes, but it isn't hard to *understand*. Not for the rest of us." He lowered his hand and reached for the sugar bowl. "We all get a little crazy when it comes to our mates, even me."

"Thanks." Jude was the calmest man in the group. Kent hadn't been there long, so it was no shock that he hadn't seen the bear shifter get rattled yet, but he had a feeling he never might. "That means a lot."

Jude raised his mug in acknowledgment, then took a sip and headed off through the house.

Checking his phone, Kent decided it was time to go. He wanted to allow plenty of time for traffic, because he wasn't about to let some little thing like being late keep him from seeing Alessia again.

By the time he'd shot through town and parked the car he'd borrowed from Gabe, Kent was twenty minutes early. It would give him a chance to acquaint himself with the area and think about exactly what he wanted to say.

But Alessia was already there. He sensed her before he saw her. Kent moved past the carefully groomed lawn and skirted the trees, heading straight toward her the same way he had the previous day when he'd ended up across the street from Russo's. It felt different this time, knowing she was there to meet him. He felt her inside him, speaking to his wolf, and his wolf was most certainly speaking back. Was she calling to him, or telling him to go away and never come back? He wish he knew.

He reached the end of the landscaped lawn area, where a white pergola perched to form a lookout. The place was dark, but he spotted her silhouette just on the other side of it.

"It's dangerous out here, you know," he said as he stepped around the pergola and joined her on the sandy point. Cliffs descended sharply from where they stood, and the waves crashed below.

Alessia didn't turn to look at him. She stood with her arms crossed in front of her chest, her wavy hair blowing in the sea breeze. She didn't acknowledge him at all, and at first, Kent thought she hadn't heard him. "It doesn't *feel* dangerous," she finally said. "I'm trying to decide if I like that or not."

His arms twitched with the need to reach out and pull her close, to make any hurts or doubts or worry disappear. If it were only that simple... "Why is that?"

"Because it would have felt dangerous last week. I probably wouldn't have even dreamed of doing it. I would've stayed on the other side of the little wall at the front of the pergola, just like a good girl should. But everything is different now. It feels different. It looks different. It sounds different. It even tastes different."

He inched closer. She could have shoved him off the cliffs if she'd wanted to. It would've been less painful than having her be angry with him. "Is it a bad kind of different?"

She took her time answering once again. "No, I don't think so. I'm just not used to it. But it's made everything I do, even the simple everyday things, feel so strange." She scratched the inside of her arm.

Kent frowned, concerned for her. She wasn't the happy woman he'd seen the day before. She was solemn and serious, yet he sensed that inside, she was just like the waves that threw themselves against the hard rocks below. "Are you all right? Physically, I mean?"

Alessia's shoulders heaved as she sighed. "Essentially, but I did want to ask you about something. I, ah..." She trailed off and scratched her arm again.

"What happened?" He no longer hesitated, stepping forward and grabbing her arm. She didn't fight him, allowing him to turn her arm over and inspect the other side of it. He skimmed his fingers along her smooth skin, but it felt perfectly normal.

"It's fine now," she said, pulling her arm back gently. "But last night at dinner, I was suddenly in need of a wax."

Her mention of being at dinner conjured an image of Alessia out at some fancy restaurant with another man. It made his muscles tense until they hurt. "Dinner?"

"I met with my grandparents." She shot him a look, as though she'd known what he was thinking. "Good thing it wasn't in public because I damn near panicked."

"I'm sorry. We didn't know what to expect with all this." He gestured to encompass the bite, the mix of his DNA with hers, and all the implications that went with it.

"I know. I still don't even know what that meant, but it was strange.

I realized I couldn't just stay away from you, no matter how pissed I am, because you're the only one who can help me." She shoved her hands in the back pockets of her jeans as she scowled out at the ocean.

"Of course, I'll help. Anything you need. But Alessia, there's something I have to tell you first."

She shrugged for him to continue.

Kent scratched his cheek. He'd rehearsed this about a million times, and it came out a little different every time, but he still wondered if it would be good enough. If Alessia wanted to, she could leave and never come back, and he'd never have any idea what had happened to her. He had to be cautious, but hiding things wouldn't help. "I got overwhelmed by you the other night. It wasn't just the sex, even though that was enough to make any man lose his head."

She let out a small laugh.

It encouraged him to go on. "I'd said a few things about it after I'd bitten you, but I think I should be more clear on what it means to be a mate."

Alessia kicked the sandy ground under her feet. "That sounds so primitive."

"Exactly. It is. For shifters, it's not just about how our human sides get along. It's about the way the animals inside us connect. It isn't anything logical or reasonable. Think about being able to live purely by your gut instinct, only going by what feels good. That's what it's like for a shifter to meet his mate, even if he still has human responsibilities." No, none of that sounded right. It wasn't wrong, but he'd meant for it to come out a lot better than that.

Alessia glanced at him now. Her eyes were the same color as the sea in the dim light, and they were just as wild. "So, that's why I'm suddenly feeling better with you around? God, even when I'm so angry that I've contemplated punching you square in the face, I want you to be near me."

"Alessia," he breathed, wondering if he could trust his ears. "You don't know how good it feels to hear that."

He could hear the words catch in her throat when she said, "Actually, I think I do. Kent, I can't get you off my mind. I think about you constantly; it's like you're living in my head. A friend suggested I'm different because of what I went through with Marco, but I know it's so much more than that. I'm terrified. I don't know the first thing about being a shifter, or even half of one."

Kent felt himself moving toward her, leaning, desiring, but he pulled back. She was feeling the same things he was, and he could take comfort in that, but right now, she didn't need a lover. "The first thing about being a shifter is learning how to shift."

"That sounds really hard. And painful." Alessia rubbed the spot on the inside of her arm. "If it hurts as badly as this did, then I'm not sure I want to shift at all."

He nodded. "It does hurt a bit at first. Your body has to get desensitized to moving and stretching like that. Eventually, though, it's not nearly as bad. We can practice right now if you want."

She tipped her head at him, her scent so intoxicating, he wanted to pull her to the ground and claim her all over again. "How are we going to do that?"

"I'll guide you through it, and if we're successful, we can go for a run. You'll love it. It feels so much different as a wolf."

"I can imagine." Alessia smiled. "Tell me what to do."

Kent shut his eyes and took a deep breath. His wolf was always there, always too close to the surface, but she had yet to find hers. "Think about the most inward, secret part of yourself. Imagine a wolf living inside you, because trust me, it's there. You just have to give it the chance to come out. Relax your body and breathe deeply. Let it take over." If he'd tried this a week ago, his wolf would have shown himself immediately. Kent found that by standing next to Alessia, even as he deliberately tapped into his lupine side, he could control it with ease. He opened his eyes.

Alessia had her arms relaxed at her sides. She was purely human as far as Kent could tell, and just as he was about to suggest something else, she stumbled backward. She cried out as she grabbed her stomach.

"It's all right, Alessia." Kent dove to keep her from falling, hoping he could ease some of her pain. "I'm right here, and there's no way you can mess this up. Just let it come."

She spasmed in his arms. "It hurts!"

"I know. It'll be over soon. I promise." He knew how disorienting it was to make the switch, yet what a release it was after the transition.

Alessia's teeth ground together as the two sides of her warred. Hair exploded along her arms and down her legs, but it was gone again a moment later. Her ears pointed to the night sky, but then quickly shifted back down. Kent saw her eyes change, and the moment they looked into his, he felt something click deep inside him.

"Come on, baby. It's all right. You can do it."

"I can't. I can't!" Alessia squeezed her eyes shut, and they were their typical green when she opened them again. Everything was completely human again, and she sagged in Kent's arms. A tear ran down her cheek and sank warmly into his shirt. "What does this mean?"

He lowered to the ground, holding her on his lap. He could sense the wolf inside her, but it wasn't as strong as he'd hoped. While he knew it would take time and practice for her to figure out the extent of her powers, it didn't look good. "You may very well be a halfling," he admitted, though it stabbed a knife through his heart to do so.

"So, I'll always be like this?" she sobbed. "Don't get me wrong. There are times when it feels amazing. I love being able to look at a tree and see every individual leaf. But then this...with the shifting...I just can't...It's so frustrating!"

"I know, and I'm sorry." He buried his face in her hair and listened to the waves. "There's a possibility that I could make you a true shifter if I marked you more deeply."

Silence closed around them for the longest moment.

"You mean, you'd have to bite me again?"

"Yes." The idea was one that strangely turned him on. He had felt horrible about that first nip, even though he'd only just drawn blood. To sink his teeth more deeply into the sweet flesh of her thigh was a thought that gave him pleasant chills.

"I'll think about it."

"Alessia."

As she turned to face him, Kent felt as though they were the only two people on the planet. He knew nothing but her, and he never wanted it to be any other way. "If I were to do that and completely change you, there could be no less than a permanent bond between the two of us. I'm already going crazy every second I'm without you, and I don't know if I can survive being apart from you once you make the full transition. Does that make sense?"

"Yes."

He felt relief hit him. He wasn't always the best with words, but he needed to be on the same page with her. "Whatever you decide, I'll always be here for you. To help you, to protect you, whatever you need.

I know I can't possibly be forgiven for what I've done to you, but I'll spend the rest of my life trying to make up for it."

She reached up, her fingertips stroking his face as she lifted her head.

Kent met her halfway, feeling first the softness of her lips and then the velvet heat of her tongue. Her hair was soft and warm against his arm, and her scent mixed headily with the ocean breeze. His wolf gave a huff of satisfaction as Kent felt her arms tangle with his. She pressed her body against him, telling him so much without a single word.

He ran his hand down her leg, feeling her warm thigh beneath the denim. No one had ever felt so good or so right.

11

ALESSIA STARED UP AT THE CEILING FOR A LONG MOMENT, BLINKING AND trying to remember what day it was. Everything that'd happened the night before had felt like a dream. She couldn't possibly have stood there on the edge of the world with Kent, attempting to turn herself into a wolf and sobbing into his arms when she couldn't. Everything had been cast in shades of blue, with the breeze playing in her hair. It couldn't have been real.

She reached over and found only rumpled sheets, but she smiled when she realized they were still warm. Kent had a certain heat about him that she liked. The scent of coffee drifting through the air told her he was considerate, too.

Throwing on a robe, not even caring if he saw her with bedhead, Alessia peeked out into the kitchen. She found a shirtless Kent standing at the stove, lifting a pan of perfectly cooked scrambled eggs and emptying it onto two plates next to buttered toast and crispy bacon. "You certainly know your way around a kitchen, don't you?"

He looked up with a smile. "When I need to. I hope you don't mind. It's noon and I'm starving, and I figured you'd be, too."

"Definitely." He could've poured her a bowl of Rice Krispies and she would've thought it was sweet. There was something about being around him that she was really starting to like. The logical part of her brain thought it was a little crazy that this wild man who'd shown up at

Russo's would end up rescuing her and sleeping in her bed within a span of a few days. She didn't care what the logical side of her thought, though, because the wild spirit inside her was far too happy.

After eating, they retreated back to the bedroom. "Mind if I take a shower?" Kent asked.

"Of course." The thought of his hard, wet body made her tingle, and she almost invited herself to join him, but Alessia wasn't ready to dive back into the physical side of their relationship. The night before had been a reminder that there was more between them than just sex. He'd held her most of the night, and she'd melted into his protective arms. He was incredibly tempting, but Alessia wanted to know more about their relationship than how it felt to be skin-to-skin.

When they'd each showered and dressed, Alessia turned to Kent to ask him if he had any plans for the afternoon. She'd be heading into the pasticceria—much later than usual—but they hadn't talked much about what he had going on with the Force. "Do you have any—" She turned her head toward the bedroom door and held up a finger. The tiniest muscles in her ears contracted, picking up a thud from the living room. "Did you hear that?"

Kent had just finished tying his shoe. She could see him perking up and paying attention as well. "We're not alone. Are you expecting anyone?"

She swallowed and shook her head.

"No roommates?"

"Just me."

Kent stood and reached for the bedroom door, but it burst open.

The wood shattered as it slammed back on its hinges, revealing a familiar face. Alessia gasped, certain she was seeing a ghost, but then she realized the man in the doorway was slightly shorter than Marco.

"Who the fuck are you?" Kent had his fists up and his feet poised for battle.

The man tipped his chin up as he barked a laugh. "Antonio Cipriani, a name you'll get familiar with as I slowly choke the life out of you. You killed my brother, asshole." Two other men flanked the intruder.

"Get out of here!" Alessia moved closer to Kent. Why did she have to live this nightmare twice? "You and your family have already caused enough trouble. We're done with the Ciprianis!"

"Sorry, Ms. Russo. I'm going to have that bakery when I kill you, and I'll have my revenge when I kill *him*." He nodded toward Kent.

Her heart drummed a beat so loud, it echoed in her ears. These wolves were hungry for blood, and there were three of them. Kent was good, but she wasn't about to let anything happen to him. "You will not! You'll have to go through me first!"

Alessia stepped in front of Kent. Her nerves fired rapidly with electricity, and for the first time, she felt the inner animal Kent had referred to. It was there, pacing, a little scared, a little excited. It would be there for her. She could do it this time. Alessia let out a breath.

And promptly fell to her knees as her feet morphed inside her shoes. Her shoes flew off as her shoulders fell forward. She let out an anguished breath as she fought hard to push the rest of her wolf out into the public eye. Alessia needed it. She needed the strength and determination that came with it, the qualities she'd seen in Kent that she'd wished she had herself. She knew they had to be there, but they failed to show more than a tiny patch of fur.

Laughter filled the air as Antonio and his goons charged further into the bedroom. "What the hell was that? If the only thing we have to deal with is a little extra fur in the air, then I don't think this is going to be a problem. Come on, boys."

A hand latched around Alessia's arm and swept her behind Kent. "Stay back," he growled.

She didn't have time to be hurt or angry. Antonio changed right before her eyes, throwing himself down on all fours as sharp teeth descended from his gums. Fur erupted all over his body as his bones reconfigured themselves. The most terrifying part was watching his face pull and stretch to form a muzzle, one that snapped angrily, ready to fight. His men growled behind him, their hulking bodies barely fitting through the doorway.

Kent had changed, too. Alessia gasped as she saw the dark wolf at her side. He was huge, far bigger than she'd imagined a man-turned-wolf could be. His hackles were raised, an obsidian ridge along his back. Those eyes were the same ones she'd seen when he'd defeated Marco, that silvery-blue hue that had been so strange, yet captivating.

As if someone had rung a bell to start a fight, everyone sprang into action. Alessia stepped back as she saw Antonio's pack come around to the side, heading for her. Kent jumped in front of her, but Antonio was already after him. He crouched slightly before springing in the air and landing on Kent's back, his fangs white against Kent's dark fur.

Alessia heard a scream and realized it was coming from her. She couldn't just stand idly by and watch as the man she cared for was torn into pieces, and the other two wolves wouldn't let her. They thought of her as a joke, she knew, and they would take their time. After all, Alessia couldn't hurt them if she was merely a human. Snagging the lamp from the bedside table, Alessia popped the cord out of the wall and swung it in front of her as a weapon.

The one on the left lunged as Alessia swung. The lampshade crashed into the wolf's face, sending shattered glass all over the floor as the bulb broke. Her effort turned his head, but it didn't stop the weight of him from crashing down on top of her.

Alessia stumbled back against the bed, grateful that it kept her from falling to the floor. She swung again, feeling desperate. This was going to be the end of her. She'd been warned all her life about walking alone on the street at night and being aware of her surroundings, but no one had ever warned her about shifters. If they had, would she have been more prepared? The frustration built inside her and exploded as she put all her effort into her attack.

The incredibly heavy lamp was an old thing her grandmother had given her when she'd moved out. Blood exploded from the wolf's mouth as it crashed into the side of his muzzle, sending a spray of red flying through the air. He screamed, an inhuman yelp like she'd never heard before, and reeled backward.

Alessia tightened her grip on the lamp, but she didn't get a chance to use it again. Kent had dispatched Antonio and was now in front of her, his teeth sinking into the enemy's fur. He was far bigger than the thug, and he shook his opponent off his feet with one violent yank of his head. The two of them tumbled to the ground together. Small crimson puddles soaked the carpet as they rolled over, teeth thrashing. Snarls and growls filled the room, and Alessia couldn't tell which noise came from whom. She still clung to the lamp, just in case, but Kent didn't need backup.

The other wolf had the advantage for a moment, but he had underestimated Kent's strength. The darker wolf chucked him into the dresser, sending bottles of perfume scattering in a rain of glass. The Cipriani wolf fell to the floor and Kent was on him, using his teeth to rip through his throat and end him for good.

Kent backed up toward her, his head swiveling from side to side as he looked for more enemies. The room was quiet. Two wolves lay dead on her carpet, and the other one had run.

Just as Alessia reached out to put a gentle hand on Kent, he began his shift. He slowly stood as his body changed, and Alessia watched his chest heave with the effort. She dared to lay her hand on his back, to feel the changes that were happening inside him. His bones cracked and twisted. His heartbeat stopped and started again. This massive, glorious wolf, with blood dripping from his jaws and soaking his dark fur, slowly became the man she was used to seeing.

He stood angrily in front of her with his fists curled. "I'm sorry, Alessia."

"Sorry for what? If anyone should be sorry, it's me. I couldn't do a thing." Even as scared as she was, Alessia was also angry with herself. "I was even stupid enough to give myself away as a halfling. The one that got away will probably be more than happy to spread that gossip."

"Maybe, but it's my job to protect you. You shouldn't have to lift a finger." He reached out a hand to help her up from the bed.

She swatted it away and stood on her own. "I can't expect you to always be the dashing hero." Alessia sighed. "I'm sorry. I'm just upset with myself."

Kent offered his hand once again, and when she took it this time, he led her out into the living room. "It's all right. Really. But if we're being logical about this, I'm the one who has all the training. I'm the one who's on the Force, and I should've expected them to find us here. Shifter groups—whether we're talking about clans of bears or packs of wolves—always look out for their own. It's not a surprise that Antonio would've wanted revenge."

Alessia glanced over her shoulder. "And now, someone will be looking to avenge Antonio."

"It's very possible. The safest place for us to be is at headquarters." Kent moved to the front door, which the Ciprianis had closed behind them, and locked it to avoid any surprises. "You can take a few minutes to gather your things, but we shouldn't stay here."

FML. Alessia frowned. *So much for opening the shop today.* She grabbed a bag from the rack on the inside of the closet door. With two dead wolves lying in her bedroom, there was no way she could've stayed in that apartment any longer than was necessary, and she definitely couldn't have spent the night. The Force's command post was an even worse option, though. "Couldn't I just get a hotel room? Or stay at my grandparents'?"

"I want to know you're safe, and the only way I'll actually know that is if I can see you," Kent replied. "Why? What's wrong?"

She sighed again, something that had become quite the habit for her over the last few days. There was just always so much to think about. "I don't think the rest of the Force wants me there," she admitted. "Don't get me wrong. Everyone looked concerned, and Emersyn was trying to be helpful. Still, I don't think they approve of me."

"They just don't know you yet," Kent countered. "Give them a little time, and remember that they don't let just any human come through the door."

"You dragged me in there," Alessia pointed out.

"It still counts," he insisted as one corner of his mouth lifted in a mischievous smile.

Damn it. He was sexy as hell, and he knew how to turn it up when she wanted to argue with him. "Fine, but let it go on record to show that I don't approve of this at all."

"So you approve of sleeping in there tonight with a couple of wolf-skin rugs?" Kent pointed to the bedroom door, where one tail could be seen.

Alessia shuddered, wondering how they were going to get the mess cleaned up. With a sigh, she packed a few outfits and some items from the bathroom before following Kent out the door.

The last time she'd been at headquarters was just after Kent had bitten her. She'd been scared and felt sick, so she hadn't bothered to appreciate the place. Fear still thundered through her, but she slowed down enough to take in the sleek architecture and clean, modern styling inside. Despite so many people being there on a regular basis, it looked fresh and open. Since Kent had already called ahead on the drive and explained everything to Amar, they went straight up to Kent's room.

"Alessia, I know this whole thing is kind of a mess, but I want to do everything I can to make it better. Make yourself at home. The rest of the Force members are a lot more like you than you think. Even I'm starting to learn that, and I didn't think there was anyone quite like me." He gave her a sheepish smile.

Alessia could see the hope written on his face. Kent had made a pretty big blunder, but he'd also done far more for her than anyone else she'd known. He'd risked his life for her more than once. She was thrilled to know there was someone in the world willing to do it, but

Alessia knew she needed more. "Thank you. I need to ask you about something."

He took her bag and set it on a bench before sitting on the end of the bed. "All right."

Pressing her fingers together, Alessia hoped she was making the right decision. "When I asked to meet you at Point Fermin Park, I knew I didn't know enough about being a wolf, but I was starting to like the idea. There was just the edge of something in my awareness, the tiniest advantage that felt inhuman and also completely natural, like being one with nature itself, even when I wasn't trying. It was incredible."

She moved to sit next to him. When he turned and put her hands on his waist, she knew the words that were about to leave her mouth were just as natural of a progression as what her body craved to do. "Then today, that feeling came back again. It was this intense need to fight, to protect, to go balls-to-the-wall crazy, and damn the consequences. To say I was frustrated when I couldn't shift would be the understatement of the year. I never want to feel like that again."

Desire was thick in his eyes as he lifted one hand to touch her cheek. "And?"

"I want you to mark me. Fully. Make me like you." Alessia leaned forward and found his lips. She kissed him deeply, pouring her heart and soul into it. She could tell him with words, or she could tell him with her body.

Kent understood as his hand slipped under the hem of her shirt, spreading wide as it roved slowly and possessively along her back. His tongue plunged deep inside the heat of her mouth as he pressed her close, and Alessia could feel his muscles shake as he fought to control them.

That wild passion made her feel irresistible, turning her on even more. Alessia lifted her arms to let Kent strip her of her shirt, but then she moved in to pull at his clothing until she ran her palms against his rippling stomach. Her fingers felt like magic as she released his fly and found the hardness that was yearning for her, and his resulting gasp of appreciation only encouraged her to explore more. She slithered out of his grip as she slid down to her knees in front of him to take him into her mouth.

To her surprise, Alessia felt that lupine feeling swirling inside her. It felt different than it had when she'd wanted to fight Antonio, but in a good way. It urged her, demanded that she continue, issued ultimatums if Alessia didn't satisfy this deepest need. Through this inner animal, Alessia could sense Kent's wolf and its lust for her.

Kent writhed as his hands twisted in her hair. "Alessia," he breathed, "if we go any further, I can't promise that I'll be able to control myself. And I meant what I said about marking you."

Her nipples hardened as a jolt of electricity shot through them. She remembered. She would be his mate. She would belong to him, and he to her. It was a serious bond, one she would have to honor. Alessia lifted her head. "Does that mean you want to do it?" she asked huskily.

His thighs tightened, his member throbbing in her hands. "God, yes."

She was no wolf, not in the way he was, but Alessia was no longer at the helm. Her subconscious was running the show, and it had no inhibitions. Dipping her head, Alessia scraped her teeth on the inside of Kent's muscular leg, just where he'd bitten her before.

A roar filled the room as Kent sat bolt upright. His strong hands latched on her arms and dragged her up onto the bed, ripping off her remaining clothing. Her jeans slammed against the wall as he thrust them aside and ripped her panties from her waist. Kent's hands dove underneath her to grip her fleshy backside as he sank his teeth into her thigh.

All the air left Alessia's chest. The sheets twisted in her grasp, but it was a pain she wanted, a pain she enjoyed because she understood what was going to come with it. She forced herself to breathe again just as Kent pulled back.

He sank inside her. Alessia pulled him down on top of her, wanting to be as close as possible as she moved her hips in time with his. Kent was no longer just some strange, bearded man at Russo's. He was not even the knight in shining armor who had pulled her from the grip of a dangerous man. He was her mate. Their possession of each other was complete, and she wrapped her legs around him. Everything she'd ever needed, physically and emotionally, was right there. Alessia buried her face in his shoulder.

They simply fit together, and it didn't take long for everything they'd been building between them to converge as a spring of electricity in her core. Alessia pushed against it as Kent pushed back, and she kissed his throat as a burst of white shot through her vision.

Kent found her lips, kissing her as she came. He pounded her against the soft mattress, urging newer, higher planes of existence from her. Alessia's body clenched around him, calling to him, and his roar thundered in her bloodstream as he expanded inside her.

Afterward, they lay together in a meld of flesh that Alessia didn't want to untangle. She lay her head on his shoulder and played her fingers along the hardness of his chest, listening to him breathe.

"Does it hurt?" he asked.

She tipped her head back so she could see his face. Despite the ecstasy they'd just achieved together, worry knitted his brows.

"You have a good way of making me forget things."

12

KENT WOKE UP, BUT HE DIDN'T OPEN HIS EYES. HE USED ALL HIS OTHER senses to pay attention to the room around him instead. In the furthest reaches of the house, he heard the gentle thuds of kitchen cabinets opening and closing along with the lilt of voices as the rest of the Force made breakfast and got ready for the day. Right next to him, though, Kent focused on the gentle rise and fall of Alessia's breath. She was right there in his bed with him. His muscles were already relaxed from a good night's sleep, but he sank into the mattress even more knowing she was only a few inches away. He could smell her, the scent of warm heat, flowers, and a touch of honey. All his life, he'd heard other shifters talking about the way their mates smelled as though they were experiencing the finest perfume in the world, but he'd never understood it until now.

Slowly opening his eyes, Kent saw her lying there on the pillow. Her hair, with its countless natural highlights, was an untamed tangle of a halo. She had one hand tucked underneath the pillow, and her lashes rested peacefully against her cheek. A shard of glass from the lamp had cut her the night before, leaving a thin red line just along her jaw, though he hadn't noticed it at the time. Even that tiny wound pained him. If he'd done a better job, she wouldn't have it. If Kent could save her even the smallest of injuries, then he wanted to do it.

Under the sheets, he burrowed his hand across the bed until he grasped her fingers with his.

Alessia stirred. When she opened her eyes, they met his gaze directly. "Do I look any different?"

He laughed, pushing himself up on his elbow and leaning over to kiss her. "You look gorgeous, so no."

"Trying to butter me up for round two?" She playfully slapped his biceps. "As much as I'd love to spend the day in bed with you, I suppose I should start getting ready for work."

"Do you *feel* any different?"

She rolled onto her back, assessing herself as she stared up at the ceiling. "I don't think so. I'm hungry, but I almost always wake up that way."

"Maybe you've been a wolf all this time and just didn't know it yet," he teased. Kent kissed her again. "I want you to be honest with me. Did I hurt you?"

Her eyes creased as she smiled up at him. "Don't ask me that. I don't need you beating yourself up because of something I asked you to do. I might not know you all that well yet, and I certainly want to know every detail, but you're too hard on yourself."

"Still." Kent frowned. In the heat of the moment, the natural drive that had pushed him into sinking his fangs into her exquisite flesh had stopped him from worrying about the pain. She'd asked him to mark her, and he'd been more than happy to fulfill the request. In the light of morning, though, it was harder to remember that he'd done it not only because he'd wanted to, but because she'd wanted it.

"I wonder how long it'll take for me to find out if it worked," Alessia mused. "I dreamed about it a few times last night, imagining what it would be like. I've only had a small taste, but my gut tells me that's not quite like the real thing."

"Maybe not, but we can arrange for some time to find out. We'll work on it, but you have to be patient with yourself. Don't give up if it doesn't happen the first time." He easily recalled how upset she'd been at her two failed attempts, and he didn't want her to go through that again. She probably would, simply because shifting took a lot of control, but he knew he'd do everything in his power to help.

"I won't. What are you doing?"

Kent sat up in bed and pulled the covers back. Though her bare, voluptuous curves were incredibly tempting, he focused on her thigh and gently examined the wound. Deep purple bruises had settled in like halos around the tooth marks, which had scabbed over neatly. "We can have Emersyn take a look at it and make sure there's no chance of infection or anything."

She twisted her mouth. "Um...I'll think about it. How do you think the rest of them will feel about our decision?"

Kent thought about his short conversation in the kitchen with Jude, when the bear had told him that even he went a little nuts when it came to his mate. "I think it'll be fine. It's not the normal way things are done, but nothing about this house is normal, anyway."

"Maybe not, but I'm starting to get a little more used to it."

He knew she'd had reservations about going there at all. "How so?"

"I went down to the kitchen at about three in the morning. I woke up absolutely starving and ended up meeting Melody, who was up for the same reason."

Kent smiled just thinking about Alessia bonding with another member of the household. With so many Force members and mates living in close proximity, and the in-house bookkeeper and daycare provider to boot, it was always a possibility that someone might not get along. If she had at least one friend there, then that was a start. Kent knew he could never let her go back to her apartment. "I don't know her well myself, but she seems nice."

"Yup. And she makes one hell of a Swiss omelet," Alessia agreed. "We sat down there and talked for probably half an hour. Just small talk, but it was nice."

"Do you think you could see yourself here?" Kent dared to ask. He'd allowed himself to fantasize about staying there himself, being part of the Force permanently, and having his life back on track. Having Alessia at his side would mean that he'd truly changed his life for the better. She would help give him all the things he'd never be able to find on his own, and he could only hope that he could return the favor.

"I'm not going to give you an answer on that because I'm afraid you'd hold me to it," she said with a little laugh.

"I just might." He kissed her chin, her forehead, the tip of her nose. "And I'm also going to take that as a yes."

"How can I say yes when you haven't asked me yet?" she teased.

Kent laughed, his heart aching as he realized just how long he'd gone without this. His life would've been completely different if he'd only met her a long time ago.

His inner reflections broke off when he heard someone shout down below. Kent tossed the sheets back and leaped out of bed, throwing on his clothes.

"What is it?" Alessia was getting up, too, her eyes wide as she searched for her clothes. "What's happening?"

"I'm not sure, but I don't like the sound of it. Things never get loud around here, at least not that I've seen." His adrenaline had activated, urging him to hurry. His short stint on the Force was reminiscent enough of military life that he automatically knew when it was time to get up and get moving. He could only hope he was wrong, but he had to find out. "Stay here."

"No way. I told you that I'm done hiding, Kent. I can hold my own." Alessia yanked a shirt down over her head, and her face was determined when it popped through the neck hole.

"I suppose the stubbornness of a wolf has already settled in, or perhaps you had it anyway," he remarked as he put his hand on the doorknob. He pressed a finger to his lips and opened it, creeping out into the hall with Alessia at his back.

Several shouts rose up the stairs. They were urgent, slightly alarmed, but not panicked. Kent only caught voices he recognized, which made him feel better about the situation. He waved over his shoulder for Alessia to follow him.

Gabe ran up when they reached the bottom of the stairs. "You're up! You're going to want to see this for yourself." He brought Kent and Alessia to one of the windows on the front of the house.

Kent was full of questions, but his time with the Delta Force had told him that hearing about something wasn't always the same as seeing it. How many times had he been briefed on a hostage situation, only to find that it was a lot more complicated or horrifying once he arrived on the scene?

Flicking the curtain aside, Kent spotted two men whom he instantly knew were Cipriani wolves. The pack had a look about them, and it was one he didn't like. They stood in the front yard, glaring up at the house. He wasn't surprised to see them, but he wasn't pleased, either. His sense of foreboding grew when he spotted the hostages they'd brought along. Mateo and Isabella Russo were on their knees in the grass, their hands bound behind them.

"Shit."

"Shit is right," Amar said as he came into the living room. He was dressed in a pair of athletic shorts, having probably gotten up early to work out. "Everyone who's going to stay and be a part of this needs to get into the conference room. Anyone else needs to head to the panic room with Melody and Lucas." His eyes rested directly on Alessia.

She lifted her chin. "I'd like to stay. This is my problem and my fault, after all."

"You understand that you could be risking your life?" Amar spoke only to her, not even looking at Kent for his opinion or permission.

"Yes."

"Very well, then. To the conference room."

Kent looped his arm through Alessia's elbow. "You don't have to do this, you know. We have no idea if or when your shifting ability will kick in, and even if it does, you're not used to running around on four legs. The others explained they had a safe room installed for this kind of situation to make sure they could keep Gabe's baby and any other innocents safe, should they need to fight. No one will think any less of you if you go."

Alessia shook her head. He could see the fear in her eyes, but his wolf could sense the resolve inside her. "No. I said I would do this, and I will."

"You saw what was out there, didn't you?" Kent had hoped to keep this from her, but he knew the truth.

"I did this, and I'm going to help fix it."

They sat at the large conference table, and Amar began immediately. "The Ciprianis are at our door and all around the building. The alarm picked up on them right away, but their main concern isn't with getting in the house. They want Alessia, and they plan to kill both her and her grandparents."

For the first time since he and Alessia had made love, Kent felt his wolf threatening to lose control. "We're not giving her up," he growled, "and we're not letting them harm the others, either."

"No, we're not," Amar agreed, "but we've got ourselves one hell of a problem on our hands. Raul, you said you have some information?" He looked toward their communications guru.

Raul nodded. "I do. I've been trying to pull up everything on the Ciprianis since this operation began. It's no shock that they haven't signed up to be on the shifter registry or even requested logins for The

Shift. I actually had more luck digging up shit on them while I was on guard duty at the Russos' home. These wolves are like the shifter mafia. They don't let anyone else into the pack unless they come in as mates. Since Kent has already taken out the eldest son, Marco, and the second son, Antonio, I'd hazard a guess that this little stunt is being headed up by Carmelo Cipriani." He pressed a button and pulled up an image on the flatscreen. "Carmelo isn't quite as careful as his other family members, apparently. He's already been in trouble with the human government for robbery and assault, among other things."

"A man who's third in line to be the head of the family is going to do something desperate to prove his place now that he's got a shot," Jude observed.

"I'd say he already is, considering he's holding two senior citizens hostage," Reid remarked. "This seems like a little more trouble than is necessary over a bakery."

"You know how territorial packs can get," Raul reminded him. "It's not about the value of the real estate or even what they want to do with it once they have it. It's all about control, and the Ciprianis want it."

Amar nodded and looked at Kent. "This was your mission to begin with. I'll give you the first chance at finishing it if you'd like."

"There's nothing I'd like better." The Ciprianis had already threatened his mate twice. Now they were threatening her family as well as the place he called home. Even the other Force members, who could hold their own, were under the threat of the Ciprianis, and Kent wasn't about to stand for that. "We need to make sure we use everyone's best abilities."

Amar looked interested. "And how do you propose we do that?"

"You're a dragon. You have wings, which gives you an advantage the rest of us don't have. You can see further, act faster, and attack from further away. You head up to the roof and use it as your base. You can dive down and attack or help wherever it's needed. You won't be much good in the house with your size. No offense."

"None taken at all," Amar assured him.

"Do we have any pairs that are particularly adept at working together?" Kent asked, feeling as though he was right back on the Delta Force again. He'd learned to exploit the best aspects of every soldier, no matter what it might be. Even a man who was terrified to be in battle had something to offer.

"Reid and I," Jude volunteered. "We're brothers, after all."

"Emersyn and I are more than happy to team up," Gabe said, speaking of his mate.

Kent nodded. The two brothers were also both bears, which meant they would be a bit intimidating for the wolves at the door. The bear and panther duo of Gabe and Emersyn would also be one hell of a threat. "Great. You said we've got Ciprianis surrounding us on all sides?"

Raul nodded and pushed a button, changing the image on the screen. "Here's a drone shot."

Kent glanced up at the TV, but it was just as he'd suspected. They were surrounded, but there weren't that many of them. "If the Ciprianis know anything about us, then they have a good idea as to our numbers. If they're a fairly small pack, then what we see here may very well be every bit of manpower they have. Still, we need to be prepared for a secondary attack. Amar, you'll be our main lookout for that. I want Jude and Reid at the back of the house. Gabe and Emersyn, you're on the west side. We don't have a door on the east side of the house, and I want everyone to have a place to retreat. Raul, you'll come to the front with Alessia and me."

"If we're dealing with wolves, then shouldn't we throw someone at them they don't expect?" Reid questioned.

Kent shook his head. "I think the Ciprianis are reckless, but they don't completely ignore the facts. They know we're a motley crew, and it'll throw them off even more if three wolves march out to meet them. Besides, I don't want them to feel intimidated and do anything stupid to the Russos when they're greeted with something unfamiliar."

"How do we get my grandparents safely away from them?" Alessia asked. Her knuckles had gone white where she gripped the edge of the table.

Kent gritted his teeth. It wasn't going to be easy. There was a good chance they wouldn't be successful at all, depending on the patience of the Cipriani pack. "I'll start negotiations with them. Raul, since you'll be with me, I'm depending on you to get the signal to the others when it's time to attack."

Amar clapped his hands. "Right. Let's go!"

The Force shot up from the table, and Amar thundered up the stairs. Gabe and Emersyn moved out toward the garage. The doctor already resembled a panther by the time she left the main part of the house. Jude and Reid exchanged a meaningful look of brotherhood before they headed to the back.

"You ready for this?" Kent asked. He was used to battle. At one point, his life had been nothing *but* battle. Alessia, however, was used to running a pasticceria, paying bills, and wondering what her weekend plans were. Kent had never knocked the life of a civilian, but he knew it just wasn't the same.

"Let's do this." Her jaw was set and she had a fire in those emerald eyes.

When Kent unlocked the door, he had Alessia on his right and Raul's wolf on his left. His heart lurched once again at seeing the poor Russos, but he tried to keep his eyes off them. They were the goal, but the Ciprianis hadn't brought them there with the intention of giving them up.

"So, you're the one." Carmelo was a scarred man, his face pock-marked and slightly twisted. His lower lip stuck out slightly as he sneered at Kent. "You whacked both of my cousins."

"And you've come here to thank me?" Kent teased.

"Wiseguy." Carmelo took a step forward, leaving two of his men standing further behind him with the Russos. "I should, perhaps. I wouldn't have had a chance at leading this pack if Marco and Antonio were still around, and I know I can do a better job than either one of them. They were too arrogant, believing they could lead us simply because of their heritage."

"And you?" Kent asked. "What do you want?"

Carmelo grinned, an ugly picture. "You can't use your words to win this time. I'm not here to negotiate or quibble. Give the woman to us now, and we'll leave you alone. If not, you and all your little friends will go up in flames."

Kent felt his wolf flaring up inside him. He pushed it back down, at least for the time being. "You know I can't do that. I'm sure there's some sort of deal we can work out here. You don't want the blood of a couple of innocent senior citizens on your hands."

"Like that fucking matters to me." At a nod from Carmelo, one of the goons near the Russos shoved his knee into Mateo's back. The old man toppled forward, barely catching himself on his bound hands before he hit the ground.

The deep growl Kent heard didn't come from his own throat. He turned just in time to see a wolf leap from the ground at his side, the pale gold of her fur mixed with the slightest mottling of gray. Her white fangs glistened in the morning sun as she leaped over the Russos and went straight for the throat of the man who'd kneed her grandfather.

Kent shifted, giving himself over to his wolf. It was angry and bloodthirsty, frustrated at being held back so much. He hadn't planned to start the battle yet. He'd wanted a chance to get the Russos to safety before claws started flying, but he also understood. Alessia had seen her loved ones in trouble. She could fully shift now, and she might have had no choice but to take on her wolf form as her anger boiled.

Dropping to all fours and knowing that Raul had already given the word to the rest of the Force through their telepathic link, Kent shot forward toward Carmelo. He was in mid-shift, his wolf form covering him in pale, silvery hair. Kent's jaws clamped onto the enemy, driven further into the skin by the force of his inertia. Carmelo brought his shoulder forward, knocking Kent back. It'd been a quick move and a smart one, making Kent stumble slightly to the side, but the former soldier recovered quickly. He heard Alessia behind him, fighting. He needed to get to her. He couldn't leave his back open in order to do it, though.

Carmelo was big, but he wasn't a trained fighter. He stood with his front paws splayed, prepared for the next attack instead of taking it for himself. Kent dodged to the other wolf's right and then the left, faking him out and making Carmelo turn his head to the side, leaving his throat exposed. Kent went for it and felt the satisfying crunch of gristle as he bit down hard and tore back. Blood stained the silver fur, dripping to the ground and shining like rubies in the sunlight.

Carmelo staggered in the grass, determined to get back up and launch another assault. He lurched forward, his teeth showing, but he'd already lost too much blood with the chunk Kent had torn out. Carmelo fell, never to get back up again.

Kent turned to Alessia. Raul had leaped in to help her, taking down the other goon, but not before her back had become streaked with blood. Kent could hardly distinguish her wounds from the red he saw as he discovered his mate was injured. A wolf hidden in the bushes chose that moment to emerge and instantly regretted it as Kent took him down with one quick shake of the neck.

A massive shadow blotted out the light as Amar landed on the front lawn in full dragon form. His black wings absorbed all the sunlight and turned it into fire as he joined Kent and took out several more Cipriani wolves who'd come to join the fray. The air smelled of singed fur as he blasted them with his fire.

Kent needed more information as to what was happening around the rest of the house, but he didn't have the link with the rest of the Force. He might, however, have one with Alessia. His wolf was strong and it reached out for her as he dove low to take out the feet of another attacker. *Are you all right?*

Kent? Her voice sounded strange, and he knew she wasn't used to being able to speak from inside her head. *Yes. I'm tired, but I'm all right.*

I'll help you get back into the house as soon as I can. He crunched and twisted with his teeth, tasting blood and dirt and fur.

Don't worry about me. I'm getting my grandparents to safety.

When he had a moment to risk looking over his shoulder, Kent saw the beautiful gold wolf gently taking Isabella Russo by her bound hands, working her way to the house. Relief hit him. She wasn't a fighter like he was, and he didn't expect her to be. But she'd held her own and gotten what she wanted. *Don't shift back for a while. You'll heal faster in this form.*

A blast of fire from Amar blocked Kent's view of Alessia, but he had to believe she was all right. Wolves streamed in from the bushes, pouring around them. The ground thundered as two bears came charging around the side of the house, their roars echoing against the side of the building. Kent gave momentary concern for guarding the back side of the property, but he also knew Jude and Kent were well-trained. They wouldn't have left their post unless they felt a need.

Kent looked up and saw what he hadn't been privy to. Another charge of wolves came flooding in through the front gate. Amar had probably seen them and called for backup. Kent gladly charged into the fray. He kept Alessia on his mind as he ripped and pulled and dragged and snarled, his chest completely soaked in red as he fought to get back to the spot where he'd last seen her. Everywhere he looked, he only saw the enemy. *Alessia?*

It took long enough for her to respond that Kent had time to dodge through Amar's legs and tumble to the ground with a large black wolf who'd been about to go after the dragon from the back.

I'm here. I'm okay.

It wasn't enough for him, not really. Kent fought in a blind rage, letting his body do what it did best as he focused on the bond he felt inside himself. He'd turned Alessia into what she was now, but the way he felt was simply an exponential version of what he'd already felt when he'd first seen her. They belonged together, whether they were fighting or making love. He slammed a wolf down into the grass and slashed his throat from one side to the other, proving to himself as much as to anyone else who cared to challenge him that he would do everything and anything to protect his mate.

When he stood, panting, Kent realized there were no enemies left to battle. Dead wolves lay scattered all over the lawn, some of them burned to a crisp and others covered in blood. His comrades were shifting back to their human forms, and Amar clapped a hand onto his shoulder.

"I'd say we did it," the Alpha said proudly, "or rather *you* did. It was a great plan, one worthy of a Force member. The Cipriani pack has been wiped out and will no longer be a threat."

"I didn't anticipate the second wave of them coming right up to the front," Kent admitted. "I thought they'd be a little more cunning than that."

Amar leveled a look at him. "Don't lambaste the enemy for being stupid, especially if it works out in our favor. Now go find your mate, because I know that's the only thing you're really thinking about."

He wasn't wrong, and Kent soon found Alessia and her family at the front of the house.

"Alessia?" Isabella questioned as she sat on the front step and stared at the golden wolf at her side. "That's you, isn't it? Oh, Mateo! Help me get these things off!"

Kent stepped in, flicking his pocket knife out and slicing the bonds neatly. "It's her," he confirmed, wondering how he would explain it all to them. They knew about shifters, but finding out their granddaughter had been turned into one sounded like an uncomfortable conversation.

With her hands freed, Isabella buried them into the scruff of Alessia's neck. "*Que bella.*"

Mateo joined his wife, a tear spilling over his cheek as he touched Alessia's ears and nose. "Absolutely beautiful; I couldn't agree more. Just look at you! So strong and fierce, just like we always knew you were."

Kent smiled. Maybe this wouldn't be nearly as hard as he thought.

13

ALESSIA PACED. SHE'D BROUGHT A THERMOS OF HOT TEA LACED WITH honey and lemon juice. It'd always been one of her favorite hot drinks as the weather got a bit cooler, and the chilly night seemed like the perfect time for it as she and the other women waited. Her wounds had healed, and she felt more alive than ever now that a wolf was living inside of her, but she still worried for Kent.

"Come sit by the fire and enjoy yourself," Penny said, gesturing at the seat next to her. She was Raul's mate, and Alessia was quickly learning just how kind she and the others were.

"I'm trying. It's just hard to be away from Kent for even a moment." She sat on a log. The Force had all agreed to initiate Kent without waiting for the rest of his probationary month to end. The magical ceremony involved had been explained to her, and she knew it would give him the telepathic link with the rest of the members. This would mean an entirely new life for him. Kent had sat with her and told her every detail about his past, and she couldn't imagine him starting the next stage of his life in any better way than officially joining the Force. Still, she knew he was hard on himself, and she hoped everything went well.

"It's like that at first," Annie admitted. "Jude and I could hardly stand not to be touching each other. It's a nice little honeymoon period, and a part of you will always be reaching out for him, but you'll both get used to it in time."

"How is your bakery doing?" Katalin asked. Kent had explained that Amar's mate was a vampire, and she certainly looked the part with her dark hair, pale skin, and red lips. There was even a bit of an accent that hinted at her Hungarian background, but Katalin now survived off of custom-formulated protein drinks, not blood.

"Honestly, it's better than ever," Alessia admitted. "My new senses do a lot to help me when I'm baking, and I've just got so much energy. It's like it spills over into the customers, and I have more and more loyal patrons who come in every day. Even my grandmother has decided she retired too early, and she comes in a couple of days a week." There were some days when Alessia thought her grandmother just wanted to keep an eye on her, concerned now that she was a shifter, but Nonna truly enjoyed getting her hands back into the dough again. Alessia and Kent had both talked with the Russos for a long time about her new status as a shifter, and they'd been nothing but accepting.

Mali, Reid's mate, blew the flames off her marshmallow. "I think they're coming."

Amar emerged from the woods with Jude, Reid, Emersyn, and Raul in tow. Gabe and Kent brought up the back, their heads bent together as they talked. They all took their places around the fire and continued roasting hot dogs and marshmallows as though this were nothing more than a camp-out among friends, but Alessia was relieved when Kent split off from Gabe and joined her at the outer reaches of the fire.

"How did it go?" she asked, taking both his hands in hers and looking up into his eyes. She could tell that he'd very recently been a wolf, the scent of it still thick and pleasant on his skin. "Do you need something to eat?"

"It was great." He ran his hand down her arm. "I'm not hungry, though. I just want a chance to run freely through the woods with my mate at my side, if she's willing."

"Absolutely." Alessia turned toward the fire, seeing that everyone else was occupied and happy. "I don't think we'll be missed."

Kent tightened his grip on her hand and pulled her toward the trail. The trees blotted out the natural starlight, but Alessia could see just fine as she followed him, her feet moving more quickly as they increased to a trot and then a run. She felt the crisp burn of air in her lungs as she let her human form go, flying forward on newly formed legs and trusting her wolf paws to catch her. She took in every sound and taste and smell as though it were something brand new, still so fascinated by this aspect of her life.

I love this! She ran shoulder-to-shoulder next to Kent, her feet pounding the dirt and her tail streaming out behind her. Could life possibly get any better than seeing her strong wolf next to her, knowing she had a successful business and a family who loved her? She was a wolf now, but she was still Alessia. In many ways, she felt as though she was finally the person she was meant to be.

The two of them darted up a hill and jumped over a log, leaving the trail behind. They dodged one way and then another around bushes and underbrush, sending the local animals skittering off behind the trees. She felt the wind rush around her ears and through her coat, and she loved the way her muscles bunched and released as she ran. This was ecstasy.

Stopping on a ridgetop, Kent poised himself to overlook the valley below and the stars above. He let go of his wolf, straightening his back and shaking out his arms. Alessia followed suit, thrilled that they had the choice to run through the woods as animals, but could still sit together out there in the middle of nowhere as people.

"Are you sure you're all right?" she asked as she came to stand next to him. "I'm still getting used to being inside your head, but I could swear you felt a little distant."

"I've just been thinking a lot." He wrapped his arm around her waist, warm against the cool night.

"About?"

"About how nice it is to be part of a family again." He pulled her close as he looked up at the stars. "It's funny, my wolf is what should've brought me closer to other shifters. I walked away from everything I'd ever known when I was younger, thinking the Army would fix it. That obviously worked out the complete opposite of how I thought it would. But now, being part of the Force and having you at my side, it's like everything is right. It's all the way it was supposed to be. I just had to wait long enough, and I wasn't exactly patient."

Alessia laughed and snuggled closer, putting her arms around him.

"I know exactly what you mean. I think I would've been a lot happier with my life up until now if I would've known what was going to happen."

"And your grandparents? Are they really okay with this new side of you?"

"I told you they were."

He nodded. "Yeah, but I still worry. It has to be a lot to get used to. I guess it was a little easier for them since they already knew about shifters. Regardless, it has to be quite a shock to see their baby as a big, proud she-wolf."

Alessia slapped his chest playfully. "You keep talking like that and you'll make me think you like me or something."

"Or something." Kent pulled her close and pressed his mouth to hers.

Alessia kissed him back, smiling around their liplock when she felt him pulling her down to the ground. They'd made love countless times since the battle, and she never wanted it to end. Being with him was like finding the other half of her soul. She hadn't realized it'd been missing for the longest time, but now that she knew, she couldn't imagine ever being without him again. They were as permanent as the stars in the sky and the ground beneath their feet, destined to be together.

In moments like this, when he held her in his arms and they explored each other's bodies, Alessia knew distinctly what it was like to be both a human and a shifter. She felt her human side and his as she looked into his eyes, or when she felt his breath on her neck as he descended his kisses down her body.

But the wolves were always there. They did a dance of their own, trapped as they were inside their human counterparts. Alessia's wolf was so much closer to the surface than when she'd first discovered it, and she was pleased to know how easily it reached out to Kent's. They connected in the way of the animals, knowing each other without even speaking, needing each other, yet taking solace in solitude. Kent had made this part of her, and Alessia treasured it all the more because of it.

As she lay in the arms of her mate, his skin pressed against hers and the stars overhead, Alessia adored how they could be one with the wilderness. They weren't afraid of anything there, knowing they were the most dangerous creatures in the woods.

His chest rumbled against her cheek as he spoke. "I'd searched for so long, I'd started to believe I would never find you. It may have taken forty years, but you were so worth the wait. God, I love you."

"I love you, too." She cuddled in closer. "All of you."

———

SANTA SOLDIER BEAR

SPECIAL OPS SHIFTERS: L.A. FORCE

1

"I'm a little nervous about showing up like this." Roman glanced away from the busy rush-hour traffic and down at the Santa suit he'd put on at Amar's behest. He'd always said he'd do anything for a fellow soldier, but this was a little much. The crimson velvet outfit was rimmed in brilliant white fur that was far too warm for southern California.

"Don't worry about it," Amar said in his headset, the voice familiar from his days in the service. "We decided to have this party to really kick off the Christmas season, and I promised the rest of the Force that there would be a surprise. It'll be a blast."

"Dude, easy for you to say. You're not dressed in a getup like this," Roman growled. He followed the GPS's directions, turning onto a road lined with palm trees and impressive homes. It was a far cry from what he'd gotten used to between his time in the Army and the time he'd spent in Wyoming. "When you said you wanted me to come down to spend Christmas with you, I didn't realize you'd be suckering me into playing Santa."

"Come on, don't be such a stick in the mud. I didn't want you to be alone for the holidays after everything that went down this year."

Roman paused, knowing what he was about to say, but he let it go.

"You'll have fun," Amar promised. "Are you almost here?"

"Yeah, I think so. This is one hell of a place." He pulled his rented truck to a stop in front of an enormous modern home. Covered porches stuck out at all angles, taking advantage of the stunning view. From the maps Roman had looked at earlier, he knew it butted up close to some of the nature preserves in the area, making it a great spot for shifters. The house was far different from the ranches and farmhouses he was used to seeing back in Wyoming, where he'd moved six months ago. It didn't look much like Christmas, either, despite the giant plastic candy canes sticking out of the flowerbed along the walkway, but he was happy to spend time with Amar. It would be good to see him and to meet this Special Ops Shifter Force that he'd talked so much about.

"I see you out there. Just wait a few minutes, then come straight through the front door. I'll make sure it's unlocked."

"If you say so. I hope this goes well, but you owe me either way." The last thing Roman wanted was to be the center of attention, but there was no way to avoid it. Everyone would be looking at him, whether he was just Amar's friend or Santa.

"Big time. Now get your ass in here." There was a click as Amar hung up.

With a sigh, Roman hopped out of his truck. The rental agency had looked at him strangely when he'd turned down the sedans and coupes they'd offered. Even though he didn't have hay or fencing materials to haul around right now, Roman was used to something a little more functional. He opened the back door and pulled out the velvet bag full of packages, praying no one drove by. Even though he didn't know anyone in L.A., he'd still rather be seen by as few people as possible in this getup. Tugging on the hat that matched the outfit, he headed for the front door and ambled in as Amar had asked.

Roman got past the festive wreath on the front door, covered in jingle bells that greeted him merrily, and headed straight into the massive open floorplan. Someone had gone all out with the decorations. Garland twined down the banister, and white lights twinkled from every horizontal surface. A colossal Christmas tree dripping with ornaments reached up to the highest point on the ceiling, and a pile of perfectly wrapped presents had already been placed under it. The stockings along the mantel looked as though they'd been hung with plenty of care, showing their owners' names printed in silver glitter. The scent of cinnamon and pine permeated the air, and old holiday music filtered through the room.

Heads turned to stare, and Roman remembered who he was supposed to be. He might as well make the most of this. "Ho ho ho! I hear there are some good boys and girls here tonight!"

"Santa?" A little face peeked out from behind the leg of a dark-haired woman, his blue eyes full of wonder, hope, and a little fear.

The boy's mother looked around the room. Getting a wink from Amar, she took her son's hand and brought him over. "Yes, sweetie. It's Santa."

Roman bent down to look at the boy. He tipped his head from one side to the other, pretending to think. "You're Lucas, aren't you?"

"My name!" Lucas squealed. "That's me!"

As ridiculous as he'd felt in the red, fur-lined outfit and big boots, seeing the delight on Lucas's face made it all worth it. His chest heated with a warmth that had nothing to do with the costume. "I hear you've been a very good boy this year. You know, Lucas, I'm pretty sure I have a present for you in this bag."

The boy didn't waste time, darting over to an empty wingback chair near the fireplace and patting the seat. "Sit, Santa! Sit!"

"*Please* have a seat," his mother corrected gently.

Roman did as the boy asked, sitting and digging through the bag until he found a gift labeled for Lucas. "My elves and I have been keeping a close eye on you, so I know you deserve this, buddy. Here you go!"

Lucas grabbed the box and immediately fell to the floor as he ripped off the paper. His face illuminated with glee as he tore a strip from the end of the package. His tiny fingers went searching for further purchase to continue the unveiling of his gift.

Everyone was staring, but Roman felt a specific set of eyes on him more than the rest. He dragged his gaze through the room, trying to be casual as he looked. His chest tightened as he spotted a gorgeous woman near a buffet table. Her curly red hair had been tamed into a high bun, a sprig of holly stuck festively in the side, but Roman could tell it was wild and unruly when she let it down. Her tortoiseshell glasses made her look prim, but the pale brown eyes behind them were intriguing. As beautiful as her face was, Roman couldn't help letting his eyes drift down to take in the gentle curves of her slim body. His polar bear fluxed and swelled inside him, and if he'd let it rule, he would've been at her side in a flash.

"I believe Santa brought gifts for everyone else, too," Amar said, dragging Roman's attention back to the real reason he was there. He gestured toward the overflowing bag of gifts.

"Of course!" Roman tore his gaze away from the redhead and began pulling more presents out of the bag, glad to focus on something besides that temptress across the room. He lifted a small box wrapped in green paper and tied with a gold bow. "Emersyn?"

The boy's mother took the gift, giving Amar a smile. "That's very kind of you, Santa."

"Merry Christmas." Roman's cheeks burned under the ridiculous white beard. He'd spent his entire adult life in the service, and while he'd pulled plenty of crazy stunts, none of them had made him feel like the spotlight was on him as much as this. Had Amar told anyone else that he'd set this whole thing up? Were they all wondering who this mysterious stranger was? It'd be easier if he could've just come in, said hi, had some eggnog, and blended into a corner somewhere. He was just there to visit, after all, not to play the jolly old elf from the North Pole.

Purposely, Roman retrieved a specific package from the bag. "This one is for Amar."

He came through the crowd, one hand in his pocket and a big smile on his face. "It's good to see you, Santa."

Roman shook the package in his hand, holding onto it tightly. "I'm not sure you actually made the good list this year, little boy," he warned.

"Sit!" Lucas was only halfway through tearing the colorful paper off his toy train, but he stood and eagerly patted Roman on the knee. "Sit, Uncle Amar!"

Emersyn pressed a hand to her lips, not quite covering her smile. "I think he wants you to sit on Santa's lap and tell him you've been good. He's already been to the mall once, and it's made quite the impression on him."

Lucas nodded eagerly and patted Roman's knee once again.

Roman knew how serious Amar was. He was never the type to head out on a weekend of leave and party until it was time to report for PT on Monday morning. He was the only one who ever came back sober, as far as Roman could remember. He was a stodgy old dragon, and if he was going to make Roman act like a fool in front of these strangers, then he'd have to do the same. He patted his knee, right next to where Lucas's warm little hand still rested. "Come on, Amar.

Perhaps you've done some good that my elves aren't aware of. Why don't you tell me about it? Santa is always ready to listen."

To the rousing cheers of the rest of the party, Amar sat. "I'm going to get you for this."

"You already did," Roman reminded him.

Amar leaned in close, concern wrinkling his brow. "Have you talked to Elizabeth at all?"

Roman let out a low growl, just quiet enough that no one besides Amar could hear it. He was already embarrassed enough. His relationship with Elizabeth hadn't been all that long ago, but it wasn't something he wanted to talk about. If he had it his way, he'd never speak about that time in his life again.

Amar raised a brow. "Point taken."

A blonde woman came through the crowd with her camera held out for pictures. "Smile, Amar! This one's getting framed and put on the wall."

Amar smiled broadly and put his arm around Roman's shoulders for the first shot. In another, Roman shook his gloved finger while Amar pouted. Though he'd felt strange about doing this little Santa gig, Roman quickly forgot how ridiculous he felt and started enjoying himself. It was a little easier to have all eyes on him when he was disguised with a hat and beard.

"Okay, okay," Amar finally said, getting up and gesturing toward the big bag. "I think it's someone else's turn. Katalin, my love, Santa told me he has something for you."

"Is that so?" A striking woman appeared at his side, smiling up at her mate. Her dark hair and eyes were a steep contrast to her porcelain skin and ruby lips. Amar had explained to Roman that his mate was a vampire, but seeing her in the flesh was entirely different than hearing about her. Katalin didn't look like a blood-sucking creature of the night in the slightest.

Roman fished through the bag, finding a slender box wrapped in gold paper. He handed it over, and though the gift said it was from Santa, Katalin only had eyes for Amar as she removed the glittering diamond tennis bracelet.

"I guess this means I've been good this year, too," she commented with a little smile as Amar fastened the bauble around her wrist.

Amar pressed a kiss to the back of her hand. "Very."

Roman turned away from the scene that somehow reminded him

of Gomez and Morticia. He pulled out a gift for someone named Gabe, who'd been helping Lucas open his toy train. The man took his present, but he only posed next to Santa for a quick photo before he returned to his son. When Raul and Penny stepped up, Roman could sense how close their mated bond was. He shoved down the bubble of raw envy in his gut and smiled while they stood on either side of him for their photo. Next came Jude. Roman never thought he'd meet someone even more solemn than Amar, but Jude chose not to do a photo at all—even when his mate, Annie, tried to pressure him into it. Reid practically launched himself into Roman's lap and pulled Mali along with him, the two of them squealing and laughing like kids as they made faces for the camera. Next came Kent and Alessia, who held hands even while accepting their presents.

As Roman passed out the gifts and became an entertainment source for the adults more than the child in the room, he felt far more in the Christmas spirit than he'd expected to be. He'd doubted his decision to come to L.A. for the holidays more than once, but at that moment, it felt right. He had no doubt that the group Amar had adopted himself into was a good one. They were all sorts of shifters, yet it was clear they had a close sense of family. Roman felt a small pang of jealousy as he pulled the last gift from the bag and read the tag. "This one is for Melody."

His world stopped as that gorgeous redhead glided across the room. Her cheeks turned pink as she accepted the package. "Thank you," she said as her eyes lifted to meet Roman's.

The Christmas tree could've caught on fire at that moment and Roman wouldn't have noticed. He felt his inner polar bear stirring, restless, and hungry. It surged toward her, sending adrenaline blasting through his veins. She'd been intriguing from across the room, but as she stood mere inches away, she was the most magnificent creature he'd ever encountered. Roman could sense her very soul, smooth and cool, yet warm and cozy, like a fire on a midwinter evening. He opened his mouth, feeling as though he was supposed to say something, but apparently, he'd forgotten the English language.

"Sit on his lap and we'll get a picture!" someone called.

"Oh, um..." Melody hesitated, looking from Roman to her friend and back again. "We really don't have to do that."

"Come on!" another voice urged.

"I'm sure Santa wouldn't mind," Amar said with another wink.

Damn him. If he had any idea what had been going on in Roman's mind, he wouldn't have said that. Actually, he would've. The dragon could be mischievous like that, and Roman wouldn't put it past him to push his friend into something he thought was good for him. He didn't want to make Melody any more uncomfortable than she was, though. "It's entirely up to you."

"Sit, Mel'dy!" Lucas was at Roman's side once again, quite the little coordinator for being the youngest in the room.

Melody glanced at the boy, and her shoulders visibly sagged as her heart melted and she gave in. "All right, but just for a second."

Roman put out his arm as she bent down and perched on his knee, a smile pasted onto her face. "I'm so sorry," she whispered through her teeth.

"It's quite all right." God, she had no idea just how all right it was! Roman had to wonder why he'd never thought about dressing up as Santa for a Christmas party before if this was the way to get hot chicks to sit on his lap. He could feel the strength of her muscles and the softness of her curves as she braced herself against him, looking this way and that for everyone who wanted to snap a photo. Roman didn't know her at all, but it was clear that the crowd was having just as much fun with Melody as they had with Amar.

"Smile! No, like you mean it!" Penny called out.

"Aww, you blinked!" This came from Annie, who frowned at her phone. "Quick! Let's try again."

"Scoot in closer! Let's get one of those funny, cuddly shots," Alessia said, gesturing with her hand. "Kind of a 'Santa, Baby' vibe."

"I'm sorry," Melody whispered as she scooched further onto his lap. Her bottom inched up closer, moving from his knee to his hip.

"Not a problem," Roman said through his teeth. But it was. All the air had squeezed out of his lungs, leaving him in a vacuum. His polar bear was going wild inside him, inciting his human body into a riotous state. He was hardly in control at all, and there was a little less room in his costume now that his body started responding to the sexy woman sitting on his lap. If the situation had been different, if they hadn't had an entire room full of people staring at them, he would've stripped her bare and devoured her right then. The thought only made his pulse race faster, and he felt like a teenager trying to figure out how to get up from his desk in the middle of class without everyone noticing what he was carrying around in his pants.

Several more photos were snapped. His muscles were stiff and achy as he fought to control his body, but he thought he was in the clear as some of the eagerness died down. This was the last gift to be handed out, and soon, the party would be directed toward some other activity. Roman didn't know what that would be, and he didn't care—as long as he could get out of there with some of his dignity intact.

Then Emersyn shook her head. "I'm not getting the right angle. Can you turn to the side a bit?"

Melody did as she was asked, pressing her behind right up against his rock-solid erection. She stiffened, her back straightening quickly.

Damn it. There was no getting away from it now and no taking it back. She knew, and she didn't seem too happy about it. Roman waited just long enough for someone to take the picture, knowing that too quick of a reaction would only make things worse.

"You know what, I think Santa's done for the night." Roman scooped Melody up off his lap. Even for that brief second, she felt perfect in his arms. He had to let that thought go as he grabbed the empty velvet gift bag and held it strategically in front of his tent. He waved erratically as he headed for the front door. "Merry Christmas to all, and to all a good night!"

He barreled toward the door, feeling heat rising in waves off his skin. Melody had noticed, but had anyone else? Would she tell them? He didn't want to know. Escaping out the front, Roman raced over to his truck, wondering why he'd ever agreed to come to L.A. for a visit in the first place—and how he was ever going to go back inside that party and face Melody again.

MELODY STOOD IN FRONT OF THE LONG MIRROR IN HER ROOM, PULLING the sprig of holly from her hair and unwinding her bun. The tiny piece of greenery had been something she'd intended to stick in a wreath as she worked on the Christmas decorations at Force headquarters, but it worked so well as a hairpiece, she couldn't resist.

She'd already changed into flannel pajama bottoms with reindeer prancing all over them and a snug cotton t-shirt, and she sighed happily as she set the holly on the dresser. "I just love Christmas. I love that warm, fuzzy feeling it gives me inside."

"Even when you're frantically trying to pick out gifts for everyone?" Emersyn asked from the bed, peering over the screen of her laptop. Her hair had been carefully curled for the party, but she'd swept it back into a braid for the evening.

"It's not that bad." Melody grabbed her tablet and flopped onto the bed next to her, kicking her feet up into the air. "After all, there's still plenty of time for online shopping if you really don't want to get out."

"It's not that I don't want to," Emersyn corrected. "In fact, nothing sounds better than just taking a long day visit every mall and store in the city and fill the car up with gifts. I wouldn't mind taking in all the sights and decorations, too, but I just don't have the time. My work at the clinic gets absolutely crazy around the holidays. I don't even know if I'll have much time for Force missions over these next two months."

"That bad, huh?" Emersyn was actually Dr. Emersyn Cruz, and in addition to the work she did with the Force, she ran a clinic in one of the lower-income neighborhoods. She was very passionate about her work, and Melody knew she often stayed there late at night as she helped those who were the worst off. It was because of her work that Melody had begun watching Emersyn's son Lucas, back before either of them had ever even heard of the Special Ops Shifter Force.

"Yeah, but it's like this every year. And every year, we get a bad outbreak of the flu or something else along those lines. I just don't like seeing anyone in pain, you know?"

"I know." Emersyn had one of the biggest, most giving hearts of anyone Melody knew, and it was just one of the many reasons Melody liked her so much. "Oh, check this out. Lucas is really into trains right now. Do you think he'd like this?" Melody turned her tablet around to show the adorable set of train pajamas she'd just found.

Emersyn shook her head, but she was smiling. "Sometimes, I think you know him better than I do, Mel. I don't know what I'd do without you."

"Oh, I don't do anything special," Melody countered. "Lucas and I just hang out while I do my work."

"The very important work of not just caring for Lucas, but keeping the whole Force running smoothly," Emersyn replied with an arched brow.

"I just balance the books." Melody's cheeks were burning. She couldn't believe her luck when Emersyn had secured her a spot at Force HQ, working as both the in-house daycare provider and their bookkeeper. She didn't hate getting to live in a sprawling, spectacular home for free, and she loved the excitement of being so close to the Special Ops vets who fought to keep the many shifter clans in the area safe.

"Bullshit. Even Amar gushes over how organized you are, and you know he's not the kind to let the light bill slip by unnoticed. It's because of you that we have all the groceries and supplies we need. You're the one who did all that insane Martha Stewart Christmas decorating. You were even the one who had the roof repaired last month after the storm. It's like you're the mother to this whole house, and you're amazing at it. Don't let yourself believe anything less."

Melody smiled at her friend. "I'm a firm believer in getting things done, that's all."

"Speaking of getting things done, are you going to do anything about *Roman*?" Emersyn challenged.

Her cheeks heated all over again at the mention of the handsome stranger. "Check out this sale on pocket knives. It's for a limited time, so I'd better stock up while I can. I think the guys will like them."

With one quick movement, Emersyn reached over and snatched the tablet out of Melody's hand. "I'm sure they will, but let's talk about Roman first. There was a connection between the two of you. I could tell."

"Well, I mean, he's a good-looking guy. I could see that, even with the Santa costume on." As a matter of fact, Melody hadn't been able to get that gorgeous face out of her mind all night. She'd gotten a glimpse of Roman after he'd come back in the house, when he'd ditched the big red suit and had brought in his suitcase to get settled in. His hair was dark, and he kept it in a short enough style to keep the curls from being too unruly. It matched the short beard that clung to his face and had been hidden completely by the Santa beard not long before that. Then there were those eyes...

"Yes, that part is obvious. But is there more than that?"

"I mean, I could tell he was, um, definitely attracted to me," Melody admitted. She'd been so shocked when she'd scooted over and discovered that her body hadn't been the only one reacting to their close proximity. "The hard evidence was right there, if you know what I mean."

The two women descended into a fit of giggles.

Melody put her hands to her face, feeling embarrassed for Roman. "It was all my fault! I was practically wiggling around on his lap, trying to accommodate all the pictures everyone wanted to take, and I practically sat right on it!"

"No wonder he got up and left," Emersyn replied, still laughing. "If the other guys know, they're probably giving him hell for it right now."

"Don't get me wrong. It's incredibly flattering. I just wasn't really thinking about it, because I was already feeling put on the spot just by having to sit on some random hot guy's lap." Melody swept her auburn curls out of her face and then wanted to pull them back down again just so she'd have something to hide behind.

"Even grown men can't help those things sometimes," Emersyn said. "Still, I swear I sensed something more than just a physical attraction between the two of you. As soon as you were close to each other, there was this little bubble that surrounded you, and you were the only ones in the room. Is there something you should be telling me?" Emersyn grinned as she tapped her fingers on the edge of the tablet.

Melody hesitated. Emersyn was her best friend. There was no one else in the world she would've rather talked to about this. After all, the connection Melody had felt to Roman had been intense. He was a complete stranger. She didn't know him at all, yet she'd distinctly felt her inner snow leopard wake up and try to leap straight out of her chest. She'd wanted to curl up on his lap and purr, imagining his strong hands stroking through her fur. Melody had never had that sort of reaction to anyone before. She knew what it could mean, but what if she were wrong?

Even if Roman was her mate, she couldn't just upend her life in L.A. She had obligations to the Force, which were important enough, but she was also committed to watching Lucas. Emersyn had just told her how vital she was to everyone there, and Roman lived all the way up in Wyoming, according to Amar. There were too many things to think about, and she was too tired to mull it all over.

"No, nothing's going on there. I was just in a good mood because I had a little too much to drink. We had a great Thanksgiving, and I'm glad everyone agreed to let me do this Christmas kickoff party. I mean, who knows what Christmas itself will end up looking like."

"That's true enough," Emersyn agreed. "I've thought about that a lot, actually. I'd like Lucas to have as traditional of a holiday as possible, but what if a mission comes up? What about all my work at the clinic? Things don't stop just because a date on the calendar says to."

Their conversation turned away from Roman and back to shopping and planning. Melody showed Emersyn the Christmas wrap she'd recently picked out, and they joked about getting all the members of the Force to dress in matching holiday pajamas for a cute photo.

That part of the conversation made her mind immediately drift back to Roman, wondering what might have gone differently if they'd met some other way. What if he'd walked in and was just introduced as Amar's friend? Would they have found a way to talk at the drinks table or near the tree, getting to know each other while feeling that distinctive connection? Or would he have just been another person she met for a brief moment before he had to return to Wyoming, never to be thought of or seen again? Was there some element of destiny in the way they'd met? Melody shook her head. She'd had too much eggnog to begin with. She just needed to wind down and forget about it until she could think rationally.

"Okay. I'm not even going to look at the total of my online cart, so I'm checking out and heading to bed." Emersyn shut her computer and glanced up. "You all right?"

"Hm? Oh, yeah. Just tired. And a little hungry, surprisingly. I snacked a whole lot, but I didn't really eat a meal." Having made very little progress with her own shopping, she turned off her tablet and set it on her nightstand. "I think I'll head downstairs and raid the fridge."

Emersyn stood and stretched, bracing her feet on the floor and arching into the air like the pantheress she was at heart. Melody had often thought one of the reasons they were so compatible was because they were both felines. "I wouldn't be surprised if some of the others are doing the same. Everyone seems to eat at midnight around here."

"It's not exactly a normal work schedule," Melody agreed. "What about you? You hungry?"

"Nah. I'm heading to bed." She tucked her laptop under her arm.

"I'll be doing the same soon." Melody shoved her feet into her favorite slippers. "I'll check on Lucas before I go to bed."

Emersyn had been heading for the bedroom door, but she turned around and leaned on the frame. "You really are amazing, Melody. You treat my son like he's your own, and no matter how much he interferes with your work, you just roll right along like everything is peachy. Seriously, I don't know how this place would function without you." She padded down the hall to the room she shared with Gabe.

Yeah, but I don't want to think about that right now, Melody thought.

As she descended the stairs, Melody was overcome with the homey feeling of Christmas. The white lights she'd strung along the banister, around the Christmas tree, across the mantle, and on several shelves were the only lighting in the main living area of the house, and they cast a warm, cozy glow that was instantly reflected in her chest as she stepped off the last stair. She hesitated on the last step, just standing there and taking it all in. She slowly moved toward the kitchen, trailing her fingers over the garland on the sofa table. A scrap of something on the carpet caught her eye, and she stooped to pick it up: a piece of wrapping paper from Lucas's gift. It was just a piece of trash now, but it'd brought him so much joy just a few hours ago. Her heart ached for just one more hug from the little boy, but it would have to wait until morning.

Melody didn't bother turning on the light in the kitchen. She knew this place like the back of her hand, and the miniature silver Christmas tree she'd put smack in the middle of the counter gave off plenty of light. It was early in the season, but her favorite Christmas song popped into her head as she opened the fridge, and she couldn't help but sing along. "Santa, baby..."

There'd been tons of food for the party, and she slowly scanned each shelf as she tried to decide what she wanted to eat. Her mouth watered just from the thought of it, and once again, her mind circled back to Roman. "Been an angel all year..." It was late and she was alone, so she allowed herself to move to the music that was consuming her head. A fantasy of Roman in a *much* smaller version of that Santa costume floated through her mind as Melody pulled out a plate of deviled eggs and bent down to get Raul's famous ham from the bottom shelf. "So hurry down the chimney tonight!" She shut the fridge door.

"If you insist."

Melody shrieked before slapping her hand over her mouth and doubling over. "Holy shit, you scared me! How long were you standing there letting me make a fool out of myself?"

He smiled, and the twinkle in his dark eyes wasn't from the Christmas lights. "Long enough. I thought I'd come down for a midnight snack."

Though she had somewhat recovered from the scare, Melody wasn't sure she'd ever recover from seeing Roman standing there like that. His plaid pajama bottoms weren't too dissimilar from what she wore, but his tight-fitting undershirt showed off his sculpted muscles. It was too easy to imagine what it would be like to press her hands against that shirt and feel the heat of his skin through it. Her tongue curled in her mouth as she took a step backward. "Well, there's certainly plenty here."

"So you don't mind if I join you?"

Could he tell that she no longer knew how to breathe? He'd probably seen her shaking her ass in the air, singing a song full of innuendo. Her only hope was that he couldn't read minds and had no idea she'd been thinking about him the entire time. "Sure. Of course. I was actually going to see if there were any good holiday movies on TV, if you'd like to join me for that, too." God, what was she saying?

Roman reached past her with one long, brawny arm and picked up the platter of ham. "That sounds great."

Melody wanted to kick herself as she led the way into the living room. What would they watch? Where would they sit? They'd have to sit close together to share the food. Wait, did that mean anything significant if they were sharing their food? No. She was overthinking this. Just because Roman had incited a feeling inside her that she'd never experienced, one that could be... No. It was just a midnight snack. That was it. It didn't have to mean anything.

"Do you have a favorite?" Roman asked as he set the platter on the coffee table.

"Huh?"

"A favorite Christmas movie."

"Oh. I don't know if I could choose." Melody racked her brain for even a title of a Christmas movie. She loved this time of year, and the movies were a big part of it. There was nothing better than settling in on a cool night to relax and watch an old flick, even if she'd already seen it a hundred times. So why couldn't she come up with even one? "It's hard to say. I like so many of them. Christmas is probably my favorite time of year."

"Then I'm surprised you live in L.A."

"What do you mean?" Melody settled in next to him on the couch, the table in front of them loaded with food. She tried not to think about how close his muscular thigh was to hers.

"It doesn't feel very Christmasy around here. I mean, other than inside the house itself. You guys must've really gone all out when you hired a decorator. If I didn't know there were palm trees swaying in a warm breeze outside, I'd think I was at the North Pole." Roman gestured widely to take in the garland, lights, and baubles.

"We didn't hire a decorator," Melody replied with a laugh. "I did this."

Roman had sat back against the cushions, but he sat up and braced his elbows on his knees. "Really? By yourself?"

"Well, sure." Her face flushed as he looked so intensely into her eyes. She let her own gaze take in his high cheekbones, the long line of his nose, the hardness of his jaw. His dark hair was rumpled, probably from being under that ridiculous Santa hat earlier. The reminder of their initial meeting sent a tingle of energy through her nipples, and she was glad they hadn't bothered turning on the lights. "It was a lot of work, but I'd gladly do it all over again."

"It doesn't bother you to put in all that effort, only to have to take it all back down in a month?" Roman grabbed a slice of ham off the platter, rolled it around a deviled egg, and downed it.

"No way. I love the feeling of Christmas, how it makes you think about home and love and even just being lucky to have a roof over your head and people to be with during the holidays. It's so cozy and warm, and I love the contrast of winter darkness with the twinkling lights. I find it incredibly..." She stalled, realizing the word she was about to say was 'romantic.' That wouldn't work in this situation, not when she was so close to a man like Roman.

"Idyllic?" he filled in for her.

"Yes, you could say that." Melody picked up the remote and turned on the TV, skipping all the available streaming services and opting for plain old antenna television. It was part of the nostalgia for her, remembering when she was a kid and had to catch her favorite movies while they were on. "Oh, *It's a Wonderful Life* just started. Does that work for you?"

"To be honest, I've seen it about a hundred times. In one of the places where I was stationed, a lot of our personal belongings got stalled in transit. Someone had a scratched DVD of this, and it was all we watched, even while we were out in the middle of the desert."

Melody held her finger over the button as she turned to him. Her snow leopard was swirling like an arctic wind inside her, blasting her from the inside out as she admired him. It wasn't just his looks, though she certainly appreciated those. It was the rumble of his voice. It was the way he moved with such ease and confidence. It was the strength and patience he exuded and the fact that he didn't seem to be aware of any of that. "Want me to find something else?"

"No, actually. It'd be nice to see it without a bunch of lines across the screen from a bad DVD." He put his hand over hers to push the remote down.

Her throat tightened completely as a shiver ran up her spine, making goosebumps explode over the back of her neck. This man had an effect on her unlike anything she'd ever felt before. She folded one foot under her knee, trying to anchor herself in reality instead of the fantasies that wouldn't leave her head. "I just have to warn you, I always cry when he finds Zuzu's petals in his pocket."

Roman laughed and scooted a little closer to her, his eyes shining. "You can lean on my shoulder if you need to."

"I just might." Melody smiled as she reached for the ham. This was proving to be the best midnight snack she'd ever had.

3

THE MOVIE WAS GOOD, BUT ROMAN WAS HARDLY PAYING ANY ATTENTION to it. His polar bear had been on a rampage when he arrived at Force HQ, but sitting there with Melody had soothed it. If he listened to his inner animal at all, then that meant... No. He had to stop himself from shaking his head to rattle the thought from his brain; he didn't want to distract Melody from the movie. But he knew it couldn't be. He would just enjoy the time he had left there—with her—and make the most of it before he headed back to Wyoming.

Melody sniffled as she wiped a tear from the corner of her eye. "I'm sorry. I told you I would cry. It's always the kids that get to me. Even though George Bailey takes up most of the movie, there's something about seeing him hug his kids with such love and joy at the end that I just can't get past, no matter how many times I see it." She reached forward to get the remote off the table.

Roman admired the long lines of her body as she did so. It was as though his eyes were addicted to her already, lingering on the wild red curls of her hair, the smattering of freckles on her cheeks, and even the way her fingers rested against the soft fabric of her pants. "What about you? Have any kids of your own?"

She rolled her shoulder. "No, and at this point, I kind of figured I wouldn't have any. But I *am* the chief caretaker for Lucas when I'm not doing the bookkeeping for the Force. That little nugget is an absolute dream."

He could see the warmth in her smile when she spoke of the boy. It ignited something inside him, but Roman knew better. He pushed it down again, reminding himself that his night with Melody could be nothing more than casual. "So, that's what your role is in the Force?"

"I'm not really a member of the Force, not in the same way the others are," she explained, sitting back against the couch cushions. The white twinkle lights illuminated her face, making her look as angelic as the tree topper. "I usually refer to myself as being Force-adjacent."

"But you live here, I assume," Roman countered. "It's because of you that Gabe and Emersyn can do their jobs, and I'm sure they appreciate having a numbers person around to balance the books. That's not for everyone." He didn't know why he had such an urge to make her feel she was just as vital as the Force members who physically fought for shifters all over L.A. Amar had explained how everything worked in the Force. He'd even hinted at recruiting him, but he wasn't meant for city life.

"It's still not really the same." She bit her lip, but the corners of her mouth turned up.

Damn, she was cute. His bear swelled inside him when he looked at her, loving every second of being so close to her.

"Shit, it's not like I'm out there doing anything heroic," Melody continued. "Besides, I get the better end of the bargain. I get a little work done, and I get to hang out with Lucas. It means that I at least get to feel like a parent sometimes, even when I'm not. What about you? Any kids?"

It was an innocent enough question. There was nothing wrong with it. Still, Roman felt that trigger pull inside him. His polar bear roared as he recalled the way he'd been wronged. It still hurt so badly, even months later. The tip of his tongue wiggled against the inside of his teeth as he considered whether or not to answer her. He hardly knew Melody, and it wasn't fair to just spew out his life story and expect her to be able to handle it. "No," he finally said quietly. "No kids."

If she'd noticed his hesitation or the tension that had suddenly built inside his muscles, she didn't let him know. Melody adjusted her position on the couch, inching her knee a little closer to his thigh.

"There's just something so magical about kids and the way they absorb everything around them," she mused, gazing up at the ceiling. "Even when we don't think they're paying attention, or we think something must be beyond their grasp, they just turn around and *know*. Like Lucas did this afternoon when he wanted everyone to sit on your lap."

It was too warm in the room. Did everything in L.A. have to be so damn hot? He craved the cool air of Wyoming to ease his soul. It wouldn't make him forget about Melody, though. As much as he wanted to turn and run from this situation, to save himself from looking like a fool, he knew their inner beasts would never let them ignore what had happened. Roman ran a hand through his hair. "Yeah, I guess we need to talk about that."

She turned away, but he could see the smile in the profile of her face. "We don't have to. It was just one of those things."

"If you mean the mere attraction of a man to a woman, then yes." Roman moved closer to her, longing to feel the silky smoothness of her skin under his hand. "But I think there was much more to it than that."

Turning just enough so that she could look at him, Melody raised an eyebrow. "Was there?"

"I think you know." God, he hoped she did. But in everything that Roman knew about shifters, these things weren't simply one-sided. He couldn't have that sort of reaction without her because *she* was part of the equation. The way his bear had gone berserk was a direct reflection of how her animal side was reacting. "There was something far more between us; something neither of us can control."

"I see," she said with a quirky little smile, reaching over and brushing cookie crumbs off the leg of his pants. "So if a girl just wants to sit on Santa's lap and tell him what a good girl she was all year, it has to mean something?"

"Absolutely. Especially if she shares her food with him. And especially if he has a far better time just sitting on the couch with her watching Christmas movies than he ever thought he would." He found himself leaning closer and closer to her as his polar bear urged him to close the distance between them.

"And if she might have felt the same thing, what do you think she should do about it? I mean, considering that they live in completely different parts of the country?" Melody had turned now so that she faced him.

Her face was so close to his, close enough that he only had to lift his hand to touch her cheek. Roman longed to tell her that none of that mattered if they were mates, but he knew it did. There was always something that jumped in the way of happiness, no matter what fate might be trying to say to the contrary. Did Melody want him to just brush off these feelings? Roman couldn't do that.

"You and I both know that a shifter can wait an entire lifetime, just hoping for the chance to run across the one person they're meant to be with. I'm not saying I know what to do about it, but I do know it's there." He swallowed, hardly believing those words were escaping his mouth.

She swallowed. It was a simple motion, but the way it moved her throat was tantalizing. Roman wanted to sink his teeth into it, to reach out with his tongue and touch her skin. He wanted to be a part of her, and he wanted her to know what it was like to be a part of him.

"Are you joining the Force?"

Did she know that Amar had talked to him about it? Roman didn't doubt how tightly knit everyone in that household was, so he wouldn't be surprised if Amar had mentioned it to the rest of them. His old buddy had tried hard, but Roman knew that Sheridan, Wyoming was his true home. He could never be happy in a place like L.A. "No."

Melody swallowed once again. Her lips moved, and for a moment, he thought she might kiss him. Instead, she swayed back ever so slightly. The increase in distance was so slight, but it was like a knife in his heart. "Well, at least we've had tonight," she said quietly. "I've had fun with you, Roman."

He felt as though he'd been trying to hold water in his hands and could only stand by helplessly as he watched it leak through his fingers. Melody was special. She was magical. She was like that Christmas wish that people always talked about in the movies, something you hoped would come true, but you never thought would. All he knew was that he wanted to keep a hold of her as long as possible. "Me, too."

"I'd better put all of this away." Melody reached forward, taking a plate in each hand.

After allowing himself a moment to see the curve of her backside as she stood, Roman joined her in cleaning up.

The two of them operated in a symphony of kitchen noises as they rinsed plates, covered leftovers, and returned everything to the fridge. Even though it felt like an anticlimactic end to what had been a promising evening, Roman found that the simple act of kitchen work was pleasant as long as he got to do it with Melody at his side. He liked the way her hair responded to her motions as she rinsed a dish. He certainly didn't mind seeing her bend over to load plates in the dishwasher. There was something authoritarian and domestic about her as she arranged items in the fridge. It was when he could stand back and realize that everyday chores were turning him on that he knew for sure he'd met his match.

"Thanks again," Melody said when they'd finished up. "I'd better be heading to bed." She wiped her hands on a towel and turned to leave.

As though someone else was controlling his body, Roman's hands were suddenly on her hips. He spun her around, pulling her close against him as he pressed his lips to hers. Roman expected her to pull back and slap him. He deserved it for just grabbing her like that without permission.

Melody stiffened in surprise, stepping backward as she caught her balance, but then melted into his embrace. Her hands slid up his chest, across his shoulders, and around to the back of his neck as her lips grew pliant and welcoming.

He dared to flick his tongue into the warm depths of her mouth, exploring, needing to know more of her. Roman knew his erection from earlier in the day had returned, but he was no longer embarrassed by it. He drove it against her, wanting her to know that she wasn't just some fluke. It wasn't just that he was a lonely vet who happened to find the comfort of a woman. No, this was his mate. He didn't know what it would mean for their future, and at the moment, he didn't care. Roman tightened his grip, locking his hands around her lower back, and held her close. He would've stood there and kissed her until the sun came up, and if that's all that he could've had, then he would've gladly taken it.

But Melody had other ideas in mind. She broke their liplock and pushed back against his chest. One hand slid down the inside of his arm to his hand, her fingers interlocking with his as she smiled up at him. Her brown eyes glittered as she turned away, pulling him along with her.

Not daring to ask questions, Roman followed. They moved through the house on bare feet, two souls who'd waited so long to meet each other. Melody could've guided him down to the pits of hell and he would have followed. But she led him up the stairs, down the hall, past the room where Amar had arranged for him to stay, and into a different bedroom. He knew it was hers without even asking, just by its scent. The white and gold accents were the same warm, inviting colors of the holiday she loved so much. Being there in her room, where she slept, where she dreamed, lit him on fire.

As soon as she closed the door behind them, Roman had her in his arms once again. He cradled the back of her skull in his hand as he kissed her hungrily, letting his tongue meld with hers as excitement shot up from his groin.

Her hands found the hem of his undershirt, and she stripped him of it, tossing it to the side as though it were completely inconsequential. Melody's eyes widened as she took in the sight of him shirtless, reaching out to touch the solid planes of his chest.

He closed his eyes to linger in the experience of her fingers on his skin, but he soon opened them again. Roman wanted to see her. She looked tempting enough in her fitted tee and pajama bottoms, but he wanted more. Slowly, carefully, he pulled her free of her clothing and reveled in every inch of her flesh, from the curve of her breasts, to the smoothness of her stomach, down to the arc of her hips and even the length of her legs. In the dim light, he found freckles to match the ones across the bridge of her nose, and he kissed every one of them. She laughed, and sometimes she moved away as his beard tickled her, but she never retreated from his arms.

The two of them tumbled to the bed together, not even bothering to pull back the covers. Melody trapped him with her legs, her knees clutched around his hips as she pulled him down toward her. She wanted him, and he wasted no time giving her what she craved. He buried himself inside her, and just the way they'd moved with such harmony in the kitchen, their hips moved with the same sense of synchrony. When he retreated, she advanced. When he pushed forward, she pulled back. Roman knew nothing of music, but he couldn't help but think of it when it came to her. She was the song to his soul, the one who knew the tune to his very being.

Roman could feel the tension build inside him, like a wire being slowly twisted. Scooping his hands around her backside, he tossed himself to the side and rolled over, pulling her on top of him. She laughed and clung to his shoulders, her curls tickling his face until she got control of herself and pushed up.

Melody arched her back as she took him in as deeply as she could. Her toes curled against the sides of his legs as she tossed her head back and braced her hands on his shoulders. She was taking what she needed from him, and Roman was ready to give it. He moved his hips in time to hers as he took her nipple into his mouth, circling it slowly with the tip of his tongue. Roman's hands clung to her ass, and she groaned with pleasure as his fingers sank deep into her flesh.

Her eyes closed and mouth slackened as her core tightened around him, inviting him to join her on the journey of pleasure she was flying on. She gripped his shoulders hard as she came, tiny gasps escaping from her throat.

Roman let himself go, and a shudder of pleasure whipped down his back as they pushed each other ever higher. His bear's roar rose from his throat as he plunged himself yet further inside her, wanting to feel even the tiniest spasm from within her. She was his. It might only be for now, but she was his.

4

MELODY WOKE SLOWLY AND PEACEFULLY, STRETCHING THROUGHOUT THE length of her body before she even opened her eyes. She knew without looking that Roman was there next to her. She could sense him. It wasn't just his scent or the way the mattress felt different at having a second person in the bed. Her body simply *knew,* and she liked that sense of knowing. Even so, she dared to open her eyes and take a peek.

He lay on his back, his face serene. She took the time to enjoy the way his hair fell back against the pillow and how his eyelashes looked much longer when his eyes were closed. He had beautiful lips, and a small thrill shot through her stomach as she remembered what they felt and tasted like. Though perfectly relaxed, she could see the outline of every muscle in his incredible body. Melody had no idea how long he'd been out of the service, but it was clear that he still kept in shape.

Her snow leopard purred with contentment as she watched him sleep. Roman was the kind of man she could've easily just tumbled into bed with for a one-night stand. Melody was pretty sure she could've done that and not regretted it for an instant, but she still preferred the way things had actually gone. She closed her eyes once more as she relived their evening on the couch, discussing the correlations between the world of George Bailey and the current world they lived in... eating to their hearts' content... slowly moving closer to each other both physically and emotionally... It'd felt so real and so mature, like a relationship she could truly be comfortable in.

No. She couldn't call it a relationship. Roman was scheduled to go back to Wyoming once the holidays were over. He had a life up there, and she couldn't ask him to change that any more than he could ask her to leave the Force. It would never work. She'd also noted that hardness that'd taken over his face for just a fraction of a second when she'd asked if he had any children. Even if their locations weren't a problem, that part would be. Roman didn't seem to want children, and Melody couldn't see her life without them.

Furrowing her brow, she tried to concentrate only on the good parts. She did have a beautiful naked man in her bed, after all. There wasn't anything pressing on the schedule for the day, and her ears had yet to pick up on anyone else being up and out of bed. *He probably won't mind if I wake him up for a repeat of last night...*

Pushing herself up onto her elbow, she leaned across the bed to stroke his inner thigh when a baby's cry split the air.

Roman's eyes flew open, and he was up and off the pillow. "What was that?"

Melody's body had also reacted to the sound with an instinctive drive that she'd never been able to understand. It was the same feeling she had every time she was in a store and heard a child cry for its mother. It sparked a physical reaction that demanded her to help, even though she had no child of her own.

She'd bounced off the mattress and was frantically searching for her pajama bottoms. "It's just..." She was going to say it was just Lucas, ready to wake up and start the day. But Emersyn's boy had outgrown crying when he woke up. This was the sound of a younger baby, and it was coming from much further away than the nursery down the hall. "I don't know."

Roman yanked on a shirt, but it wouldn't go past his shoulders. He ripped it back off again and tossed it to her. "I think this is yours."

Melody had already put on a different one, but having found her pants, she slipped them on as well. "I'm going to check on Lucas first."

"I'll go with you." He was at her back as soon as she had her hand on the doorknob.

She had it covered and was more than capable of peeking in the baby's room, but Melody didn't argue. Something had changed in the air, and she could sense it just as she'd been able to sense Roman was at her side without seeing him. Was she simply becoming more perceptive now that her body had tapped into knowing what it was like to have a mate? There was no time to think about it.

Racing down the carpeted hallway, Melody knew before she even opened the door that it wasn't Lucas. It wasn't his cry. But who else would be making that noise? She looked in the nursery just to be safe. He was in his crib, just as he should have been. His dark hair was tousled from sleep, but his lashes lay peacefully on his cheeks. His breathing was even, and he most certainly wasn't crying. Fortunately, he hadn't been woken up by whoever was.

Melody shut the door quietly. "This is very strange," she murmured as she began moving through the house.

"No other kids live here, do they?" Roman asked.

"No, just Lucas." She headed down the stairs, realizing she was following an innate sense more than she was trusting her hearing, though she could certainly hear better than most humans. Her body moved with the litheness of her inner cat as she swept down the stairs and into the living room. The Christmas lights that had looked so welcoming the night before now only looked like clutter as she tried to figure out what was happening. "It's coming from outside."

"Hold on, I'll look." Roman reached for the door handle.

But Melody had it first. She had to see what was there. A child was crying, screaming practically, and it needed someone. It needed her. Pounding her code into the electronic lock, she flung open the front door.

The volume of the baby's wailing increased exponentially, filling the air. Melody hardly heard it as she looked down, seeing a car seat on the front porch. The handle was still up, and a yellow blanket covered the top of it. She immediately knelt and pulled the edge of it back to find the red, pinched face of a baby, screaming so hard, its tiny tongue was vibrating.

"You poor sweet thing!" Scooping up the entire carrier, Melody turned and brought the child inside.

"I didn't see anyone else out there," Roman said as he closed the door behind her.

Melody's heart swelled with sadness. "Who could leave you like that?" she gently cooed to the screaming baby. It blew her mind that something like that could still happen in this day and age, yet there the little girl was. With expert fingers, Melody deftly pulled the blanket out the rest of the way and unfastened the buckles. "She's hungry, and her diaper is more than full," she said as she lifted the squirming bundle free. Melody turned to Roman. He looked completely lost, standing there with his pajama pants on backward and his hair a rumpled mess. His eyes were wide, and he moved his hands as though he were ready to take some sort of action, but he didn't know what it was.

"Do me a favor and wake up Emersyn. There's no telling how long this poor little thing was on the porch, and she'll need to be looked over. I'm taking her into Lucas's room to get her cleaned up, then I'll be back down here to make her a bottle." Melody pulled the little girl close and headed for the stairs.

"Sure." Roman raced up ahead of her, clearly glad to have something to do.

Melody smiled as she slowly headed upstairs, pushing the tip of her finger into the baby's palm. The little girl gripped it tightly, her tiny knuckles turning white. "That's right. You go ahead and be angry. You have every right to be. How could anyone do such a terrible thing?" Turning down the hall, Melody opened the door to Lucas's room. The screaming baby might very well wake him, but they'd just have to deal with it. This child had to be taken care of.

"Here you go, sweetling," Melody cooed as she laid her out on the changing table. "I'm so sorry. I know these diapers aren't quite the right size, but they're better than nothing for now. I'll go out to the store later to get you something that fits you a little better. And some clothes, too. For right now, I think I have some clothes Lucas has grown out of. He won't mind if you borrow them." Anytime she'd dealt with little ones, she'd always chattered at them about what she was doing. She'd later read that it was good for their language development, but Melody enjoyed doing it regardless.

"Who's that?" Melody turned. Lucas was standing in his crib, gripping the side of it with one hand and pointing at the newcomer with the other. "You have a baby, Aunt Mel'dy?"

"No, it's not my baby," she admitted, though even speaking that simple truth broke her heart a little. The baby was calming down now that she had a clean diaper on, and Melody was already falling in love with her. There was just something so enchanting about babies. It was like they could reach inside and touch her heart with their tiny fingers.

They were so soft and warm and sweet, the kind of qualities you didn't always find in adults.

"Who's baby 'dat?" Lucas pressed.

She couldn't blame him. He'd just woken up to find a new child in his room. But that was a very hard question to answer at the moment. "Well, she's just a baby I'm watching for a little while."

"You not gonna watch me?"

Clothed in an old onesie that sagged off her little behind, Melody lifted the girl off the changing table. She cradled her against her chest and brought her over for Lucas to see. "Of course I'll still be watching you," she assured him as she reached out to touch his shock of dark hair. "Nothing between us will change. This little girl needs my help right now, that's all."

"Name?"

Lucas had always been inquisitive. Most of the time, Melody admired that about him. She loved to see how bright and interested he was, but right now, it was making her life harder. Melody hesitated. If there had been any sort of note in the baby seat, she hadn't seen it. She'd have to go back and check. For the moment, perhaps it was best to just make something up. "Her name is..."

"Ruby," said a voice behind her.

Melody turned to find Roman standing in the doorway. He held up the yellow blanket that had been wrapped around the baby, and Melody could see there was a name embroidered on it. "Ruby," she repeated as she gazed down at the sweet little bundle. With her dusting of blonde hair and her big blue eyes that were still full of tears, having a name to attach to that precious little face just made Melody fall for her even harder. "Such a pretty name."

"I can play with Ruby?"

"Maybe later. Right now, she needs some breakfast." And a thorough checkup. Melody hadn't noticed anything wrong with Ruby—not even a diaper rash—but she knew it was best if the doc had a look at her. "Roman, will you please help Lucas out of his crib and bring him downstairs? My arms are kind of full."

He hesitated before taking a step forward. Roman moved to the side of the boy's bed and reached in, helping him down to the floor. He let go once Lucas was on his feet, but the tot immediately reached back up. Lucas held his hand as naturally as if Roman had been his father as they headed out of the room.

Despite the strange situation she'd just found herself in, Melody smiled as she headed back down the stairs to the kitchen. Roman was a big guy, a burly soldier, the type of man who'd probably killed and saved numerous lives during his career in the service. He exuded a quiet strength that Melody admired, but she couldn't help but find it a little funny that he seemed intimidated by a toddler. Not everyone had spent their teen and college years babysitting, though.

"I know, Ruby, I know," she crooned as the baby began screaming all over again. "I think I've got a bottle in here somewhere for you." Working with one hand and holding Ruby with the other, Melody quickly flipped through the cabinets. She was grateful that Lucas had only recently stopped using a bottle and that they'd stashed them away instead of getting rid of them just yet. There was even an unopened can of formula, much to her relief. "Almost there, baby girl. Almost there."

"Melody!" Emersyn came rushing into the kitchen with her arms out. "Roman told me what happened. Unbelievable!"

The room suddenly got much quieter as Melody gave Ruby the bottle. "I know, but here she is."

"Was there a note or anything?" Emersyn asked as she began looking Ruby over.

"Nothing," Roman confirmed as he joined them, still being guided by Lucas. "Sorry. It took us a minute to get down the stairs."

Melody clamped her lips together and looked back down at Ruby. She knew Lucas still took the stairs one at a time, and she would've given anything to watch Roman have to do the same.

"I didn't find anything on or in the car seat, and I checked the front porch thoroughly," Roman continued. "Do you have any surveillance cameras set up?"

Amar joined them just then, and he, too, came over to study the little girl. "I'll have Raul check through the feeds. Anything that has to do with tech immediately goes to him." He rubbed the back of his neck. "Of all the problems we've had to solve, I never would have thought we'd be presented with one like this."

"Is it possible that someone just left her on the doorstep of a nice house in the hopes that she'd have a good life?" Melody asked. It was the kind of thing you saw in old books or movies, but not the kind of thing that happened in reality.

"We'll figure it out soon enough," Amar assured her. "Melody, can I ask you to take care of her until we do?"

"Already on it, Chief," she assured him. Melody braced the bottle as she grabbed a cloth to wipe a dribble of formula from Ruby's chin. She felt awful that this adorable creature had been taken away from her mother and left with strangers, but her heart secretly soared.

"Great. I'll get everyone together, and we'll have a meeting in one hour." Amar strode purposefully from the room.

"I'll wait until she's done eating, then I'll take her into the exam room," Emersyn said. "She sure is a cutie."

"I'm not going to argue with that." Melody smiled down at the cherubic face. She hadn't asked for a baby for Christmas, but it looked like she was getting one anyway.

5

ROMAN STEPPED OUT THE BACK DOOR. IT HAD BEEN LESS THAN AN HOUR since he and Melody had found that child on the doorstep, though it'd felt like a lifetime. The world was heaving and changing underneath him, and he couldn't do anything about it. He belonged back in Sheridan. He knew that without even a trace of doubt. It was the one place he'd found that he really belonged, and the solitude of the rural Wyoming community was good for him.

But then he'd had to come to California and meet Melody. Roman walked out past the pool, gazing into its blue depths as he recalled the night before. He'd been unable to sleep in a new place, and the temptation of all those leftovers from the party had been irresistible. He hadn't counted on finding something—or rather, *someone*—even more irresistible when he'd wandered into the kitchen. Roman smiled, remembering how she'd been swinging her ass from side to side as she sang, with hardly a care in the world. That was the beginning of all this change, but it was a change that was much easier to fall into.

He'd been so comfortable with her as they sat on the couch and watched that old movie. Roman couldn't remember a time in his life when he'd found that level of ease so quickly with someone. That was just one of the many reasons he knew Melody was his mate. He could see himself falling for her just as easily as he'd fallen into bed with her, disrupting his entire life just to be with her. He knew, though, that it wouldn't work if either of them had to give up what they loved.

That notion had been driven home as soon as he'd seen Melody dive into action with Ruby. She hadn't delayed for half a second when she'd seen that child on the front porch, nor had she shown any reluctance to take care of her simply because she wasn't biologically hers. In fact, the way Melody carried Ruby around, cooing and fussing over her, it was hard to believe she wasn't the baby's mother.

Roman shoved his hands in his pockets and tried to appreciate the scenery of the landscaped backyard, but it was too difficult to concentrate. All he could see was the beatific look on Melody's face as she gazed at Ruby. There had been an instant connection between the two of them, and Roman wasn't sure how he felt about it. It was something akin to jealousy, but there was so much more to it. It was his own history that was affecting him, a history that was still too fresh for him to just brush off. He was crazy about Melody, but he couldn't possibly give her what she needed. He scuffed his foot in the grass. They'd already decided that it wasn't going to work out for him, and there was no point in lamenting over it now.

"Roman?" Jude stood at the back door, a cup of coffee in his hand. "The meeting's just about to start. Amar said you'd probably want to sit in on it."

"Thanks." Roman's lips began to form a protest, explaining that he wasn't part of the Force and had no reason to be at that meeting, but his feet had a different plan and began walking across the grass toward the house. "I don't want to intrude on anything, though."

Jude lowered his chin slightly, his pale eyes penetrating as he looked into Roman's. Jude had a certain sense of gravitas about him that suggested he knew far more than he said. "You're not. Any friend of Amar's is a friend of ours. Come on in, man."

Roman followed Jude inside. He'd been on some crazy missions during his time in the service. He'd done things that most civilians couldn't even imagine, yet sitting in on a meeting was making him more nervous than heading to war with a Glock 19 in his hand. That feeling was only magnified when he saw Melody step into the conference room ahead of him. It was one thing to sit in on the Force's briefing, but it was only going to be harder now that he knew Melody was there.

The conference table was a long behemoth of polished wood with comfortable chairs arranged around it. With the fresh paint and a flatscreen television on the wall, the room looked like it belonged in a corporate office building instead of the headquarters of a shifter-based team of soldiers. Roman almost thought he should be wearing a suit to attend this meeting versus his t-shirt and jeans.

Amar took his place at the head of the table. "All right. I think we all know by now what's happening, but let's run through all the facts. We've got a child in our custody, and I want to get this figured out as quickly as possible. I'm sure the parents are worried to death. Melody, let's begin with you since you were the one who found Ruby."

She sat to Amar's right with the baby on her lap, holding her as naturally as if she'd been taking care of the child from the day she was born. Melody had managed to find time to get dressed and pull her hair into a ponytail. The cinnamon curls burst from the back of her head, and several wild tendrils escaped the fastening and fell to frame her face. Roman thought her hair's unruliness was quite the contrast to the calm, organized way Melody had acted when it came to Ruby.

Lifting her eyes and glancing at him for a moment, Melody told her side of the story. "Just after I woke up, I was still lying in bed and heard a baby's cry. I knew that it couldn't have been Lucas. I mean, I've spent enough time with him that I just know. I checked his room anyway, but he was sound asleep. Then Roman and I found Ruby outside."

Roman raised a brow at this last sentence, but he merely nodded in response. "Did you see any sign of another person out there? Any indication that someone might've been watching from nearby?"

Melody's head had fallen forward to look at Ruby once again, her cheeks glowing. "Honestly, I couldn't say. I was too focused on the baby to notice."

"Roman?"

Looking to his old friend, Roman felt called out. He'd just slept with Melody right there at Force headquarters. It felt like a betrayal to Amar's clan, but he knew he wasn't being called to the carpet for that. They needed to find this child's parents, and that was the only thing that really mattered. "After Ruby was brought inside, I took a look around. I don't know your neighborhood the way you do, but I didn't see anything that looked out of the ordinary."

Amar gave another nod, and if he was upset with Roman for his nighttime activities, he gave no indication. "Right. Raul, you installed security cameras for us not too long ago. Were you able to find anything?"

The wolf shifter stood up, his cell in his hand. He used it as a controller to project several images up onto the television. "I've been through all the footage as thoroughly as I can, and I used a few software programs to enhance the images. Unfortunately, as you see here, whoever did this was very careful to disguise themselves."

Roman ripped his gaze away from Melody to study the screen. A robed figure, shown in several different still shots, came up the walkway and deposited the car seat on the porch. Whoever it was had taken great pains not only to swathe themselves in thick clothing that completely disguised their figure. With the head covered as well, Roman could hardly tell if he was looking at a man or woman. "That doesn't help much."

Raul shook his head. "No, it really doesn't. I've got some pretty sophisticated facial recognition software, but I can't exactly use it if there's no face."

"What about the city cameras? Can you trace this person by tapping into those?" Amar was firing questions just as quickly as they could be answered. Roman could see why he'd been chosen as Alpha of this group, though it hadn't surprised him in the first place. He'd always acted as a natural leader out in the field.

"I tried," Raul admitted. "Our cameras indicated this person approached from the west and left that way, too. I used the time stamp and direction to patch into the appropriate city cameras. They're a little glitchy, so some of the information I have is mere inference, but there's a good possibility this person came from one of three clans." He switched the image on the screen to a map with three green dots indicating the clans' locations.

"It's so strange," Melody mused. "Why would someone leave a child on our doorstep?"

Amar leaned forward, bracing his elbows on the table. "I think we can take a safe gamble that whoever did this is a shifter, and they must know this is our headquarters. As the Force has gained more and more recognition, it's not surprising, nor is it something worth completely repressing. At least we know that someone—whoever this person is— likely came to us for help. I only wish I knew more. Emersyn, do you have any medical findings on the baby?"

Sitting next to Melody, Emersyn shook her head. "Nothing pertinent. As far as I can tell, she's a shifter. I haven't seen any signs yet as to what species. She seems to be in perfectly good health, other than she might've missed an early morning meal. Melody has already taken charge of getting her cleaned up and fed, and at this point, she's no different than any other baby."

"Yes, thank you for stepping in, Melody," Amar added. "It's very much appreciated."

"I'm more than happy to do it," Melody admitted as she contemplated Ruby once again. Her eyes were so soft, her smile so genuine. "I feel bad for her because this obviously isn't the perfect situation, but she's a complete angel."

As Melody lifted a hand to brush back Ruby's soft, blonde hair, Roman felt another pang of regret ripple through his chest. She'd told him how she loved children, and it was obvious now that he saw her in action with a little one. He could see this wasn't just something Melody said because she thought it was expected of her as a woman. She adored that child in her arms, even though she had no ties to it. She would do anything for Ruby.

It broke his heart. Melody was his mate, and he knew that. It made him entertain ideas like finding a way for the two of them to be together, no matter where they lived. But a child? The idea thickened his throat. He couldn't do that. He couldn't be a father, not after what'd happened.

"I've scanned The Shift thoroughly, but I haven't found any posts or even hints about a missing child," Raul was saying as Roman returned his attention to the meeting.

"The Shift?" Roman asked.

"It's a news app with a social media aspect I created for shifters only," Raul explained. "With the help of the geniuses over at Taylor Communications, anyway. Shifters can only activate it if they have an access code generated by their Alpha, which would have to come from us first. It helps us build our registry of shifters in the area, plus it keeps out any prying eyes. Normally, it's a pretty good source for leads."

"The lack of information isn't comforting," Amar replied. "If someone were missing this child, I would think they'd have something to say about it. Unless, of course, something had happened to them."

"I certainly hope that last part isn't something we'll have to worry about," Jude said quietly.

"Agreed," Amar said with a nod. "Our first line of business is to track down the parents, no matter what their status is. We'll start by getting in touch with the three clans who could be tied to this incident and see if we can arrange peaceful meetings with them. In the meantime, let's keep our eyes and ears open for any other hints that might point us in the right direction, whether it's something online or in person." He hesitated, tapping his fingers on the desk. "If the parents can't be located or if we find they're dead, we'll cross that path when we come to it. You're all dismissed."

Roman made his way out of the conference room, though a few others held back to talk with Amar. He felt the urge to act building in his muscles once again, feeling as though he needed to do something to make this situation better. Unfortunately, he didn't know what that was. He also didn't know how he was going to deal with the problem of Melody.

"How's she doing?" he asked as she stepped out of the conference room behind him.

When she looked up at him, he was unsure if the kindness in her eyes was actually for him, or if it was from looking at the baby. "As well as can be expected. She's young enough that she might not know a major difference, especially if she's used to being dropped off with a sitter regularly. As long as someone's taking care of her, she should be content. Lucas was a lot like that. He still is, actually. He sees everyone here as one big family. Even though I'm technically the one who watches him, he's still just as happy as a peach as long as it's one of us. He's with Mali right now, and I'm sure it doesn't bother him a bit."

"The Force members sure are a tight-knit group," Roman observed, "even those who don't actually live here." Why did he feel a little envious of that? He had his own clan up in Sheridan. It wasn't a family he'd been born into, much like what the Force had going on there in L.A., but they were good to him.

"We really are," she agreed. "I didn't have a big family growing up, so it's great to always have someone to lean on."

He felt yet another crack form in his heart. This woman was utterly perfect. Even if she suddenly agreed to go to Wyoming with him, he'd be moving her to the middle of the wilderness where she didn't know a soul. She was strong, and while he had no doubt she'd be able to handle it, she still wouldn't be happy. "The Army was kind of like that," he said for lack of anything else. "I was closer to some than others, but you always had your brothers at your back."

"Yes, and that sense of camaraderie is thick around here," she said with a smile. She looked down as Ruby stretched and wiggled in her arms, turning her head toward Melody's chest and making tiny noises of distress. "Looks like it's time for another bottle."

He watched her head toward the kitchen, on the verge of asking if she needed any help or what he should do, but he knew there was nothing. This was Melody's life. This was her way of being, and she didn't need him to get involved. It was better if he stayed out of the picture as much as possible. The real question was how long he'd be able to do that for.

6

EMERSYN LET OUT AN EXASPERATED SIGH AS SHE RUSHED AROUND THE
exam room at headquarters, packing up a few supplies she needed for
the day. She'd swept her dark hair back into a braid, but tiny strands
were already pulling free. "I'm never going to get out of here on time."

"The clinic will be there when you get there," Melody reminded
her calmly as she lifted Ruby into her arms. "You worry too much."

"Maybe so," she said with a flick of her fingers in the air as she tried
to remember what else she was supposed to get for the day. "It's just
that every day I wake up and think I must have missed something
when it comes to Ruby's health. I just feel like there should be something wrong with her if someone was going to leave her here, you
know?"

"I do," Melody admitted. She'd thought about it several times
herself, but every time she looked at or took care of Ruby, the little girl
seemed completely fine. "It's all really strange. I guess I see this as just
a different kind of babysitting job. I'll take care of her until her parents
come for her, whenever that may be."

Emersyn paused in her frenzy and looked Melody in the eye. "Mel,
you know it's probably not going to be the kind of thing where we get
to keep her, right? I mean, even if we discover that her parents are
dead, there's probably a relative who'll want her."

"Oh, I know that. Of course." Melody shifted Ruby in her arms. She hadn't admitted it to anyone, and she'd hardly been able to admit it to herself, but she would've gladly raised Ruby as her own. She didn't care if she shared blood with her or not.

"And you're sure you're going to be okay watching both Lucas and Ruby today? The two of them are going to be a handful."

Melody shook her head, setting her red curls bouncing over the shoulders of her light sweater. Several of the other women had helped out since Ruby arrived, giving Melody time to take care of her other duties, but she was looking forward to having both of the little ones to herself. After all, that's probably how things would be from now on until they figured out what to do with Ruby. "It won't be a problem at all. I've got a big day of activities planned, including heading over to the L.A. Zoo Lights."

Emersyn lifted an eyebrow as she stowed an extra pack of syringes in her medical bag. "You're a braver woman than I am. Maybe Amar ought to have you out running missions instead of running the homestead."

"No way," Melody replied as she lightly tapped the tip of her finger against Ruby's nose. "Then I'd miss out on all the fun."

When Emersyn had gone and the rest of the Force was going about their day, Melody launched into the endless series of events revolving around caring for two little ones. She fed snacks and cleaned up after them. She mixed formula and washed bottles. The small layette she'd ordered for Ruby was delivered, and Melody delighted in washing up all the dear little outfits so she could play dress-up with the new baby. She taught Lucas to be gentle with their houseguest, and she answered his questions about her as patiently as she could. It was difficult when she knew so few of the answers, but fortunately, he was far more interested in their evening plans.

"Zoo?" he asked as he spun a wooden block in his hands, examining the colorful sides.

"No, it's not quite time to go to the zoo yet. We have to wait until it gets closer to dark." Melody stood up from the floor and stretched, wondering when she'd gotten old enough that her knees felt so terrible after sitting cross-legged on the carpet.

"Dark?" He ran to the sliding glass door and peered out.

"Yeah. How else are we going to see all the pretty Christmas lights? I think Ruby will have fun, too. Don't you?"

Lucas marched over to where Ruby sat peacefully in the bouncy seat Melody had dug out of the attic, playing with an oversized set of plastic keys. He twisted his mouth and tipped his head from side to side. "Yeah, I guess so."

"It's been a long time since we've been to the zoo, but this will be a bit different. We won't see the same kinds of animals we normally do. They'll all be asleep."

Roman happened to walk into the room just then. "You're going to the zoo at night?"

Her heart lifted as soon as she saw him. Melody didn't want to have that reaction. She wanted to feel the same way about him as she did any other man in this household, like she was seeing someone familiar and kind but nothing more than a friend. Her body, and especially her snow leopard, didn't seem to share the same desire. "Yeah. They have a big Christmas light event at night, and I'm going to take the kids. I thought they'd have fun."

"Are you going by yourself?" He stood next to the couch with his hands on his hips as he surveyed the disaster area that the living room had become after an entire day of entertaining two children.

Melody laughed. "Since when is it impossible for one adult to leave the house with two children? I can handle them."

"I'm sure you can, but I'm not sure you should."

She didn't like the dark look that had come over his face. It was as though he were completely somewhere else in his mind. "What do you mean?"

"This is a big city, and I'm sure an event like that draws a decent crowd. Plus, you'd be out after dark by yourself, trying to find your car in the parking lot..." He trailed off as he lifted his hands in the air in turn, weighing all the possible, horrible options. "And we don't know what Ruby's circumstances are," he added.

Though she wasn't exactly sure what he meant by that, Melody didn't mind a little company. It would be a good excuse to spend more time with Roman, which had been difficult since they'd discovered Ruby. She'd hardly talked to him at all, and though things had been amicable after their night together, she didn't want anything to feel awkward. "Sure. You can come if you want to."

When they arrived at the L.A. Zoo an hour later, Melody quickly found a place to park and hopped out of the car, heading for the trunk. She whisked out one of the strollers and opened it with a snap. "I'm so excited! I have to admit I enjoy the lights just as much as the kids do, or maybe even more so since I understand all the work that goes into them. The weather is absolutely beautiful for this!" The temperatures had dropped into the fifties, making it just cool enough to bundle up and feel the coziness of the season without having to worry about keeping the kids warm.

Roman didn't appear to be enjoying himself at all as he tried to figure out the stroller. He shook the handle as he bent over and ran his hand down the side. "Is there a button or a switch or something for this thing?"

Melody reached over. She grabbed the handle and the button next to it, and the stroller popped open with a flick of her wrist. "Don't look at me like that," she said with a laugh. "I've been doing this for a while, so I'd better be familiar with the equipment. I'll get the kids."

When she had Lucas and Ruby buckled into their respective strollers, Melody was pleased to see Roman wrap his thick fingers around the handles of Ruby's. He looked a little apprehensive, but it was clear to her now that he just didn't have much experience with kids. She couldn't knock him for that, and she certainly had to admire him for trying.

They meandered along the paved pathway as Lucas waxed ecstatic over all the sights and sounds. "Look! Lion!" he shouted, pointing at the large, illuminated decoration that stood proudly along the path. "Look, Ruby, look!" Her name came out more like 'Wooby,' and it positively melted Melody's heart.

"Good job, Lucas. That is a lion. And what's that over there?" She knelt next to the stroller and pointed, directing his eyes to a polar bear. It was a completely different experience than coming to the zoo during the day and seeing the live animals, but that was one of the things Melody loved about it.

"Bear!" Lucas squealed.

Roman smirked, leaning close to Melody as they moved on. "You know, I'd think there would be certain species he'd be less interested in seeing, considering he sees them all the time."

Melody stopped herself from leaning into Roman's warmth. Their soul-bond was hard to ignore, no matter how much logic she tried to apply to it. The night air, the bright lights, and even just seeing him watch the fascination on Ruby's face only helped cement just how incredible he was inside her heart. The man didn't know a damn thing about kids, and he was under no obligation to go there with her, yet there he was.

"You'd be surprised," she admitted. "Lucas says his favorite animal is a bear. When I ask him why, he just points to himself. I think it's kind of great that he can relate to the animal world so well, but I do have to really keep an eye on him when I bring him here during the day."

They made their way toward a canopy of trees. The mirror balls that dangled from the branches enhanced the numerous lights that surrounded them. "He gets a little too enthusiastic?" Roman asked.

Melody bit her lip, trying not to laugh. "When he was really little, he was too young for it to matter all that much. As he's gotten a little bit older and more self-aware, he's figured out who he really is at heart. Of course, living at headquarters means that he doesn't have to hold back his animal self. You combine all that, and you've got a little boy trying to jump over the railing and get as close to the real bears as he can. There was no way he could actually get to them, because of the way everything is set up here, but that didn't stop him from trying."

"Did he think he should be living with them or something?"

"You know, I think he wanted them to come home with us," Melody giggled. It was hard to keep the conversation quiet, but she didn't want Lucas to think she was making fun of him. "He couldn't really tell me because he was so upset. I can laugh about it now, but at the time, I was glad it wasn't a busy day. There weren't too many people around to see him throwing an absolute fit over not being able to take the bears home."

"That's pretty cute," Roman admitted. "I have to say, I thought these two would be too young to enjoy this, but they seem to be having a good time. Look." Roman nodded down at the little girl in the stroller.

Ruby had been swaddled in a thick knit cap and a fleece coat, and Melody had tucked a thick blanket around her in the stroller. She'd shown a good temperament so far, and even being wrapped up like the Abominable Snowbaby hadn't fazed her. She turned her head from side to side, her eyes wide as she followed all the moving, shimmering lights.

It was a sweet scene, one that Melody would be sure to gush about to Emersyn, but she found herself far more focused on Roman. The soft, colored lights bathed and softened his face. He was a handsome man in any light, but the way he looked at Ruby completely changed his features. This wasn't just a man who'd seen the suffering of war and had moved off to the Cowboy State to bury that past. This was a man who felt, who wanted to feel.

He brought out the feline side of her, and Melody wanted to rub her cheek against his shoulder affectionately. She wished she hadn't been so reserved when they'd had that time together on the couch, with the rest of the house asleep. Yes, they'd ended up in bed together, but she longed for something even more intimate. How nice it would've been to twine her fingers between his, to cuddle up against him and lean her head on his shoulder while they watched the movie, to stretch and snuggle and be completely comfortable with each other. The sex had been incredibly hot, but Melody knew it could go even deeper than that if they could get past everything else that was in their way.

"Isn't she something else?" Roman murmured, nodding at Ruby. "She must've been through a lot over the last couple of days, but she still manages to chill out and enjoy all the lights. I know she doesn't think about things the same way we do, but still. I might have a hard time if I were in her position."

The warmth in Melody's cheeks had nothing to do with the sweater she'd put on for their trip. Roman was showing her, in all the little ways, just how real of a person he was. She'd expected something different, someone more distant, when Amar had told them he was coming.

As they moved on toward the Twinkle Tunnel, Melody directed their little party over to the side. "Okay, I think it's best to stop off for some diaper changes before we get any further. I don't want to get inside that tunnel of lights and regret it." She bent down to unbuckle Lucas from his stroller.

"Um, what should I do?" Roman asked softly.

She looked up at him, seeing the sheer terror in his face. He was trying. He'd already done a lot, considering that neither of these children was related to him biologically. "I'll just run in with Lucas, and then I'll come back to swap them out. You can stay here with the strollers if that works. Then I won't need to worry about our stuff."

Roman looked somewhat relieved, and Melody hid her smile as she took Lucas into the restroom. "Are you having fun?" she asked the little boy. The bright lights overhead were a contrast to the darkness outside, and she squinted against it.

"Yeah!" he replied enthusiastically. "More lights?"

"Oh, yes," she said as she opened the diaper bag. "Lots and lots and lots of them!"

When they emerged, she found Roman right where she'd left him. He was squatting next to Ruby's stroller, her tiny fingers wrapped around one of his as he cooed to her sweetly. Melody hated to interrupt the little tableau, and she caught the slightly self-conscious look on his face as she approached. "Ruby's turn!"

Back in the bathroom, Melody put the little blondie on the changing table and began removing all the wrappings she'd put on her to make sure she stayed warm. "I hope you're having a good time, sweetling. You are just the most adorable little thing. I know you seem to be doing okay, but I worry about you so much." She bent down and kissed her on the forehead.

Her hands deftly performed the tasks she'd become so used to over the years without thought. There wasn't anyone else in the restroom at the moment, and she quickly found herself chatting to Ruby the way she always did with babies. "You know, I can tell you this because I know you won't tattle on me, but I'm just crazy about that man who's pushing your stroller. It's too easy, when we're out here with you kids, and the weather and the lighting is all so perfect, to think that the two of us are a couple. I mean, the way I'd like us to be." She smiled as she began putting Ruby's clothes back on, grateful that the restroom wasn't too chilly for her. "I think he'd make an awfully good father himself, considering the way he pays attention to the two of you."

She was full of warm thoughts as she emerged, but her blood ran cold when she didn't see Roman or Lucas anywhere. The things he'd said at headquarters earlier about not knowing where Ruby came from or who might be after her kicked in with a shot of adrenaline, and she held the baby closer to her chest as she moved through the dim light. There were people everywhere, but she didn't see the familiar set of his shoulders.

A dark figure loomed toward her on the left, and Melody quickly turned. It was Roman, pushing both of the strollers.

"Oh, thank goodness! I didn't know where you'd gone!" she gasped as she clutched at her chest.

"Sorry. We decided to pick up some hot chocolate. Here." Roman handed her a covered paper cup.

Her fingers touched his as she took it from him. Why did he have to go and do yet another thing to make her feel this way about him? It was hard enough that their inner beasts were fighting so hard for the two of them to be together, but little things like this made it even more difficult to resist. "That was very kind of you."

"I thought it would be a nice treat," he said, his dark eyes meeting hers over the rim of his cup.

"Look! Bear!"

Melody glanced down to see that Lucas was clutching a sippy cup from the zoo's gift shop.

"They had some souvenir kids' mugs, and he went nuts for them," Roman explained. "I figured Ruby wasn't old enough for one, so I got her this." He reached under the stroller and pulled a stuffed bear with a Santa hat out of a bag.

"You're so sweet," Melody said genuinely. As they continued through the Twinkle Tunnel, made their way through a huge, lit-up storybook scene, and enjoyed a forest full of snowflakes and snowmen, Melody felt herself being lulled into a sense of family and belonging. Her snow leopard was content, gently kneading away at her heart, and almost sleepy as they reached the end of the light tour and headed for the parking lot.

"So, what did you think?" Melody asked as they pulled up next to the car and she unbuckled Ruby from her stroller.

Something about Roman had changed. His shoulders were tense, and his hands were fisted at his sides. He stood with one foot forward, as though he were ready for action. "Do you smell that?"

"Um, we *are* at a zoo," Melody joked as she opened the back door and prepared Ruby's car seat by pulling the straps out of the way.

"No, it's something else."

Just then, a figure burst out from the shadows at the edge of the parking lot. Melody turned just in time to see someone reach into the stroller and snag Ruby straight out of it. Melody screamed. She dove for the stranger, who was nothing more than a dark shape in the night. Her razor-sharp claws shot out from the tips of her fingers, her body acting instinctively, but she only snagged Ruby's blanket as it fell to the ground.

Scrambling, Melody latched onto Lucas as her mind tried to sort out what was happening. The captor turned to disappear into the trees, but Roman was after him. His feet pounded into the soft earth as he shot off into the night.

"You okay, baby?" she asked, her voice trembling as she impatiently shoved the stroller buckles aside to get to Lucas. She was terrified by what had happened to Ruby, but the important thing at the moment was to get Lucas in the car and make sure he was safe.

Pulling him up into her arms and snuggling his warm little body to her chest, Melody felt the cold metal of a knife at the back of her neck. "Give me the baby." The voice sent a shiver of horror down her spine.

It also activated her snow leopard, along with the parental instincts that Melody so rarely got to tap into, but she was in public; she had to restrain her big cat for the time being. She kept Lucas latched tightly to her torso as she punched her elbow backward, hearing the satisfying sound of air forcibly leaving the perpetrator's lungs. Immediately, Melody struck with her opposite foot before turning around and swinging a kick through the air. She didn't care where it landed, as long as this asshole understood he was not going to get away with this.

Her elbow and the first kick had made the culprit double over, so her final kick swept right across the side of his face. His head whipped to the side, and he kept the momentum going as he took off into the darkness.

"Melody!" Roman called, jogging back toward her with Ruby in his arms. The dim light showed a scratch across his face, but otherwise, he looked intact.

Tears flooded her eyes as she saw the duo. "Oh, thank God! Is she okay?"

Ruby clung to Roman, and tears shined in her big blue eyes, but Roman nodded. "Yeah. That shifter was fast, but not a great fighter. He or she gave up quickly."

Melody's hands shook as she put Lucas in the car and reached for Ruby. "Holy shit. I can't believe that. Who would do such a thing?" She would hold back as long as she could, not wanting to scare the children any more than they probably already had been, but that was just too much.

"That's the problem. We don't have any way of knowing." Roman packed the strollers into the trunk, shut it with a slam, and took the driver's seat.

It was her car, but she didn't feel like arguing. She didn't care about the logistics, as long as they got back to headquarters. "I guess not."

Roman's hands clung tightly to the steering wheel as he backed out of their parking space. "This is exactly what I was talking about, Melody. For whatever reason that Ruby is on our doorstep, it's possible that she and anyone else around her are in great danger. You can't just go running off through the city without a care in the world."

She'd been ready to sink into the passenger seat and just close her eyes until they got home, but she straightened and turned to face him. "Excuse me?"

"You heard me. You need to be more careful. Something horrible could've happened just then. You need to call Amar and tell him about this."

"Since when are you in charge of anything?" she challenged, her adrenaline quickly funneling away from fear and toward anger. "You've been in town all a few days, and you think you can just order me around? Like I'm some idiot who doesn't know how to watch out for children?"

"Don't get all defensive on me. Amar needs to know about this. I smelled those guys, and I knew they were shifters. This obviously has something to do with Ruby." He pounded his fist into his thigh.

"Of course, but do you seriously think I need you to tell me that? Or to come down on me like I'm some sort of dumbass who doesn't understand all the possibilities? I might not be an official part of the Force, but I'm sure as shit going to do everything I can to protect these kids!" She slapped her hand over her mouth, realizing she'd cussed twice in front of the little ones now. Turning, she was relieved to see Lucas asleep in his car seat.

"Yes, you are going to do just that by staying home and keeping them as far out of harm's way as possible. I wouldn't be able to forgive myself if something happened to them." He triggered the turn signal with an angry flick of his hand.

"You?" she spluttered, unable to fathom how or why he'd suddenly come to decide that Lucas and Ruby were his responsibility instead of hers. If it had just been the two of them in the car, she would've ripped him up one side and down the other, telling him to take his polar bear ass straight back to Wyoming where he belonged. But the children were asleep, and they'd had a traumatic enough evening without seeing two grown adults fighting like children.

Instead, she crossed her arms in front of her chest and turned her head toward the window, though she hardly saw any of the lights or decorations of the city as they made their way back. As angry as she was, she could at least be grateful that Lucas and Ruby were safe. And that Roman wouldn't be joining the Force.

7

"I'm not going to push you into participating, but I'm glad we've got a mission happening while you're here. It's a good chance for you to see what things are really like for us." Amar smiled, looking completely at ease behind the wheel of his sedan as they pulled onto the highway.

As much as it had felt like Christmas the night before, with the lights, festivities, and hot chocolate, the brilliant morning light and the palm trees made Roman feel like he was on a tropical vacation. He wasn't particularly in the mood for one, though. "Yeah. That's true."

"It should be a pretty easy operation today. The Alpha of this clan isn't exactly known for his pleasant disposition, nor for cooperating with other clans in the area, but he agreed to the meeting readily enough," Amar continued. "We'll just sit down with him, have a chat, and see what he has to say. Of course, you'll still want to be ready in case shit goes sideways."

"I always am," Roman said with a half-smile.

"What's eating you?" Amar asked after a moment of silence. "You've been a bit off ever since you and Melody got back home last night."

Roman let out a long breath. Ever since he'd arrived, he'd been trying to decide how to talk to Amar about this, but he'd have to do it eventually. "I know Melody is my mate."

His friend let out a light laugh. "I had a feeling. The air practically crackles between the two of you."

"Yeah, well, it doesn't anymore. She got so pissed at me last night." It was impossible to avoid each other, even in that huge house, so he'd seen her at breakfast. She'd turned away from him with a stiff jaw as she made a bottle for Ruby, and not a single word had been exchanged. "I don't understand it."

"What did you do?" Amar pressed.

"What do you mean, what did I do?" Roman's muscles bunched in his shoulders. "Why do you think it's my fault?"

Amar shrugged as he changed lanes. "Because you're a man, and us men are usually the ones doing stupid things, as far as women are concerned. You got Ruby back, but what else did you do?"

Roman flicked his fingers in the air. "Nothing, man. I just told her she needed to be more careful, and that until we got this figured out, she and the kids needed to stay at headquarters. I told her to call you, and since I was the one driving, that only made sense."

"Hold on," Amar said, putting his hand up. "You've already hit the nail on the head. You told her she has to stay home?"

"Well, she does! It's not safe to have those kids out in public, not if someone could be after Ruby. She's got to be more careful." How could Melody not see that?

His friend pressed his lips together and sighed. "While there's certainly some sense in what you're saying, I have a feeling you said it in the wrong way. You know, the kind of way that suggests she's weak and can't fend for herself."

"But she's not," Roman countered. "I saw her take down the second attacker, all while having a kid in her arms. She definitely stood her ground." His fight with the first assailant had been easy, and he'd witnessed Melody making quick work of the second one as he came back to the car. The fire and determination inside her were easy to see, even in the darkness. It was admirable, even a little sexy.

"But you made her believe you felt the opposite," Amar pointed out.

"It scared the hell out of me to know I hadn't been right there for her when she'd needed me the most," he admitted. "I thought it was supposed to be so easy and natural when you found your mate, like everything else in the world just fell into place, and you lived happily ever after. Of course, I'd been dumb enough to think I'd found a happy ending before. I guess I'm just a fucking sucker." He braced his hand on his forehead.

"Don't be so hard on yourself. What Elizabeth did to you was wrong; there's no doubt about that. You're allowed to take time to deal with it, and you're even allowed to be mad, but you can't let it dictate the rest of your life." Amar glanced at Roman before returning his eyes to the road. "Trust me, man. I knew Katalin was the one, but when I spent all those years searching endlessly for her, it made me a shell of a man. After all those centuries, I was lucky enough to find her somehow, but I still have to wonder how different my life might've been if I hadn't let the trauma of losing her get to me."

Roman wanted to argue, simply because he was angry about how much he'd screwed up everything with Melody. He'd hated seeing the way she'd dismissed him once they'd gotten through briefing the others the night before. A close call like that should've brought them closer together instead of further apart. They should've spent the night in bed together, holding each other and talking about how grateful they were to be all right. It didn't matter that they'd already dismissed the idea of any sort of real future as a couple. The coldness with which she'd turned away from him that morning in the kitchen was enough to haunt him until the end of his days.

He sighed. "That's easy for you to say since you were able to find her again and be together. It's not going to be like that with Melody. Even if it were, I can't give her what she really wants."

"Which is?"

"Children." She'd told him that, but Roman had seen it for himself in a way that was absolutely undeniable. Melody didn't just want to be a mother, she *needed* it.

"Ah. And so we're right back to Elizabeth once again, aren't we?"

Another sigh. How could Roman just let go of everything he'd been through? It hadn't been easy to have a steady girlfriend when he was in the service and overseas. Roman came back as often as he could, though, and even when doubts about long-distance relationships crept into his mind, Elizabeth always found a way to assuage them.

Then there'd come the moment she told him she was pregnant. Roman had been over the moon at the news. He'd been getting close to his discharge date, and this would've been the perfect way to start his new life as a civilian. He was daydreaming about all the things he would teach his son any time he wasn't on duty.

"She absolutely killed me inside," he said into the silence that had fallen between them. "My father had spent a lot of time with me growing up. He taught me how to fish, hold a gun, open a door for a lady...all that guy stuff. I soaked up everything I could from him, and he was my hero. I can't tell you how badly I wanted to be that for my son, too. I was going to be there for him, and I was going to be the good father that so many kids don't get to have. I felt awful about not being able to be home for the birth, but I told myself it would be all right because as soon as I was out of the service, I'd be there all the time. Every damn second."

"I know." Amar patted him on the shoulder. "I'm really sorry, man."

"Don't be. It's my own dumb fault for believing her. We had a few mutual friends who'd tried to warn me about her in the beginning, but I was too in love to listen. What gets me the most is I was stupid enough to fall for it." He gritted his teeth, still clearly remembering how his heart had soared at seeing little Aiden on video calls from Elizabeth. Roman had thought he was the most precious thing in the world, and his love for the baby surpassed even what he'd felt for Elizabeth. Without having even met him in person, Roman had dedicated his entire being to this child. And then he'd gone home for the last time.

He'd been so nervous, even though he'd told himself how stupid that was. Aiden was a baby, and he wouldn't have any idea how significant of a meeting he was about to have. It would be the start of the rest of their lives together, and the time Aiden had spent without his father would simply be something they reminisced about over the dining table in the future.

But Roman had known right away that Aiden wasn't his. He could smell it on him. This was some other man's kid. Elizabeth had denied it, of course, and she'd even thrown it back in his face. She'd lambasted him for being irresponsible enough to have a child when he couldn't even be stateside for Aiden's birth, as though it hadn't been her fault, too. Finally, when he'd insisted on a DNA test to prove it, she'd caved.

"So much for my life as a family man," Roman continued. "I was so angry and so hurt, but more than anything, the emotional scars left me jaded about ever being a father. All that hope, all that joy, everything I'd built out in my head about raising a son... just to be gone like that in a matter of seconds? Man, I just can't deal with that kind of pain. Not now, not ever. How can I possibly try to continue things with Melody when I know she could never really be happy with me?"

Amar tapped his fingers on the steering wheel. "You want my opinion?"

"You're going to give it to me, anyway."

"You're damn right I am."

Roman ran a hand over his head. "I guess you're going to tell me not to let the past get in the way, but I don't see any way around it. I've already messed up as it is by exploding on Melody at the zoo. It's better if she thinks I'm an asshole."

"Do what you want, but you can't escape fate. Whatever is meant to happen will happen." Amar flicked on his turn signal and veered onto the exit ramp.

"Yeah, speaking of that, there's something we need to talk about." He rubbed a finger alongside his nose, unsure of exactly how to broach this. "I don't want to upset you as Alpha of the house, but Melody and I slept together." Roman braced for a possible detonation from Amar. He didn't want to disrespect the Alpha, nor his house-mates. Roman was trusted as a guest, and he couldn't have kept his dick in his pants for even the first 24 hours?

But the other man shrugged. "I know how strong our inner beasts are, and there's no denying that the two of you have some sort of connection. These things happen. Besides, I have a feeling Melody would kick your ass if you tried anything she didn't approve of."

Roman grinned despite himself. He wanted to feel moody and dark, and maybe even a little sorry for himself, but the way Melody had defended herself and Lucas at the zoo had been incredible. Without shifting, she'd still managed to transform into a kickass fighting machine. Melody had gone from the sweet, happy woman he'd curled up and watched a movie with into a protective mother who'd stop at nothing to keep the child in her arms away from her assailants.

"Here we are," Amar announced, pulling Roman back into the present moment. They stepped out of the car and wound through the heavily landscaped walkway toward the front porch of a two-story home. Amar tipped his head back to examine it. "It always interests me to see the different ways clans live. This one seems to have a bit of funding, but they're not over the top like some of the others I've seen. At least they're not living in poverty, which is always a problem."

"I guess we can safely assume, just like our time in the service, that whether you're dealing with rich or poor, it's just as likely that someone's up to no good."

"You bet."

Roman was excited to go in and get this done. Though he had no intention of joining the Force, he needed something to keep his mind off Melody. Unfortunately, the Alpha of this clan had very little to say.

"I appreciate that you've taken the time and effort to come all the way out here," Mr. Morefield said with mock sympathy as he puffed on a cigar behind his desk. "I mean, this must be a major event if the SOS Force is involved. I can't, however, give you any clue as to what's going on in the case of this child. We prefer to keep to ourselves as much as possible. It's the much safer way to run a clan, as I'm sure you can agree."

Amar nodded. "And you're sure you haven't heard anything about either a missing or a found shifter child?" He'd been careful not to give any specific information as to where Ruby was, and he hadn't even spoken her name.

"All I can tell you is that we're all present and accounted for. I'll be sure to contact you if I find myself in need of your assistance." With a wave of his arm, they were dismissed.

"He's lying," Roman said through gritted teeth as soon as they were out the front door. "The bastards who attacked us at the zoo had a very distinct scent, and I picked up on it here. These guys are definitely involved."

"We haven't had any trouble out of this clan just yet, but I've heard a few rumors that they might not always operate on the up-and-up. Their territory butts right up next to another clan's, which is bound to cause some trouble eventually if it hasn't already."

They ducked through an arbor overgrown with vines and rounded the edge of a flower bed, where a woman was on her hands and knees working the soil. "He's lying to you," she said quietly.

"Ma'am?" Roman stopped.

She glanced behind her, toward the house, but she was shielded from view by a large bush. "Don't look down here! If they see you talking to me, I'll be in more trouble than I even want to think about." She clutched her hands in the rich soil.

Roman and Amar played along, turning to look at each other so it would look to anyone else as though they were standing on the sidewalk and having a conversation. "What do you know?" Roman asked.

"They took the child," she whimpered, a tear dripping off her jawline and into the dirt. "They didn't say anything about it, and I'm not privy to Mr. Morefield's scheme, but I heard it crying in the night. I knew it wasn't ours, and I couldn't bear the idea of it being taken away from its parents."

"So, you were the one who left her on our doorstep?" Amar asked, glancing down the block.

"No. I couldn't get away, but I sent someone who could. I would've done it myself if I could have. As it is, I may be killed just for talking to you." She wept harder, her dirty hands on her knees now.

"You can come with us," Amar offered. "We can give you shelter until this whole thing is over with. Our vehicle is just over there, and we could be there in just a few seconds."

She shook her head emphatically. "I can't. I have obligations here. I had to tell you. As a mother myself, I had to do what I could. It wasn't even safe to risk giving the baby back to its own clan, but I believe it belongs to the one to the east of here. Please, just go before it creates more trouble for all of us."

The two men moved on to the vehicle, but as Roman climbed into the passenger seat, he couldn't help but think of Melody. This woman had gone against her Alpha at the risk of her own life because she knew how Ruby's parents must have felt. She had no obligation to Ruby's parents when it came to clan or blood, and Ruby's clan might very well have been their mortal enemies, but none of that mattered. It was just like Melody, who cared so much for children who weren't of her own womb. That was a deep kind of love that couldn't be denied.

8

"Eggs?" Lucas asked eagerly from his chair at the breakfast table.

"You want more?" Melody asked as she scooped a bit onto his plate. "You've got a good appetite this morning."

Lucas pointed at Ruby in her highchair. "Eggs, Ruby?"

"Yes, she might like some, too." It was hard to know what Ruby was used to eating, but Melody followed her instincts as best as possible. She put a spoonful of scrambled eggs onto the tray and watched as Ruby scooped them up in her fingers. The baby dropped more of them onto herself than into her mouth, but she gave a coo of pleasure as she ate.

"She likes eggs!" Lucas said triumphantly.

It was adorable, but Melody was having a hard time throwing herself into the typically happy work of childcare. As she served juice and milk and wiped up spills, she couldn't help but think about what a royal prick Roman had been. She didn't care about his past with the military. It didn't give him the right to make her feel as though she were too incompetent to take care of these children. She'd certainly kept Lucas out of harm's way, hadn't she? Hell, the whole incident might not have even happened if Roman hadn't been there in the first place. She would've known she was there on her own at night, and she wouldn't have let her guard down for a second. She had always been vigilant, even before there was any known threat.

"Mel'dy mad?" Lucas asked, scraping the last of the eggs from his plate.

She swiped a hand over her forehead, where she could feel tension building, and she forced a smile. "No, sweetie. I was just thinking about some things. Are you all done?"

He nodded eagerly, and she wiped him down and helped him out of his chair.

"Am I too late for breakfast?" Roman said as he walked into the room.

Her muscles jolted with electricity at his presence, but she quickly reminded herself that she was angry with him. Furious. She didn't want to have anything to do with him, no matter what her snow leopard said. "I thought you left hours ago."

"I did. I went with Amar to talk to a few more people. He's determined not to take any action with Ruby until we can be absolutely certain that we're putting her back in the correct arms." He grabbed a granola bar from the basket on the counter.

"That's good." Melody took a warm, damp washcloth to Ruby's face. The little girl laughed as it tickled her. Melody didn't want to smile back, because she was so damn angry, but Ruby was irresistible. At least she had her back to Roman as she returned the baby's smile. "It's important to keep her safe."

He let out a sigh as he unwrapped the granola bar that she wasn't sure how to interpret. "We think we've got a good lead on finding her parents, so it's quite possible she'll be going back to them soon."

"That's..." Melody hesitated. She knew that Ruby going home was the right thing. If this were her child, she'd certainly want her back. That was part of the problem, though. Melody had built a bond with Ruby in the short time she'd been watching her. She'd taken her in as though she were simply part of the family, and she'd continue to care for her as long as needed. "That's good," she finally said.

"Melody, I think we should talk."

She was purposely not looking at him. She didn't want to see his handsome face and get weak in the knees all over again. Melody had every right to be angry with him, and she needed to hold onto that as much as possible. That anger would fuel her strength against the demands of her snow leopard, who apparently wasn't nearly as insulted by his comments after they'd left the zoo. Even as her human side focused on its fury, her animal side longed to sidle up next to him. Melody wished she could squirt it with a spray bottle like a naughty housecat. "I don't think we really have much to talk about."

There was no response, and when she still didn't hear anything from him after she finished washing out Ruby's bottle, she turned and expected him to be gone. Instead, he stood there leaning against the pantry, his uneaten granola bar still in his hand as he looked at her. She couldn't quite read his eyes. Was he pissed? Apologetic? Hoping to wait her out until she started talking first? That last one only made her angrier, and she cared even less about what his motives were. "What?" she demanded.

"I just...I just don't think you quite understand what happened last night."

Her lashes fluttered as she blinked several times, shocked at what he was saying. "Really, Roman? You've already insulted me once. Are you calling me stupid now?"

"Outside?" Lucas asked, pointing at the back door.

Leave it to him to de-escalate the situation. "Yes, we can go outside. Let's get our jackets on." Good, this would be the perfect chance for her to avoid any further encounters with Roman.

But Lucas had other ideas. "You play?" he asked Roman. "Outside?"

Shit. Lucas was a sweet little thing. He'd already been thinking of Roman as just another part of the family, and the trip to the zoo had only reinforced that.

"Oh, you want me to play?" Roman asked Lucas.

"Yeah! Play!" Lucas flung his hands in the air and waved them around.

Roman lifted his gaze to meet hers. "Only if it's all right with Melody."

It wasn't as though she could say no. What kind of example would that set for Lucas? It was bad enough she was already arguing in front of him. "If you'd like," she said as coldly as possible.

With jackets on, they headed into the back yard. As soon as Lucas's little feet touched the grass, he shifted into the grizzly bear form he'd inherited from his father.

"That was quick," Roman remarked.

Melody spread out a blanket and set Ruby on it. "He was a slow start, and he didn't show any signs of his animal form until his first birthday. Once he figured it out, though, he wanted to do it all the time. We had to work with him a lot just to get him to understand that there are only certain times when it's acceptable."

Roman gestured to the tall fences that surrounded the backyard. They were mostly covered in ivy, making them even better barriers against private eyes. "Was all this already here?"

Melody flicked the tip of her tongue against the back of her teeth. She didn't want to explain anything to him. Nothing that happened there at headquarters was his business, especially if he thought he could butt in and just take over whenever he wanted. Still, they had an adorable little cub wandering around the yard, listening whether he meant to or not with the acute hearing of a wild animal. "There was a fence, but we decided to put in something that would keep us a little more secluded from the rest of the world."

The young cub stomped up to Roman and nudged him on the leg before taking off across the yard.

"What's that about?"

One of these days, when Lucas was much older, she would tell him the story of how he picked the one person she was absolutely furious with and begged him to play. "He wants you to play tag with him. He likes to do it in his bear form so he can run on all four legs instead of just two. You don't have to do it if you don't want to, though."

Roman gave her a challenging look before a shiver ran up his back and racked his shoulders. His skin exploded in white fur as he bent forward, his spine lengthening. His fingers thickened as his hands and feet turned to four huge paws. His face had stretched and molded to accommodate his animal form, and Melody soon found herself staring at a polar bear.

She'd known what he was, but it was entirely different to see his arctic beast standing in their Southern California backyard. Melody lived in a house full of shifters of all kinds. She should be used to seeing their animal forms emerge. Why did it feel so different to see Roman?

He was huge, first of all. His muscles rippled under that thick coat of fur, and even though his natural insulation had to be suffocatingly hot in this environment, he romped off across the yard after Lucas. Melody put her hand in front of her mouth as she watched them, not wanting Roman to have any idea how much she loved seeing him like this. It wasn't just the appeal of him, though she certainly had to admire his glossy coat and dark eyes that still carried a reflection of the man she'd come to know. It was also in the way he played with Lucas, how he dodged first one way and then the other as they stormed through the yard in a far more raucous game of tag than Melody ever normally played with Lucas. Roman knew little about caring for children's most basic needs, but he certainly knew how to entertain them.

She was distracted from her admiration by movement at her feet. Ruby sat on the blanket, her little fingers braced on the fabric as she watched the action in the backyard. She chattered at Lucas and Roman, blowing raspberries at them every time they ran past. She rocked back and forth on her backside.

"They're having a lot of fun, aren't they?" she said, smiling once again at how absolutely adorable this little person was. Roman had said they had a lead on her parents. Did they know she was safe? Did they have any clue their dear baby was being taken care of? Roman hadn't given her any details about the parents. What if they didn't want her at all?

Ruby thrust herself forward and caught herself on her arms. Melody bent down to make sure she was all right, but then she noticed the thin coat of hair on Ruby's ears that hadn't been there earlier that morning. Before her very eyes, those tiny ears continued to transform as they shifted up the side of Ruby's head. Her tiny baby fingernails that were only paper-thin in her human form emerged as thick black claws. The next thing Melody knew, Ruby was toddling in pure bear cub form across the grass.

"Good job, little girl!" Melody cheered.

Lucas and Roman turned to look, slowing down as Ruby meandered across the lawn to them. Lucas gamboled up to her and nudged her with his nose, while Roman was suddenly very careful about the exact placement of his paws.

Melody refused to hide her delight this time, and for the first time in the past day, she and her snow leopard were in agreement. She called her own arctic beast to the surface, and though her body had to compact itself for this transformation, it was incredibly freeing. Melody twisted and stretched as she melted down to her feline form, extending her claws as soon as she had them to grip the cool grass underneath her. There was a certain balance that came from having a long tail that complemented her body perfectly, making her feel far more comfortable in this form than as a human. Even her wild, unruly hair that she always sought to tame when she stood on two feet was no longer a problem. The silvery-white fur was warm and fluffy, its spots and rosettes acting as both decoration and camouflage.

With a flick of her tail, Melody trotted off across the yard to join the others. She stuck close by Ruby, wanting to make sure the little one was all right. The baby often lost her balance and rolled over onto her side, but she didn't seem to mind as she grabbed at her toes and rubbed her muzzle in the grass. Lucas charged at Roman from the other side of the yard, slamming into the side of the big white bear. Roman responded with a rather dramatic fall to the side, allowing Lucas to climb on top of his defeated enemy and make a tiny roar of victory. Ruby decided to join in on the triumph, frolicking over to nip at Roman's toes.

Melody watched with interest. Any man who was that thoughtful and sweet when it came to children couldn't really be as much of a jerk as she thought he was, could he? And he'd made the effort of buying both Lucas and Ruby souvenirs at the zoo. Why, then, did he always seem so hesitant when it came to kids? And why did he have to be so rude to her?

Lucas rolled off Roman and tried to engage Ruby in a new game of tag. As the two of them worked out the best way for young shifters to act like bears, Roman's dark eyes met Melody's. While in their human forms, their animals had been reaching out to each other. Now, it was her mind that reached out toward his like a curling wisp of magic in the December air, something so intrinsic and natural that Melody hardly even knew what it was as it was happening. But it persisted nonetheless, yearning toward its one goal.

Roman got up and strode away from the cubs, his body changing as he moved toward the back door. His snowy fur melted away as his ears returned to their human shape, and he straightened up onto two feet as his paws once again became fingers. That strand of something that had reached out so desperately, so instinctively for him slammed into a wall as he became a human again, just in time to open the back door and disappear.

The cubs looked disappointedly after him. Melody did, too, but she couldn't dwell on that. The most important thing at the moment was the children, not some man who couldn't seem to make up his mind about where or who he wanted to be. She swiveled her head, looking for something to distract them from having lost their playmate, and found a late-season flower growing along the fence line. Melody pounced toward it and purposely missed, leaving it bobbing and weaving in her wake. Lucas and Ruby batted at it joyfully.

Out of the corner of her eye, Melody watched the house. She wanted to give him the benefit of the doubt, that perhaps he'd realized he had something he needed to do with Amar for the mission or that he'd eaten some leftovers that'd been in the fridge too long. But Roman had given no explanation when he went inside, nor was there any sign of him returning. Whatever his problem was, she wasn't going to find out anytime soon.

9

ROMAN SHUT THE DOOR BEHIND HIM AND CURLED HIS HANDS INTO FISTS, digging his fingernails into his palms. All he'd wanted to do was talk to Melody a little and make her realize that he hadn't meant to offend her. He wasn't about to make up with her, not in the way that mates would if they were going to make their connection a permanent one. There was just something about her being angry with him that he couldn't stand, and he'd wanted to fix it. Roman wouldn't be staying there in L.A., but he didn't want to go on with the rest of his life knowing she thought of him as an asshole.

Then the kids had gotten involved. At first, Roman thought that might make it easier. They might soften Melody up a bit, make her more willing to listen to him. She didn't have to change her mind about him completely, she only had to know that he hadn't meant to hurt her feelings. The conversation Roman had wanted had been lost in the playtime of the backyard, and before Roman knew it, he was far too busy wrestling on the grass with the cubs to think about anything else.

Other than how striking Melody was in her true form. He wasn't sure he'd ever seen a snow leopard shifter before. They weren't nearly as common as the typical bears, tigers, and wolves. Though even his own form wasn't the most common, he knew it was nothing compared to the magnificence of Melody. Her feline was lithe and quick, side-stepping without a hint of hesitation to nudge Ruby when she got off balance. She happily twitched her tail in the air to create a plaything for the children, who seemed to get quite the kick out of chasing her. At one point, Melody pretended to stalk Lucas and Ruby from behind a bush, digging her paws into the grass and wiggling her hind end in the air. That had certainly caught Roman's attention, but the children were far more intrigued when she sprang out at them and dodged to the side as though she'd missed.

But then that little nudge had shown up in the back of his mind. Roman had recognized it instantly. Shifters of the same clan shared a telepathic link, one that allowed them to communicate with each other when in their animal forms. He had the same thing with his clan in Wyoming, and it was what made a clan truly feel like a family. Roman had always heard the stories of fated mates who experienced the same thing and how their bond formed that connection just like blood ties did. For the longest time, he hadn't been sure it was real. After all, he hadn't experienced that with Elizabeth. Roman had spent a lot of time convincing himself that it was little more than a fairy tale. Just as humans fantasized about romantic stories they saw on television or in the movies, shifters got caught up on some arcane notion of a particularly special bond. It was ridiculous.

Until he'd felt it coming from Melody. Roman stomped up the stairs toward his room, wishing he hadn't felt it. It was only just the softest prompt from her mind to his, something as quiet as a whisper. He'd brushed it off, choosing instead to focus on playing with the children. They were just having a good time out in the sunshine, and Roman had to be imagining things. That signal suddenly became stronger, poking a little deeper into his mind and demanding to be noticed. That was when Roman knew he had to stop it right away.

"What's eating you?" Amar asked.

Roman had hoped to avoid running into anyone else, but Amar was standing at one of the large windows that overlooked the backyard. "Why do you think anything's eating me?"

One corner of Amar's mouth lifted in a smile. "You don't really think you can fool me, do you? I've known you for too long, and I've been around shifters for too long. I doubt you fooled Melody, either, storming off in a huff like that."

"I'm not in a huff," Roman countered, though simply saying it only made him sound all the more like he was. "And why are you spying on us, anyway?"

"Me?" Amar asked innocently. "I was on my way to contact that other clan and hopefully locate Ruby's parents, and I simply stopped to watch some of my household having one heck of a good time in the backyard. That is, until you put the kibosh on it." He folded his arms in front of his chest and watched Roman expectantly.

Looking out into the yard, Roman watched as the cubs toddled after a late-season butterfly. Melody moved along behind them, stealthy and serene, with only an occasional flick of her tail. "I couldn't lead her on any longer. I allowed myself to just get lost in what was happening. It's so natural when I'm around her. But then I felt her start to get into my head. If I let that happen, then it's going to be a lot harder to turn around and head back to Wyoming when the holiday is over."

"I see," Amar said, one eyebrow raised. "I can understand, to a degree. The telepathic link is a big step, but it's also quite the confirmation of just what the two of you have going on. If you ask me—what the hell?"

He'd been looking out the window, and Roman turned to see what had caught his attention. Two large streaks of fur were bolting into the back yard, right toward Melody and the kids. Roman's inner polar bear let out a mighty roar at the mere thought of his mate and these children being in danger. It was his job—whether he wanted to admit it or not—to keep them safe, and he'd abandoned his post.

"Let's go!" Amar flew down the stairs, transforming as he moved. His deep umber skin broke apart into pieces, flipping and resetting on his body in the form of onyx scales. His spine elongated into a tail, and it whipped angrily against the floor. His face completely changed into his dragon's, complete with piercing teeth and a row of spikes on top of his head, and smoke curled from his snout. He saved his wings until he got out the door, the obsidian absorbing the sunlight. It was a sight Roman had only seen once or twice, given how much of their time in the military had to be spent as humans.

Roman was on his heels, back into his bear form as soon as his paws touched the concrete of the back patio. Adrenaline raced through his system and his lungs opened, allowing him to take in and assess even the faintest of scents in the air. He sensed the same one he'd noted before, both at the zoo and when he and Amar had gone to talk to Mr. Morefield. The bastards were back, and they were after Ruby. The only difference was that they felt safe enough to shift within the confines of the backyard, and that meant they were a far more formidable enemy than they'd been while out in public.

The two incoming enemies were bears, and with that same fetid stench coming off of them, Roman was sure they were the enemy. They were giant, with long black claws that churned up the soil as they ran, their heavy coats rolling on their backs. Their mouths gaped open, showing their teeth and the long strings of saliva that dripped from them as they anticipated the fight and their supposed victory.

Melody had noticed the threat, and she stood with her back to the children. Her ears were laid back flat against her head as she hissed, a row of fur raised all down her spine. Her yowls and hisses twisted through the air, reminding these two attackers of just who they were dealing with. Ruby sat near the fence, looking completely puzzled as Lucas stood up in front of her. He put his paws in the air and tried to look as ferocious as possible as the first assailant charged at them.

Roman closed the distance between the house and the fray, Amar in the air at his side. They wouldn't get there in time. These bears who'd intruded headquarters were after the things he wanted to protect most in the world, and even as he tried his best, he couldn't do anything to protect them. *I'm coming, Melody. I'm coming.*

He didn't know whether she heard him or not, but she wasn't going to just stand down and let the bears take Ruby. She leaped into the air as the first bear approached, sailing past his mouth and landing directly on top of his head. Her cries of anger shot through the air as her claws shredded his thick hide. Blood splattered on the grass below as she tore through his fur and skin, glistening bright and red. The bear let out a moan, but it was one of frustration as he whipped his head around and sought purchase on her. Sinking her teeth into his hide, Melody held on as the bear whipped his body from side to side, trying to shake her off like a bull rider at a rodeo. Melody sank her claws in once again as the bear's fur darkened, stained by his blood.

The second bear dodged past Melody and his comrade to get to the children, but Roman dove in front of him, forming a wall between the attacker and the little ones. Amar swept in, sending down a stream of fire, and the air filled with the acrid scent of burning fur as the bear roared his pain. Digging his claws into the grass, Roman built as much traction as possible before he barreled across the short distance. The enemy was distracted by the massive black dragon overhead, his chin turned up, leaving his throat vulnerable. There were times in war when a soldier did his best to give the foe a chance to run away or surrender, when the noblest thing was simply to stop the situation from escalating instead of slaughtering the enemy. This was not one of them. These assholes had already come after his mate once. Now he was reliving the nightmare all over again, and he'd be damned if it happened a third time.

Roman went straight for its throat, and the other bear reared back, but it was too late. Roman's teeth sank into its flesh, clamping his jaws together as he twisted, pulling backward and taking a chunk of the other bear with him. Blood spewed over Roman's white coat, tinting it pink as he went back in again and again, his mouth filling with blood as his teeth chopped and tore. A deep bellow of fear, pain, and anguish echoed through the air, and Roman realized it was coming from his enemy. He was absolutely mad with fury as he attacked, ripping and tearing, putting all his anger and frustration into it.

A clawed hand rested heavily on his shoulder. Roman turned to attack it as well, but the red that had clouded his vision cleared just in time for him to realize it was Amar. The dragon dissolved back into his human form, folding his wings into his back and standing up straight. His face was solemn. "It's over, Roman. The children are safe." He moved toward the fence, where the two cubs were shivering against the foliage, and scooped them into his arms.

Melody! Roman turned to see Melody lying on the ground. The bear's carcass next to her was proof of the effort she'd put into the fight, but the blood that rimmed the bear's mouth showed that he'd fought back before she'd killed him. Her silvery fur was contaminated with the blood of her enemy, staining it a dingy red around her paws and mouth. The parallel slashes from the bear's claws seeped fresher blood in a brilliant crimson that made him sick to his stomach.

Slowly, tenderly, Roman began licking her wounds. His heart wrenched seeing her lying there like that on the grass, panting and shivering. The light hadn't gone out of her eyes, though, and the wounds appeared to be superficial. Shifters healed far faster than humans did, and he had no doubt she would recover. That didn't make it any easier to see her like this.

Damn it! How could he have let this happen? He'd insisted on accompanying her to the zoo because he wanted to protect her. He'd even been enough of an asshole to insinuate that she couldn't protect the children herself outside of headquarters. This fight had certainly proven that Melody knew how to hold her own, and that no place was truly safe.

"We need to get her inside," Amar said. Since Roman had arrived, Amar had mostly spoken to him as a friend, but now, he spoke as an Alpha. His orders were ones to be followed, not questioned in any manner. "I'm taking the children inside. You stay here with her, and I'll send someone out to help you carry her in."

As the dragon headed for the house, Roman sucked in a staggered breath and let his polar bear go. His muscles, strength, and size could only do so much. He also couldn't risk reaching for that link that they'd both tried to use now. "I've let you down," he said to the snow leopard as he gently scooped his hands underneath her warm body. "I can't tell you how sorry I am, Melody."

She lifted her head slightly, her eyes closing in pain as he pulled her into his arms. Roman wasn't going to wait for anyone else to come and help him. Melody needed to stay in her animal form as long as possible to make the wounds heal more quickly.

He'd made so many mistakes, and there was no way he was ever going to make it all up to her.

10

MELODY OPENED HER EYES. SHE WAS IN HER ROOM, TUCKED SNUGLY INTO her bed. The miniature Christmas tree she'd set up on the dresser twinkled happily at her, though she didn't remember turning it on. The base of her spine hurt, and her head throbbed. Actually, every part of her hurt. She turned her head to look when the door opened, but that hurt, too.

"Emersyn," she said when she saw her best friend. "I need to talk to you."

"Yes, and there's plenty I need to talk to you about, too." Her face was all business as she set her medical bag on the bench at the foot of the bed and opened it. "But first, I need to see how those wounds are coming along. Bear claws can be a real bitch."

Melody cooperated as Emersyn whisked back the covers and examined the wounds on her sides. She sucked in air through her teeth as Emersyn poked and prodded with her cool fingers. The injury felt hot and swollen.

"There's a small amount of infection, but it's already working its way out of your body," Emersyn said. She pulled a thermometer from her bag and pressed it to Melody's forehead. "You don't have a fever, so I think you're just about in the clear."

"Other than how much it hurts, I guess," Melody groaned as she got back under the sheets. "Those bears were pretty determined."

"Yes, but thanks to you, they're no longer a threat. Also, thanks to you, the children are safe." Emersyn took Melody's hand in her own and looked into her eyes. "I can't tell you what it means to me that you've put your life on the line—twice now—for my son. You're incredible, Melody."

"I didn't do it alone." Melody said it to remind both Emersyn and herself that she'd had help. There'd been Amar, but also Roman. She'd seen him streaking across the yard, his white coat shining in the sun as he came to her aid. She'd felt him, too, inside her head. He'd reached out to her in the same way she'd done to him, but his effort had been far more powerful. Melody wasn't sure whether she should regret the fact that she'd been too busy to reply. "I don't know what I would've done if they hadn't been there. I need to thank them."

"That's going to have to wait a little while. You need your rest. Half the house is heading out to visit Morefield's clan. They're going to assess the situation and see what they need to do next. Gabe and I are staying here, considering that Lucas was involved in the attack. Gabe's with the children right now."

"And the kids are okay? I mean, they have to be somewhat traumatized by the whole thing. I think I might be." Tears pricked her eyes as the memory of that bear charging at her played in slow motion. At the moment, she'd operated purely by instinct and adrenaline. Now, she could slow it all down and examine every aspect of it. That bear would've killed her, and then it would've taken the children. If she'd managed to save them all from the first attacker, the second one surely would've succeeded if it hadn't been for Roman. She could still see them coming at her, their teeth bared. Worst of all, she could still feel the pounding of the earth under her feet as they charged.

Emersyn sat on the edge of the bed. "Ruby is young enough that she probably won't remember any of this, at least not long-term. Lucas won't stop talking about it, in his own way, but it seems he's rather proud of himself for protecting Ruby."

Melody smiled at that thought. "He was really doing his best to be scary."

"So I'm told. I'll leave you to rest, but don't worry. We'll get all this business with Ruby straightened out soon enough." She stood up.

Melody grabbed her hand. "I really do need to talk to you, if you have a minute."

"Of course." Emersyn sat down again. "What is it?"

Swallowing, Melody searched for the right words. Then she reminded herself that she was closer to Emersyn than anyone else in the world. Well, almost anyone. She didn't have to think; she only needed to speak. "I... I lied. I *do* think Roman and I are mates. There's this pull between us that I can't resist. I gave into it a little at first, telling myself that there was nothing wrong with the two of us just having fun. Then it started to feel like it got out of hand, and I got so mad at him. And then he was out there playing with the kids, and I reached out to him with my mind, but I didn't really mean to, and then he stormed off, and maybe that was why..." She broke off from her rambling, crying into the pillow.

"Shh. Honey, don't cry. It's all okay. I know how frustrating and strange it can be when you meet your mate."

"But I don't know what to think about it all," Melody explained, accepting the tissue Emersyn offered her. "One minute we're doing fine, and then the next, it's like he wishes he'd never laid eyes on me."

Emersyn pressed her lips together. "Like any other soldier, I'm sure Roman has some demons from his past that he's trying to deal with. I've noticed the energy between the two of you. I'm sure you'll work it out if you give it time."

Melody shook her head. "That's just the thing, Em. I tried to tell myself that it didn't matter because it would never work with the distance between here and Wyoming. He'd already told me he wasn't going to join the Force. I'm starting to feel, though, like it *does* matter."

Tightening her grip on Melody's hand, Emersyn asked quietly, "What do you want to do about it?"

"Like everything else, I'm still trying to figure it out. But I do know that I can't just give up this chance at actually settling down and being with my mate. I don't know how we would work it all out, whether we'd live here or in Wyoming or somewhere else entirely, but that means there's a chance I wouldn't be able to watch Lucas or run head-quarters. Before I even think of talking to Roman about all this, I need to know if you're all right with it. The last thing I want to do is let you down."

"Do you mean because of Lucas?" Emersyn asked. "You must've hit your head when you were fighting off that bear. I love that I have someone here whom I love and trust who watches my son. Lucas means more to me than anything, and even before you proved it in real life, I knew you'd do everything in your power to protect him. Still, he's my son, not yours. You don't have any obligation to stay here, Mel. Gabe and I would figure it out."

Melody nodded and let out a breath. In the back of her mind, she'd known Emersyn would be rational about this. That was always how she was, anyway. "I just didn't want to disappoint you. And what about Roman? Do you think I should go for it?"

Emersyn giggled. "Are you writing his name in little hearts on the inside of a notebook, because I feel like we're in high school! I went through some of that with Gabe, too. Yes, go for it. See how he really feels."

"Yeah." Melody thought about how quickly Roman had shut her down when she'd reached out to him. He'd come right back to her aid a few minutes later, and she could swear he'd been in her mind during the attack, but it still worried her. "What if he rejects me?"

"I doubt he would." Emersyn raised her brows and pinched her mouth, looking sassy. "You're one hell of a catch, Mel. The absolute worst he can do is say no, anyway. Then you'll move on, and you'll get past it. I promise. For right now, though, you rest." She patted Melody's arm, collected her bag, and slipped out of the room.

Melody lay there, staring at the ceiling. Emersyn was right. She couldn't live her life waiting for something to happen and hoping it would all work out. There was nothing wrong with standing up for what she wanted and asking if it could be possible. She wouldn't demand anything from Roman that he wasn't willing to give freely, but Melody had never been such a meek and mild woman to only take the minimum and be all right with it.

Flicking off the covers, she sat up in bed and swung her feet over the side, though the stabbing pain in her ribs made her immediately regret it. That damn bear had done a number on her. She'd heal up soon enough, but she could at least go find Roman.

The door to his room was slightly ajar, and classic rock filtered out through it. Melody smiled, realizing she'd had no idea up until this point what kind of music he liked. There was still so much to learn about him. There was so much more to both of them than just the events over the past few weeks. His visit was going by quickly, but they still had time before he was due back in Wyoming after Christmas. Melody knocked softly.

"Come in," Roman barked.

She pushed the door open to find him standing next to the bed, dressed in jeans and a t-shirt. A suitcase was spread on the comforter, already packed with a neatly folded stack of clothes, a row of socks, and a few books. Roman was in the process of folding another shirt when he looked up at her. He said nothing.

"What's going on?" Alarm bells were clanging in her head, and her heart was pounding so heavily, she could hardly hear the music anymore. "I thought you weren't going back until after Christmas."

"I've changed my mind." He turned away from her as he pulled open a dresser drawer, saw that it was empty, and slammed it shut again. He took a pair of jeans from the next drawer down.

Her throat was thick as she tried to swallow. This wasn't right. This wasn't what she wanted. She was supposed to have more time. *They* were supposed to have more time. How could they work it all out if he wasn't even in the same state? "Why?"

"There's no reason for me to stay here any longer." He put the jeans in his suitcase and crossed the room to the closet, opening the door wide to double-check that he'd gotten everything.

Roman didn't elaborate, but he didn't need to for Melody to understand. "You could've at least told me."

His eyes met hers for only a fraction of a second. "There's nothing to tell."

"Now, hold on a second." She stepped forward, wincing at the pain in her side once again, but was determined to get past it. "What, exactly, makes you think there isn't anything to tell? At the very least, I'm the one who oversees the daily functions of this house. I think I deserve to know who's coming and going."

"Fine. You do that, Melody. Get your ledger book and note that I'm leaving today, catching a plane, and heading right back to Wyoming where I belong." Roman picked up a pair of shoes from under the bed and slammed them into his suitcase.

Her eyes narrowed. "That's not what I meant."

"Then what did you mean?" he asked, throwing his hands in the air. "What does any of this mean?"

"You're not making sense." She wanted to reach out, grab his arms, and push him down on the bed. She wanted to make him sit and listen to her, to talk this through, to figure it all out in a rational way, but he wasn't going to allow it. Her snow leopard was already reacting, growling in frustration at his stupidity.

"That's fine by me, because there's not a damn bit of my trip here that has made any sense." Roman's brows were a firm line as he zipped up his suitcase. "I came out here because Amar didn't want me to spend the holidays alone. He thought I should be around him and meet all his friends so that he wouldn't have to worry about me. What he didn't realize was that I'm more alone here than I am anywhere else in the fucking world." He breezed past her toward the door.

"Can't we at least just talk about this?" She couldn't let him go without speaking her mind, but right then, she didn't know what to say. How could she tell him she was head-over-heels in love with him and wanted to find a way for them to work out when he was glowering at her from the doorway?

"I wanted to talk to you earlier today, as I recall, and you refused." Roman shook his head as he set the suitcase down. In two quick strides, he was only inches from her face, and she could feel the heat and tension rising from his body. "Melody, I can't keep doing this. There's something between us, and I don't think either one of us would try to deny that, but every time I turn the corner, there's something else standing in the way of it. Everything I do, everything I feel, and every decision I make is wrong. I'd much rather go be wrong by myself, thank you."

Arguments formed on the tip of her tongue, but they were quickly squashed by the urges of her snow leopard. As angry as she was with him, why did she want to reach out and pull him closer? Why did she want to press her lips against his and fall into bed the way they had that night after watching TV? Why did her big cat constantly remind her that there was so much more going on than what either of them could see on the surface?

No. She couldn't just let her instincts guide her on this. Where would they be if they did nothing but act the way their wild sides demanded them to? Melody wanted to end her spinster streak, but it wasn't worth it if she got stuck with someone who wouldn't even sit and have a rational conversation with her. "Fine. I guess if that's how it is, then who am I to stop you?" She shoved past him and stormed out into the hall, heading back to her room. The doorbell rang, but she ignored it. Someone else could get it.

Tears blurred her eyes, but she blinked them back as she paced cagily in her room. Roman wasn't worth shedding any tears over. He was just another dick, like all the rest of them were. If he'd wanted to be with her, then he would have tried to find a way. It didn't have to be up to her. She shouldn't have to be the one to bow down and say she was wrong when he'd been plenty guilty himself. Melody curled her fists at her sides. Maybe it was time to get out and just take a long run in her feline form. Dashing through the woods and pretending the rest of the world didn't exist sounded like the perfect prescription for what was ailing her.

She bumped into Emersyn again as soon as she left her room. "If you're here to tell me to get my ass back in bed, don't bother. I've been through enough for the time being, and I just need to get outside." Melody put her chin in the air, thoroughly expecting Emersyn or someone else along the way to caution her about the recent attack and how it wasn't safe.

But Emersyn shook her head. "You probably should be in bed, but I actually came to give you some news. Kent just called. They were able to deal with the Alpha and beta of the clan who kidnapped Ruby. Apparently, it was a scheme hatched by the two of them. They were planning on returning her in exchange for territorial rights, but her capture wasn't something the rest of the clan agreed upon. They're dealing with all of that, but the important thing is that Ruby's parents are on their way here to pick her up."

The world swirled in Melody's vision, and the edges darkened until she could see only Emersyn's face. "Are you serious?" she whispered.

A steady arm wrapped around her. "Yes. Ruby's parents had been working hard to get their baby back, but they didn't know what had happened to her or that she was here. They thought she was still in the custody of Morefield's clan, so they and their clanmates launched several attacks against the Morefields. That was how it all came to light to the rest of the bears. Mr. Morefield and his beta are being forced to step down. Ironically, it was Morefield's wife who'd told Amar and Roman about the kidnapping and had arranged for her to be dropped off here, and she's now the one who will become the new Alpha."

Clan politics might have been interesting to Melody at any other time, but not right now. The only thing she understood was that two of the people she'd come to take so much joy in were being taken away from her. There was still the rest of the Force, and her work for them, and especially little Lucas, but she still felt as though her heart was being ripped straight out of her chest. "I know it's not fair of me to say this," she sobbed into Emersyn's arms, "but I don't want Ruby to go."

"I know, honey. I know. She's meant the world to you. And you're the kindest, sweetest, most wonderful person because I know you would've taken care of Ruby for the rest of her life if that was what was needed. But her parents need her right now."

"They must be so relieved to know she's safe," Melody replied, trying to console herself. Everything hurt so badly, but her injuries were the least of it. "How long until they get here?"

"Kent didn't say, but I'm sure they're coming as quickly as they can."

Melody nodded. "I want to say goodbye to her."

"Of course. She's right down the hall in the nursery." Emersyn guided the way, and even though Melody knew it well, she still leaned on her friend for support. "Gabe, I think we need to give Melody and Ruby a minute."

Gabe looked up from where he'd been playing on the floor with the two children. He didn't question his mate as he scooped up Lucas and headed into the hall. "Let's go see if we can find a snack, buddy."

"Snack? Ruby?"

"That's okay, Ruby will get a snack later."

Emersyn touched Melody's back. "I'll give you two some time, but I won't be far. Just call if you need me." She closed the door gently behind her.

Melody grabbed a tissue from the dresser and blotted her eyes. "You poor thing. You don't want to see me this way, but I can't help it. I've just fallen in love with you so much over the last couple of weeks." She fell to her knees in front of Ruby's bouncy seat.

Ruby responded with a playful kick of her feet and a grin.

"Oh, I know. You're so young, and you don't understand the tragedy of all this. I'm so grateful for that. I'm so glad that you probably won't remember this at all, because I know it would be so hard for an older child to go through. But I'm also so terribly sad that you won't remember it, because I want you to remember me." Melody cried harder as she unbuckled the straps and lifted Ruby into her arms. "You've been a very precious little thing to me, Ruby. I hope that you'll understand that."

A gentle knock came on the door, and it opened a second later. "Melody, honey. Her parents are here."

"Okay. Let's go, sweet one. Time to go see Mommy and Daddy."

Emersyn held out her arms. "Would you rather I take her?"

"No. I need to do this myself." She knew it was true. She was heartbroken enough over Roman, and there was little she could do about it. But she could do herself the favor of being the one to hand Ruby over, to see her parents, to know she was doing the right thing. It would be a type of closure for her, even if it hurt.

Emersyn nodded. "I'll gather her things."

Downstairs, a couple was standing near the front door. Jude and Reid stood nearby, and that let Melody know that these people really were who they said they were. She knew the two brothers, who'd been orphaned as children, would never let Ruby be handed into the wrong arms. That thought made Melody realize how much comfort she'd taken in the little things that the Force offered. It wasn't just the fact that she had a roof over her head, a steady job, and a sense of satisfaction that came from getting things done. It was that she knew these people and all their little idiosyncrasies. She knew what to expect from them, and she knew she could count on them.

Jude made the introductions. "Melody, this is Allison and Matthew Wilson. Ruby's parents."

"Hi," Melody said with a forced smile as she blinked back her tears. "My name is Melody. I've been taking care of Ruby for these past few weeks."

"Oh!" Allison swooped in to take her daughter. "Oh, my sweet baby! My little princess! I've missed you so much! I've been so worried about you!"

Ruby replied with an enthusiastic coo, her arms and legs bunching in and punching out in excitement as she saw her mother again.

There were tears in Matthew's eyes as he stroked his baby girl's back and turned to Melody. "Jude and Reid told us what good care you've been taking of her. I admit we were relieved when we found out she was with the SOS Force, but it makes me feel even better to see how happy and healthy she is. We can't thank you enough." His wife was bawling too hard to even respond.

Melody understood that sentiment, as she could no longer stop herself from crying. "It was my pleasure. I know you already know, but your daughter is such a sweet, amazing little thing. And she's so cute when she shifts into her bear cub." She laughed through her tears at the memory of Ruby chasing after Lucas in the yard.

Matthew and Allison looked at each other in shock. "She shifted in front of you?"

"She sure did." Alarm bells went off in Melody's mind. She would feel terrible if that'd been the first time their daughter had taken on her animal form and they weren't around to see it. "Hasn't she done it before? She didn't seem to have any trouble with it."

"She has," Matthew replied, his thumb gliding over the back of Ruby's head in awe, as though he was seeing her for the first time. "It's just that we've found she only does it in front of those she's extremely comfortable around, such as ourselves and our parents. Even the rest of our clan hasn't seen her change before. You really are something special, Melody."

"Yes, she is," Emersyn replied for her, putting her arm around her friend once again. "We're just so glad we found you. I've gathered up Ruby's things, including her blanket. We had ordered some clothes for her, as well, so she'll have some new outfits."

"What can we do to repay you?" Allison asked.

"Not a thing," Melody said. "Having time with Ruby was enough." She turned, not waiting to see Ruby leave, not wanting to press her forehead to the window as she watched her parents load her into their vehicle and drive off to live her life. Melody would get past this at some point, she knew. She had to, and they said that time healed all wounds. But it sure as hell hurt right now.

11

———————

"You're sure this is what you want to do?" Amar asked as they sped toward the airport.

Roman was starting to regret letting Amar drive him there. It would've been easier to just get up early, sneak off before anyone else had gotten out of bed, and waste time in the lounge, but he'd felt he owed it to his old friend to do a little more than that. "Yes. I'm sure."

"But it's not even officially Christmas yet," Amar countered.

"That's true," Roman said with a nod. "And that's exactly why it's a good idea to fly right now. I can get back to Wyoming in time to wish all my cattle and horses a very Merry Christmas."

"Even with all the traffic that's bound to be at the airport? Come on, Roman. I know you don't like crowds, and we both remember how difficult it was to get stateside too close to a holiday when we were on leave." He checked his mirrors and changed lanes. "It'd be much easier if you just stayed at headquarters and had Christmas with us. Hell, stay until New Year's. We can ring it in together. It's a lot more fun doing it in a warm and comfortable home instead of in a mess hall on the other side of the world."

Roman couldn't argue with that. "I'm sure you're right. I'm sure that it'll also be nice to ring in the new year at home in Sheridan, maybe with a few of my new clanmates, lifting up beers and belching into the night in a remote cabin where we don't have to worry about women."

Amar nodded. "Uh huh."

"What?" Roman's muscles tensed. He hadn't really thought he'd get anything past his friend and comrade. Amar saw and noted everything. That didn't mean Roman wanted to talk about it.

"It's a woman thing," Amar replied.

"Isn't everything a woman thing?" Roman challenged.

Amar laughed. "Sure, I guess that's true. You could make the argument that you fought for your country, putting your life on the line because you wanted to keep the women safe. You could stretch that out and make further arguments about major life decisions being based on women somehow. That doesn't mean you made the right ones."

"You don't have to be the wise old dragon all the time, you know. You could just let me do what I want and call it good enough." Roman looked out the window, squinting against the bright sunshine and all those damn palm trees. It didn't look like Christmas or even winter around there, and he was getting tired of it.

"I could, but I wouldn't be much of a friend if I didn't call you out on your mistakes."

Roman sighed. "I already explained all this. Being a dad just isn't in the cards for me, and Melody is far better off without me. I would only get in the way of her dreams. Even if—and that's a big *if*—the two of us could work it out for a little while, it would just end up falling apart, leaving the two of us even more miserable."

Amar was silent for a long time as they floated along the expressway. Roman glanced at him a couple of times, surprised that he wasn't making any further arguments or trying to rope him into joining the Force again.

"Thanks for helping us with the Morefield clan," he finally said. "The rest of the crew and I work well together, but it's always nice to get a fresh perspective on things."

"No problem. Do you think Mrs. Morefield will do all right as the Alpha?" Roman figured it would all work out well enough, and it wasn't really any of his business, but it was easier to make conversation about matters that didn't directly involve him.

"I don't have the least bit of doubt. I admit I was a little shocked to find out the woman in the flower bed was the Alpha's wife, but after talking to her more recently, I know she'll do well. The rest of the clan, it turns out, didn't like her husband very much, but they do think quite a lot of her. She has the backing of the rest of her clan as well as the Force, so there won't be any further problems from them."

"Good. And I heard that Ruby's parents came to get her, so everything is back to normal." Roman turned to look out the window again. There had been a little chaos while he was in California, but it had all settled now. Roman would leave before any further trouble started.

Amar ran his hand across his face, scratching his fingers through the dark stubble that had recently grown in. "Did you happen to talk to Melody before we left?"

So much for keeping the conversation on other subjects. "No. I doubt she'd want to hear anything I have to say."

"Yeah, maybe you're right."

Roman snapped his head around to look at his friend.

"Well, she was really upset about Ruby going home as it was. The last thing she needs is for you to complicate things when you're just leaving anyway." He slid the car over into the drop-off lane in front of the airport. "You let me know when you want to come down for another visit. I'll be happy to have you. I might even pick your sorry ass up at the gate if you ask me nicely." He flashed a grin from the driver's seat.

"I don't know if I had the chance to tell you this, Amar, but you haven't changed a bit." Roman shook his head and laughed as he retrieved his bags from the trunk and headed into the terminal.

He made his way through check-in and security. The airport was horribly crowded. Parents yelled at each other as they tried to keep track of their children, people swayed restlessly as they queued up for overpriced coffee, and young businessmen in suits carried out their deals loudly on their phones. Roman just wanted to get past all of it and back to the peace and quiet of Wyoming, and he was grateful for the short wait at the gate.

Though he hadn't meant to, he ended up next to the window to accommodate a young couple who wanted to sit together. They whispered excitedly to each other, her hand touching his arm, his hand touching her leg. The seats were too close together for Roman to scoot his hulking frame any further away from them, but they were oblivious anyway. He spent the rest of his flight concentrating on all the ranch work that awaited him when he got back home, purposely keeping Melody from his mind.

The plane landed with a thump that woke him up. Roman had

been dreaming, but seeing the runway stream by through the window made him forget what it had been about. He was there. He was back home in Wyoming, right where he belonged. His new clan was there, and they wouldn't create the sort of drama he'd been living through over the last few weeks. It would all just be work as usual, and that was exactly what he needed.

As eager as he was to get off the plane, and even though he knew exactly where his one carry-on was stowed, his best-laid plans to get off a plane quickly never worked out. There were always too many people in the aisle, blocking the way as they stumbled over feet and purses to find their bags and get themselves together. Roman had often found this annoying. It wasn't as though it was a surprise that the plane had landed when it did; they ought to have been prepared for it. Moreover, they ought to have had a little more courtesy and organization so they could've disembarked in an orderly fashion. People, however, were much like cattle. The most you could hope for was that they'd be walking in the right direction.

Stepping into the airport, Roman was greeted with a blast of hot air and the sound of Christmas music ringing in his ears. Someone had decorated the place with cheap plastic garland and a sad old Christmas tree that should've been put out of its misery long ago. Faded gold ornaments dangled from its sagging branches.

Roman didn't want to see any of that as it was. He wasn't in the holiday spirit, but it was all the more aggravating because it made him think of Melody. If she had been there, she would've had the whole place glitzed up to the nines, with a beautiful tree, tons of lights, and little touches that would make all the difference. He thought of that sprig of holly that had been in her hair that first night he'd met her. He could easily imagine himself reaching up and taking it out, watching as her hair tumbled down in a cloud of untamed fire.

No. The whole reason he'd come back early was to get away from Melody, and that meant physically as well as emotionally. He had no place in her life, and she had no place in his. This was how it was supposed to be. Who cared that their inner animals had created such chaos? He could restore balance by force, and he would do just that.

Roman trudged through the airport, his carry-on bag slung over his shoulder. The Sheridan County Airport was much smaller than the one he'd left just a few hours ago, and he was grateful for it. He'd get his suitcase and be on his way.

"There he is!" someone called off to his left.

"Hold up your sign, so he'll see it! Nice and tall, just like that. Great job!"

"Daddy!"

Roman turned, as did everyone else in the terminal, to see a family standing in a cluster, holding up a big sign that said, "Welcome Home, Daddy!" on it. The family was all dressed in their Christmas pajamas and furry boots, and someone even had a huge velvet sack full of presents dragging along on the ground.

A man who'd just come from the gate locked eyes with the family. He dropped his bags and ran straight for them, scooping the little boy holding the sign up into his arms, swinging him around in a big circle.

Roman looked away. This wasn't any of his business. People had reunions in airports all the time. It only made sense. And he couldn't even feel sorry for himself about no one picking him up since he hadn't bothered to let any of his clan know he was coming home early. Old Henry would be thrilled when Roman showed up at home to take over all the work and care that went into running the place, though.

"Baby!"

Unable to help himself, Roman turned back toward the family. The mother had broken off from her children, her eyes soft and wet as she stepped toward her husband. She touched his cheeks, taking a long moment just to look at him before she wrapped her arms around his neck. He murmured something in her ear that couldn't be heard at this distance, but Roman could guess it was all about how much they loved each other and how much they'd hated being apart for so long.

Roman tightened his grip on his bag as he continued toward baggage claim, joining the line of passengers who stood patiently while they waited a familiar piece of luggage to come circling around on the conveyor belt. It was nice that the family he'd seen could have a relationship like that. He had no doubt they'd probably all sit down right there in the terminal to exchange presents and take a bunch of pictures that their friends and family would all pretend to be enthusiastic about.

But romantic notions like that weren't real. They were just ridiculous fantasies that people created because they sounded nice, and they believed them for as long as they could. They were just something that would dissipate over time and leave everyone disappointed.

And they were exactly what he wanted to experience with Melody.

Though it was easy to believe that romance was just fiction for everyone else and even for himself, he couldn't actually believe that about her. She'd proven it in the way she'd decorated headquarters, not because she was asked to, but because she liked it. Then there was her love for old Christmas movies, and how she didn't seem to care that the two of them were eating leftovers in their pajamas in the middle of the night, as long as they were spending time together. She'd sprung into action when she'd heard Ruby crying on the doorstep, even though at that time, she had no idea whose child it was and had no obligation to take care of it.

Roman stepped forward to grab his suitcase as he remembered the way she'd looked just before he'd left. He hadn't stopped to talk to her, knowing he was only going to make things worse, but he'd caught a glimpse of her face, swollen from all the tears she'd cried. He wanted to blame all of those tears on her separation from Ruby, but deep down, he knew it wasn't just that. He'd caused plenty of them, and she deserved better.

That last part was what had convinced him that he'd been right to change his flight and leave early. Roman loved her, and he'd known that early on, but he'd also known he wasn't right for her. He was too stubborn, too overbearing, and too damn selfish. He was also too dumb to realize what an amazing opportunity he'd passed up, and he'd made an awful mistake.

12

"YOU OKAY, MEL'DY? YOU OKAY?" LUCAS BENT DOWN IN FRONT OF Melody, his hands on his knees, and peered into her face.

"I'm just tired, buddy. You're very kind for asking, though." She smiled at him, glad to know that he truly did care about her. Someone else might think of it as a small comfort, but there was nothing better than concern from a sweet, innocent child.

"Nap?" Lucas asked, pointing upstairs.

Melody pulled him into her arms. He'd lost that baby scent that she enjoyed so much, and instead, he smelled like Goldfish crackers and Play-Doh, but she loved it anyway. "No, I don't want to take a nap right now. Maybe later."

"Mel'dy nap." Lucas headed for the couch, where he pulled down a throw pillow. He put it on the floor and put his hands on her head, slowly guiding her down toward it.

Who was she to interfere when he was trying so hard to take care of her? "That's very nice. Thank you, Lucas."

But he wasn't done. He next pulled down a soft blanket that they kept draped over the back of the couch. It took him a lot of effort to cover her, and her backside was still hanging out by the time he was done, but he looked pleased with himself. "There. Mel'dy nap."

"A very nice nap, indeed," Melody replied. "You want to lay down here with me?"

"Okay." He stretched out on the rug next to her.

Melody covered him with some of the blanket. She reached for the remote and turned on the TV, grateful for a little bit of downtime. Her separation from Roman had been much harder on her than she'd thought possible, and so had Ruby's absence. She'd considered asking Jude for the Wilsons' phone number so she could offer to babysit, but she was worried about coming off like a weirdo.

As Christmas cartoons jangled brightly on the television in front of her, she allowed herself a fantasy of what things might've been like if the world had been a different place. What if she and Roman could have actually worked things out? What if they'd never fought in the first place? Melody hardly cared whether they lived in Wyoming, California, or Timbuktu, and she imagined them living out their fictional relationship in some nondescript home that could have been anywhere. Maybe they would even have had a child or two. Roman would have gotten the hang of the kid thing. In fact, he already had a better handle on it than he realized, Melody was sure.

"Melody?"

She opened her eyes. The cartoon on the screen had changed completely. Lucas was still curled up with her, fortunately, or she'd have felt even more terrible as she looked up at Emersyn standing over her. "Hey. I guess I fell asleep. Lucas had me very well tucked in."

"I can see that."

Melody sat up, and Lucas scooted closer to the television. "I told him I was tired, and he insisted. It was really cute." She pressed her hand to her forehead, feeling drained even after her little snooze.

"You doing okay? I know the last few days haven't been easy on you." Emersyn sat on the edge of the couch and folded her hands between her knees.

"They haven't, but I'm fine. I just need to catch up on a little sleep, and I'd better do it soon. I'd planned to have all my shopping done early, but that got put on hold by...you know, so I still have a few things to pick up. And then I've still got to get everything wrapped. I have a big grocery trip to make, too." She pushed back the blanket and stood up. Black waves spiraled in toward the center of her vision, and she stumbled backward.

"Whoa. Are you sure you're all right?" Emersyn reached out to grab her hand and led her toward the sofa.

"It's just a little holiday stress, that's all." Melody looked up at her best friend, and when she saw the compassion in her eyes, it made her want to cry. She'd thought she'd run out of tears a long time ago, yet there they were, threatening to spill over once again. "I think."

"You think? Tell me everything that's happening. Don't skip a bit of it." Emersyn was back in doctor mode.

Melody knew that was not a force to be reckoned with. "I'm having trouble sleeping. I spend half the day feeling like I want to throw up and the other half feeling like I'm going to cry. I'm just stressed out."

Emersyn patted her hand and stood up. "Why don't you step into my office for a minute?"

"But Lucas—"

"He's entertained, and we'll be right in the next room. Alessia's in the kitchen, so she can keep an eye on him, too. Come on." Emersyn brought her through a doorway and into the exam room. She reached into a cabinet and fetched a small cup with a lid. "Let's start with a pregnancy test."

The blood drained from Melody's face. Somehow, even as rational of a person as she normally was, she hadn't even thought about that. "I don't think that's necessary."

Emersyn's face was challenging. "Is there even the slightest chance?"

"Well, I mean, yeah…"

The doctor forced the plastic cup into Melody's hand. "Then pee."

A couple of minutes later, Melody shifted her weight from one foot to the other as she awaited the results. "I hadn't really thought about this, you know. I mean, I always wanted children, but what if—"

"Save the what-ifs for just a minute longer," Emersyn advised, "until you know for sure. I know how much you like to plan things out, but in this case, whatever will be will be."

"Yeah. I guess so." It was impossible not to think about it, though. Melody had found one of Ruby's little pink rompers mixed in with the laundry. Her parents had shown up unexpectedly, and the item had been missed. Melody had taken it back to her room and tucked it away in a drawer, unsure of what to do with it. She couldn't possibly go visit them with the outfit as an excuse; it would hurt too much.

"Mel?"

"Yeah?"

Emersyn turned the test around so she could see. "You're going to be a mother. Congratulations."

Melody clapped her hands to her mouth. "Oh, my God. Are you sure?"

"Are you questioning my medical degree?" Emersyn retorted, laughing. "Of course, I'm sure. This is so exciting! You're going to have a little one!"

"Wow," Melody breathed. Just a second ago, she'd been making plans for the next eighteen years of her life, but in that moment, she just wanted to quiet her brain and take it all in. This was it. It hadn't happened the way she'd imagined, but it was most certainly happening.

"That's one heck of a Christmas present," Emersyn said with a smile as she put everything away and stripped off her gloves. "I'm so happy for you, Melody."

"Thanks. I—I don't even know what to think or do or say." Melody wandered out to the living room, where Lucas was still happily watching TV. She looked down at him and his adorable face. That would be her life from now on. She wouldn't just be watching someone else's child, but her own. There would be late nights and long days and tons of diapers and more laundry than she could ever keep up with. There would be times when she'd be so frustrated, she wouldn't know what to do next, but the one thing she was sure of was that she'd be the happiest woman in the world.

———

"If you don't like the color, just let me know and I'll make you a different one," Melody said.

"Are you kidding me?" Emersyn ran her hands up and down the length of the bright red scarf she'd just pulled out of the gift bag. "It's so pretty and so soft!"

"I just have to wonder when you had time to make it," Gabe added, reaching over to touch it. "You're too busy for something like that."

Melody waved off the compliments. She was already feeling a glow unlike anything she'd experienced in her life. As much as she loved Christmas and seeing her friends get their gifts, she knew it wasn't from that. It was from the miracle that was growing inside her, the one that would change the rest of her life. "Hey, I've been planning this holiday for months. And don't be too flattered. You're just my guinea pigs for learning how to knit."

"I think you did just fine," Alessia marveled as she also pulled out a scarf, hers in a pale green that matched her eyes. "I'll be wearing this all the time!"

Lucas was just as enthusiastic as the others as he took out the thick blanket she'd made for him. He immediately rolled himself up in it and pretended to take a nap on the floor, much to the delight of all the adults watching.

The morning went far too quickly, with everyone up early and ready to get started. The ring of presents around the tree that had extended halfway across the living room was soon reduced to shredded paper and boxes, all headed for recycling, as everyone gathered their prizes and took them off to their respective rooms or packed them into their vehicles to head home.

Melody lingered, touching a little glass ornament on the tree and wishing it didn't have to be over with so soon. There was a thrill to seeing all the decorations up at the end of November, but by the time Christmas came and went, most of it lost its magic.

Amar stepped into the room. "Melody, I'm glad you're here. I wanted to tell you how wonderful everything looked."

"You already told me that when I put it all up a month ago," she said with a smile as she adjusted one of the tree's baubles. "I'll give it another day or two, but then I'll get it all put up in the attic."

His dark eyes grew serious at the suggestion. "Don't you dare! There are plenty of hands here to help you, and I don't want you to hurt yourself."

"Okay, okay. You do have a point on the heavy lifting. But," she leveled her gaze at him and tried her best to look authoritative, "I'll personally be in charge of getting all the delicates wrapped and put away. I don't trust any of you brutes to do it correctly."

He put his hands in the air. "Wouldn't dream of it!" Amar hesitated, glancing over his shoulder. Melody didn't think he meant to, but she caught his eyes flick to her stomach and then away again. He rubbed the back of his neck with one hand. "I also just wanted you to know...I mean...anything you might need, we're here for you. All of us."

"Thank you. I know, and I appreciate it."

"And I'm sorry."

She'd just been turning back to the tree, but she flicked her head back around to look at him. "What do you mean?"

Amar shrugged. "I was the one who asked Roman to come here in the first place. We've always been good friends, and even though I knew he wasn't perfect, I genuinely didn't think there would be any problems. I just feel like there was something more I could've done, and I don't want you to be in a bad situation because of it."

Melody rested her hand on his arm. Amar was a formidable Alpha, a true dragon at heart who didn't get sappy about anything. It tickled her to see him show a little bit of his softer side, but she knew he was being very sincere about this. She owed it to him to return the favor. "Amar, don't be sorry, and don't feel like any of this is your fault. It hurts to think of Roman, and I can't help but think about him constantly, knowing that I'm carrying his child. It's just something I'm going to have to work through, and I know I will."

"Have you told him yet?"

Melody shook her head. "No. I wanted to give myself a little time to get used to it, to be able to find all the right words. I'll do it soon, though. After Christmas."

"Okay," Amar said with a nod. "I know it's not really my business, but he'd be devastated if he didn't know."

Melody wasn't so sure about that. She was willing to gamble that Roman would be scared or maybe even angry when he found out. The one thing she had to make sure of was that, no matter how she felt or how he acted, she wouldn't try to pull any sort of commitment out of him. "Don't worry. I'll do it."

"Thanks. Katalin and I are planning to have dinner out later on tonight if you'd like to join us."

"That's all right." Melody knew how much the two of them were in love. She didn't want to spoil their holiday together, nor was she sure she could stomach all that romance right in front of her. "I've got some other things I'm going to take care of."

Amar looked doubtful, but he turned and headed out of the room.

Melody ran her fingers over the strand of garland on the mantel and straightened the stockings hung in front of the fireplace. Most of them were just for show, but Gabe and Emersyn had weighted Lucas's down with snacks, fruit, and little toys. He would be eating out of that overgrown sock for a couple of weeks, at least.

On an impulse, Melody returned to the tree. She took down a miniature stocking ornament and brought it back over to the mantel, hanging it on top of hers. It was so tiny that it looked silly compared to the rest, but she knew what it meant.

A heavy, urgent knock sounded at the front door. Melody's instincts turned on high, her snow leopard at the ready as she crossed the room, wondering what kind of drama would be on the other side of the door this time.

Roman stood there on the doorstep. For the longest moment, his bags in his hands, he simply stared at her. "Melody."

"Roman." She glanced over her shoulder, wondering if anyone else had known he was coming. "What are you doing here? I thought you went back to Wyoming." Melody held the door open wider for him to come in.

"I did, and I felt like an absolute piece of shit for it." Roman stepped inside and tossed his bags down in the entryway. "I need to talk to you."

"All right." If he'd asked her that a few days ago, she would've told him to just shove it. But Melody needed to talk to him, too. "We can go in the living room. We just finished up Christmas and everyone is pretty much gone." Why was she babbling like that?

He stopped in front of the Christmas tree and took her hand. "I owe you an apology and an explanation."

"No, you don't—"

"Yes." His eyes were serious as they bored into hers, and he was holding both of her hands in his now. "Yes, I do. You see, I thought I found the person I wanted to be with while I was still in the military. We tried to make it work, even while I was overseas. Elizabeth told me she was pregnant with my child, and I couldn't have been more excited. Whatever problems the two of us had, I knew we could work them out because we were going to have a baby together. I fell in love with that little boy through video calls and letters and photographs, but when I got home, I found out he wasn't really mine after all."

"Oh, Roman." Melody was too emotional for this, and the corners of her eyes stung with threatening tears. "I'm so sorry."

He shook his head. "I was devastated, too hurt to consider fatherhood again. When I started feeling things with you—not just things, but big things—I knew we were experiencing something real. But if I wasn't emotionally ready to be a father, and if you were destined to be a mother, as I know you are, then I just didn't see a way to work it out."

She touched his cheek as she looked over every aspect of his handsome face.

Roman sighed, looking down for a moment. "I think, in some ways,

I know how you must've felt when Ruby's parents came to take her away from you. You had the time to get attached, and you knew there was a chance it would be forever. It wasn't fair of me to just leave you to grieve like that."

"I'm dealing with it," she replied, a small smile playing on the corners of her lips.

"It also wasn't fair of me to flip out on you after the incident at the zoo. I never meant to make you feel like you were incompetent. It just scared the hell out of me to think something could've happened to you. Then when it happened again in the backyard, I just felt that fear all over again. I had to leave, and maybe I still should, but I had to come back here and tell you."

Melody squeezed his fingers. "You didn't have to come all the way back to California just to explain your past to me."

"Maybe not, but I did need to come back to give you these." Roman reached into his pocket. He pulled out a closed fist and held it over her hand, releasing a little pile of burgundy rose petals into her palm.

"Zuzu's petals," she said with tears in her eyes. This was the best apology she'd ever gotten, though she thought she might cry all over the velvety little things. "It's Zuzu's petals. You remembered."

"Of course, I did. I can't forget a single moment when I'm with you, Melody. I know we're meant to be together, and I promise I'll stop acting like an ass if you can just give me a chance to love you the way I should." He held her wrist so delicately in his big hand, the petals vibrating between them.

"Roman." Melody fell into his arms and kissed him, her tears streaming back as her snow leopard purred its content. This was what she needed. *Roman* was what she needed. They'd had their little squabble, but that was all over now and everything was going to be different. She pulled back as she realized just how different everything really was going to be.

"What's wrong?" His shoulders sagged as she left his embrace.

Melody kept her arms resting on his, not wanting to let go but knowing she had to do this. "First, I need to apologize to you, too. You tried to talk to me about all this, and I was too stubborn to let you. I didn't make things any better, and I guess I thought it would be easier."

"It's all right, Melody."

"But there's more." She pulled in a deep breath. There hadn't been enough time to find the right words. Instead, she reached out to the fireplace and picked up the mini stocking she'd hung there next to her own. "If we're going to be together, you need to know that it won't just be the two of us."

He took a step back, but he tightened his grip on her arm as he automatically looked down at her stomach. "Are you sure?"

"Very. Emersyn confirmed it herself."

Roman took the tiny stocking from her hand. Tears glistened in his eyes as he ran his thumb over the glittery rickrack at the top of it. "Melody, this is the best Christmas present I ever could've gotten."

They fell against each other once again. Melody roved her tongue over his, tasting him as a thrill of Christmas magic ran up and down her spine. Her body was alive as she pressed herself against him, and her snow leopard leaped inside her. This was where she was meant to be. It didn't matter what state or even what side of the world they were in, as long as they were together.

Roman scooped his hands underneath her, easily swinging her into the air and carrying her up the staircase, pausing on the landing to kiss her again. "You're so beautiful."

"Are you still going to say that when I'm as big as a house?" she challenged.

He laughed as he went up the second flight of stairs and down the hall. "You'll be the prettiest house I've ever seen."

Melody thumped the side of her fist into his broad chest, liking the way his hard muscles bounced beneath her hand. "Beast."

"You don't even know." Roman shouldered open her bedroom door. He held her high over the bed, making it look as though he would simply drop her in place, but he lowered her gently to the covers and kissed her forehead as he kicked the door shut behind them. He pushed her back down as she started to sit up. "No, you need to relax."

"I'm plenty relaxed," she argued with a smile.

"Not the way I want you to be." He took off her shoes and placed them on the floor next to the bed. Next came her socks, her pants, and her festive sweater. His lips pressed hotly against her cooling skin as he traced a curving line along the top of her breasts, dipping down between them as he unclasped the front closure of her bra. He moved down along the lines of her stomach, kissing her navel as he slowly slipped off her panties. His hands moved back up her legs, squeezing tightly and releasing the tension in her muscles.

Melody moaned softly, not having realized until then just how knotted up she'd been. "Oh, that feels good."

"And I'm just getting started." Roman worked his way up and down her legs. He rubbed down her arms and even swept his hands over her breasts before asking her to roll over.

Melody complied instantly, unable to get enough of this. "You're going to spoil me," she said, her voice halting in the middle of it as he straddled her from behind and worked the knots out of her neck.

"That's the point, isn't it?" His fingers dug pleasantly into her flesh and up onto her scalp.

Goosebumps erupted all over her skin. "That means I'll have to find a way to spoil you, too."

His breath was warm against the back of her neck. "Don't worry. I'm sure you'll figure it out." Those magic hands roved down her backside and to her legs once again, and he dropped kisses all the way.

"There's something distinctly unfair about this situation," Melody remarked as he finally let go of her. She rolled over and sat on the edge of the bed, taking a moment just to put her hands around him and lean against him. He felt so solid and strong. She was always trying to be strong herself, but it was nice to know she wouldn't have to be the only one. His skin was warm and inviting, radiating heat through his clothes. "I think I just want to get you naked to cuddle in bed with me all day," she said as she slowly began unbuttoning his shirt.

"I'm up for that, but I can't promise you I'll behave myself. Not with such a gorgeous woman at my side." He ran his fingers through her hair as she pushed his shirt back from his hard abs and ran her hands over his chest. His dark hair narrowed into a promising trail at the waistband of his jeans, and she unbuckled his belt to see just where it led. Melody skimmed her palms over his backside as she removed his pants and his boxer briefs.

Naked, the two of them moved backward onto the bed together, their skin sliding pleasurably against each other as they got between the sheets, and Melody felt her spirit lift to new heights she'd never experienced before. Roman held her close as he made love to her, worshipping every part of her body with his hands and his mouth, murmuring how much he loved her in her ear. The best part was that she actually believed him. She'd spent far too much of her life thinking she would never truly be loved by someone, that the fairytale endings were for everyone but her, yet it was happening right before her eyes. Her body ripened in his hands as he pulled her close, his hardness insistent against her inner thigh.

"I love you, Melody," he said with one more kiss, his rough palms on either side of her face as he looked into her eyes. "I've loved you from the minute I saw you, and I don't ever want to let you out of my sight again."

"I love you, too, Roman. So much."

He plunged into her then, and as full of passion she already was, Melody discovered there was even more. She surged and rolled with him, her hips moving of their own volition to keep time with his, her hands continually finding some new, exciting plane of his hard body to explore. The morning light streamed through the window, illuminating their bodies and making a gleaming halo around his hair as he pleasured her. Roman moved so carefully, yet she felt the intensity and desperation in his shaking muscles as he sought to claim as much of her as he could.

Melody closed her eyes, letting the rest of the world melt away as she gave herself over completely to this feeling. She focused on the way his body felt inside hers, throbbing in perfect harmony with her heart, and how both her human and snow leopard sides reveled in the soul connection between them. Her breath caught in her throat as her muscles wound up like a spring, clenching tighter and tighter until she could hardly even breathe.

Roman must have felt it, too, because she felt his girth expand, filling her even more. That was enough to push her over the edge, making that knot of muscle melt in an instant as she let go. She clenched her jaw and clawed at his back as their flesh spoke to each other in an ancient exchange they couldn't control.

Her mind buzzing and her muscles quivering, Melody curled up in the crook of his arm as Roman pulled the covers over the two of them. She listened to his heartbeat, knowing that soon enough, they'd both be listening to another heartbeat that was developing in her belly. This had been the perfect Christmas.

13

"ROMAN! HAVE YOU FINALLY RETURNED TO US?" AUSTIN STRODE forward through the terminal and embraced his clanmate. Roman recognized him immediately, with his lantern jaw, piercing eyes, and signature Stetson. "And I take it this is the lovely Melody. I hope that little charter plane wasn't too interesting of a ride." He swept off his hat and kissed her hand.

"It's nice to meet you," she said, blushing a little.

"Old Henry said to tell you everything's fine at the ranch," Austin said as he took Melody's bags from her.

"I hope he didn't have too much trouble taking care of my part of things," Roman hedged. He'd hated to ask anyone to do that much work for him, but he couldn't exactly just leave all the livestock to fend for themselves.

Austin shook his head. "I don't think he minded at all, really. He doesn't have an excuse to get out into the fresh air as much as he'd like to these days. In fact, it also gave him an excuse to head over to my place every night and give me a full report on what he'd done."

The older bear was a beloved member of the clan, and Roman had come to like him just as much as everyone else did. "I'll owe him big for this."

Austin paused at the doors out to the parking lot. "You'd better zip up your coat, Melody. It's a lot colder here than where you came from."

"Oh, look at all this snow!" she squealed as they headed for Austin's truck. "I just love it."

Roman took her hand. He'd missed it too, and it was all the better now that he had her there with him. He chuckled at her enthusiasm. "You haven't seen much of anything yet. We haven't even left the airport parking lot."

"I don't care! I saw plenty through the plane window, but I don't think I'll ever get over all this snow. Everyone's just carrying on about their business as if nothing's happened." She slipped a little, leaning on Roman for support.

"It's just a way of life up here," Roman explained. "They're prepared for it, too. They always have the plows out on the main roads, and everyone has four-wheel-drive vehicles. This will be my first full winter here, but even I know to keep plenty of provisions on hand, just in case. It's nothing like L.A." He hoisted the bags into the back of Austin's truck and held the door open for Melody.

The two of them slipped into the back to sit next to each other. "That's exactly what I'm going to love about it," Melody replied as she buckled in. "There are a lot of great things about L.A., but I was ready for a change of scenery. Can you imagine how wonderful Christmas is going to be up here?"

Austin glanced at her in the rearview. "You like Christmas, huh? Well, then I'll give you the grand tour." He turned the truck toward Main Street, slowing down so Melody could take in all the garland, wreaths, and lights that decorated the downtown area.

"This is amazing!" Melody squealed.

Roman put his hand affectionately on her thigh. When the two of them had sat down and talked about where they'd live, he hadn't been sure that Wyoming was the right choice. Roman had known that was what he'd wanted. Though he'd originally chosen it because of his urge to be alone, he'd come to love it and the grizzly clan that had adopted him. He'd worried that Melody would choose to go back there with him not because she genuinely wanted to, but because she felt she had to. They'd talked well into the night, weighing all the pros and cons of all the decisions that rested on their shoulders. The fact that they could discuss it like mature adults instead of arguing children had told him a lot. Roman turned up the heat to make sure Melody didn't get cold. "I'm glad you think so. I was worried about taking you away from your friends."

"It's not as though we can't go back to visit. In fact, I've already convinced Emersyn that she and Gabe will need to take a vacation out here next summer." Melody leaned against him, grinning as she kept her eyes glued to the windows.

Moving out of Sheridan proper, Austin turned down a side road and headed out into the country. Roman felt himself relaxing more and more as they drove, finding comfort and familiarity in a bump or pothole here and a tree there. He'd known he belonged there the first time he'd arrived, but at that time in his life, he'd never imagined he'd be bringing his one true mate back home with him. He kept his arms wrapped around her, determined never to let her go again.

"Here we are," Austin announced as he pulled into the driveway.

"No way." Melody scrambled out of the truck before Roman could insist on helping her down. "You didn't tell me you lived in a log cabin!"

Roman had simply seen it as a house before, but everything about him had changed, including his perspective. He could see why Melody would have loved the place, with the split-rail fence around the front yard, the stone foundation, and the heavy logs that made up the home. He'd been more focused on the huge pole barn off to the side that allowed him a place to work from and keep his equipment, but Melody herself was all about home. Now that she was there, he couldn't imagine the place without her.

"It's not locked. You can head on in, and I'll be there in a second." Roman could barely finish his sentence before she'd trotted up the porch steps.

"You've got yourself an enthusiastic one there," Austin noted as he helped pull the luggage out of the truck's bed. "She seems sweet, too, not like some of the girls I've met recently."

"You must like her, considering how civil you're being," Roman noted. "I know you're not a fan of having strangers around." He'd witnessed Austin react when some tourists had accidentally come up Austin's driveway, then were promptly escorted out by the wrong end of a shotgun.

"If she's your mate, then she's part of the clan. That's different, not like these city slickers my sister wants to bring in after converting the whole damn place to a dude ranch like the Bancrofts did." He turned his head and spat on the ground.

Roman shrugged and smiled. "I had to go halfway across the country to find her, if that tells you anything."

"The bigger miracle is that you convinced her to come up here to the middle of nowhere and live with a lout like you," Austin said with a grin.

"You just go on home and be jealous, then. I've got to get settled in and give Melody the grand tour." Roman made a shooing motion down the driveway.

Austin waggled his brows suggestively. "I see how it is. I should be getting home, though. The dogs will be upset that I've left the house without them for a change." With the last of the bags out of the truck, Austin hopped back into the driver's seat and fired up the engine.

Roman leaned in the window. Everyone down at Force HQ in L.A. knew about the good news, but it was going to spread fast enough around Sheridan. "I've been so busy traveling that I didn't get a chance to tell you we're expecting a little one next summer."

"You lucky son of a bitch!" Austin clapped him on the arm and grasped his hand. "Congratulations! Man, I hope I'm lucky enough to find my mate at some point. Some of these cold nights get pretty lonely, but I guess you wouldn't know about that."

"Not anymore. I can't wait to introduce her to the rest of the clan. I think she's going to fit in well." Roman glanced toward the house, eager to get back to her.

"She will. I'll put together a New Year's Eve party up at my house, and I'll be sure to stock something non-alcoholic for her." Austin put the truck in reverse and waved as he backed out of the driveway.

Roman headed inside to find Melody standing in the middle of the living room. She looked so happy as she turned to him, her hair bouncing as she jogged across the rug to put her arms around him. "Roman, this place is great! I know it's past Christmas, but I can already see just how beautiful we can make it next December. I love the open floor plan and all the wood, and there's plenty of room for the baby."

He nodded as he pulled her into his arms. Roman couldn't remember ever having such a sense of home and family, and they'd only been there for a few minutes. "There's a room right next to the master bedroom that's perfect for a nursery."

"Perfect, just like you." Melody kissed him, and then she kissed him again.

He pulled her closer, deepening the kiss. The house was cool from being unoccupied for the last month, but he felt his own body heating up. He'd been looking forward to having some alone time with her. "I can't wait to show you the place. This house is on clan land, and all the ranching area that expands between the houses is shared by all of us. I also can't wait for them to meet you, but first, I'd like to give you a very detailed tour of that master bedroom. I plan on the two of us spending a lot of time in there, at least as much as we can before the baby comes."

She bit her lower lip as she looked up at him, but she backed away and let go. "We can do that soon enough, but there's something I've got to do first."

"What's that?"

Melody bent over toward one of the suitcases he'd just brought in and unzipped it. "I think your house is absolutely lovely, but I'd like to start giving it my own touch when it comes to décor."

Roman blinked. "All right."

She stood, holding a small jar in her hands. Melody confidently crossed the room and put it on the mantel.

Stepping closer, Roman saw that it was full of the rose petals he'd given her when he'd come back to L.A. "That's nice, but I think it needs something more."

"Really?" It was Melody's turn to be surprised.

"Definitely." He unzipped his own bag and removed the tiny stocking. "It might be past Christmas for this year, but I don't mind having a little something put up." He hung it on a hook just beneath the jar full of petals. "What do you think?"

She slipped her arms around him once again, a gesture that was natural to them already. "I love it, and I love you. I think it's time to check out that master bedroom you mentioned."

Roman took her hands and led the way, eager to start their new life together.

THE END

If you enjoyed *Santa Soldier Bear*, get ready for Austin's story, the first book in the Wild Frontier Shifters series! Read on for a sneak peek of *Her Rancher Bear*.

AUSTIN

"Ow! Dammit, Roman! You get my fingers with that hammer again, and you'll be pushing up daisies out in the pasture," Austin warned, holding the barbed wire in place.

"I said I was sorry," Roman grumbled. "Maybe if your big ol' paws weren't in the way—"

"You know what they say about big hands."

Roman shook his head. "Whatever you say, man. Can we wrap this up already? I've gotta go check on Melody. She's about to have that baby any day now."

Austin tucked the fencing pliers into the back pocket of his jeans and stood back, looking at their work as Izzy and Dizzy chased each other around a fencepost. His mother's two Boston Terriers loved coming along for the ranch work, whether Austin wanted them there or not. They did have their purpose, but more often than not, they were underfoot. "I suppose that'll do for now."

"For now?" Roman rested his hand on the nearest fencepost, surveying the row of freshly-repaired posts along the cattle pasture. The grass had turned green and lush under the Wyoming summer sun. "I know I haven't been in this business for generations like you have, but it looks pretty damn good to me."

"It does," Austin agreed. Roman was right. He'd come into

ranching and into their clan about a year ago when he'd left the military. He'd proven himself to be a hard worker and a family man, one who'd seen the temptations of city life, yet still returned to the place he now called home in Sheridan, Wyoming. Austin had to give him credit for that, and for always being willing to help. He did like to rib him for not being a rancher, born-and-raised, but Roman gave him hell right back when he accused Austin of never seeing a single blade of grass outside of his own territory.

"There's nothing wrong with the fence at all," Austin continued. "I'm sure it would stand the test of time if left to its own devices. But I'm not convinced that the Bancroft clan wasn't behind this. Ever since they opened that damn dude ranch, they've been trying to sabotage everything we have going on here." He wanted to spit every time he thought about it.

Roman rubbed his lips together. "Sounds like a big problem."

"It is."

"Have you talked to Levi?" The Alpha of their clan also happened to be the local sheriff.

Austin pulled in a deep breath. "A little. He knows what's been happening, but I don't have any actual proof. I told him I could handle it. He's probably got enough on his hands dealing with that brother of his."

Roman chuckled. "Wade got himself in trouble again?"

"That's what I understand. I never should've listened when Shawna suggested we turn this place into a dude ranch. She insisted the numbers were on her side, and I didn't see any way out of it." He pulled in a deep breath as he wondered what his ancestors might think of the commercialized, touristy operation they were now running. At least it was a lot more rustic than some of the other ranches that catered solely to city slickers. The Crawford Ranch was still a family-centered place that focused on raising cattle and doing things the old-fashioned way, just how he liked it. He didn't like having nosy humans roaming around his territory, and he absolutely hated it when they wanted to follow him around and see how the work was done, but the money it brought in was hard to argue with.

Checking his watch, Roman gestured to his truck parked nearby. "I'd better get going. I don't want to be away from Melody any longer than I need to be right now."

"Sure thing. Keep me updated. And thanks for the help." Austin turned to Gunner, his chestnut gelding who patiently waited nearby. He swung easily up into the saddle and headed back down to the barn, Izzy and Dizzy keeping up in the dust clouds behind him. It'd been a long, hot day. Austin was already behind on his daily chores, and as he got closer to the center of operations, he remembered he was supposed to have guests coming that afternoon.

He cursed under his breath. He didn't have time for this. He spent far too many hours showing tourists around and coming up with activities to keep them entertained, as if they weren't grown-ass adults who could take care of themselves.

On top of the many other jobs he had at the ranch, making sure the guests didn't get bored was the worst. He removed Gunner's tack and gave him a good rubdown while the two dogs competed over a hoof clipping from the last time the farrier had been there. Austin shooed them toward the house before he headed for the outdoor shower stall at the back of the barn. He was covered in horse dirt and cattle mud, and if he didn't track it into the house, he'd have one less thing to take care of.

Austin stripped off his clothes and tossed them aside on a nearby bench, but he carefully hung his Stetson on a hook on the outside wall of the shower. He stood directly under the showerhead as he turned on the spigot, not bothering to wait for it to heat up. There was something about that first spray of bitterly cold water that woke him up and reminded him of just where and who he was. He was a rancher. He was a survivor. He was out there in the middle of nowhere, with no one around, and that was just the way he liked it.

Grabbing a bar of soap, he began washing away the dirt, along with his worries about opening the family ranch to strangers, letting his concerns go running down the drain in the center of the concrete shower floor. Sure, these folks could bankrupt him if they did something stupid, but they could also make his family a good living if they brought all their friends. In the moment, he was happy to not think about any of it.

He stiffened as he felt someone watching him. No, it was something deeper than that. Something affected him all the way down to his core, making his inner grizzly raise its head and pay attention.

A long whistle sounded behind him. "I knew we were coming out here to see how they raise cattle, but they obviously do a hell of a job with their cowboys, too."

Austin rinsed the soap out of his eyes and glanced over his shoulder to find three ladies standing there, staring at him in shock. "Shit!" He grabbed a towel from a nearby hook and wrapped it around his waist. These must have been the guests that were supposed to be staying for the week. "I didn't expect you for another few hours."

The woman in the middle's cheeks were flushed, her lips slightly parted, but the gaze from her deep green eyes was unwavering. She didn't bother to check out his rugged physique as the other women were doing, choosing to stare deep into his soul instead. Not a strand of her deep golden hair was out of place, and her fitted dress suggested she thought she'd be spending the afternoon at a luxury hotel instead of a farmstead. She blinked as though she were coming out of a trance and then looked away.

"I...I'm sorry. Our earlier plans fell through, so we went ahead and came right here. We didn't find anyone up by the house, so..." Her voice was deep and velvety, and it sent a quiver of energy through Austin's stomach.

He returned her level stare, only vaguely aware of the other women standing there. He wasn't particularly modest, having grown up in a rural area where getting things done was the important thing, and there was no room for shyness. Regardless, he knew he'd feel naked under her gaze, even if he were fully clothed.

"Don't be sorry, Harper," purred the woman to her left, the one who'd initially spoken. She openly eyed Austin's broad chest without a hint of impropriety showing in her eyes. "If you ask me, this is going to get the Crawford Ranch a five-star review."

"Oh my god, can we just go?" asked the third woman, shielding her eyes and edging away from the scene. "This is so embarrassing!"

Either Harper simply wasn't impressed, or she was too cool to let him know. She kept her gaze carefully averted as she edged away. "We'll go now. We're looking for someone named Austin."

"Well, you've found him." Tucking in the corner of his towel, Austin sighed and grabbed his hat, gesturing around the corner of the barn toward the house. "You can head into the lodge and I'll be there in a moment." He couldn't help himself as he stared at the blonde. His inner grizzly was stirring, impatient, eager to get closer to her. He stepped out of the shower, meaning to head toward the back of the house, but he brushed past her on his way.

Austin could hear the other women giggling and arguing as they went around to the front, but he could still feel Harper's eyes on him.

No doubt, this was going to be a long week.

———

Find *Her Rancher Bear* on Amazon in ebook and paperback. Also available in Kindle Unlimited!

ALSO BY MEG RIPLEY
ALL AVAILABLE ON AMAZON

Shifter Nation Universe

Marked Over Forty Series

Fated Over Forty Series

Wild Frontier Shifters Series

Special Ops Shifters: L.A. Force Series

Special Ops Shifters: Dallas Force Series

Special Ops Shifters Series (original D.C. Force)

Werebears of Acadia Series

Werebears of the Everglades Series

Werebears of Glacier Bay Series

Werebears of Big Bend Series

Dragons of Charok Universe

Daddy Dragon Guardians Series

Shifters Between Worlds Series

Dragon Mates: The Complete Dragons of Charok Universe Collection
(Includes Daddy Dragon Guardians and Shifters Between Worlds)

More Shifter Romance Series

Beverly Hills Dragons Series

Dragons of Sin City Series

Dragons of the Darkblood Secret Society Series

Packs of the Pacific Northwest Series

Compilations

Forever Fated Mates Collection

Shifter Daddies Collection

Early Novellas

ABOUT THE AUTHOR

Steamy shifter romance author Meg Ripley is a Seattle native who's relocated to New England. She can often be found whipping up her next tale curled up in a local coffee house with a cappuccino and her laptop.

Download *Alpha's Midlife Baby,* the steamy prequel to Meg's Fated Over Forty series, when you sign up for the Meg Ripley Insiders newsletter!

Sign up by visiting www.authormegripley.com

<u>Connect with Meg</u>

amazon.com/Meg-Ripley/e/B00Z8I9AXW
tiktok.com/@authormegripley
facebook.com/authormegripley
instagram.com/megripleybooks
pinterest.com/authormegripley
bookbub.com/authors/meg-ripley
goodreads.com/megripley